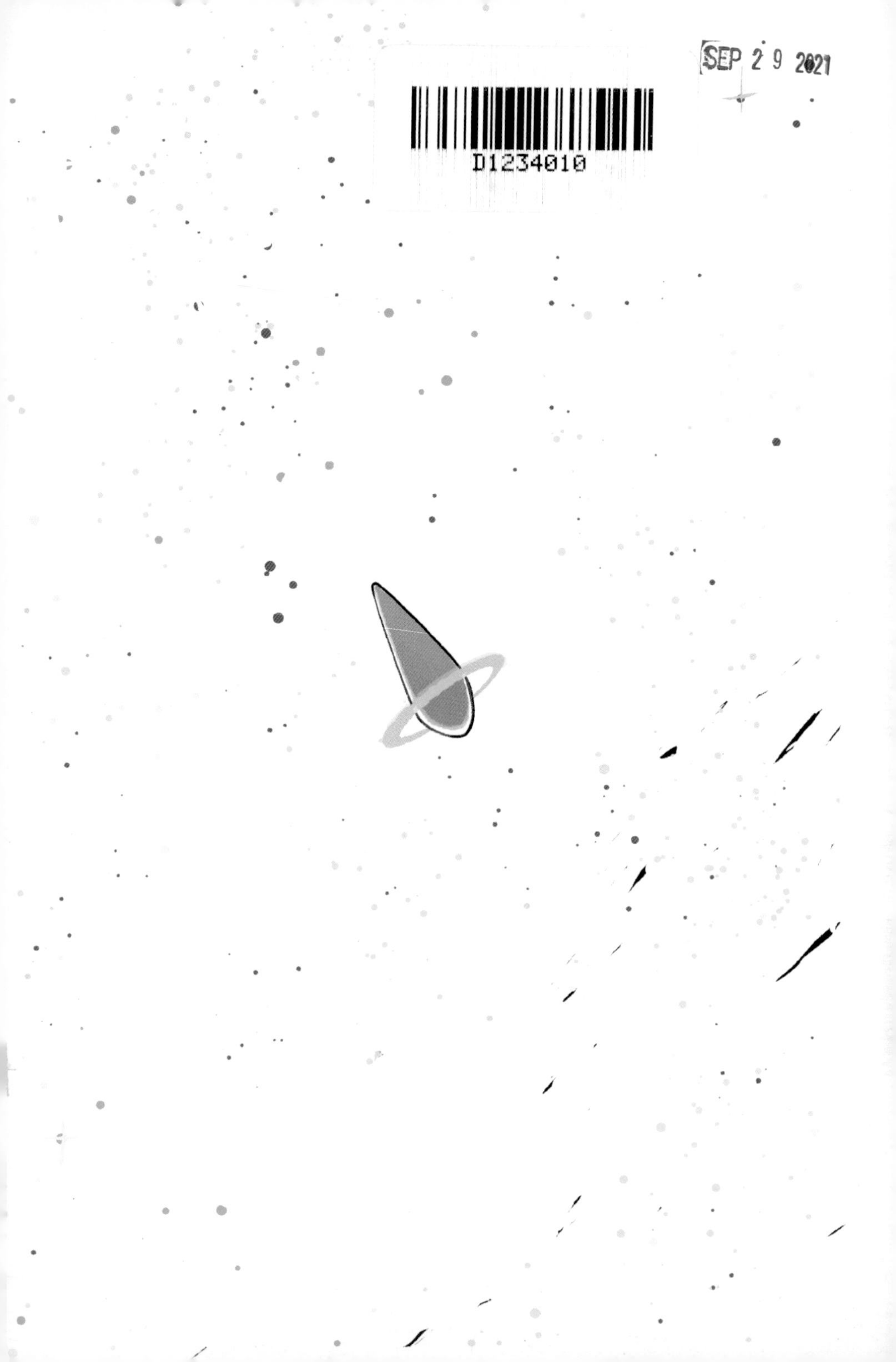

Stephen McCranie's

SPACE BOY

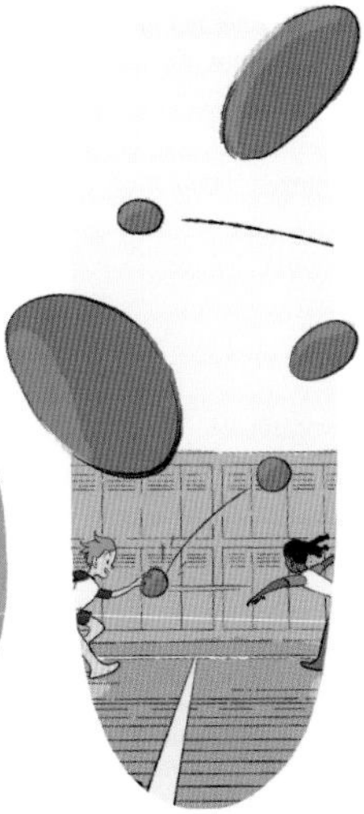

VOLUME 10

Written and illustrated by
STEPHEN McCRANIE

DARK HORSE BOOKS

President and Publisher **Mike Richardson**
Editor **Shantel LaRocque**
Associate Editor **Brett Israel**
Designer **Anita Magaña**
Digital Art Technician **Allyson Haller**

STEPHEN McCRANIE'S SPACE BOY VOLUME 10
Space Boy™ © 2021 Stephen McCranie. All rights reserved. Dark Horse
Books® and the Dark Horse logo are registered trademarks of Dark Horse
Comics LLC. All rights reserved. No portion of this publication may be
reproduced or transmitted, in any form or by any means, without the
express written permission of Dark Horse Comics LLC. Names, characters,
places, and incidents featured in this publication either are the product
of the author's imagination or are used fictitiously. Any resemblance to
actual persons (living or dead), events, institutions, or locales, without
satiric intent, is coincidental

This book collects *Space Boy* episodes 144–159, previously published
online at WebToons.com.

Published by Dark Horse Books
A division of Dark Horse Comics LLC
10956 SE Main Street | Milwaukie, OR 97222
StephenMcCranie.com | DarkHorse.com

To find a comics shop in your area, visit comicshoplocator.com

First edition: June 2021
ISBN 978-1-50671-884-2
10 9 8 7 6 5 4 3 2 1
Printed in China

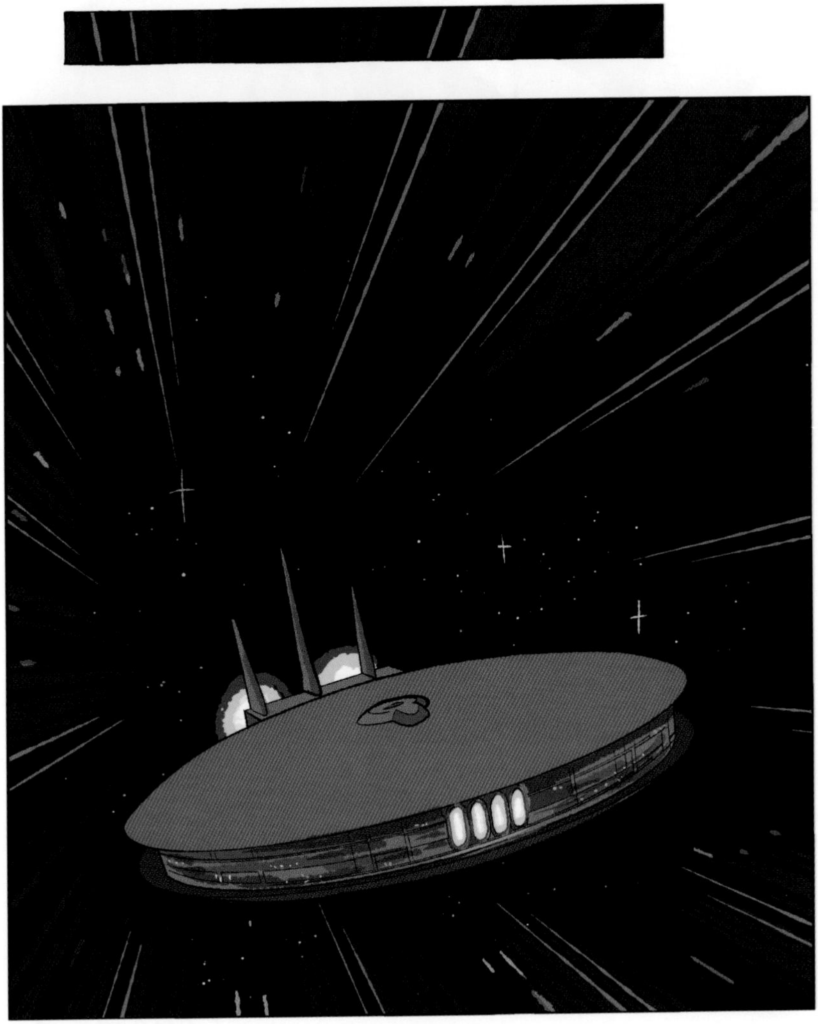

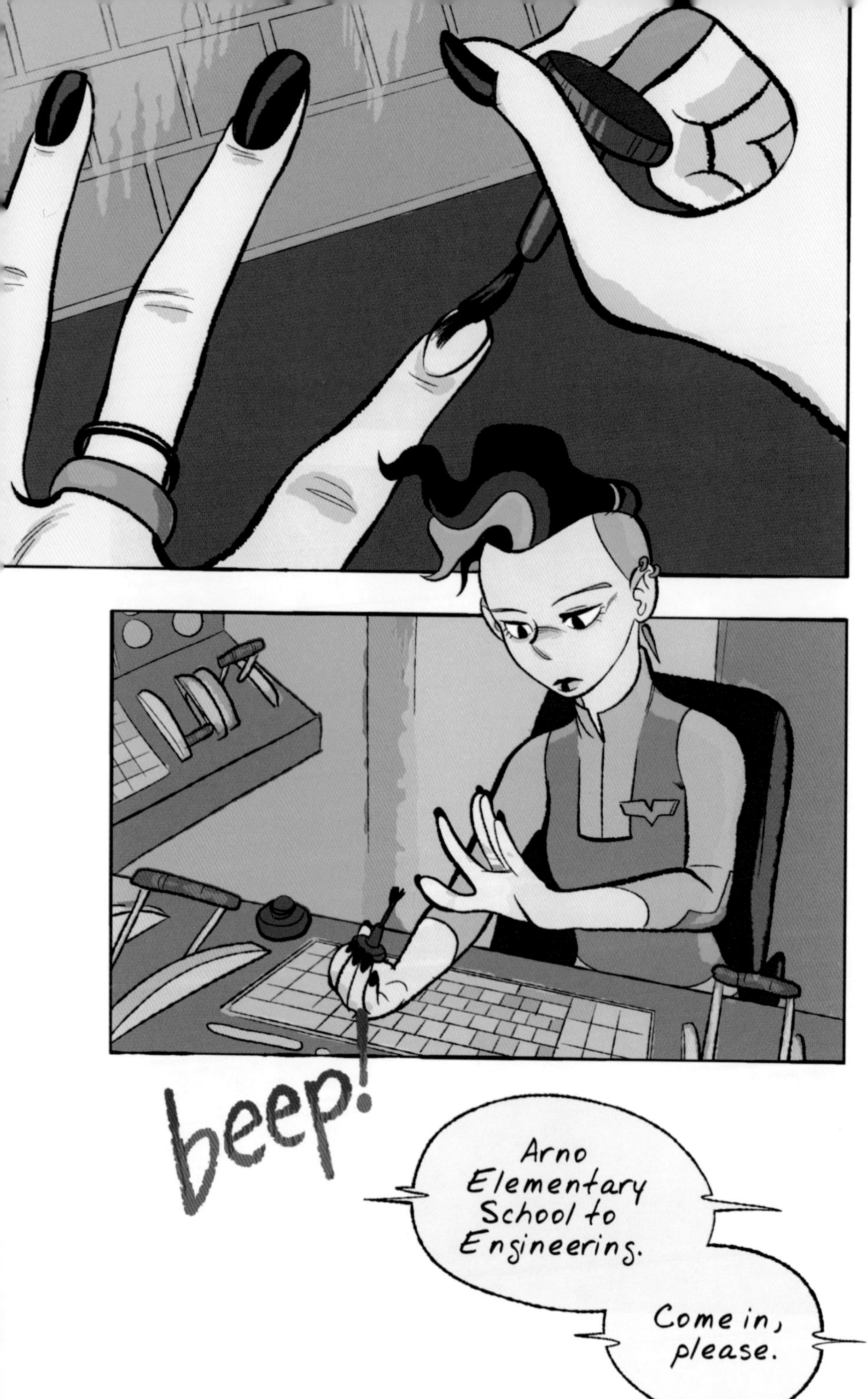
beep!
Arno Elementary School to Engineering.
Come in, please.

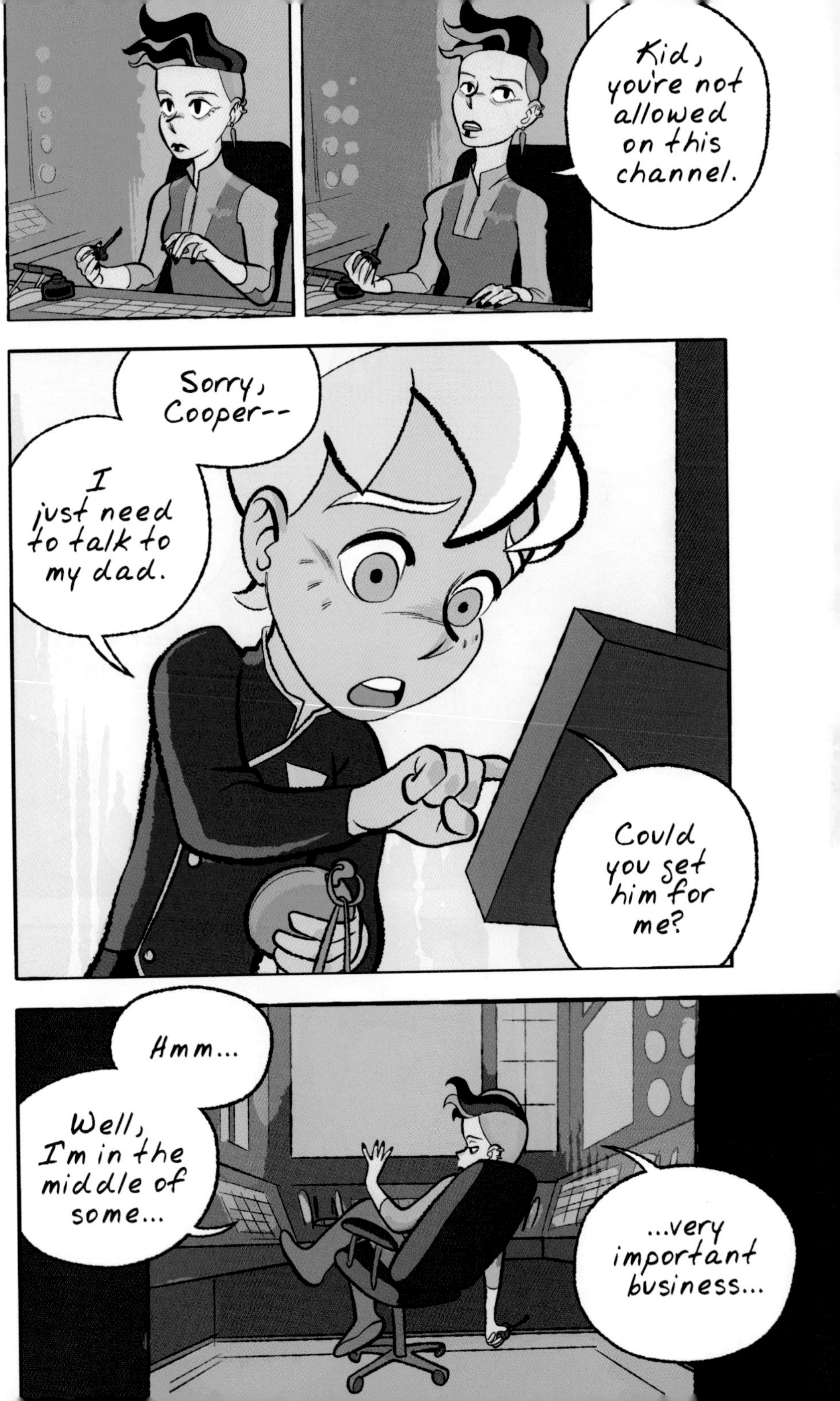
Kid, you're not allowed on this channel.
Sorry, Cooper--
I just need to talk to my dad.
Could you get him for me?
Hmm...
Well, I'm in the middle of some...
...very important business...

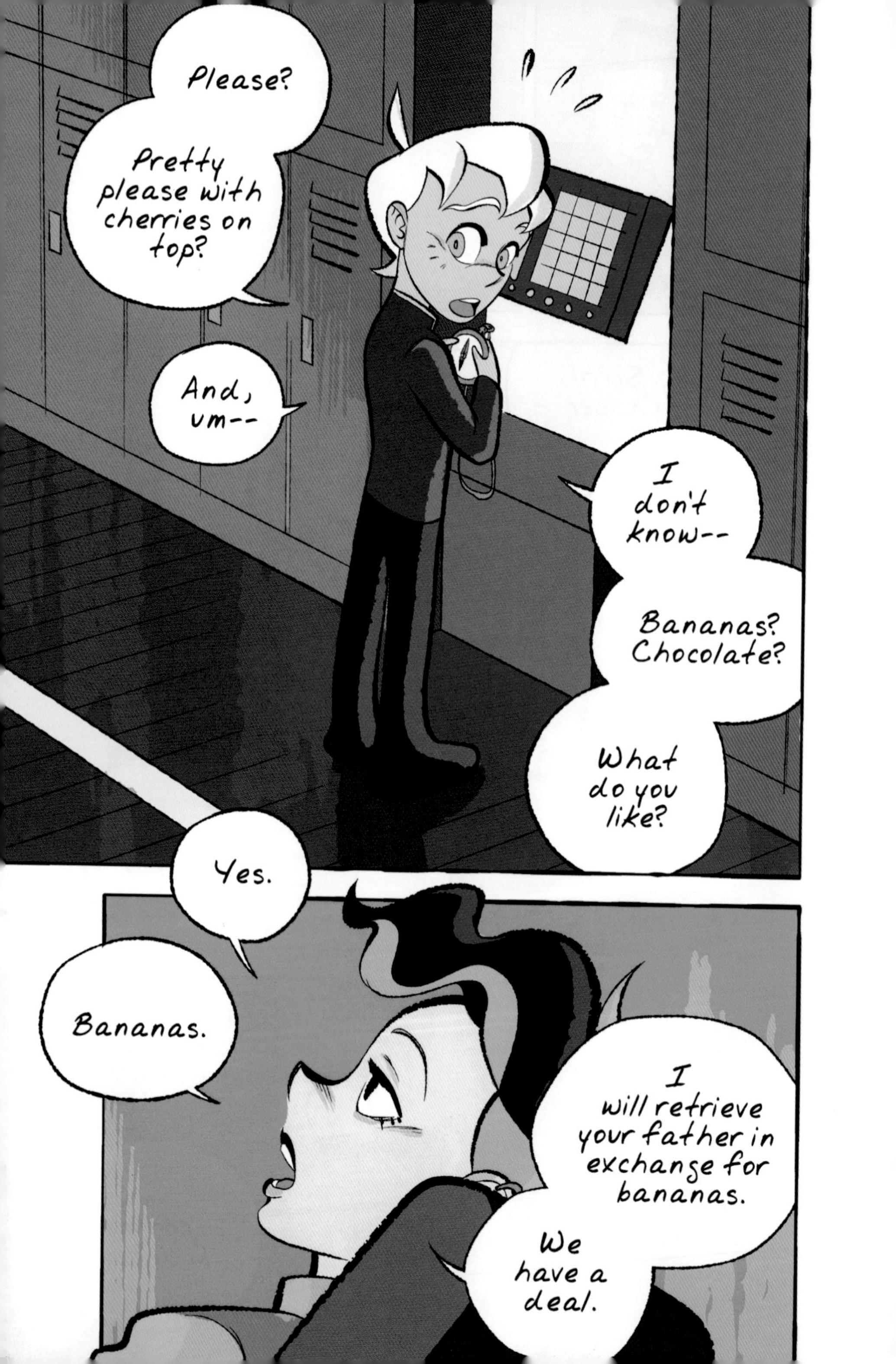
Please?
Pretty please with cherries on top?
And, um--
I don't know--
Bananas? Chocolate?
What do you like?
Yes.
Bananas.
I will retrieve your father in exchange for bananas.
We have a deal.

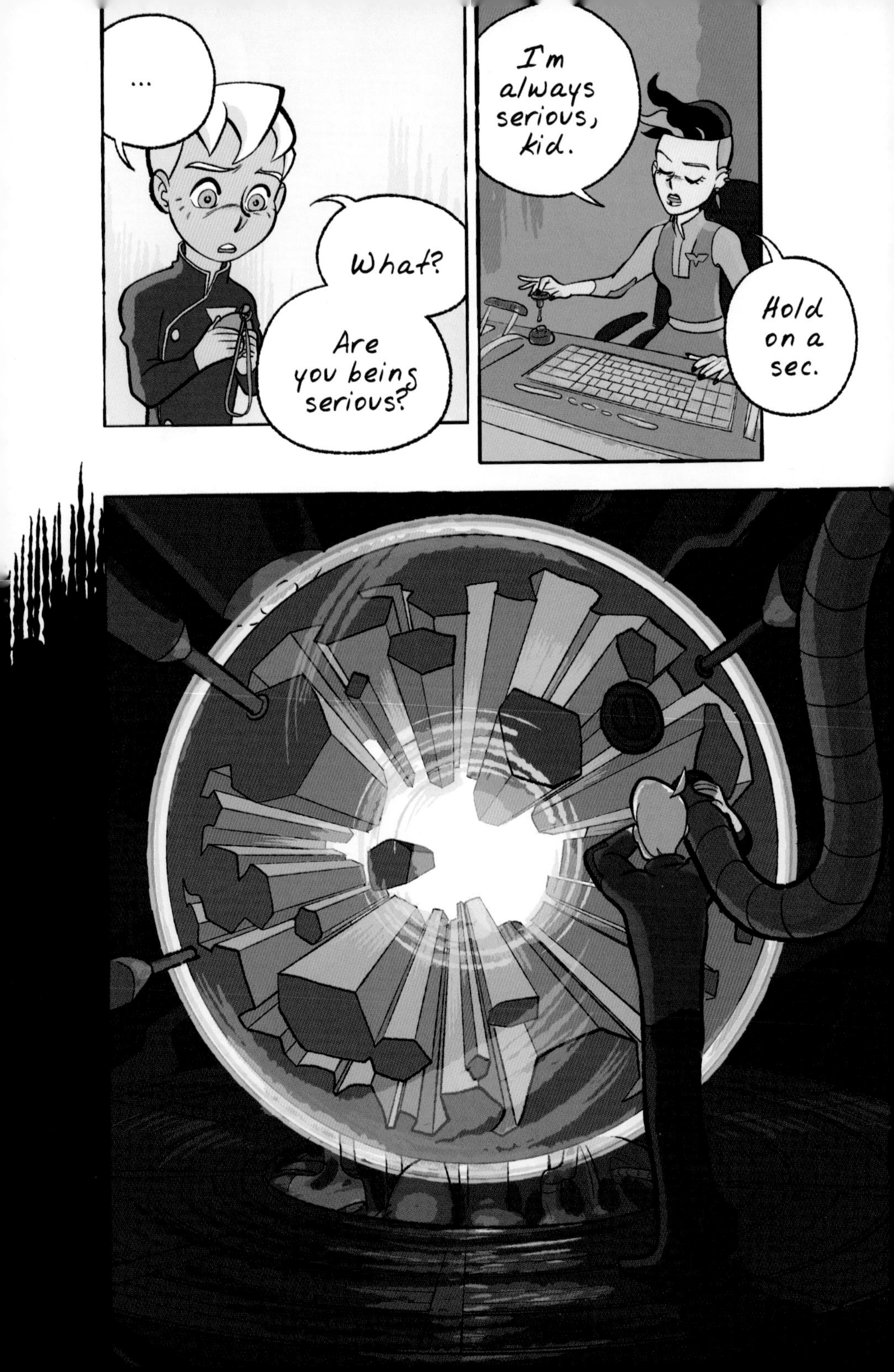
...
What?
Are you being serious?
I'm always serious, kid.
Hold on a sec.

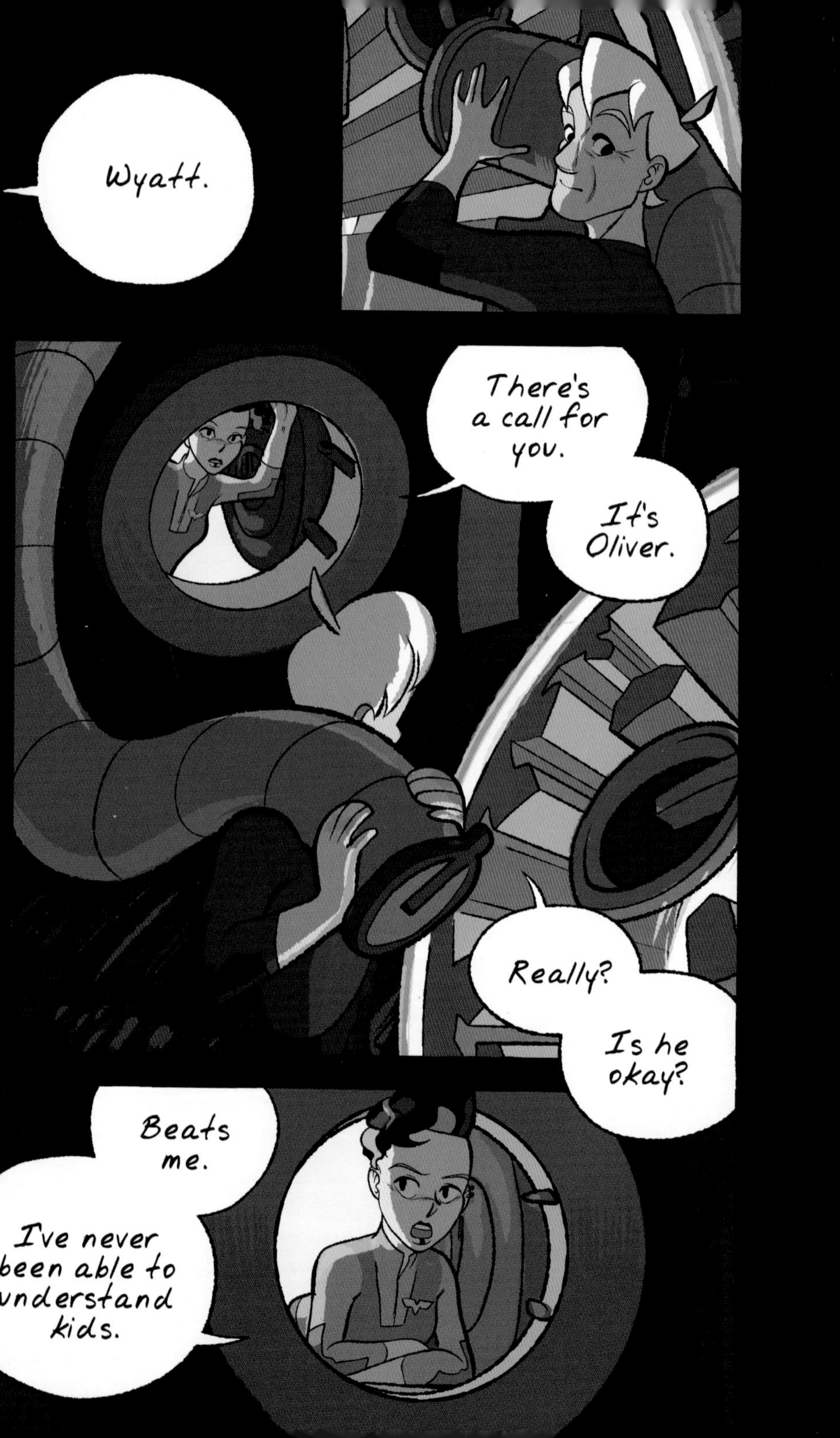

Wyatt.
There's a call for you.
It's Oliver.
Really?
Is he okay?
Beats me.
I've never been able to understand kids.

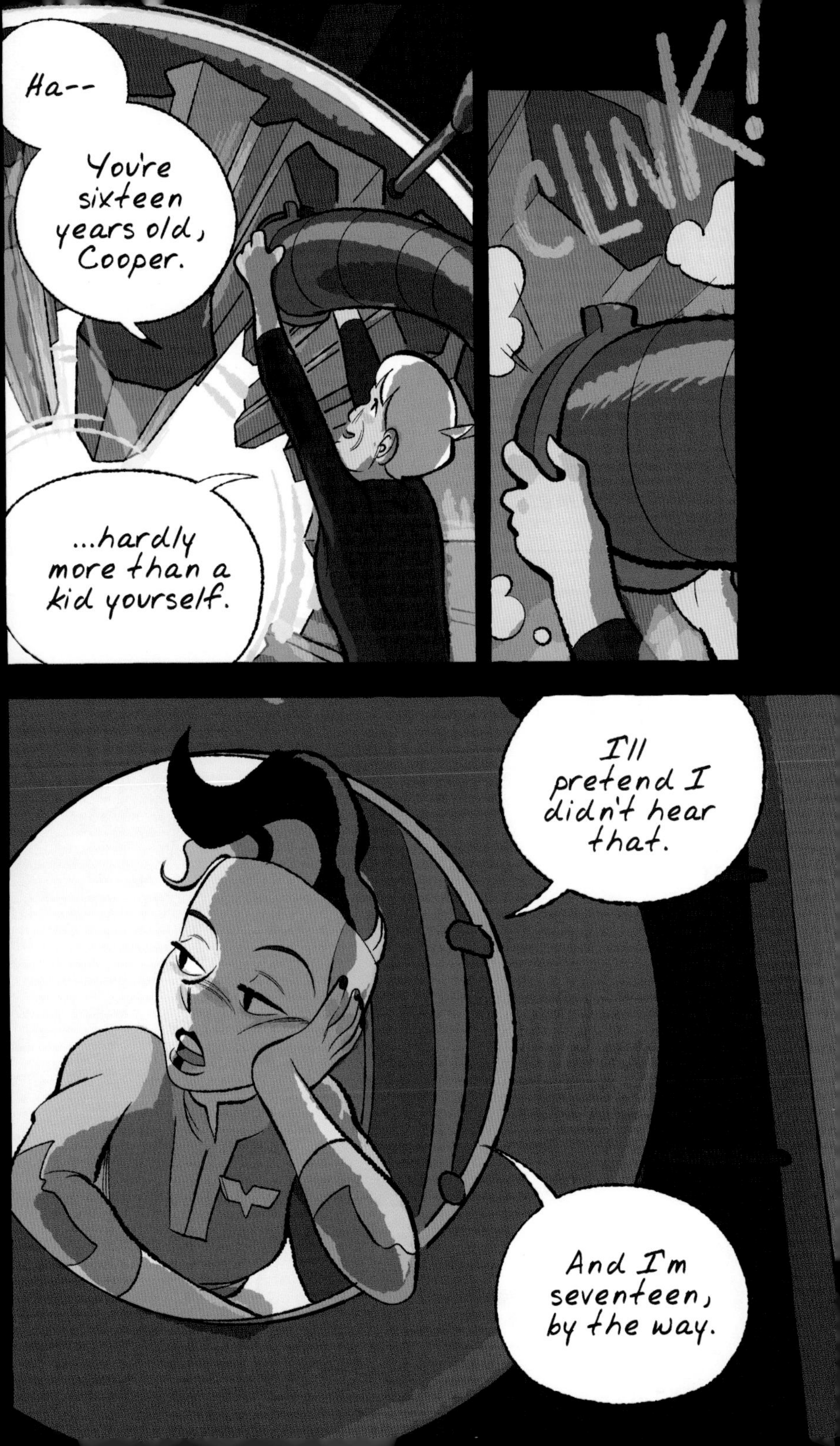
Ha--
You're sixteen years old, Cooper.
...hardly more than a kid yourself.
CLINK!
I'll pretend I didn't hear that.
And I'm seventeen, by the way.

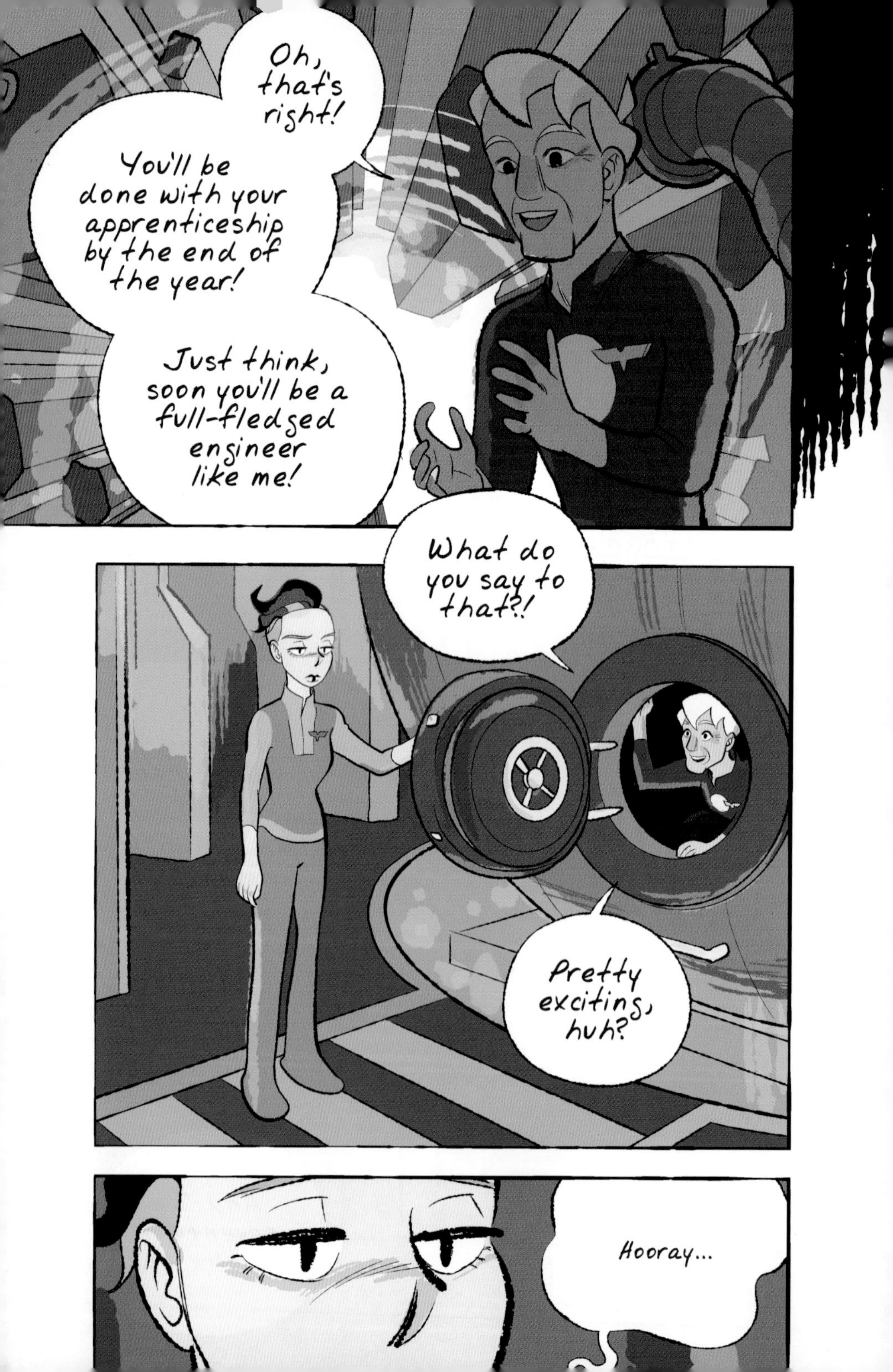
Oh, that's right!
You'll be done with your apprenticeship by the end of the year!
Just think, soon you'll be a full-fledged engineer like me!
What do you say to that?!
Pretty exciting, huh?
Hooray...

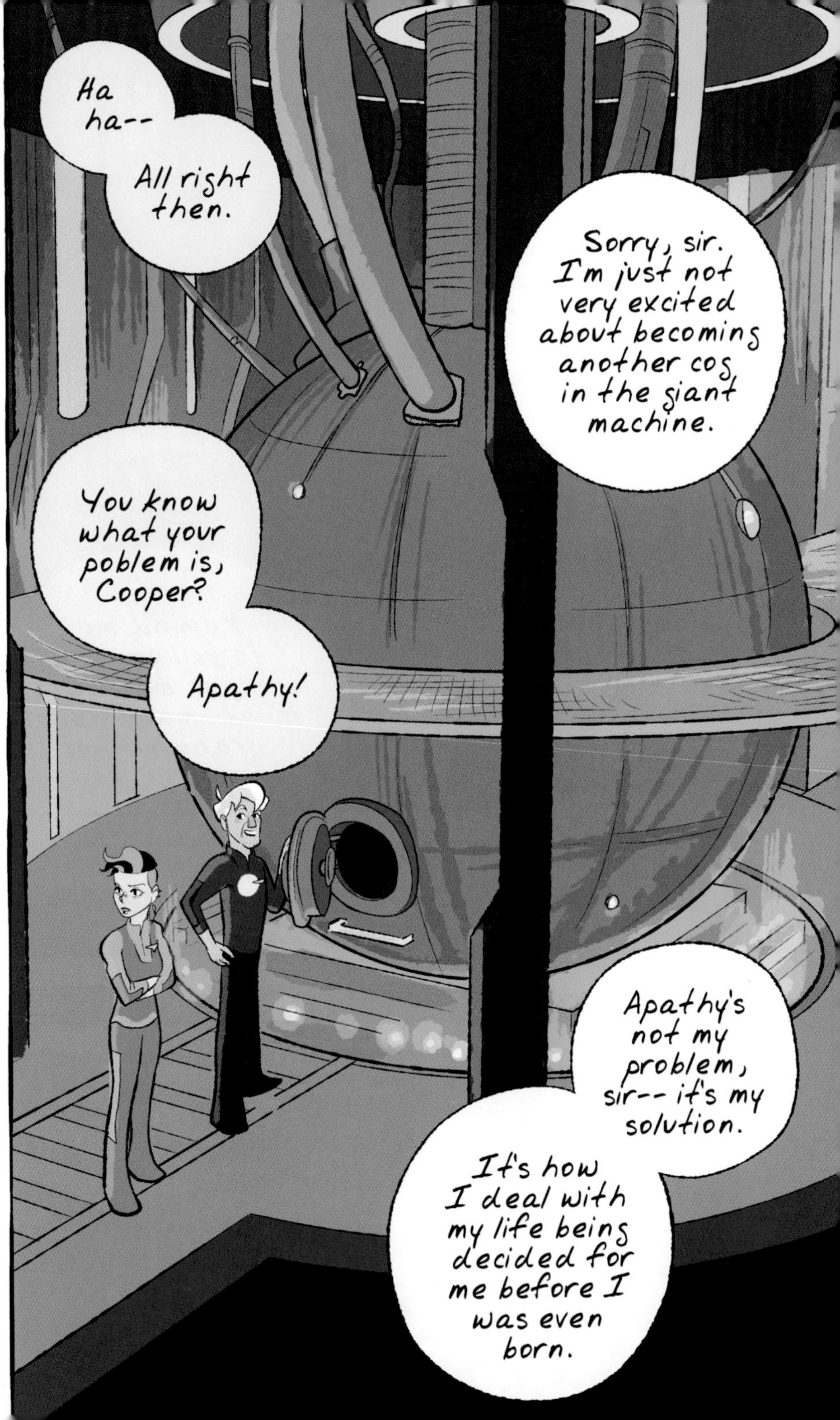
Ha ha--
All right then.
Sorry, sir. I'm just not very excited about becoming another cog in the giant machine.
You know what your poblem is, Cooper?
Apathy!
Apathy's not my problem, sir-- it's my solution.
It's how I deal with my life being decided for me before I was even born.

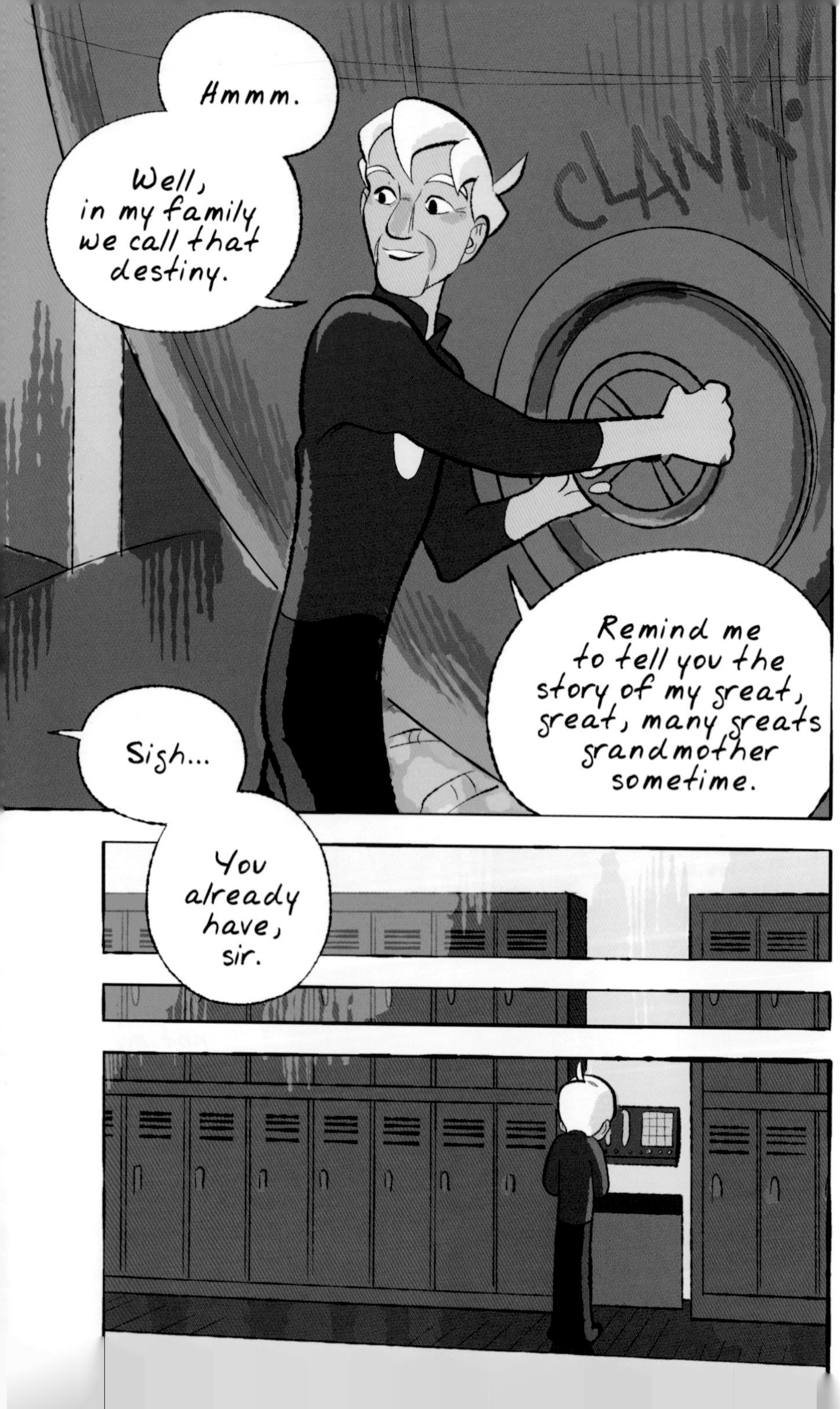
Hmmm.
Well, in my family we call that destiny.
CLANK!
Remind me to tell you the story of my great, great, many greats grandmother sometime.
Sigh...
You already have, sir.

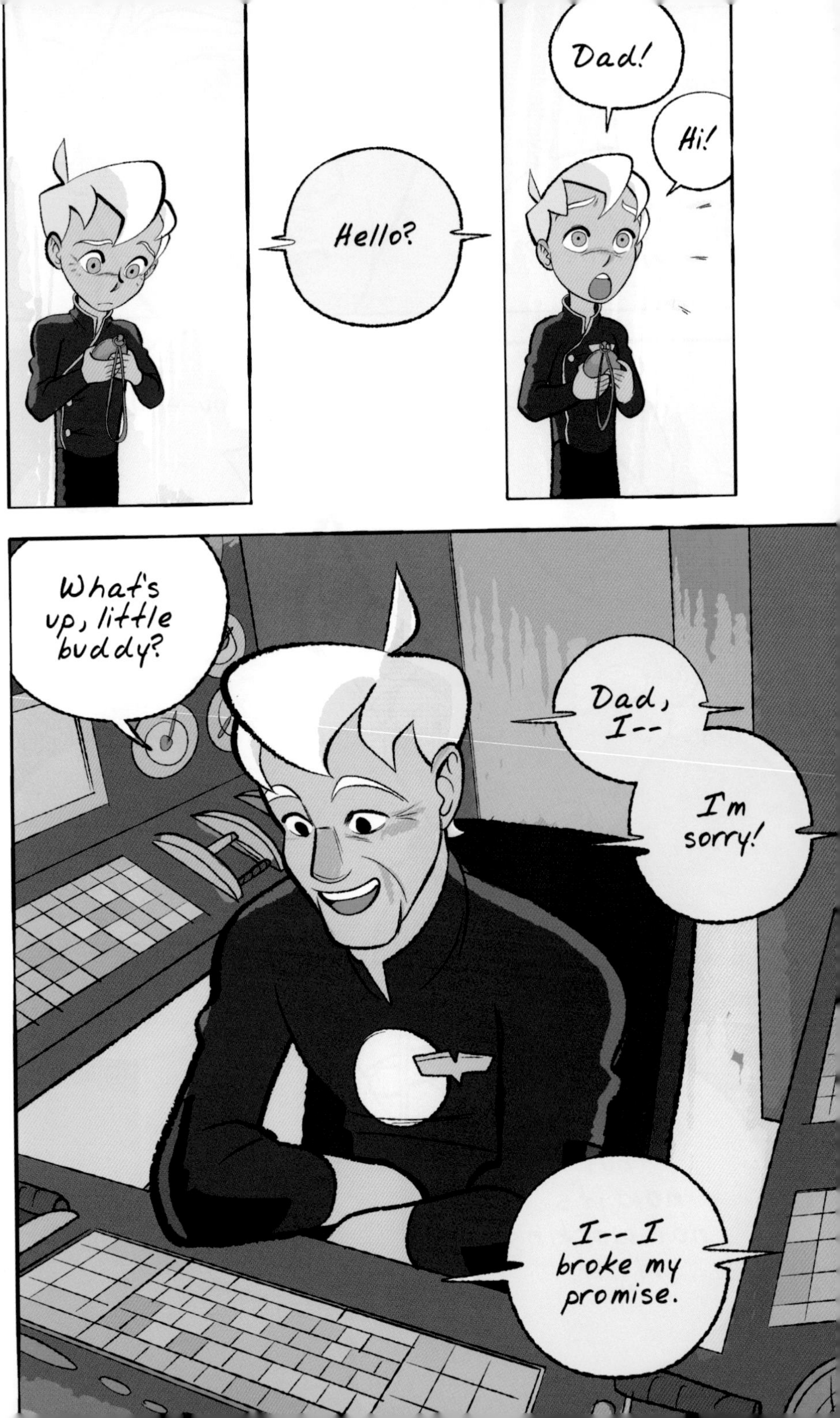
Hello?
Dad!
Hi!
What's up, little buddy?
Dad, I--
I'm sorry!
I-- I broke my promise.

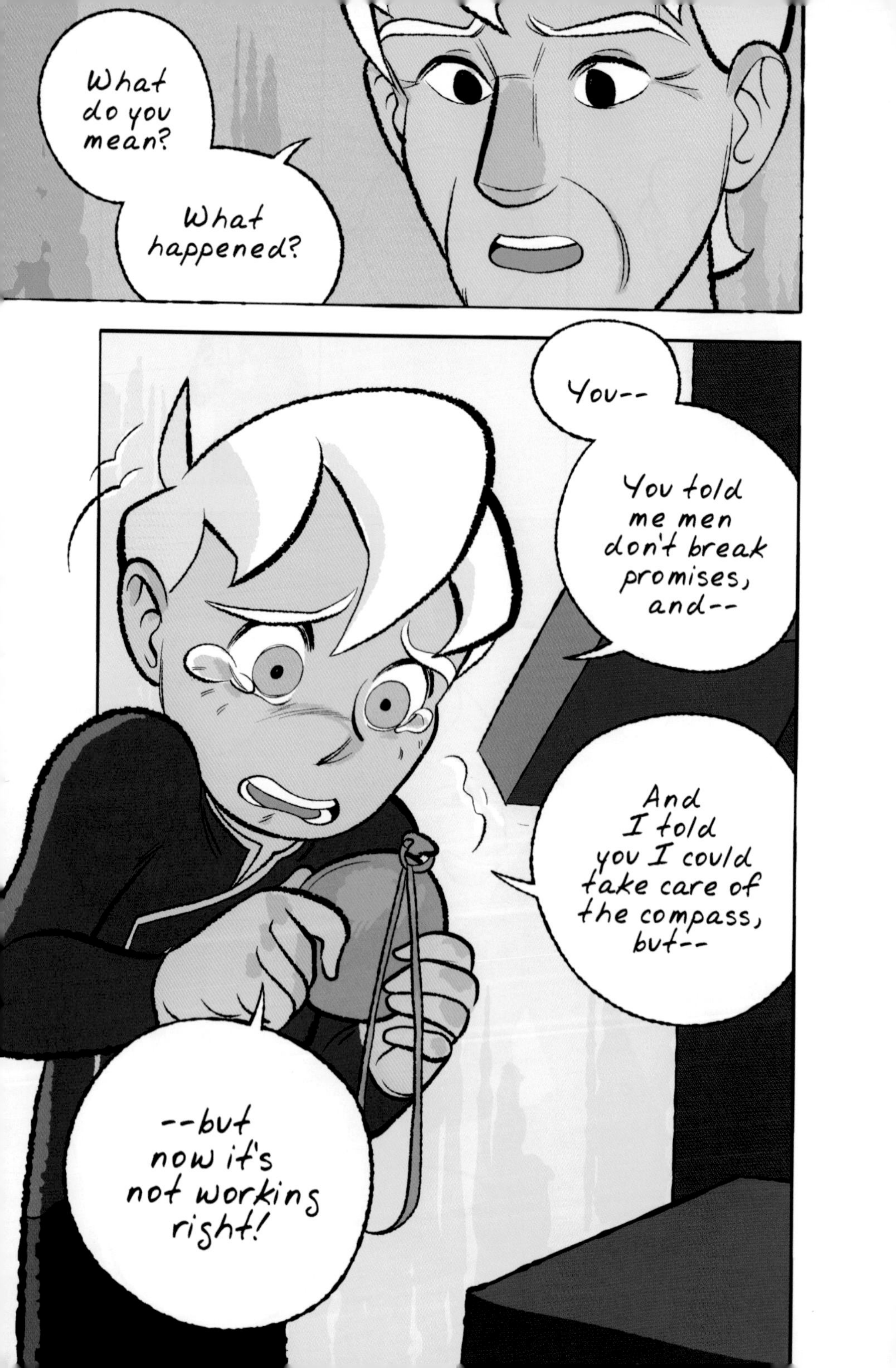
What do you mean?
What happened?
You--
You told me men don't break promises, and--
And I told you I could take care of the compass, but--
--but now it's not workins right!

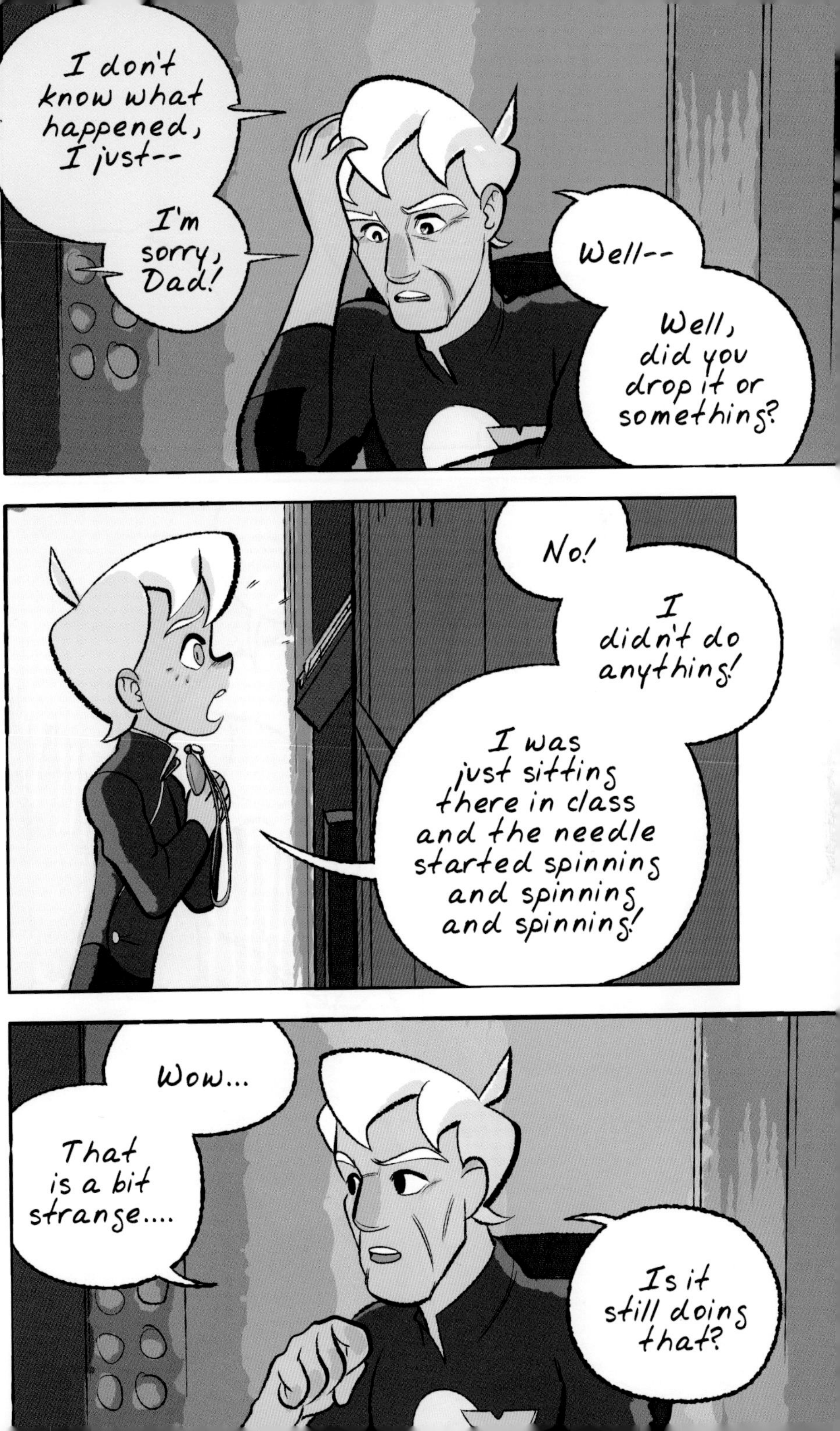

I don't know what happened, I just--
I'm sorry, Dad!
Well--
Well, did you drop it or something?
No!
I didn't do anything!
I was just sitting there in class and the needle started spinning and spinning and spinning!
Wow...
That is a bit strange....
Is it still doing that?

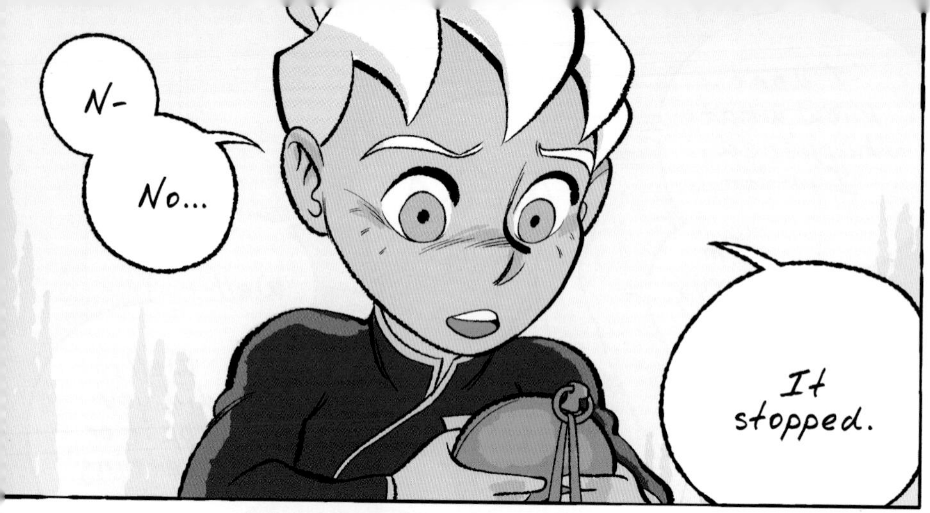
N-
No...
It stopped.

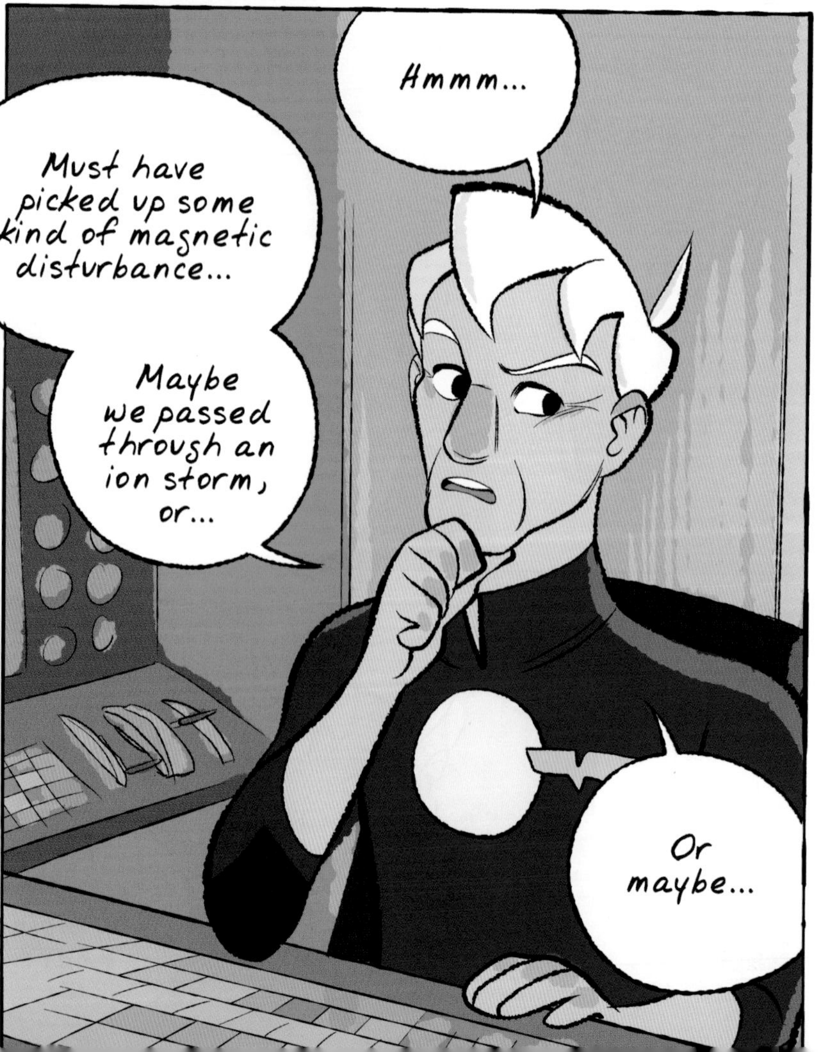
Hmmm...
Must have picked up some kind of magnetic disturbance...
Maybe we passed through an ion storm, or...
Or maybe...

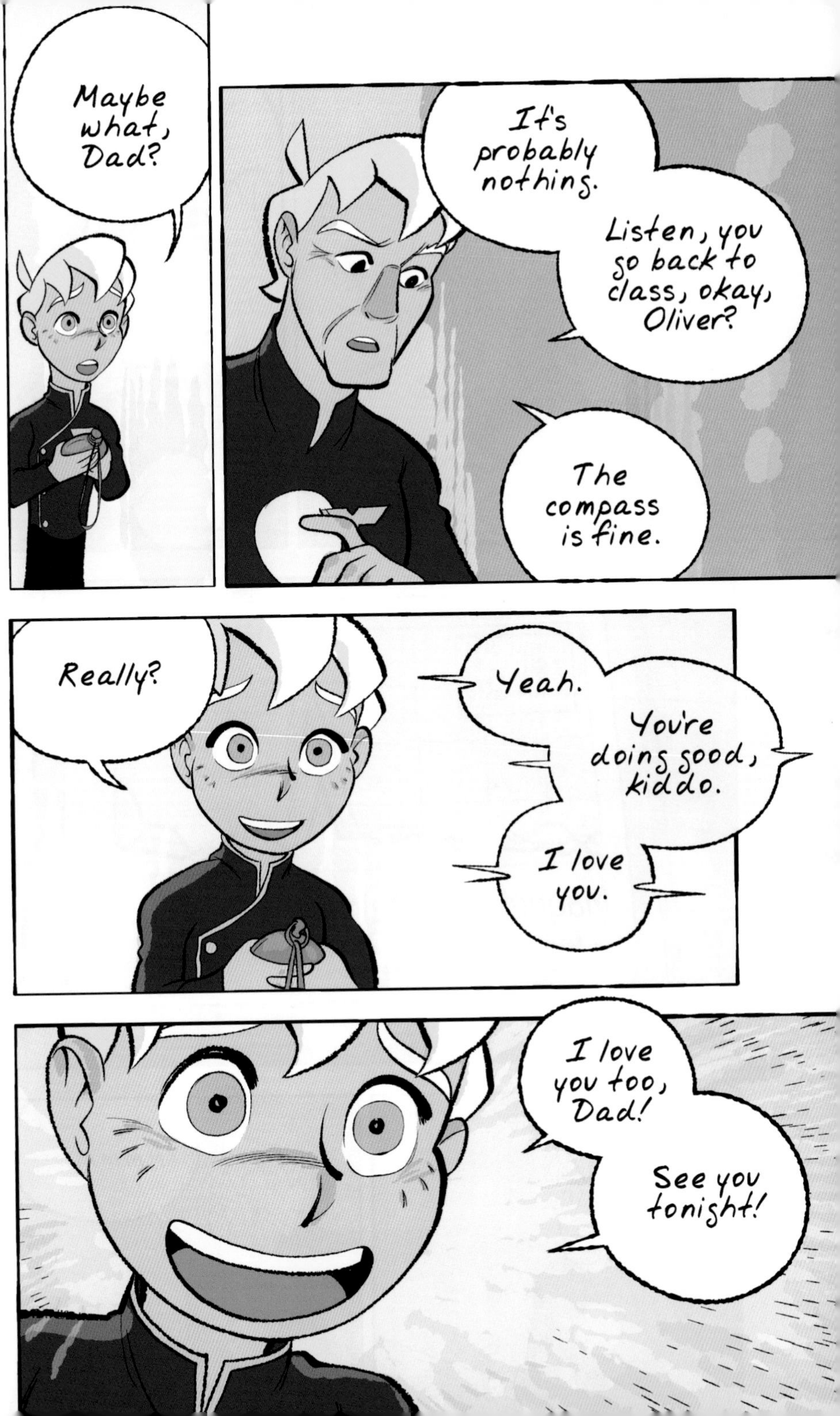
Maybe what, Dad?
It's probably nothing.
Listen, you go back to class, okay, Oliver?
The compass is fine.
Really?
Yeah.
You're doing good, kiddo.
I love you.
I love you too, Dad!
See you tonight!

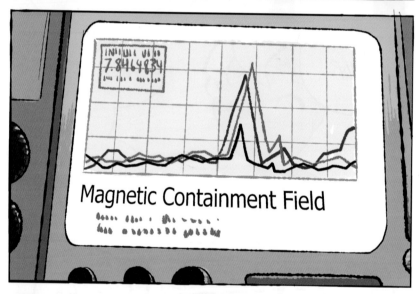

Magnetic Containment Field

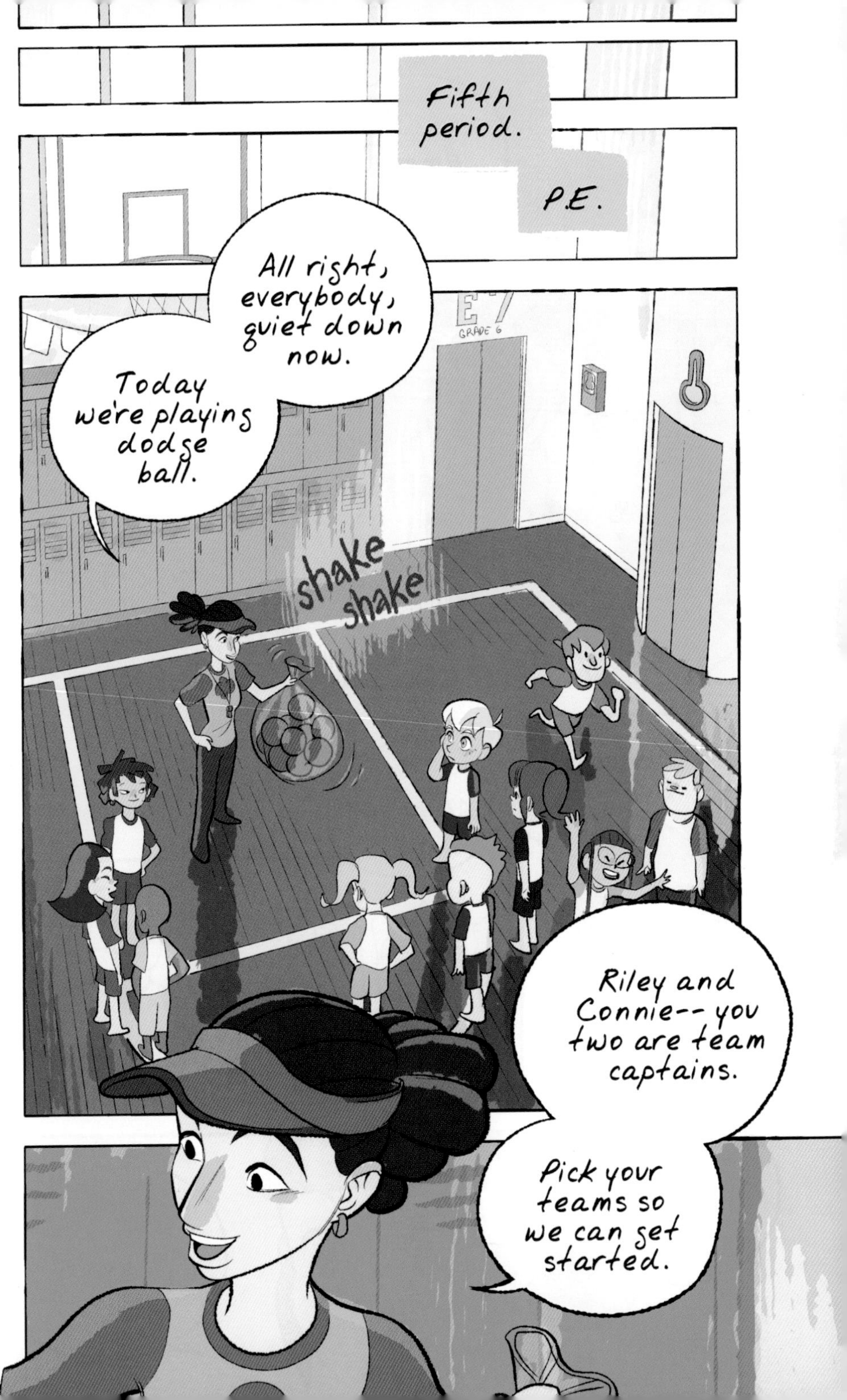
Fifth period.
P.E.
All right, everybody, quiet down now.
Today we're playing dodge ball.
GRADE 6
shake shake
Riley and Connie-- you two are team captains.
Pick your teams so we can get started.

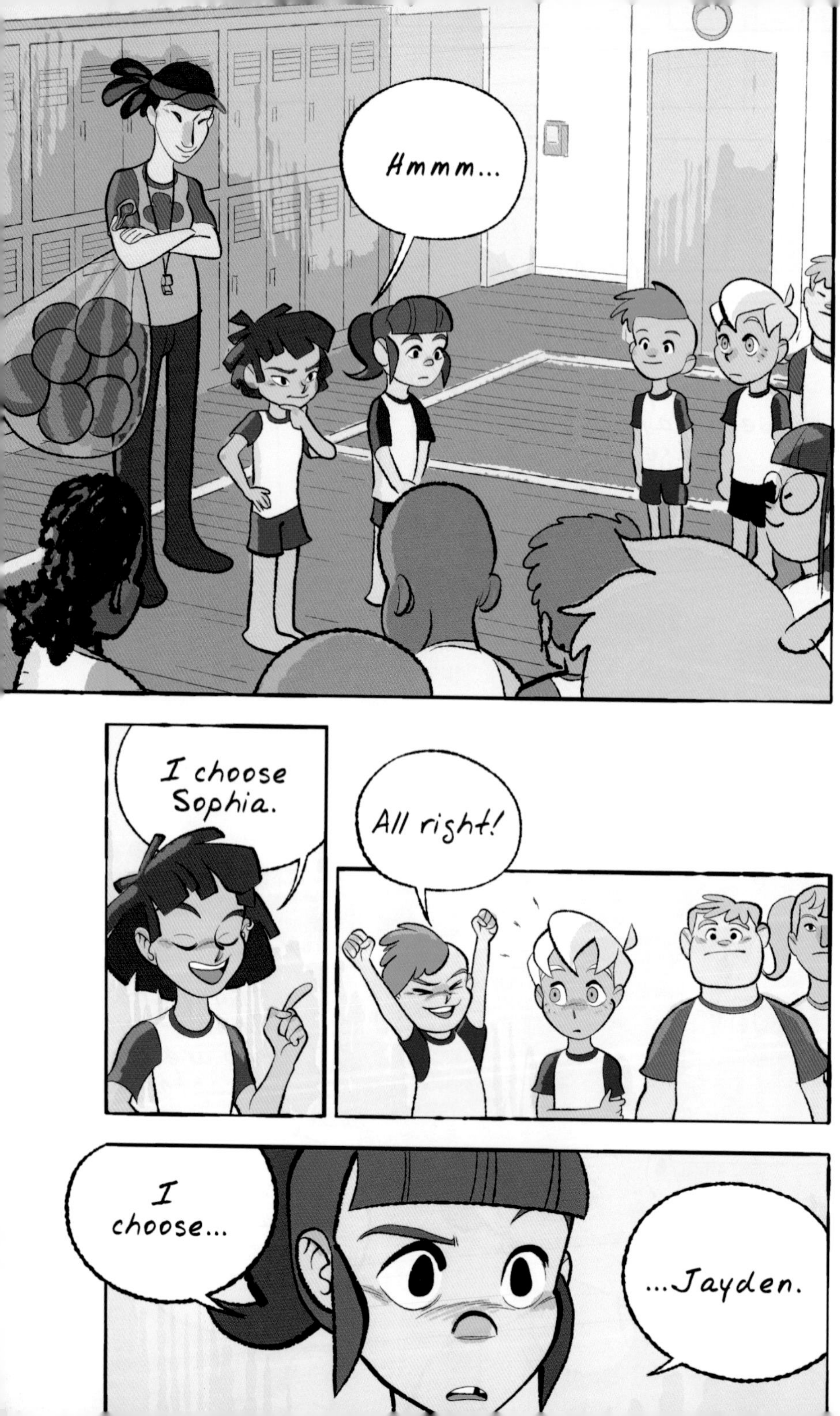
Hmmm...
I choose Sophia.
All right!
I choose...
...Jayden.

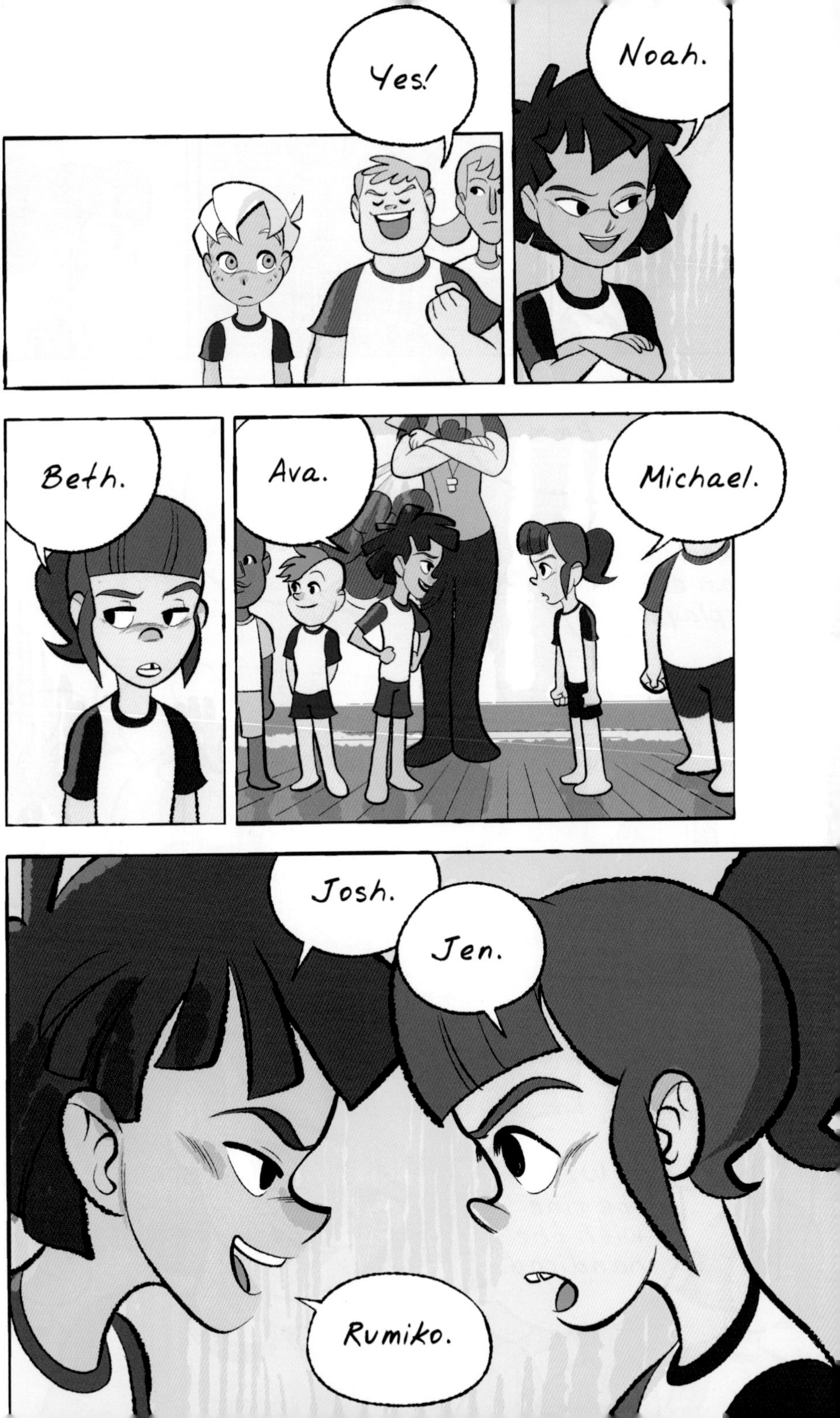
Yes!
Noah.
Beth.
Ava.
Michael.
Josh.
Jen.
Rumiko.

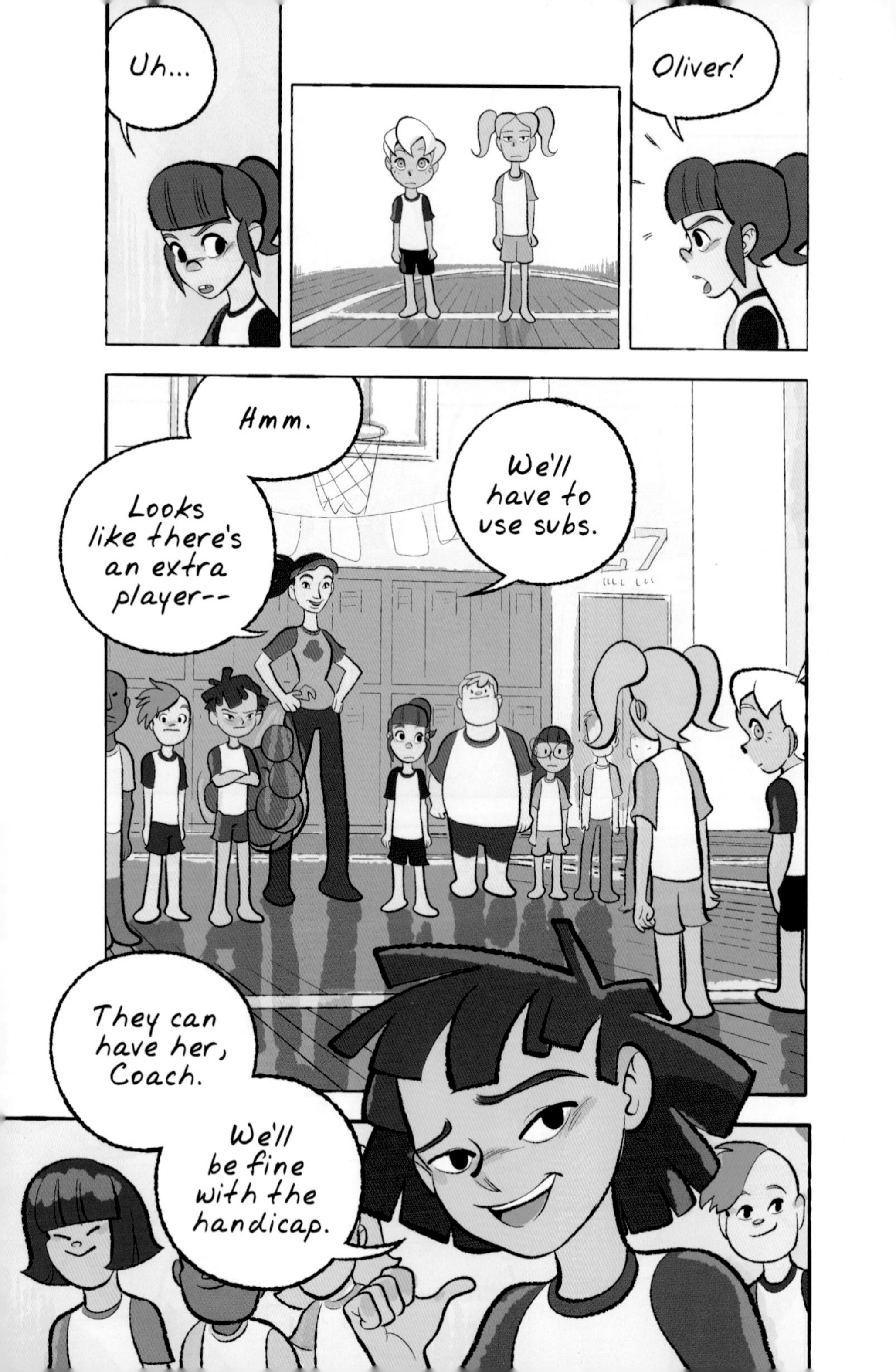
Uh...
Oliver!
Hmm.
Looks like there's an extra player--
We'll have to use subs.
They can have her, Coach.
We'll be fine with the handicap.

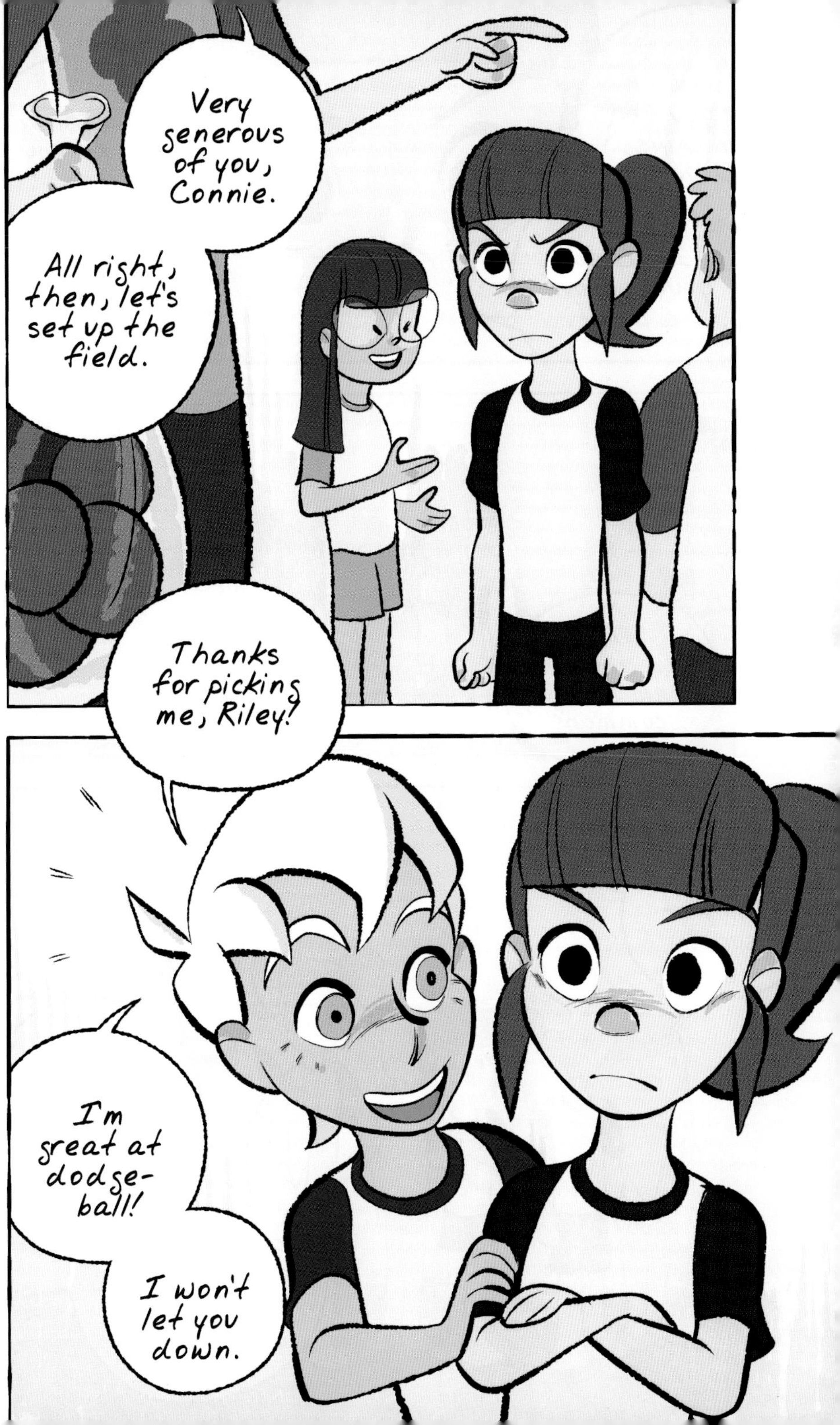
Very senerous of you, Connie.
All right, then, let's set up the field.
Thanks for picking me, Riley!
I'm great at dodge-ball!
I won't let you down.

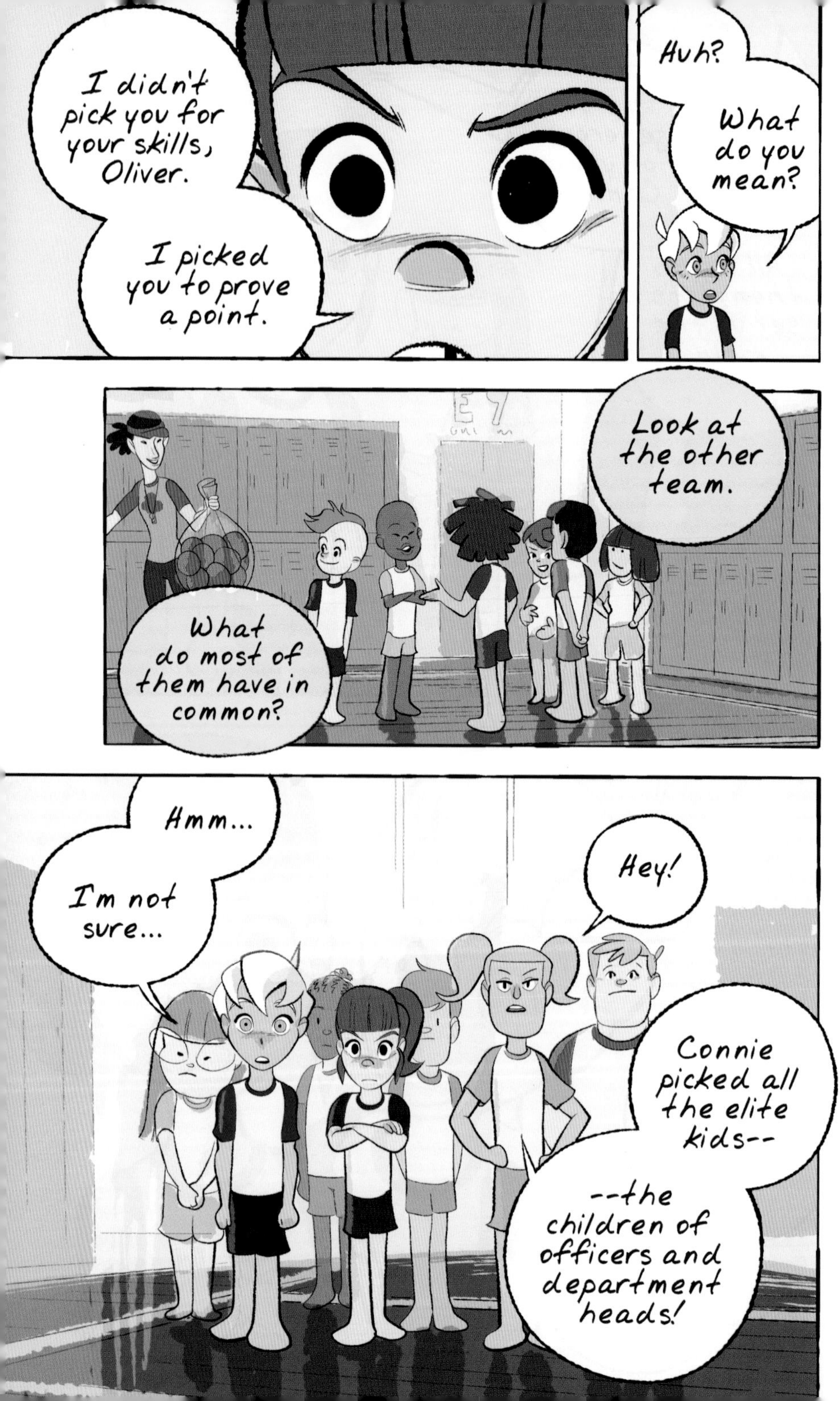
I didn't pick you for your skills, Oliver.
I picked you to prove a point.
Huh?
What do you mean?
Look at the other team.
What do most of them have in common?
Hmm...
I'm not sure...
Hey!
Connie picked all the elite kids--
--the children of officers and department heads!

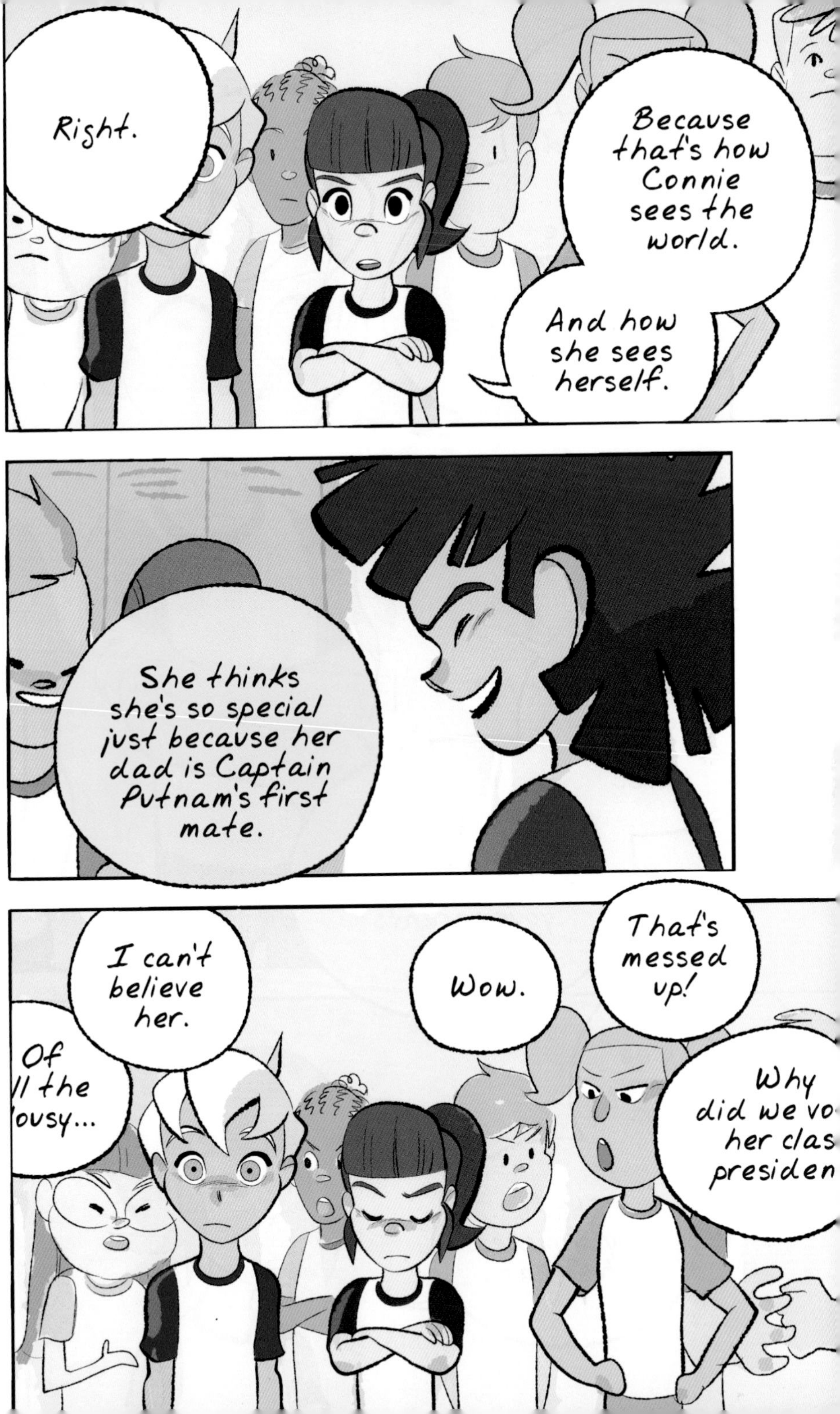
Right.
Because that's how Connie sees the world.
And how she sees herself.
She thinks she's so special just because her dad is Captain Putnam's first mate.
I can't believe her.
Wow.
That's messed up!
Of ll the ousy...
Why did we vo her clas presiden

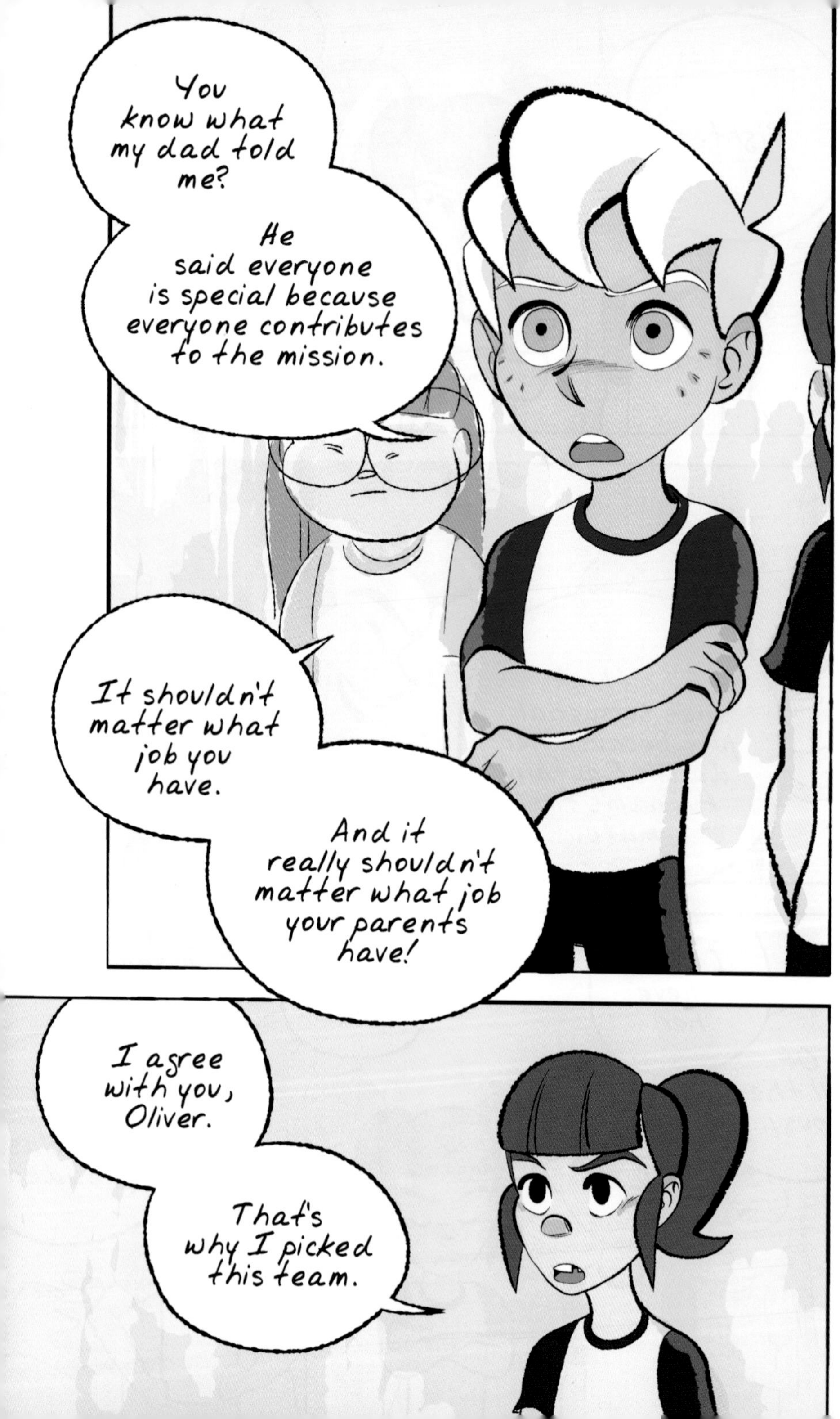
You know what my dad told me?
He said everyone is special because everyone contributes to the mission.
It shouldn't matter what job you have.
And it really shouldn't matter what job your parents have!
I agree with you, Oliver.
That's why I picked this team.

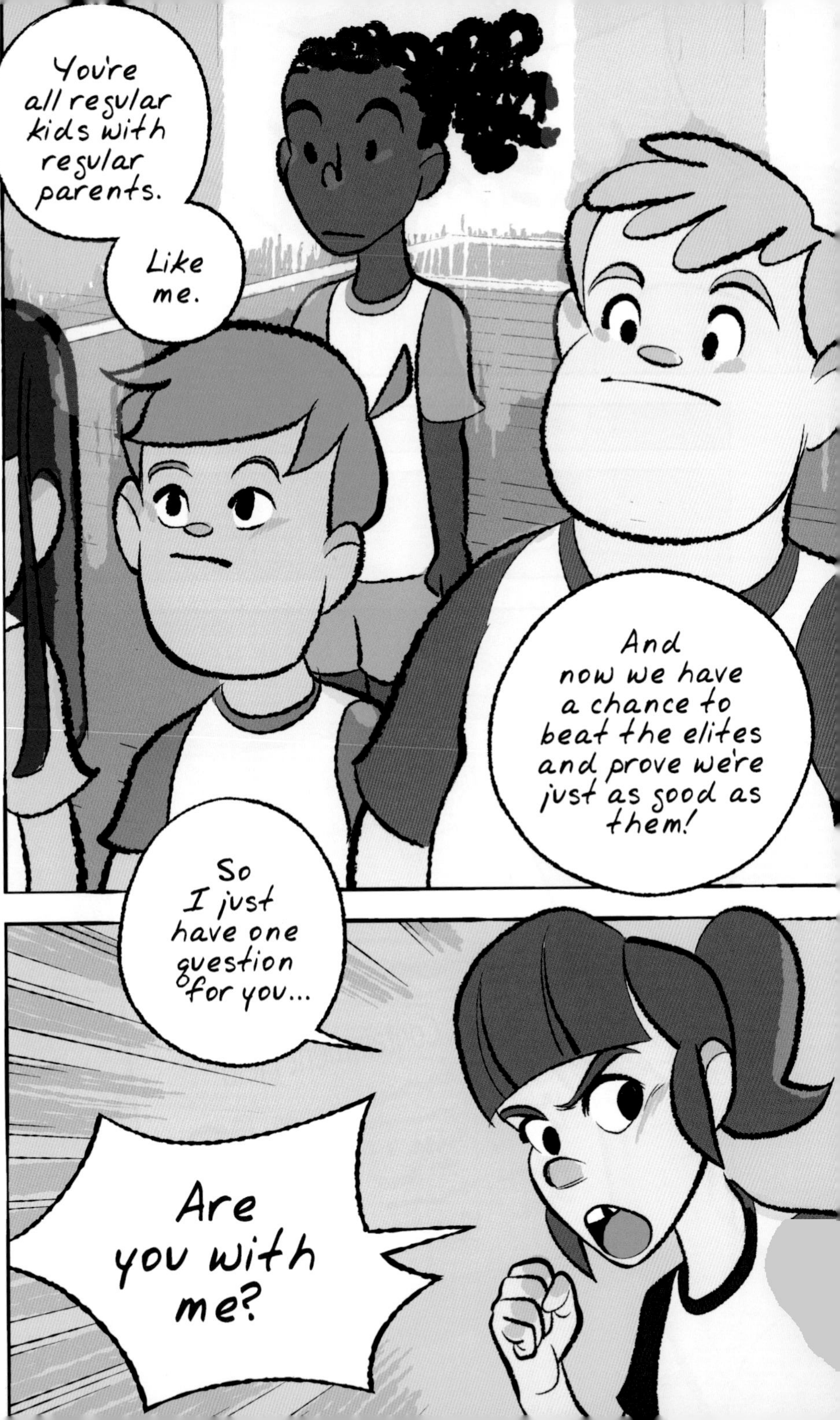
You're all regular kids with regular parents.
Like me.
And now we have a chance to beat the elites and prove we're just as good as them!
So I just have one question for you...
Are you with me?

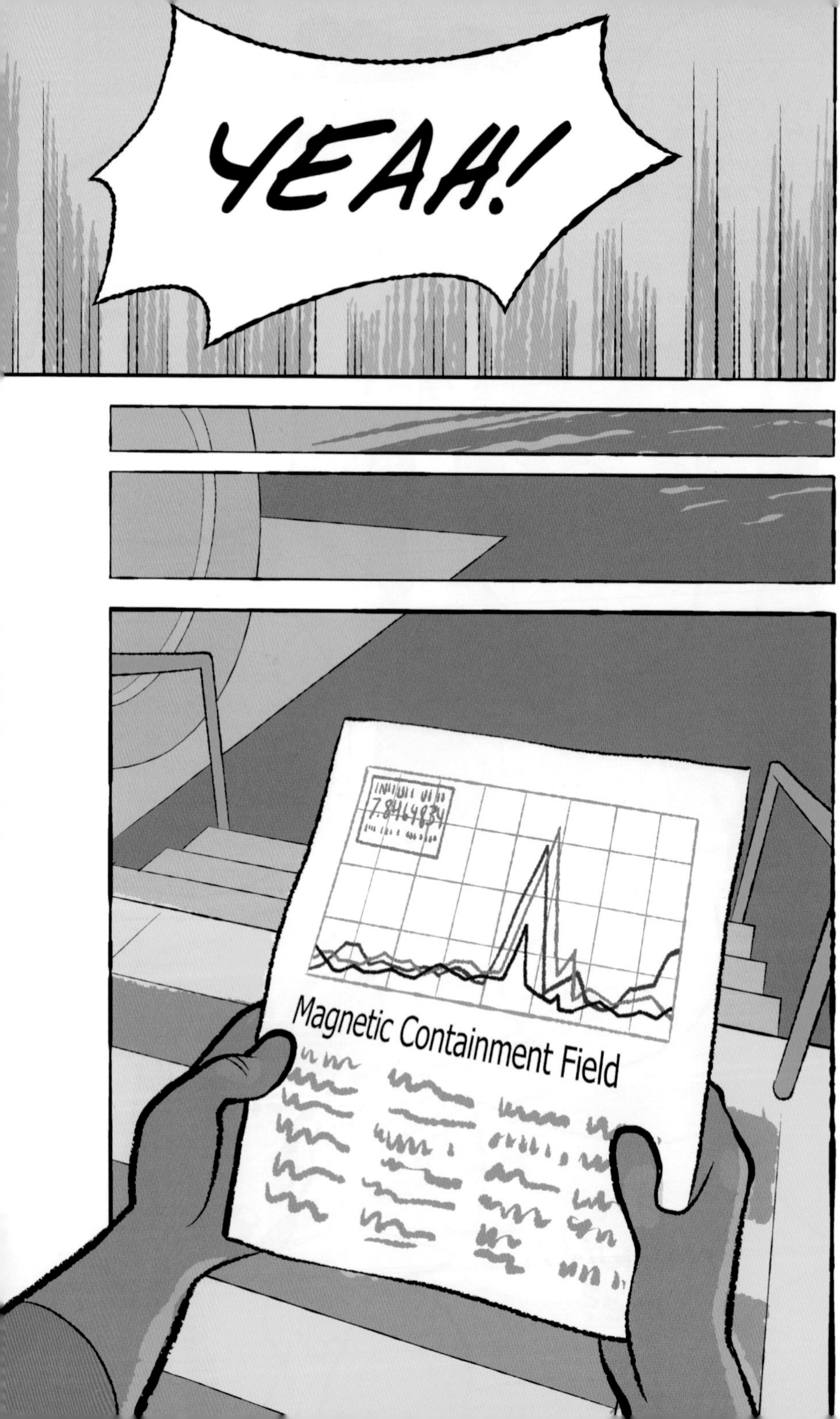
YEAH!
Magnetic Containment Field

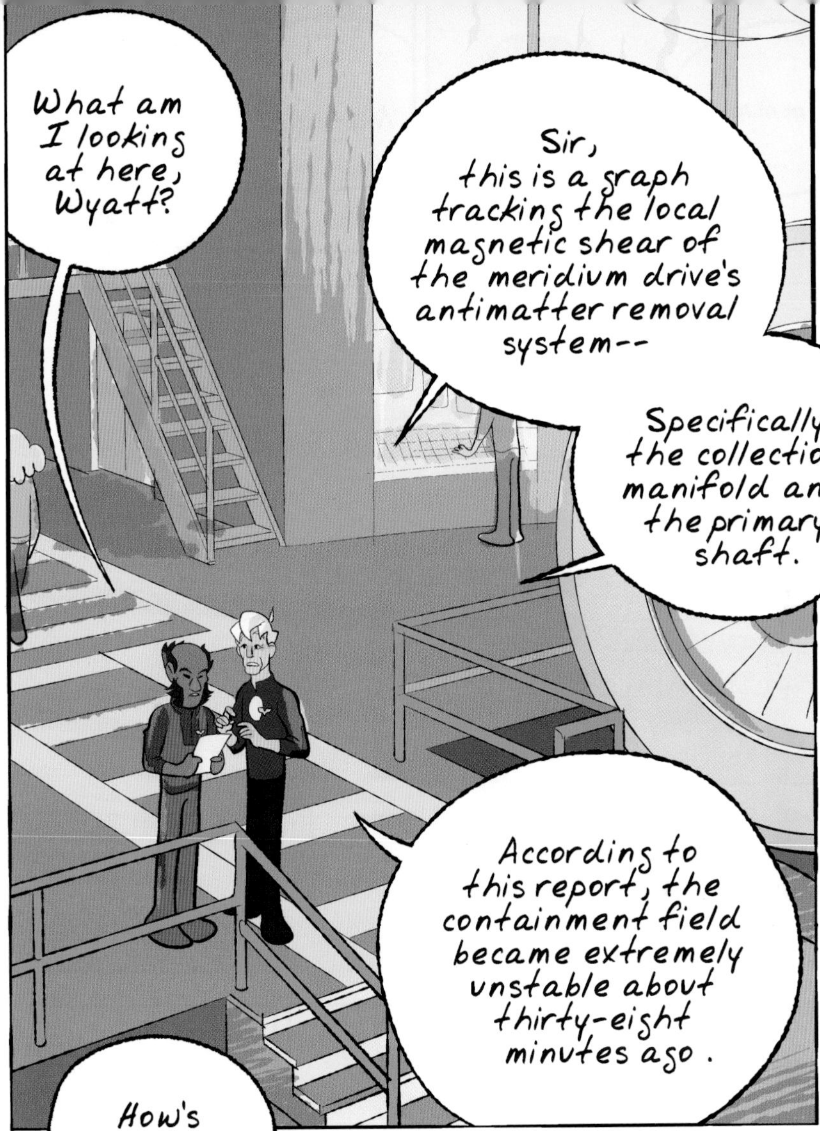
What am I looking at here, Wyatt?
Sir, this is a graph tracking the local magnetic shear of the meridium drive's antimatter removal system--
Specifically the collection manifold and the primary shaft.
According to this report, the containment field became extremely unstable about thirty-eight minutes ago.
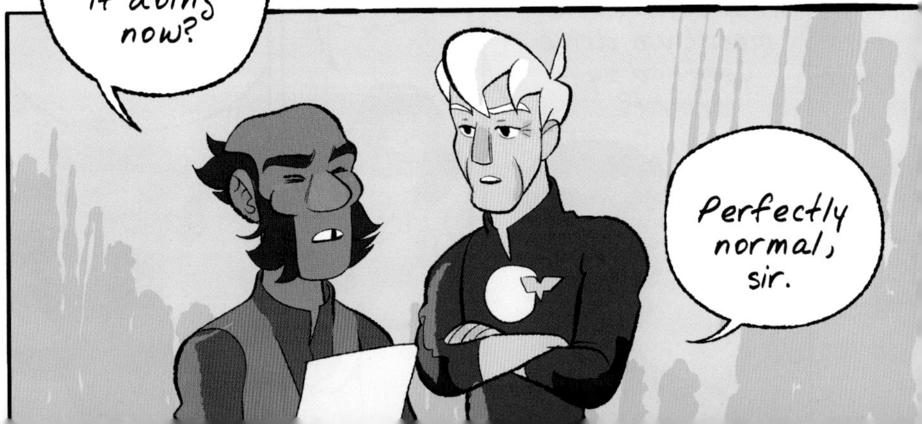
How's it doing now?
Perfectly normal, sir.

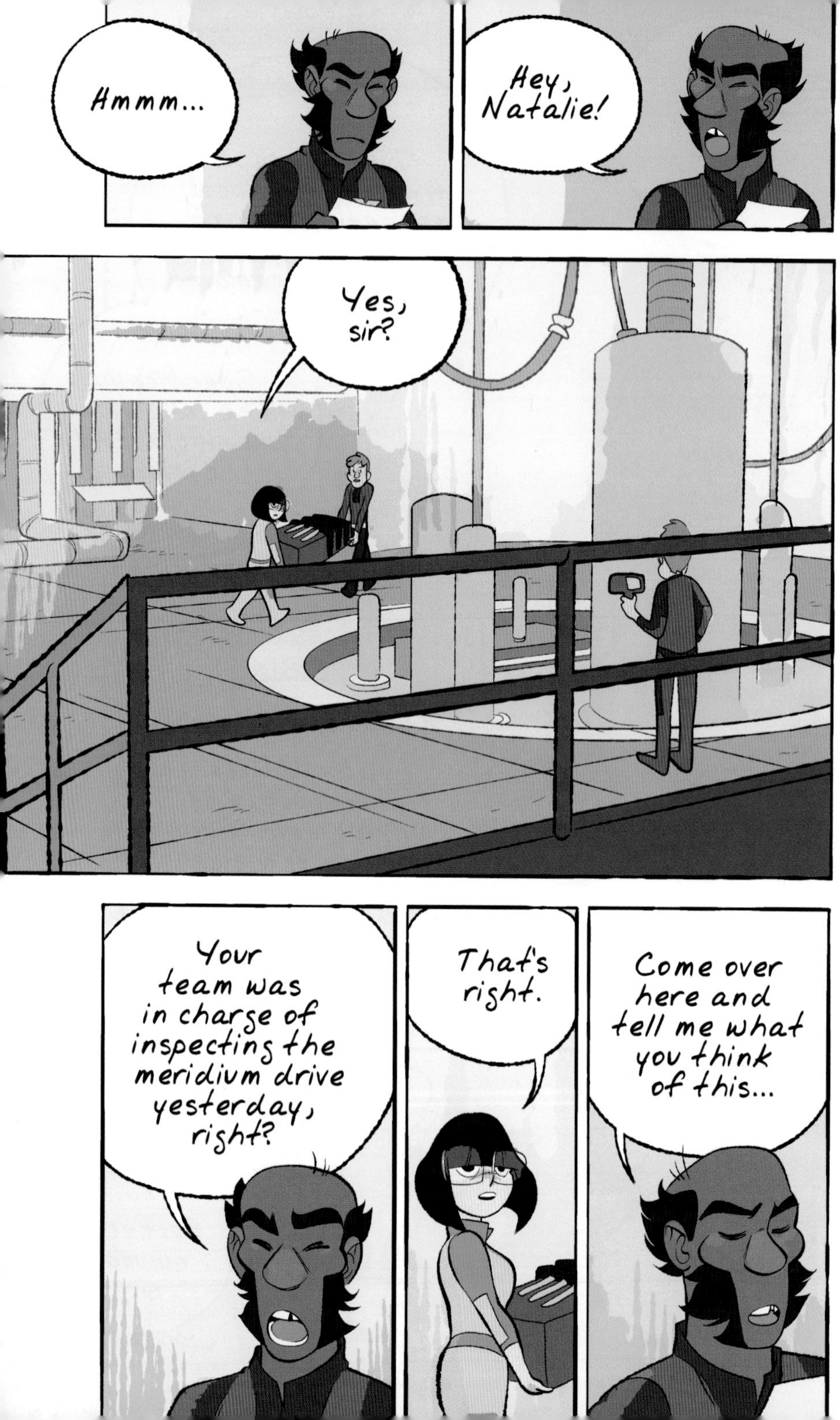
Hmmm...
Hey, Natalie!
Yes, sir?
Your team was in charge of inspecting the meridium drive yesterday, right?
That's right.
Come over here and tell me what you think of this...

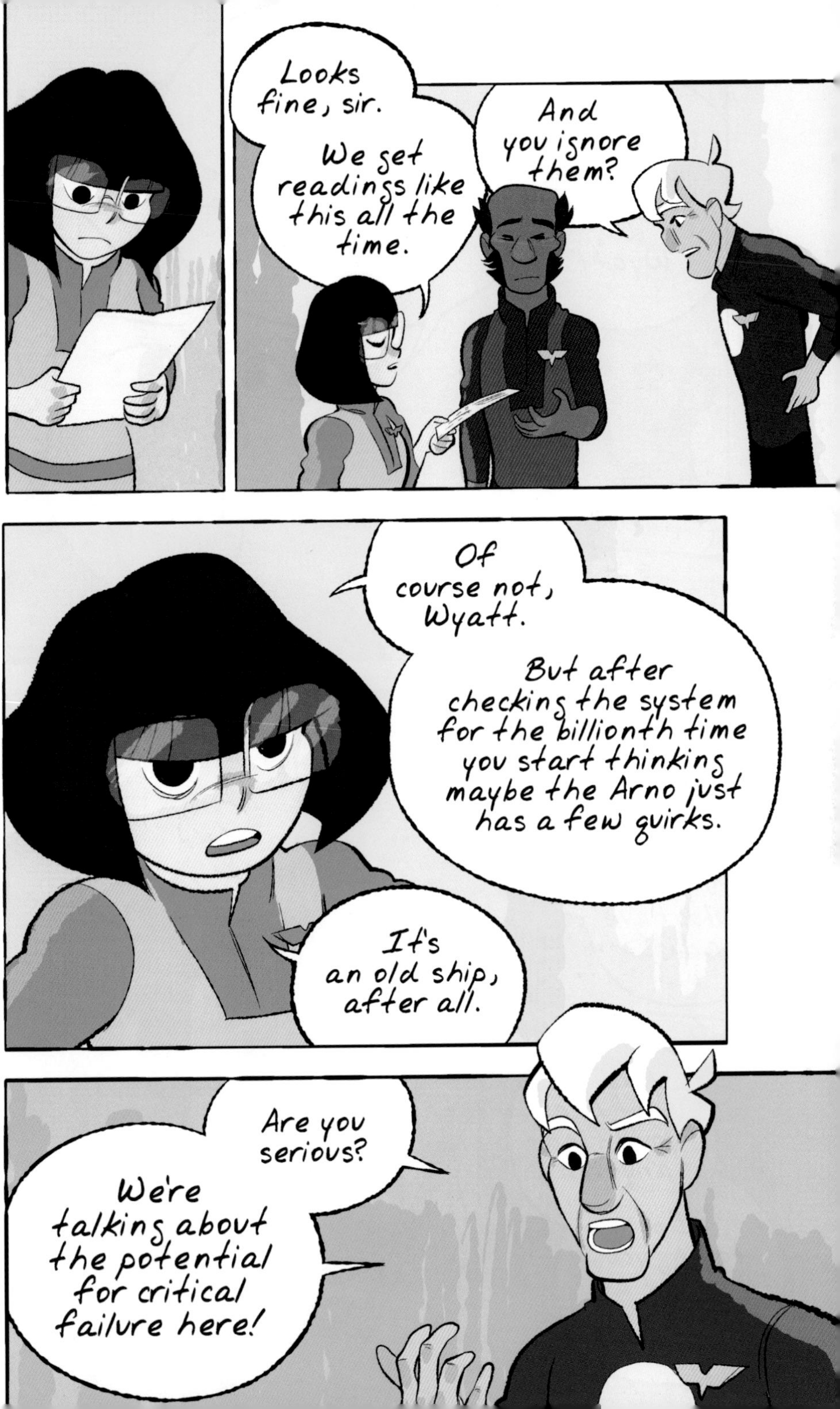
Looks fine, sir.
We get readings like this all the time.
And you ignore them?
Of course not, Wyatt.
But after checking the system for the billionth time you start thinking maybe the Arno just has a few quirks.
It's an old ship, after all.
Are you serious?
We're talking about the potential for critical failure here!

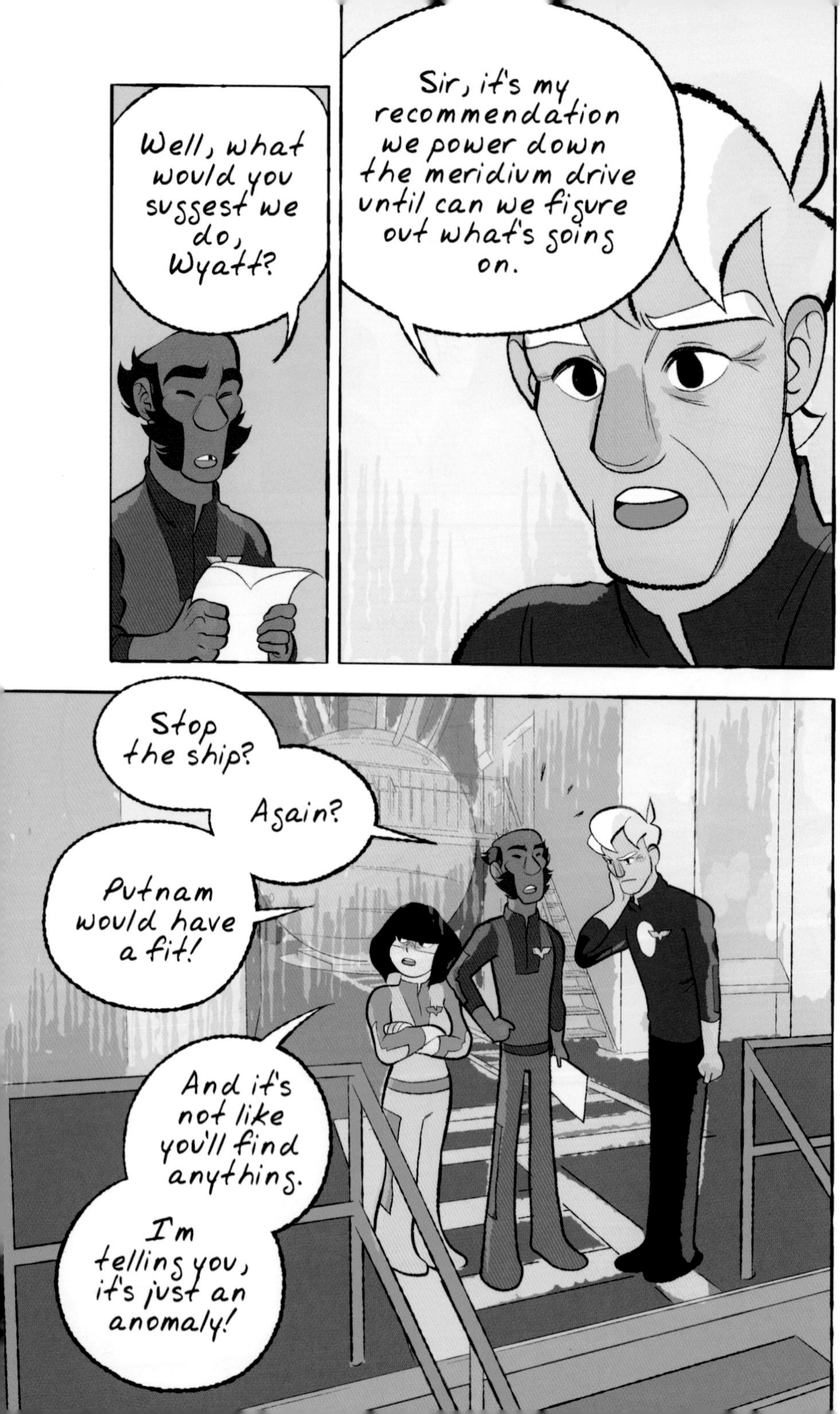
Well, what would you suggest we do, Wyatt?
Sir, it's my recommendation we power down the meridium drive until can we figure out what's going on.
Stop the ship?
Again?
Putnam would have a fit!
And it's not like you'll find anything.
I'm telling you, it's just an anomaly!

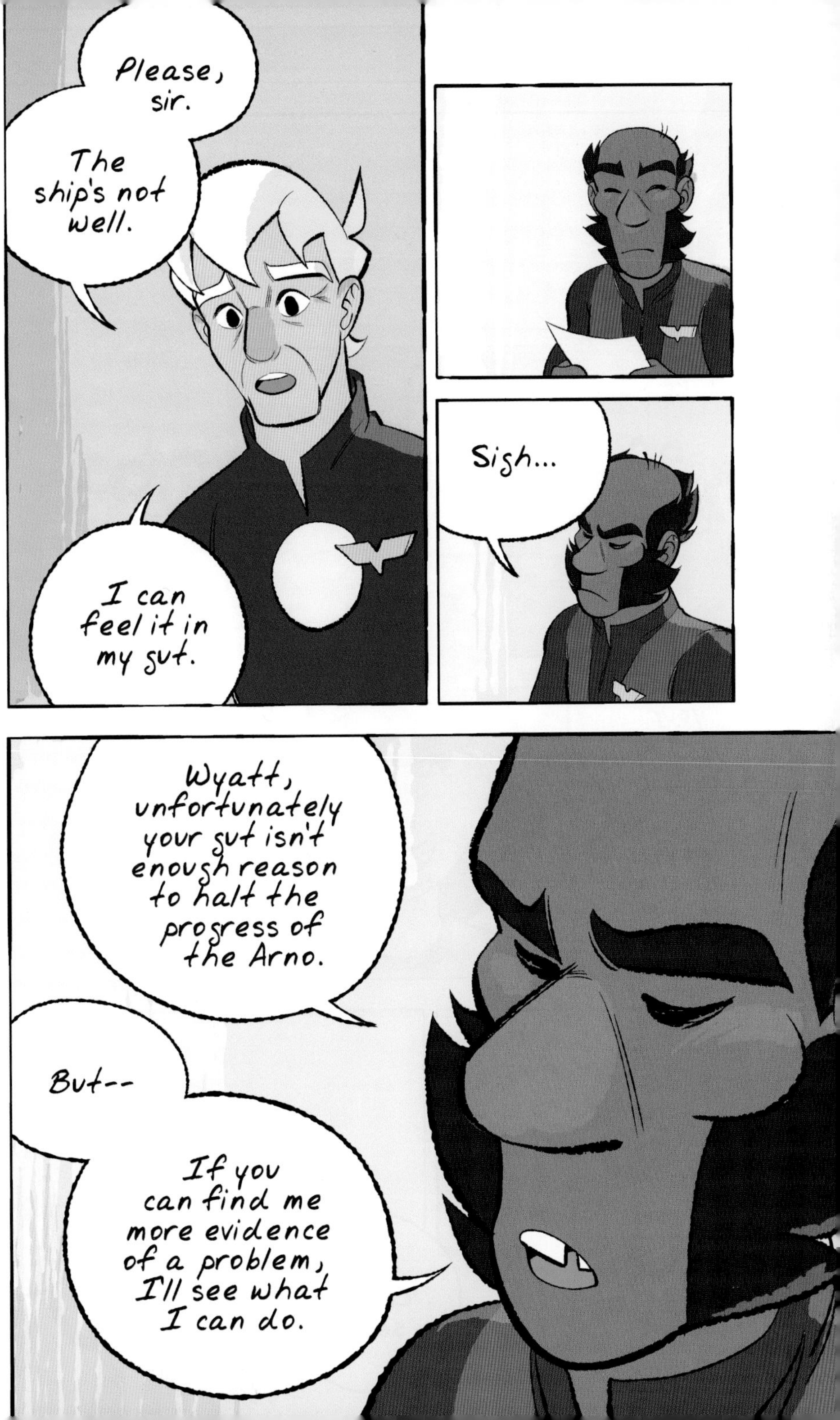
Please, sir.
The ship's not well.
I can feel it in my gut.
Sigh...
Wyatt, unfortunately your gut isn't enough reason to halt the progress of the Arno.
But--
If you can find me more evidence of a problem, I'll see what I can do.

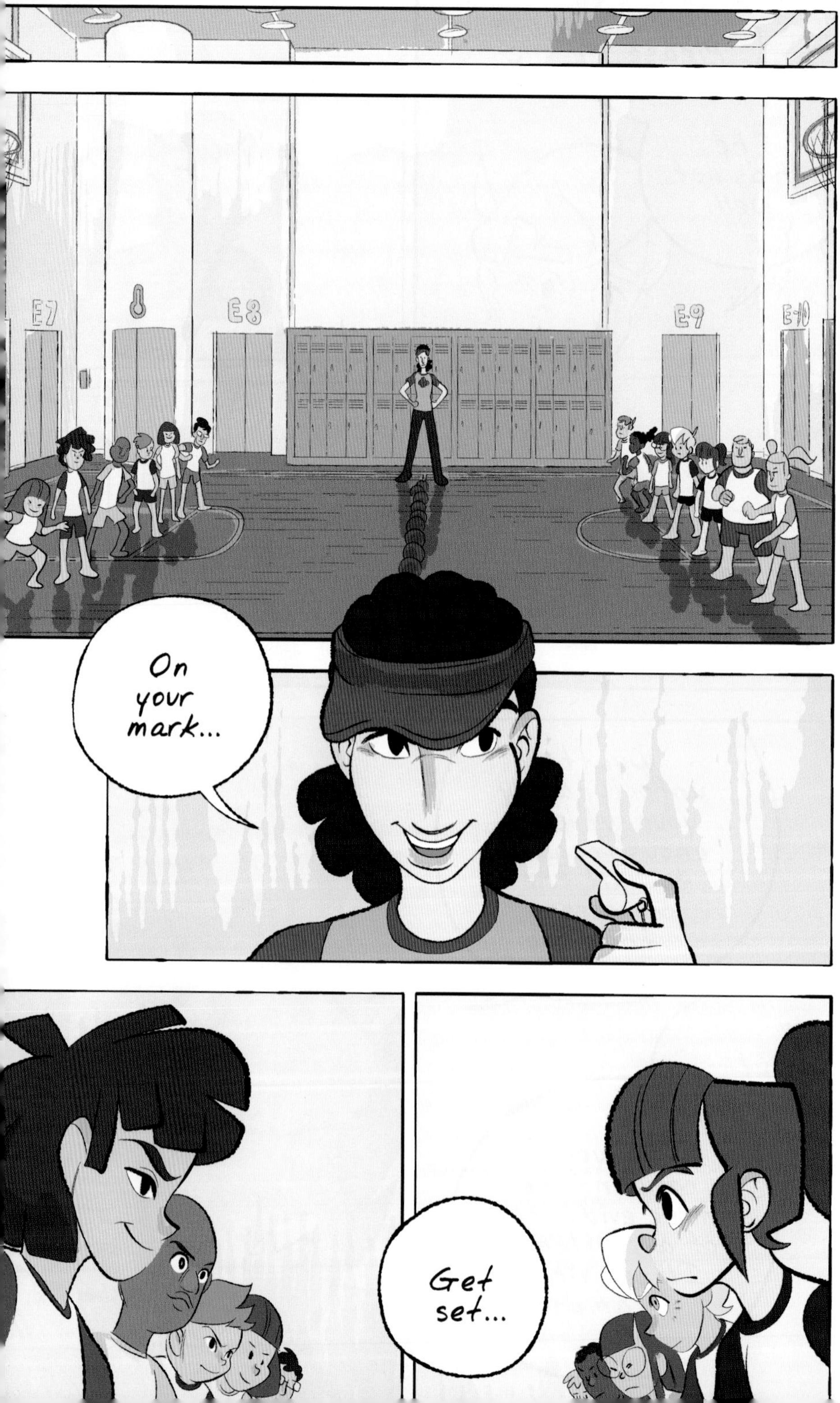
E7
E8
E9
E-10
On your mark...
Get set...

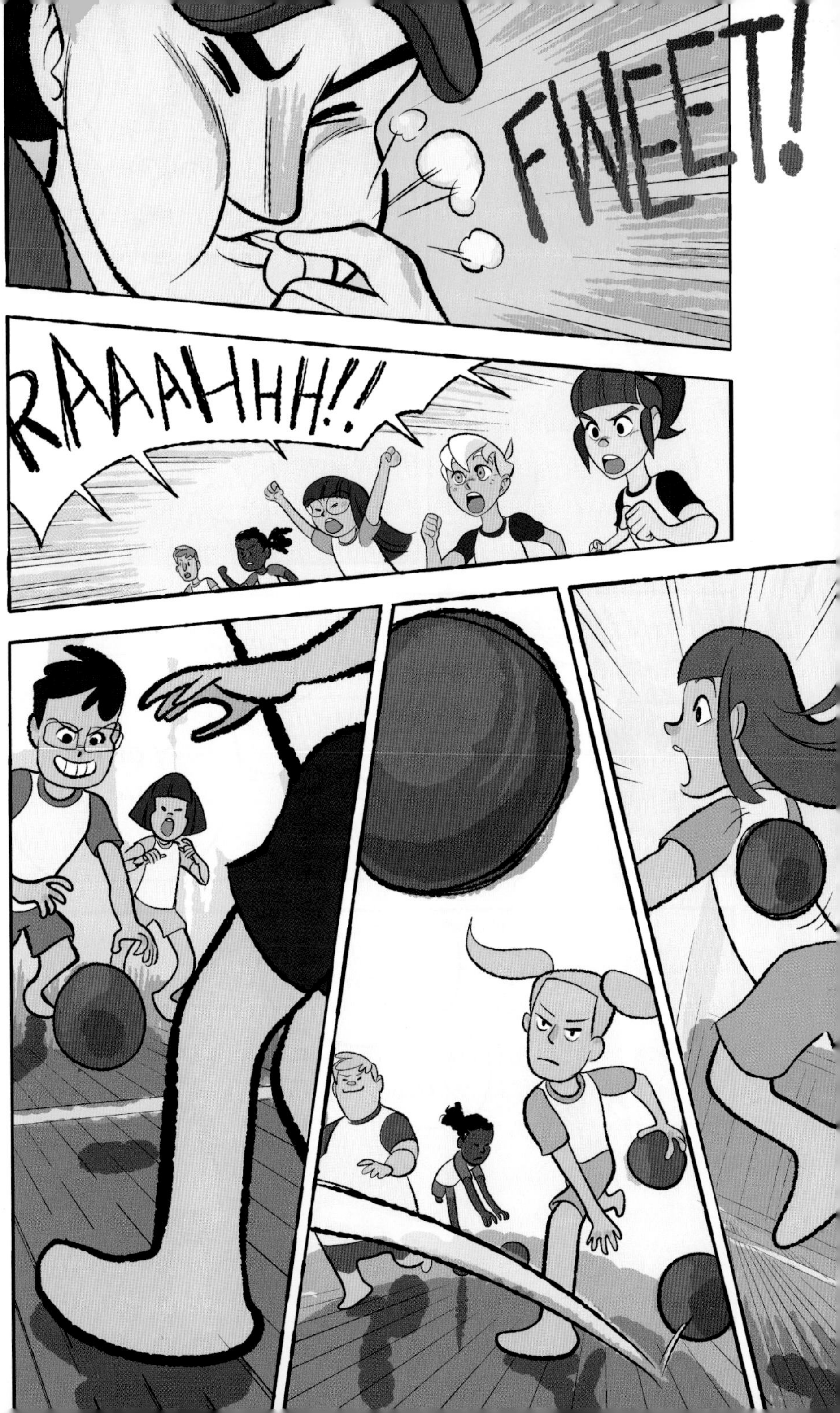
FWEET!
RAAAHHH!!

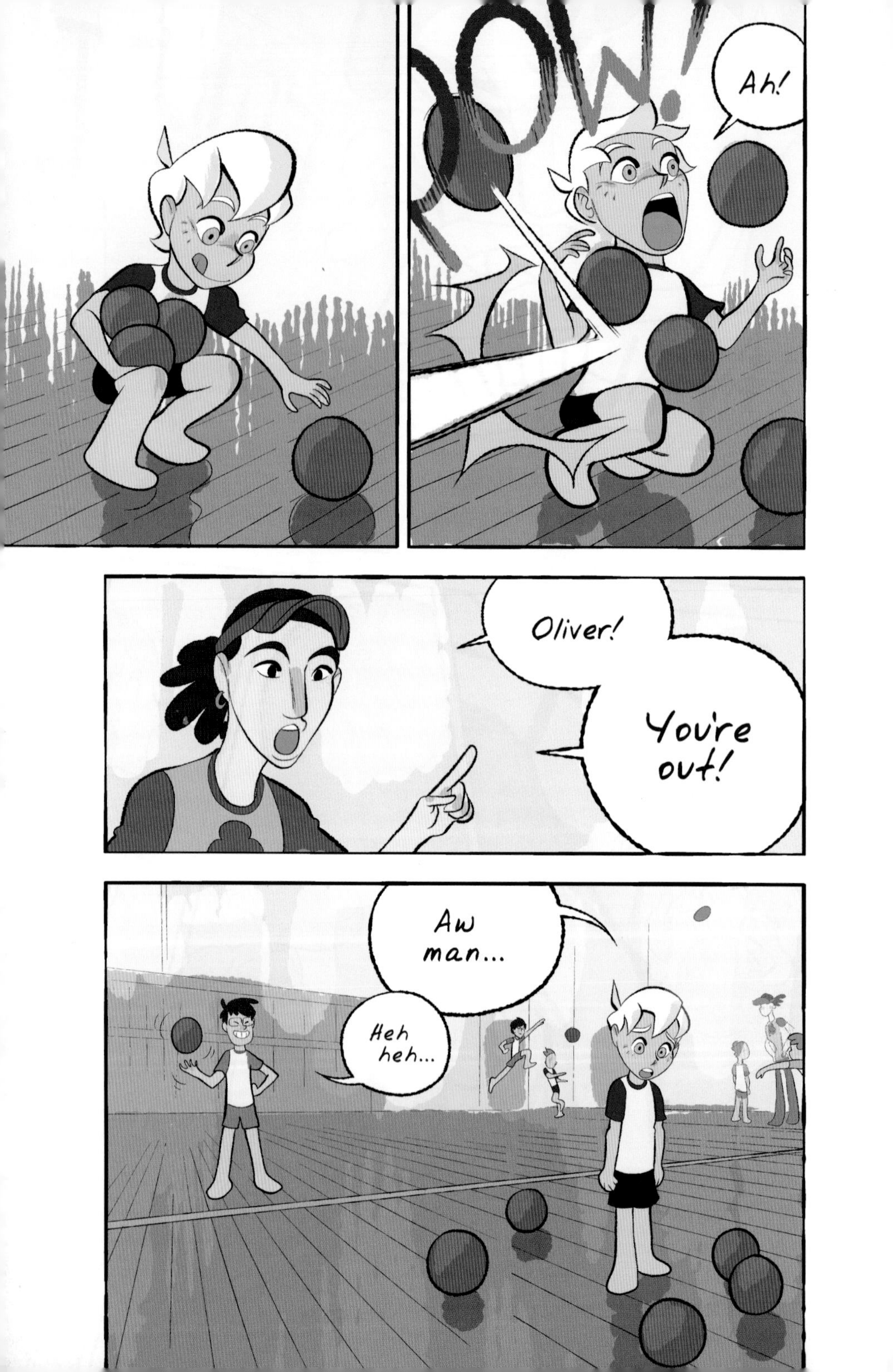
POW!
Ah!
Oliver!
You're out!
Aw man...
Heh heh...

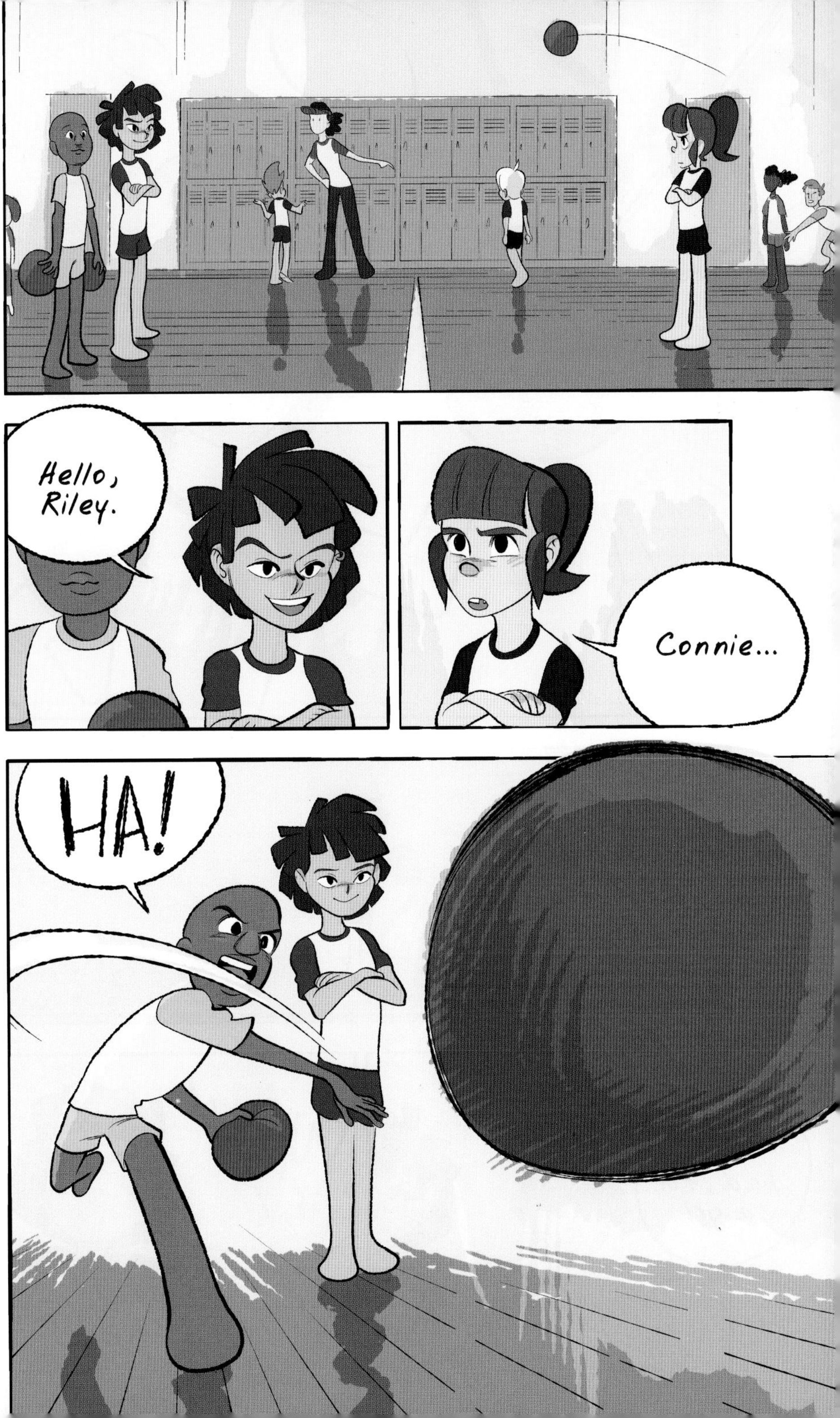
Hello, Riley.
Connie...
HA!

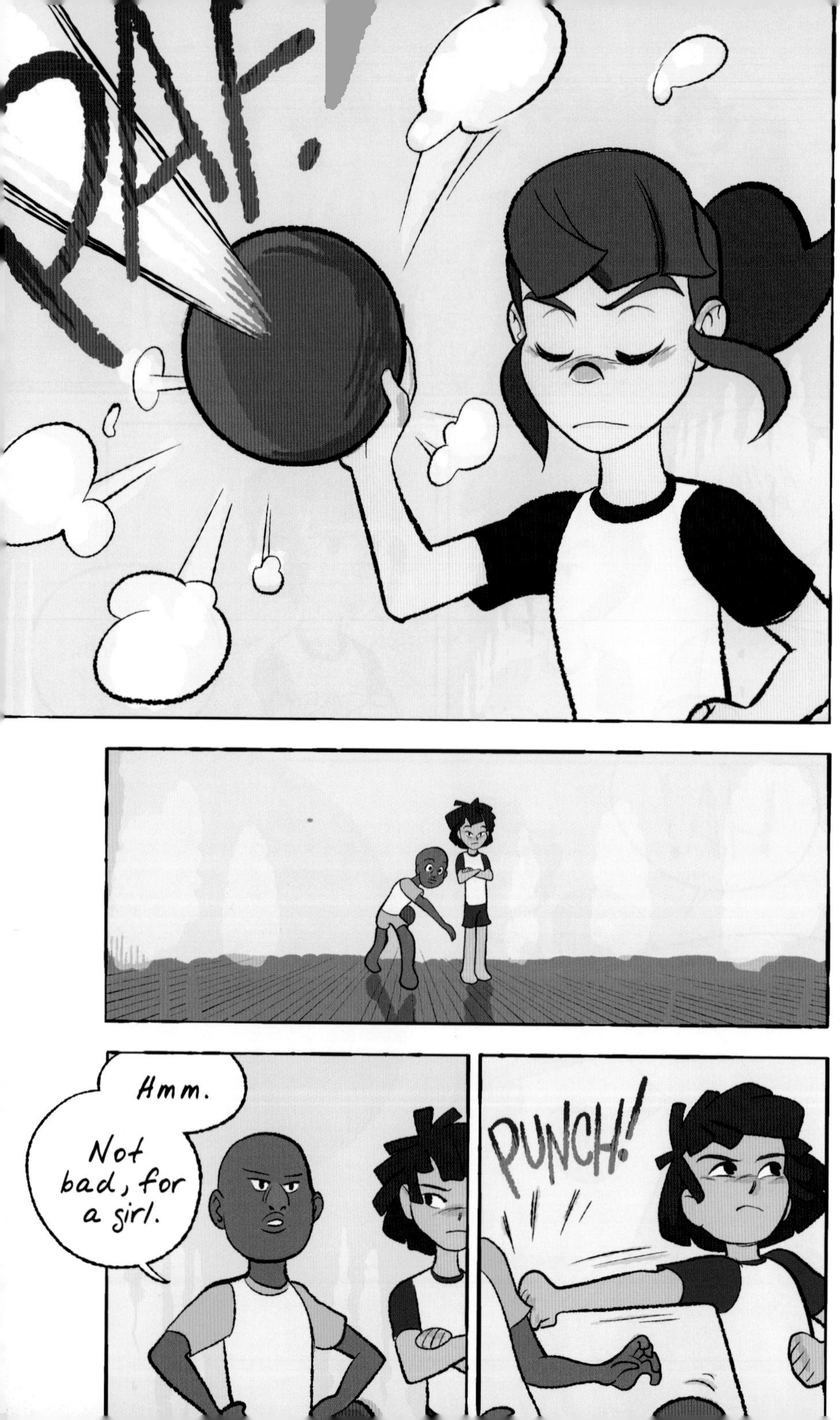
PAF!
Hmm.
Not bad, for a girl.
PUNCH!

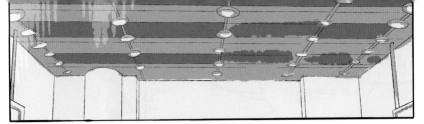

Oliver, you're back in.

Riley caught my ball, so I'm out and you're in.

Don't you know the rules?

What?

Oh... Oh, right!

Thanks, Noah!

Whatever.

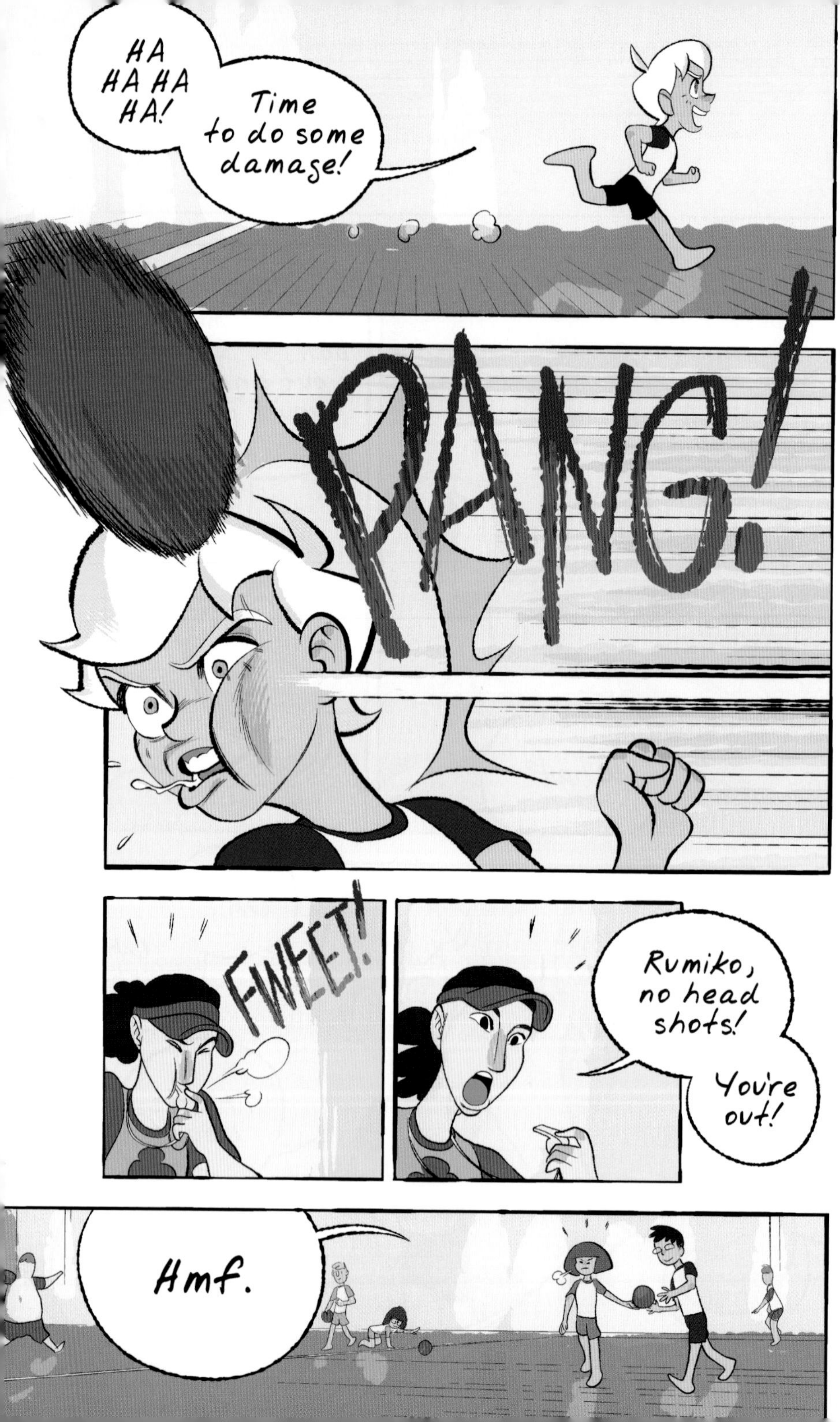
HA HA HA HA!
Time to do some damage!
PANG!
FWEET!
Rumiko, no head shots!
You're out!
Hmf.

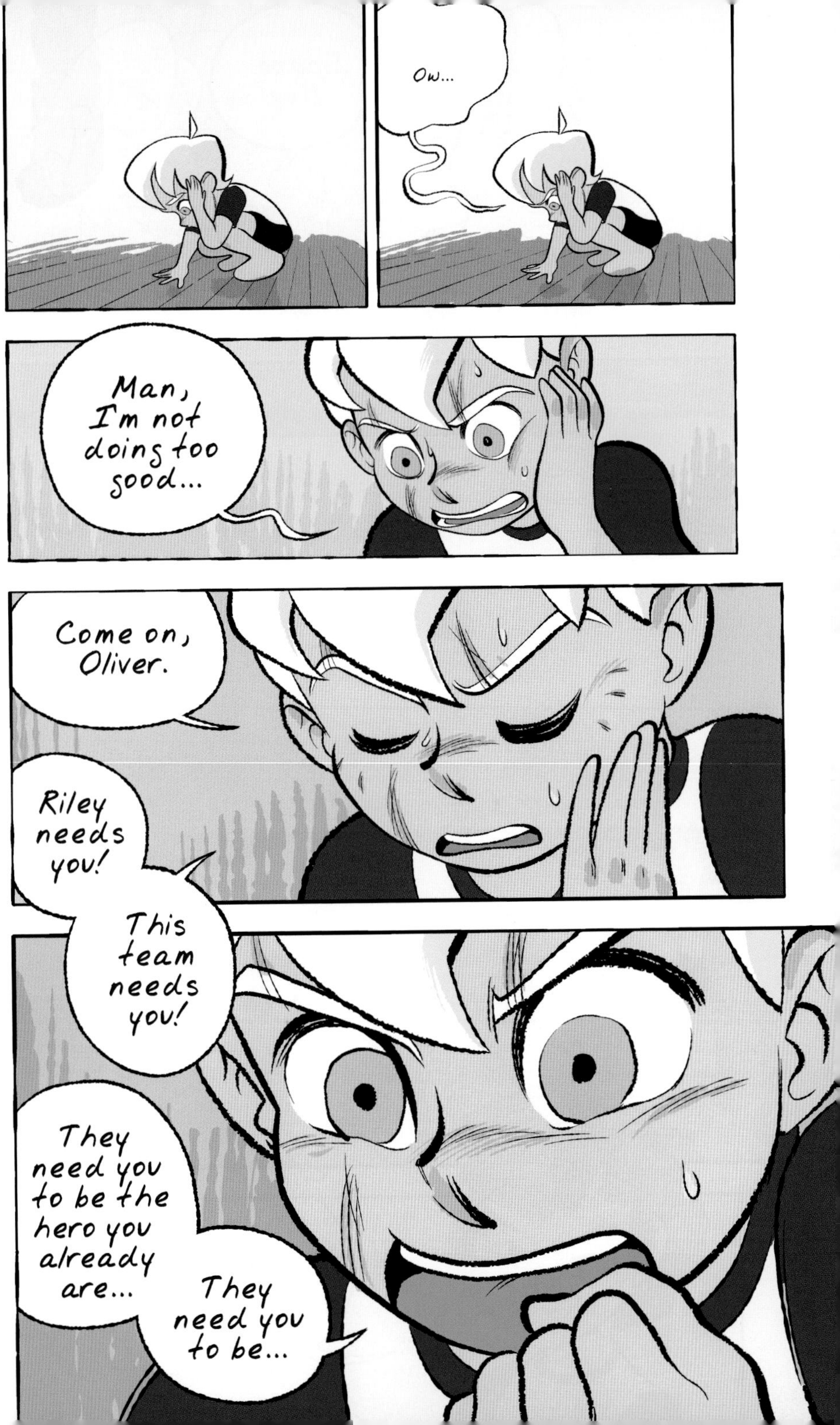

Ow...
Man, I'm not doing too good...
Come on, Oliver.
Riley needs you!
This team needs you!
They need you to be the hero you already are...
They need you to be...

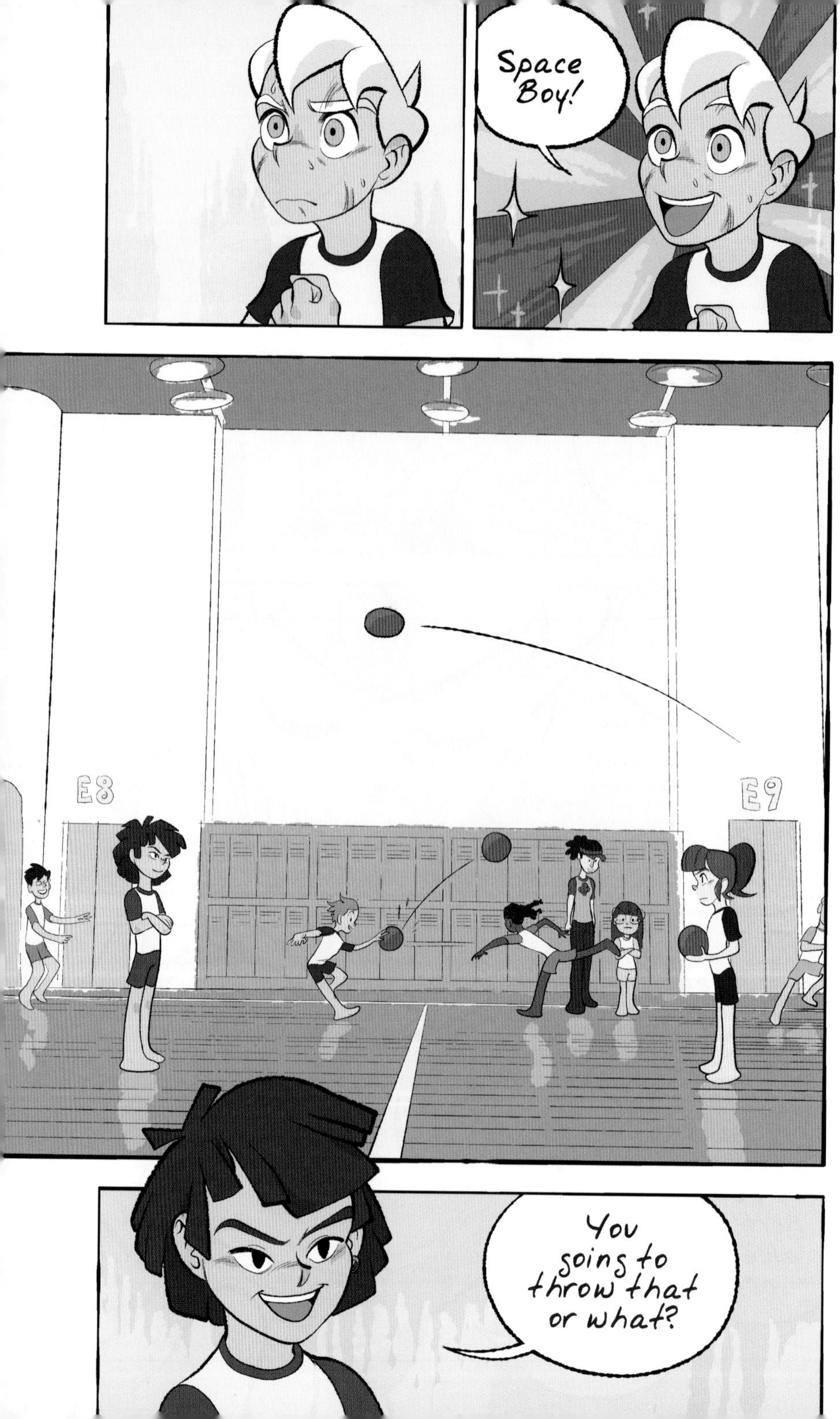
Space Boy!
E8
E9
You goins to throw that or what?

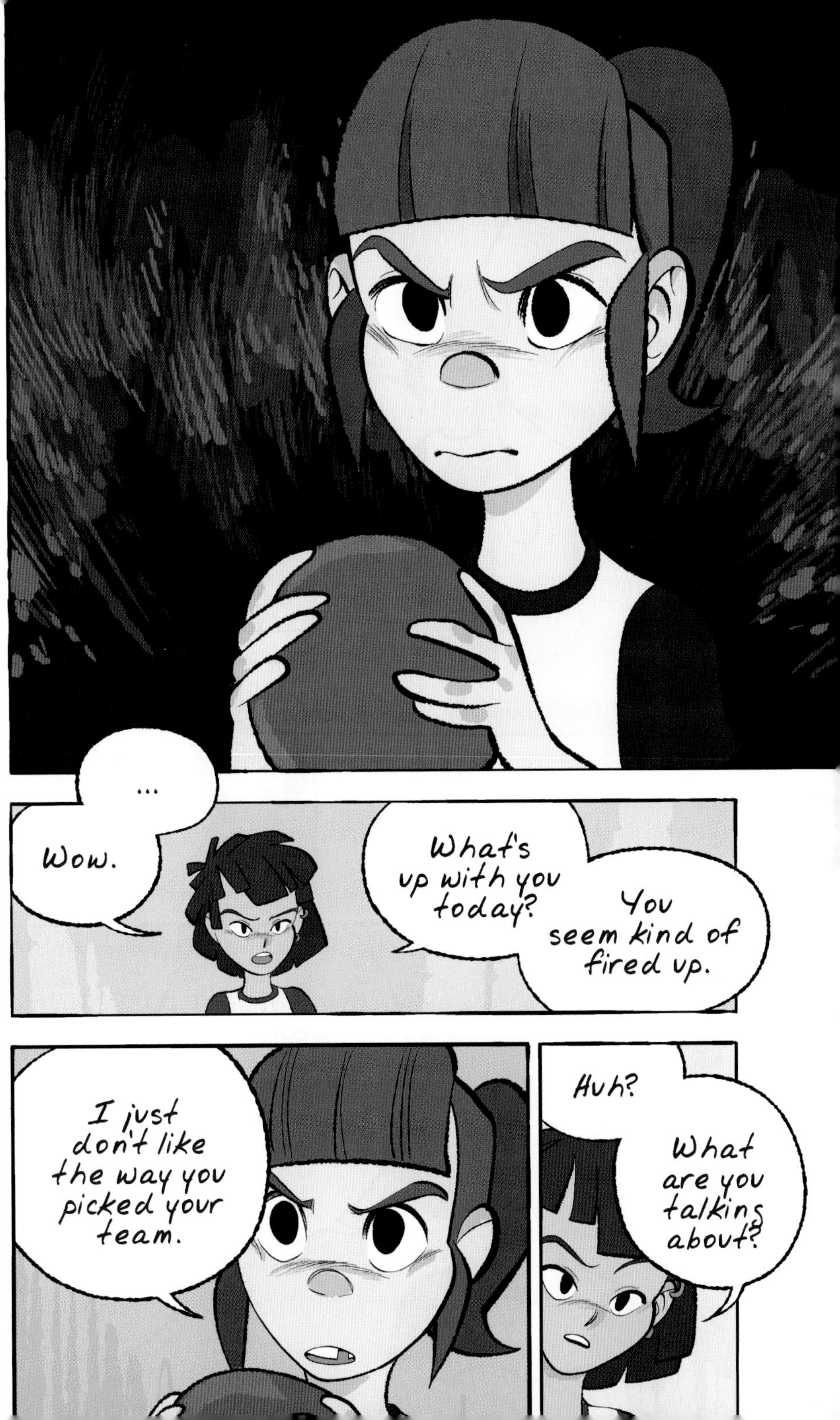
...
Wow.
What's up with you today?
You seem kind of fired up.
I just don't like the way you picked your team.
Huh?
What are you talking about?

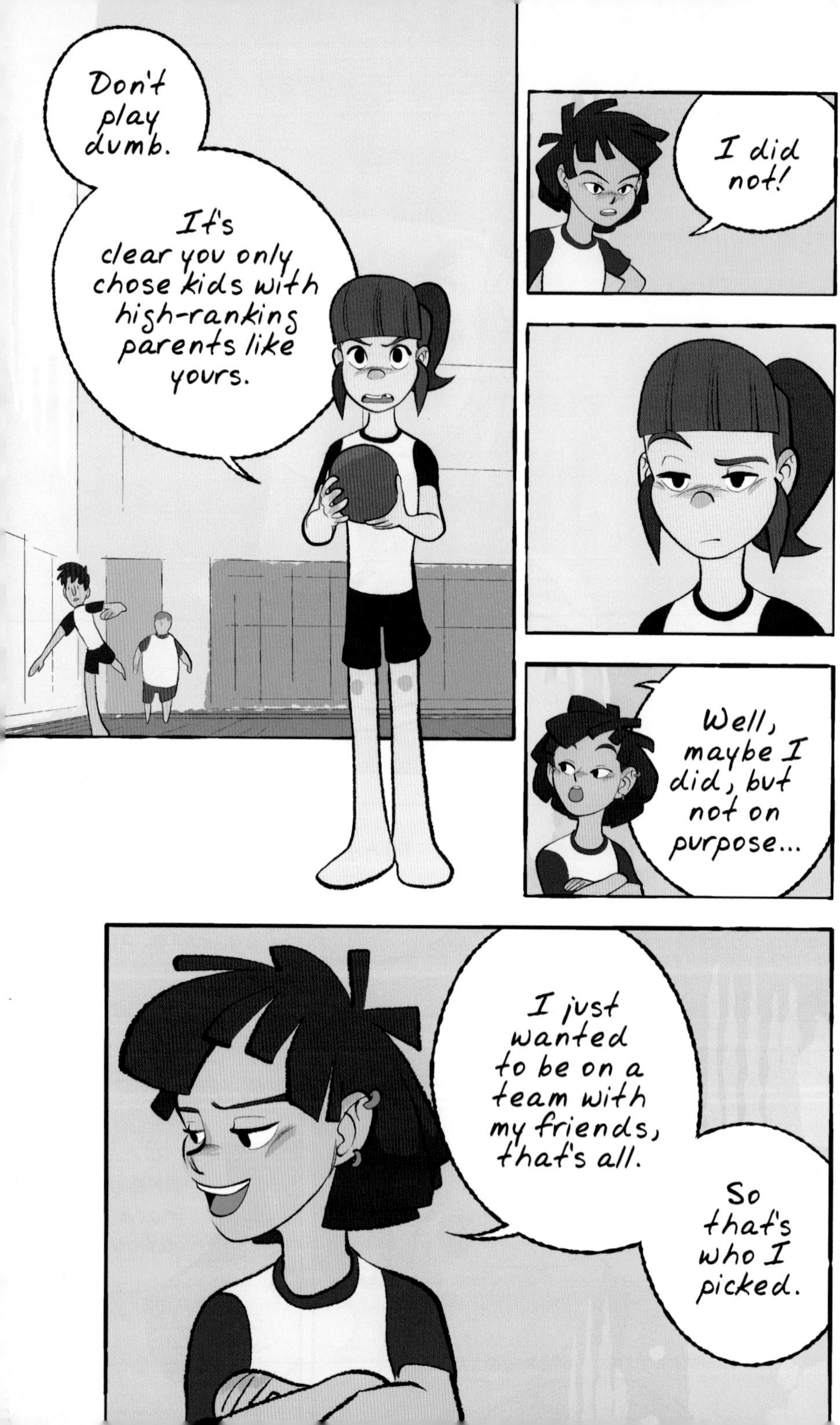
Don't play dumb.
It's clear you only chose kids with high-ranking parents like yours.
I did not!
Well, maybe I did, but not on purpose...
I just wanted to be on a team with my friends, that's all.
So that's who I picked.

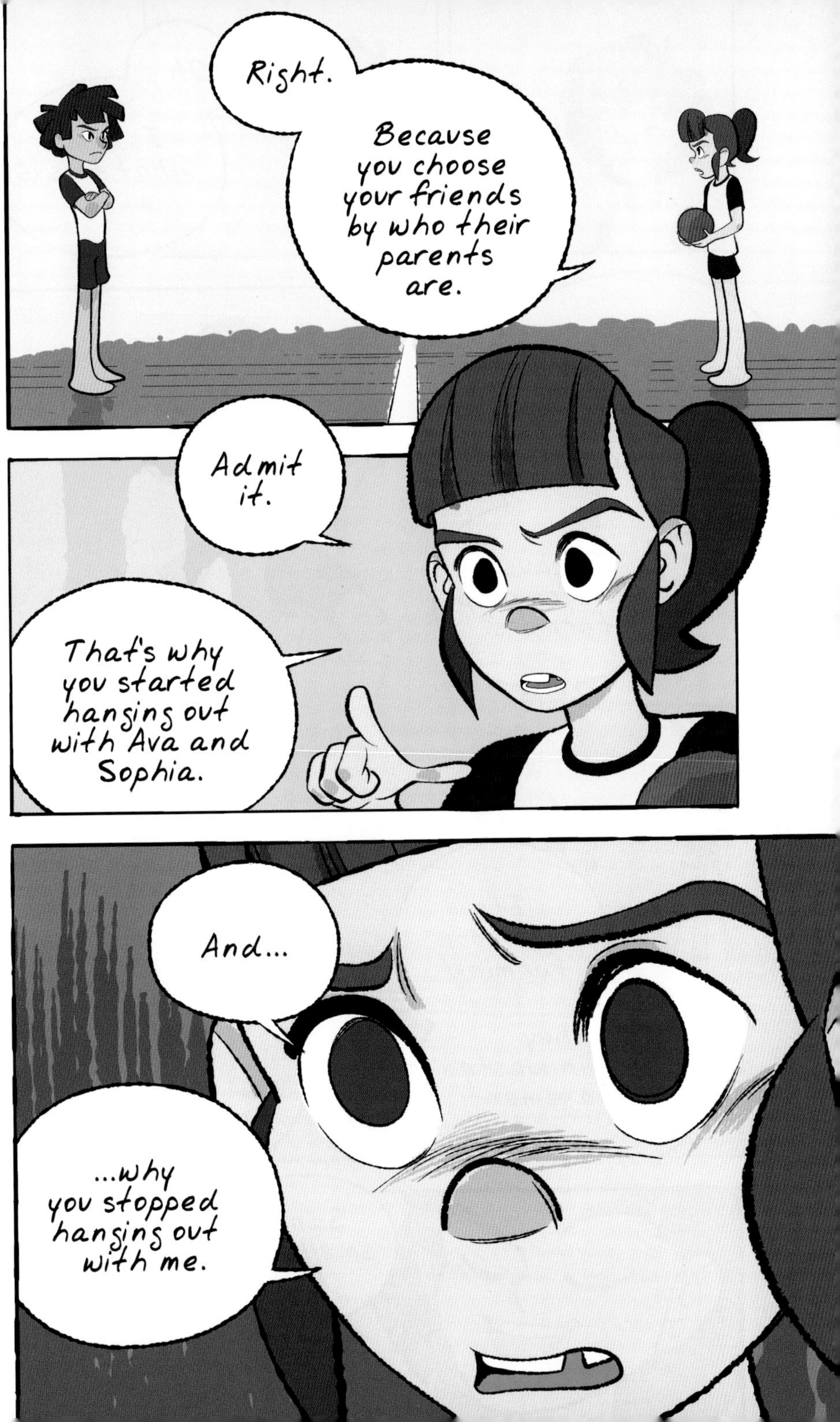
Right.
Because you choose your friends by who their parents are.
Admit it.
That's why you started hanging out with Ava and Sophia.
And...
...why you stopped hanging out with me.

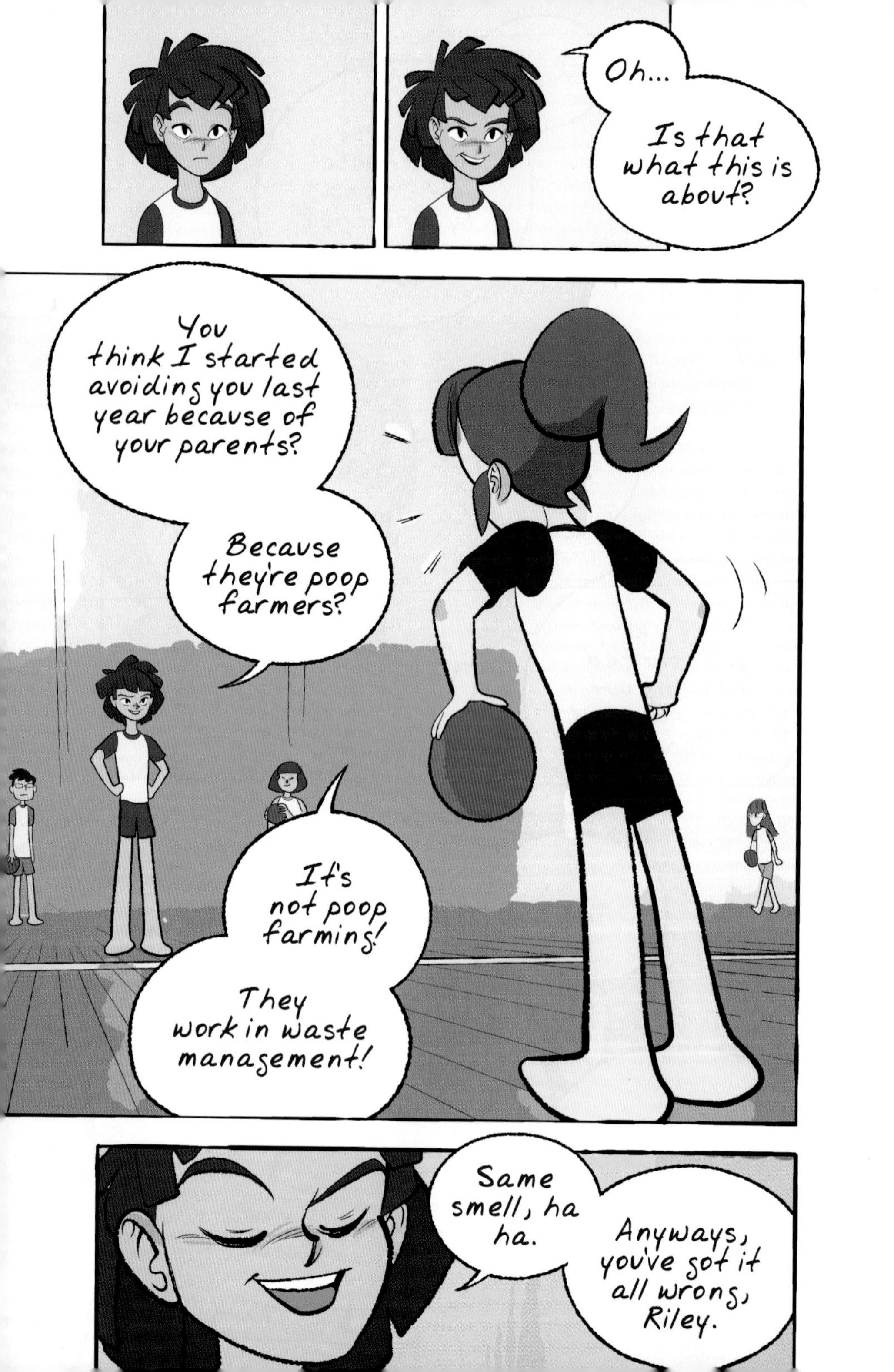
Oh...
Is that what this is about?
You think I started avoiding you last year because of your parents?
Because they're poop farmers?
It's not poop farming!
They work in waste management!
Same smell, ha ha.
Anyways, you've got it all wrong, Riley.

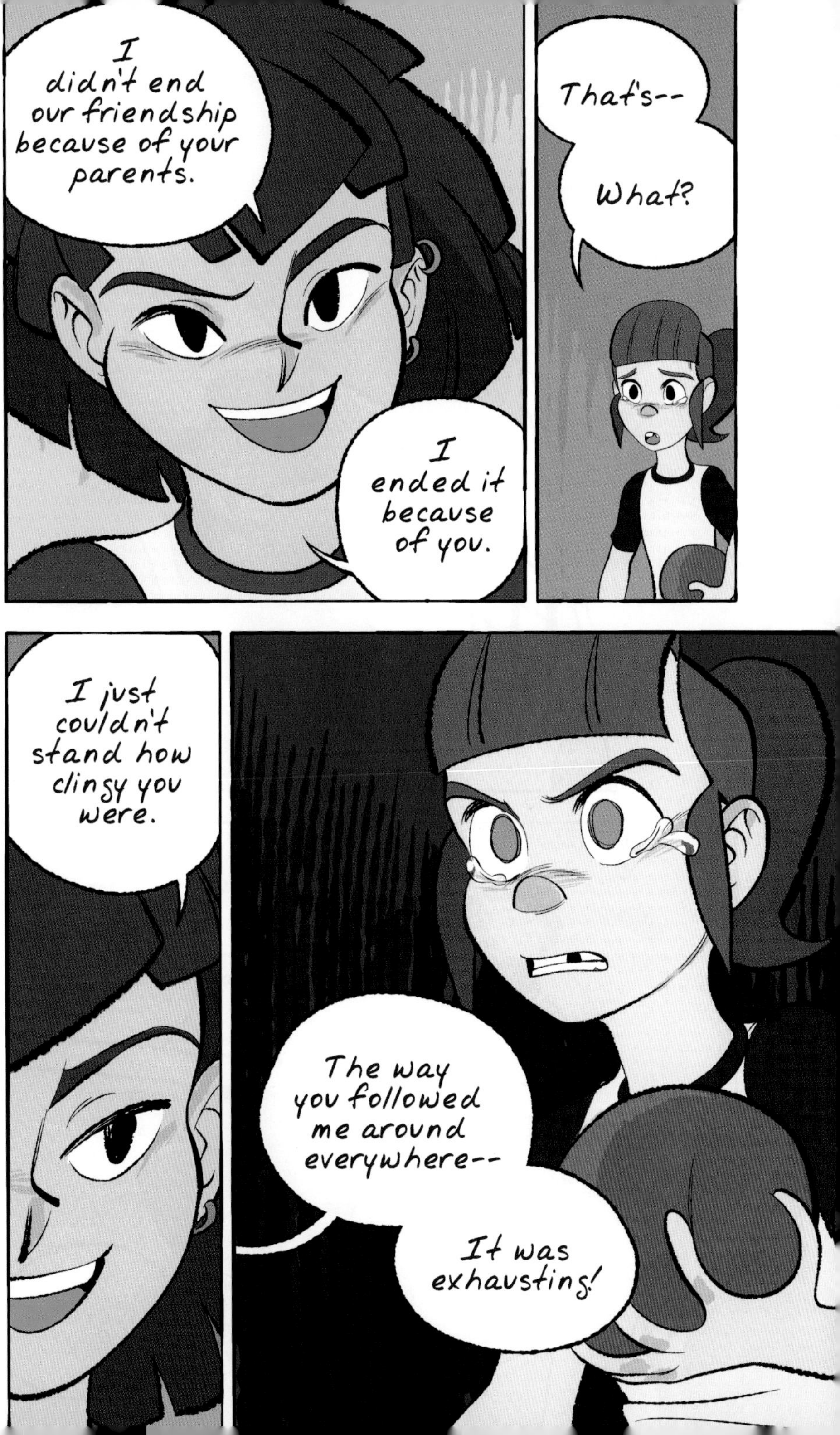
I didn't end our friendship because of your parents.
I ended it because of you.
That's--
What?
I just couldn't stand how clingy you were.
The way you followed me around everywhere--
It was exhausting!

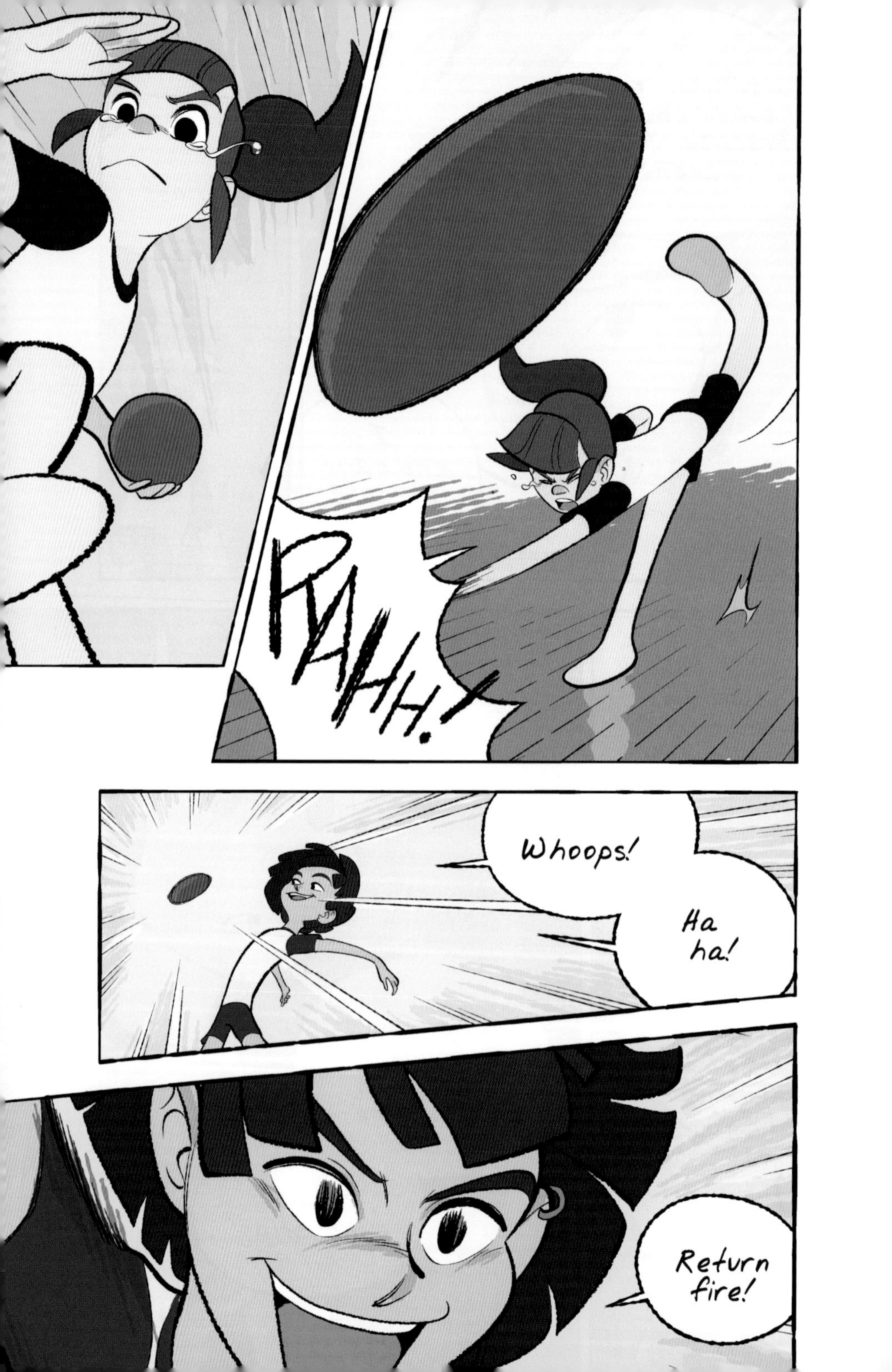
RYAHH!
Whoops!
Ha ha!
Return fire!

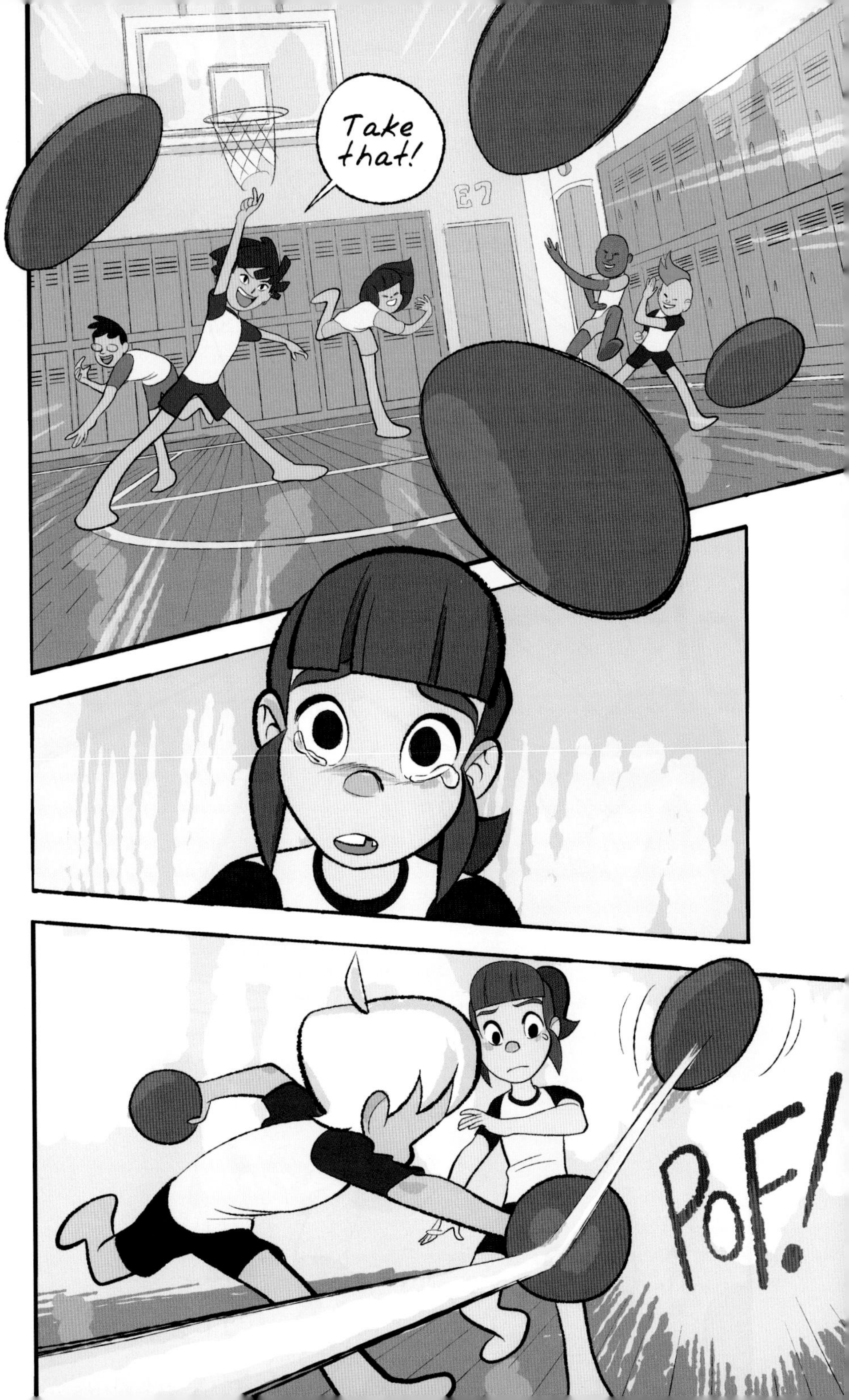

Take that!
POF!

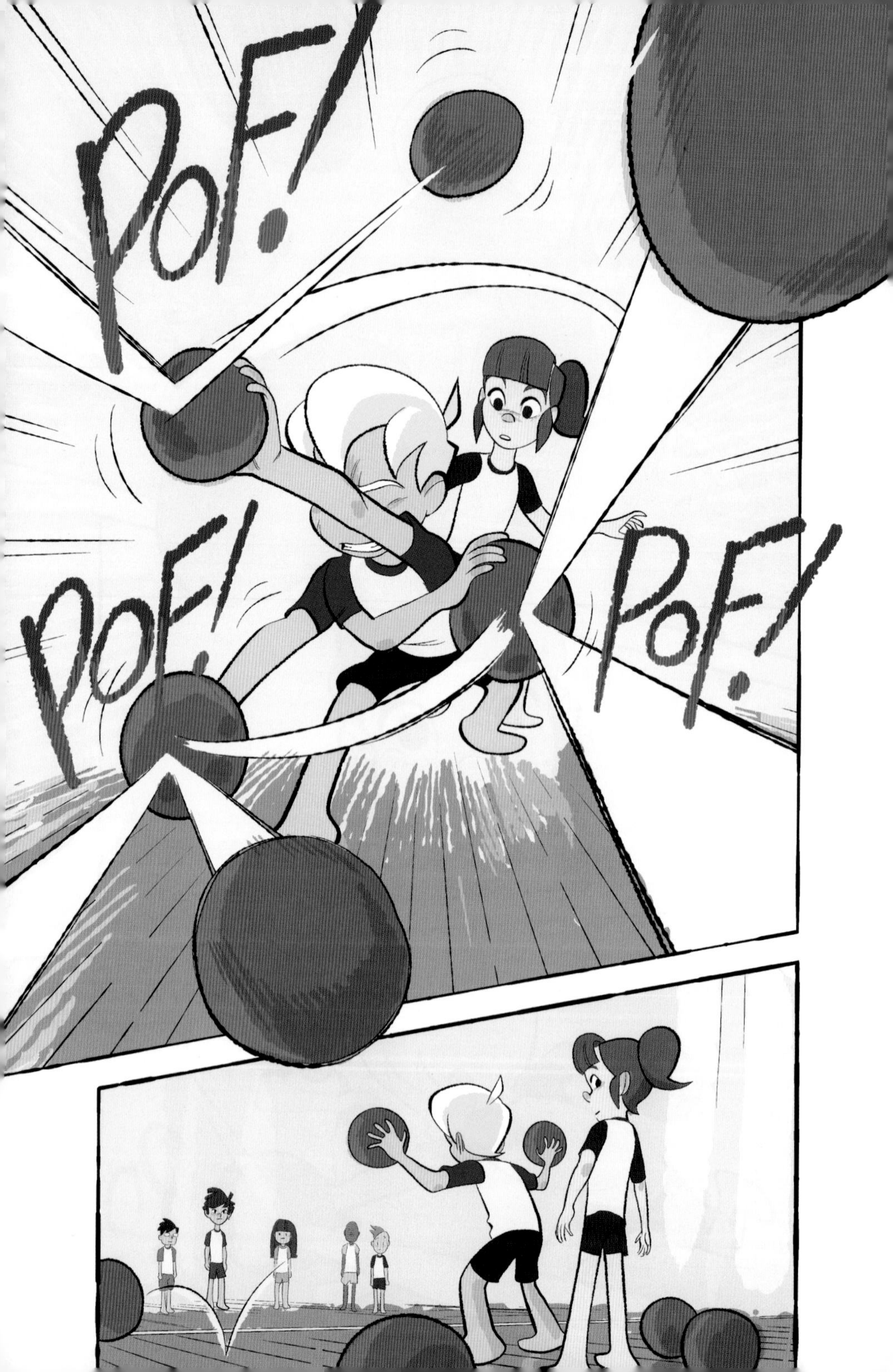
POF!
POF!
POF!

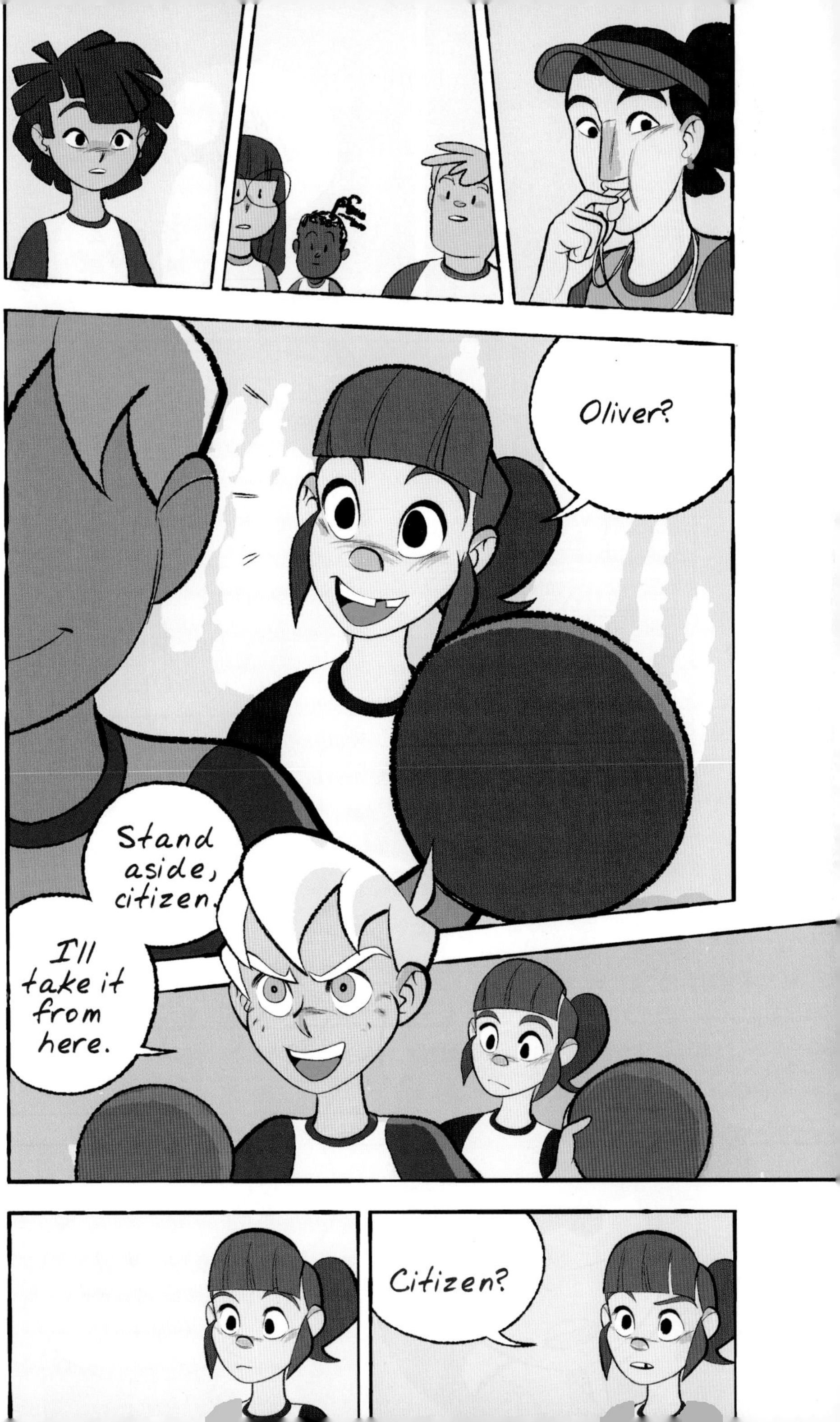
Oliver?
Stand aside, citizen.
I'll take it from here.
Citizen?

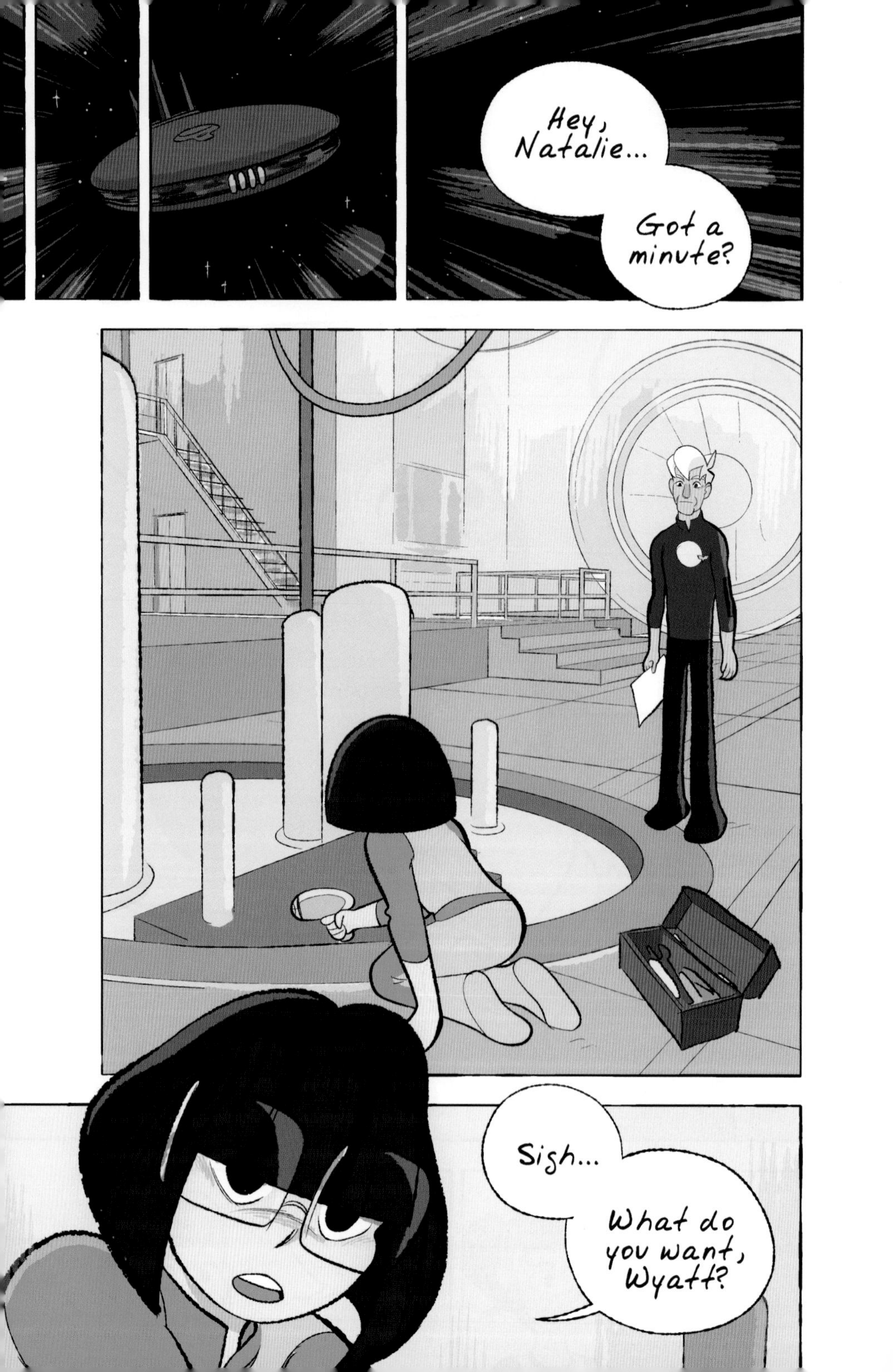
Hey, Natalie...
Got a minute?
Sigh...
What do you want, Wyatt?

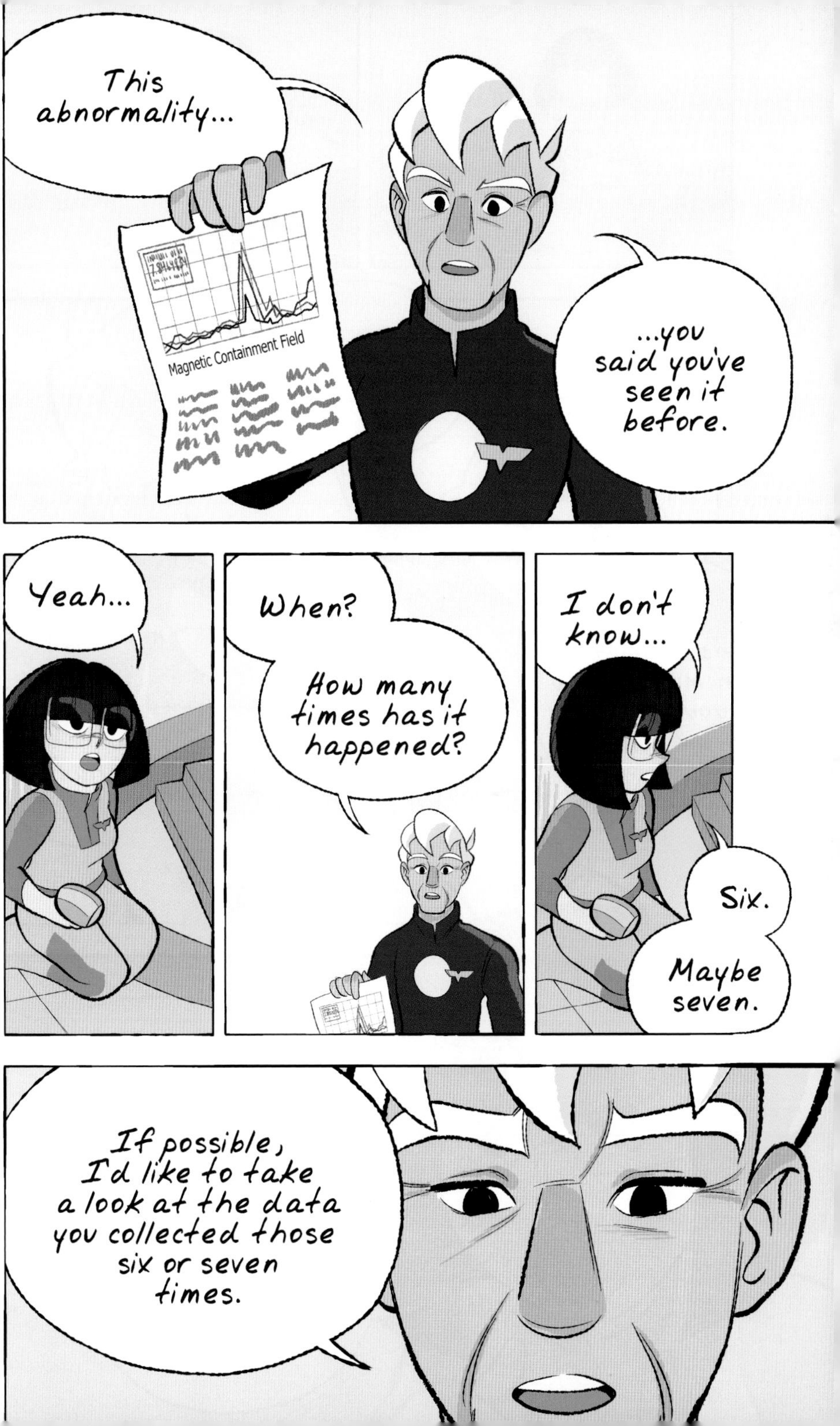
This abnormality...
Magnetic Containment Field
...you said you've seen it before.
Yeah...
When?
How many times has it happened?
I don't know...
Six.
Maybe seven.
If possible, I'd like to take a look at the data you collected those six or seven times.

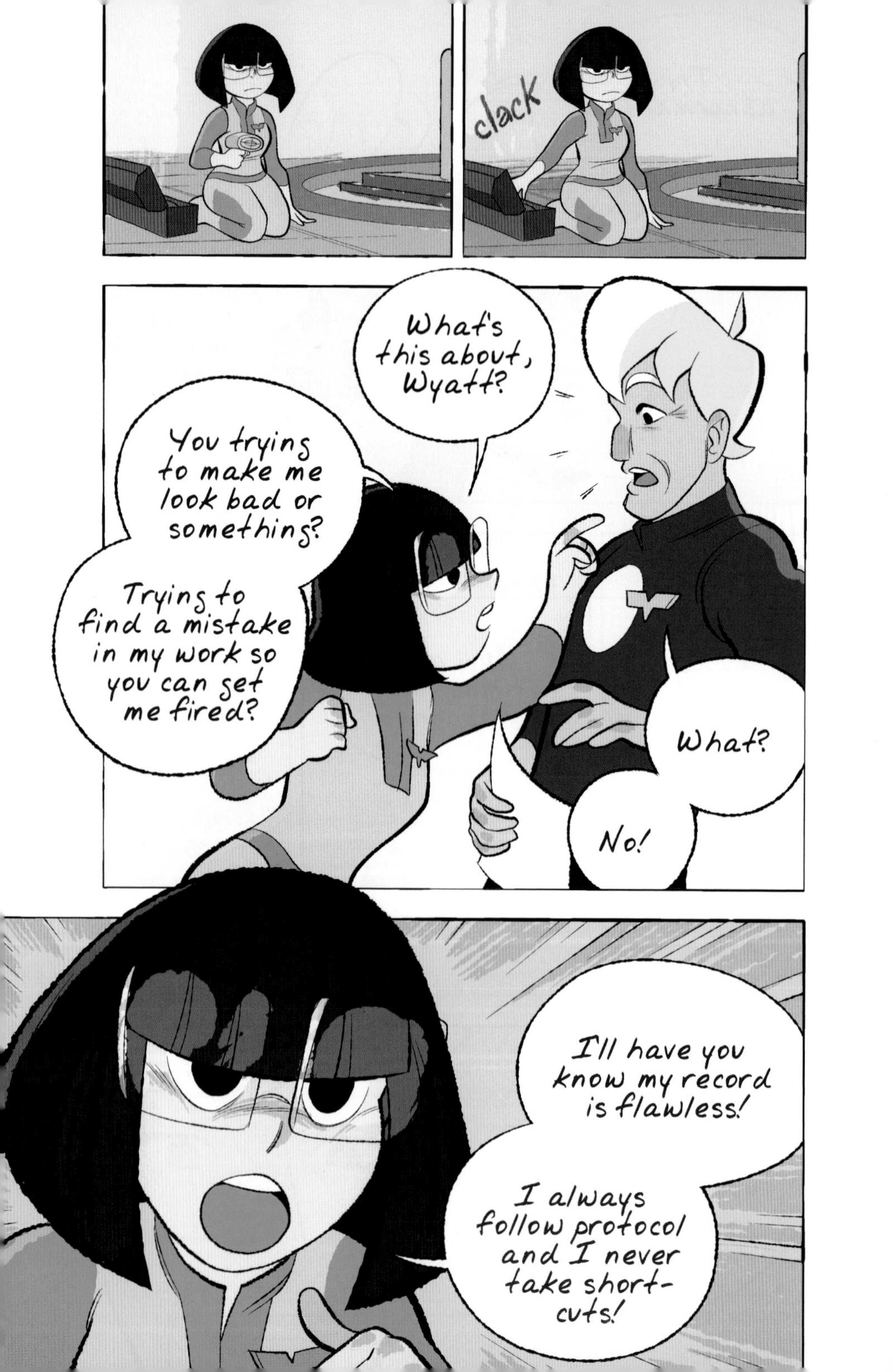
clack
What's this about, Wyatt?
You trying to make me look bad or something?
Trying to find a mistake in my work so you can get me fired?
What?
No!
I'll have you know my record is flawless!
I always follow protocol and I never take short-cuts!

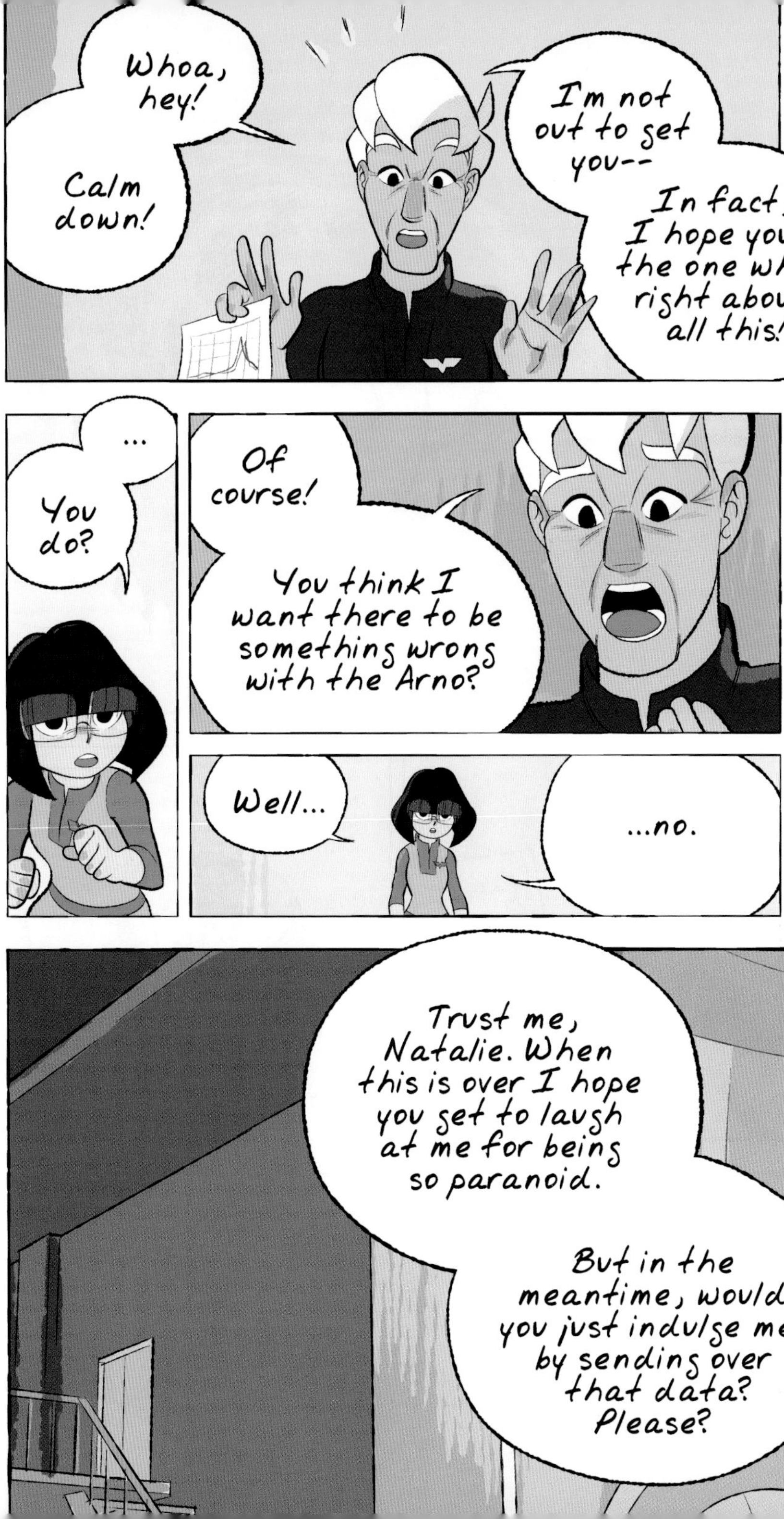
Whoa, hey!
Calm down!
I'm not out to get you--
In fact, I hope you're the one who's right about all this!
...
You do?
Of course!
You think I want there to be something wrong with the Arno?
Well...
...no.
Trust me, Natalie. When this is over I hope you get to laugh at me for being so paranoid.
But in the meantime, would you just indulge me by sending over that data? Please?

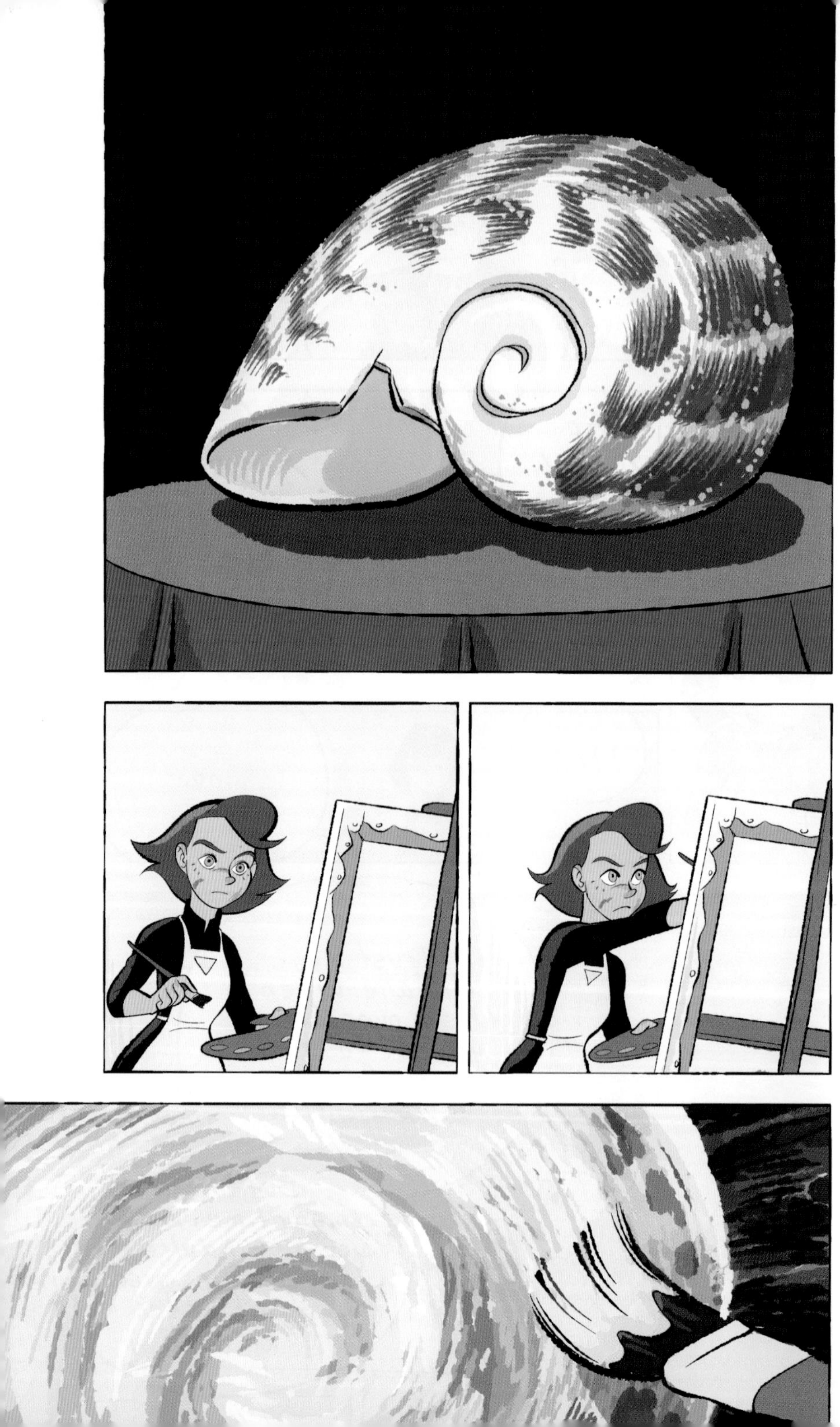

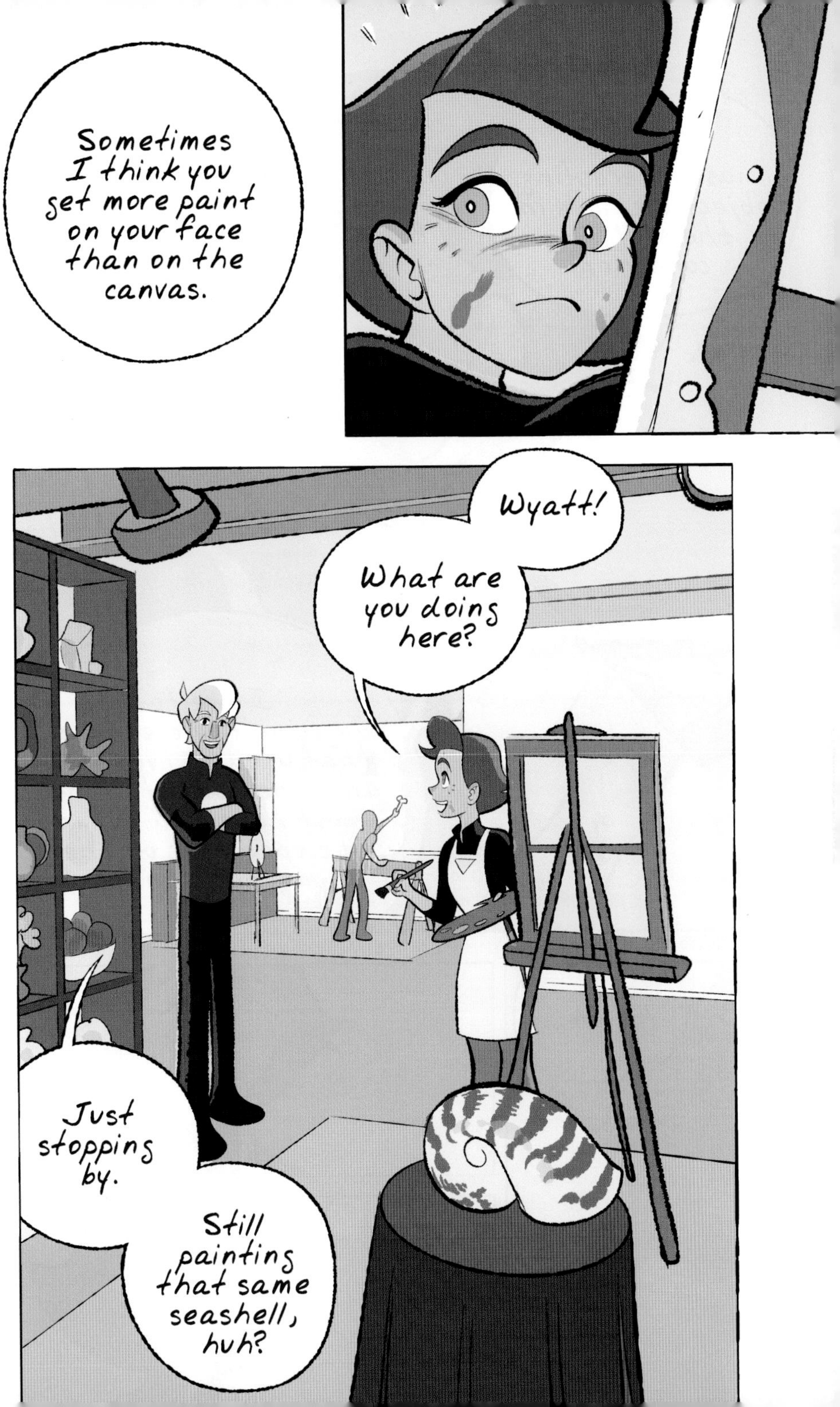
Sometimes I think you get more paint on your face than on the canvas.
Wyatt!
What are you doing here?
Just stopping by.
Still painting that same seashell, huh?

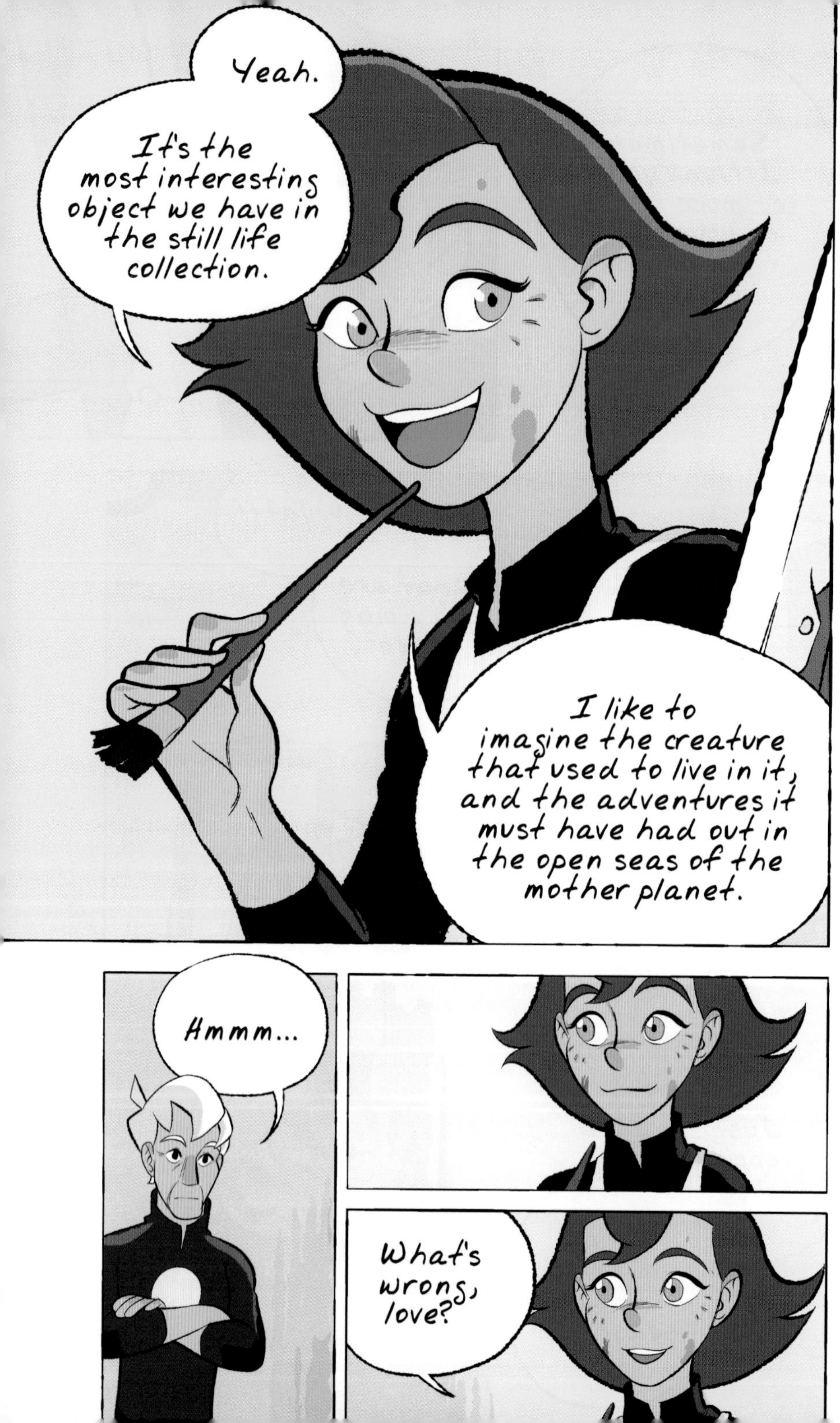
Yeah.
It's the most interesting object we have in the still life collection.
I like to imagine the creature that used to live in it, and the adventures it must have had out in the open seas of the mother planet.
Hmmm...
What's wrong, love?

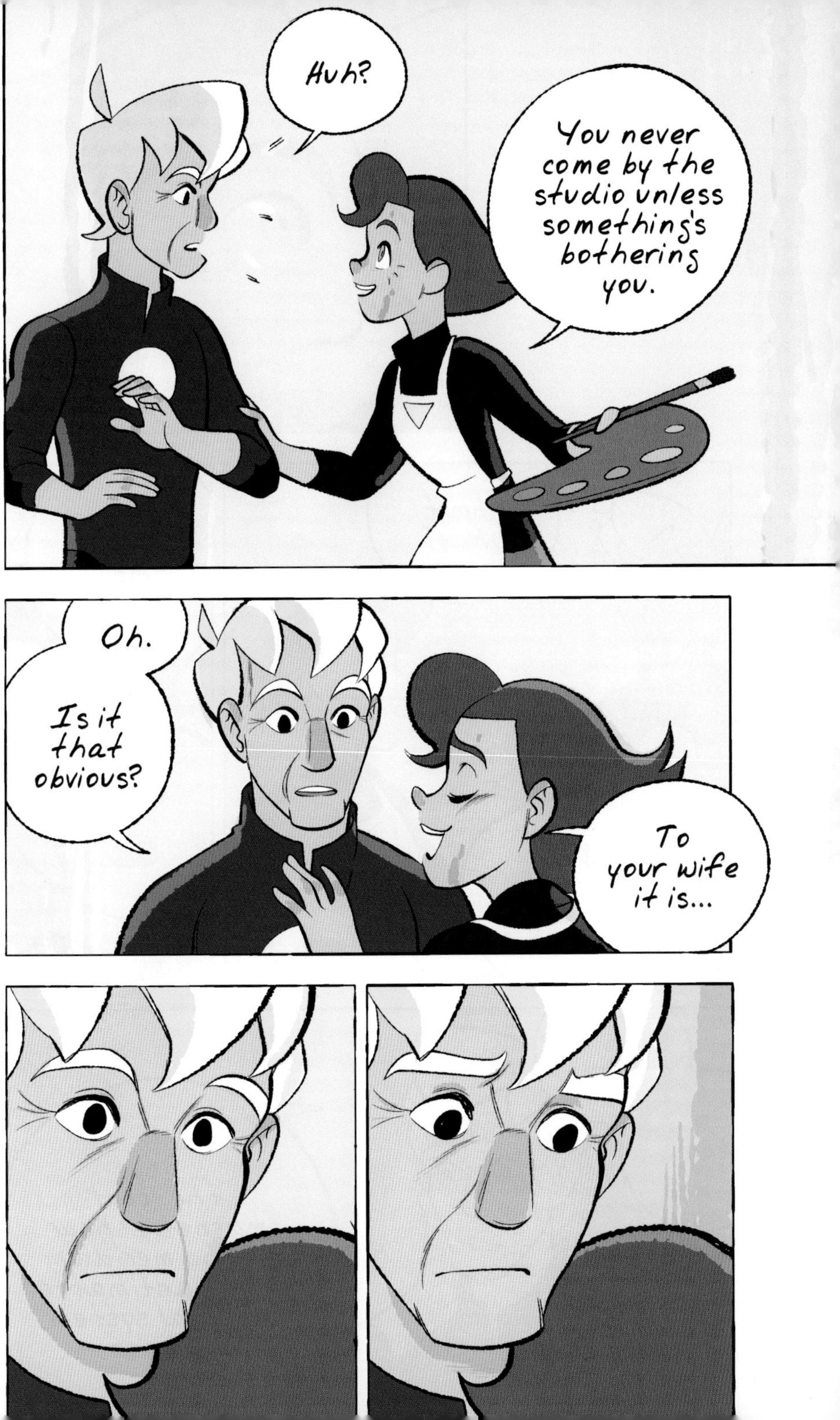
Huh?
You never come by the studio unless something's bothering you.
Oh.
Is it that obvious?
To your wife it is...

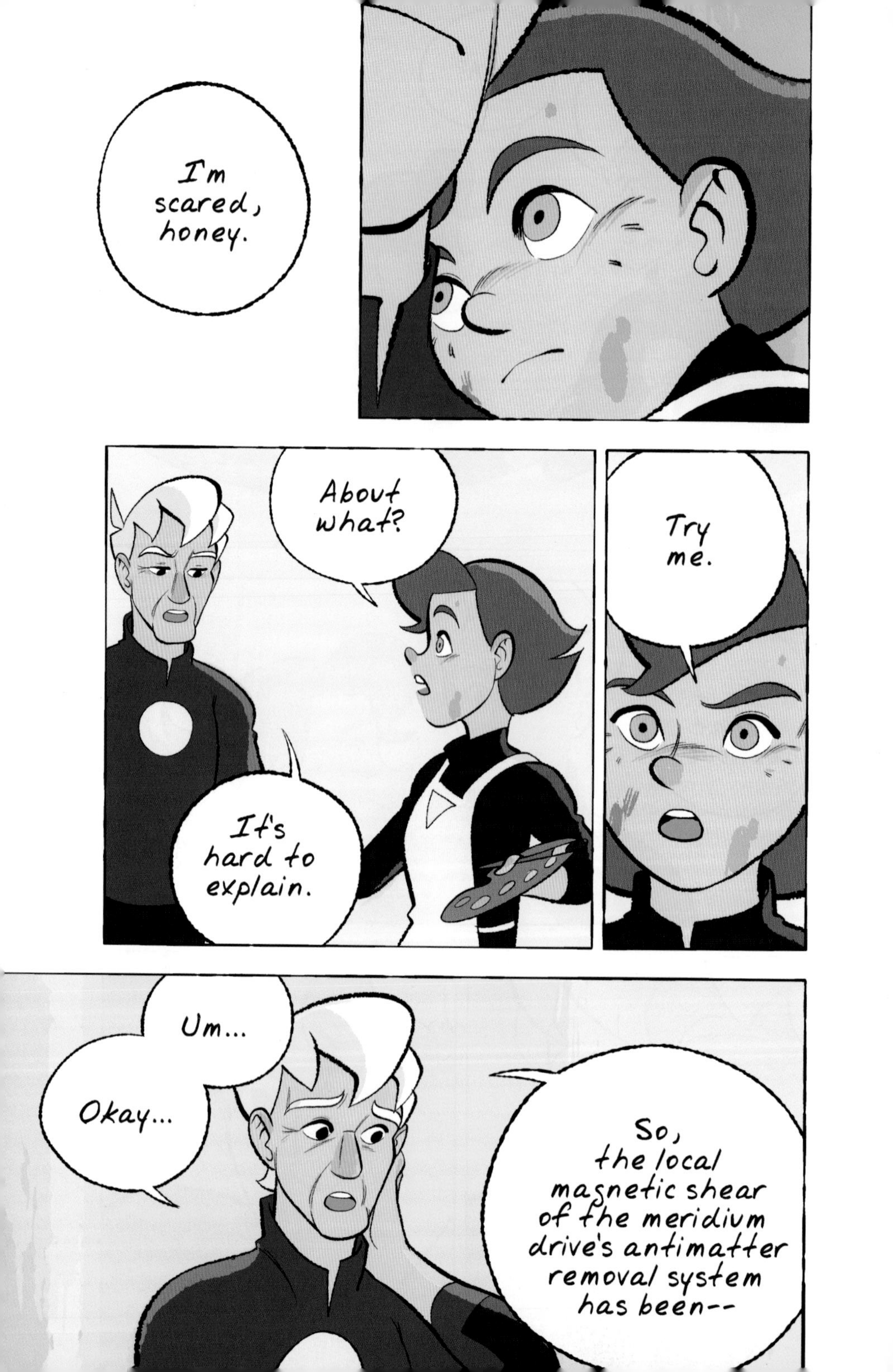
I'm scared, honey.
About what?
It's hard to explain.
Try me.
Um...
Okay...
So, the local magnetic shear of the meridium drive's antimatter removal system has been--

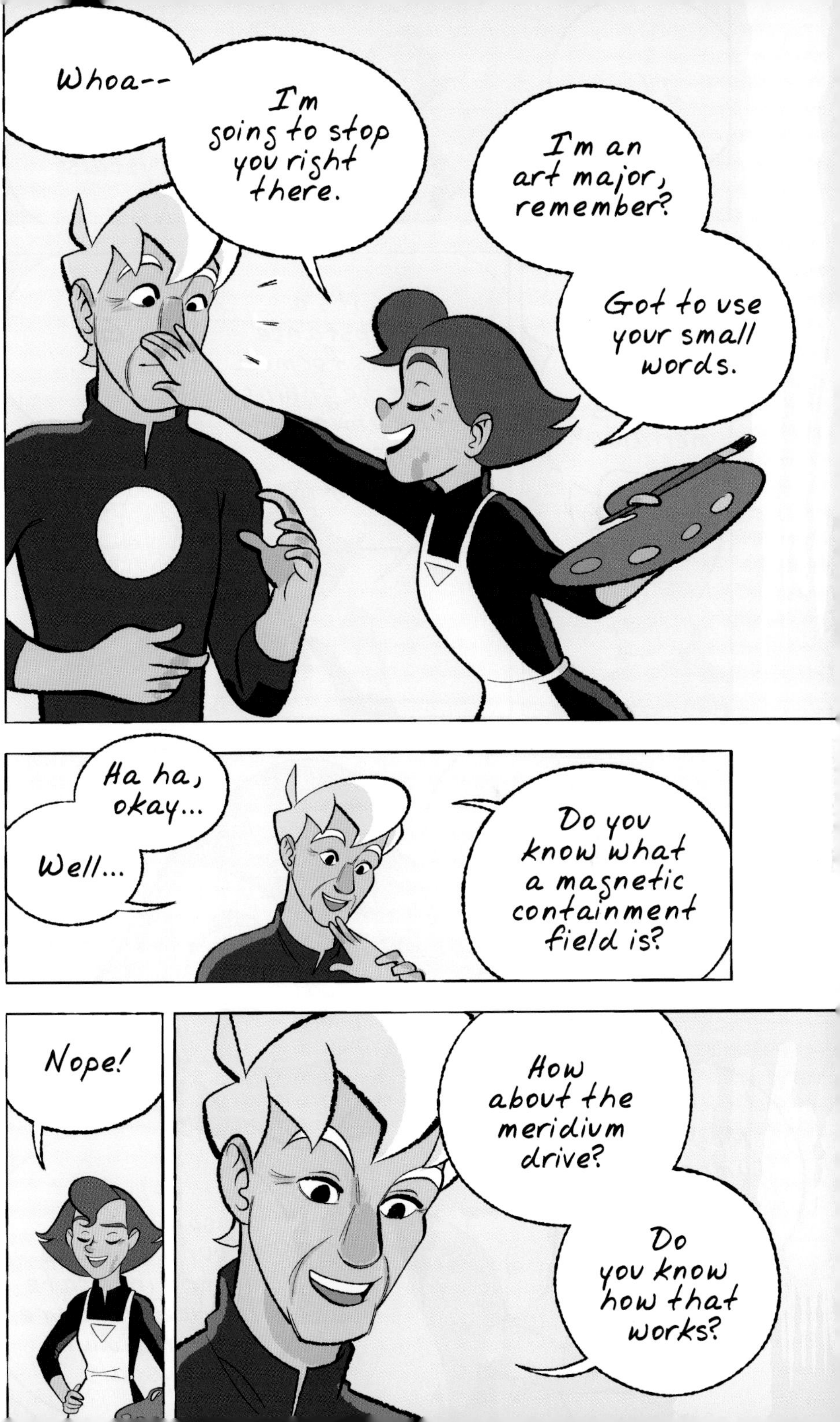
Whoa--
I'm going to stop you right there.
I'm an art major, remember?
Got to use your small words.
Ha ha, okay...
Well...
Do you know what a magnetic containment field is?
Nope!
How about the meridium drive?
Do you know how that works?

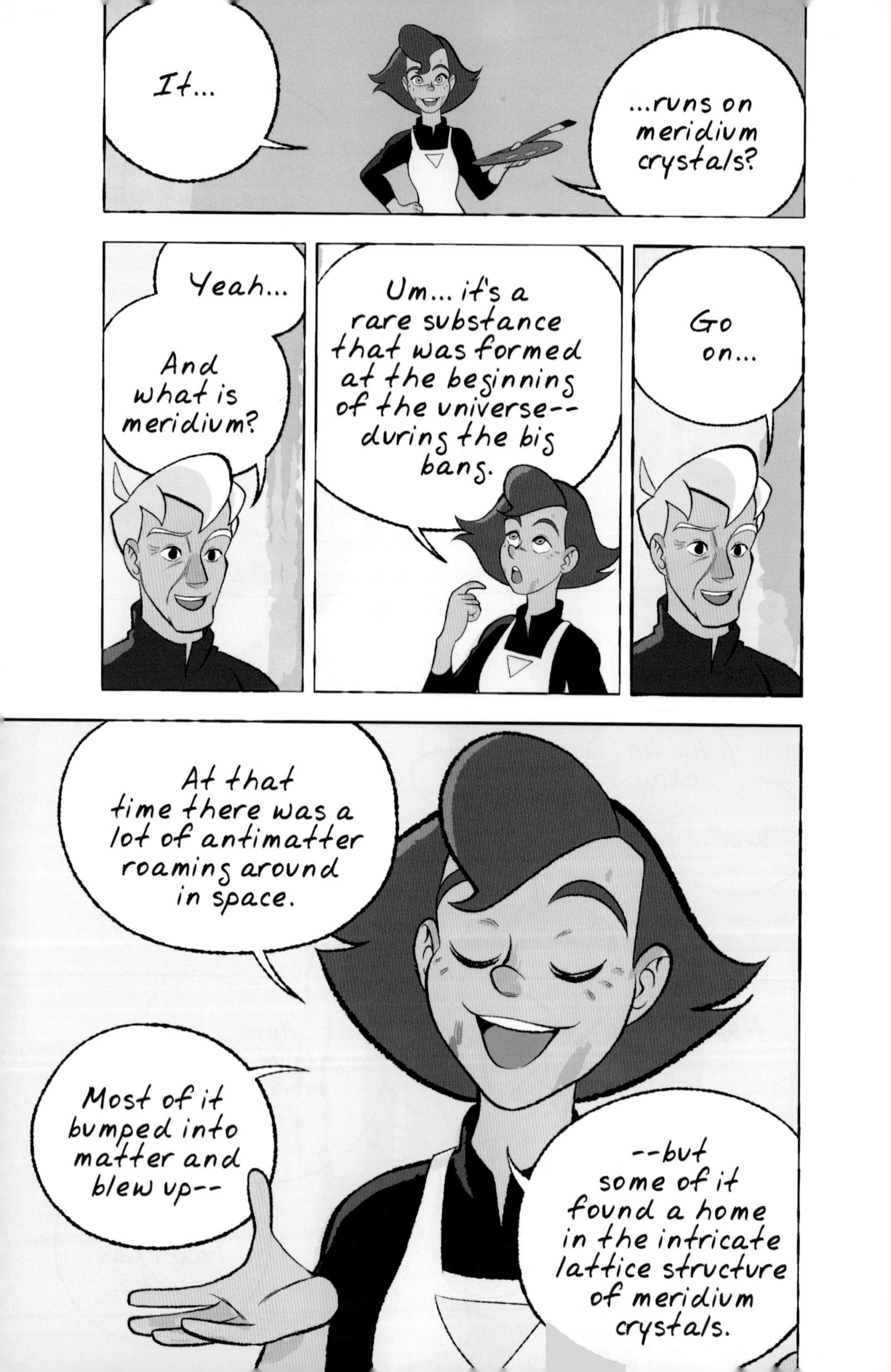
It...
...runs on meridium crystals?
Yeah...
And what is meridium?
Um... it's a rare substance that was formed at the beginning of the universe--during the big bang.
Go on...
At that time there was a lot of antimatter roaming around in space.
Most of it bumped into matter and blew up--
--but some of it found a home in the intricate lattice structure of meridium crystals.

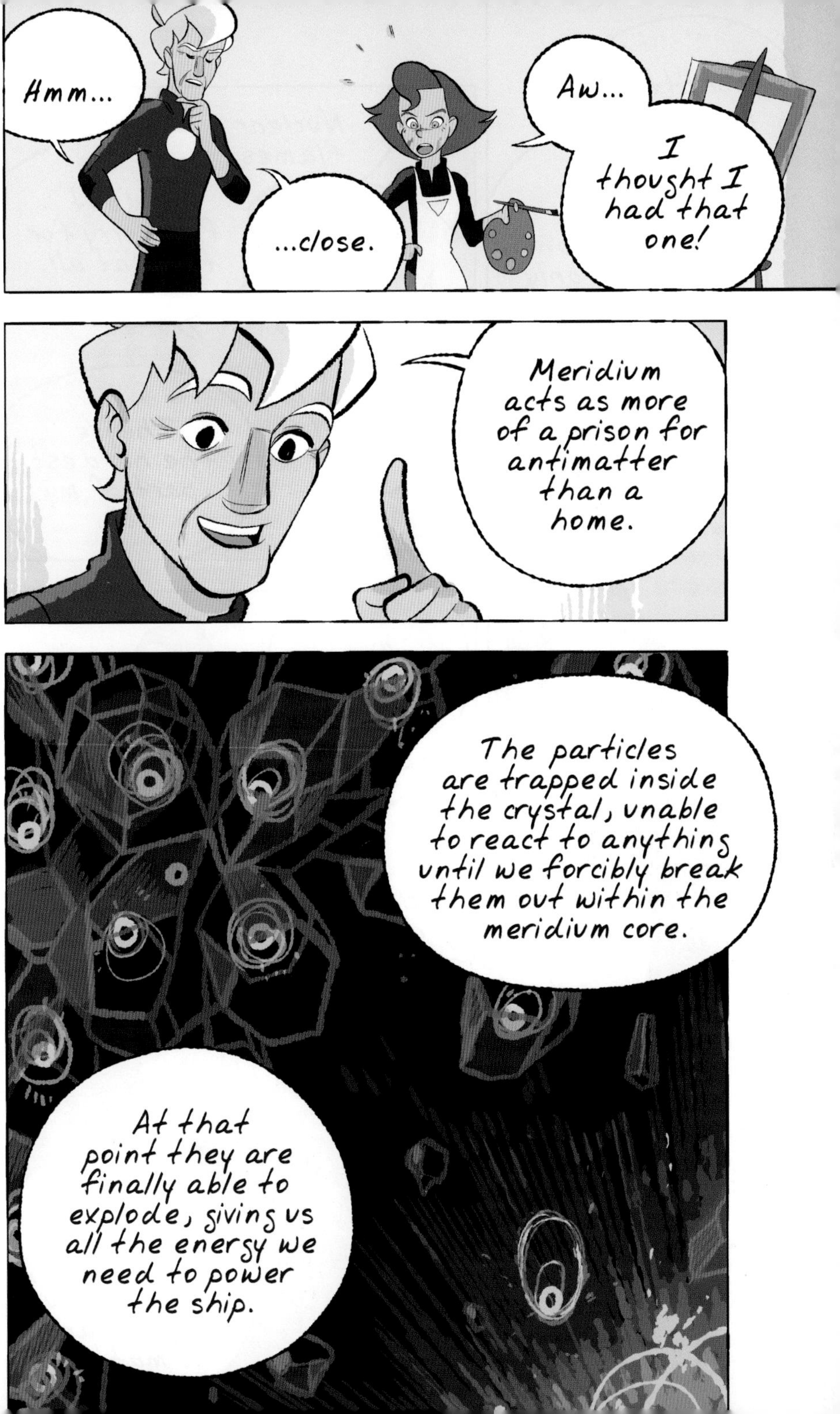
Hmm...
...close.
Aw...
I thought I had that one!
Meridium acts as more of a prison for antimatter than a home.
The particles are trapped inside the crystal, unable to react to anything until we forcibly break them out within the meridium core.
At that point they are finally able to explode, giving us all the energy we need to power the ship.

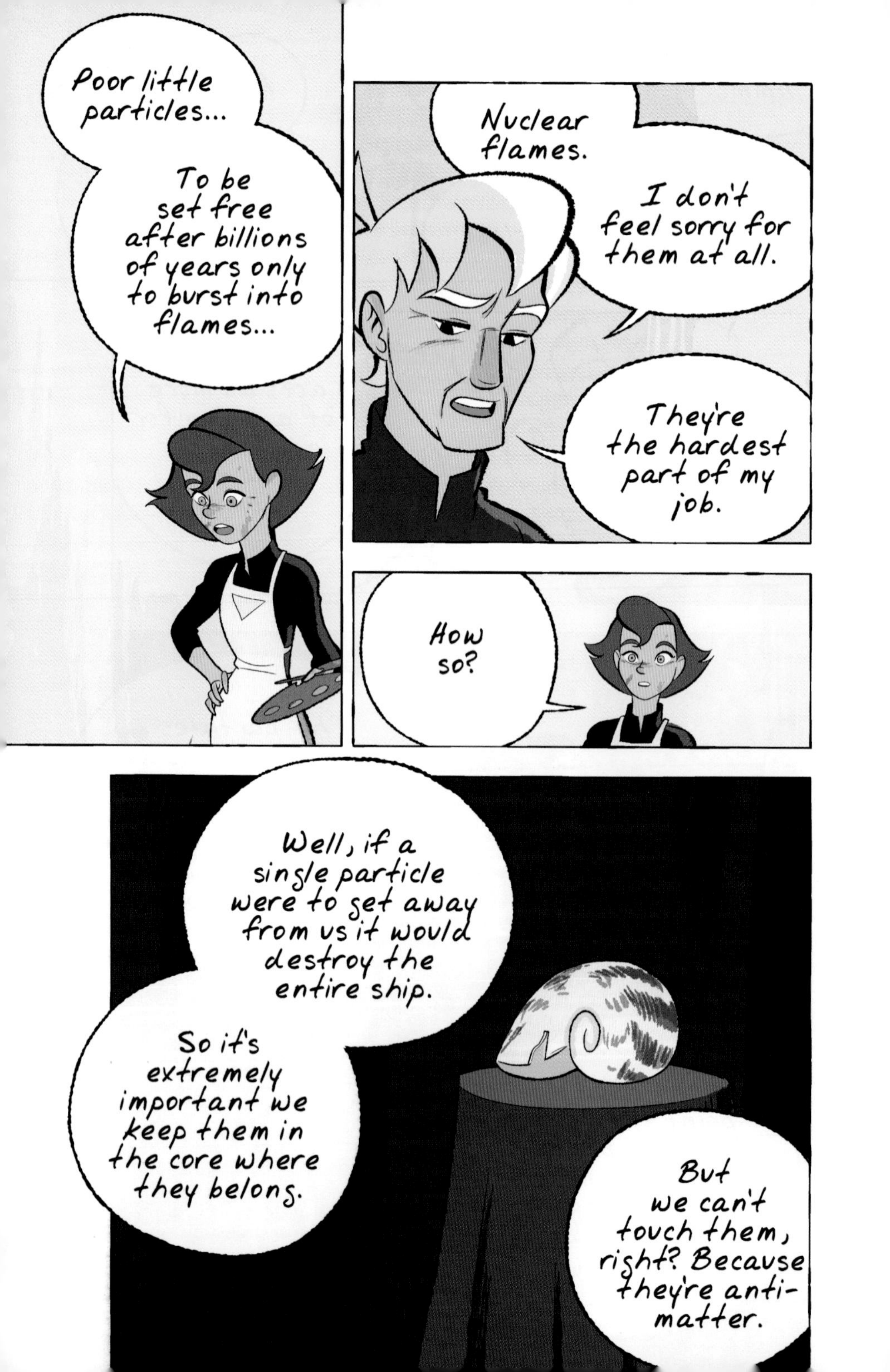
Poor little particles...
To be set free after billions of years only to burst into flames...
Nuclear flames.
I don't feel sorry for them at all.
They're the hardest part of my job.
How so?
Well, if a single particle were to get away from us it would destroy the entire ship.
So it's extremely important we keep them in the core where they belong.
But we can't touch them, right? Because they're anti-matter.

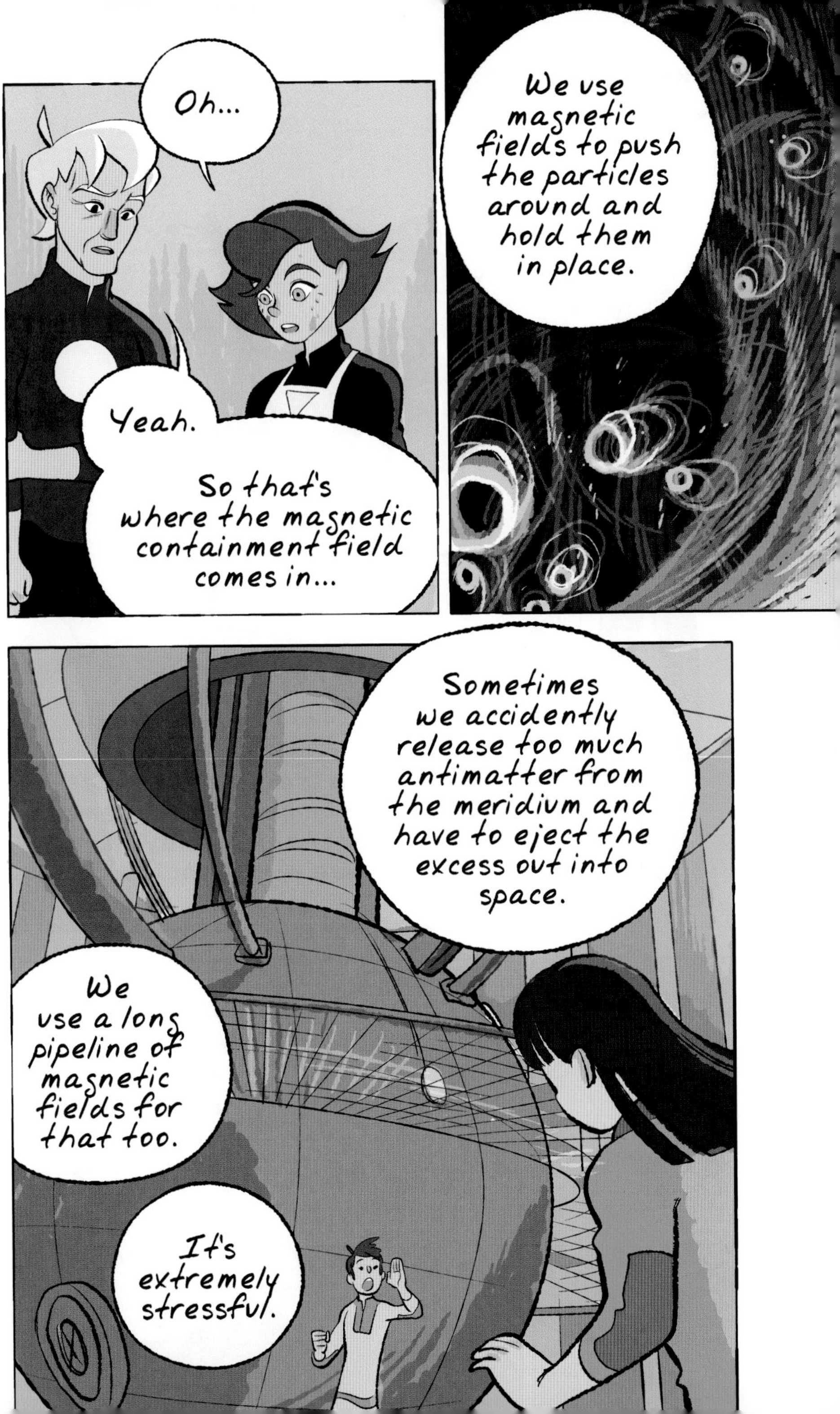
Oh...
Yeah.
So that's where the magnetic containment field comes in...
We use magnetic fields to push the particles around and hold them in place.
Sometimes we accidently release too much antimatter from the meridium and have to eject the excess out into space.
We use a long pipeline of magnetic fields for that too.
It's extremely stressful.

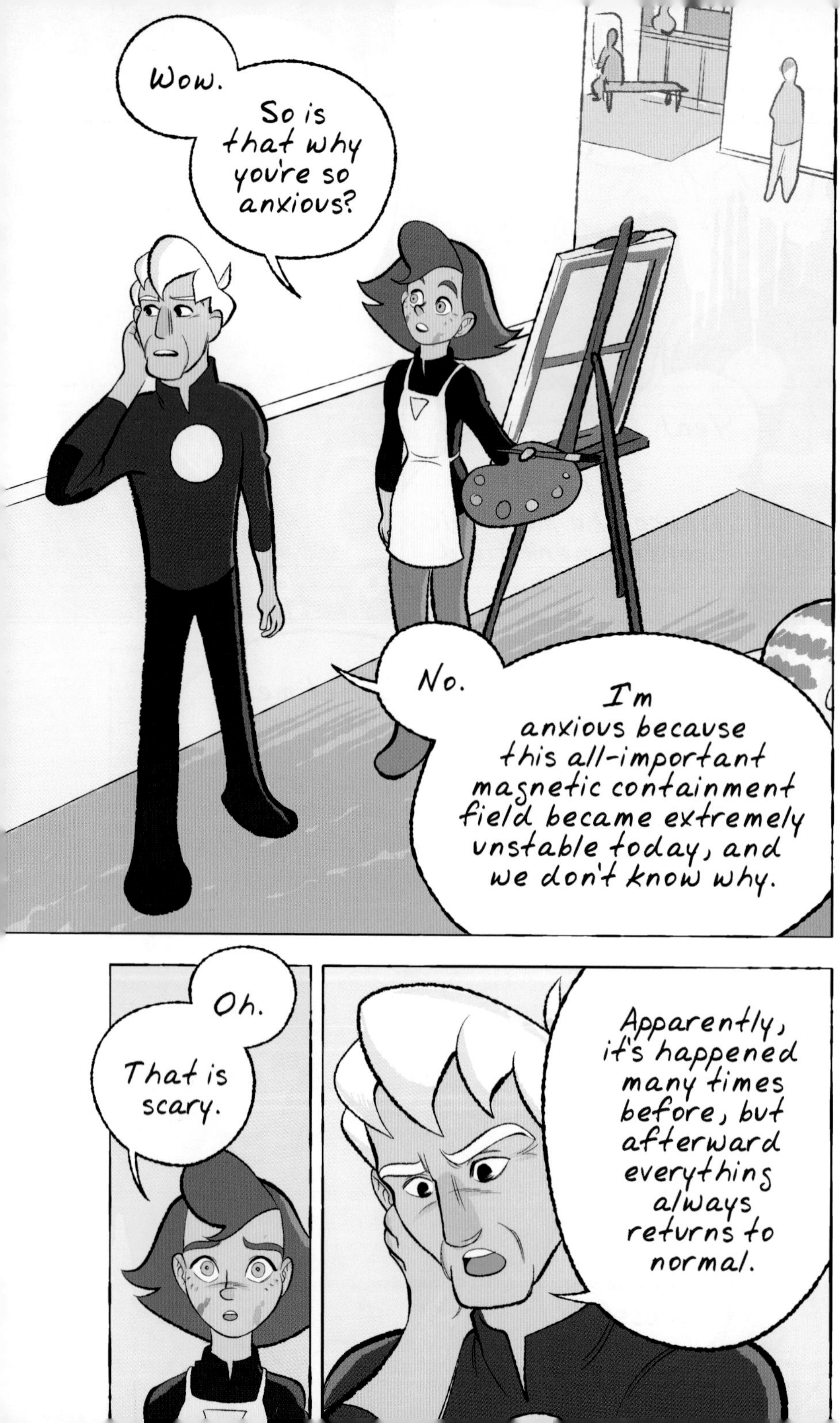
Wow.
So is that why you're so anxious?
No.
I'm anxious because this all-important magnetic containment field became extremely unstable today, and we don't know why.
Oh.
That is scary.
Apparently, it's happened many times before, but afterward everything always returns to normal.

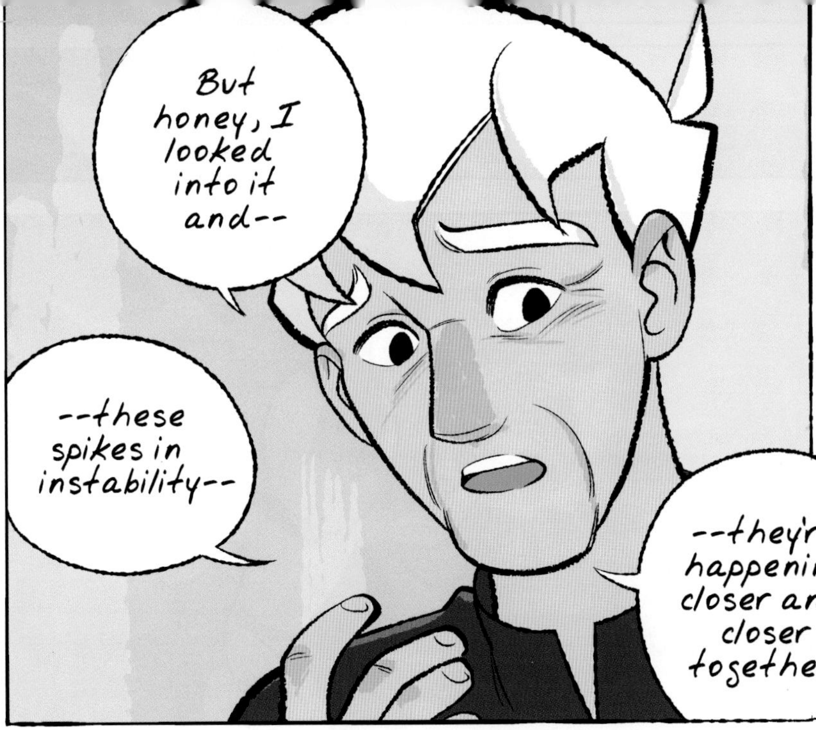
But honey, I looked into it and--
--these spikes in instability--
--they're happening closer and closer together.

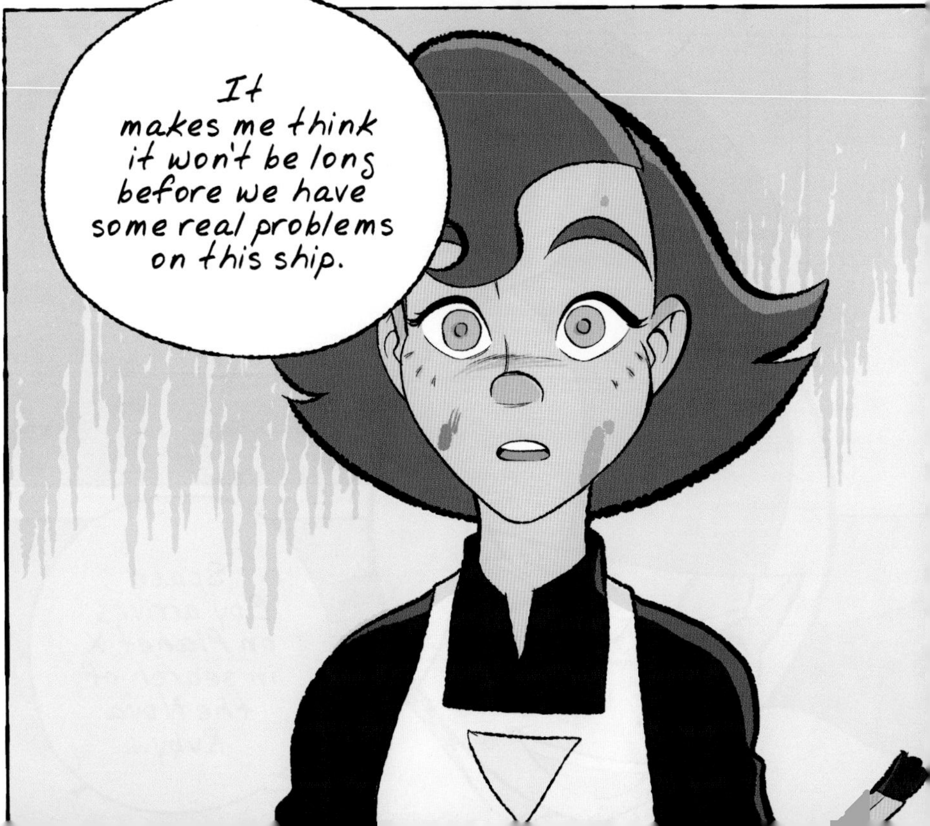
It makes me think it won't be long before we have some real problems on this ship.

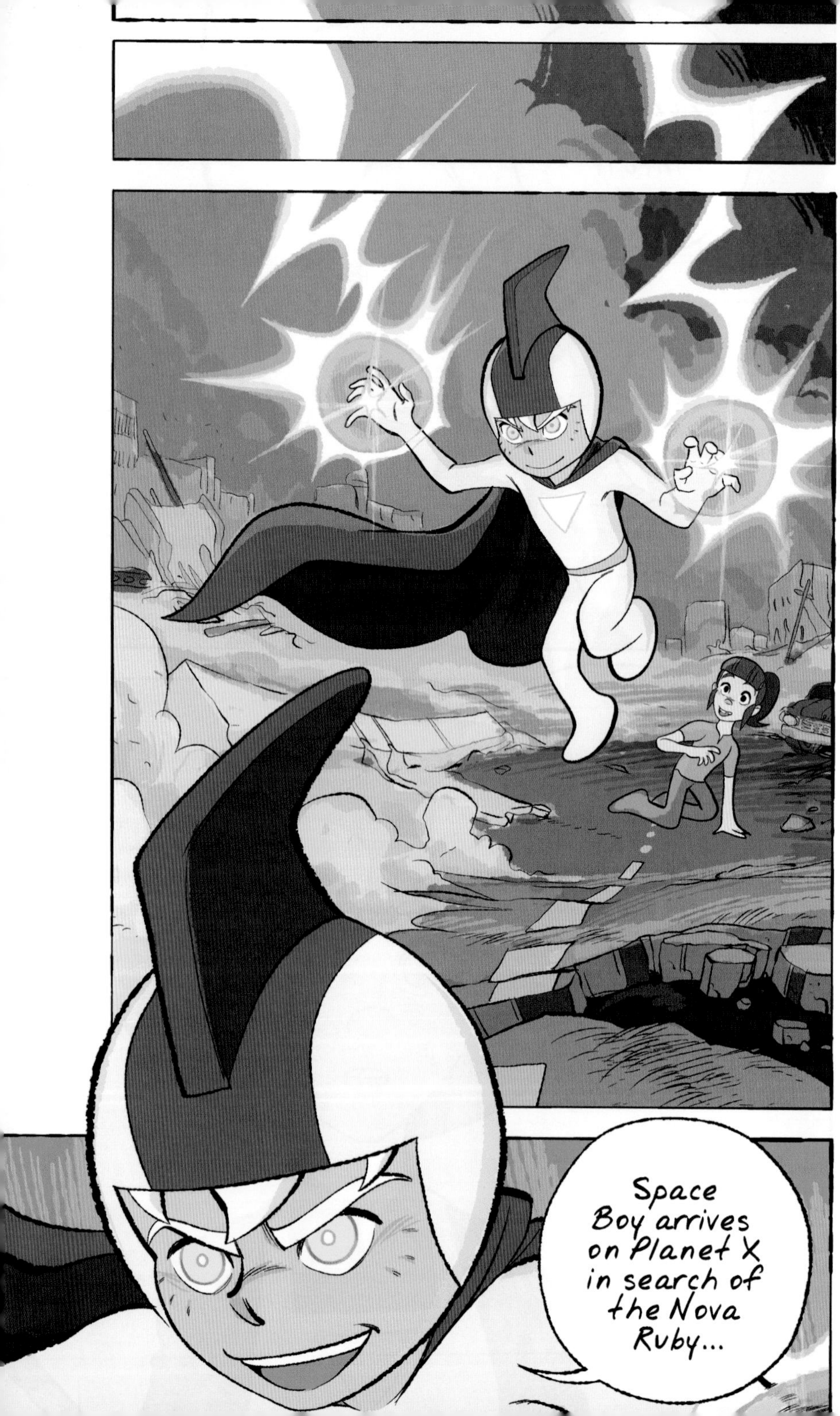
Space Boy arrives on Planet X in search of the Nova Ruby...

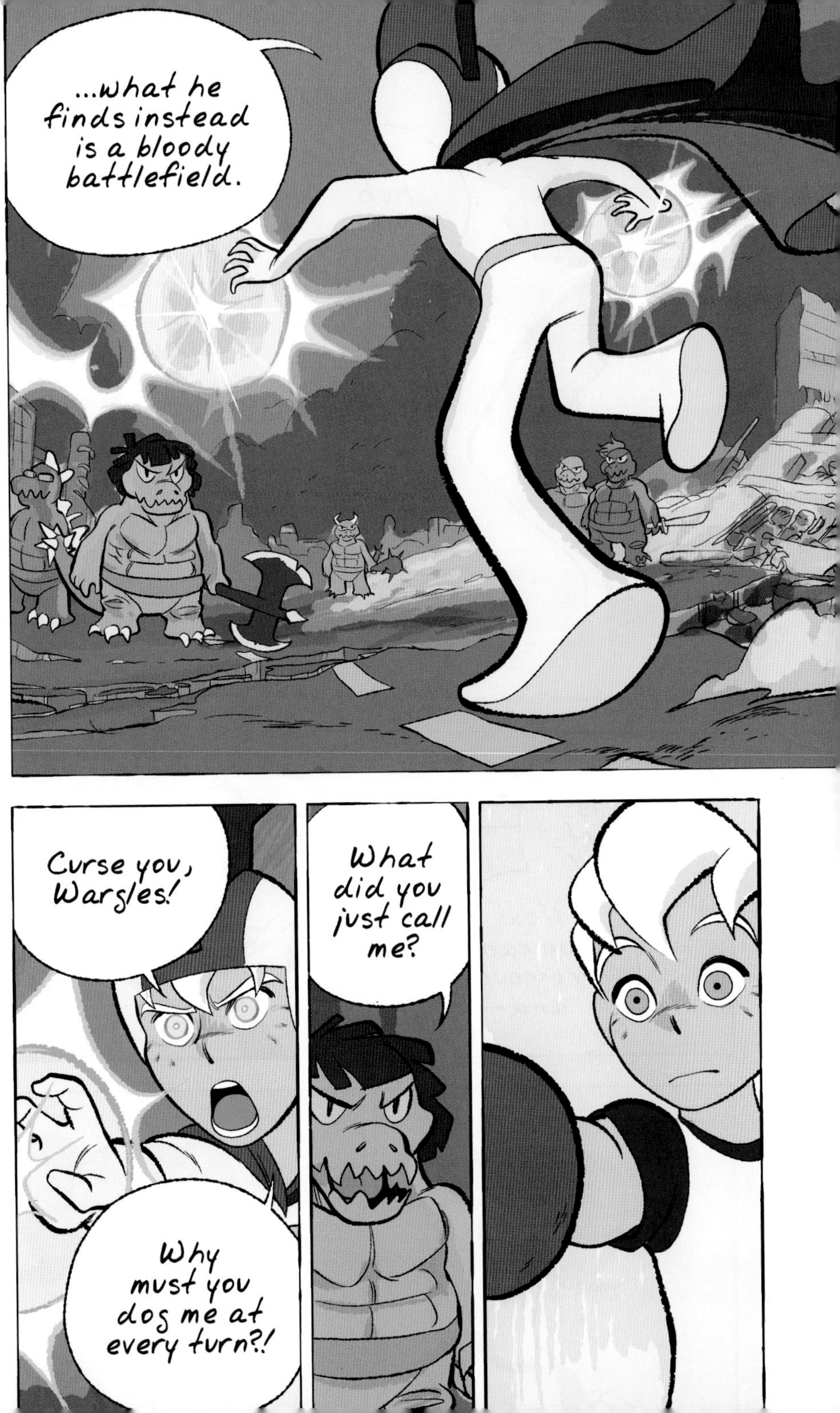
...what he finds instead is a bloody battlefield.
Curse you, Wargles!
What did you just call me?
Why must you dog me at every turn?!

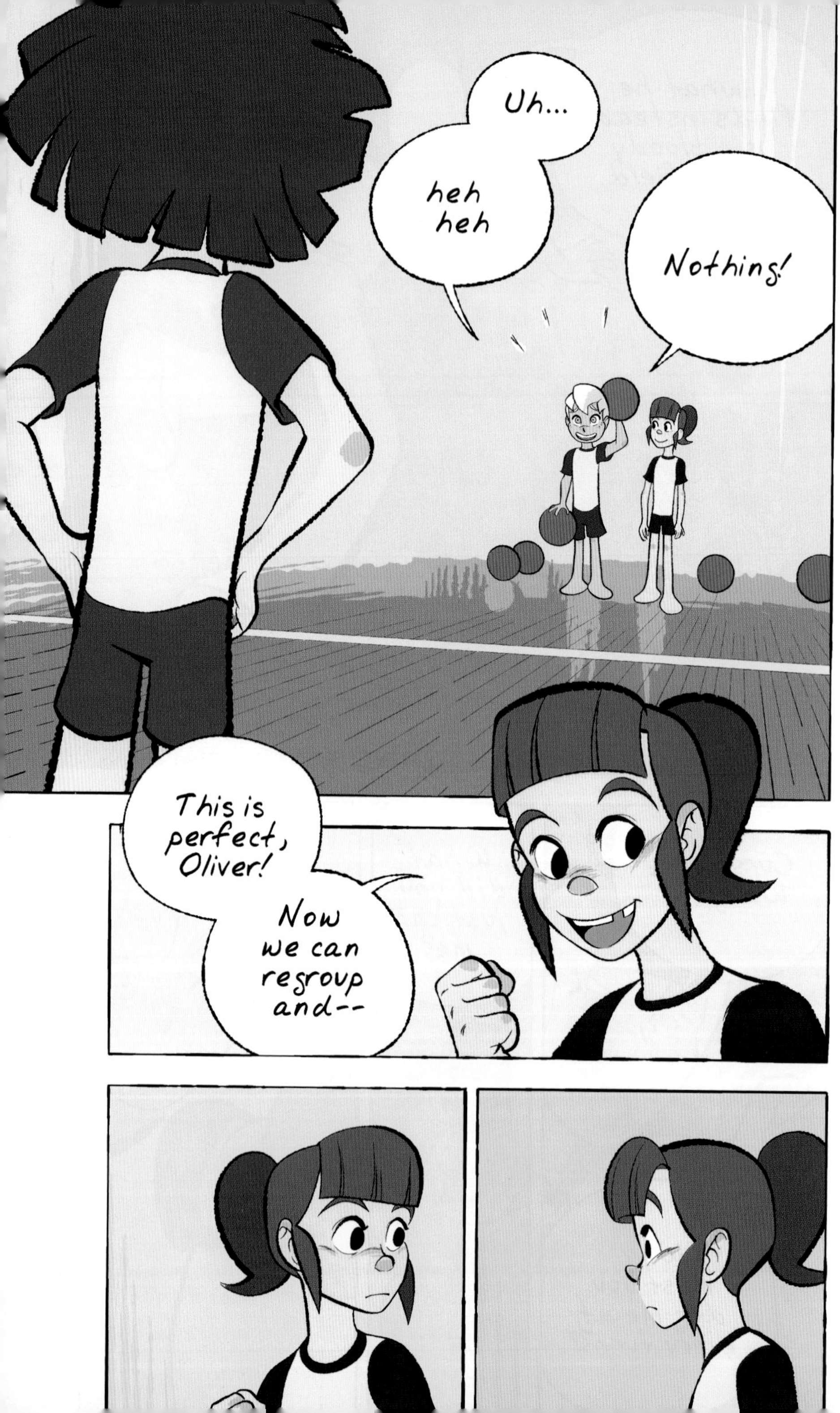
Uh...
heh heh
Nothing!
This is perfect, Oliver!
Now we can regroup and--

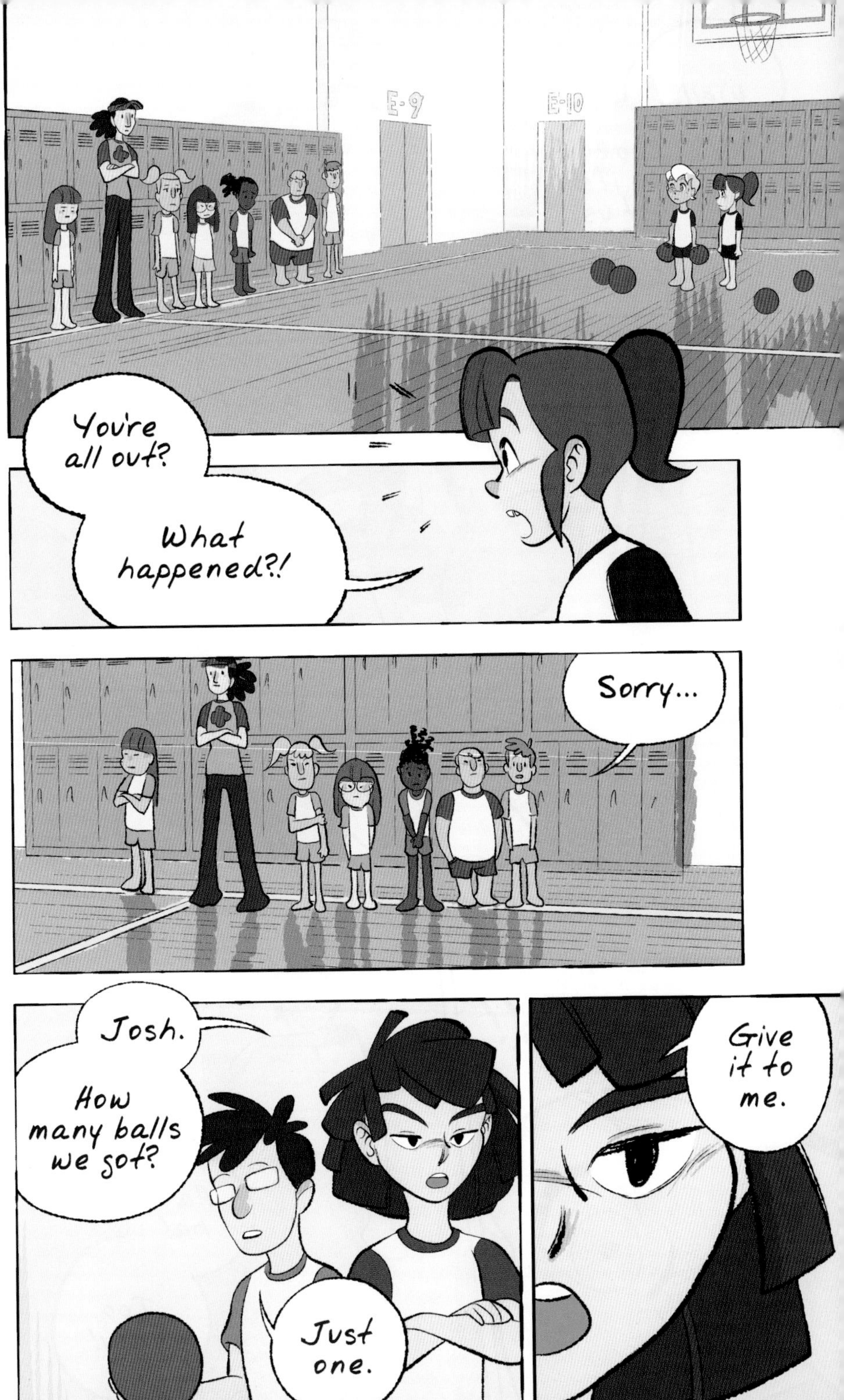

E-9
E-10
You're all out?
What happened?!
Sorry...
Josh.
How many balls we got?
Just one.
Give it to me.

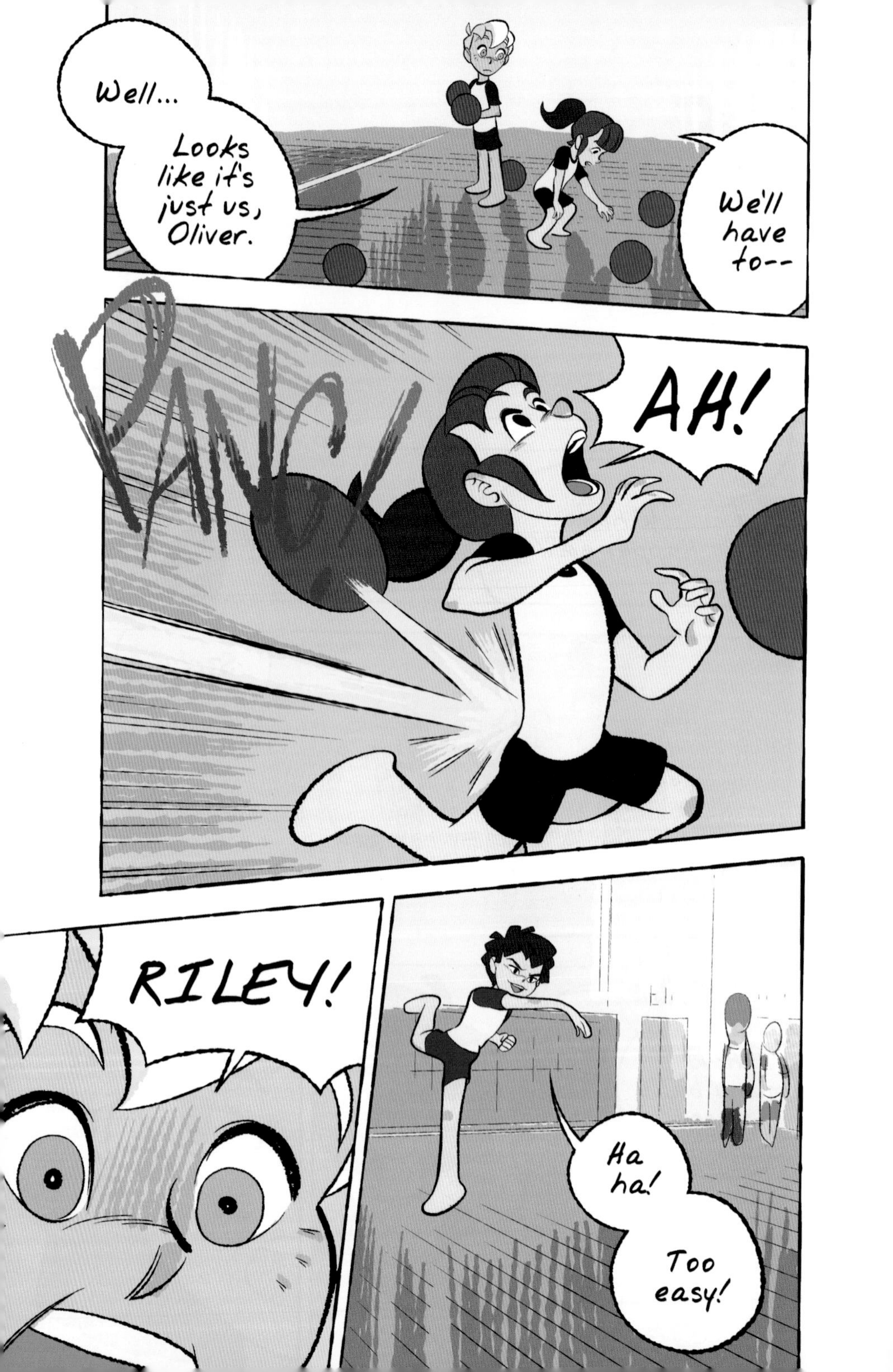
Well...
Looks like it's just us, Oliver.
We'll have to--
BANG
AH!
RILEY!
Ha ha!
Too easy!

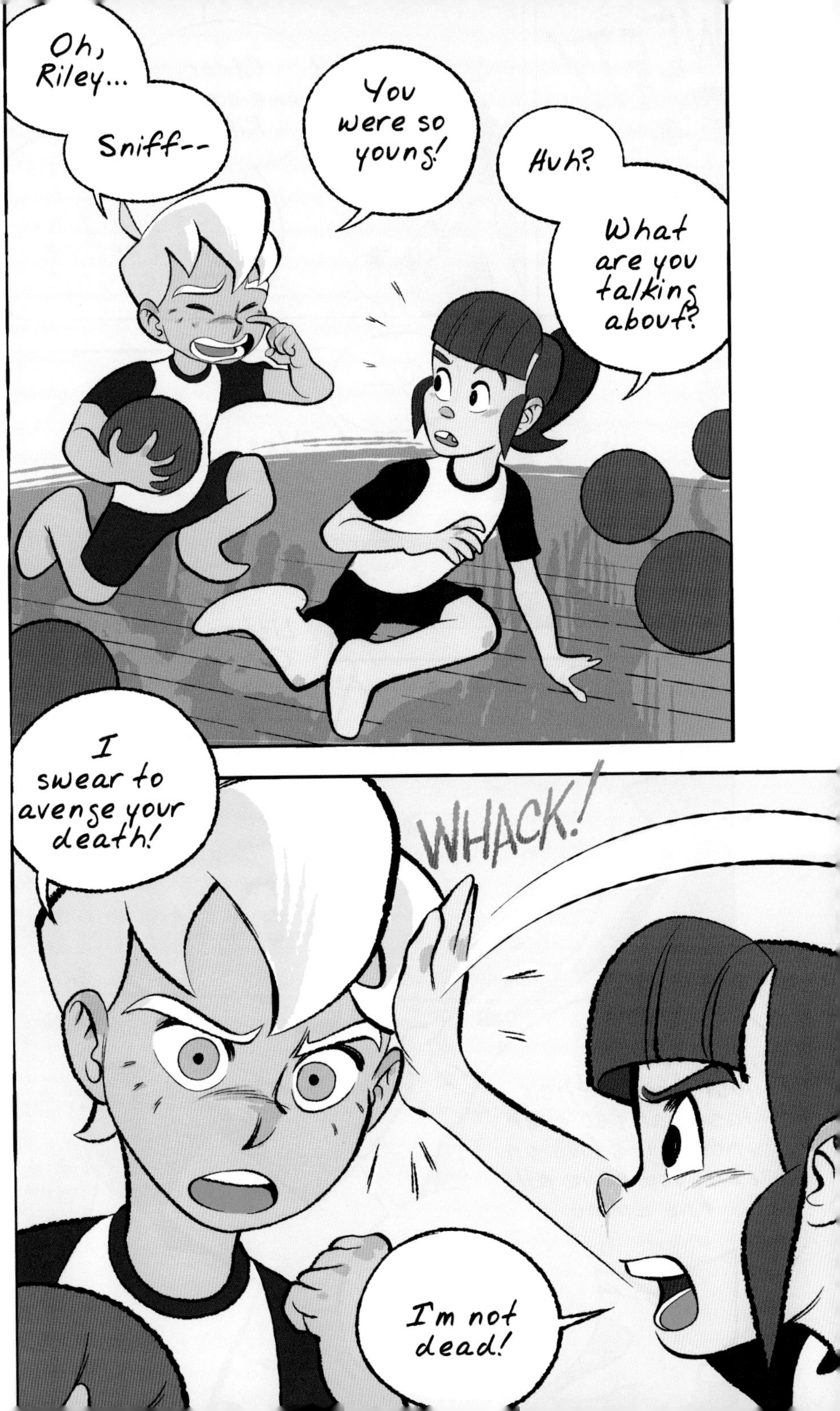
Oh, Riley...
Sniff--
You were so young!
Huh?
What are you talking about?
I swear to avenge your death!
WHACK!
I'm not dead!

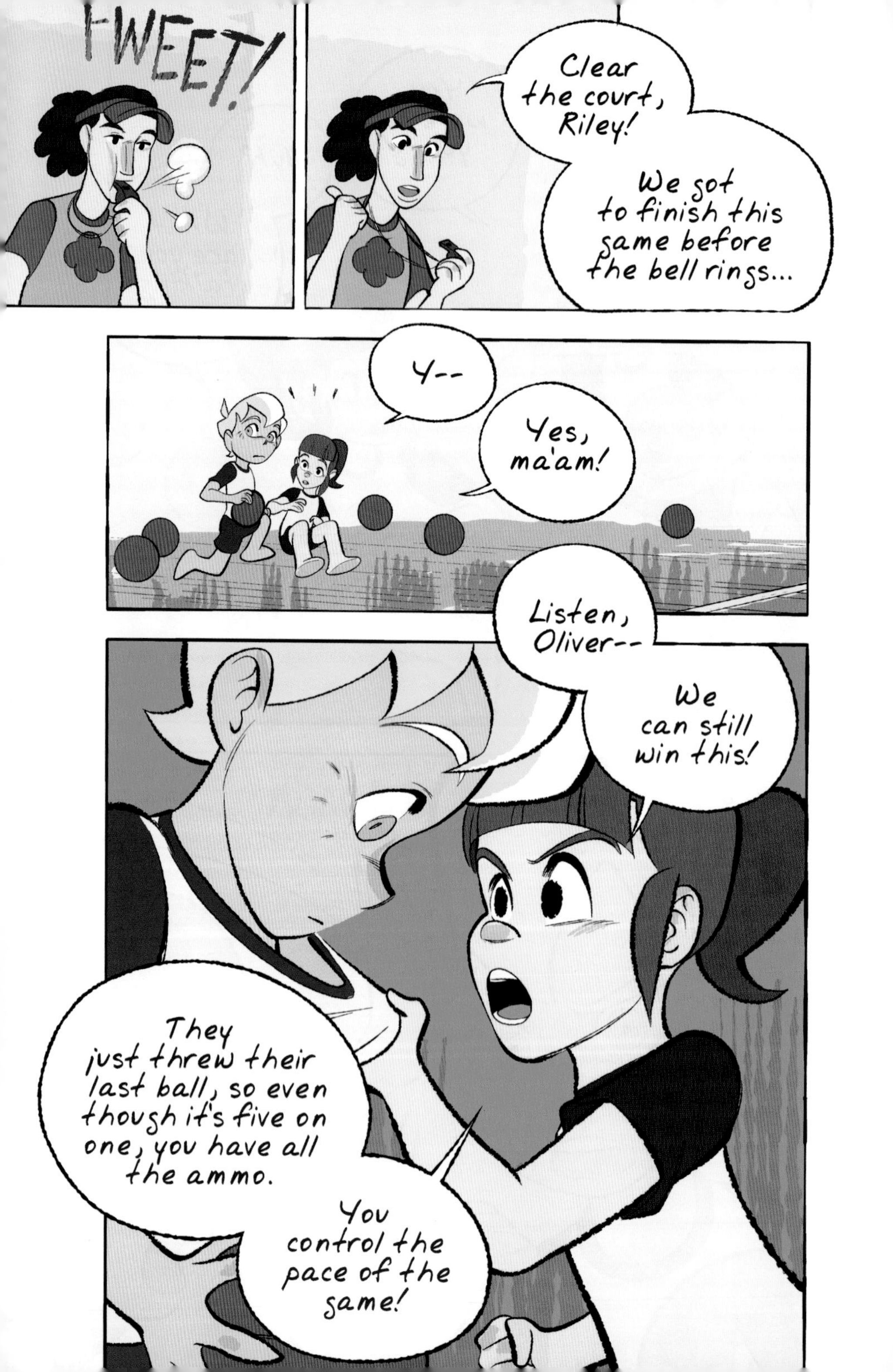
TWEET!
Clear the court, Riley!
We got to finish this game before the bell rings...
Y--
Yes, ma'am!
Listen, Oliver--
We can still win this!
They just threw their last ball, so even though it's five on one, you have all the ammo.
You control the pace of the game!

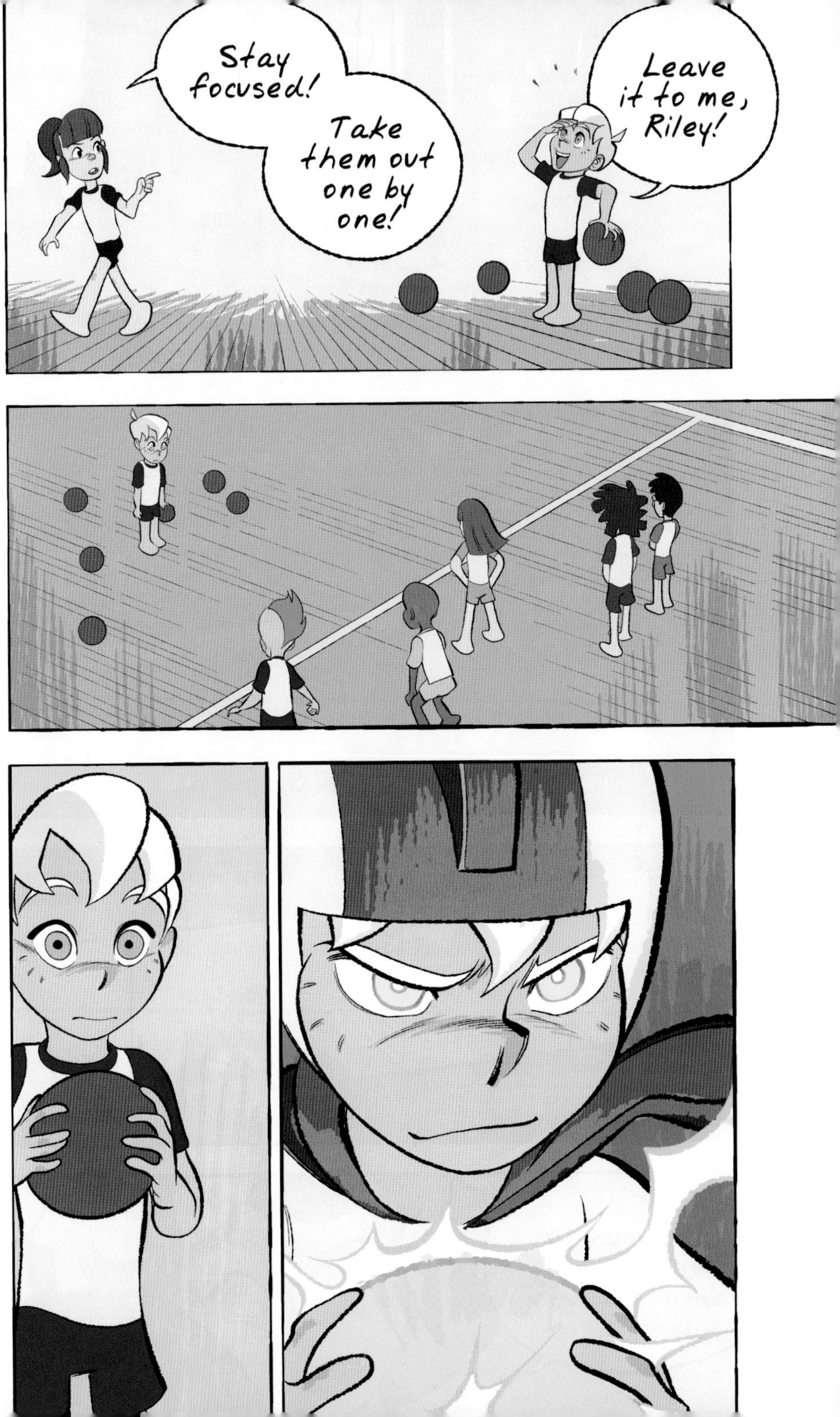
Stay focused!
Take them out one by one!
Leave it to me, Riley!

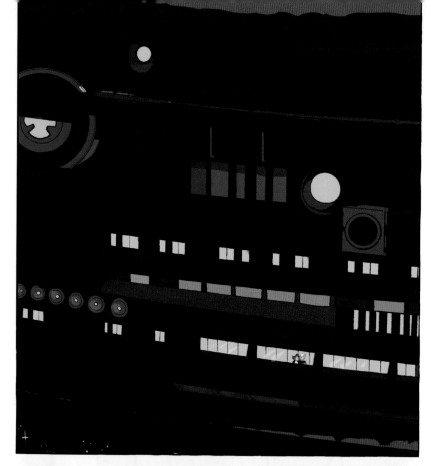

So did you tell Chief Hennins about all this?

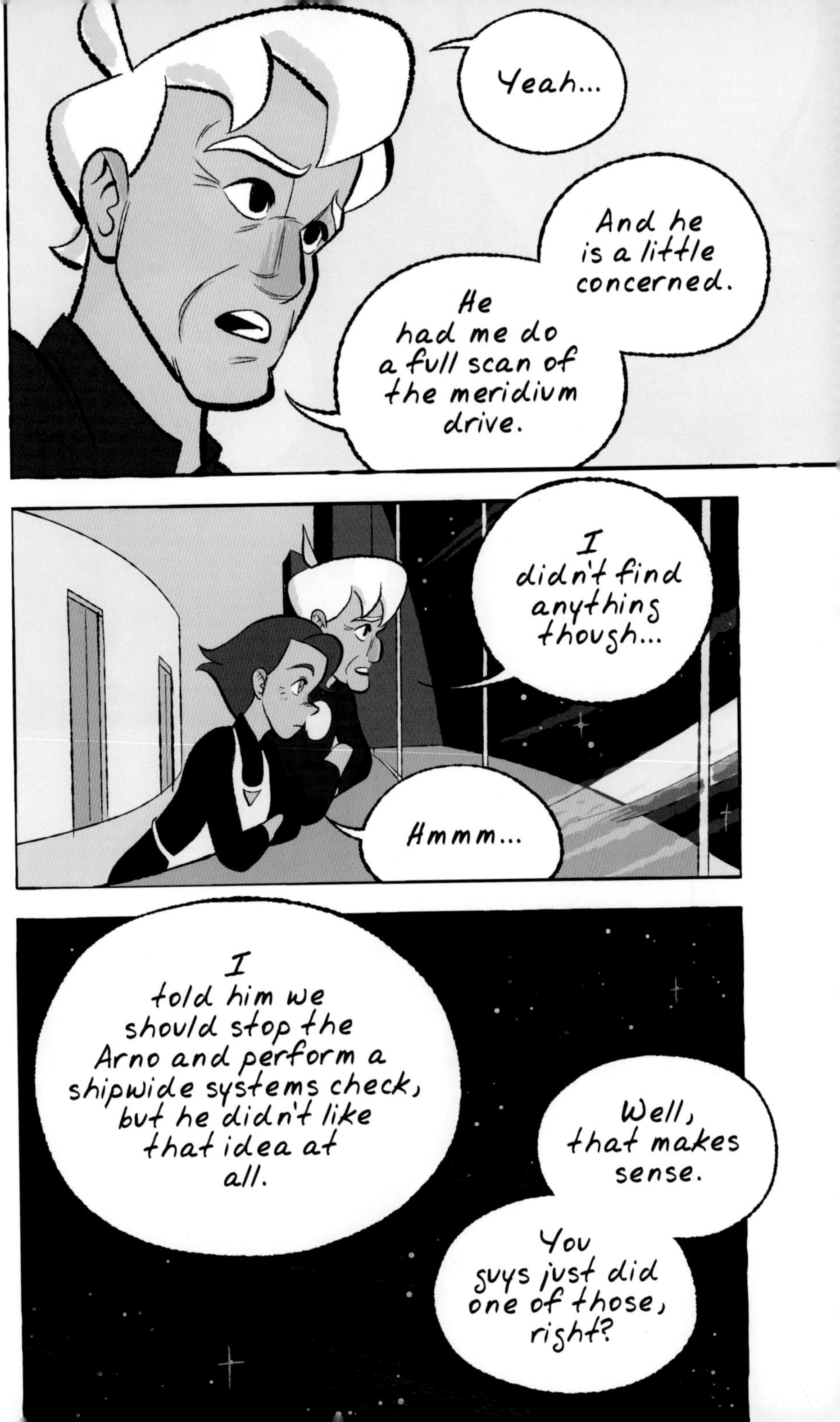
Yeah...
And he is a little concerned.
He had me do a full scan of the meridium drive.
I didn't find anything though...
Hmmm...
I told him we should stop the Arno and perform a shipwide systems check, but he didn't like that idea at all.
Well, that makes sense.
You guys just did one of those, right?

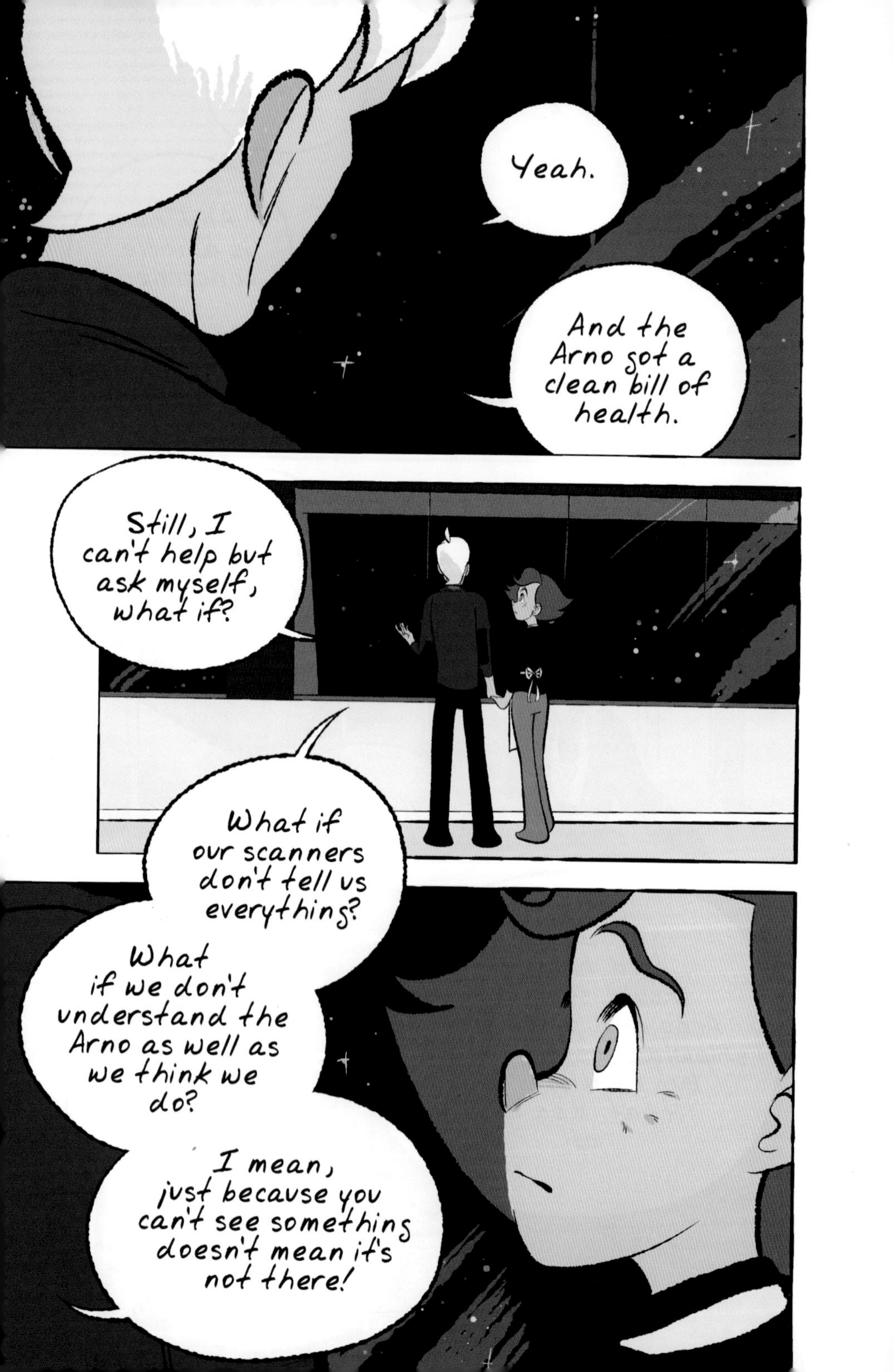
Yeah.
And the Arno got a clean bill of health.
Still, I can't help but ask myself, what if?
What if our scanners don't tell us everything?
What if we don't understand the Arno as well as we think we do?
I mean, just because you can't see something doesn't mean it's not there!

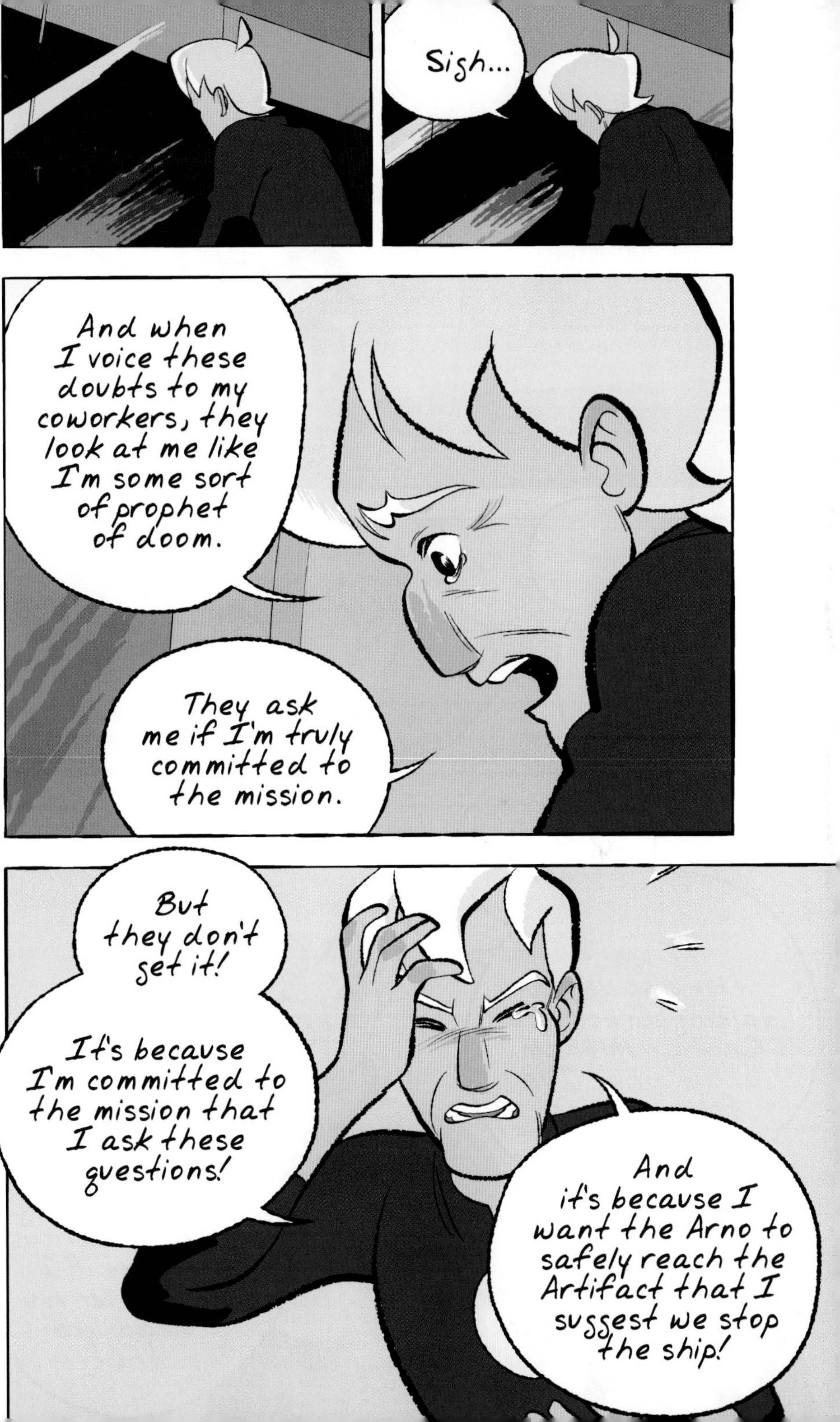
Sigh...
And when I voice these doubts to my coworkers, they look at me like I'm some sort of prophet of doom.
They ask me if I'm truly committed to the mission.
But they don't get it!
It's because I'm committed to the mission that I ask these questions!
And it's because I want the Arno to safely reach the Artifact that I suggest we stop the ship!

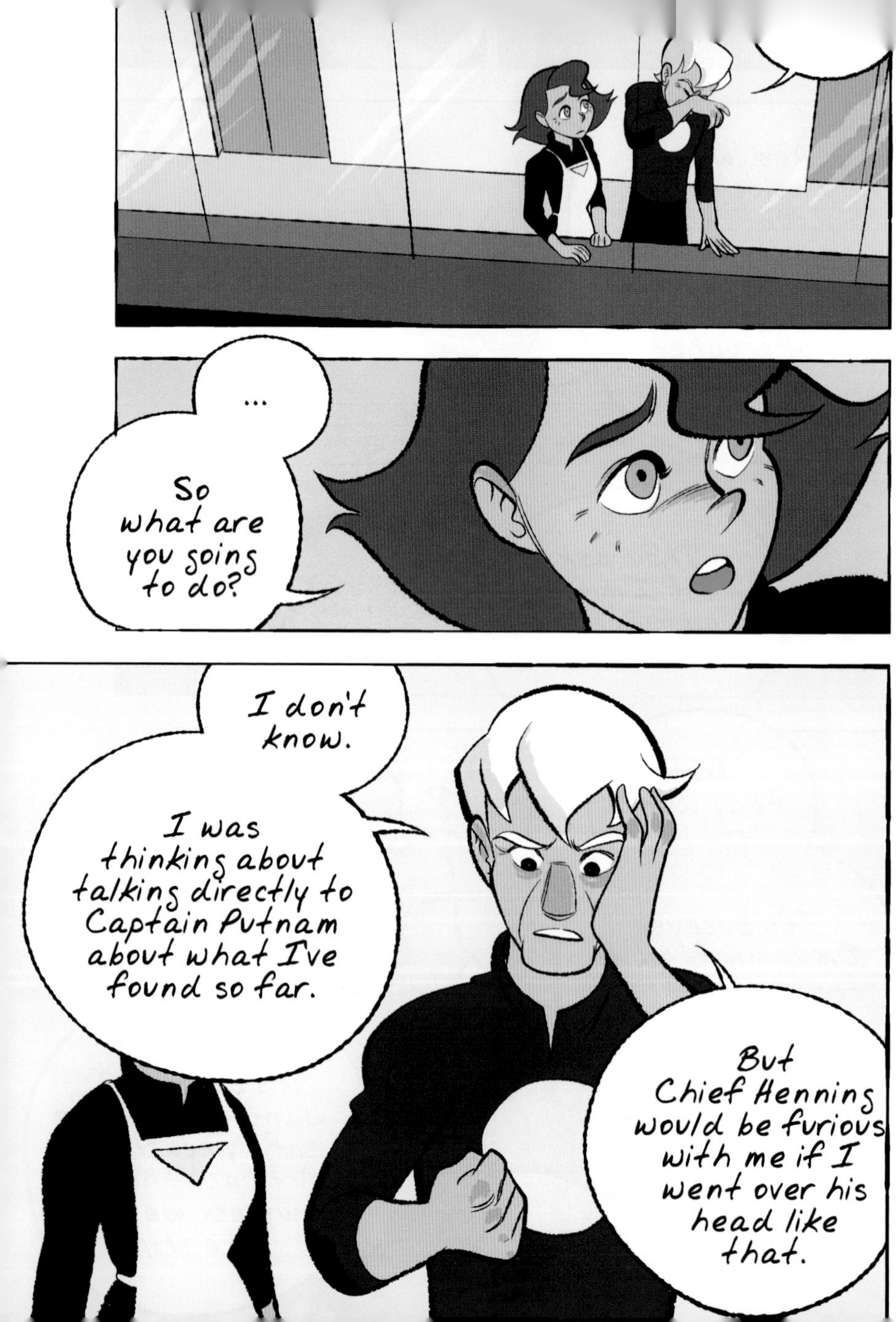
...
So what are you going to do?
I don't know.
I was thinking about talking directly to Captain Putnam about what I've found so far.
But Chief Hennings would be furious with me if I went over his head like that.

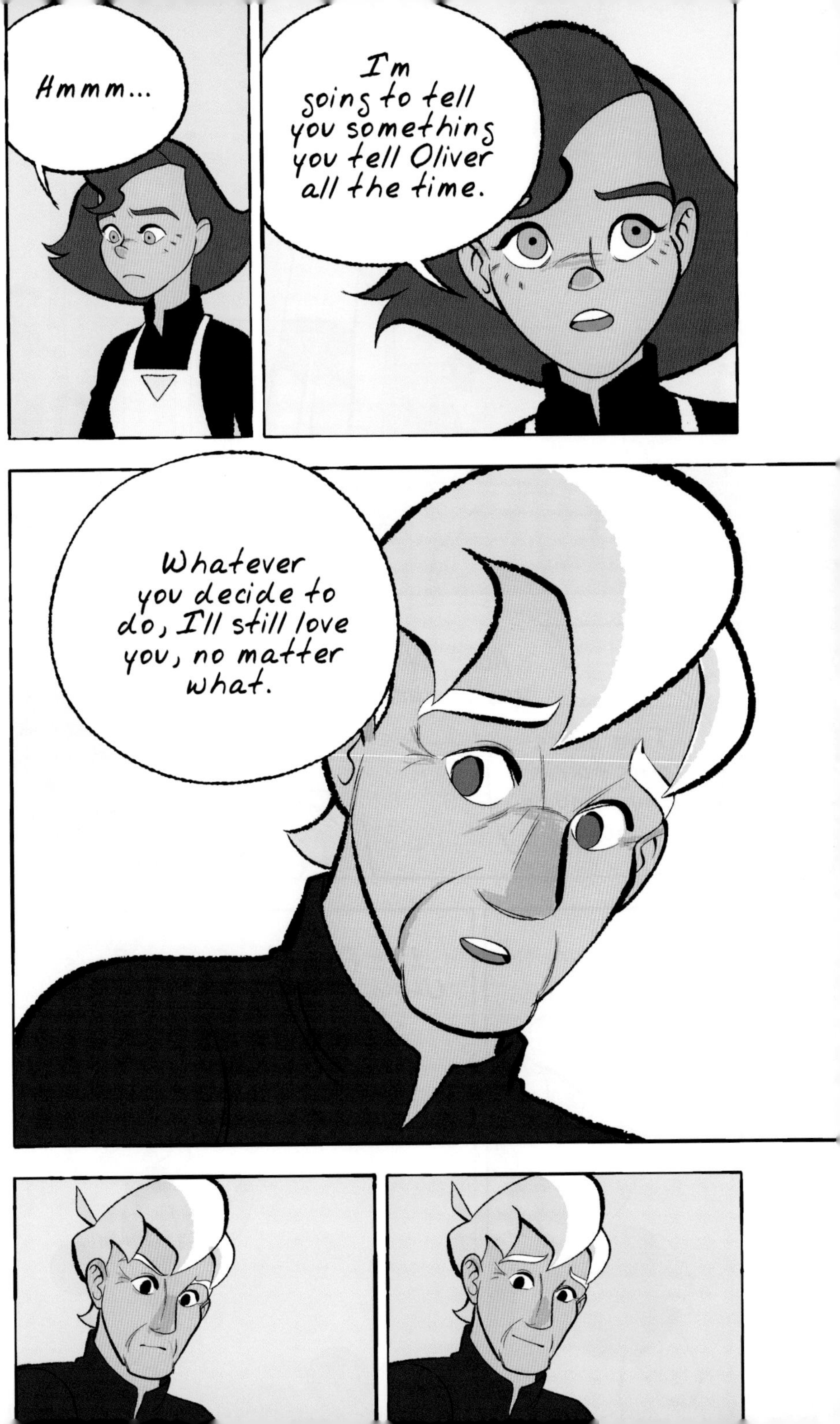
Hmmm...
I'm going to tell you something you tell Oliver all the time.
Whatever you decide to do, I'll still love you, no matter what.

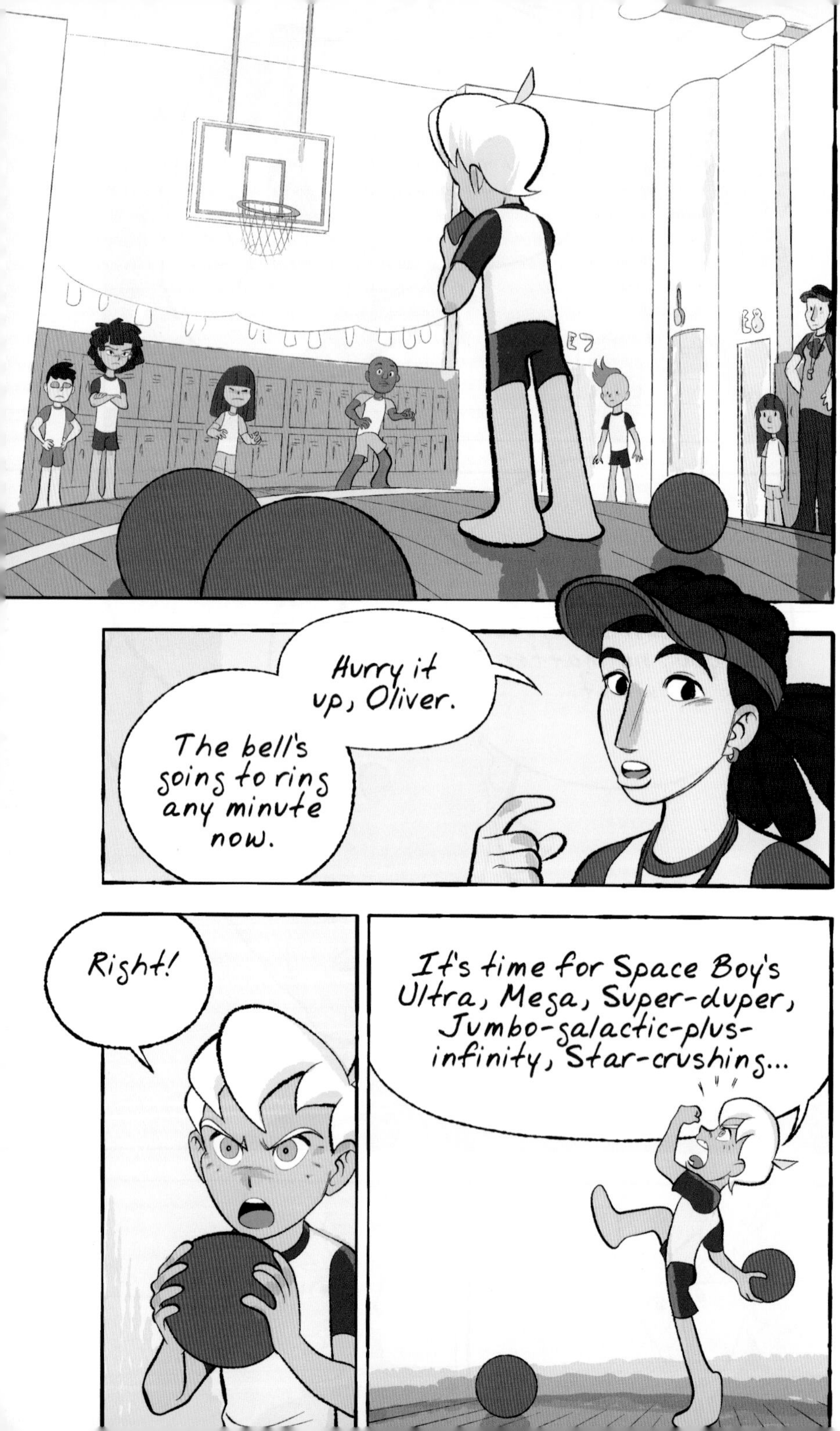
Hurry it up, Oliver.
The bell's going to ring any minute now.
Right!
It's time for Space Boy's Ultra, Mega, Super-duper, Jumbo-galactic-plus-infinity, Star-crushing...

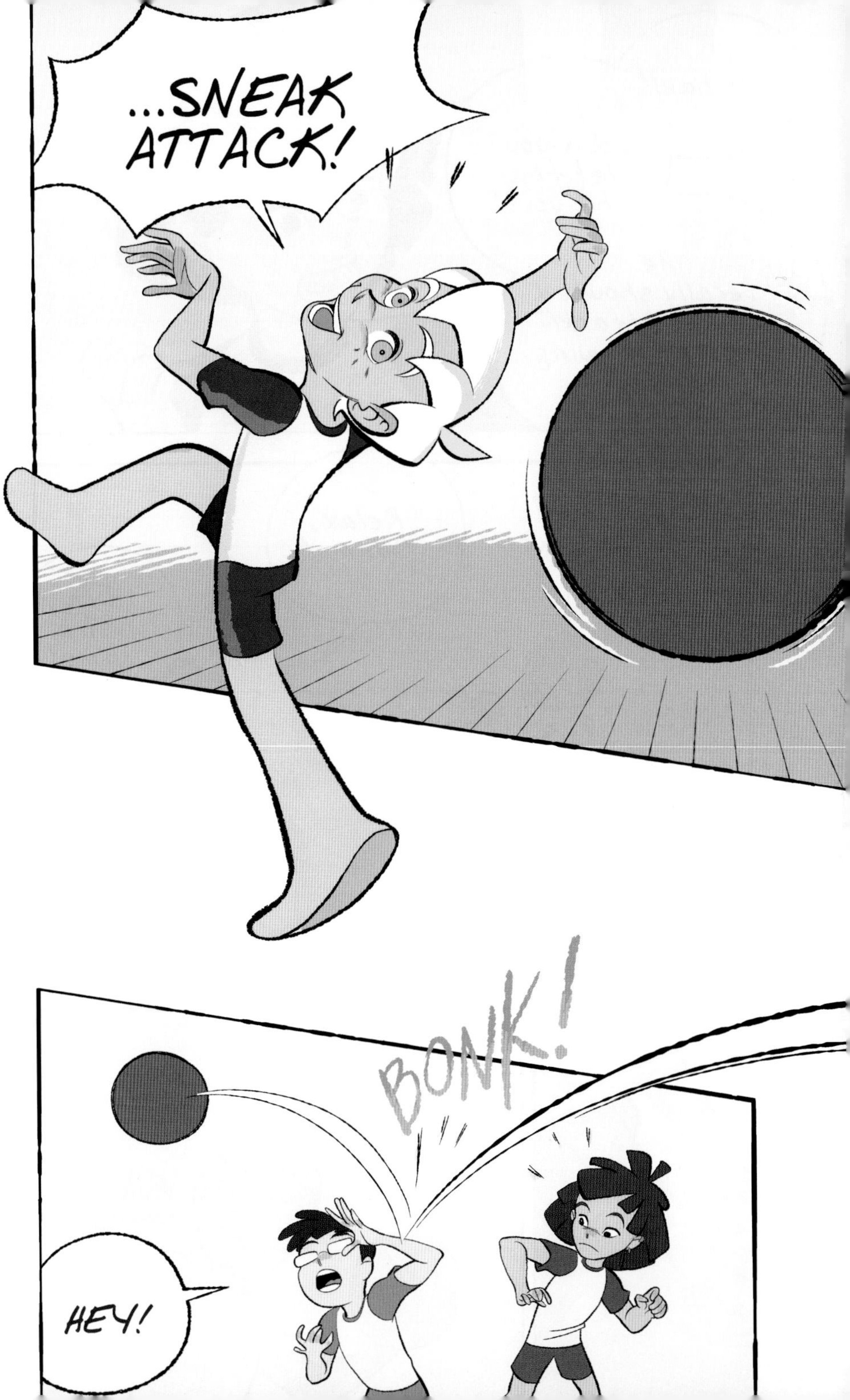
...SNEAK ATTACK!
BONK!
HEY!

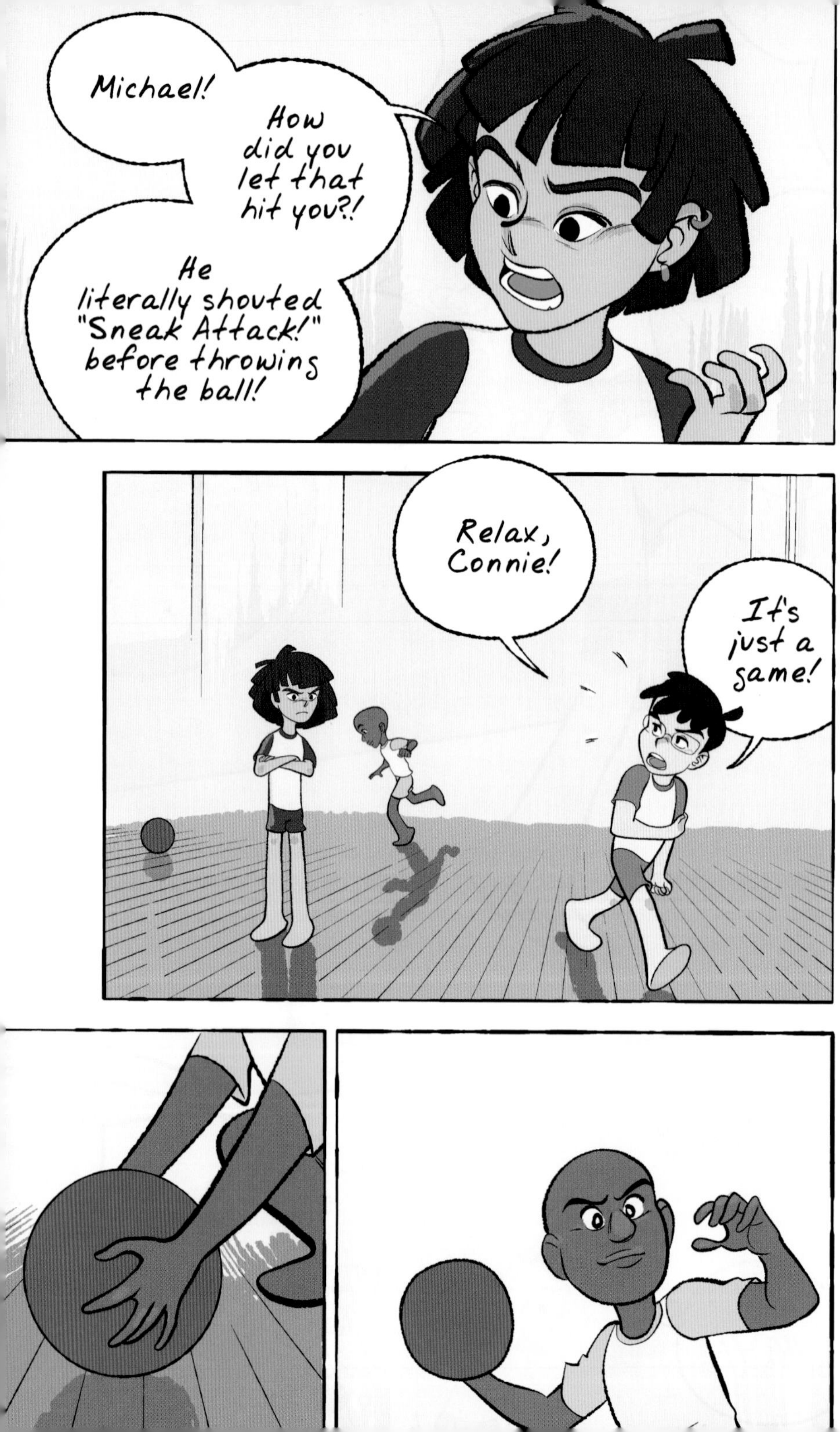
Michael!
How did you let that hit you?!
He literally shouted "Sneak Attack!" before throwing the ball!
Relax, Connie!
It's just a game!

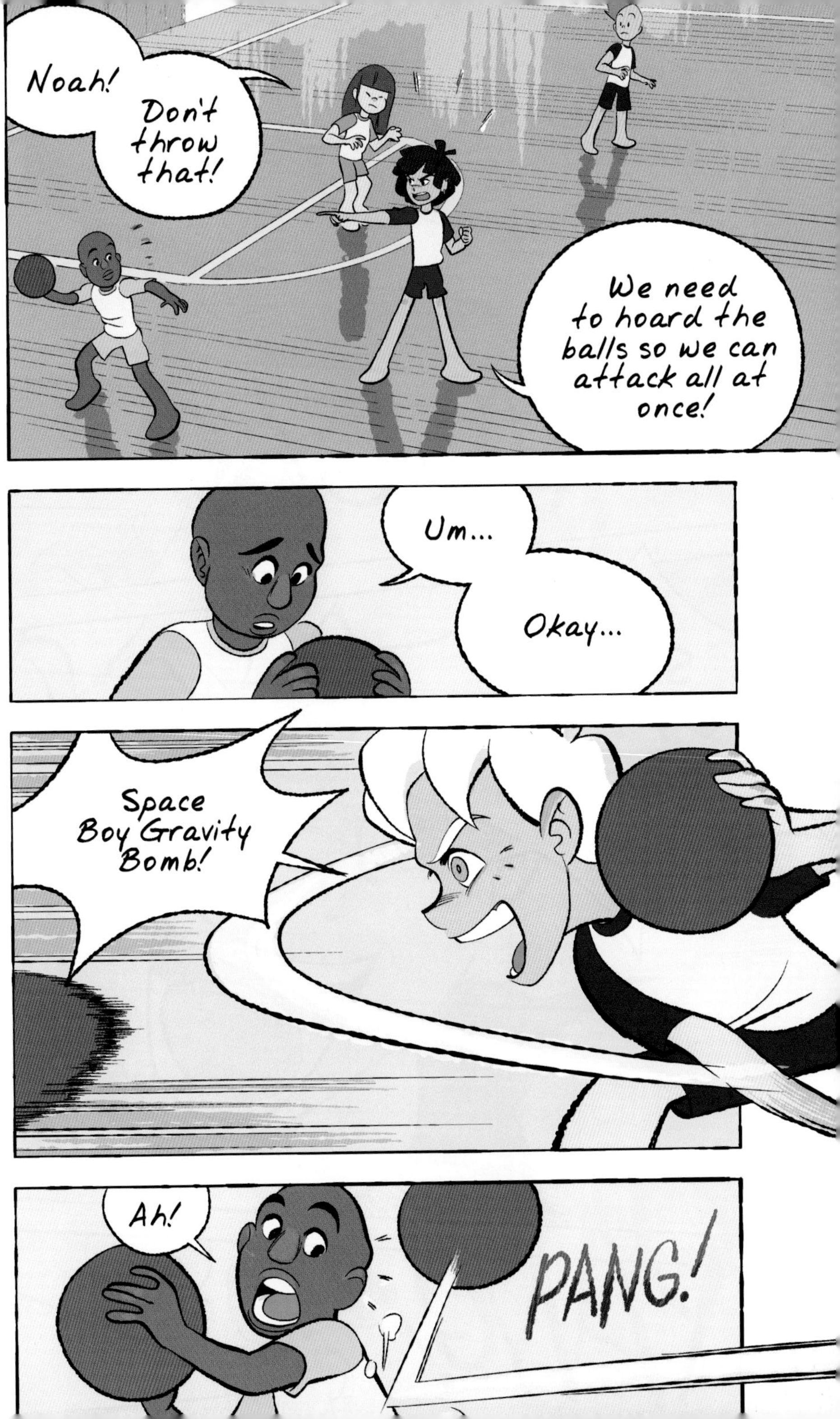
Noah!
Don't throw that!
We need to hoard the balls so we can attack all at once!
Um...
Okay...
Space Boy Gravity Bomb!
Ah!
PANG!

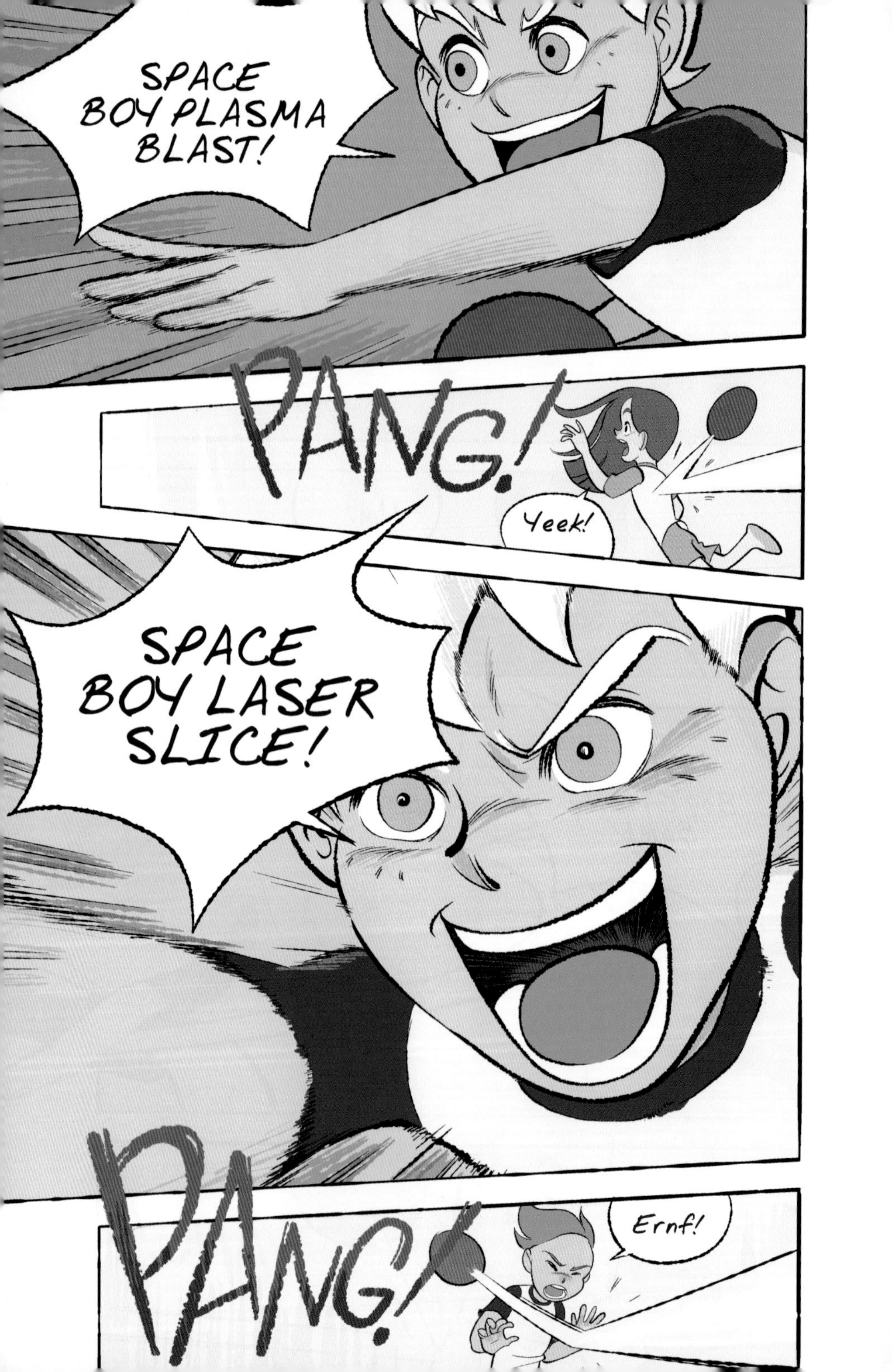

SPACE BOY PLASMA BLAST!
PANG!
Yeek!
SPACE BOY LASER SLICE!
PANG!
Ernf!

FWEET!

You three are out!

It's down to Connie and Oliver!

Wow! Oliver's better than I thought!

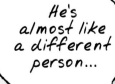

Yeah...

He's almost like a different person...

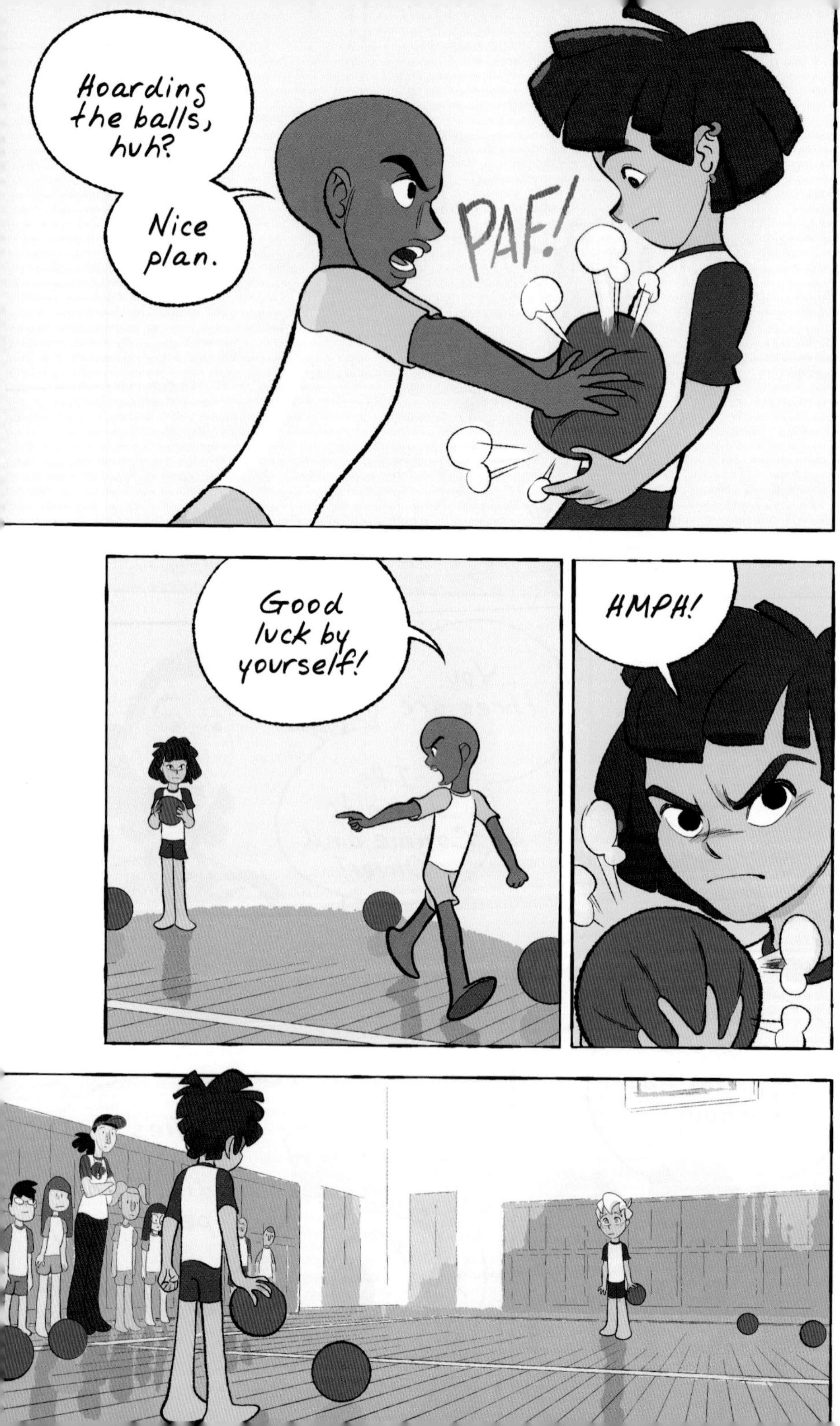
Hoarding the balls, huh?
Nice plan.
PAF!
Good luck by yourself!
HMPH!

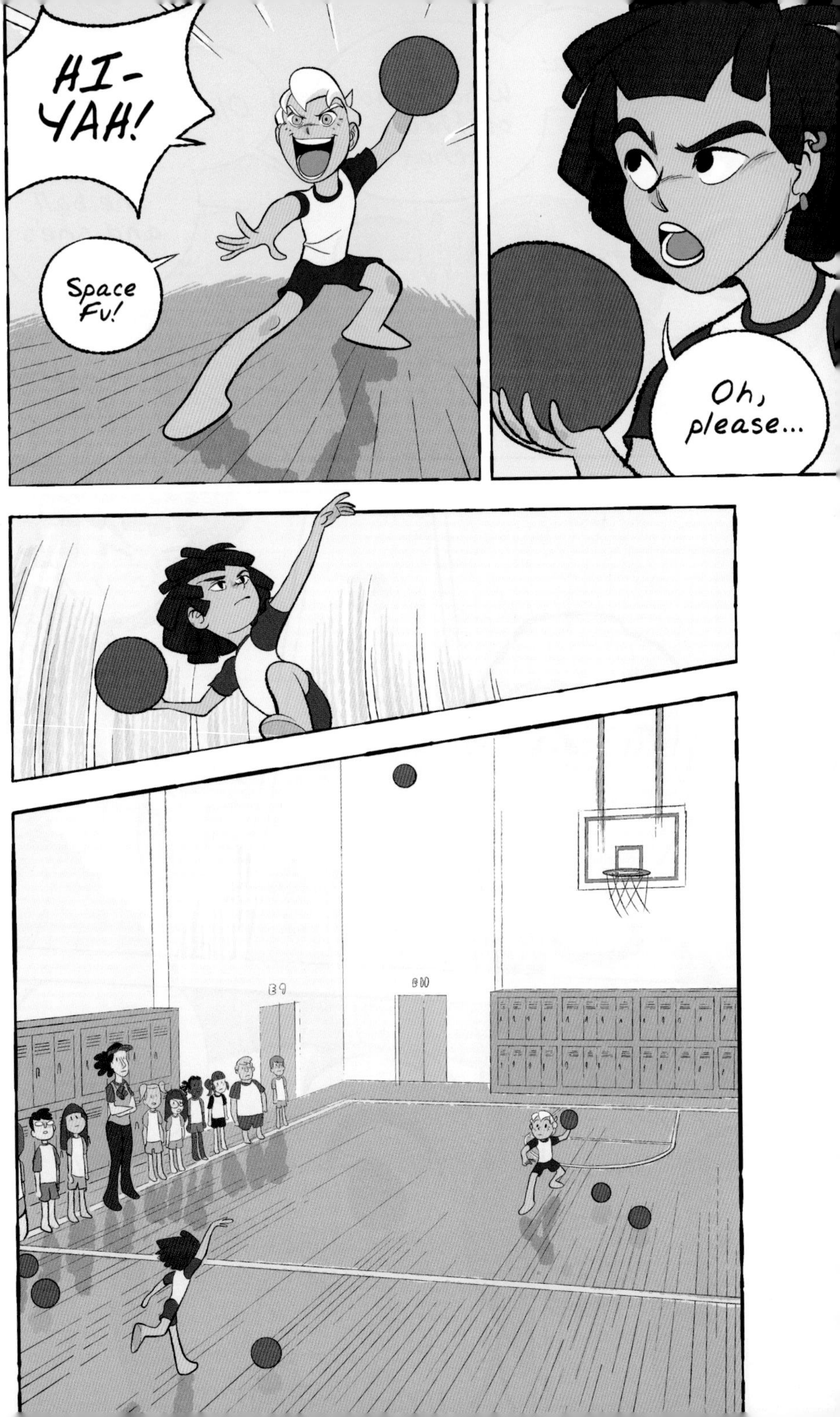
HI-
YAH!
Space
Fu!
Oh,
please...
E9
E10

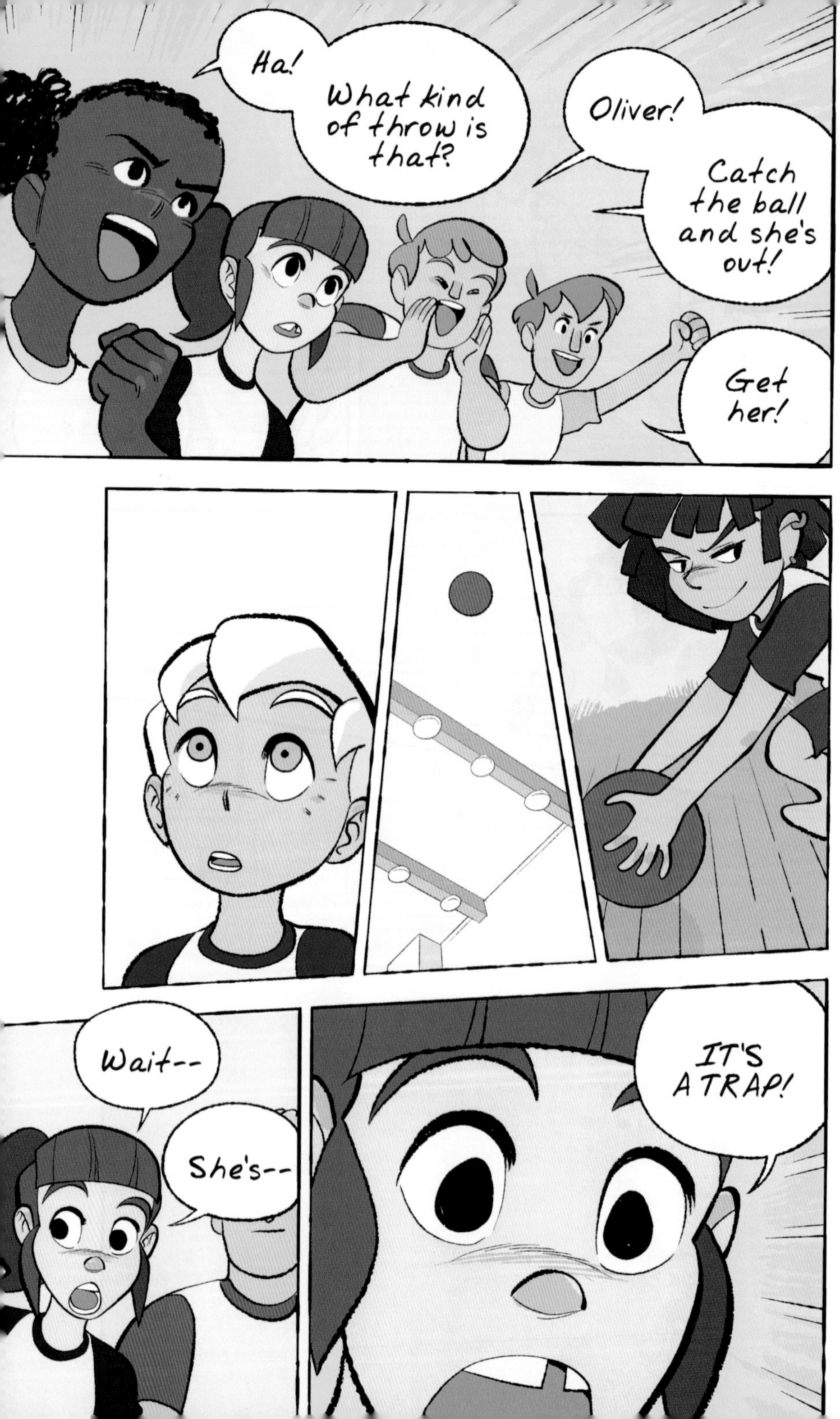

Ha!
What kind of throw is that?
Oliver!
Catch the ball and she's out!
Get her!
Wait--
She's--
IT'S A TRAP!

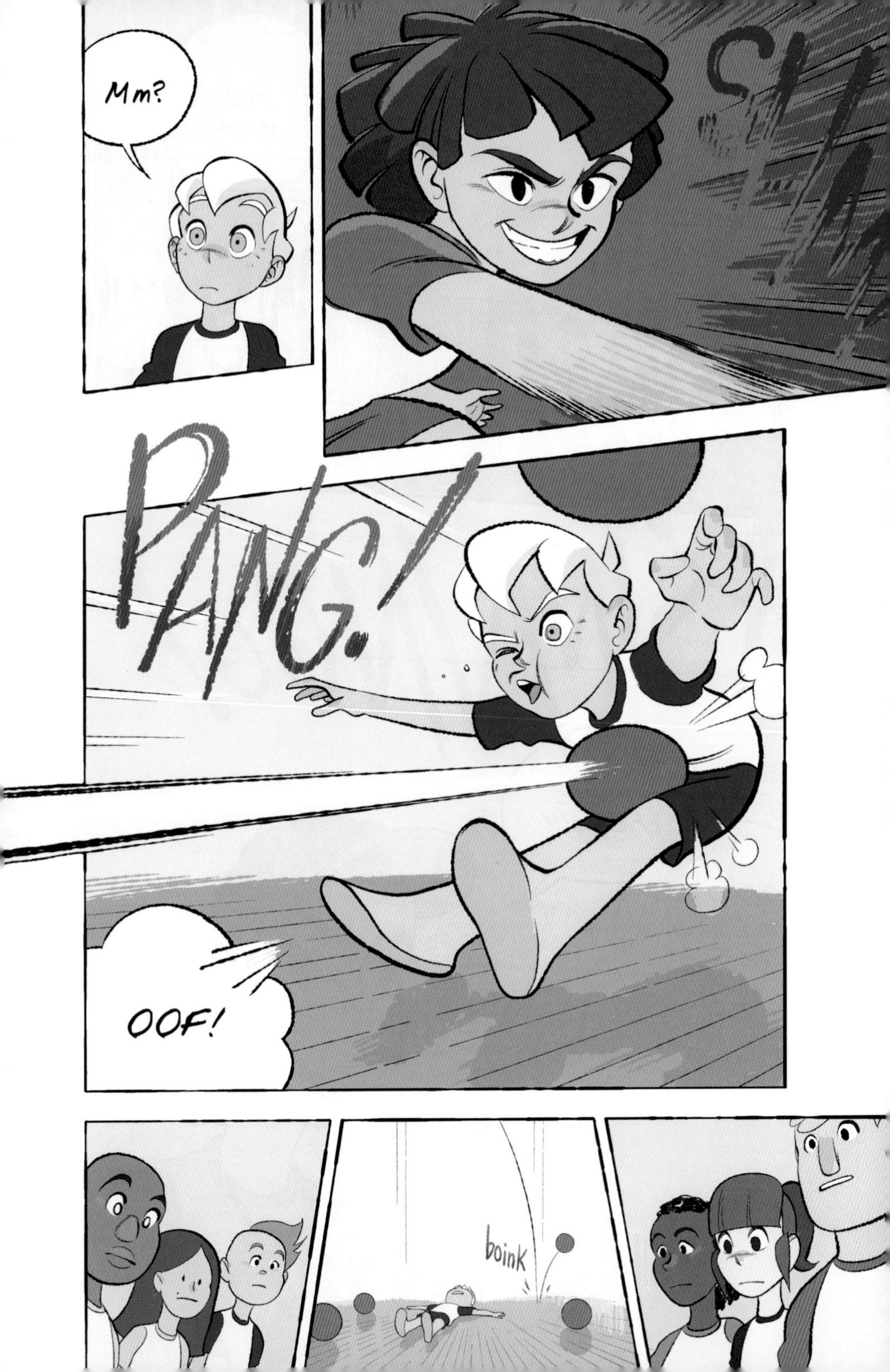
Mm?
SH
PANG!
OOF!
boink

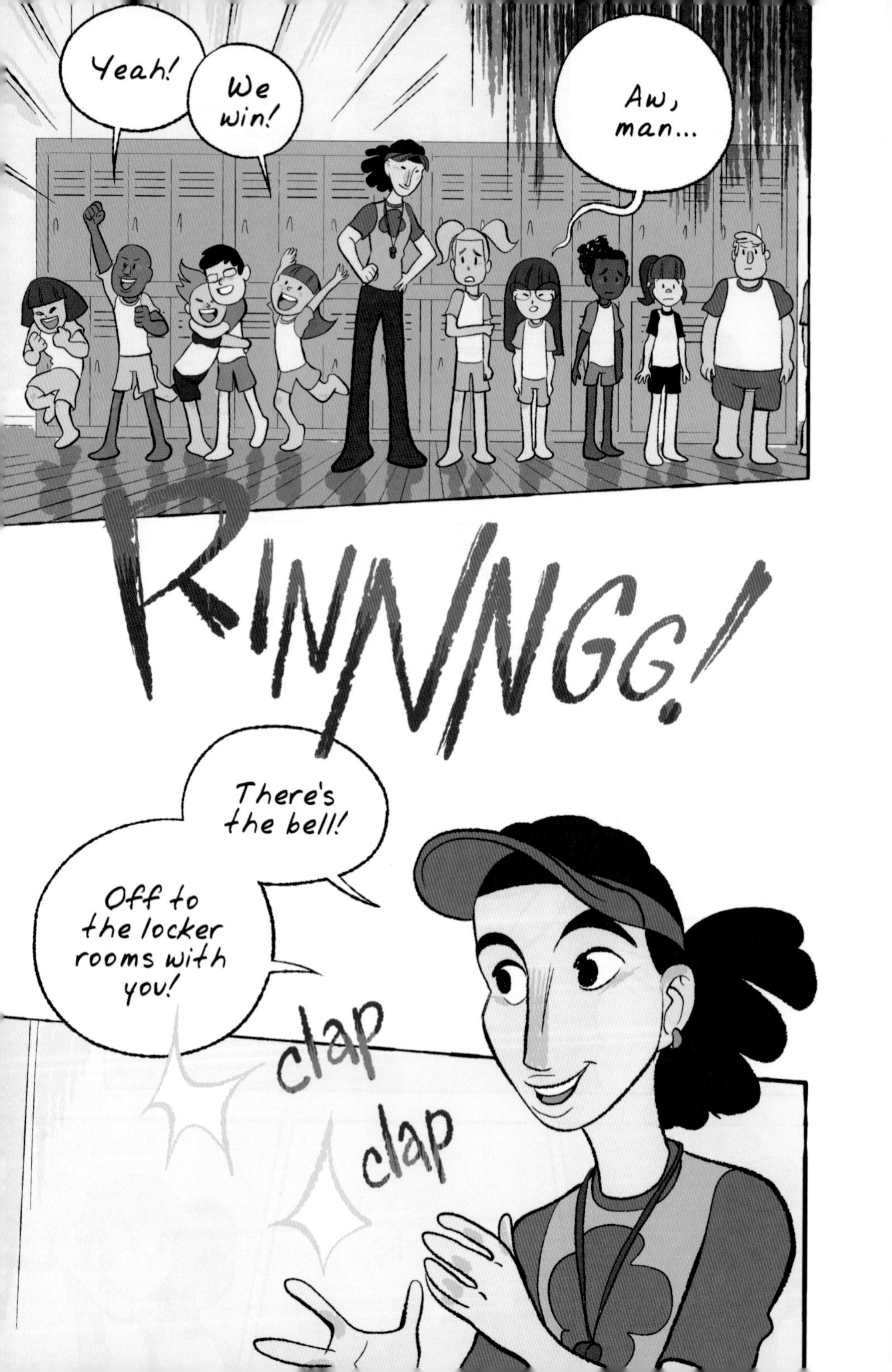
Yeah!
We win!
Aw, man...
RINNNGG!
There's the bell!
Off to the locker rooms with you!
clap
clap

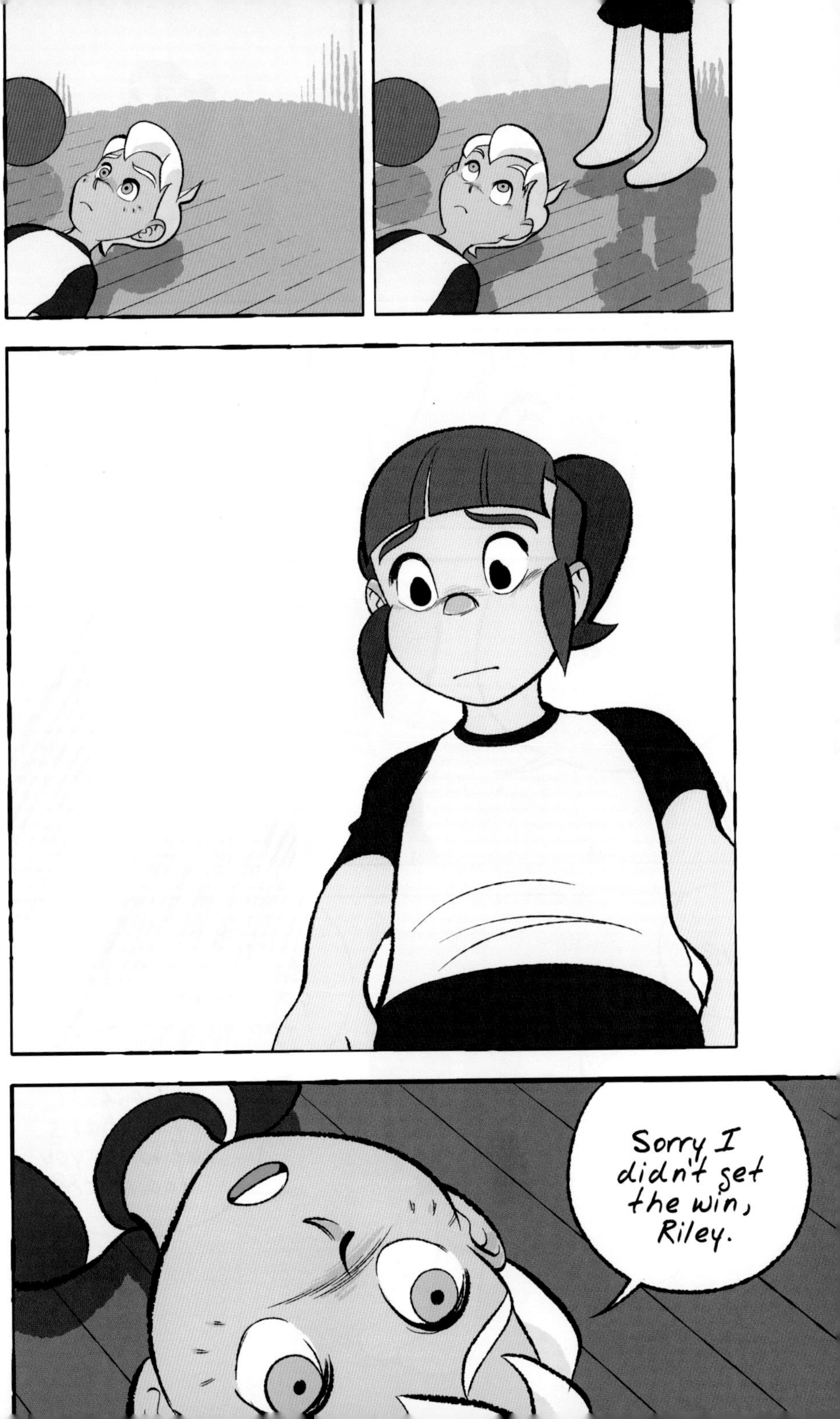
Sorry I didn't get the win, Riley.

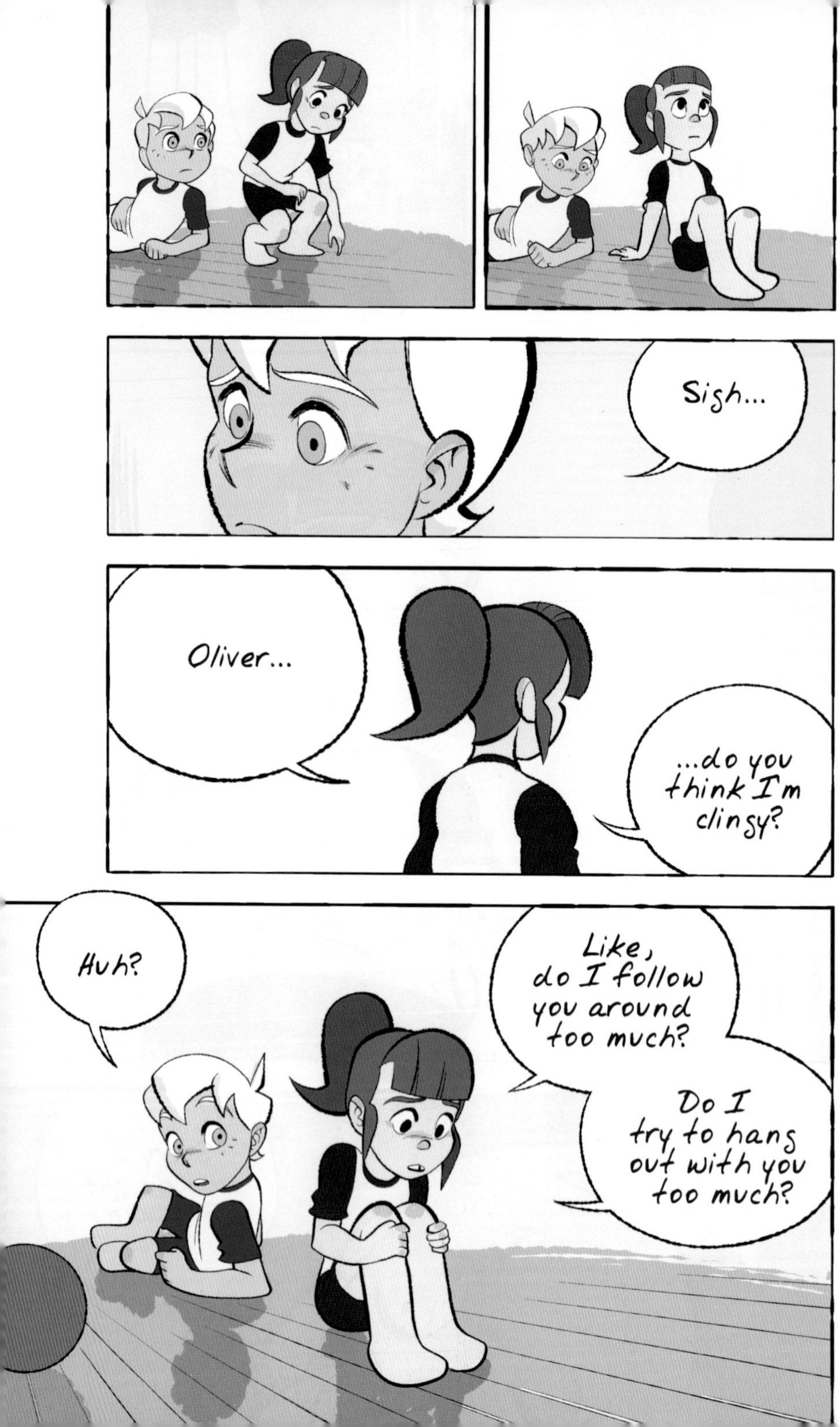
Sigh...
Oliver...
...do you think I'm clingy?
Huh?
Like, do I follow you around too much?
Do I try to hang out with you too much?

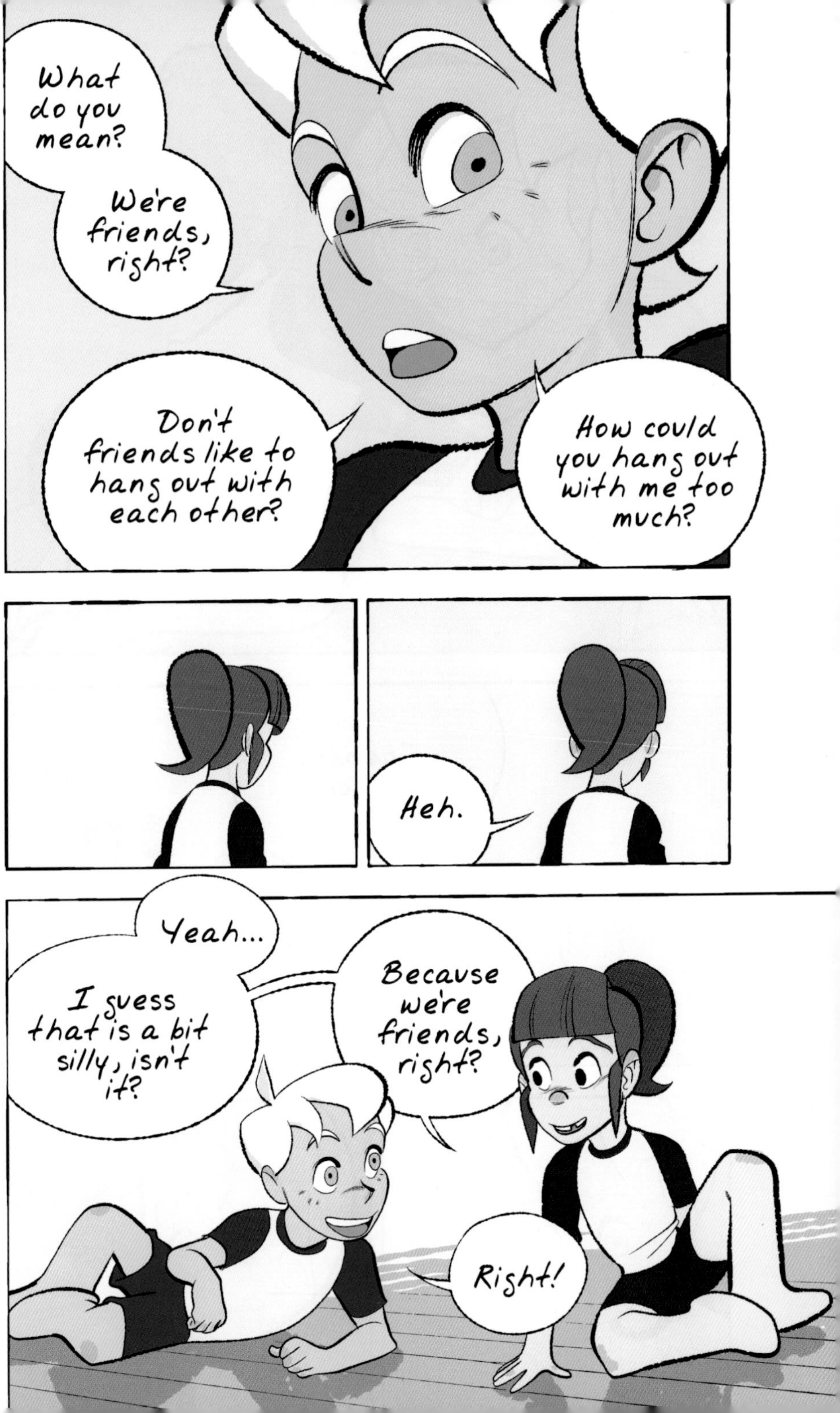
What do you mean?
We're friends, right?
Don't friends like to hang out with each other?
How could you hang out with me too much?
Heh.
Yeah...
I guess that is a bit silly, isn't it?
Because we're friends, right?
Right!

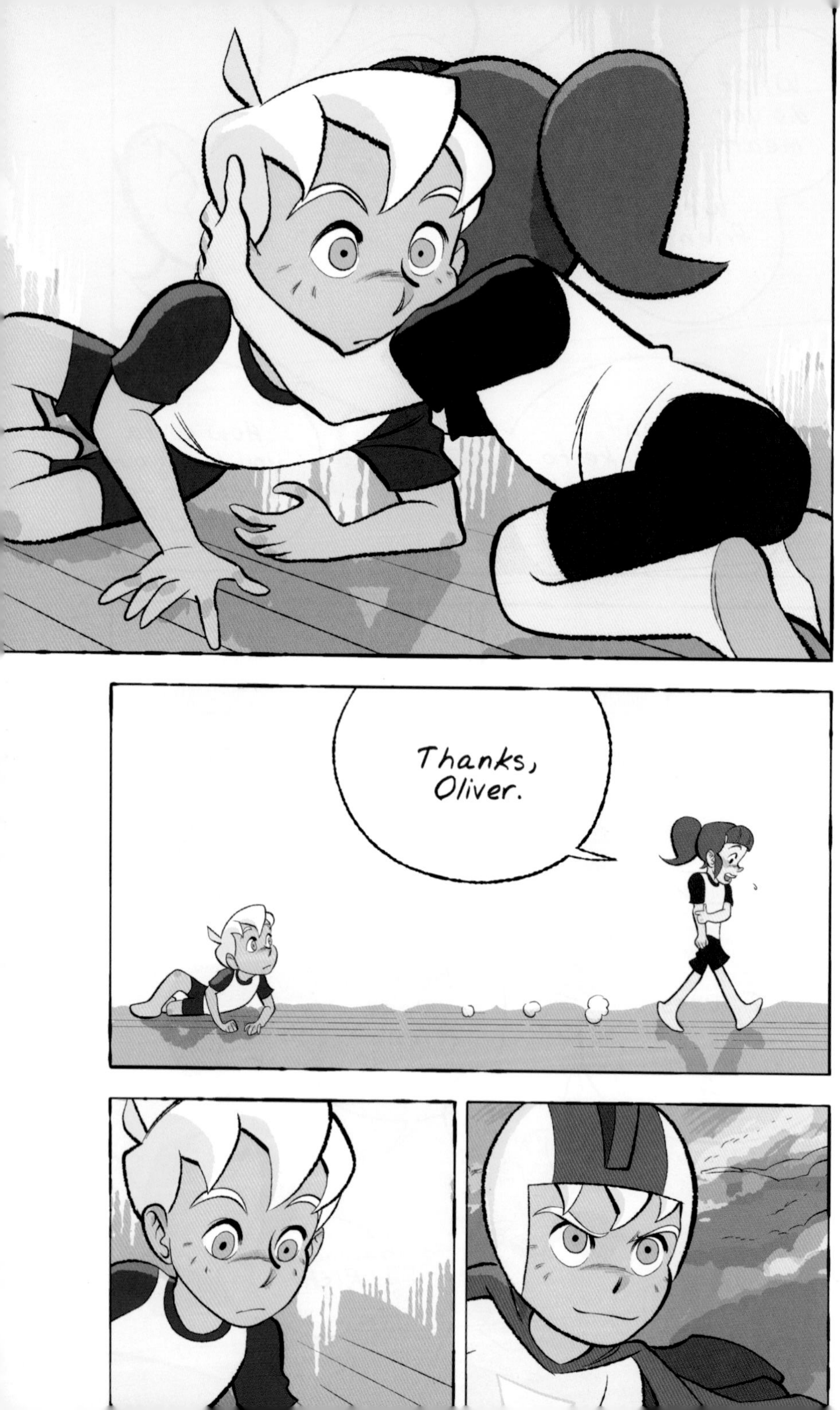
Thanks, Oliver.

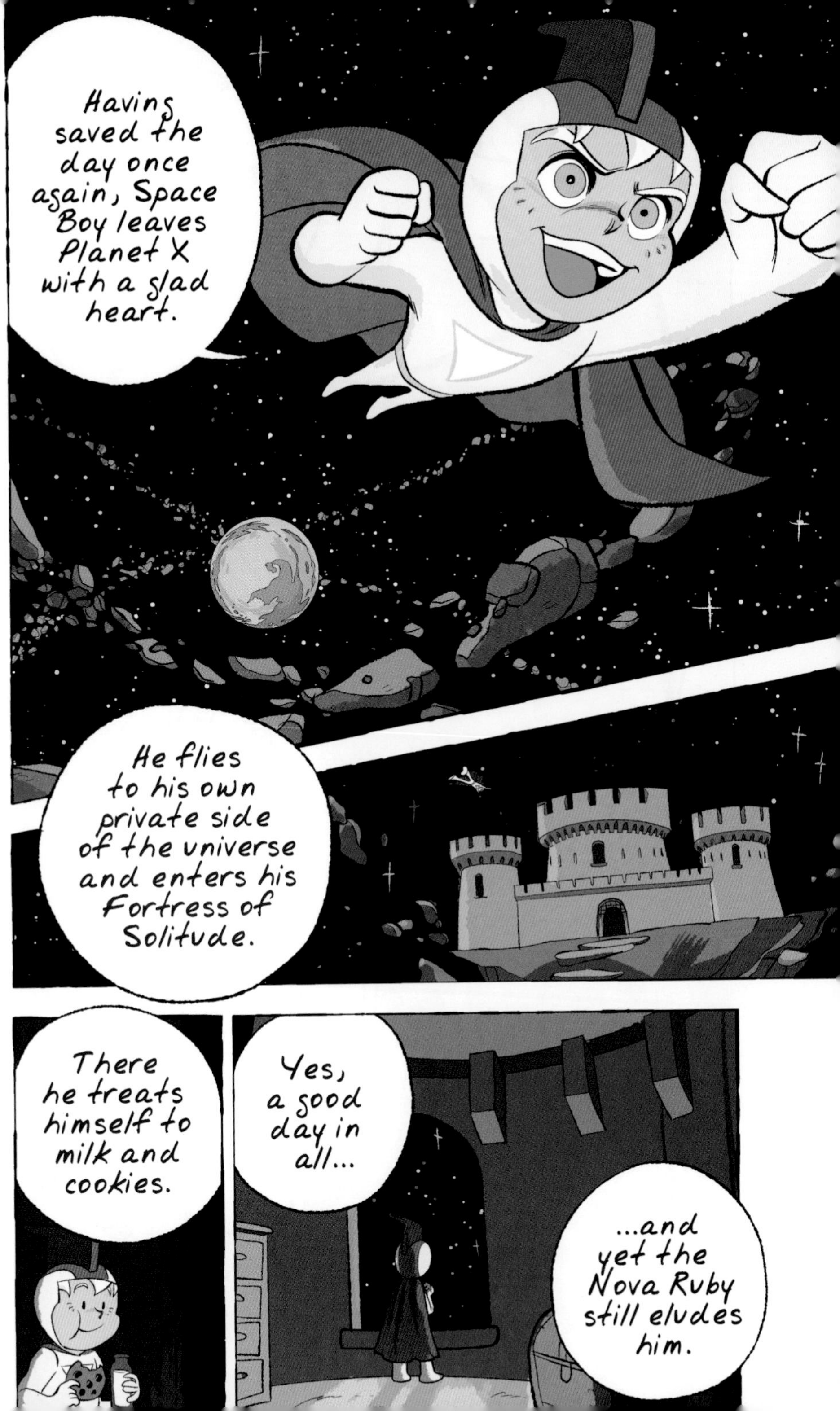
Having saved the day once again, Space Boy leaves Planet X with a glad heart.
He flies to his own private side of the universe and enters his Fortress of Solitude.
There he treats himself to milk and cookies.
Yes, a good day in all...
...and yet the Nova Ruby still eludes him.

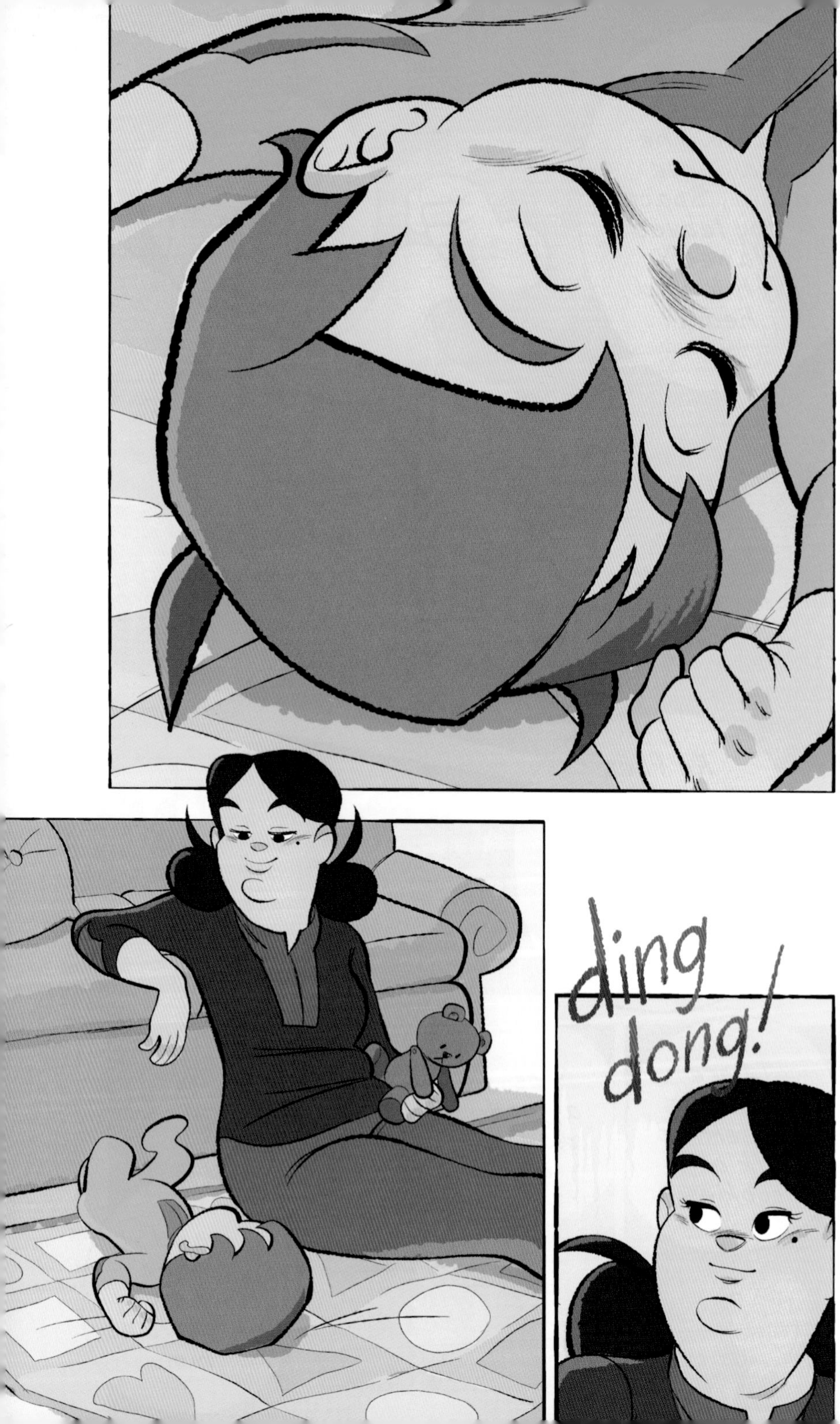
ding dong!

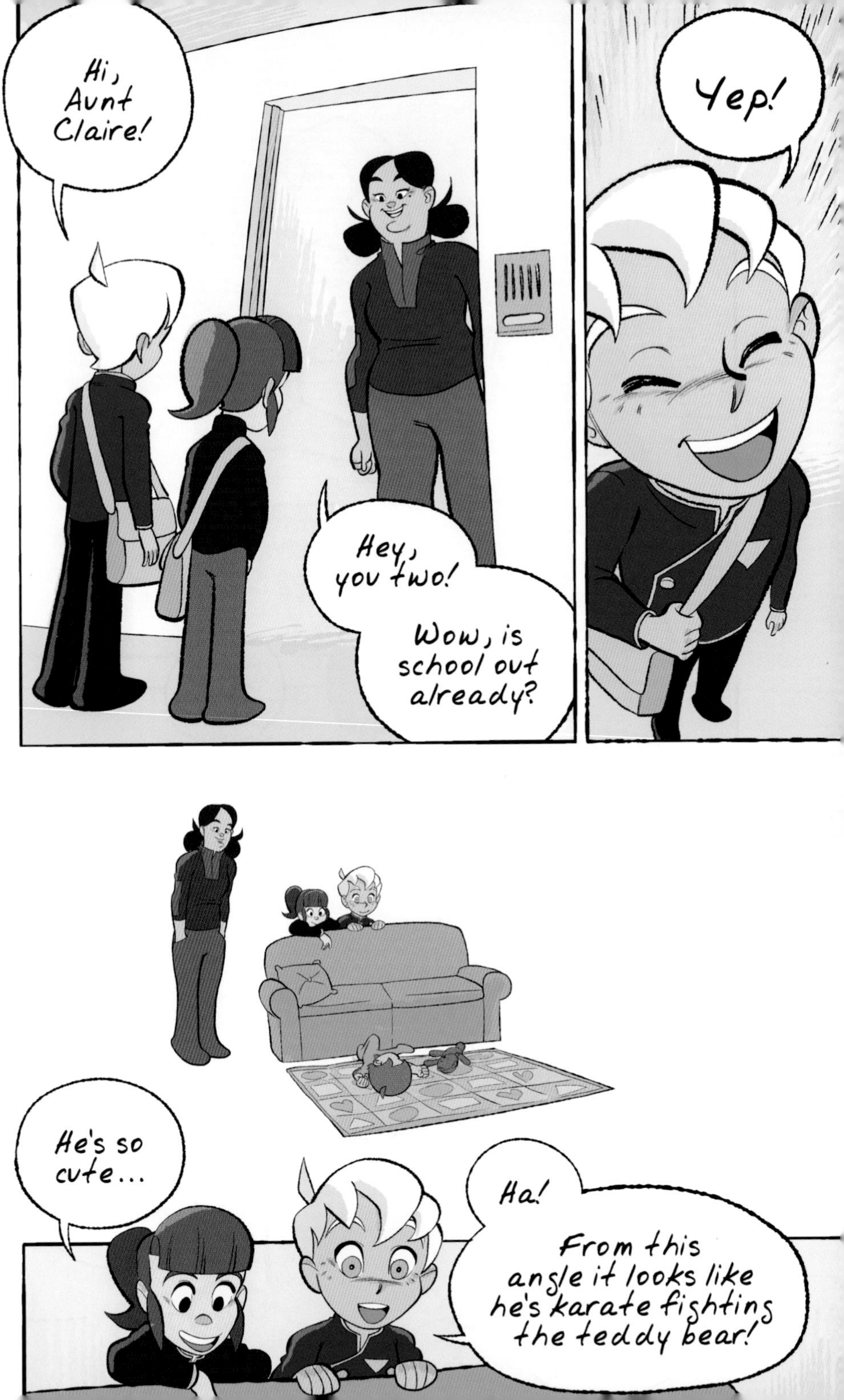
Hi, Aunt Claire!
Hey, you two!
Wow, is school out already?
Yep!
He's so cute...
Ha!
From this angle it looks like he's karate fighting the teddy bear!

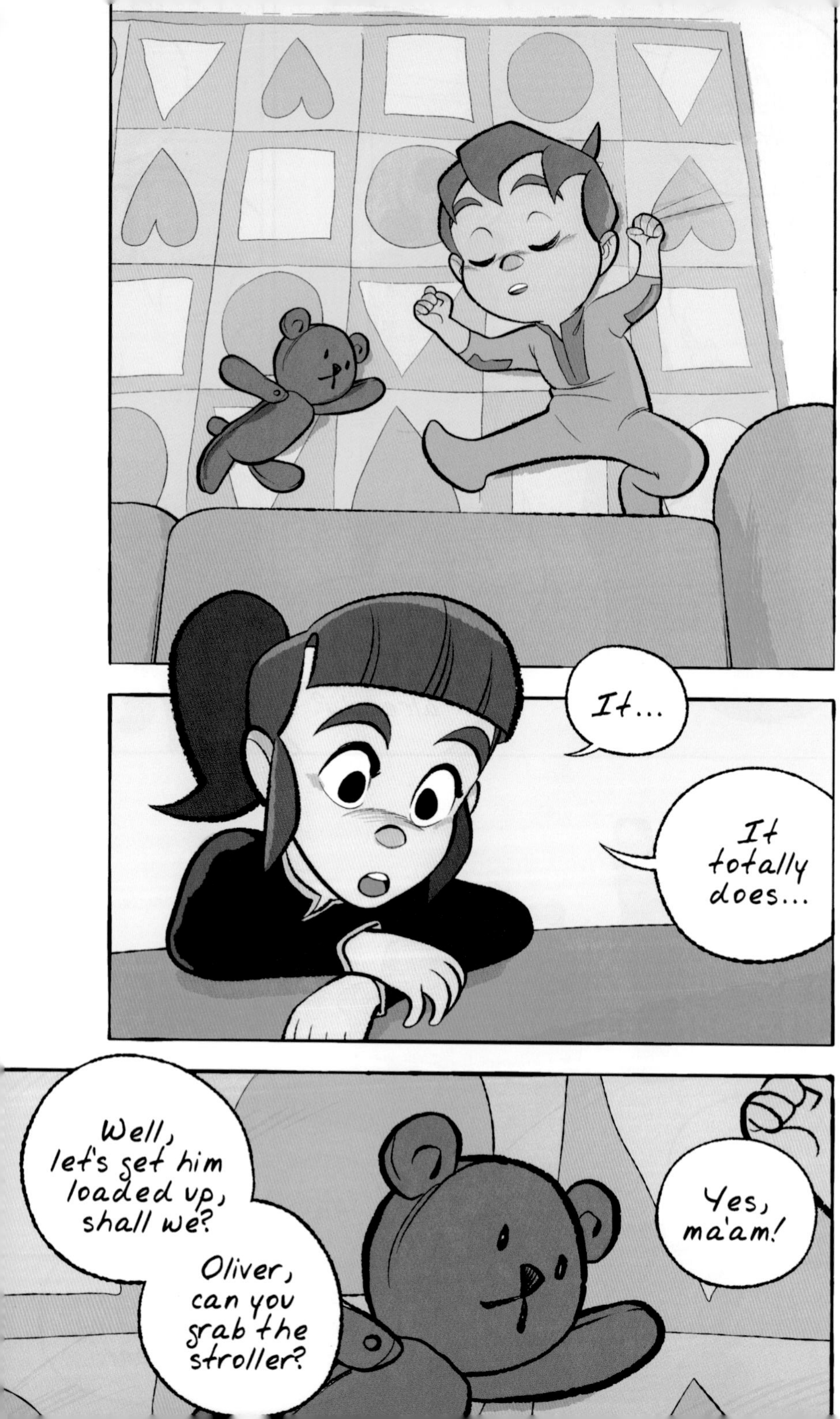
It...
It totally does...
Well, let's get him loaded up, shall we?
Oliver, can you grab the stroller?
Yes, ma'am!

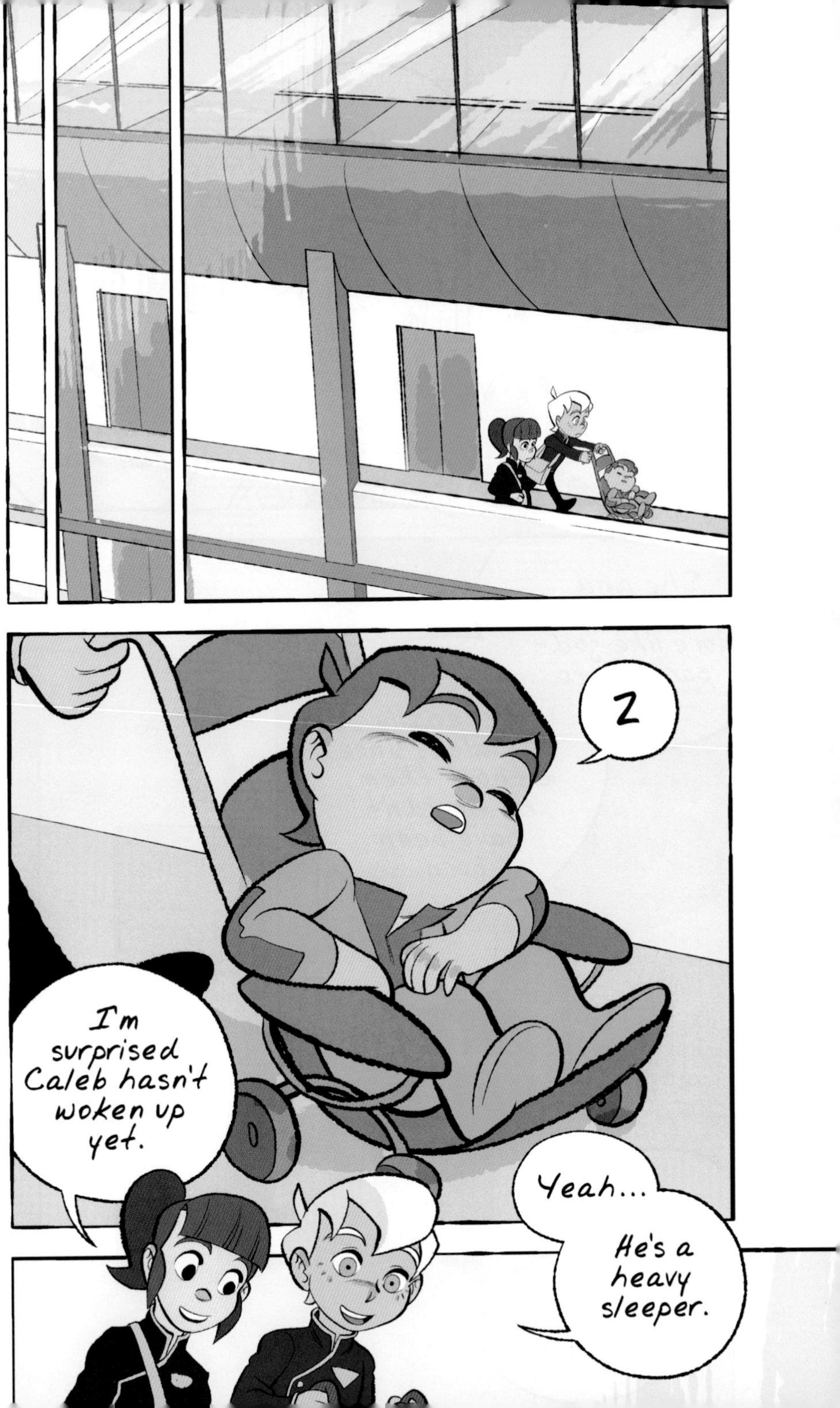
Z
I'm surprised Caleb hasn't woken up yet.
Yeah...
He's a heavy sleeper.

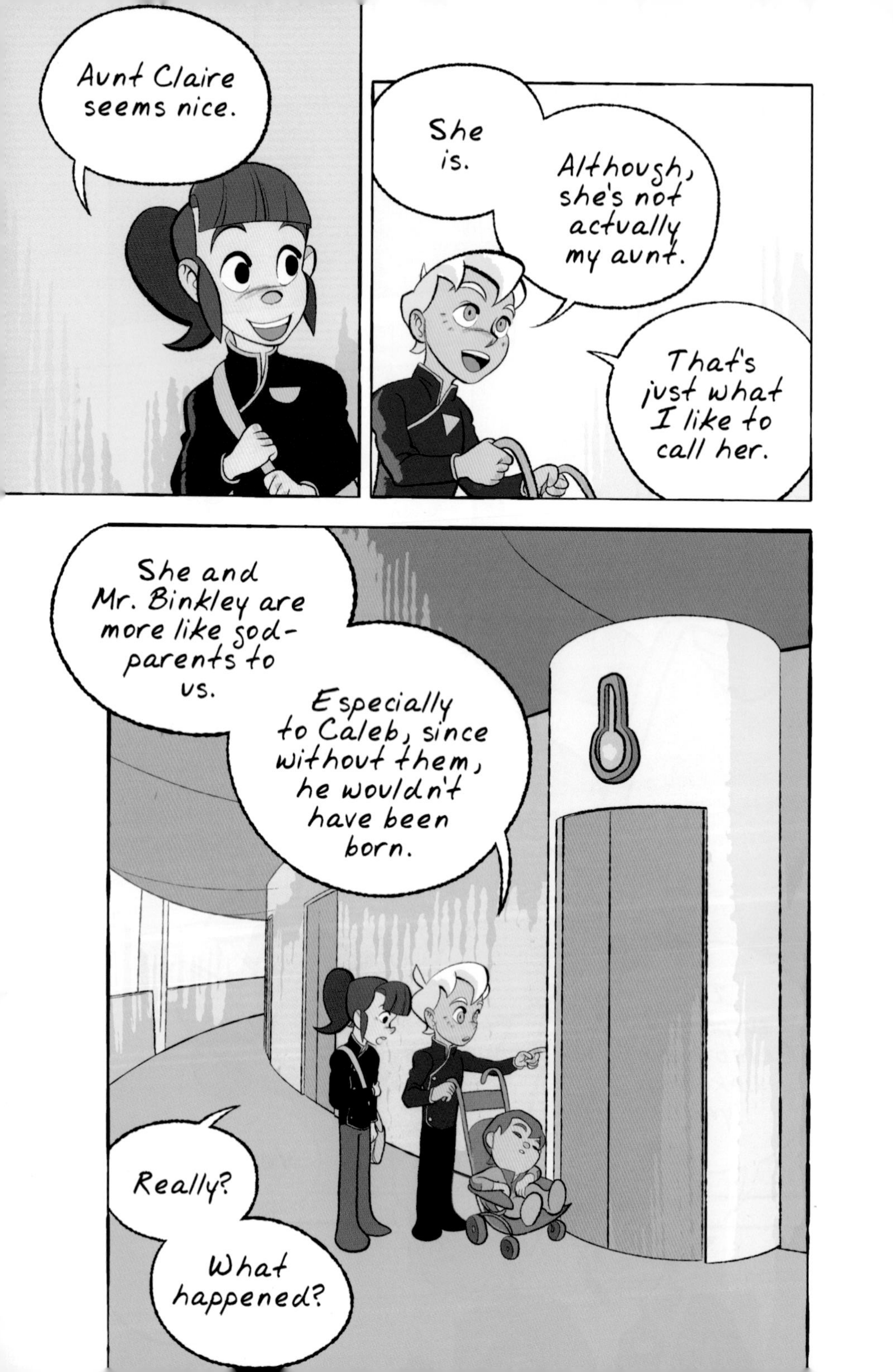
Aunt Claire seems nice.
She is.
Although, she's not actually my aunt.
That's just what I like to call her.
She and Mr. Binkley are more like god-parents to us.
Especially to Caleb, since without them, he wouldn't have been born.
Really?
What happened?

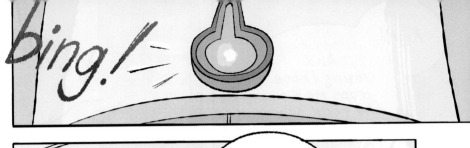

bing!

Well, it's kind of a long story, but--

Did your parents ever tell you about the blight that happened eight or nine years ago?

Of course!

My dad said it was someone from his own department who caused the blight--

They let some bad bacteria get into a batch of fertilizer and it killed an entire harvest of crops!

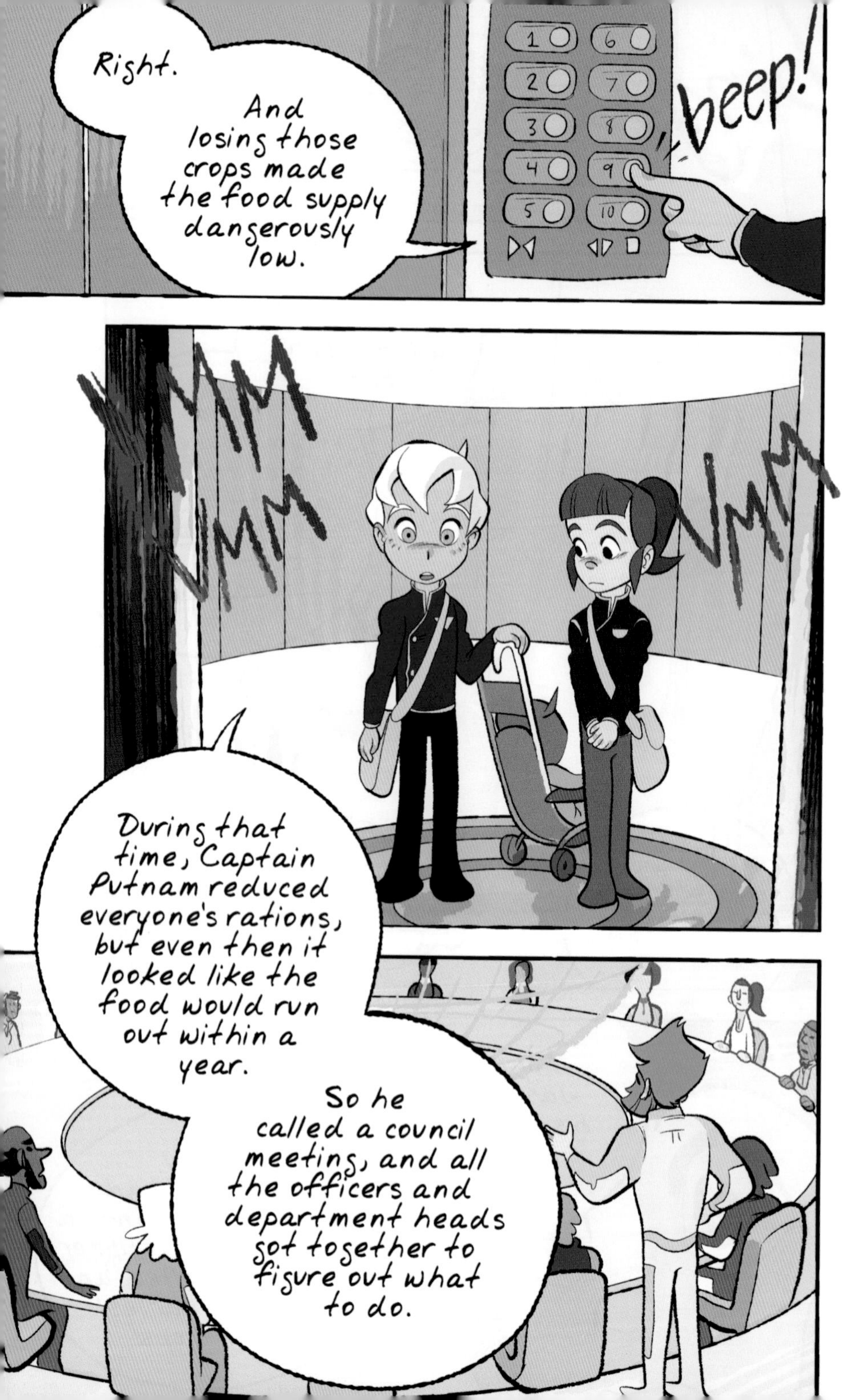
Right.
And losing those crops made the food supply dangerously low.
beep!
VMM VMM VMM
During that time, Captain Putnam reduced everyone's rations, but even then it looked like the food would run out within a year.
So he called a council meeting, and all the officers and department heads got together to figure out what to do.

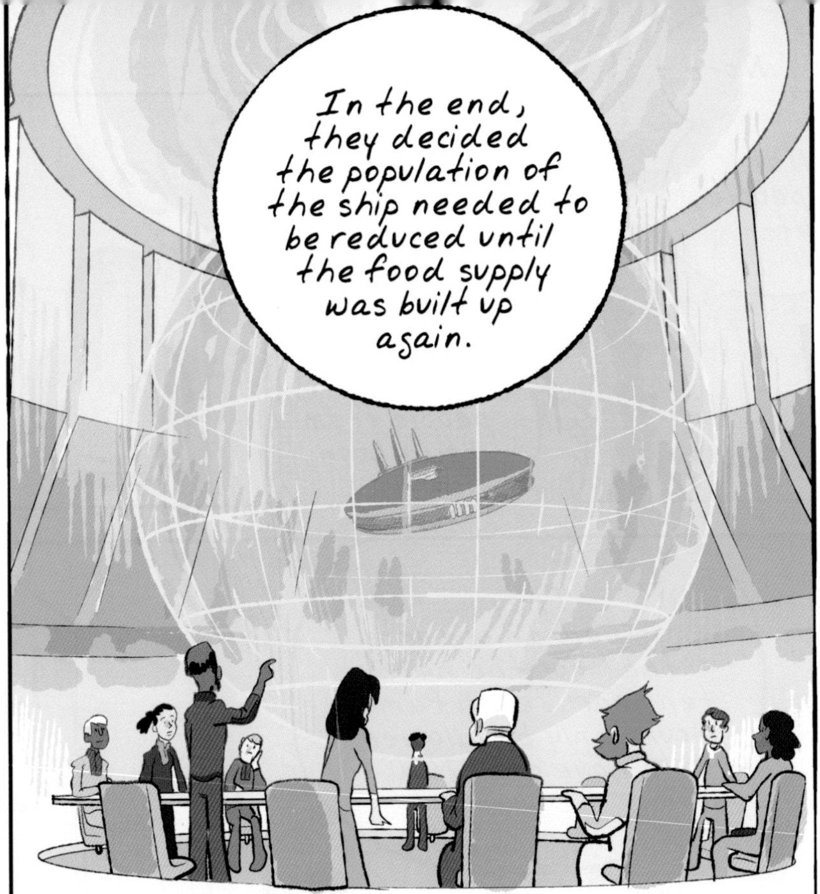
In the end, they decided the population of the ship needed to be reduced until the food supply was built up again.

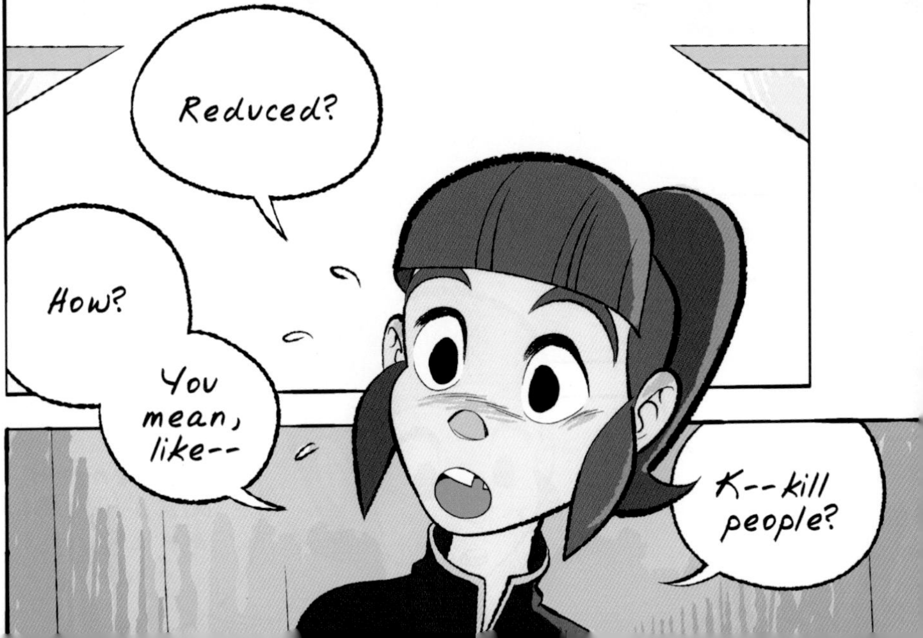
Reduced?
How?
You mean, like--
K--kill people?

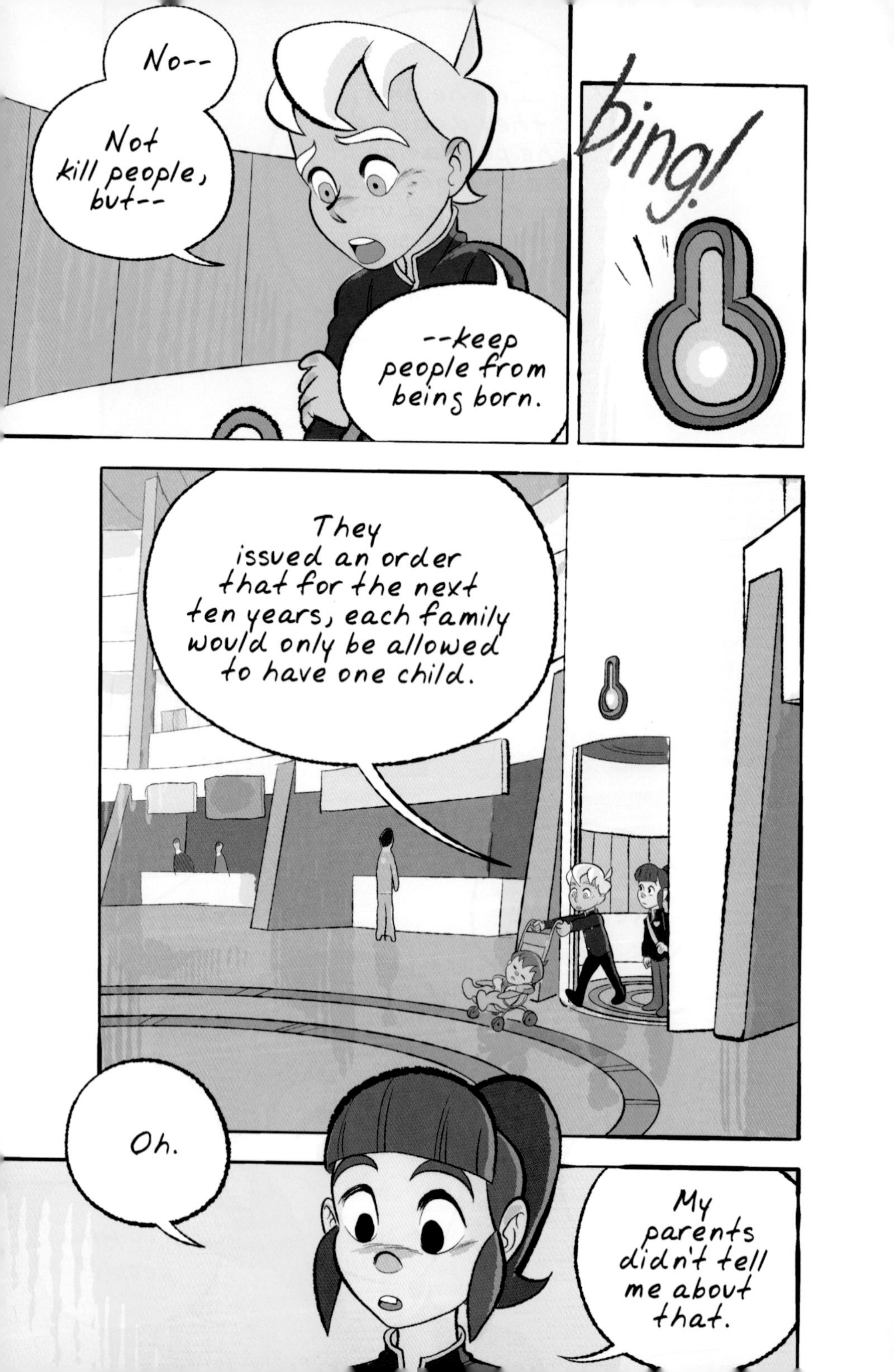
No--
Not kill people, but--
--keep people from being born.
bing!
They issued an order that for the next ten years, each family would only be allowed to have one child.
Oh.
My parents didn't tell me about that.

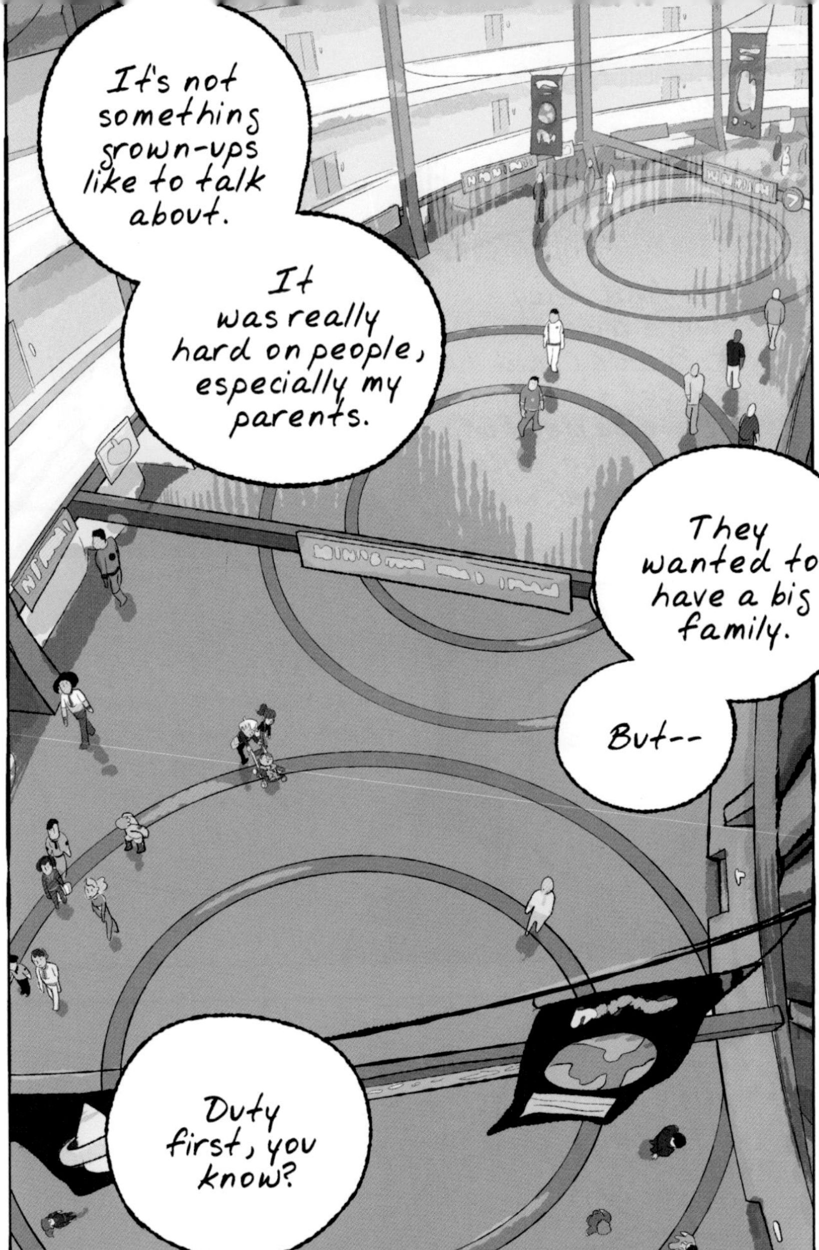
It's not something grown-ups like to talk about.
It was really hard on people, especially my parents.
They wanted to have a big family.
But--
Duty first, you know?

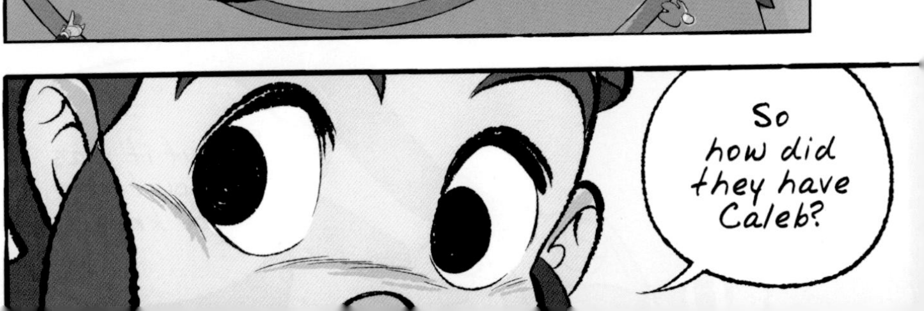
So how did they have Caleb?

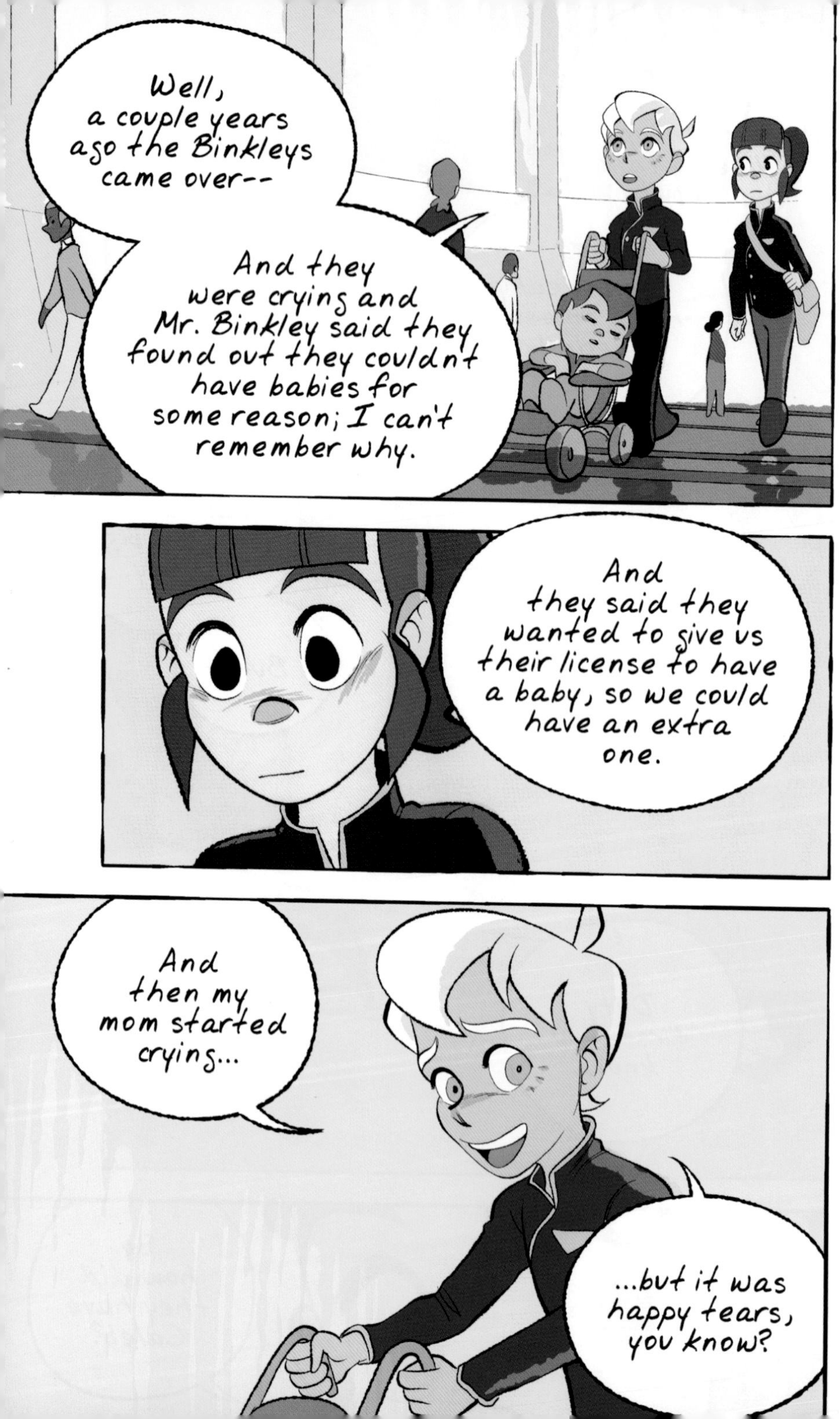
Well, a couple years ago the Binkleys came over--
And they were crying and Mr. Binkley said they found out they couldn't have babies for some reason; I can't remember why.
And they said they wanted to give us their license to have a baby, so we could have an extra one.
And then my mom started crying...
...but it was happy tears, you know?

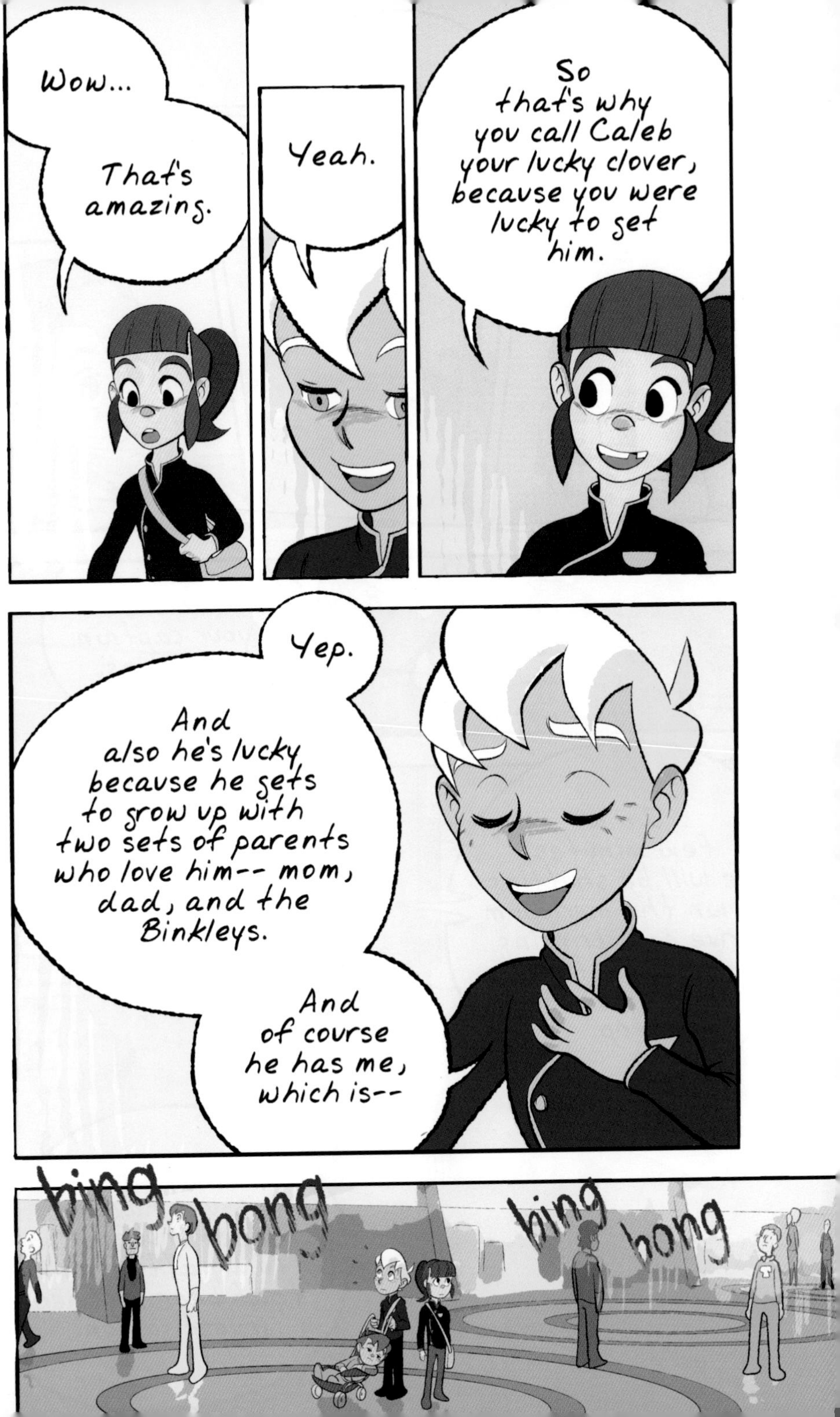
Wow...
That's amazing.
Yeah.
So that's why you call Caleb your lucky clover, because you were lucky to get him.
Yep.
And also he's lucky, because he gets to grow up with two sets of parents who love him-- mom, dad, and the Binkleys.
And of course he has me, which is--
bing bong bing bong

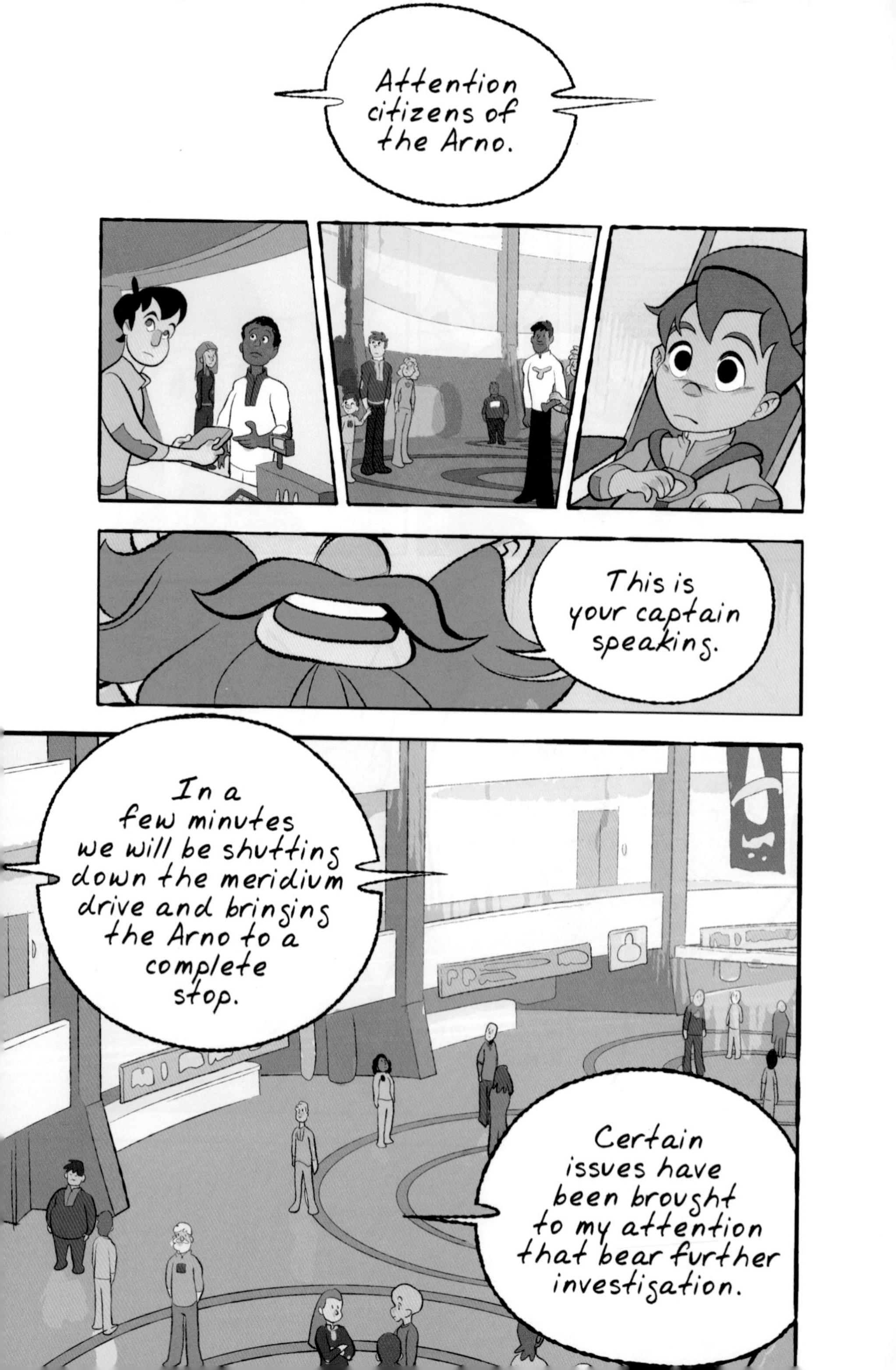
Attention citizens of the Arno.
This is your captain speaking.
In a few minutes we will be shutting down the meridium drive and bringing the Arno to a complete stop.
Certain issues have been brought to my attention that bear further investigation.

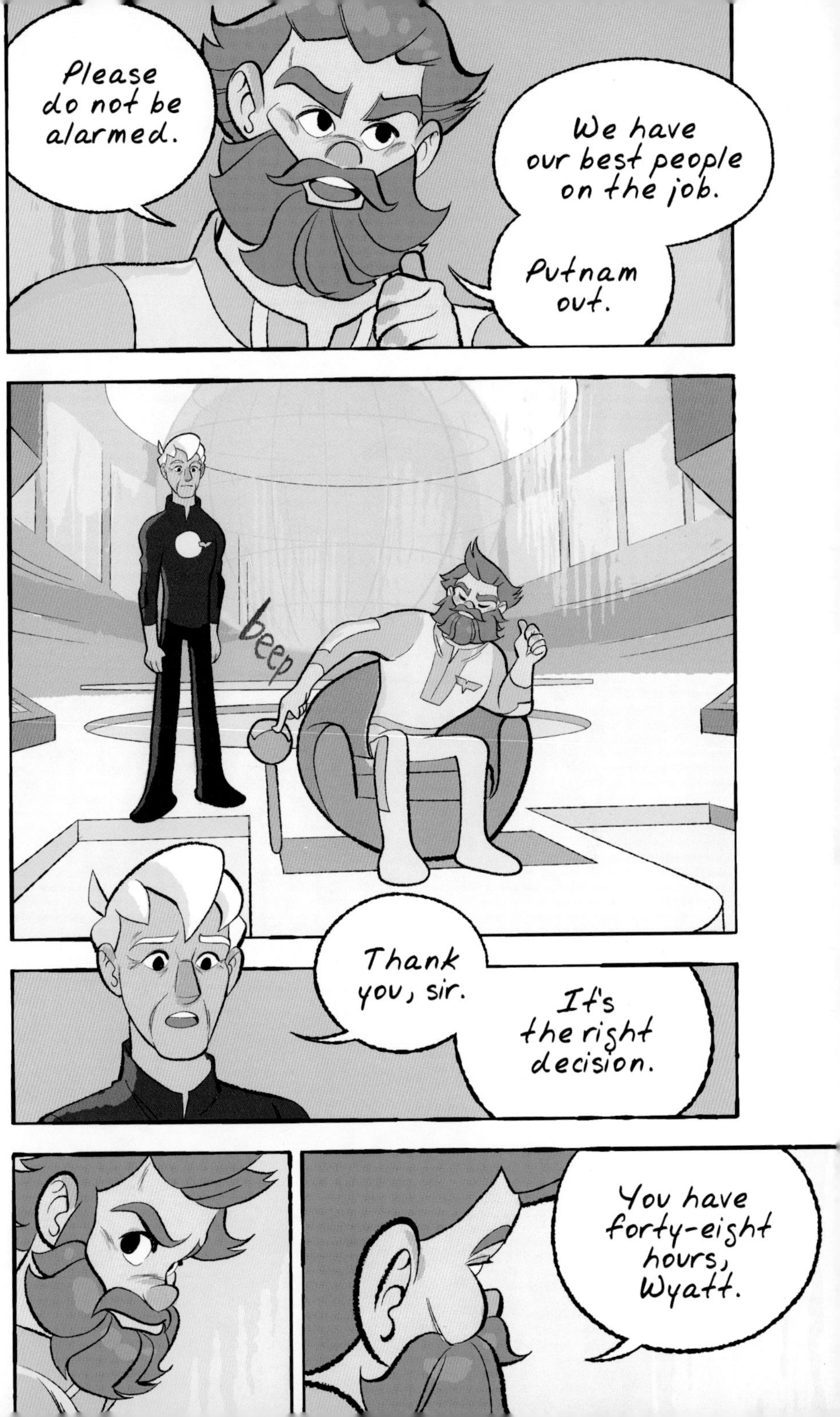

Please do not be alarmed.
We have our best people on the job.
Putnam out.
beep
Thank you, sir.
It's the right decision.
You have forty-eight hours, Wyatt.

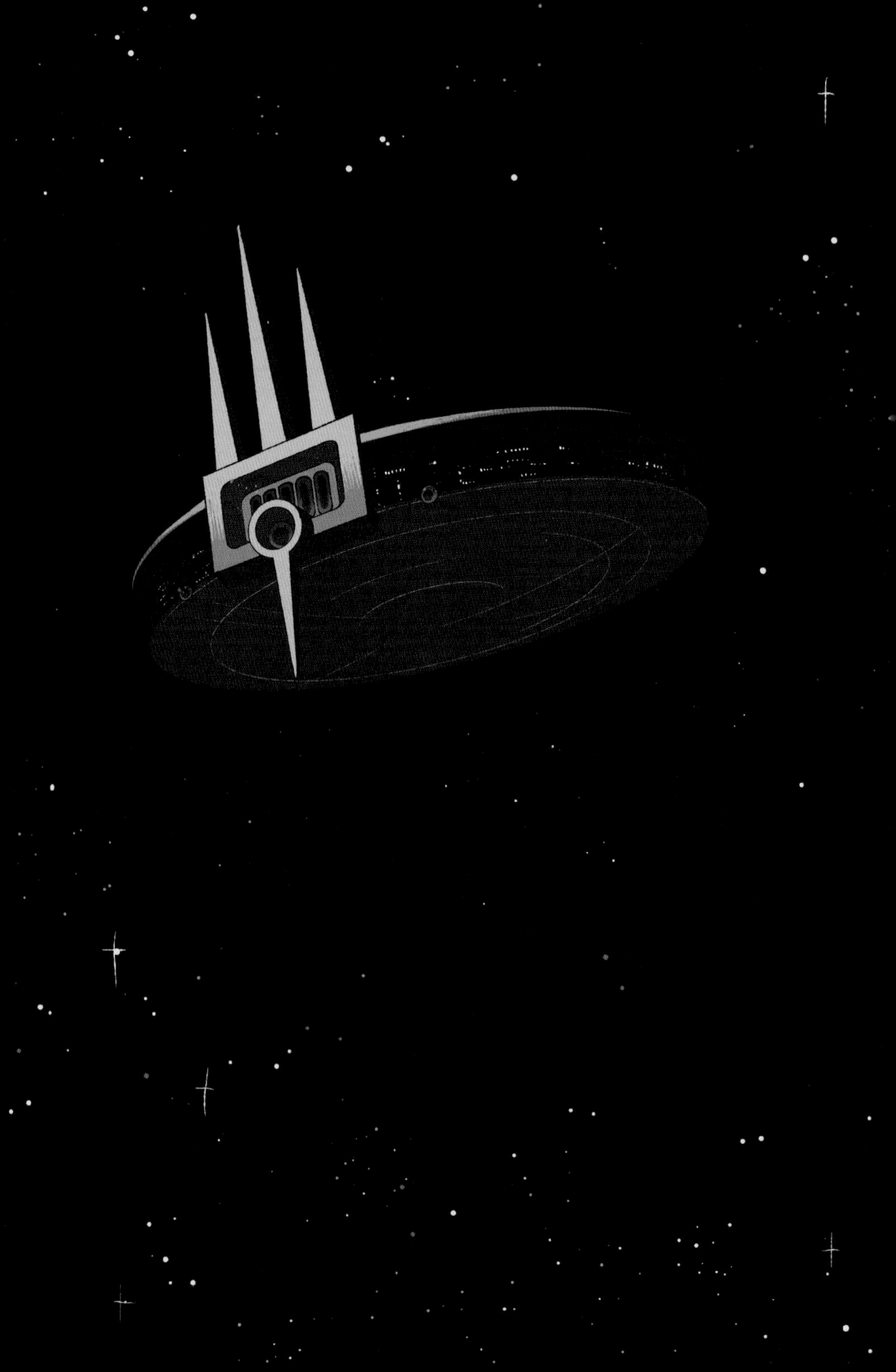

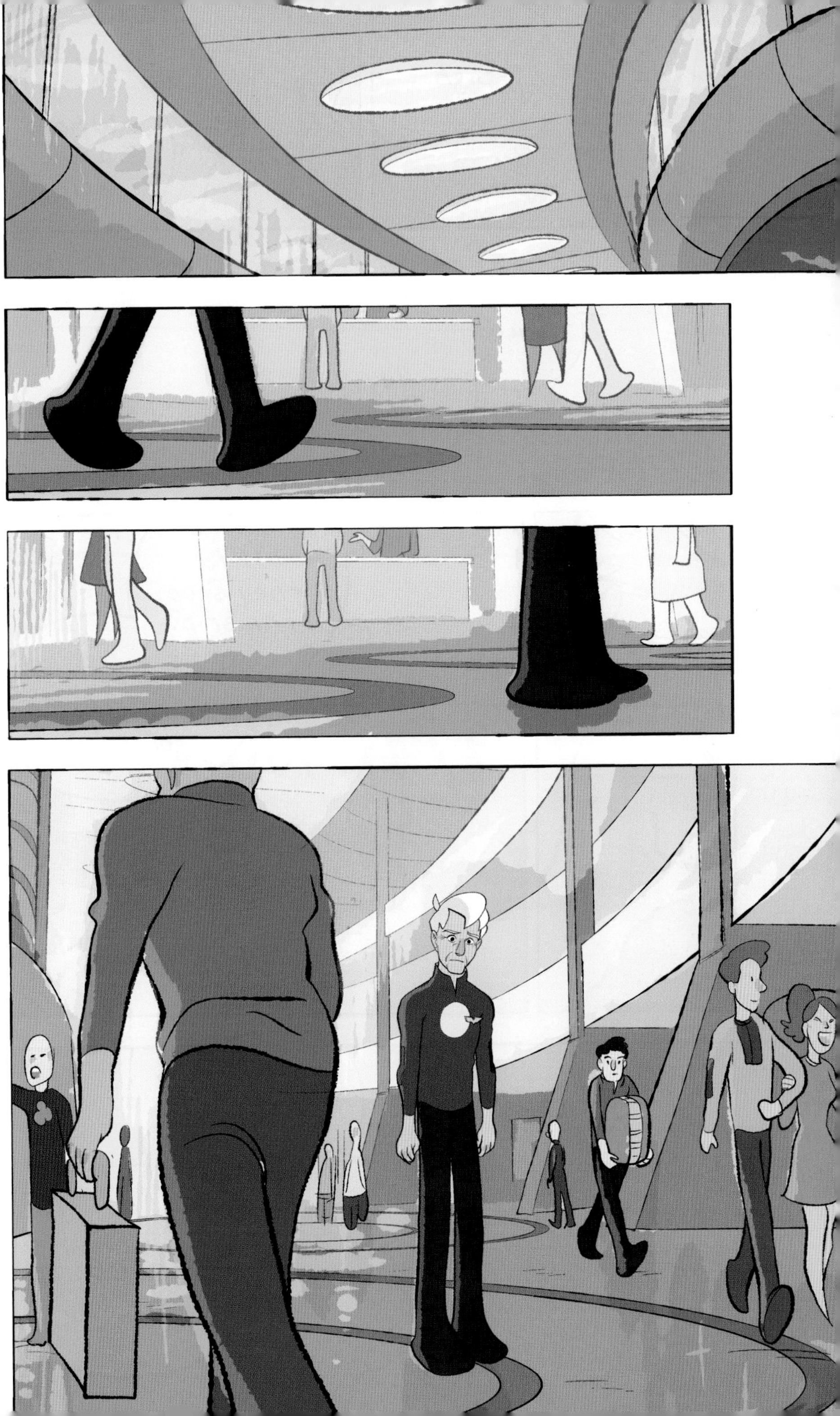

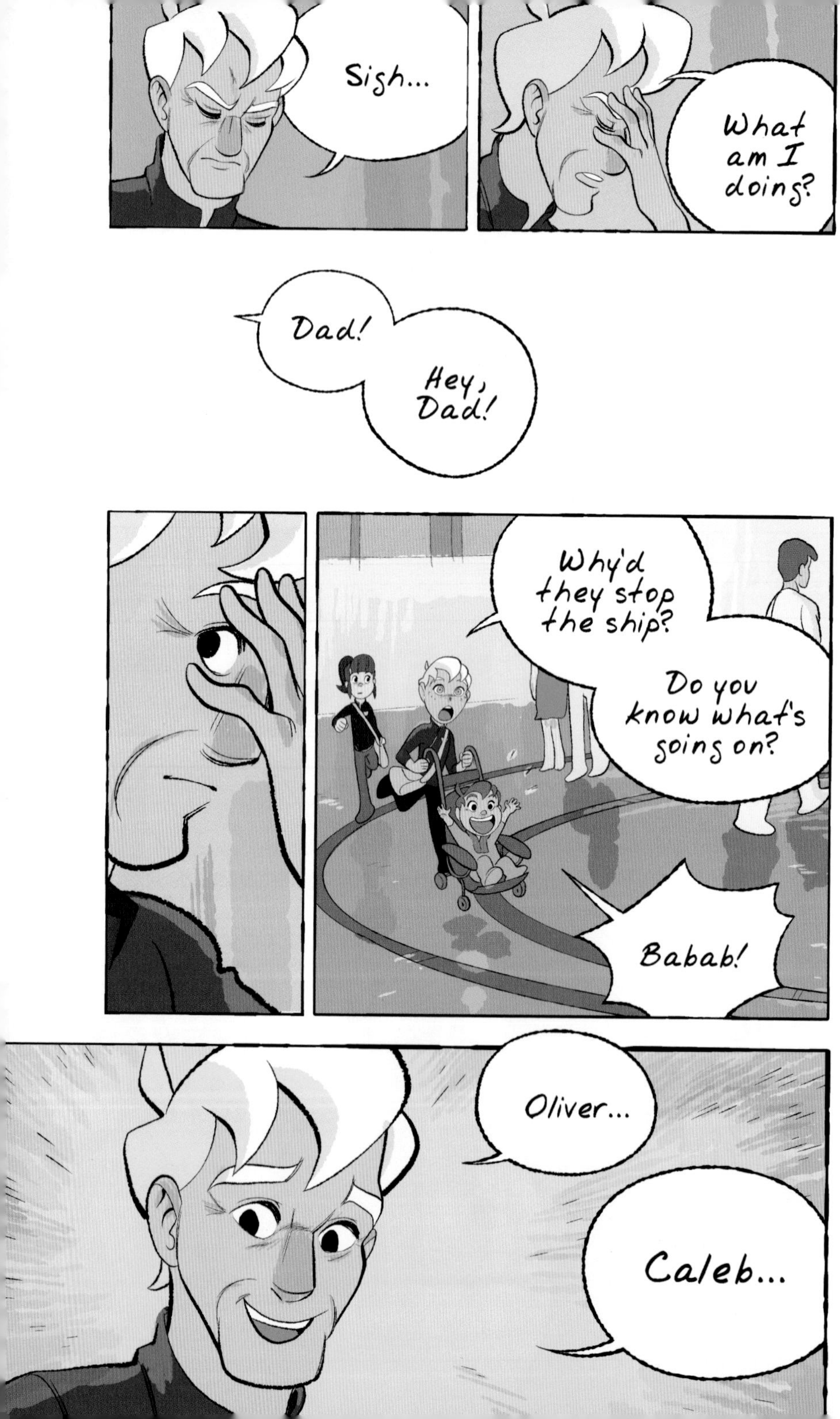
Sigh...
What am I doing?
Dad!
Hey, Dad!
Why'd they stop the ship?
Do you know what's going on?
Babab!
Oliver...
Caleb...

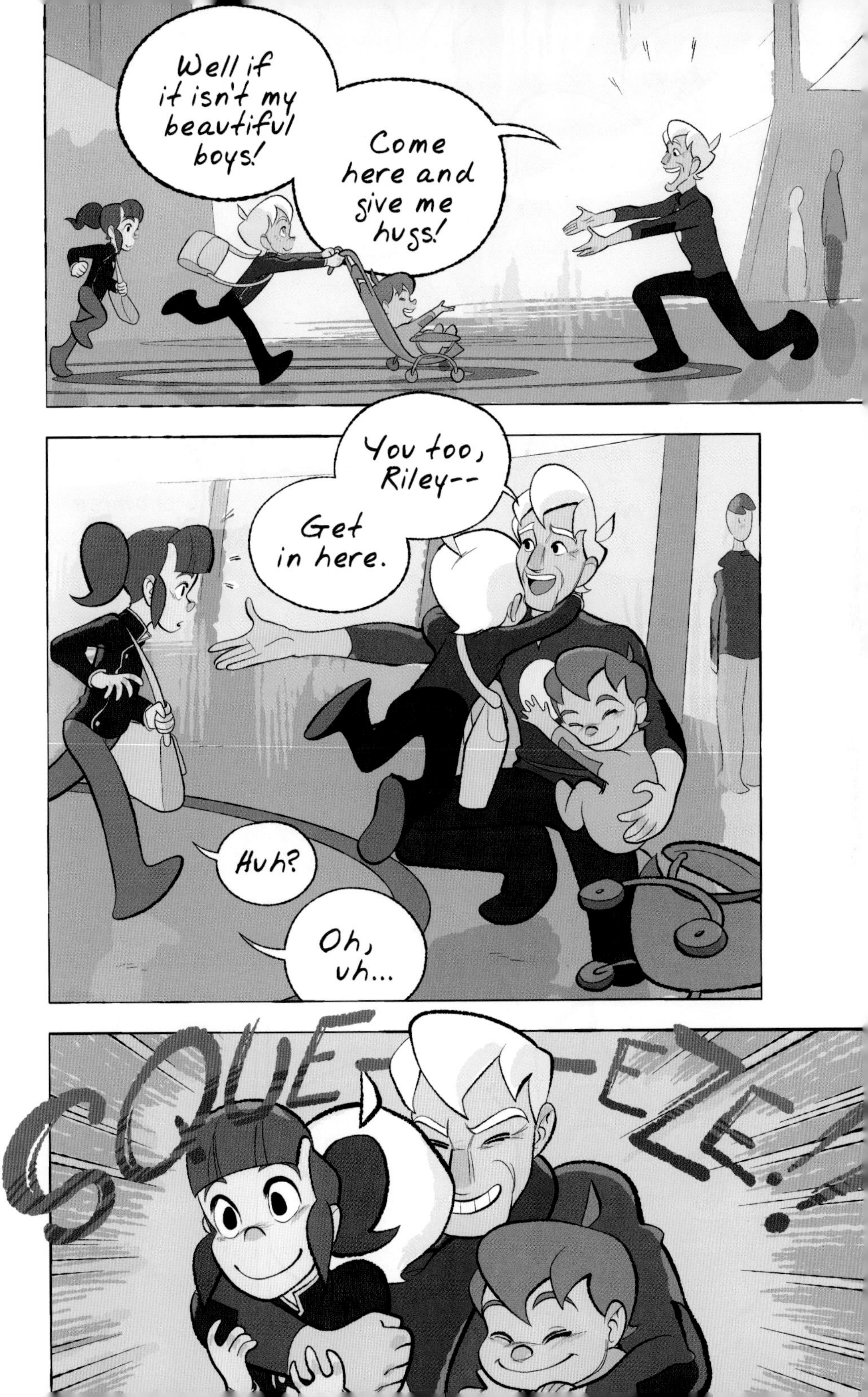
Well if it isn't my beautiful boys!
Come here and give me hugs!
You too, Riley--
Get in here.
Huh?
Oh, uh...
SQUEE--EZE!!

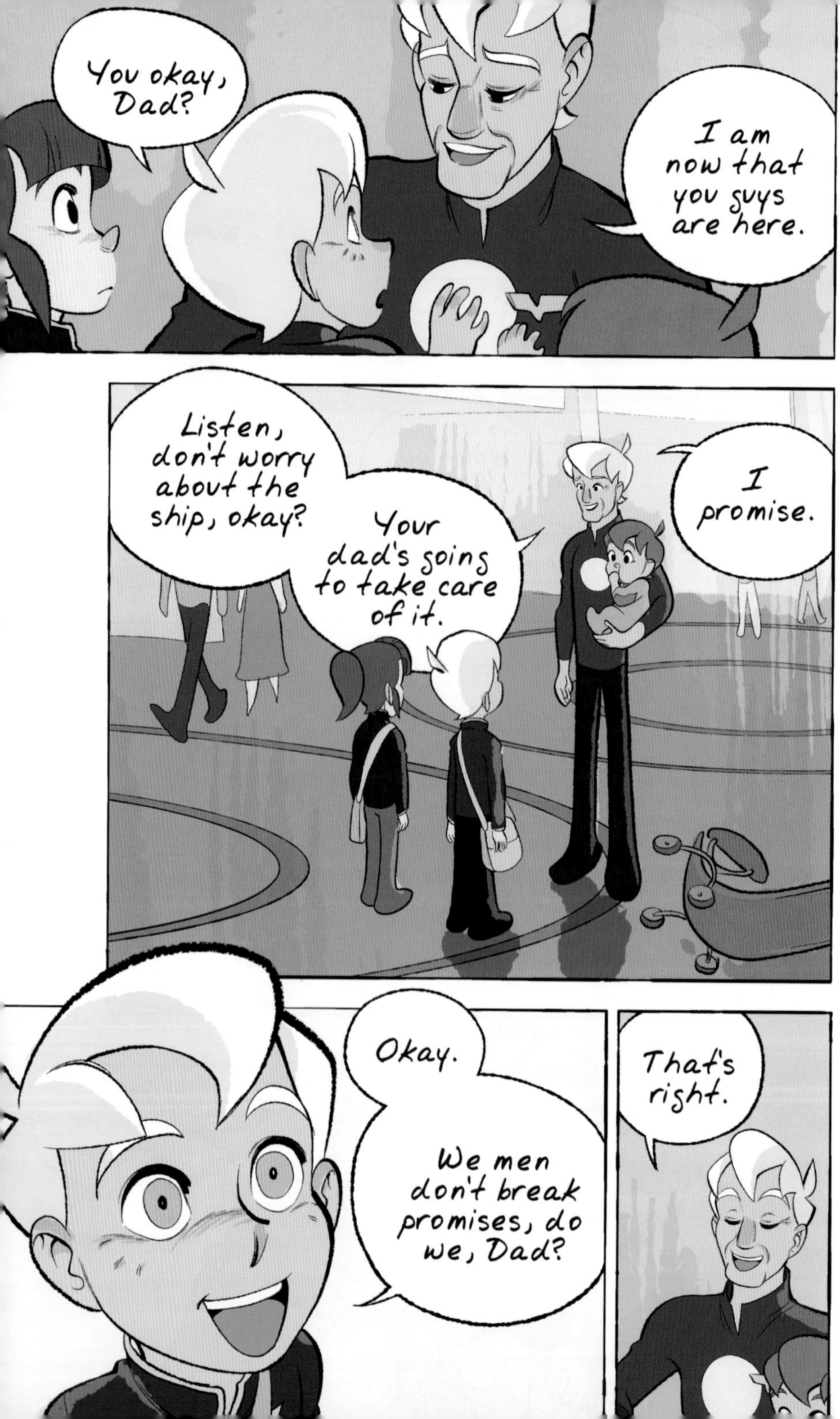
You okay, Dad?
I am now that you guys are here.
Listen, don't worry about the ship, okay?
Your dad's going to take care of it.
I promise.
Okay.
We men don't break promises, do we, Dad?
That's right.

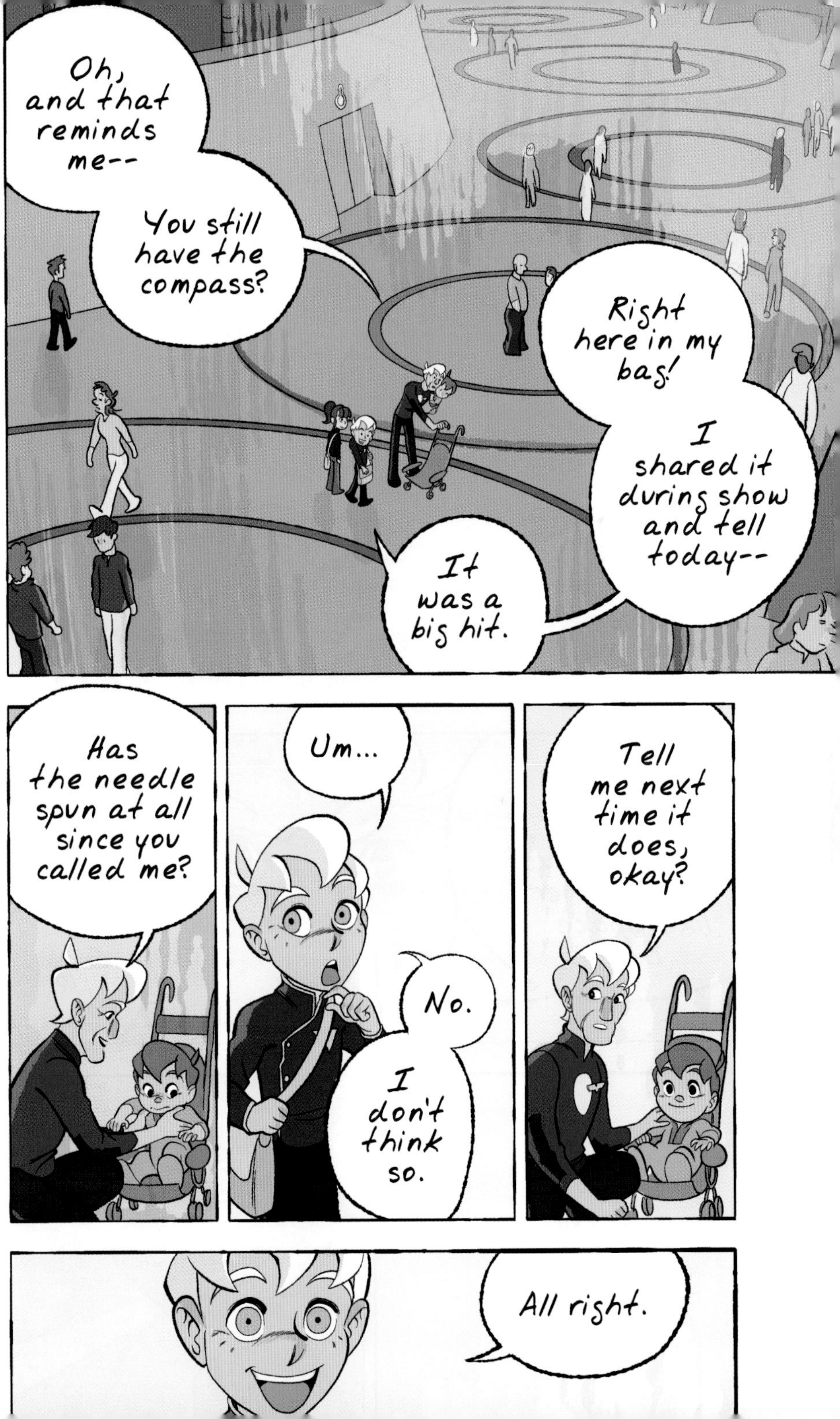
Oh, and that reminds me--
You still have the compass?
Right here in my bag!
I shared it during show and tell today--
It was a big hit.
Has the needle spun at all since you called me?
Um...
No.
I don't think so.
Tell me next time it does, okay?
All right.

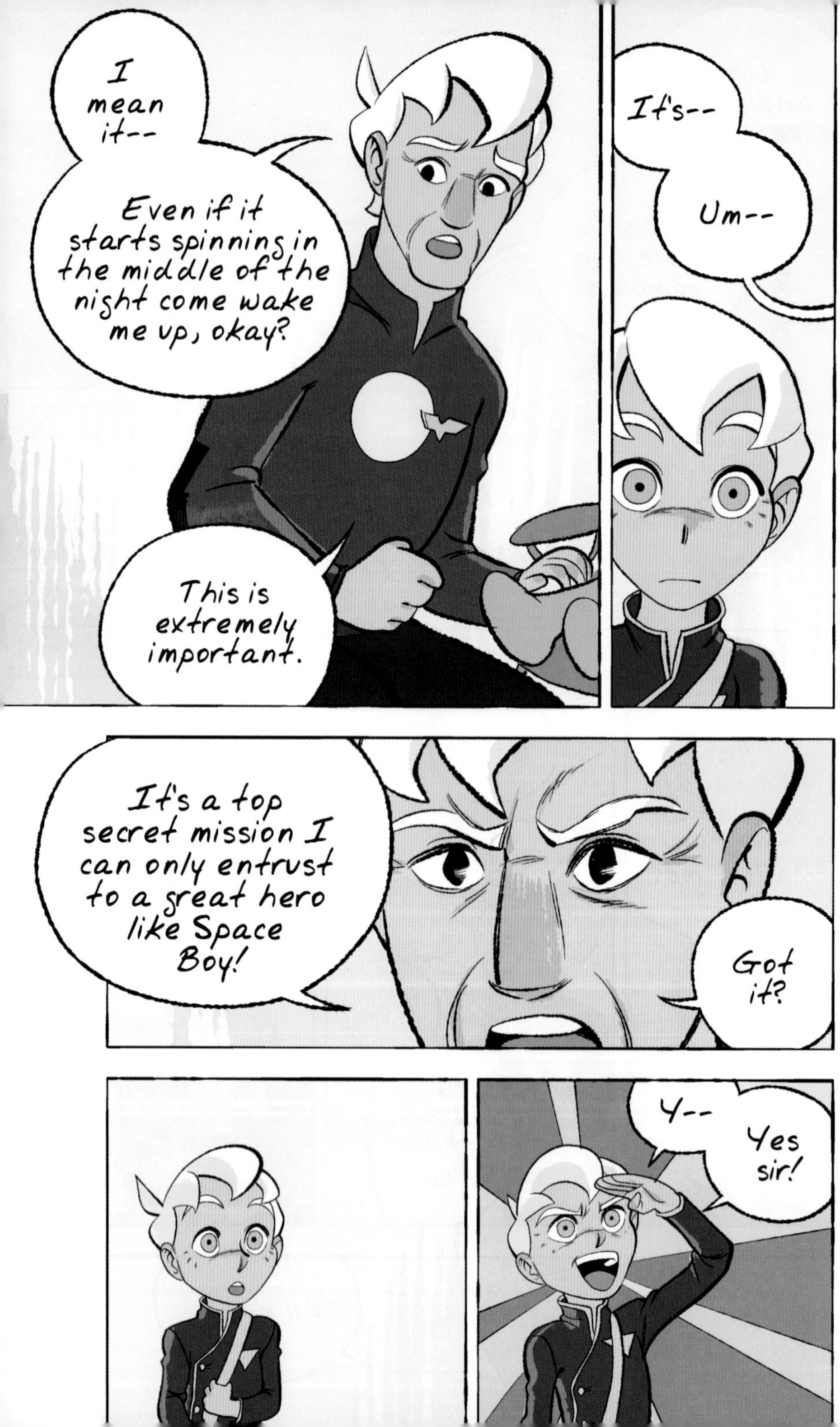
I mean it--
Even if it starts spinning in the middle of the night come wake me up, okay?
This is extremely important.
It's--
Um--
It's a top secret mission I can only entrust to a great hero like Space Boy!
Got it?
Y--
Yes sir!

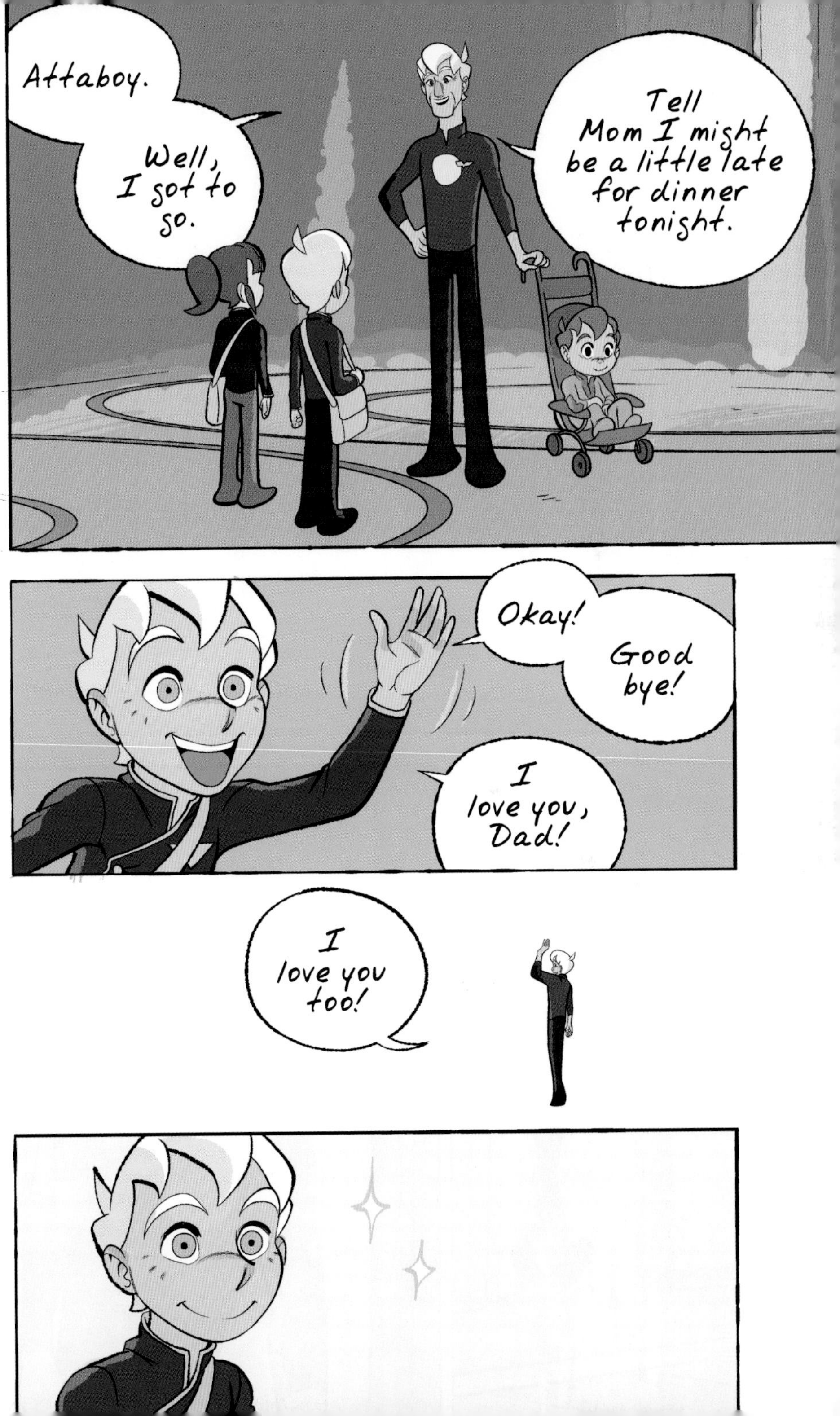
Attaboy.
Well, I got to go.
Tell Mom I might be a little late for dinner tonight.
Okay!
Good bye!
I love you, Dad!
I love you too!

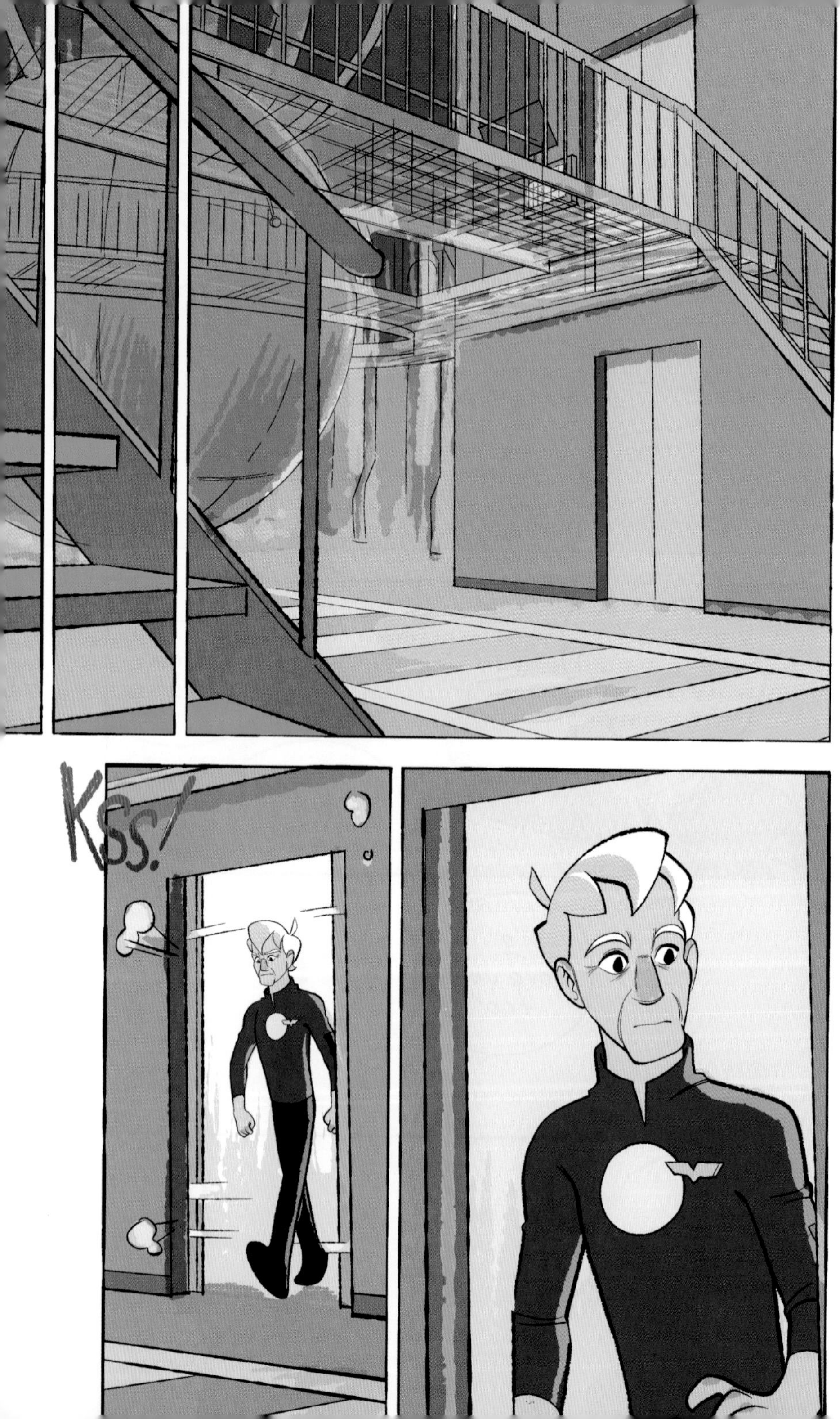
Kss!

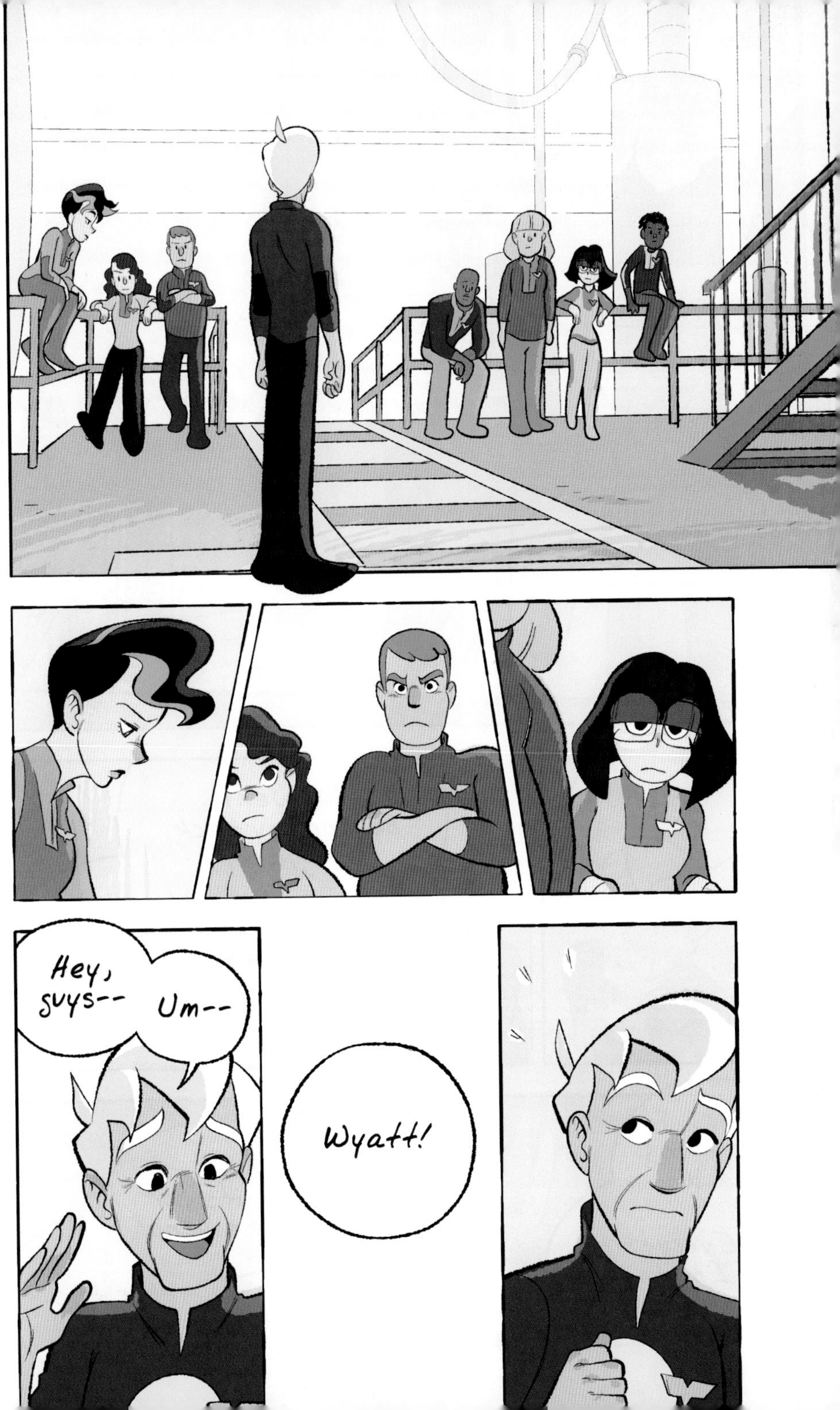
Hey, guys--
Um--
Wyatt!

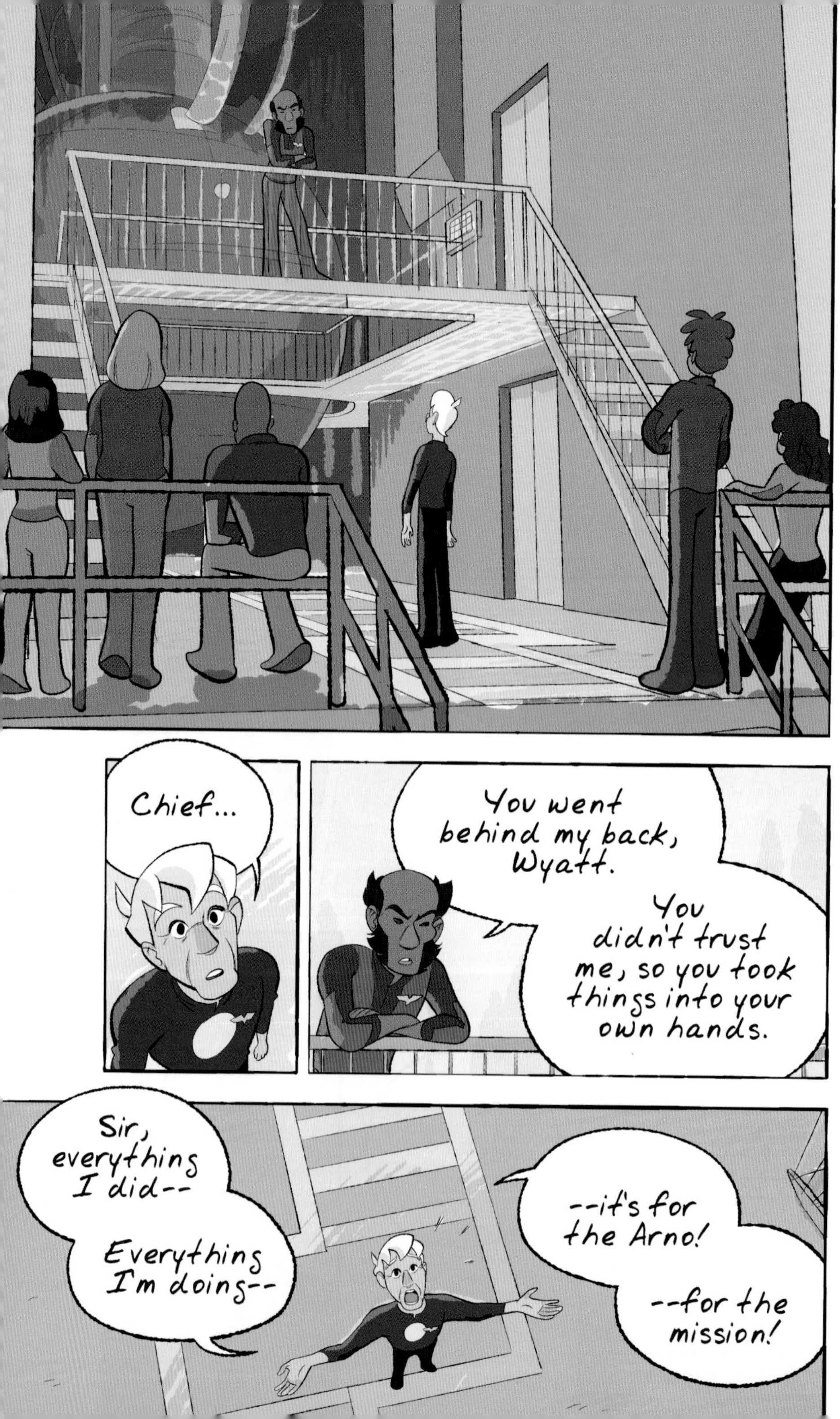
Chief...
You went behind my back, Wyatt.
You didn't trust me, so you took things into your own hands.
Sir, everything I did--
Everything I'm doing--
--it's for the Arno!
--for the mission!

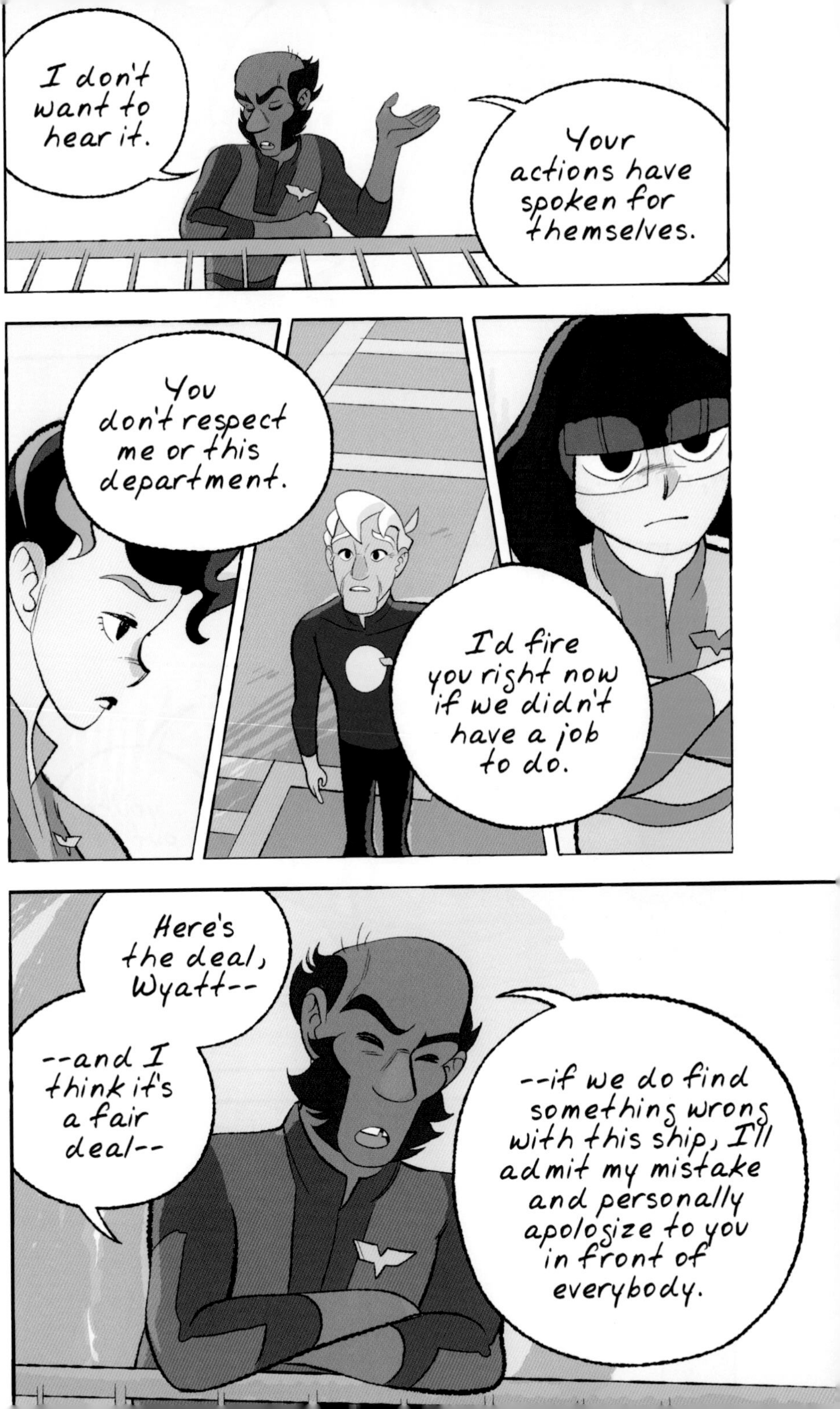
I don't want to hear it.
Your actions have spoken for themselves.
You don't respect me or this department.
I'd fire you right now if we didn't have a job to do.
Here's the deal, Wyatt--
--and I think it's a fair deal--
--if we do find something wrong with this ship, I'll admit my mistake and personally apologize to you in front of everybody.

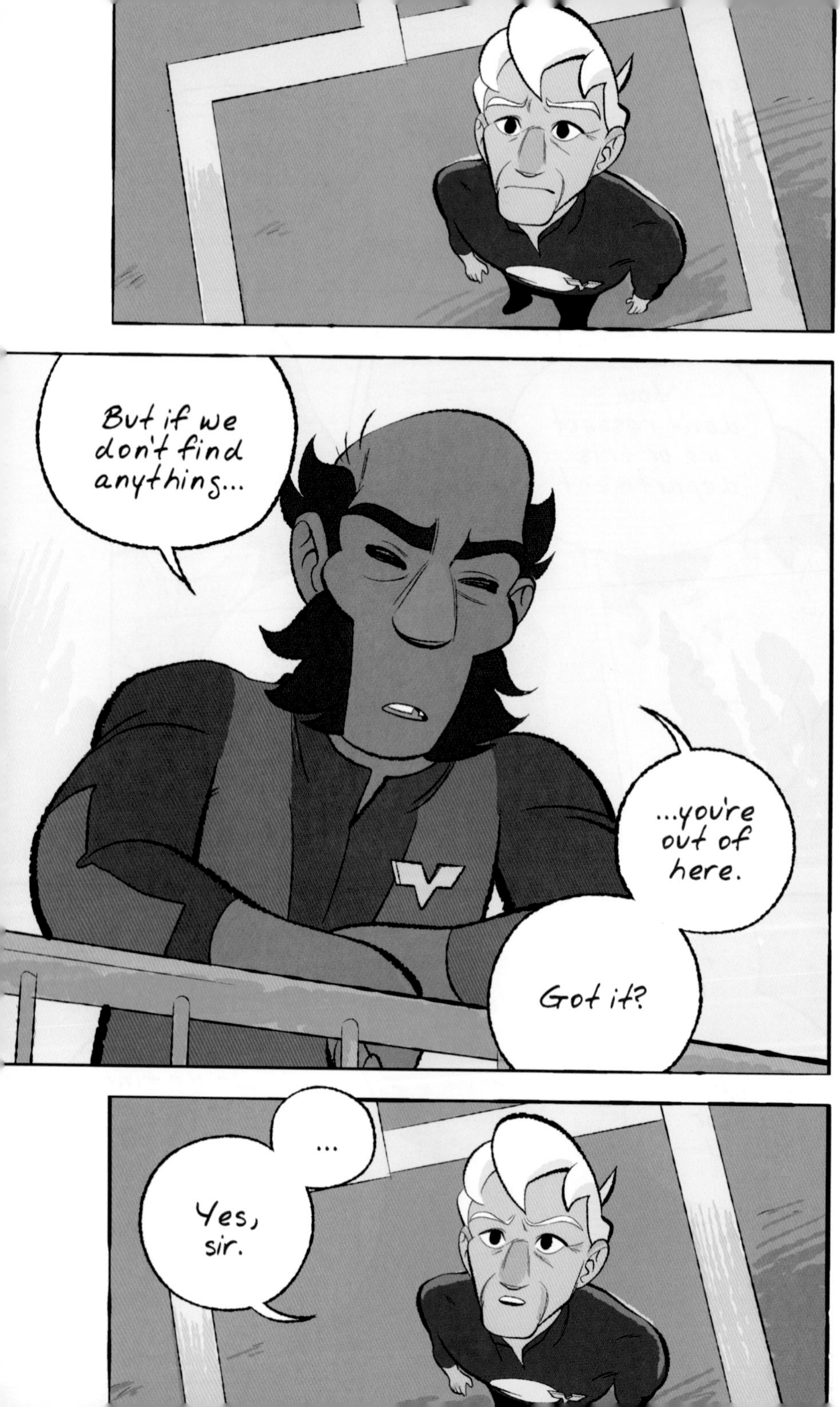
But if we don't find anything...
...you're out of here.
Got it?
...
Yes, sir.

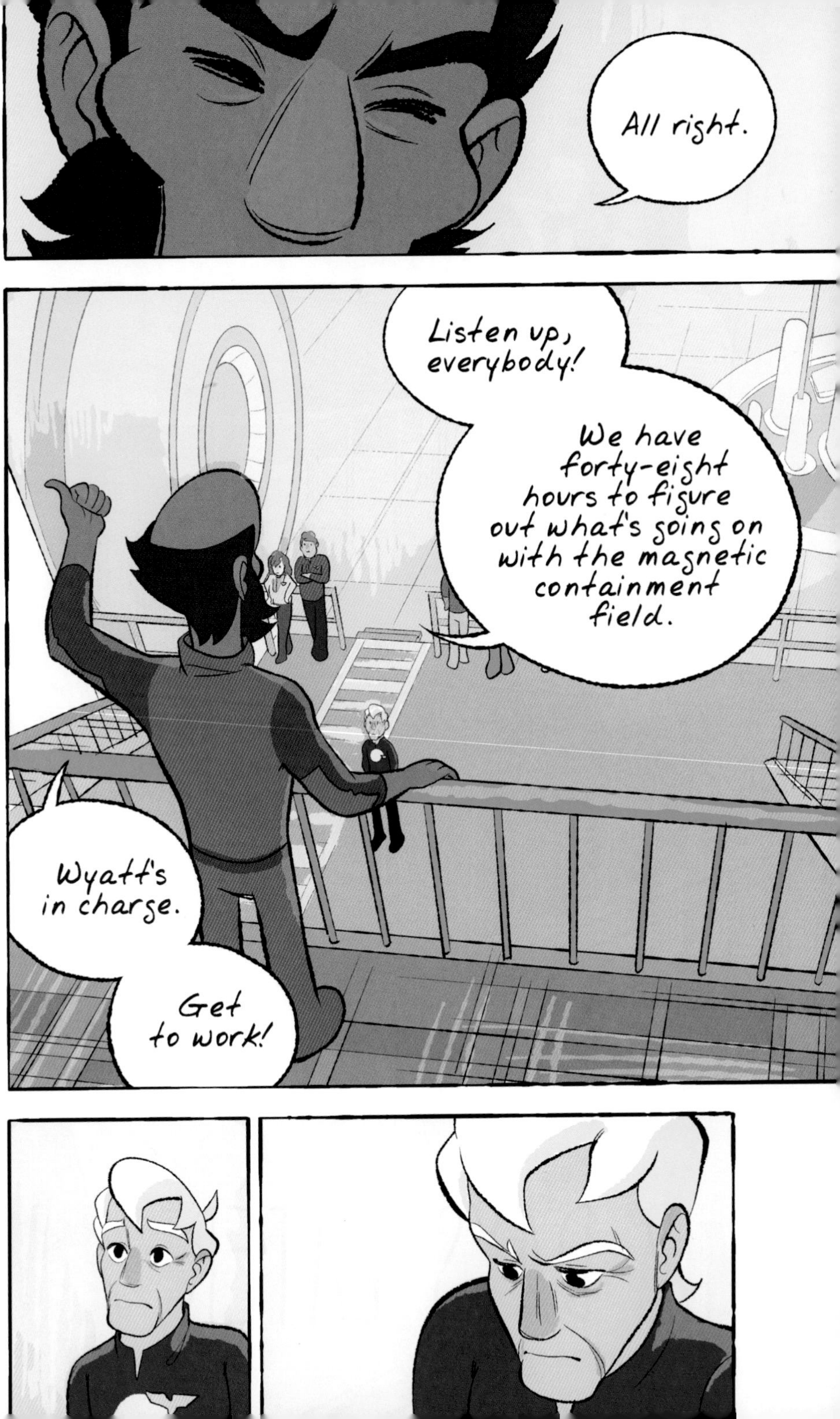
All right.
Listen up, everybody!
We have forty-eight hours to figure out what's going on with the magnetic containment field.
Wyatt's in charge.
Get to work!

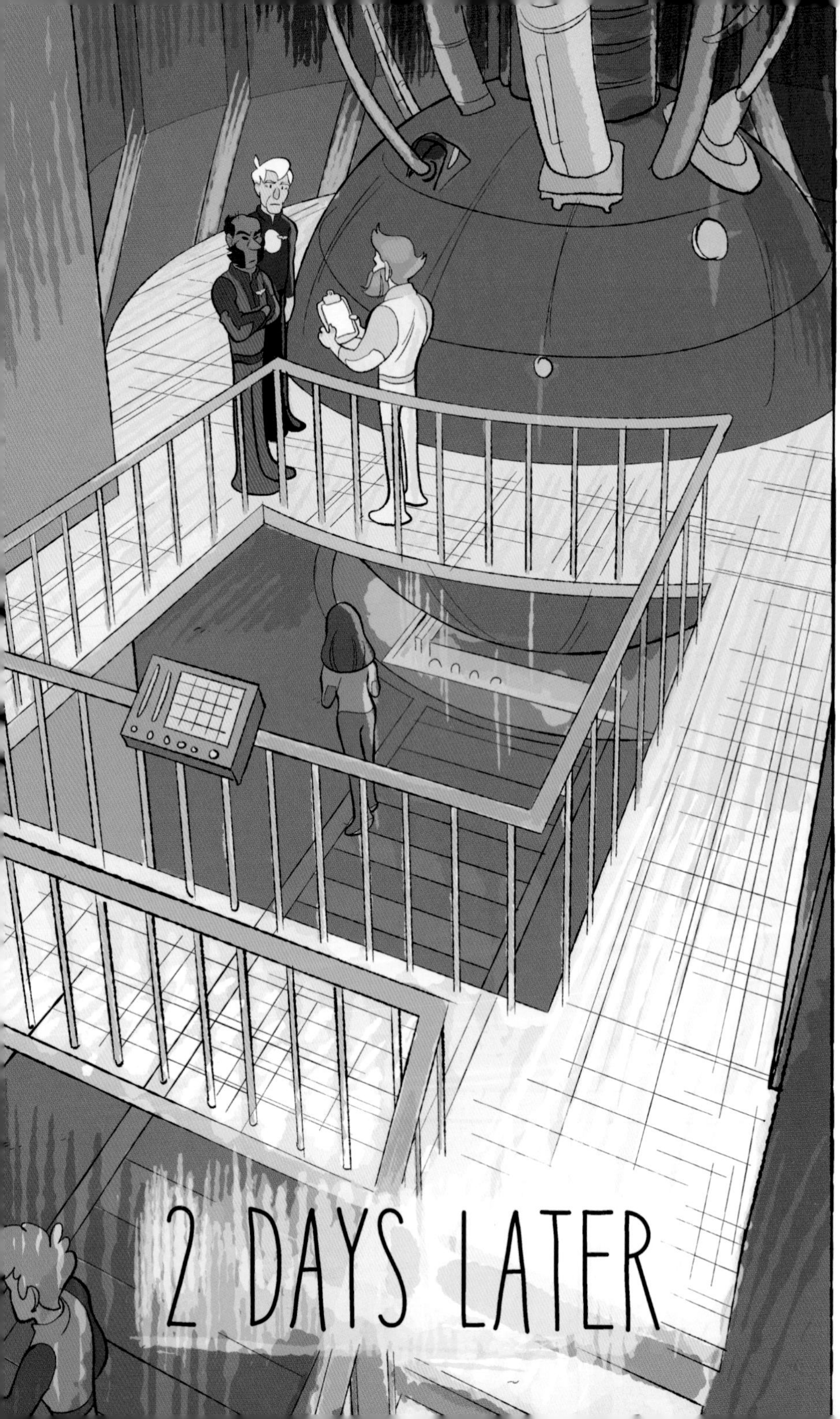
2 DAYS LATER

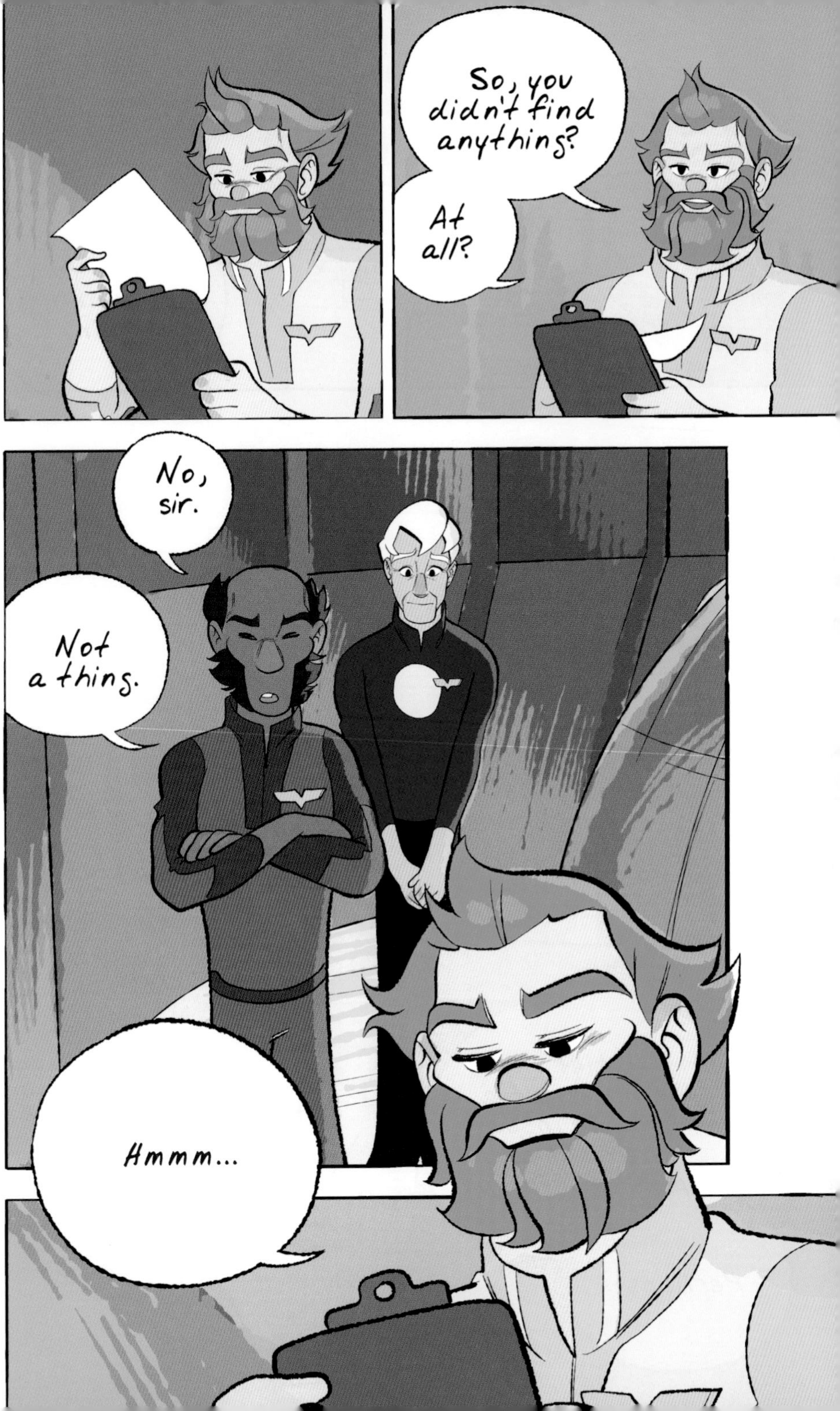
So, you didn't find anything?
At all?
No, sir.
Not a thing.
Hmmm...

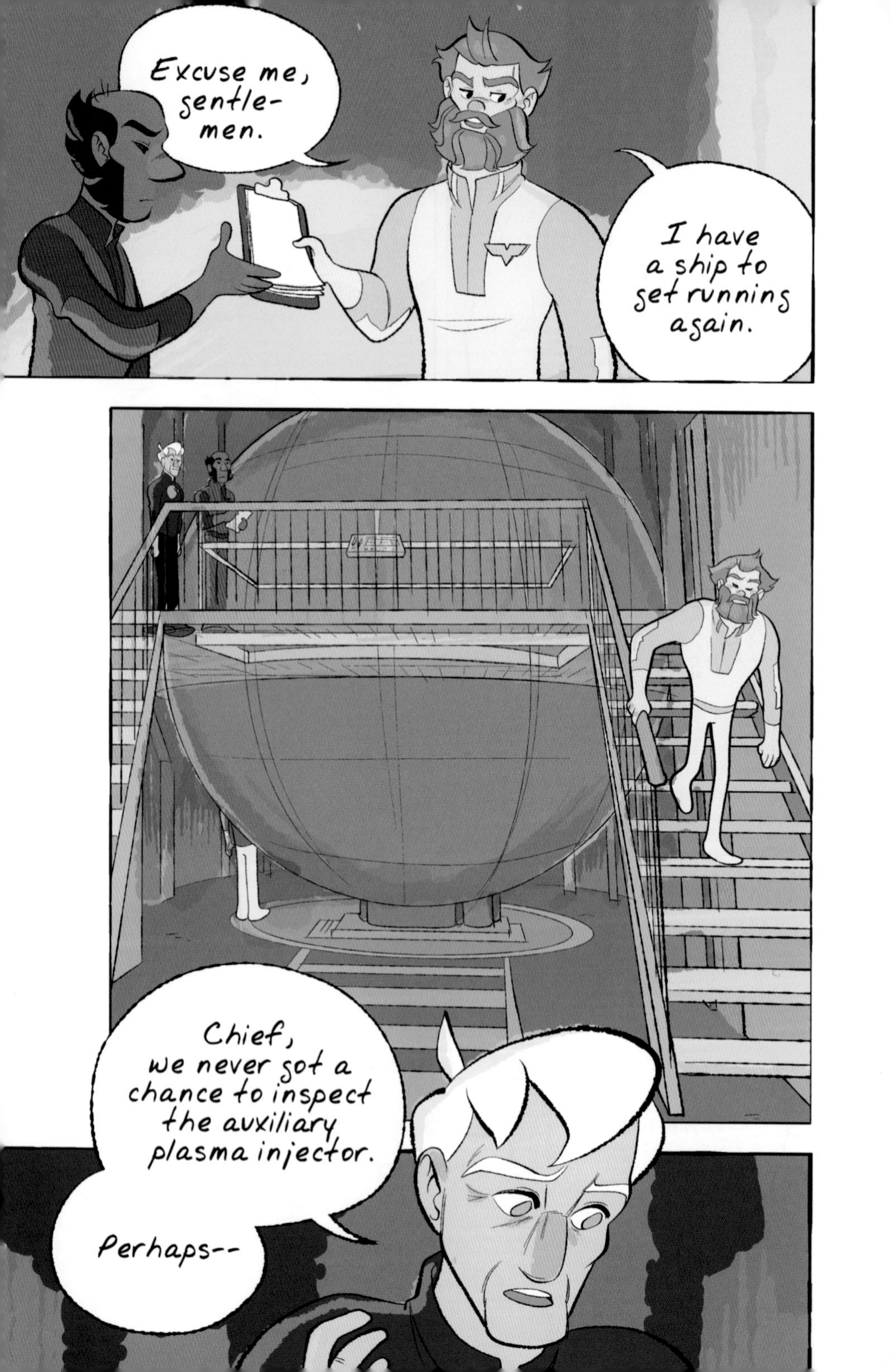
Excuse me, gentlemen.
I have a ship to get running again.
Chief, we never got a chance to inspect the auxiliary plasma injector.
Perhaps--

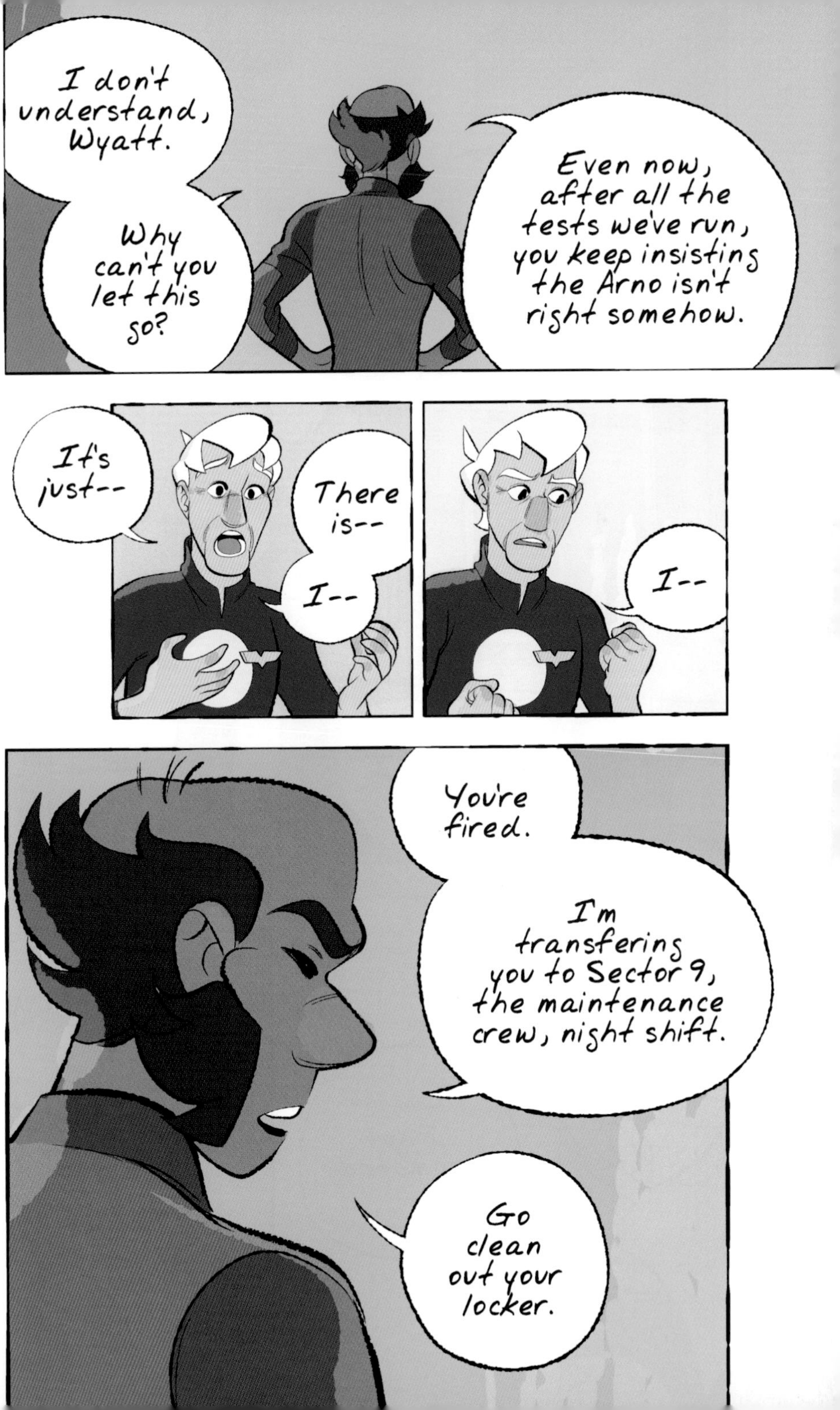
I don't understand, Wyatt.
Why can't you let this go?
Even now, after all the tests we've run, you keep insisting the Arno isn't right somehow.
It's just--
There is--
I--
I--
You're fired.
I'm transfering you to Sector 9, the maintenance crew, night shift.
Go clean out your locker.

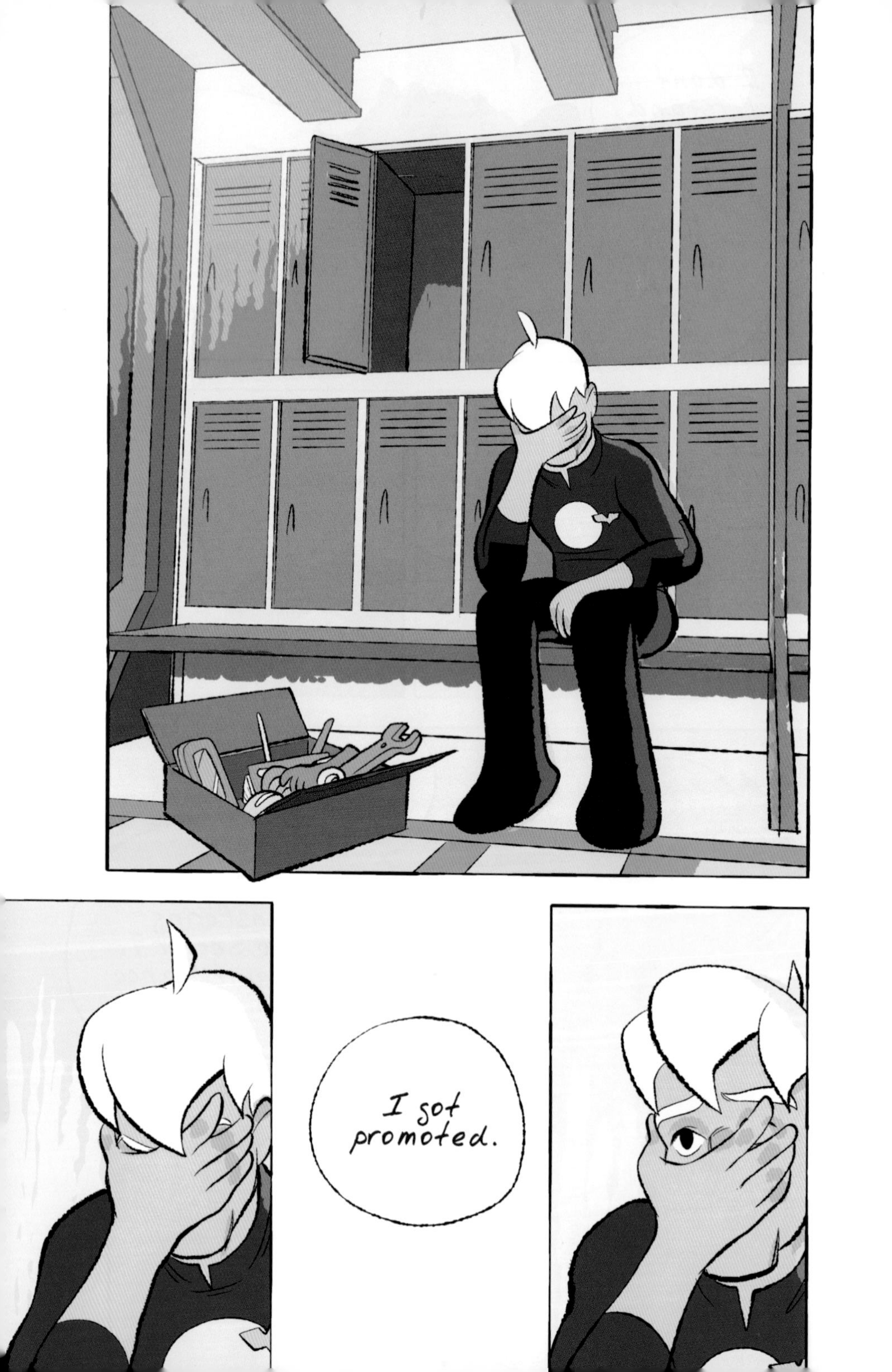
I got promoted.

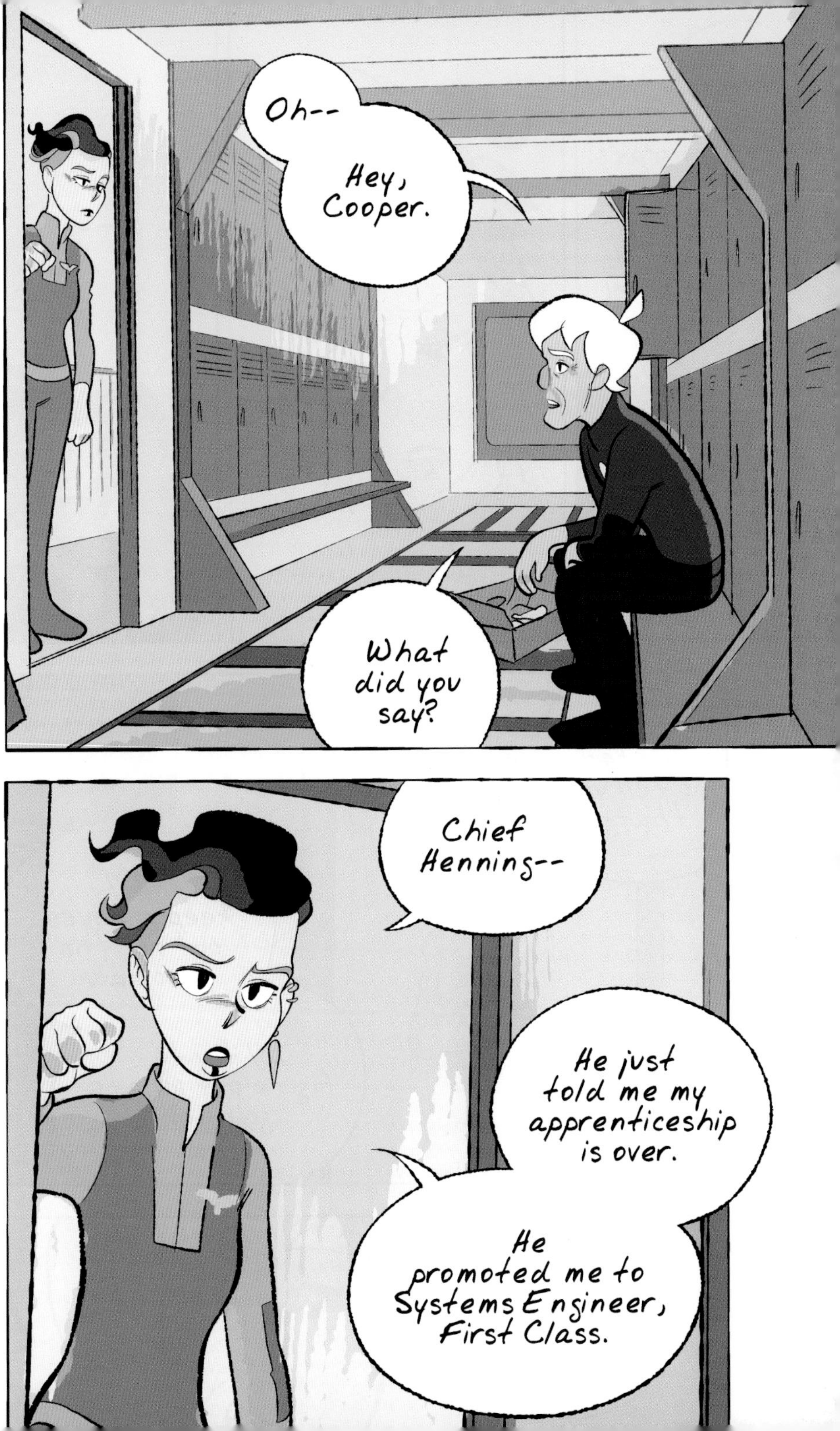
Oh--
Hey, Cooper.
What did you say?
Chief Henning--
He just told me my apprenticeship is over.
He promoted me to Systems Engineer, First Class.

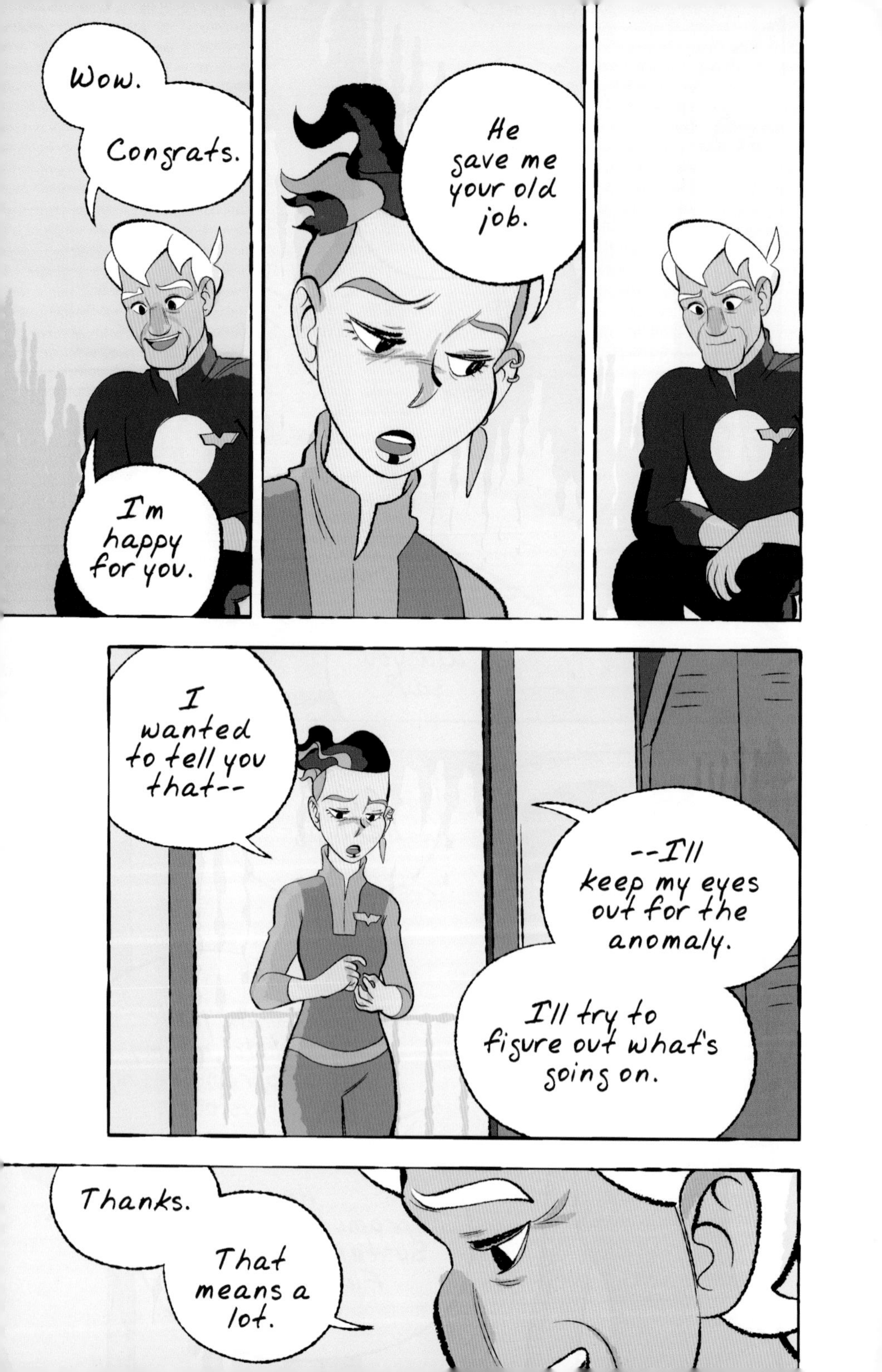
Wow.
Congrats.
I'm happy for you.
He gave me your old job.
I wanted to tell you that--
--I'll keep my eyes out for the anomaly.
I'll try to figure out what's going on.
Thanks.
That means a lot.

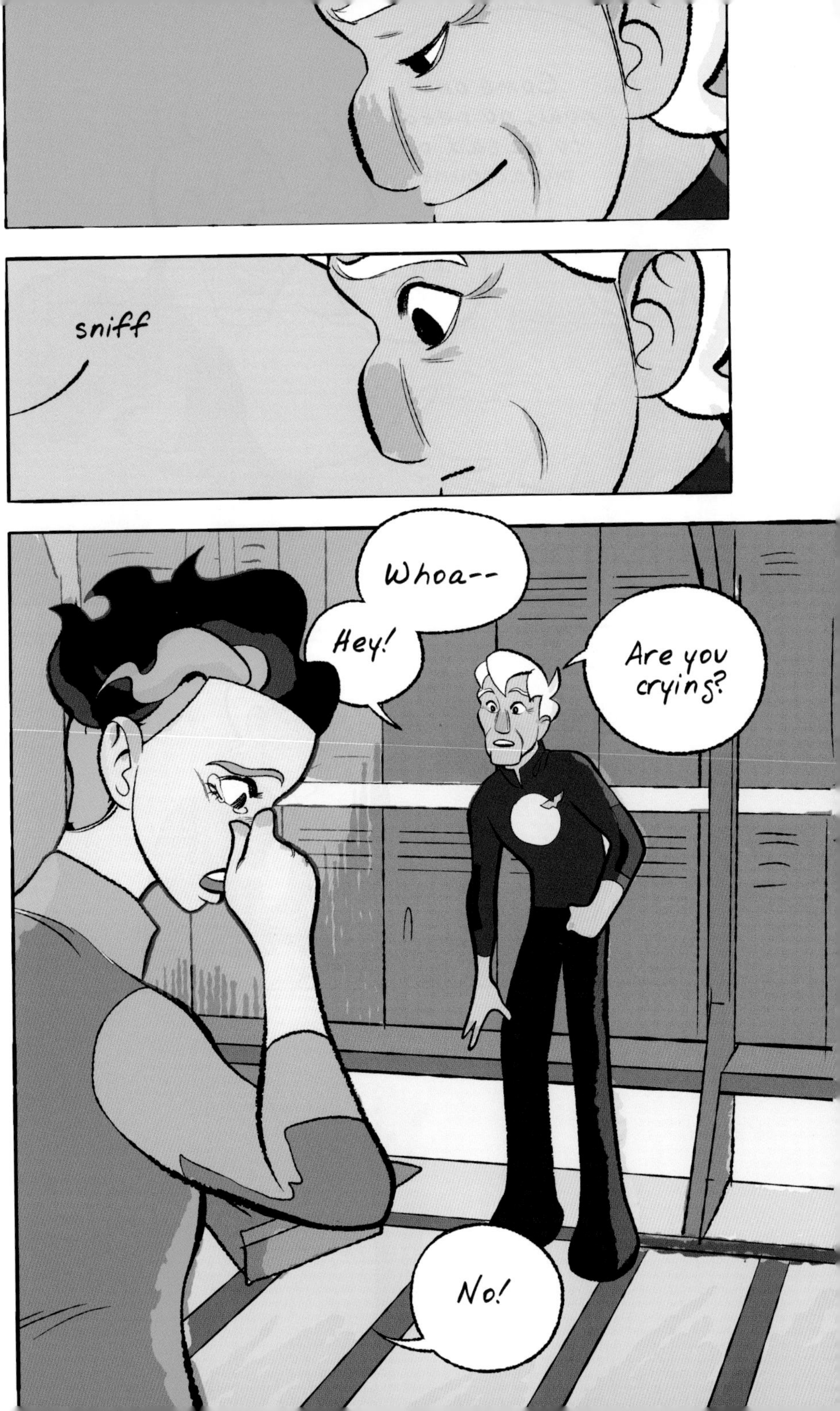
sniff
Whoa--
Hey!
Are you crying?
No!

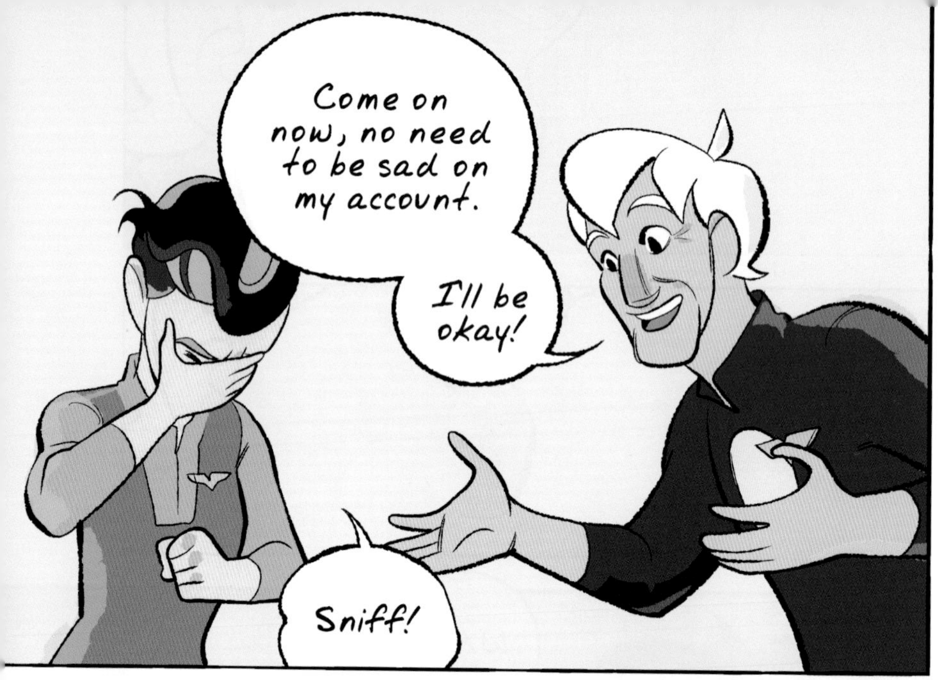
Come on now, no need to be sad on my account.
I'll be okay!
Sniff!

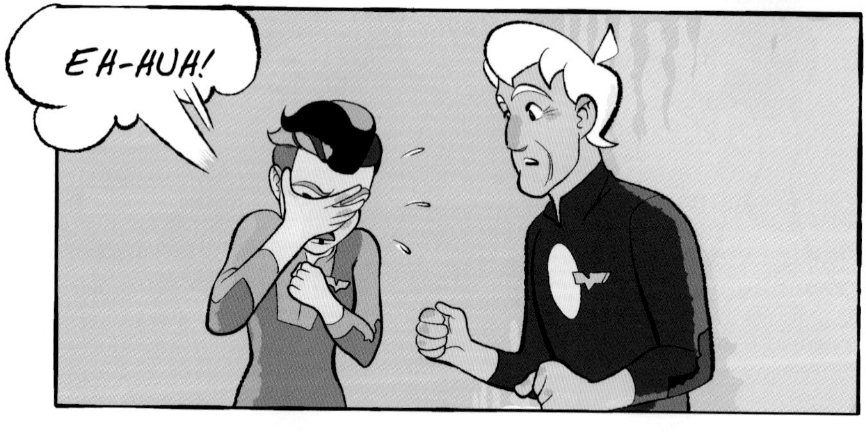
EH-HUH!

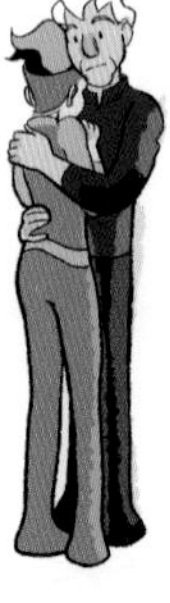

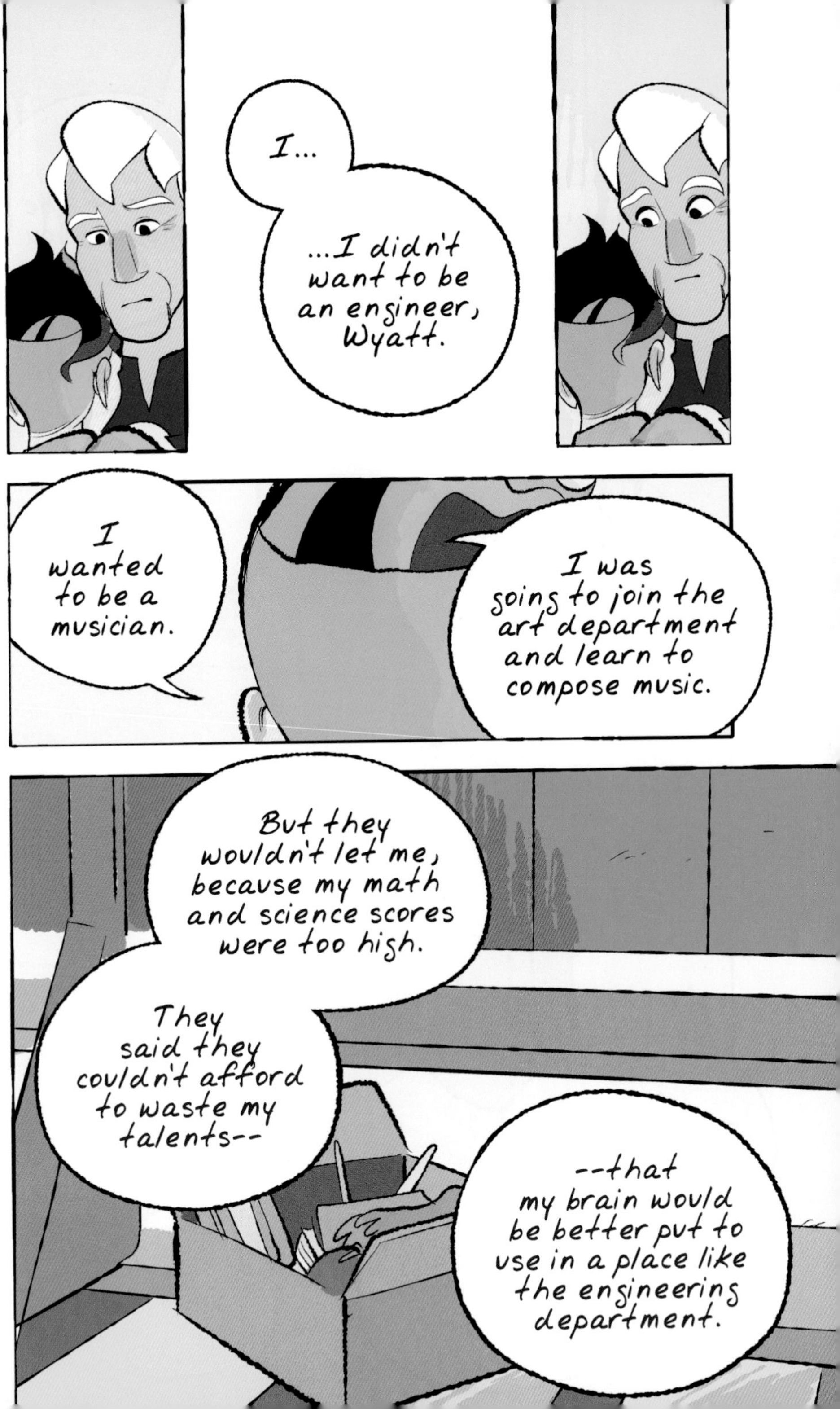
I...
...I didn't want to be an engineer, Wyatt.
I wanted to be a musician.
I was going to join the art department and learn to compose music.
But they wouldn't let me, because my math and science scores were too high.
They said they couldn't afford to waste my talents--
--that my brain would be better put to use in a place like the engineering department.

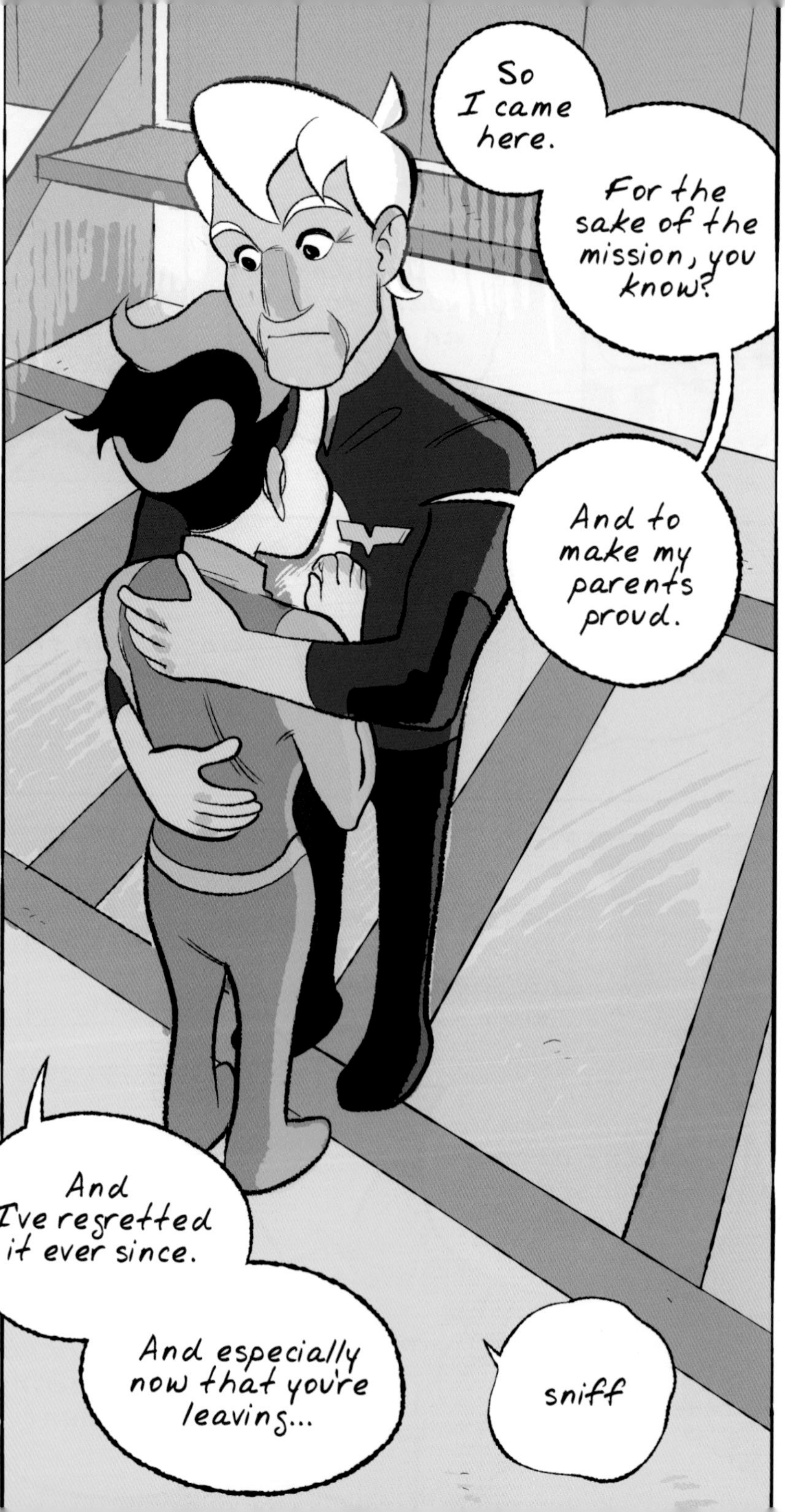
So I came here.
For the sake of the mission, you know?
And to make my parents proud.
And I've regretted it ever since.
And especially now that you're leaving...
sniff

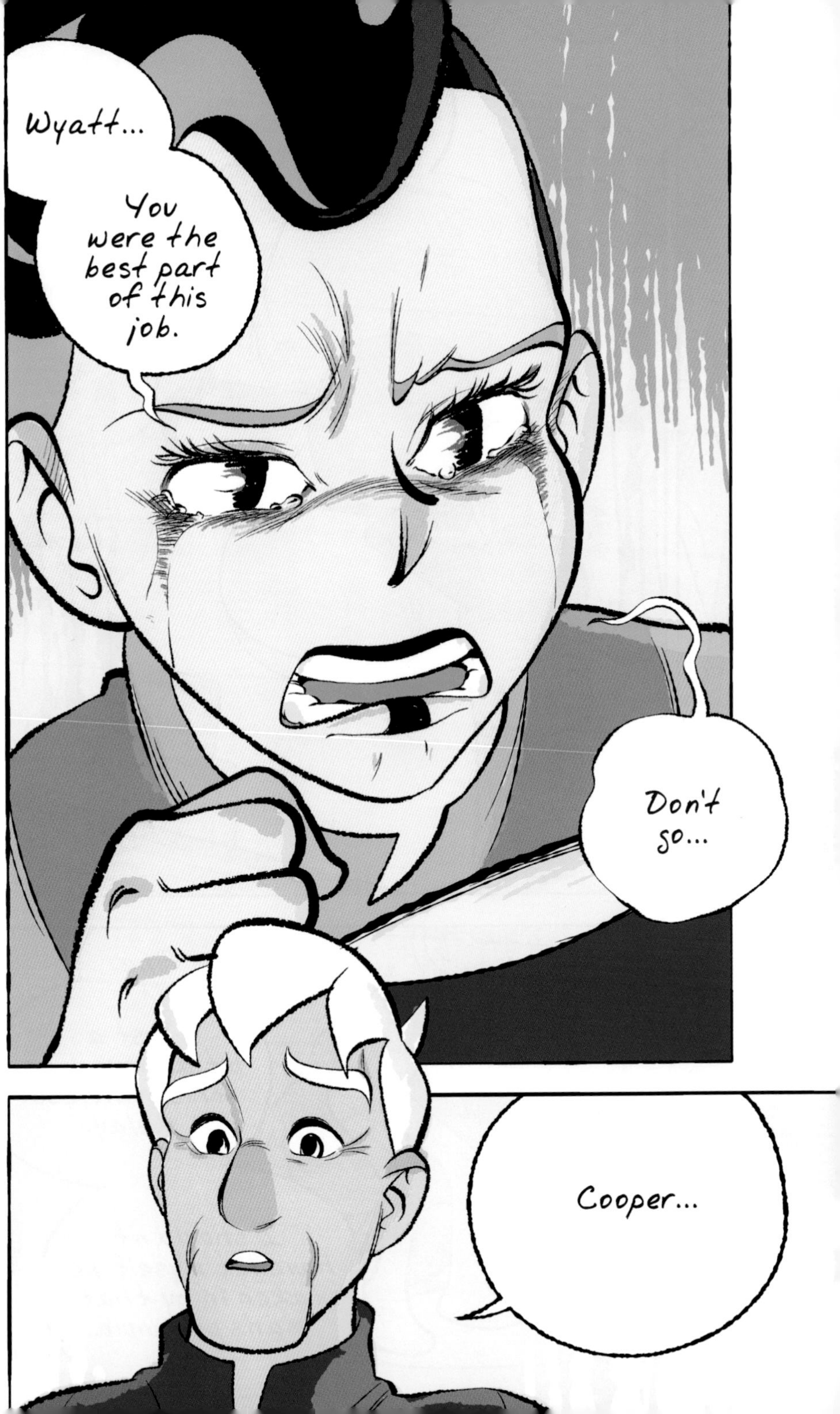
Wyatt...
You were the best part of this job.
Don't go...
Cooper...

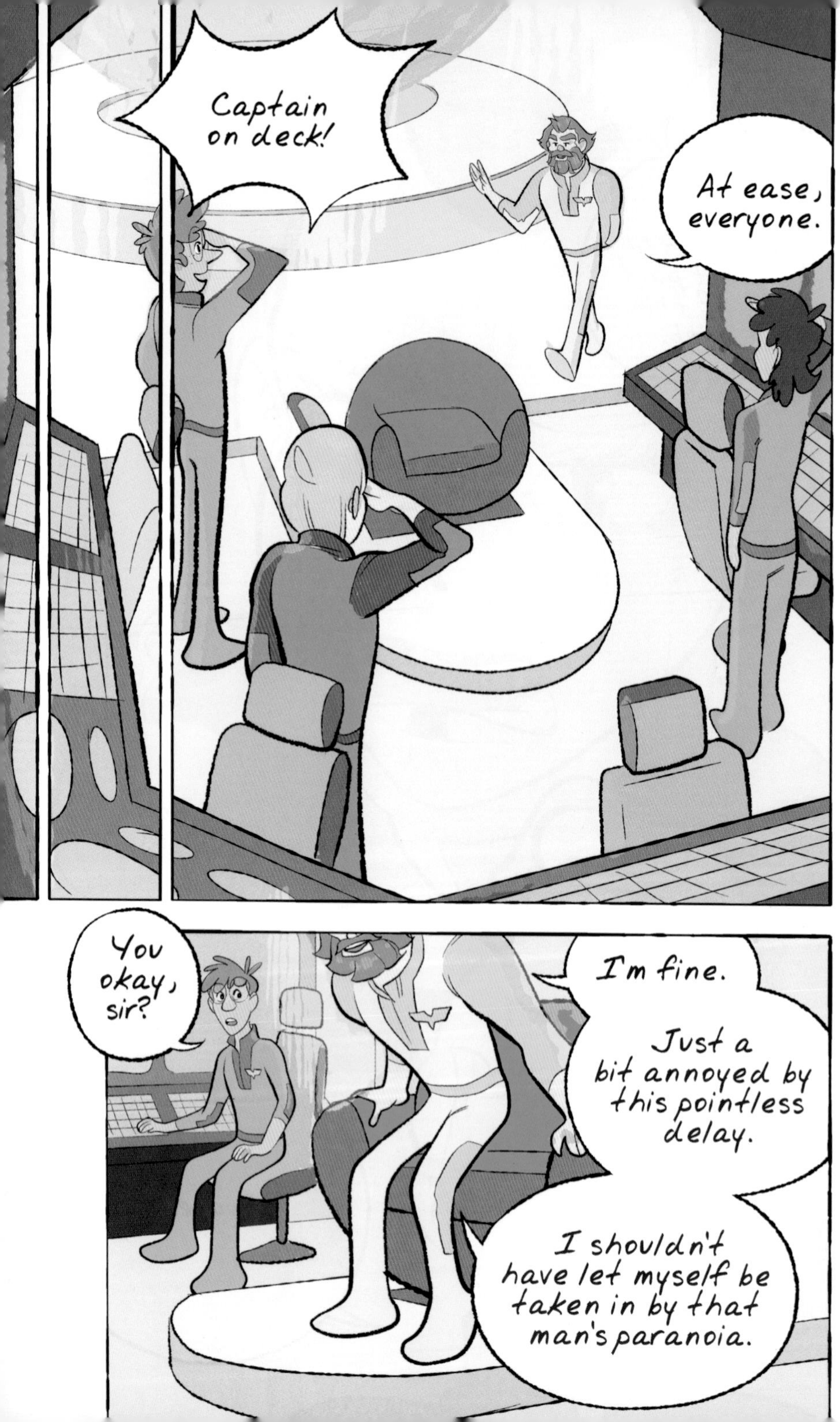
Captain on deck!
At ease, everyone.
You okay, sir?
I'm fine.
Just a bit annoyed by this pointless delay.
I shouldn't have let myself be taken in by that man's paranoia.

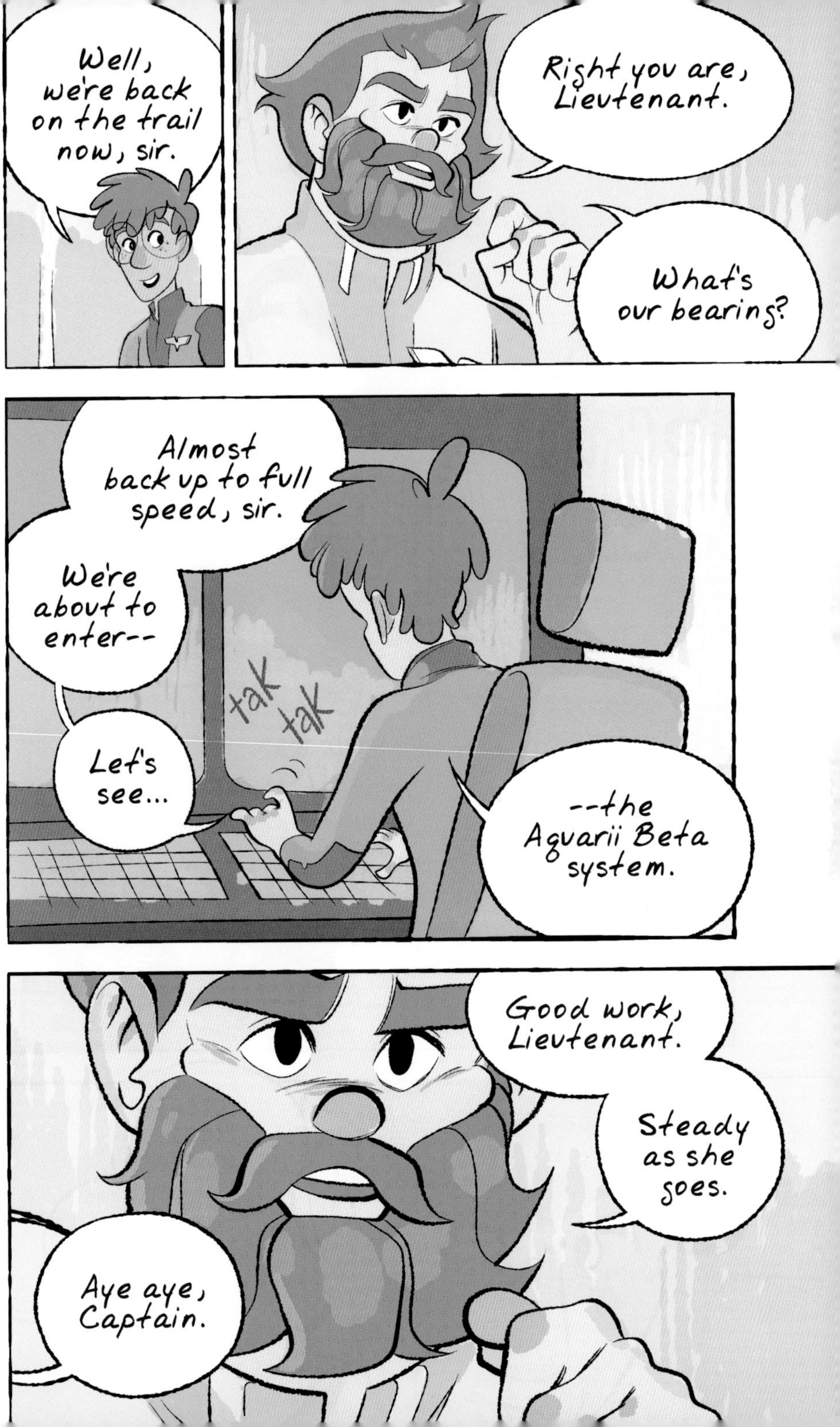
Well, we're back on the trail now, sir.
Right you are, Lieutenant.
What's our bearing?
Almost back up to full speed, sir.
We're about to enter--
tak tak
Let's see...
--the Aquarii Beta system.
Good work, Lieutenant.
Steady as she goes.
Aye aye, Captain.

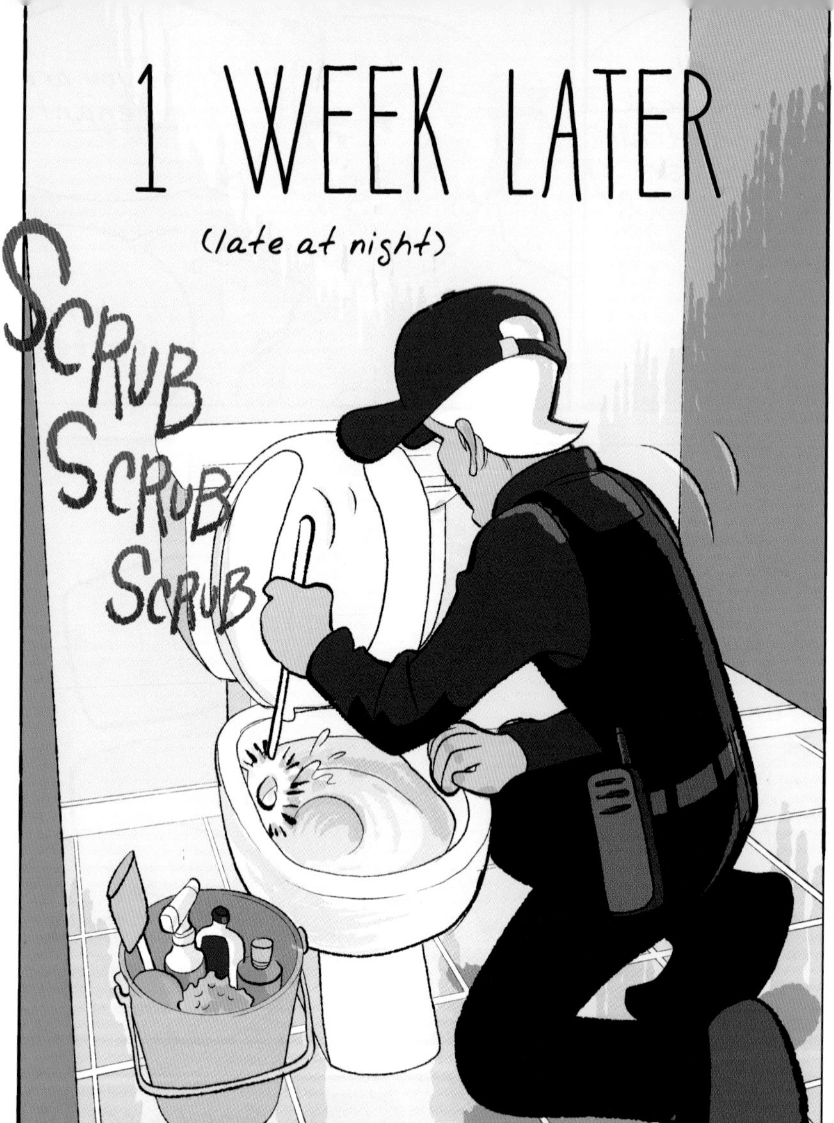
1 WEEK LATER
(late at night)
SCRUB SCRUB SCRUB

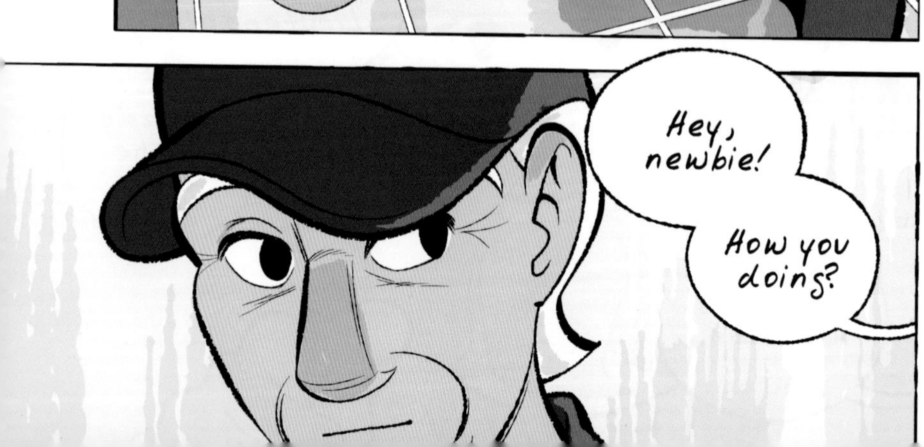
Hey, newbie!
How you doing?

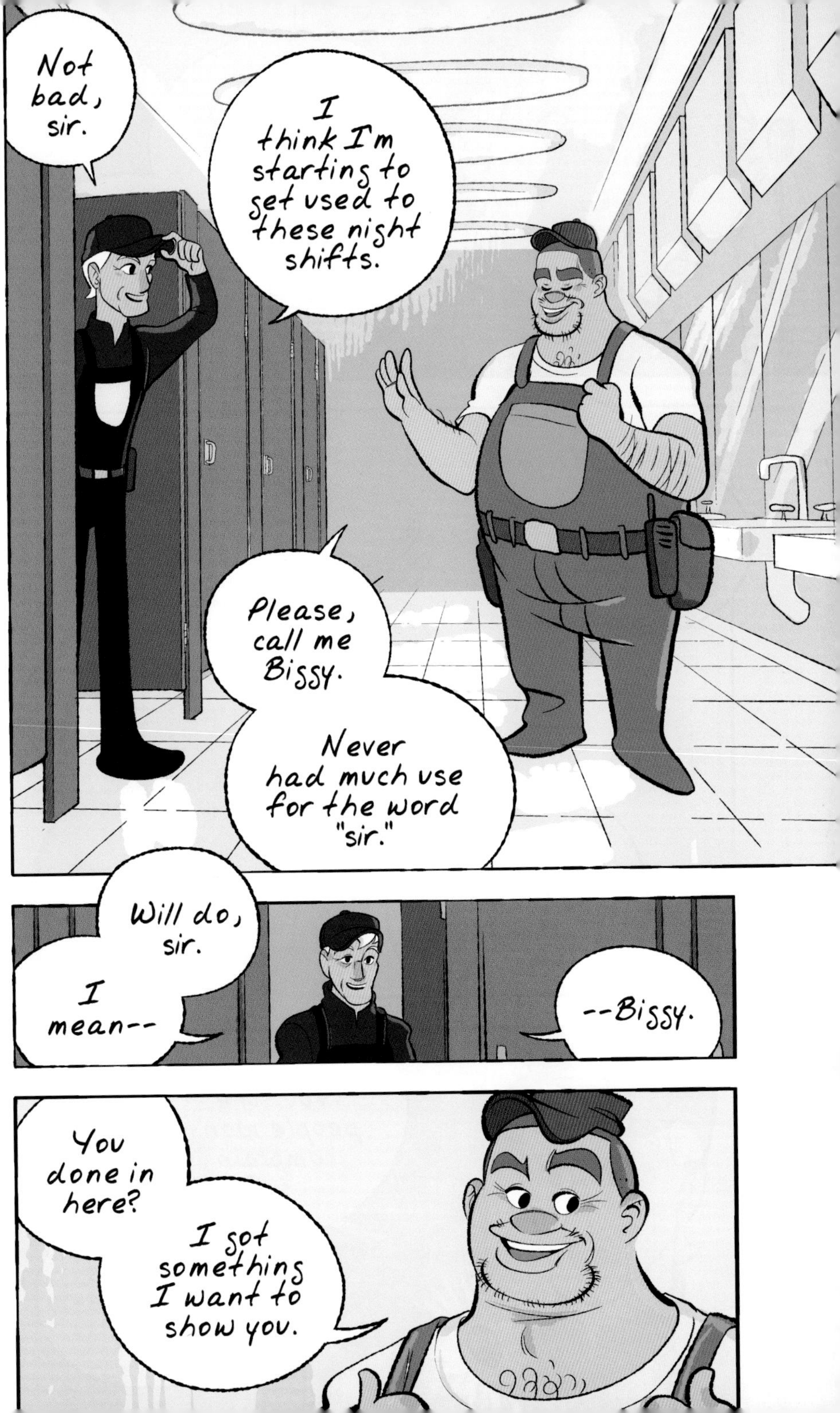
Not bad, sir.
I think I'm starting to get used to these night shifts.
Please, call me Bissy.
Never had much use for the word "sir."
Will do, sir.
I mean--
--Bissy.
You done in here?
I got something I want to show you.

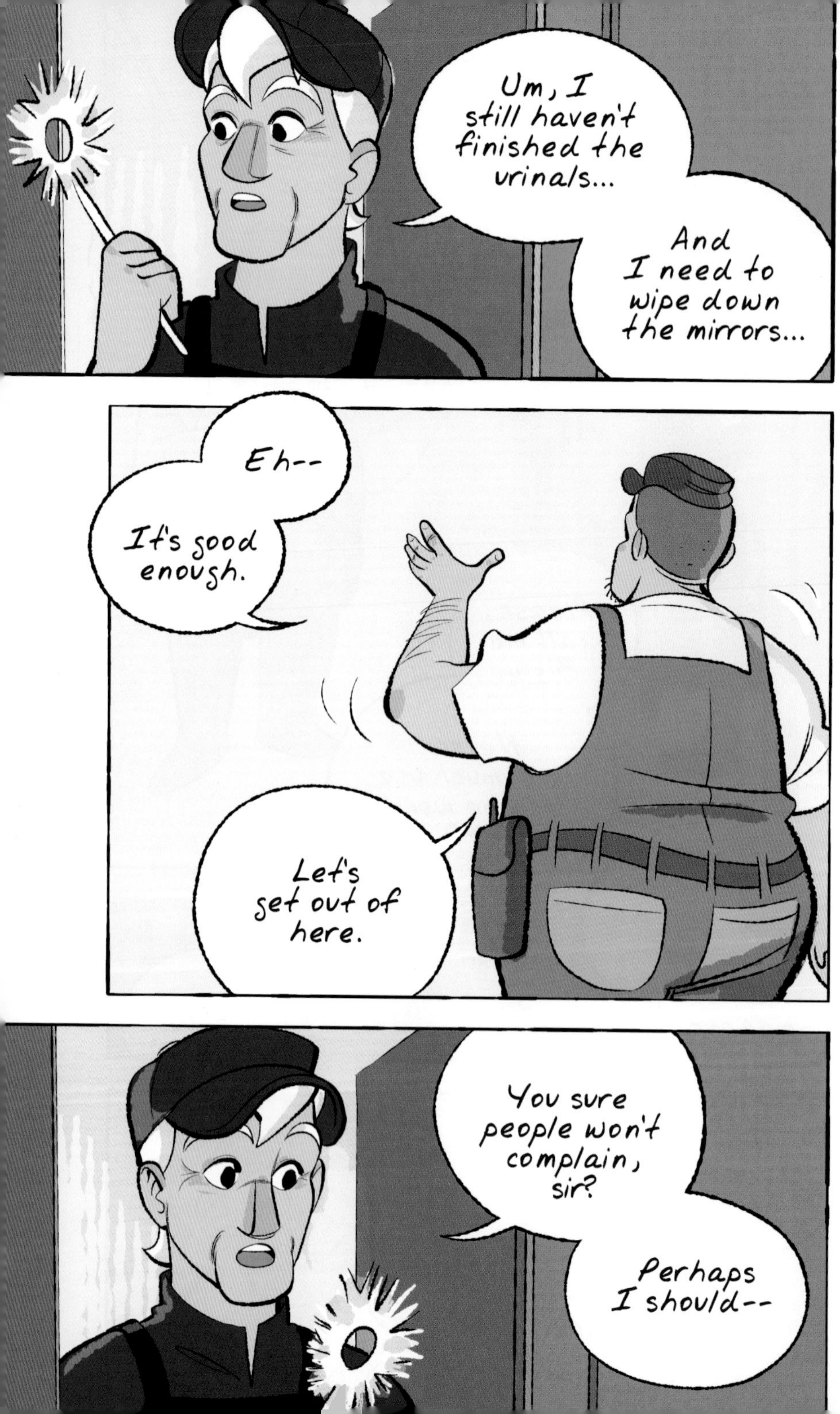

Um, I still haven't finished the urinals...
And I need to wipe down the mirrors...
Eh--
It's good enough.
Let's get out of here.
You sure people won't complain, sir?
Perhaps I should--

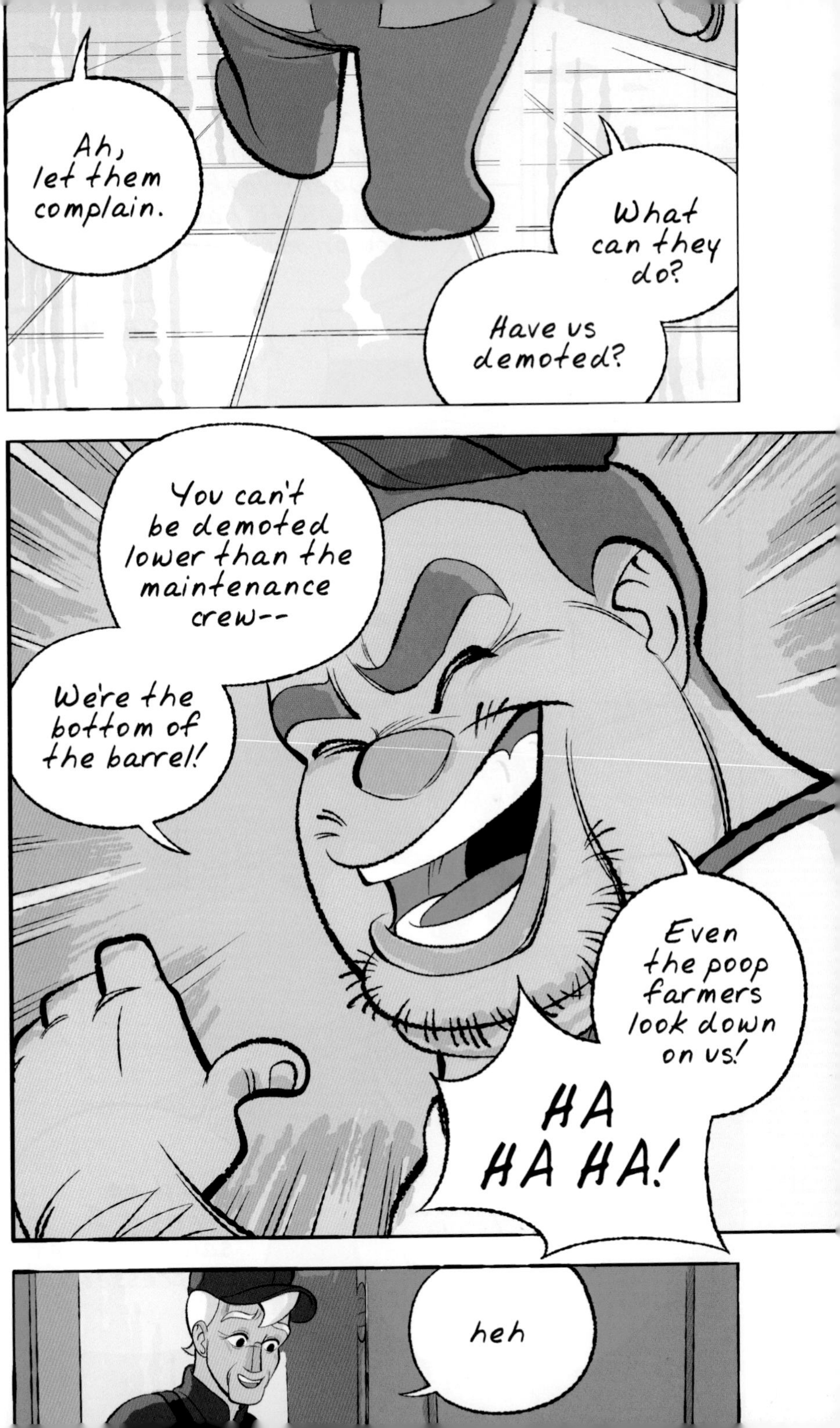
Ah, let them complain.
What can they do?
Have us demoted?
You can't be demoted lower than the maintenance crew--
We're the bottom of the barrel!
Even the poop farmers look down on us!
HA HA HA HA!
heh

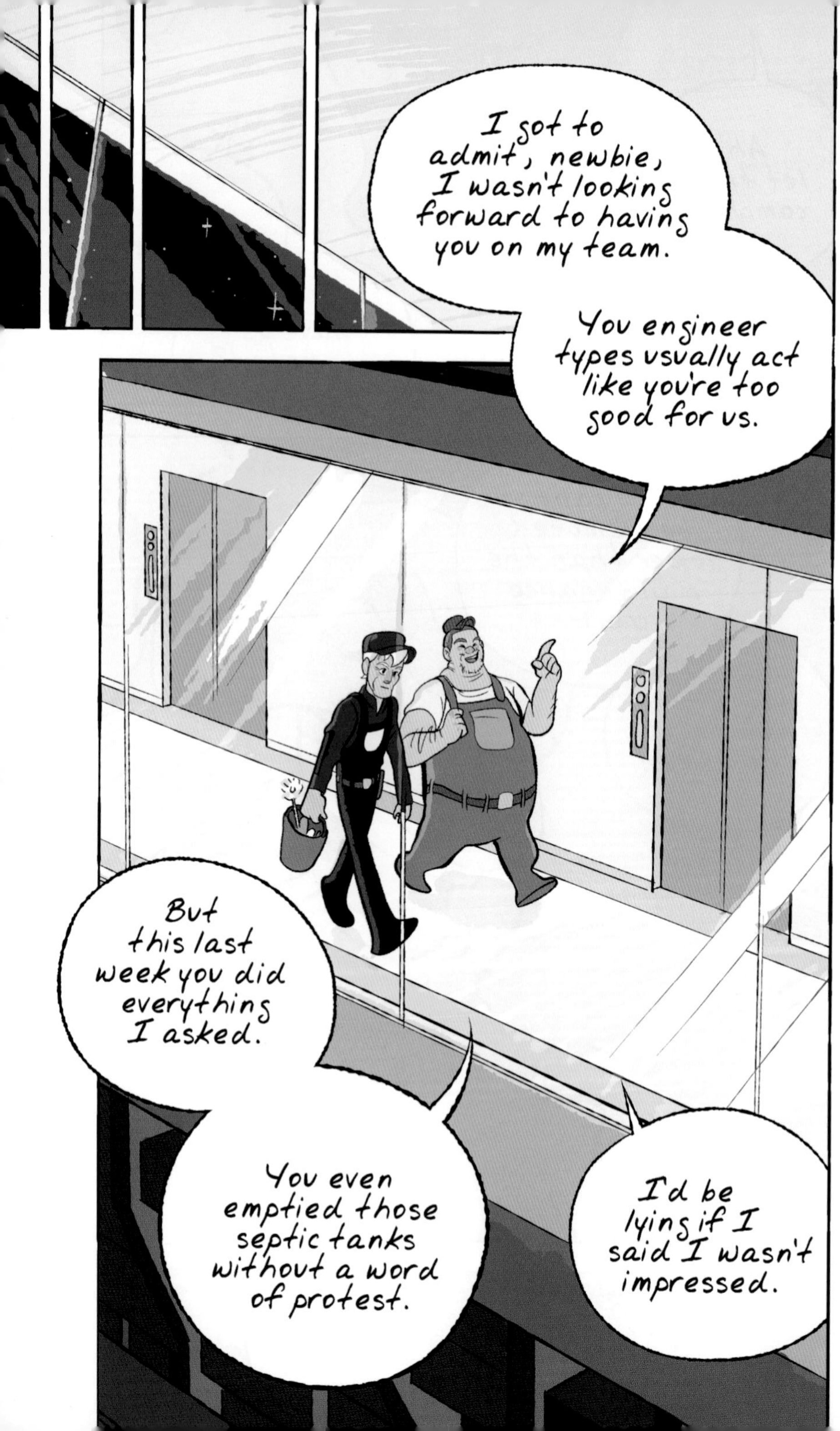
I got to admit, newbie, I wasn't looking forward to having you on my team.
You engineer types usually act like you're too good for us.
But this last week you did everything I asked.
You even emptied those septic tanks without a word of protest.
I'd be lying if I said I wasn't impressed.

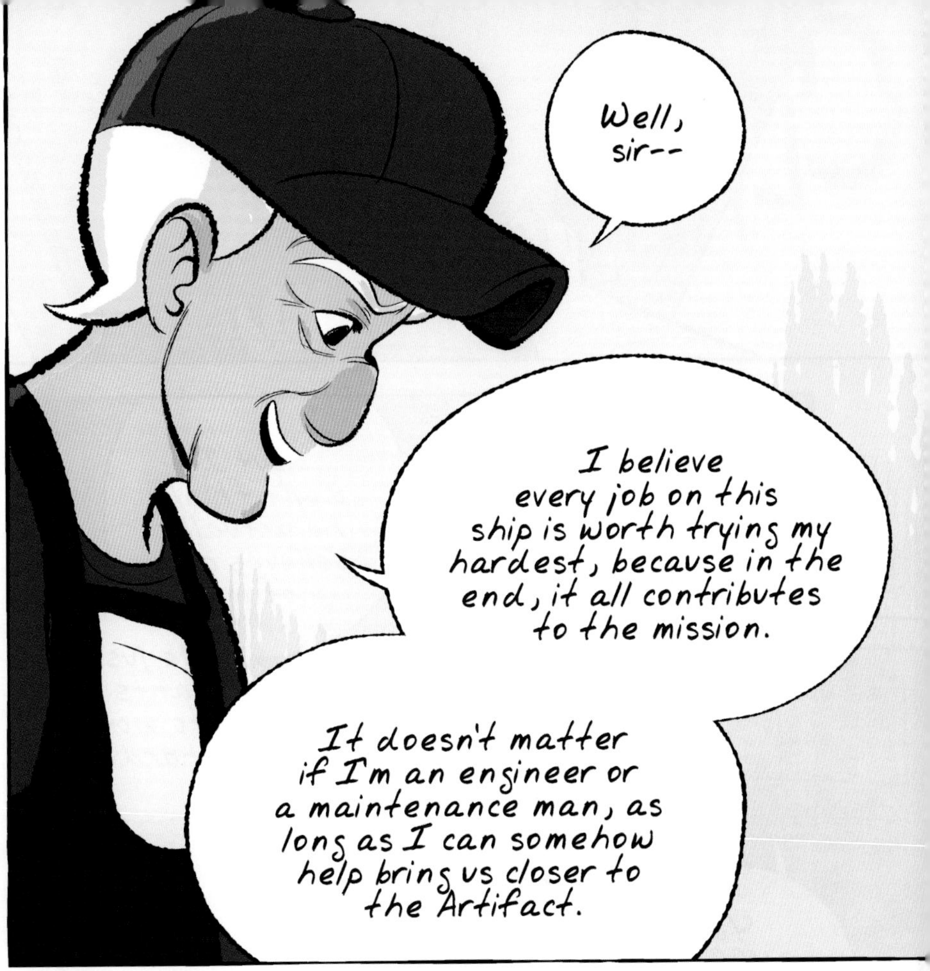
Well, sir--
I believe every job on this ship is worth trying my hardest, because in the end, it all contributes to the mission.
It doesn't matter if I'm an engineer or a maintenance man, as long as I can somehow help bring us closer to the Artifact.

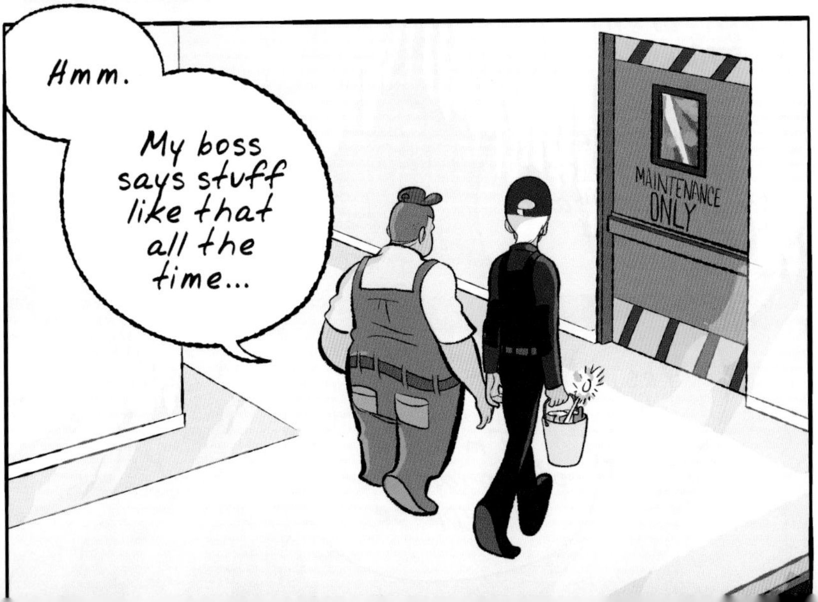
Hmm.
My boss says stuff like that all the time...
MAINTENANCE ONLY

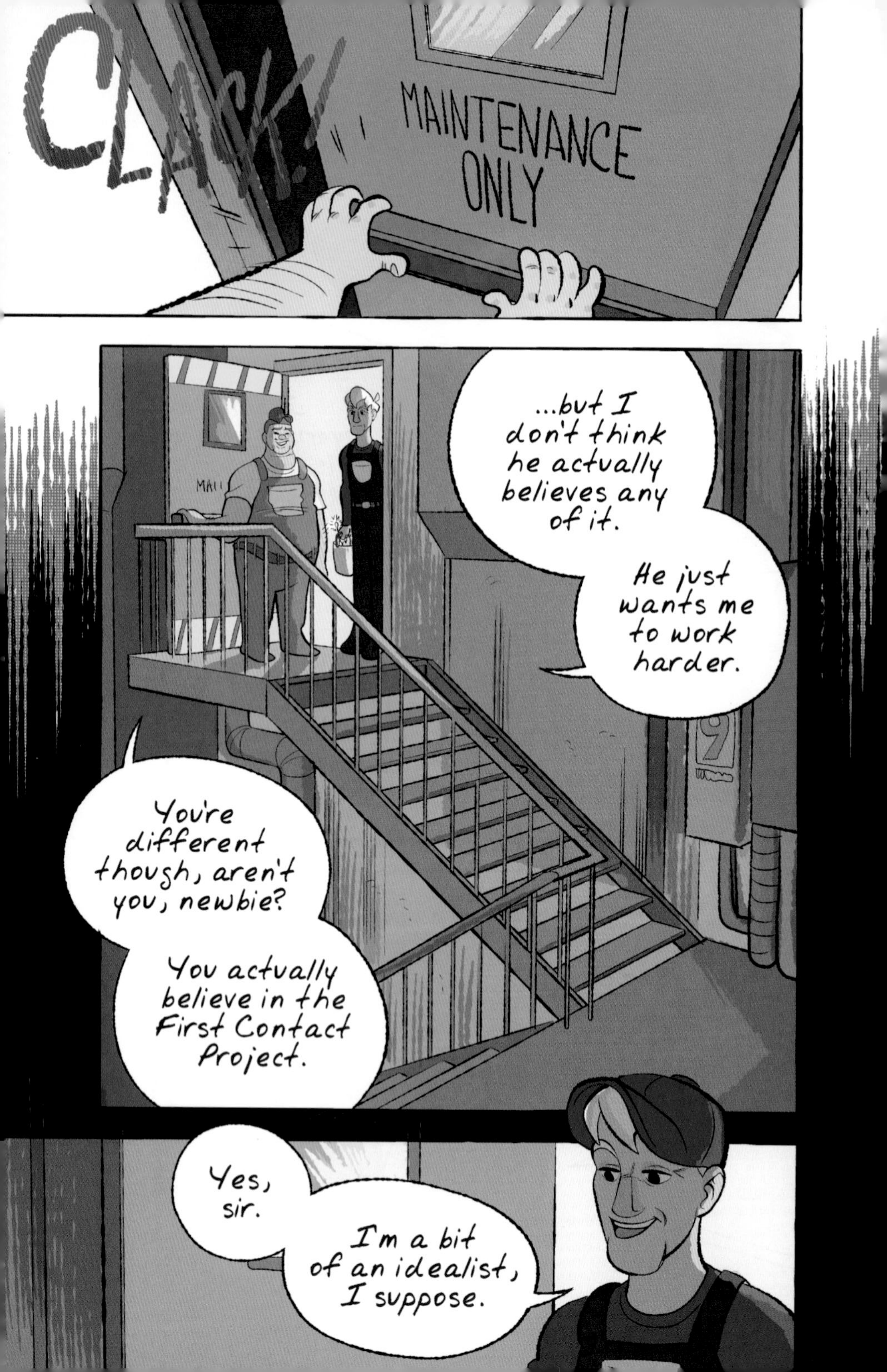
CLACK!
MAINTENANCE ONLY
...but I don't think he actually believes any of it.
He just wants me to work harder.
You're different though, aren't you, newbie?
You actually believe in the First Contact Project.
Yes, sir.
I'm a bit of an idealist, I suppose.

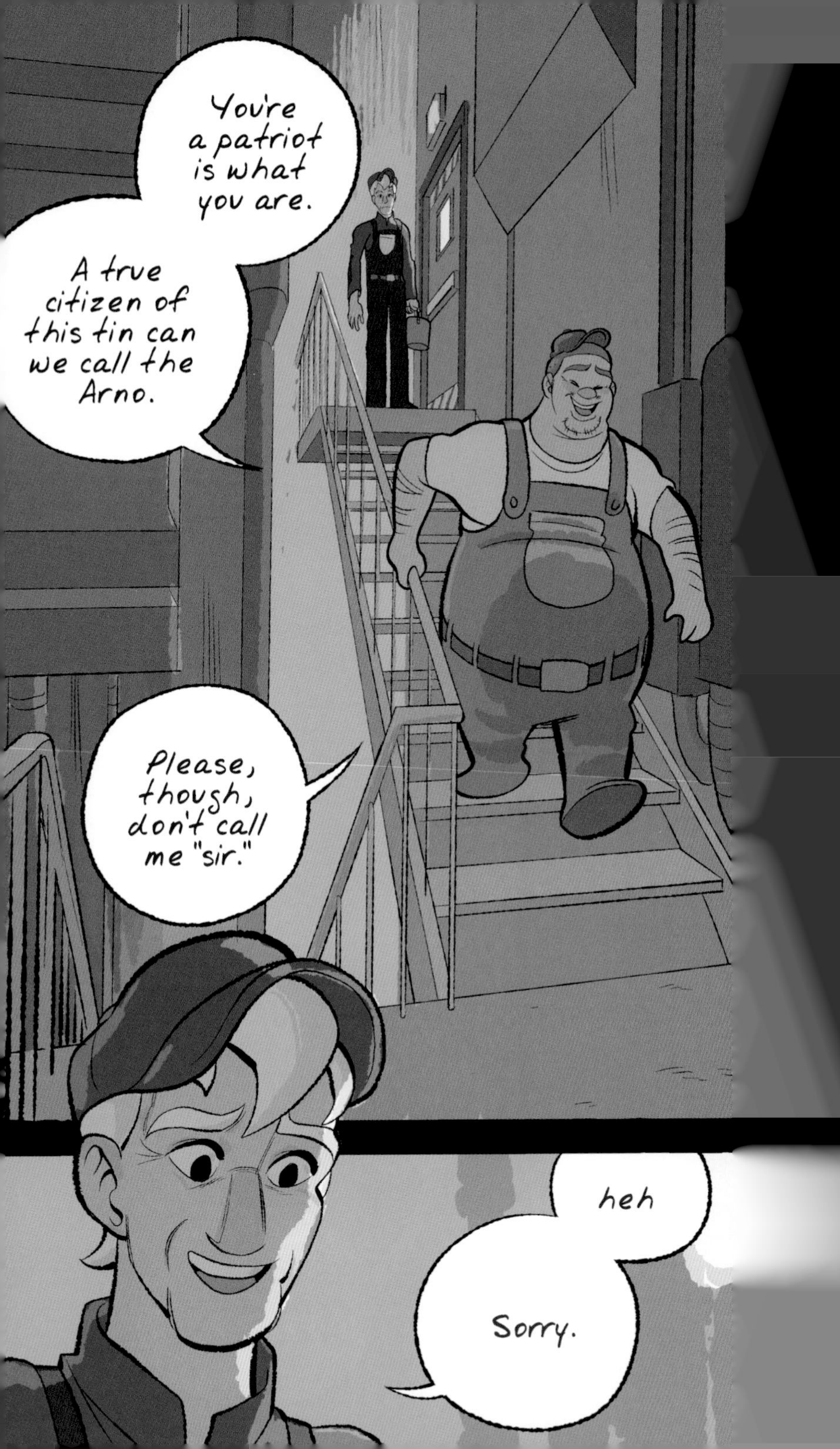
You're a patriot is what you are.
A true citizen of this tin can we call the Arno.
Please, though, don't call me "sir."
heh
Sorry.

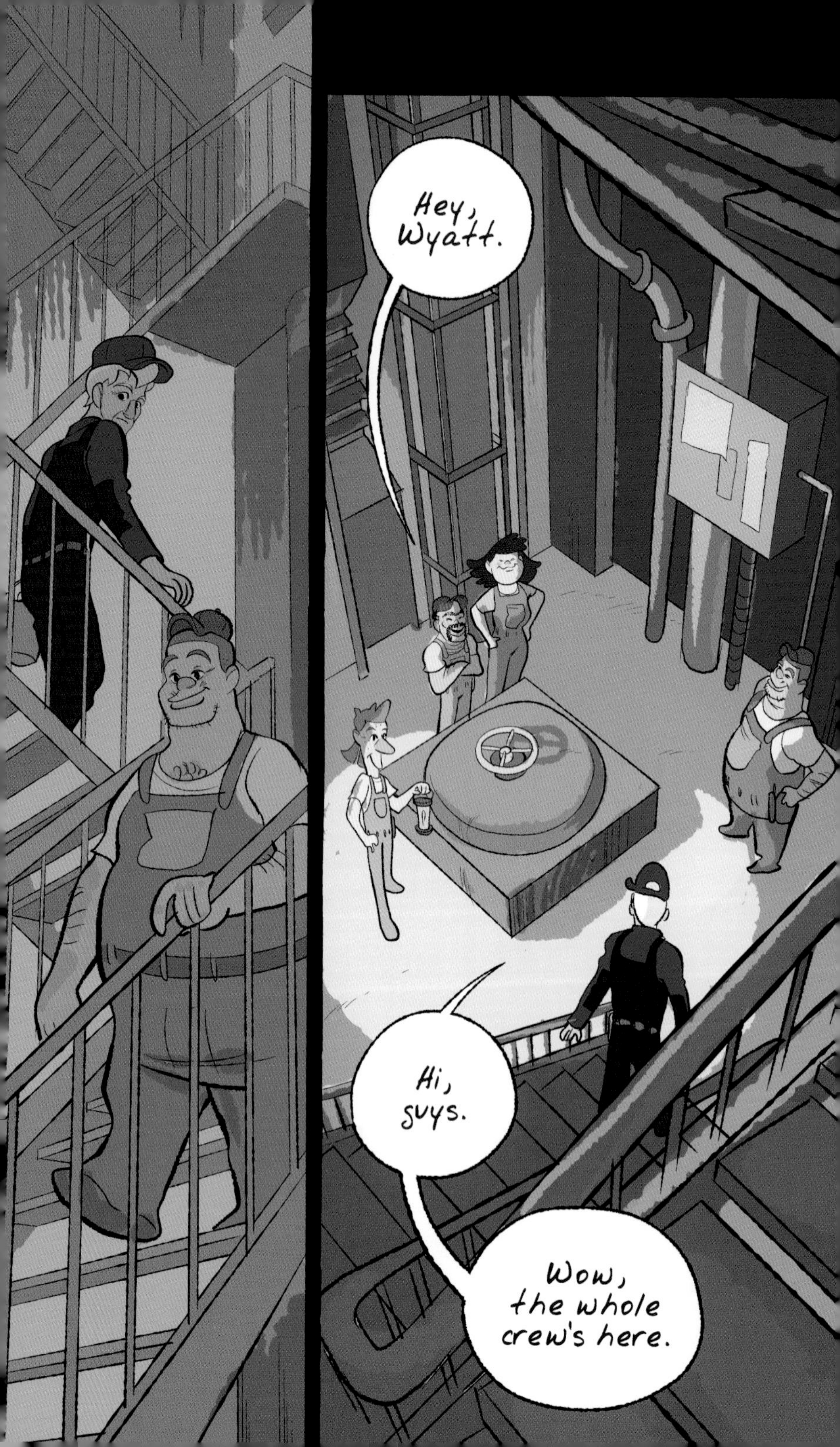
Hey, Wyatt.
Hi, guys.
Wow, the whole crew's here.

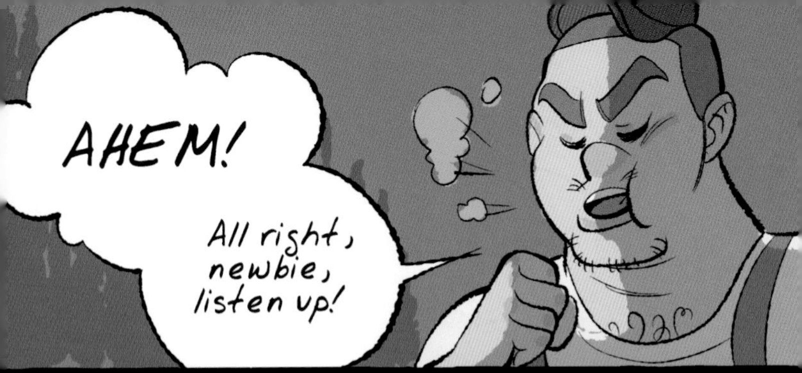
AHEM!
All right, newbie, listen up!

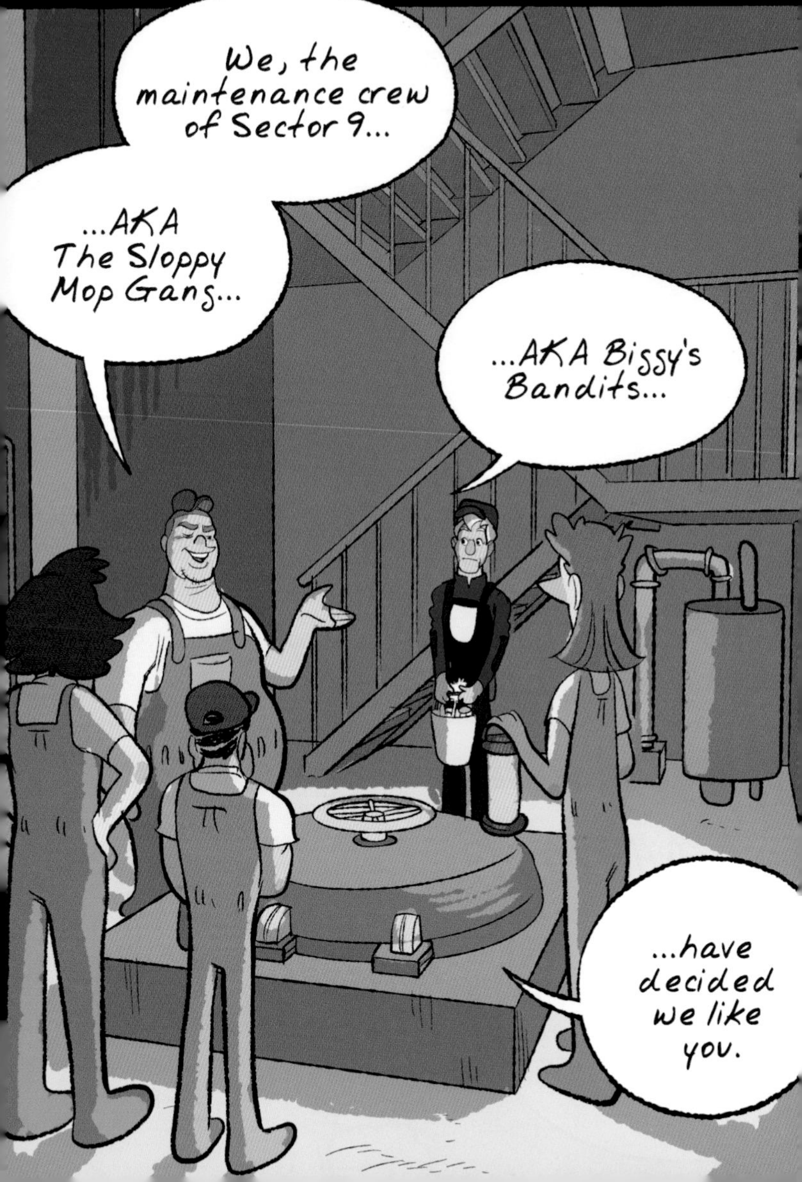
We, the maintenance crew of Sector 9...
...AKA The Sloppy Mop Gang...
...AKA Bissy's Bandits...
...have decided we like you.

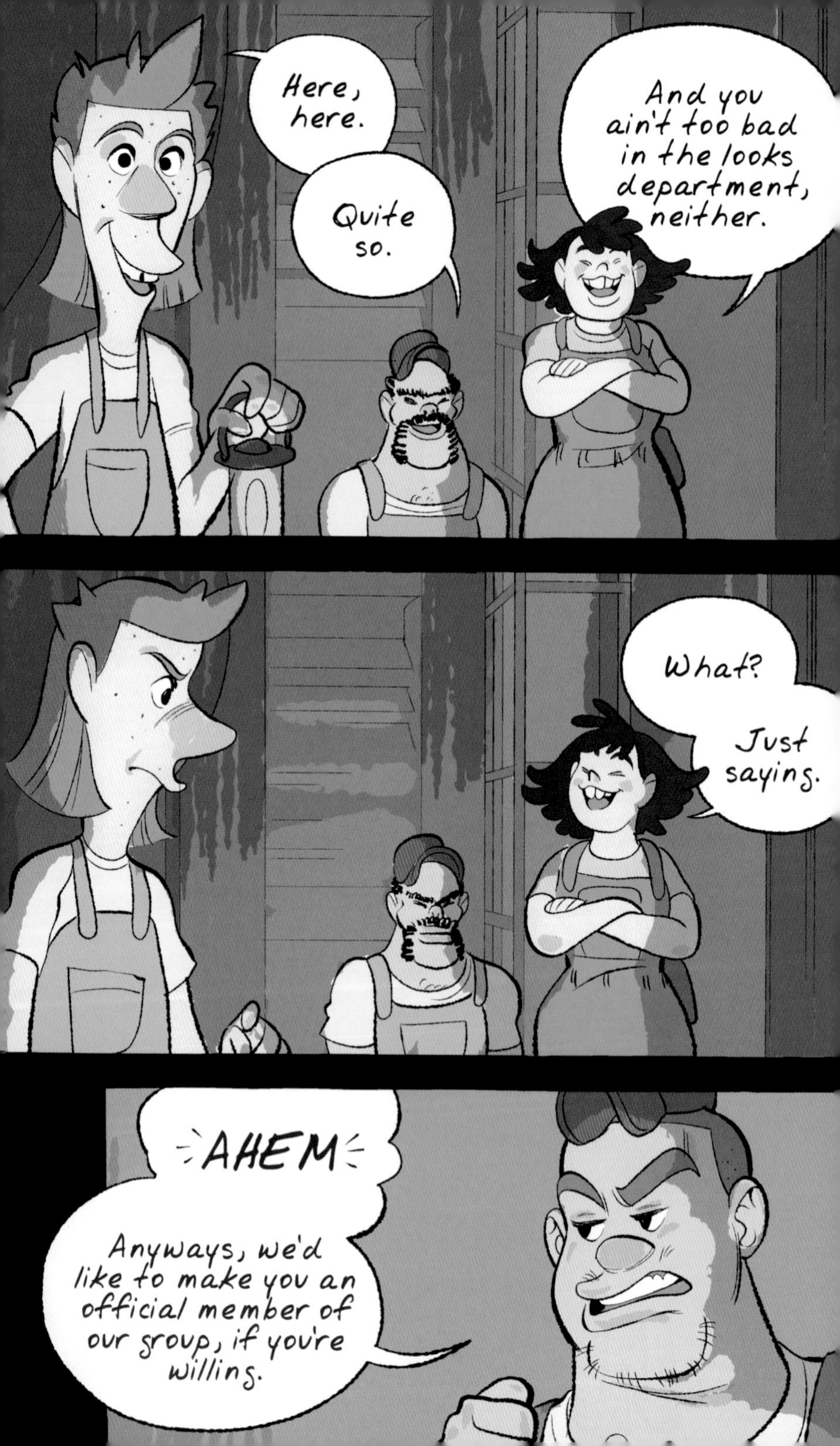
Here, here.
Quite so.
And you ain't too bad in the looks department, neither.
What?
Just sayings.
AHEM
Anyways, we'd like to make you an official member of our group, if you're willing.

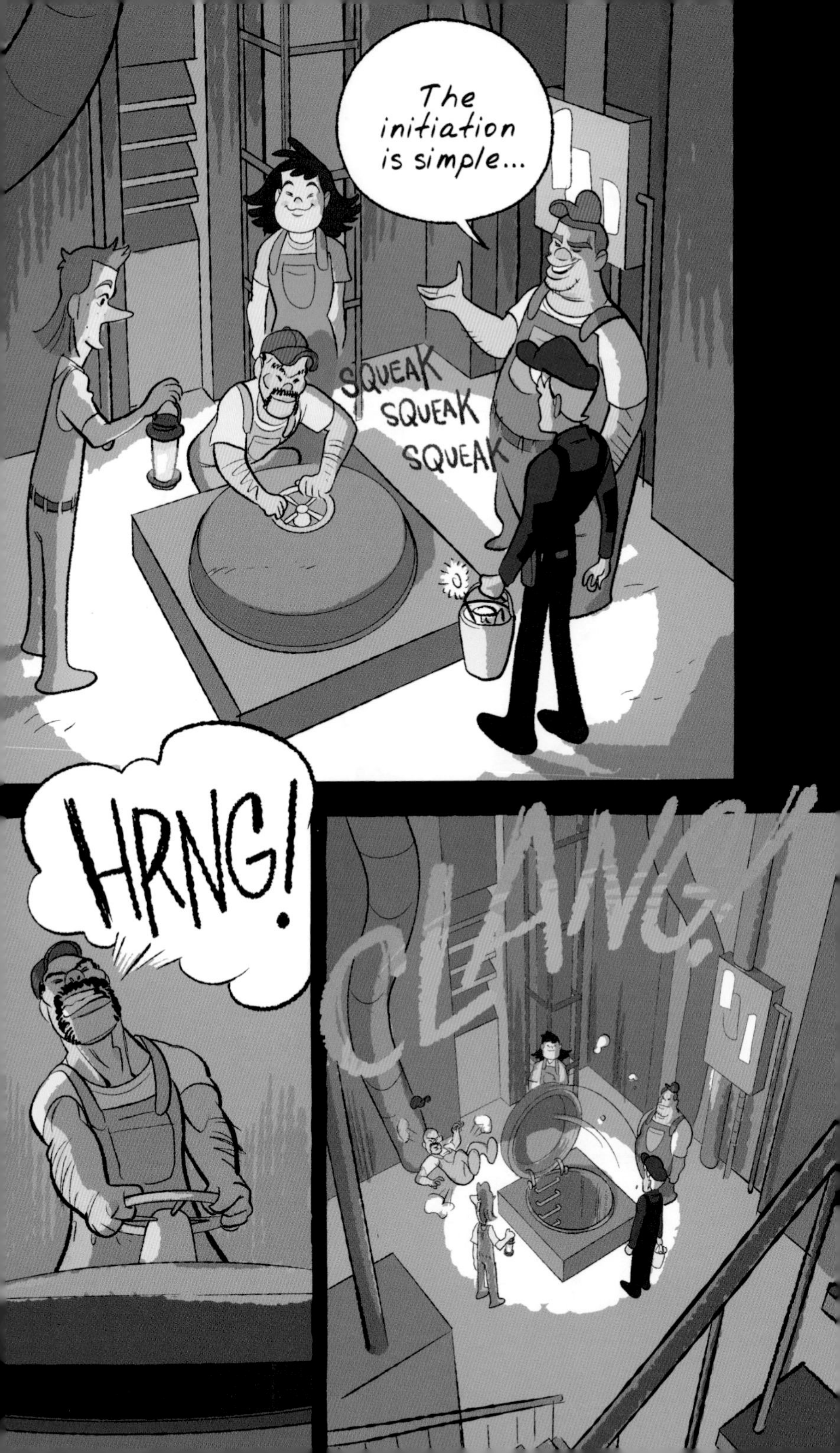

The initiation is simple...
SQUEAK
SQUEAK
SQUEAK
HRNG!
CLANG!

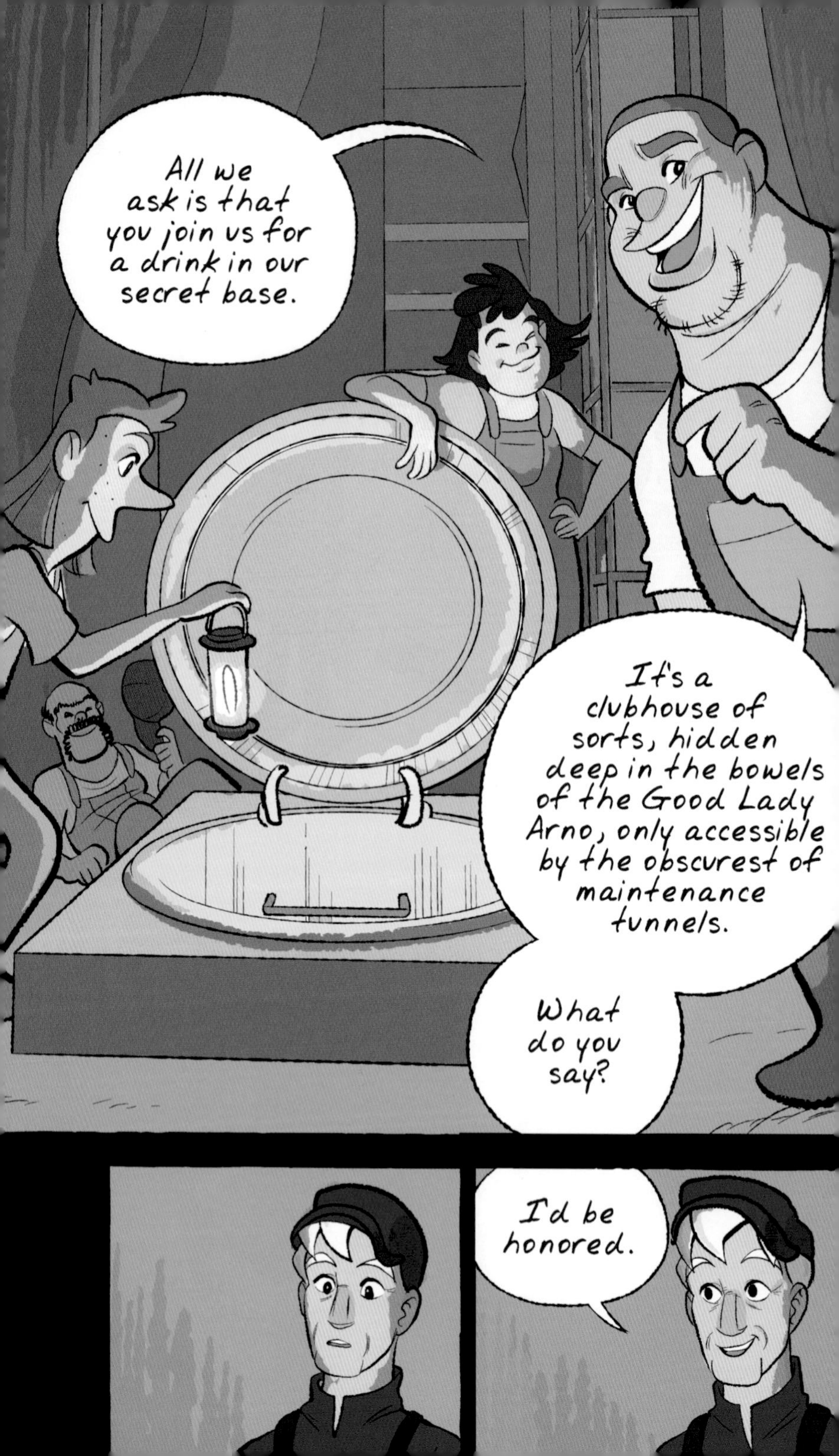
All we ask is that you join us for a drink in our secret base.
It's a clubhouse of sorts, hidden deep in the bowels of the Good Lady Arno, only accessible by the obscurest of maintenance tunnels.
What do you say?
I'd be honored.

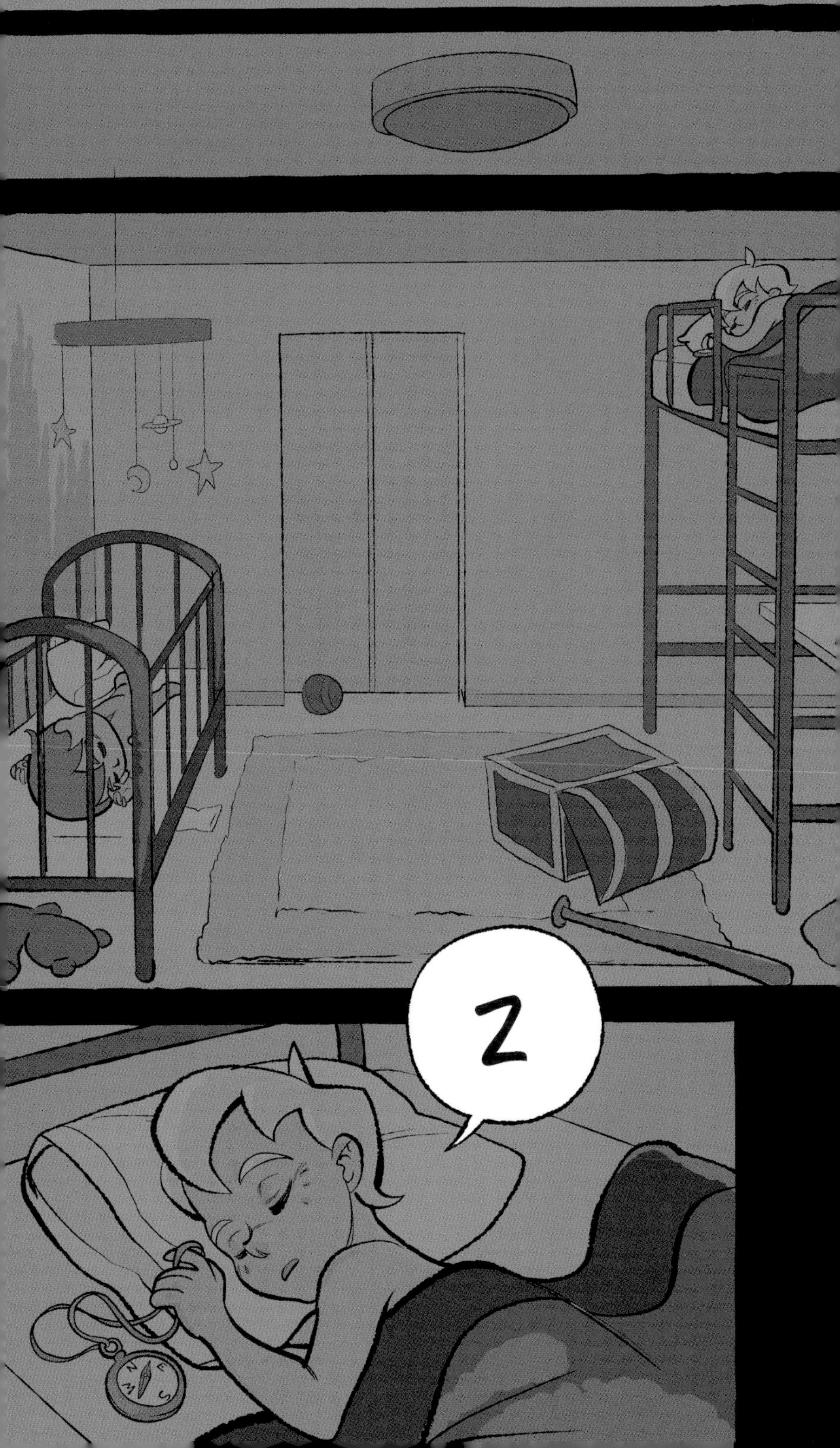

Z

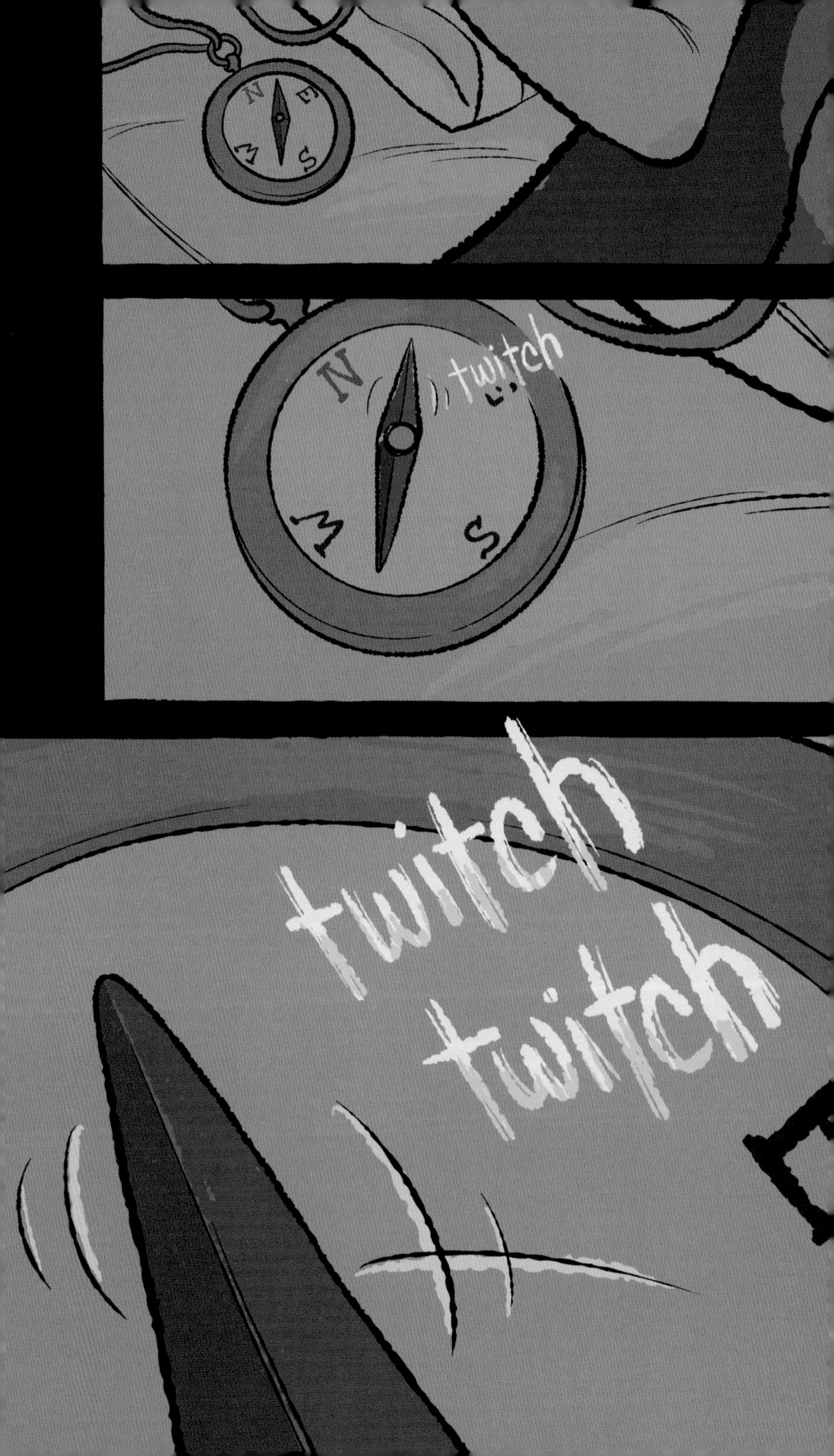
N
E
W
S
N
twitch
W
S
twitch
twitch

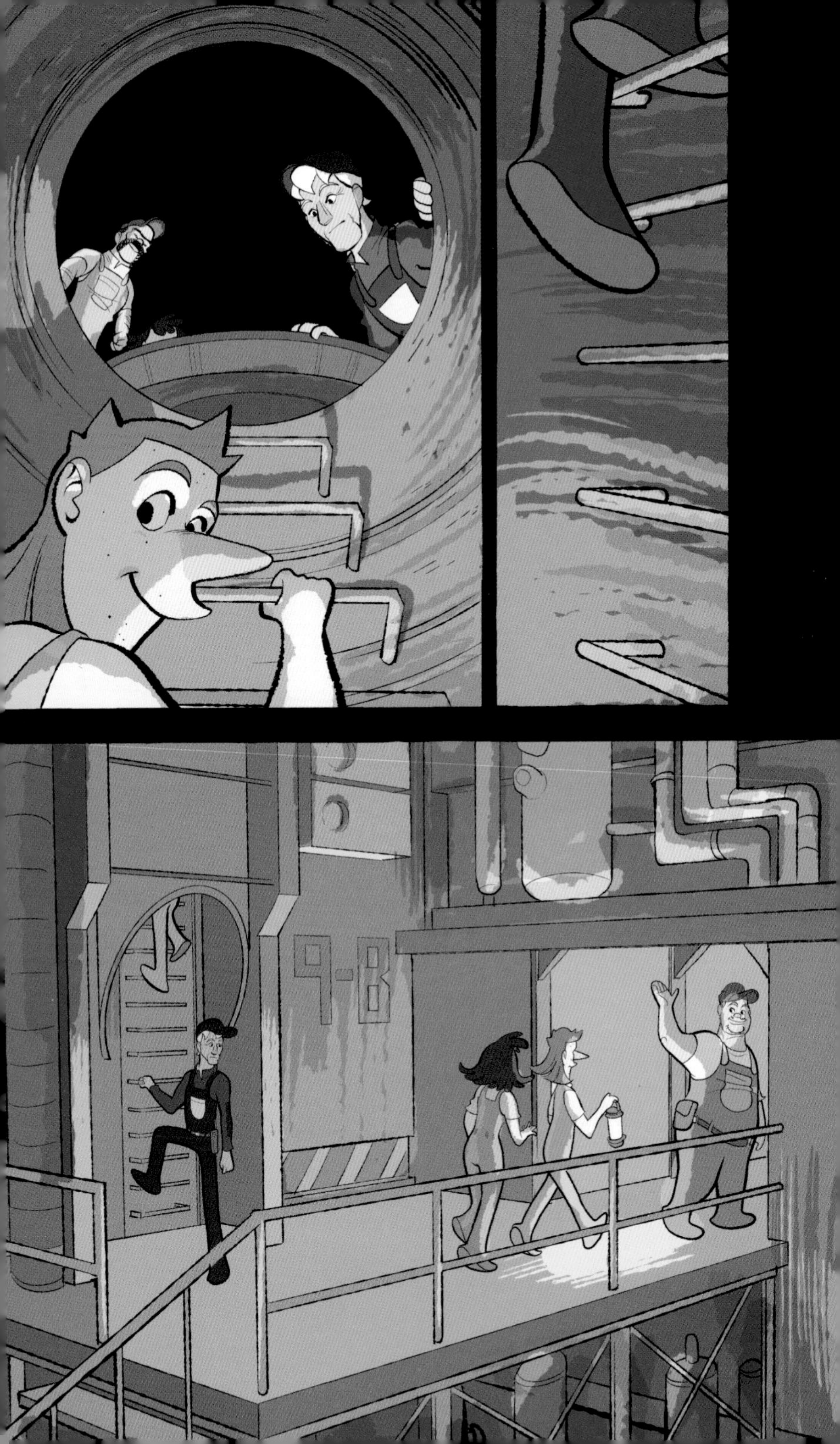
9-8

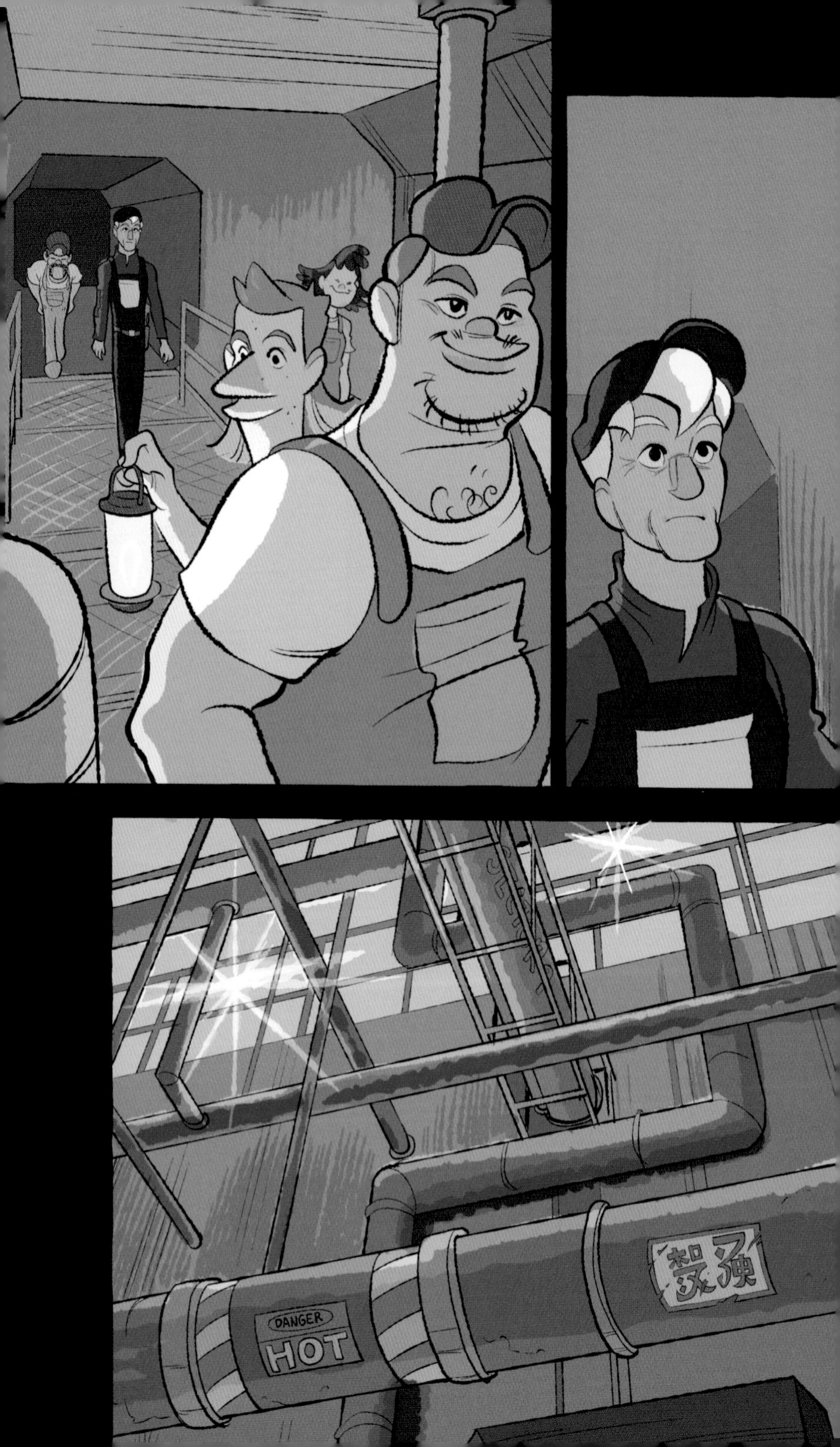
DANGER
HOT

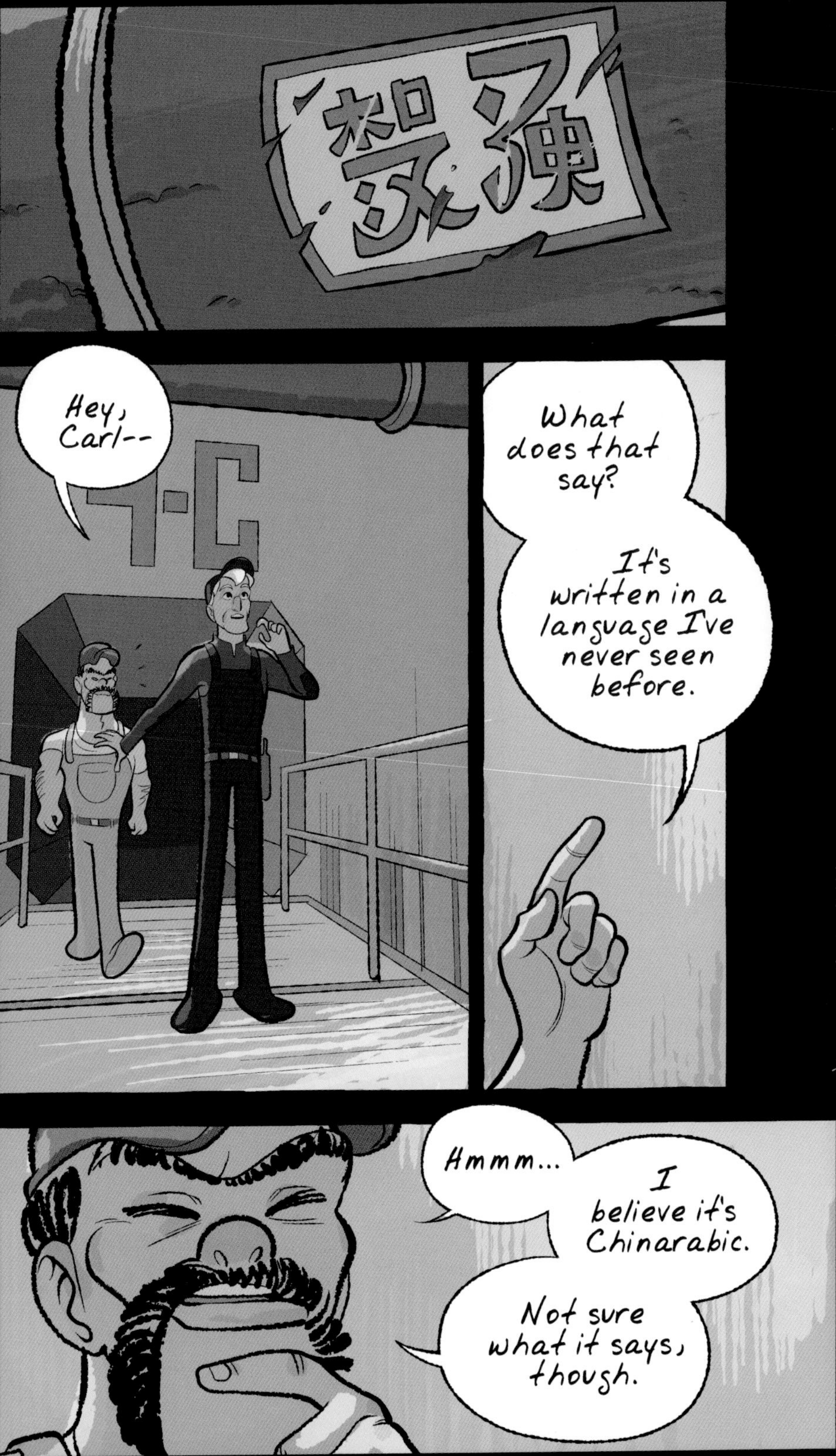

Hey, Carl--
What does that say?
It's written in a language I've never seen before.
Hmmm...
I believe it's Chinarabic.
Not sure what it says, though.

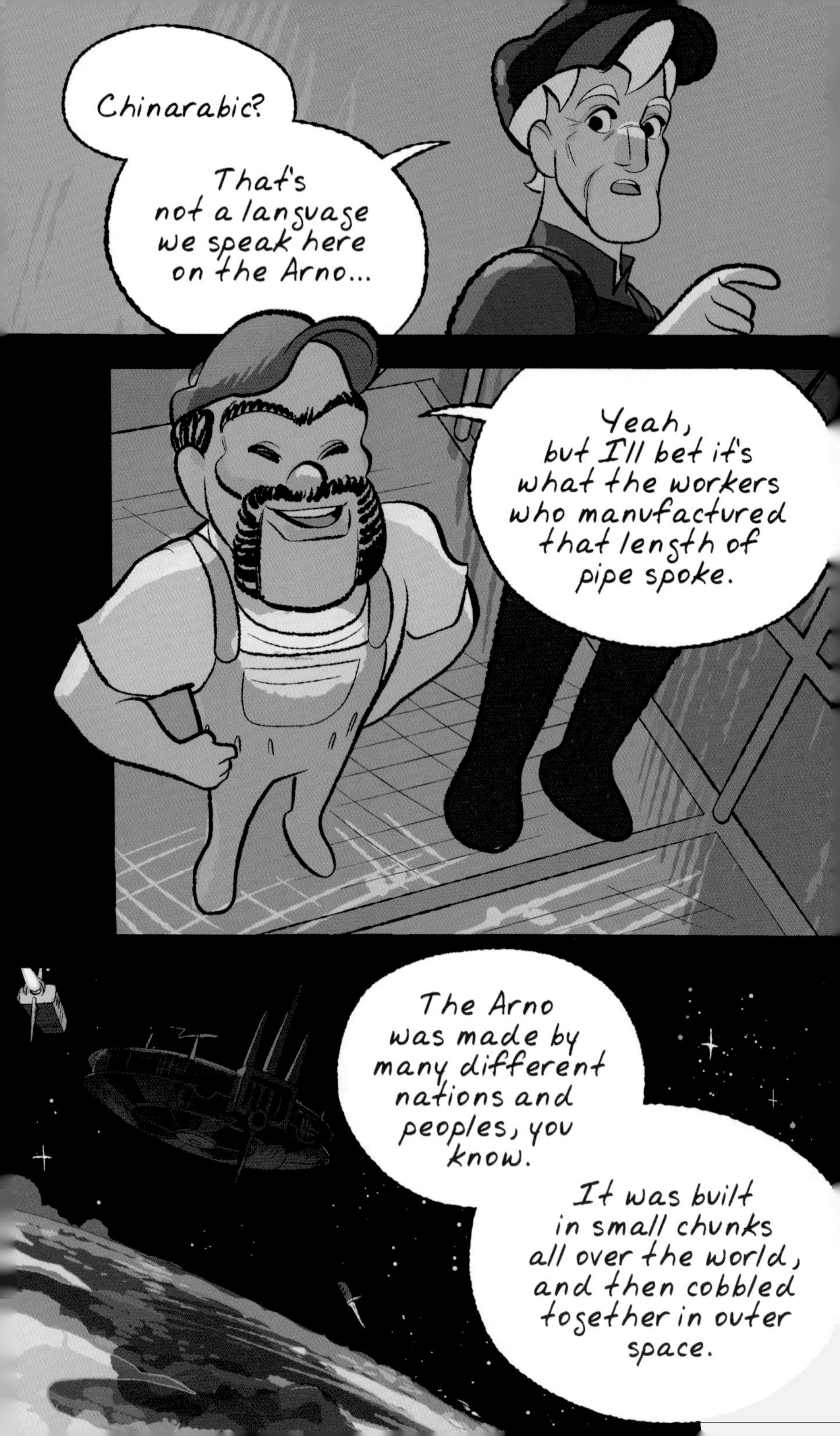
Chinarabic?
That's not a language we speak here on the Arno...
Yeah, but I'll bet it's what the workers who manufactured that length of pipe spoke.
The Arno was made by many different nations and peoples, you know.
It was built in small chunks all over the world, and then cobbled together in outer space.

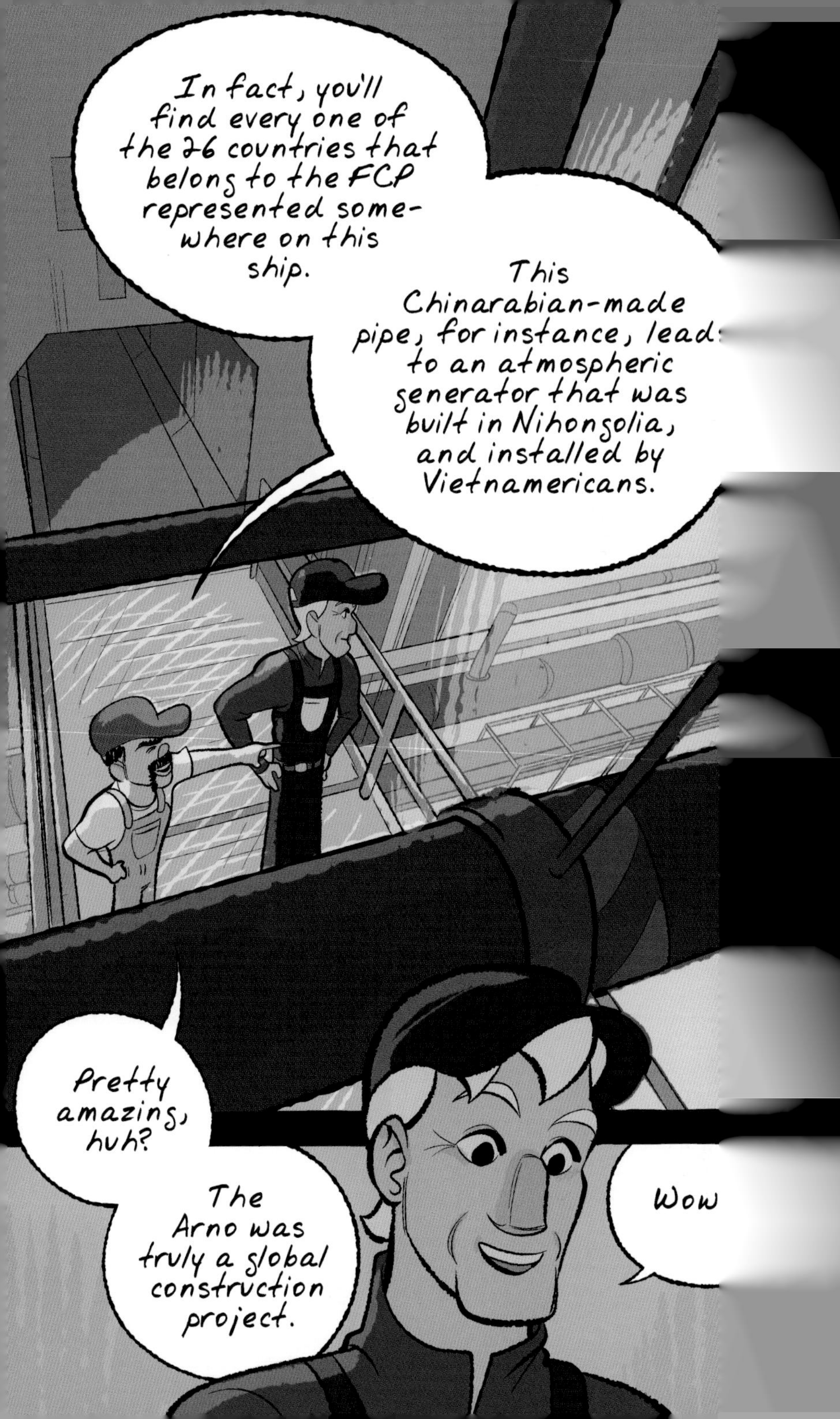
In fact, you'll find every one of the 26 countries that belongs to the FCP represented some-where on this ship.
This Chinarabian-made pipe, for instance, leads to an atmospheric generator that was built in Nihongolia, and installed by Vietnamericans.
Pretty amazing, huh?
The Arno was truly a global construction project.
Wow

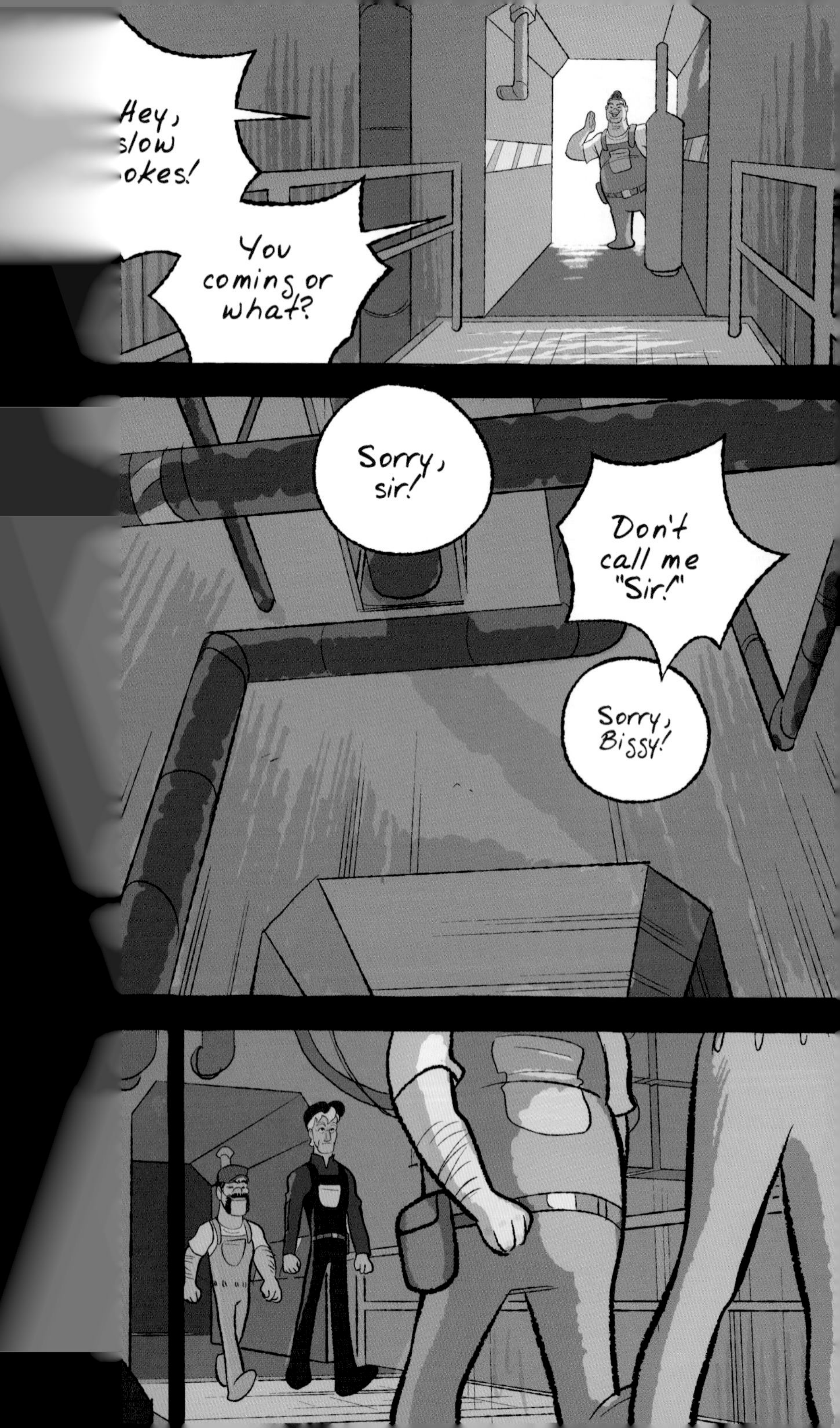
Hey, slow okes!
You coming or what?
Sorry, sir!
Don't call me "Sir!"
Sorry, Bissy!

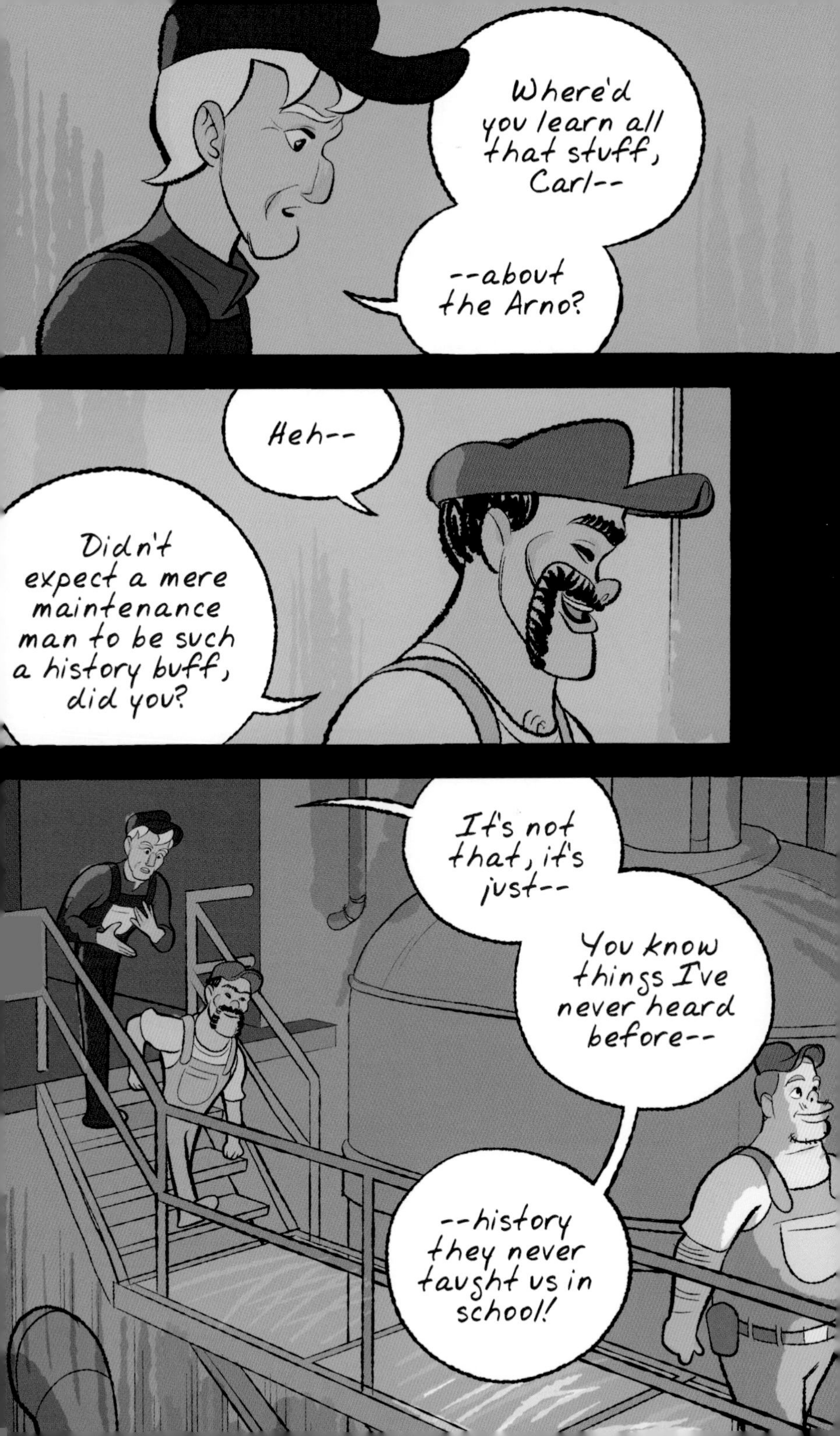
Where'd you learn all that stuff, Carl--
--about the Arno?
Heh--
Didn't expect a mere maintenance man to be such a history buff, did you?
It's not that, it's just--
You know things I've never heard before--
--history they never taught us in school!

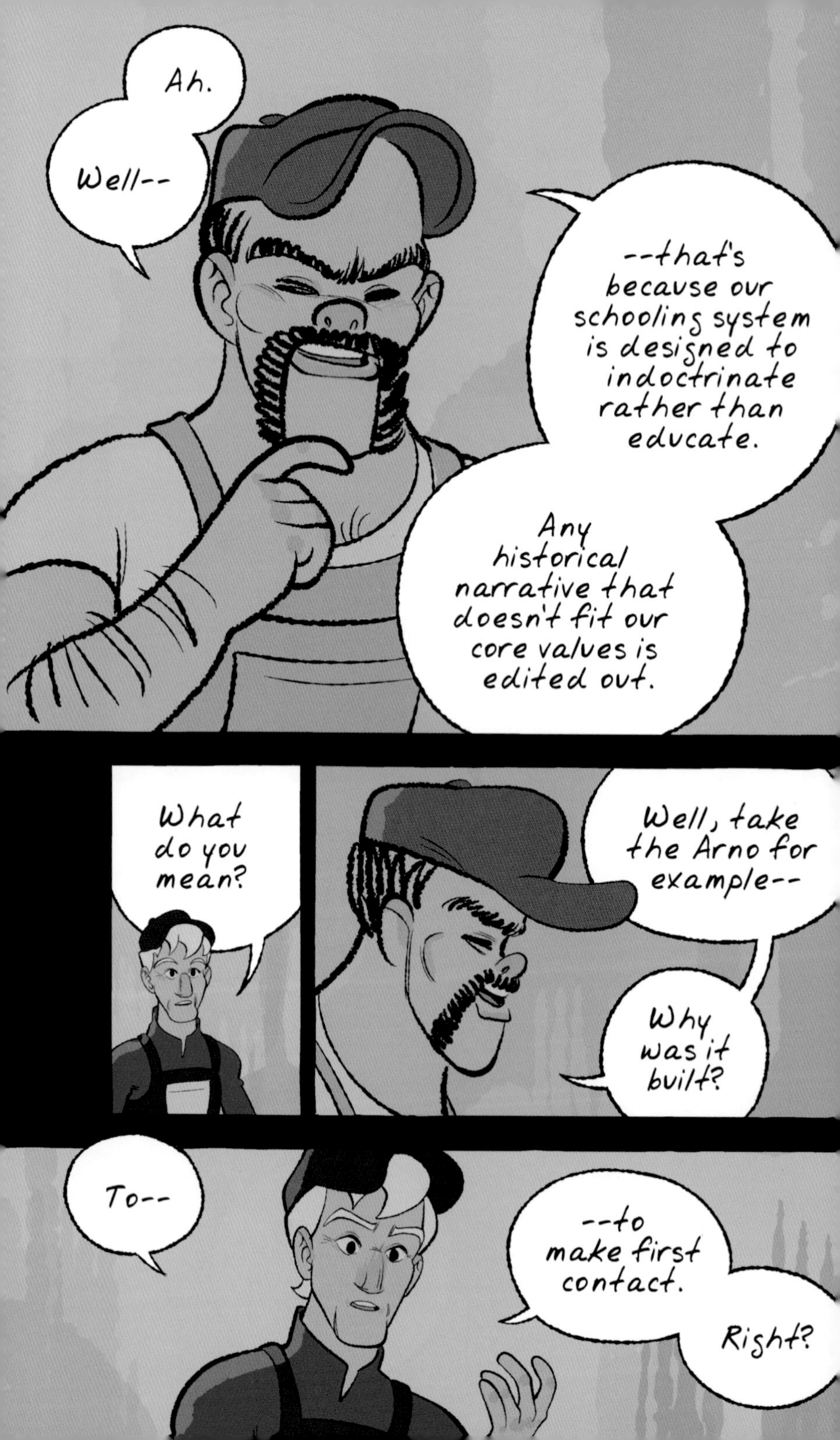
Ah.
Well--
--that's because our schooling system is designed to indoctrinate rather than educate.
Any historical narrative that doesn't fit our core values is edited out.
What do you mean?
Well, take the Arno for example--
Why was it built?
To--
--to make first contact.
Right?

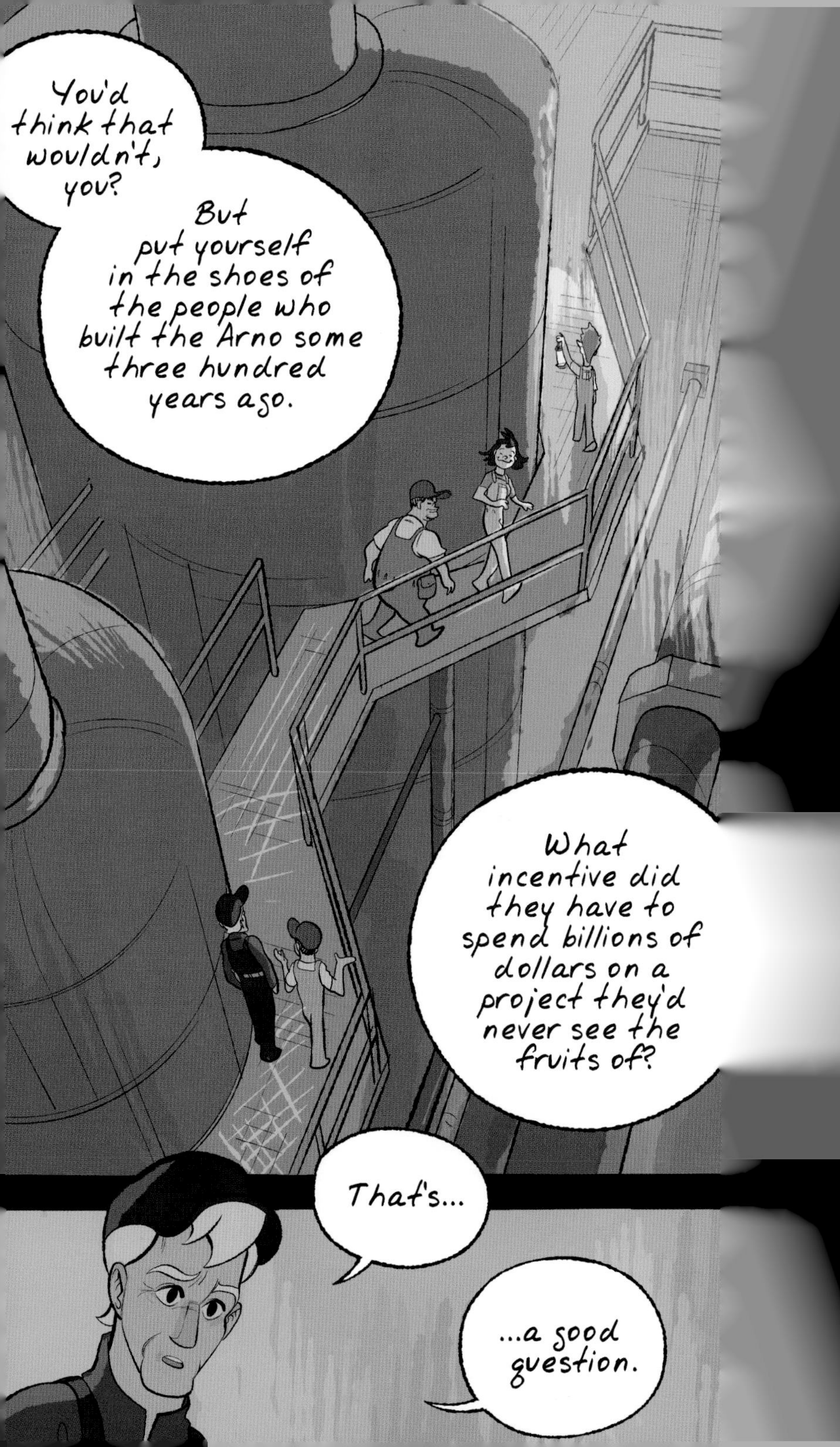
You'd think that wouldn't, you?
But put yourself in the shoes of the people who built the Arno some three hundred years ago.
What incentive did they have to spend billions of dollars on a project they'd never see the fruits of?
That's...
...a good question.

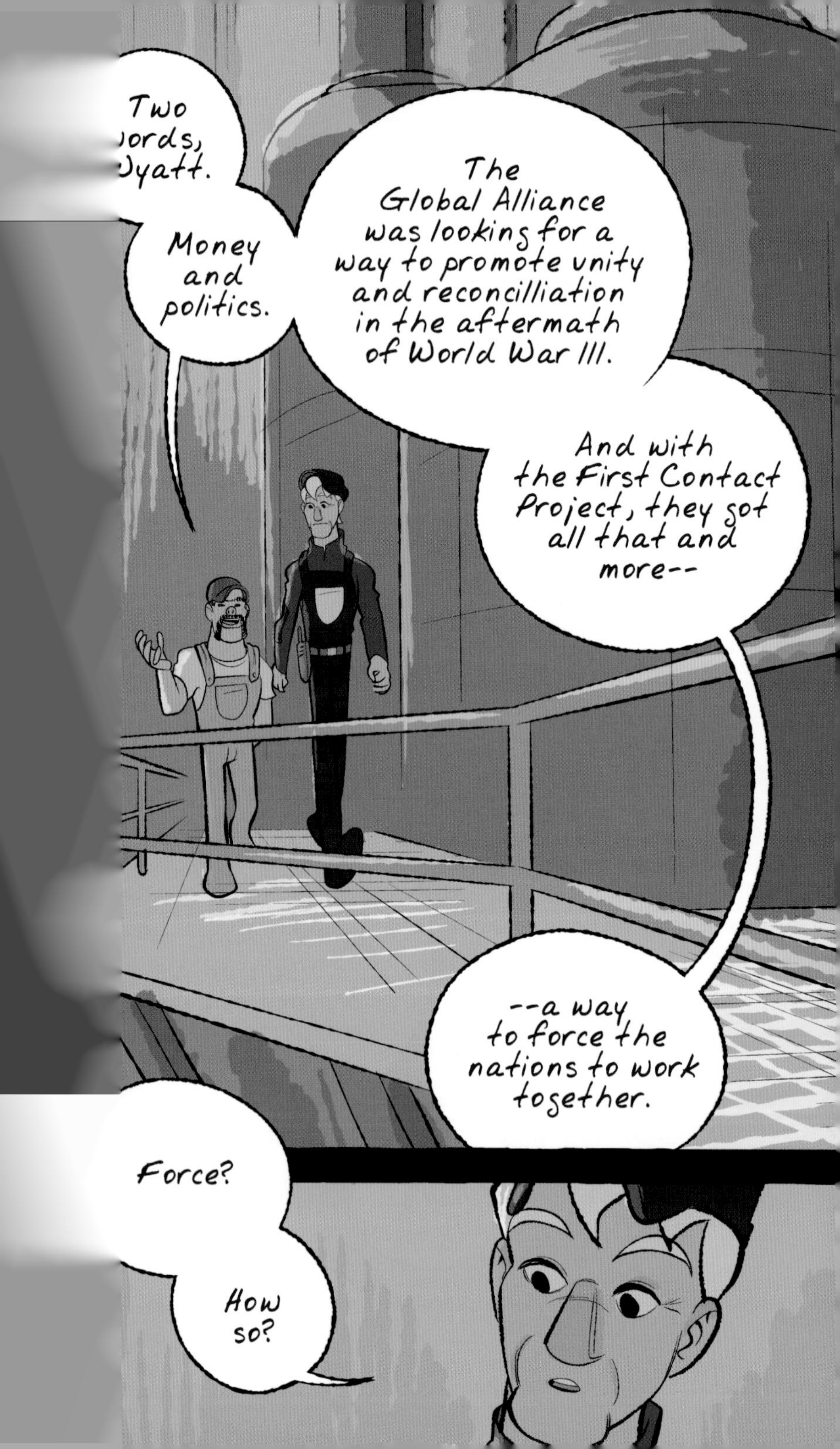

Two
ords,
Vyatt.
Money and politics.
The Global Alliance was looking for a way to promote unity and reconcilliation in the aftermath of World War III.
And with the First Contact Project, they got all that and more--
--a way to force the nations to work together.
Force?
How so?

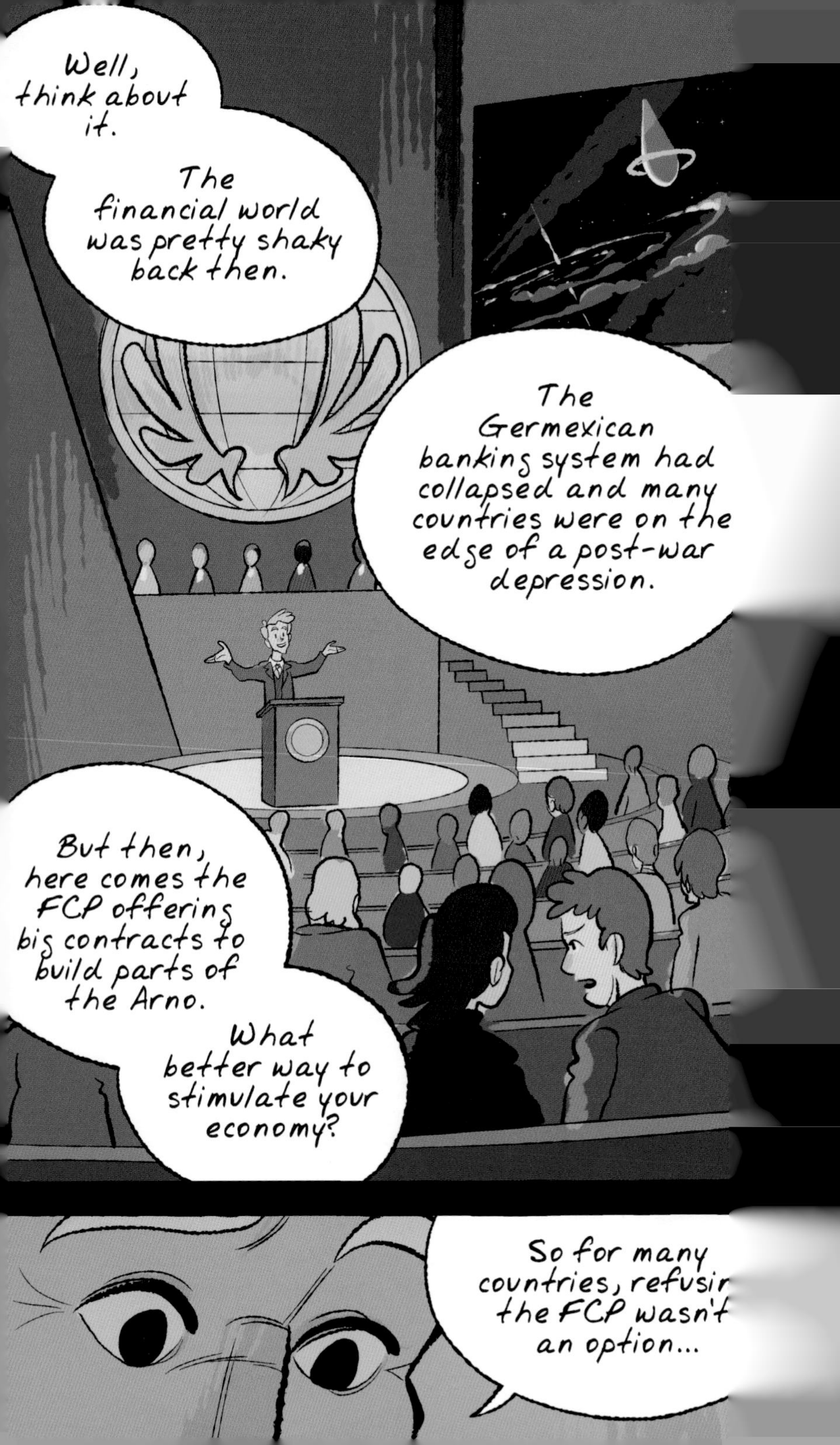
Well, think about it.
The financial world was pretty shaky back then.
The Germexican banking system had collapsed and many countries were on the edge of a post-war depression.
But then, here comes the FCP offering big contracts to build parts of the Arno.
What better way to stimulate your economy?
So for many countries, refusin the FCP wasn't an option...

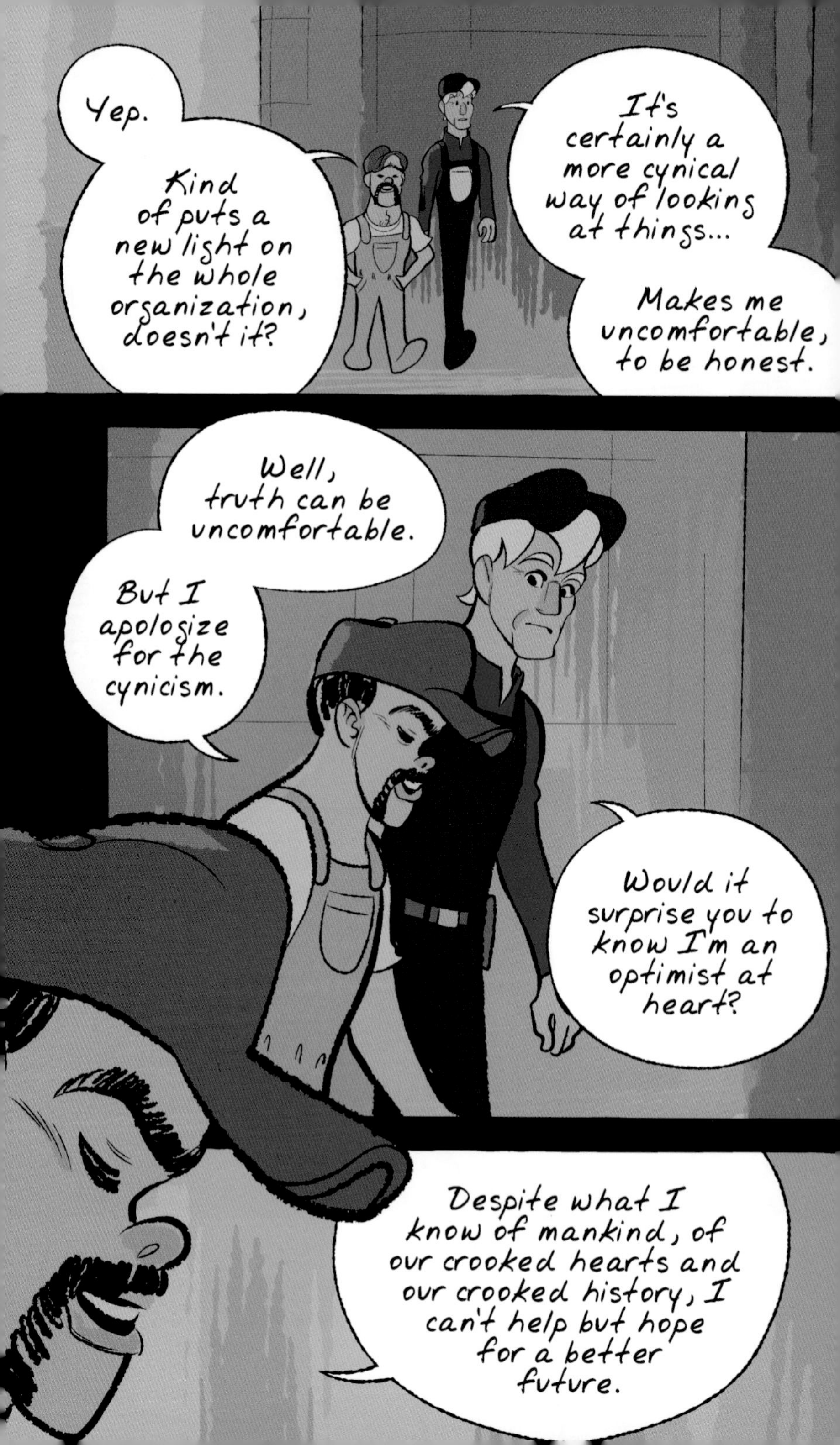
Yep.
Kind of puts a new light on the whole organization, doesn't it?
It's certainly a more cynical way of looking at things...
Makes me uncomfortable, to be honest.
Well, truth can be uncomfortable.
But I apologize for the cynicism.
Would it surprise you to know I'm an optimist at heart?
Despite what I know of mankind, of our crooked hearts and our crooked history, I can't help but hope for a better future.

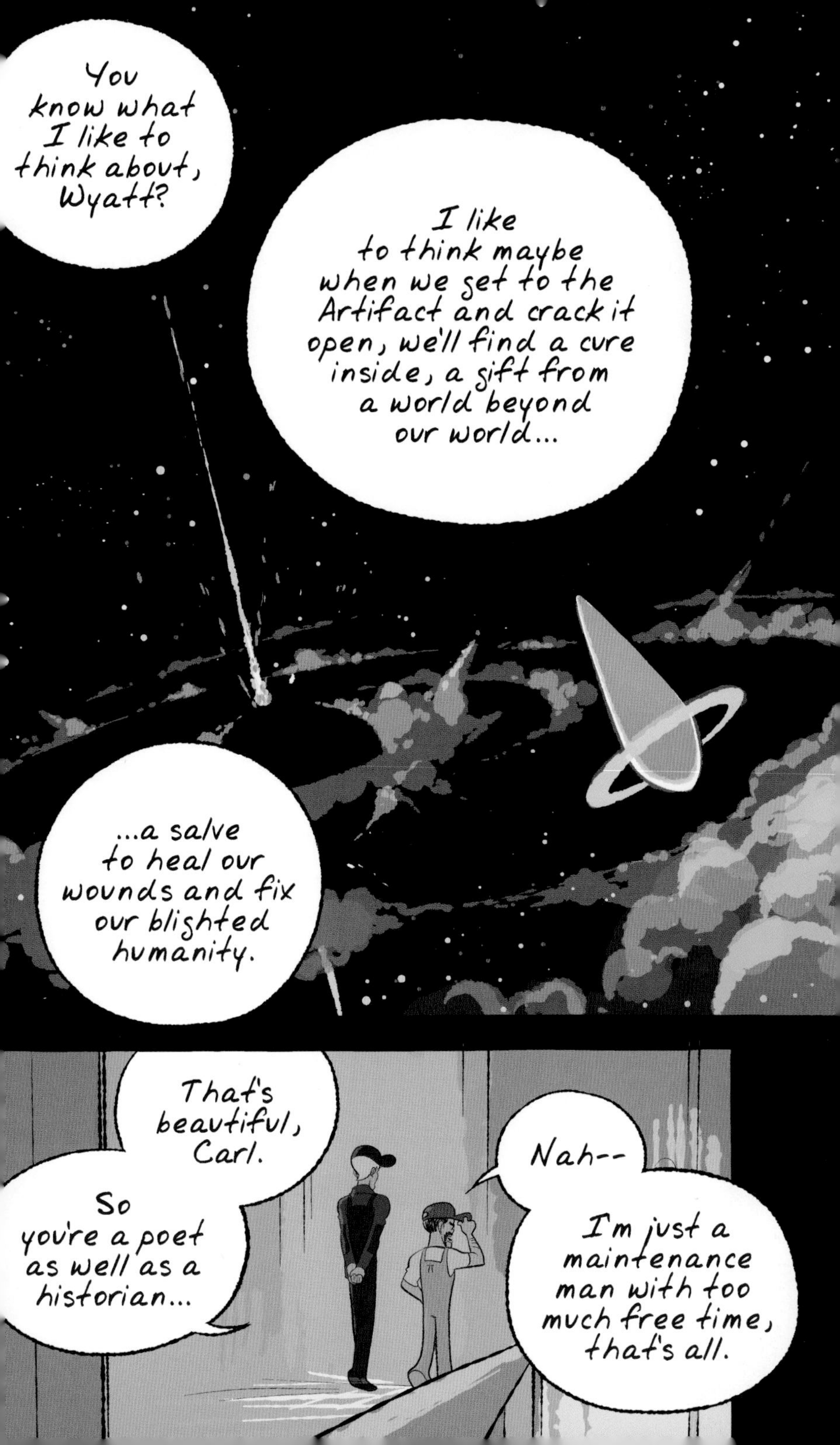
You know what I like to think about, Wyatt?
I like to think maybe when we get to the Artifact and crack it open, we'll find a cure inside, a gift from a world beyond our world...
...a salve to heal our wounds and fix our blighted humanity.
That's beautiful, Carl.
So you're a poet as well as a historian...
Nah--
I'm just a maintenance man with too much free time, that's all.

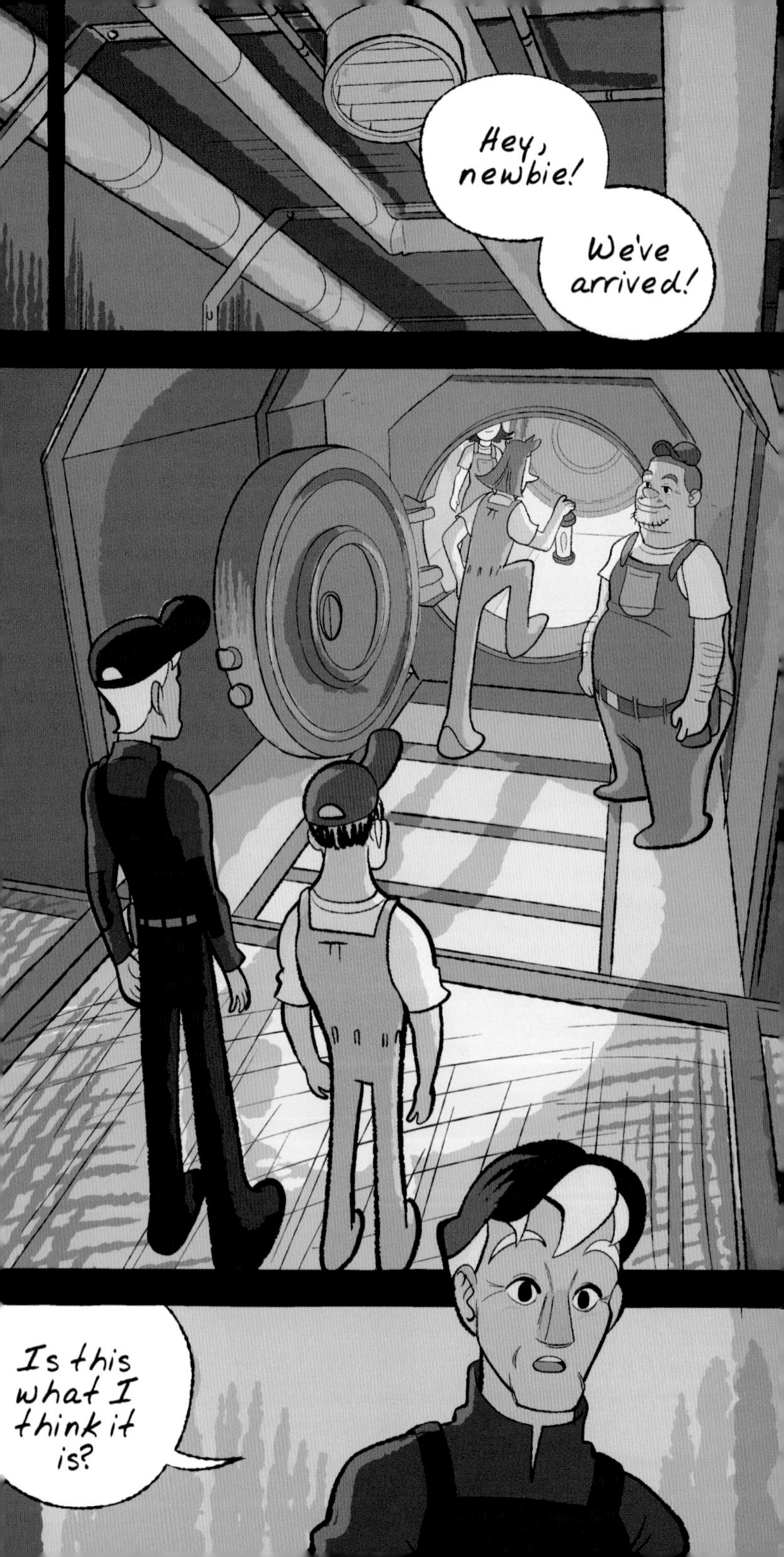
Hey, newbie!
We've arrived!
Is this what I think it is?

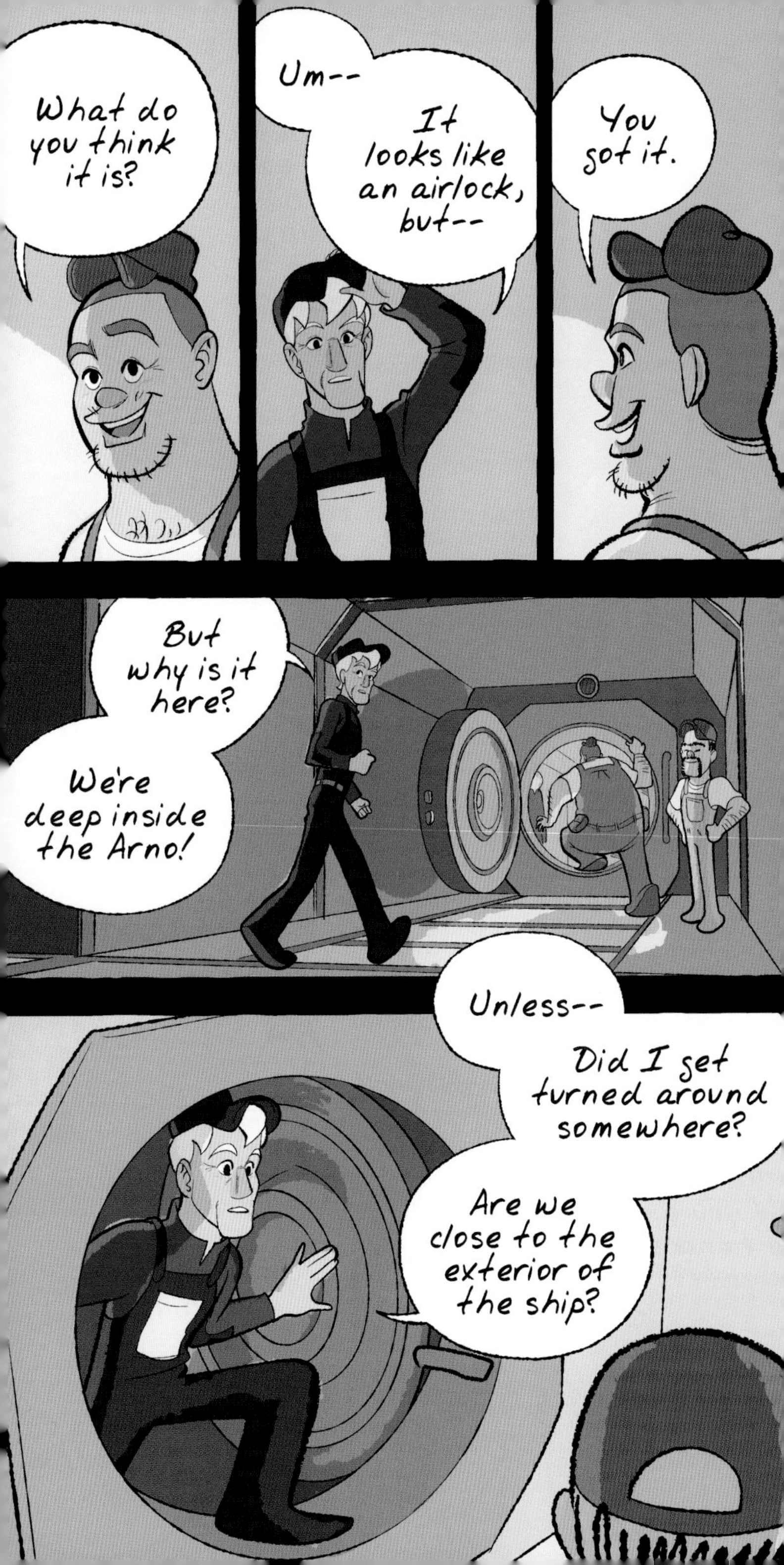
What do you think it is?
Um--
It looks like an airlock, but--
You got it.
But why is it here?
We're deep inside the Arno!
Unless--
Did I get turned around somewhere?
Are we close to the exterior of the ship?

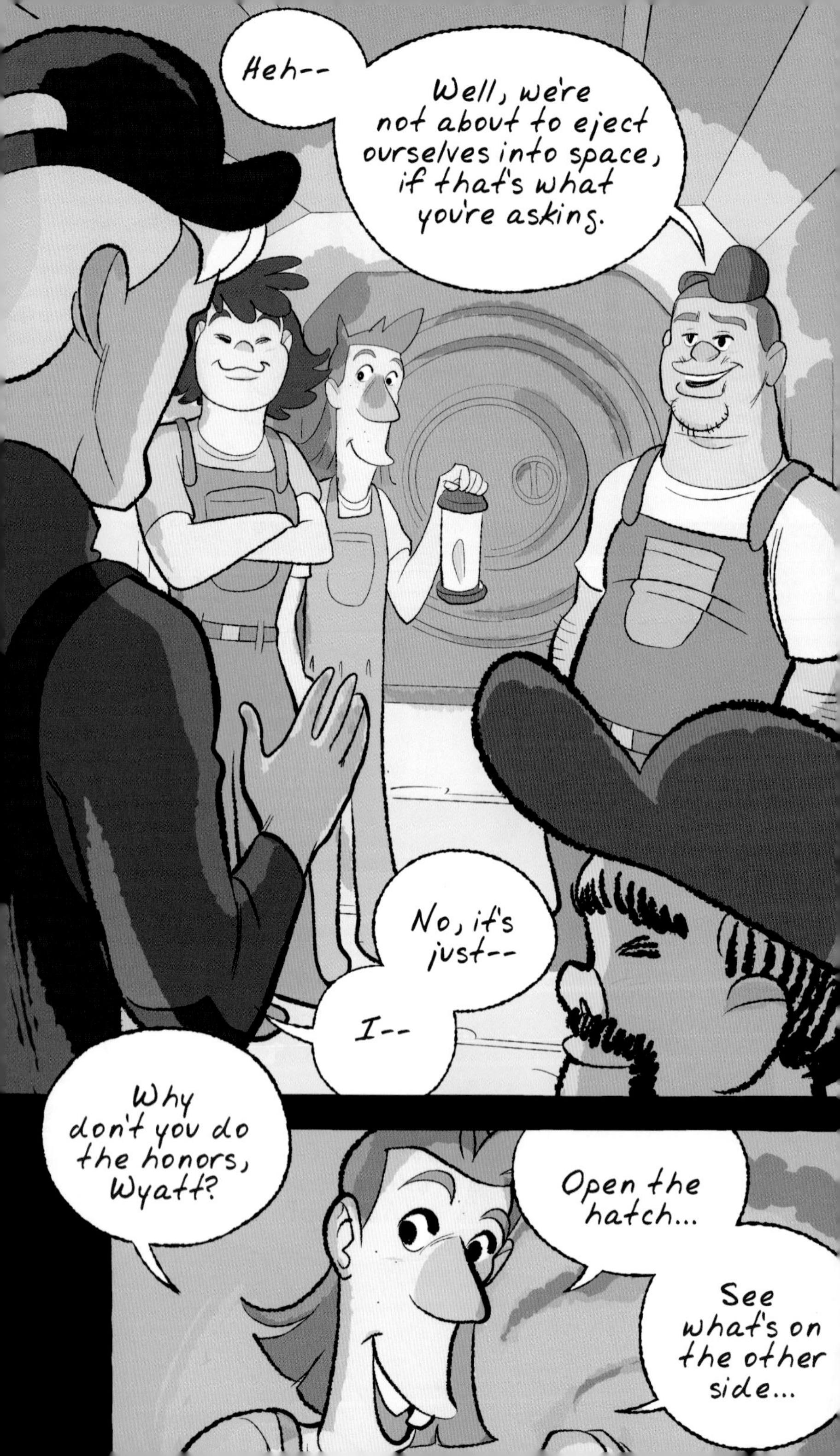
Heh--
Well, we're not about to eject ourselves into space, if that's what you're askins.
No, it's just--
I--
Why don't you do the honors, Wyatt?
Open the hatch...
See what's on the other side...

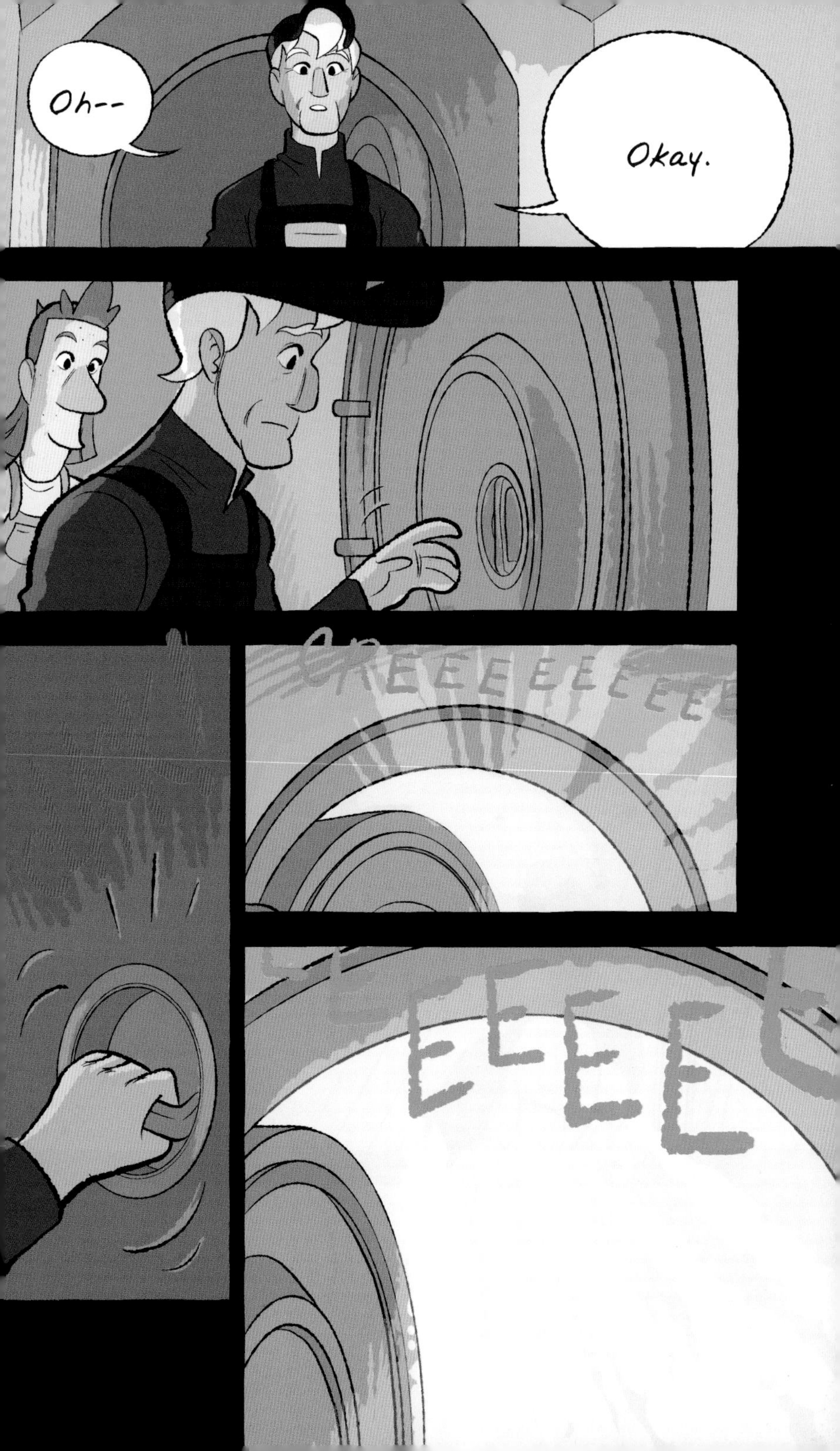
Oh--
Okay.
CREEEEEEEEEE
EEEE

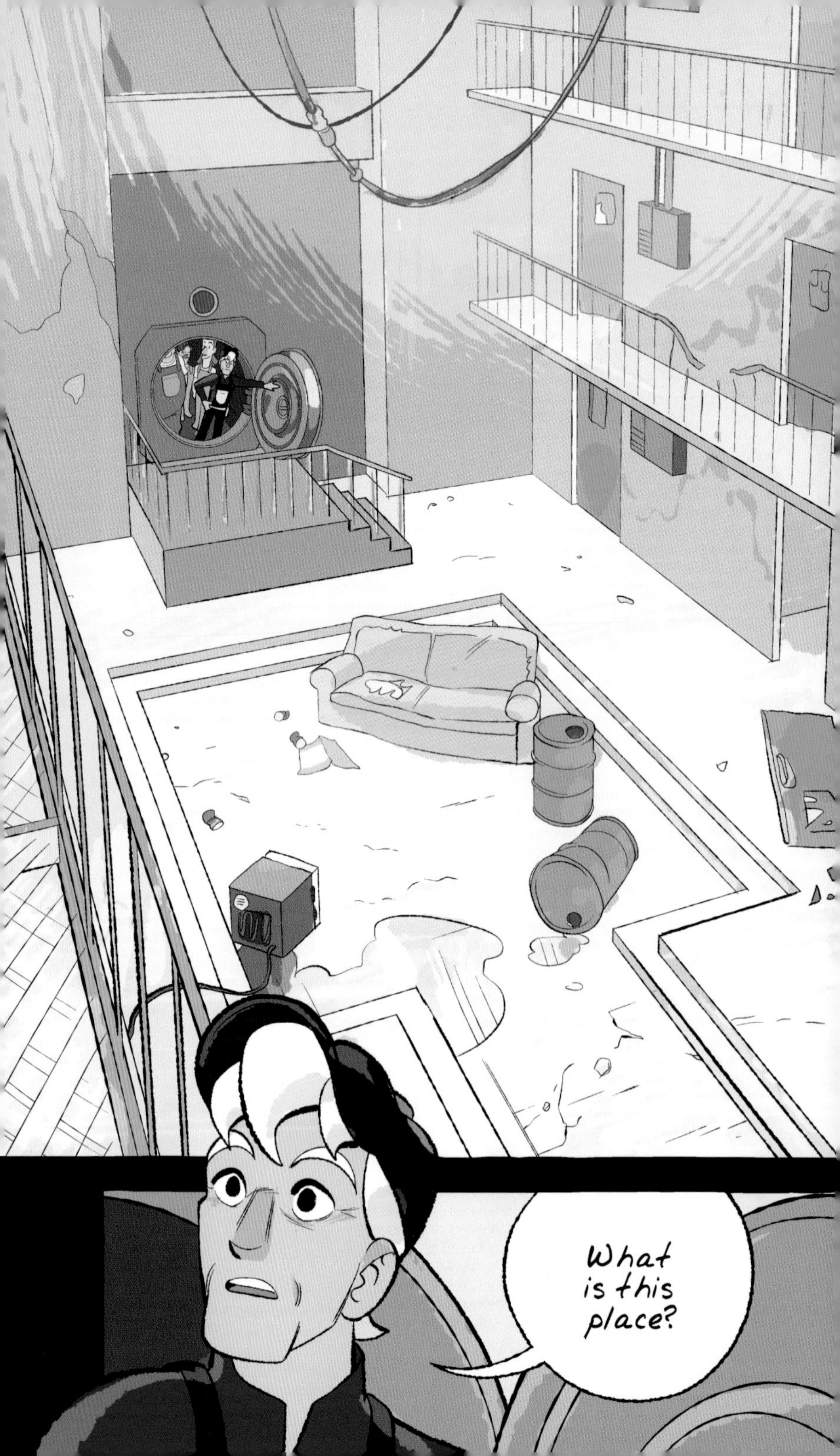
What is this place?

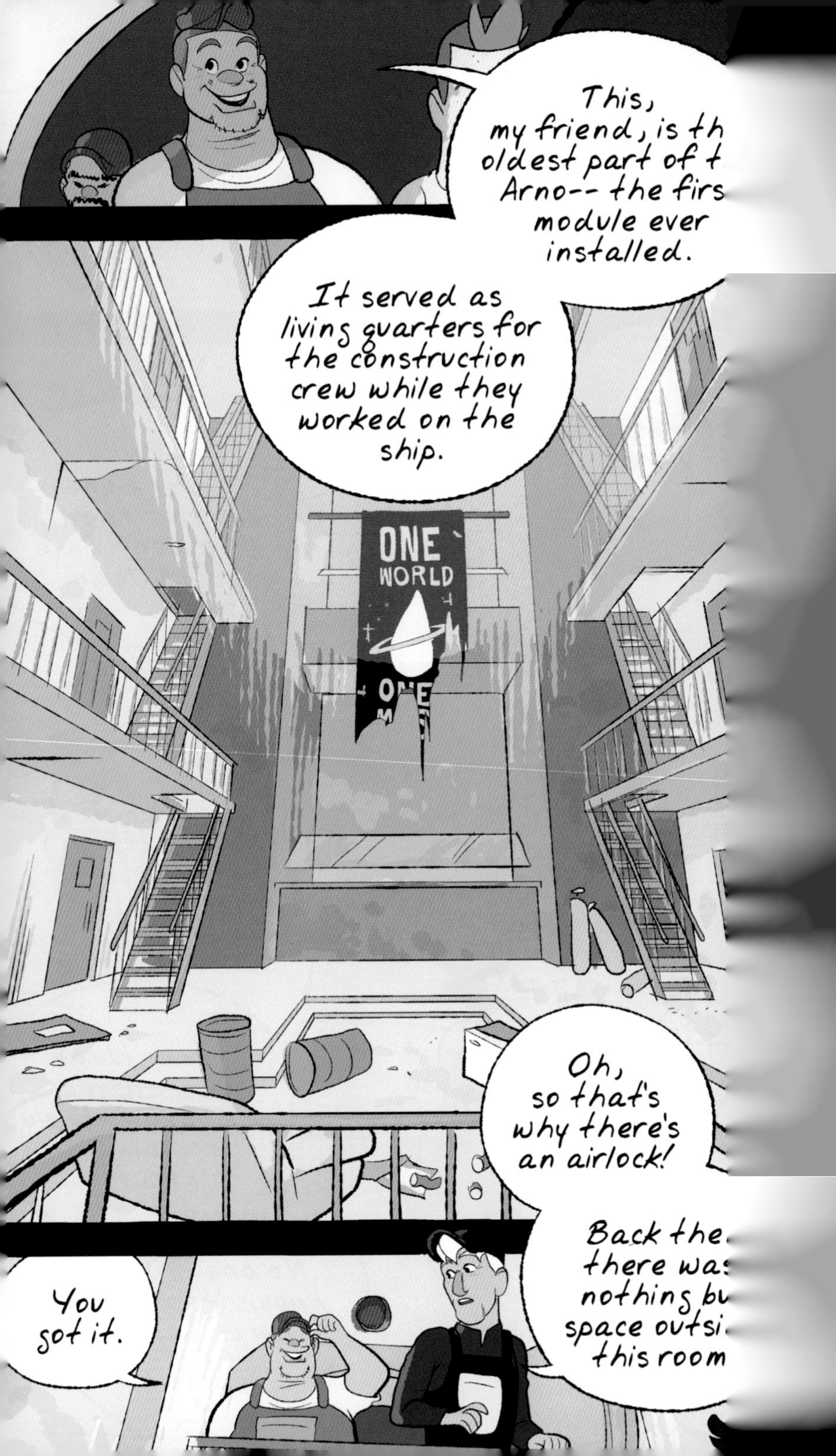
This, my friend, is th oldest part of t Arno-- the firs module ever installed.
It served as living quarters for the construction crew while they worked on the ship.
ONE WORLD
Oh, so that's why there's an airlock!
You got it.
Back the there was nothing bu space outsi this room

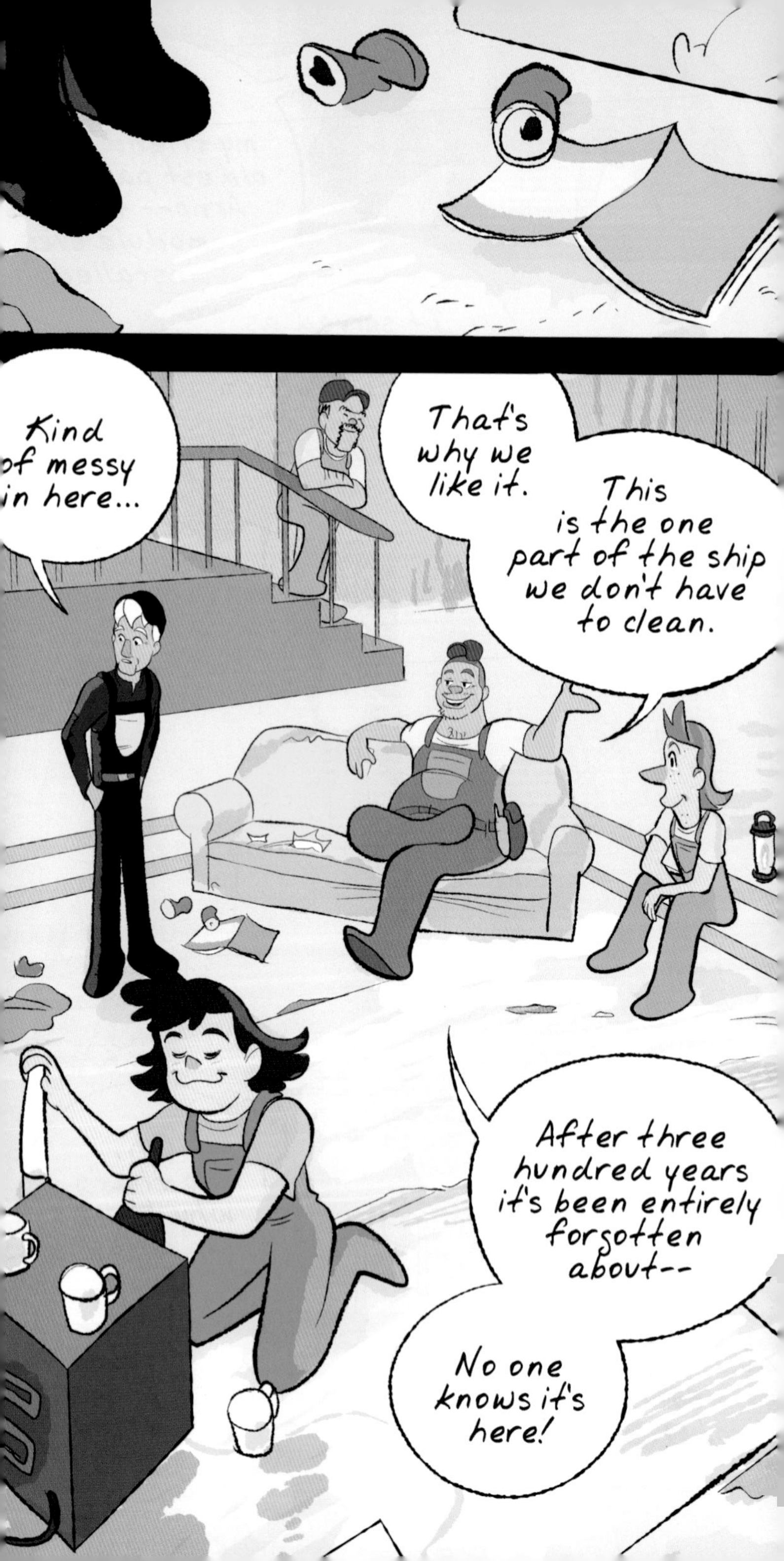

Kind of messy in here...
That's why we like it.
This is the one part of the ship we don't have to clean.
After three hundred years it's been entirely forgotten about--
No one knows it's here!

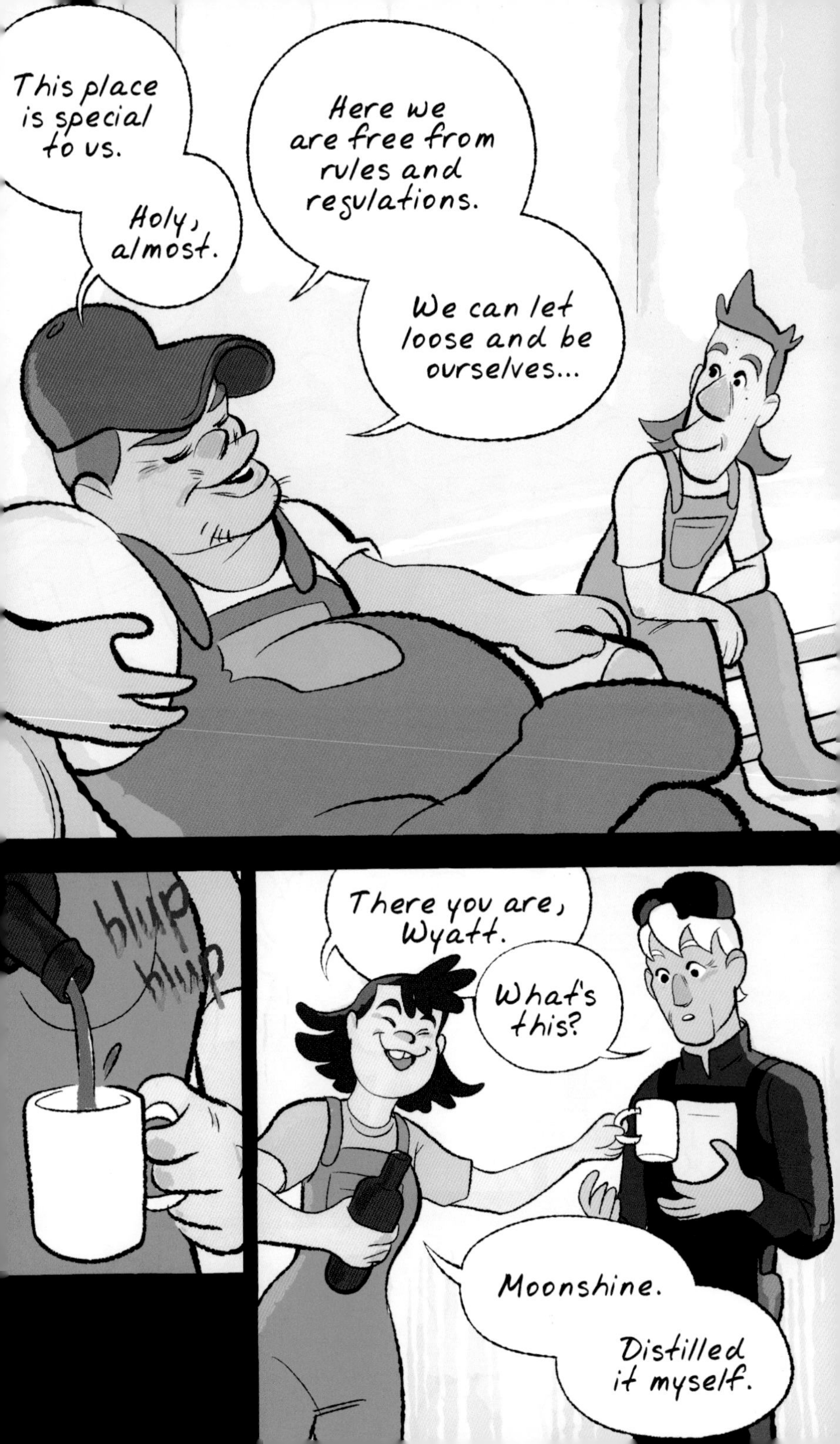

This place is special to us.
Holy, almost.
Here we are free from rules and regulations.
We can let loose and be ourselves...
blup blup
There you are, Wyatt.
What's this?
Moonshine.
Distilled it myself.

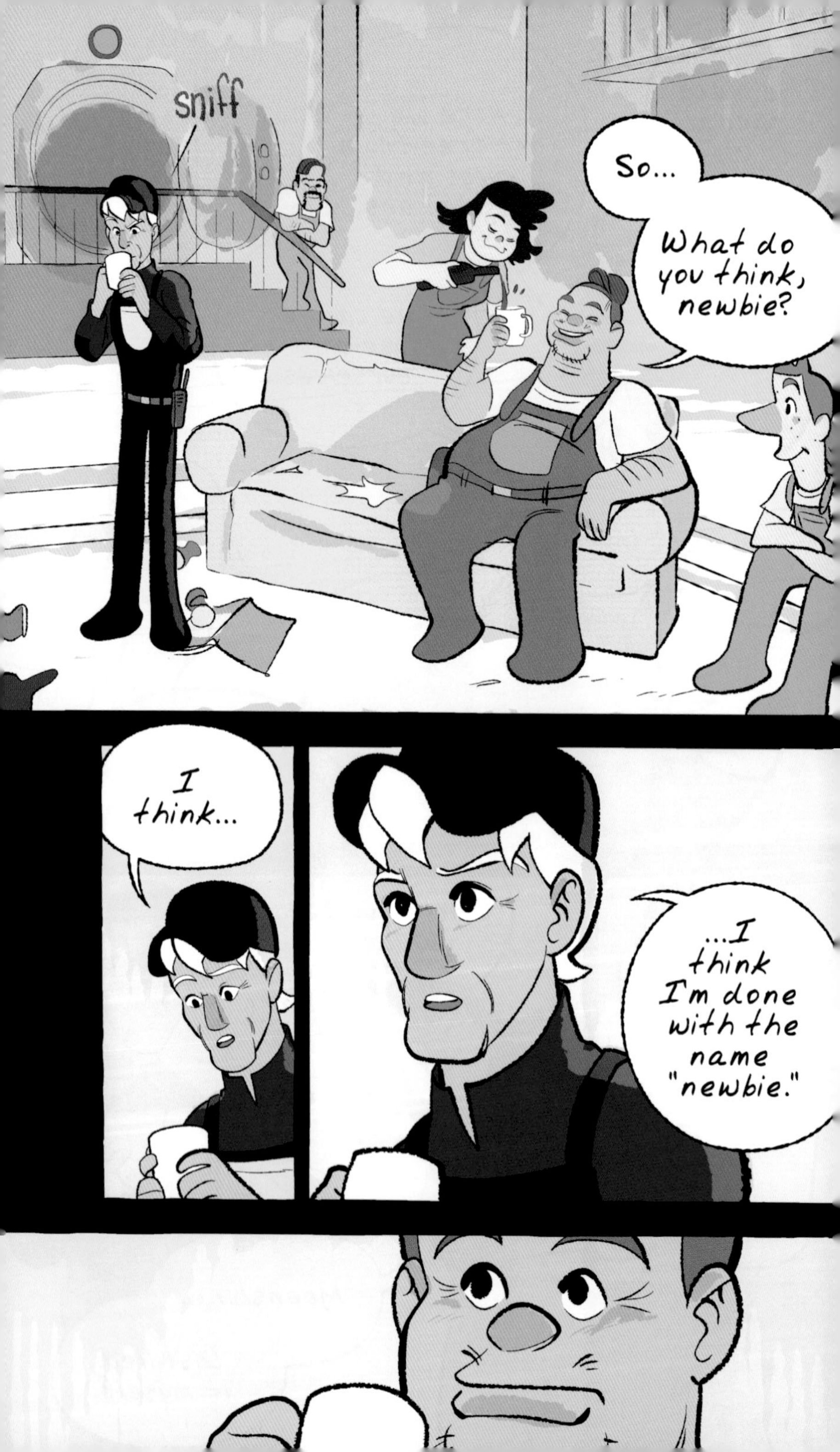

sniff
So...
What do you think, newbie?
I think...
...I think I'm done with the name "newbie."

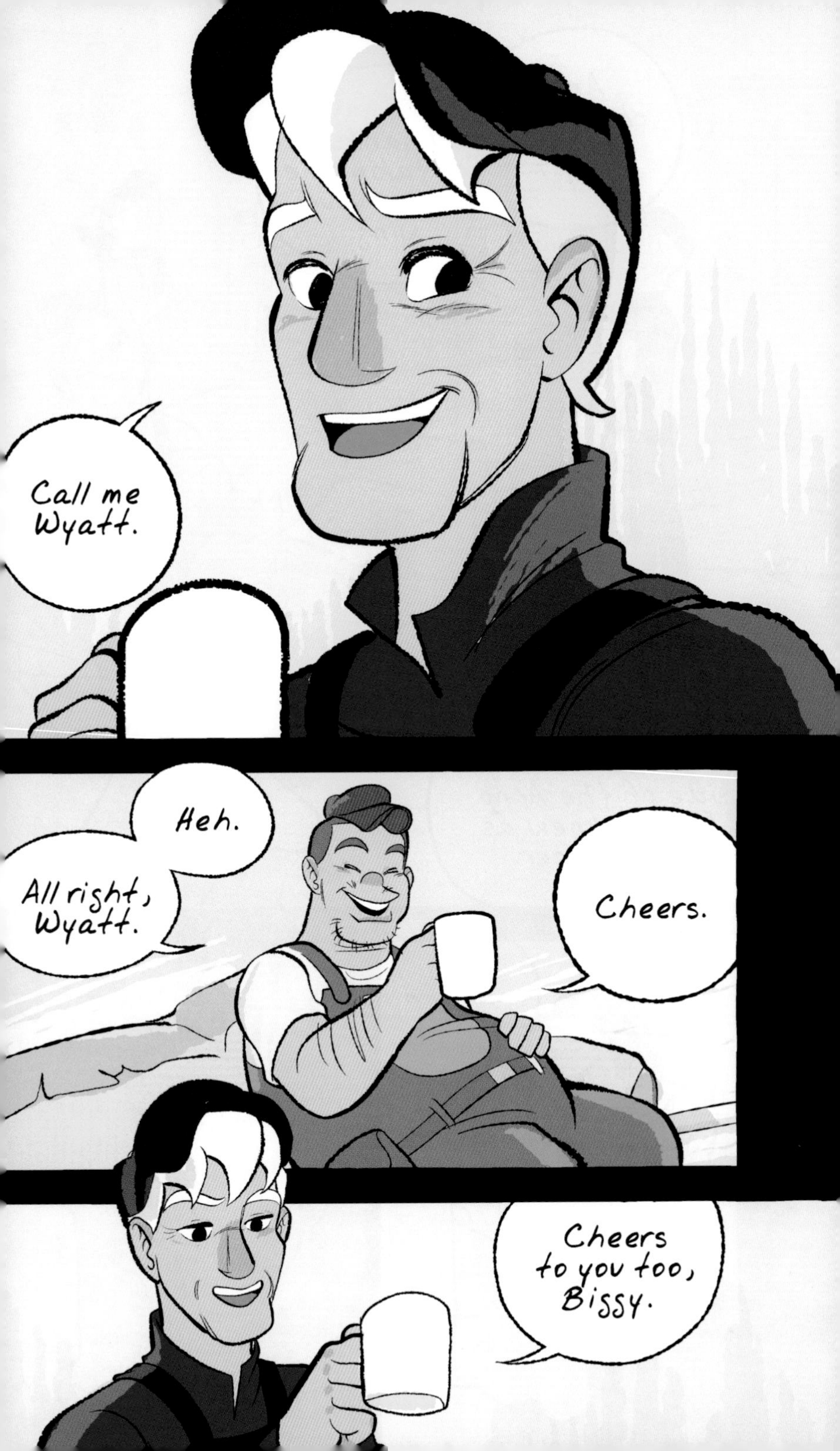
Call me Wyatt.
Heh.
All right, Wyatt.
Cheers.
Cheers to you too, Bissy.

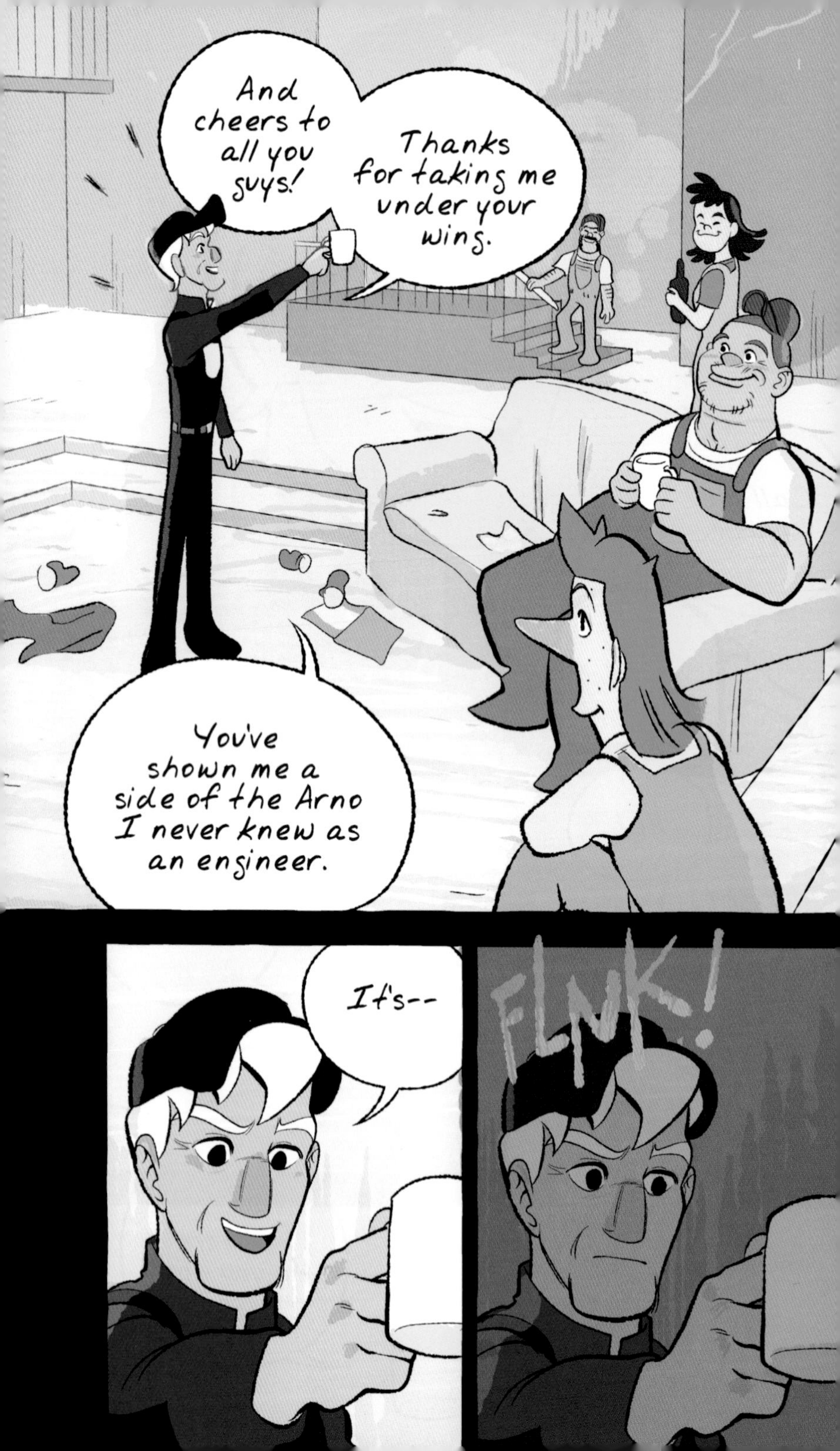
And cheers to all you guys!
Thanks for taking me under your wings.
You've shown me a side of the Arno I never knew as an engineer.
It's--
FLNK!

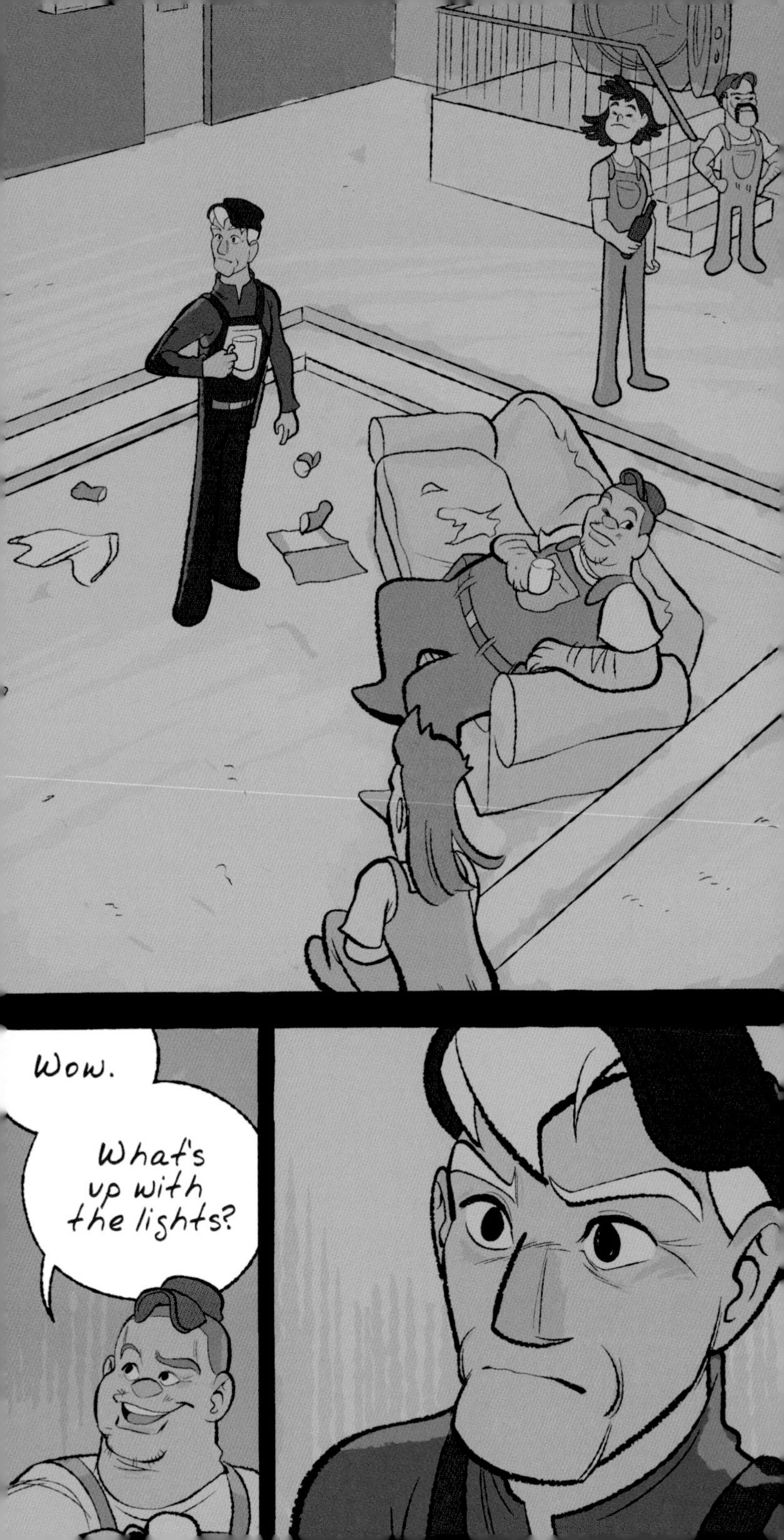
Wow.
What's up with the lights?

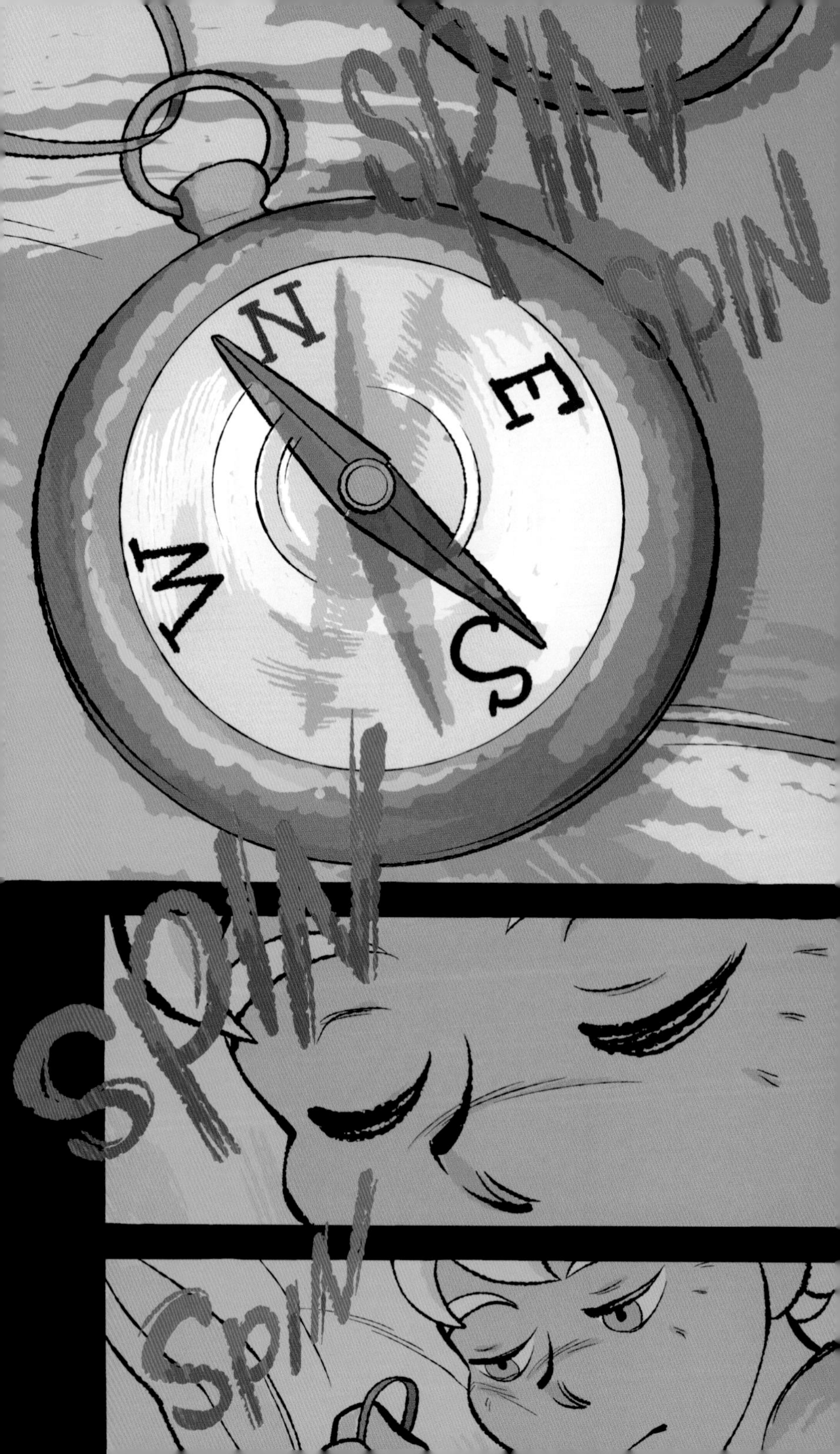
SPIN
SPIN
N
E
S
W
SPIN
SPIN

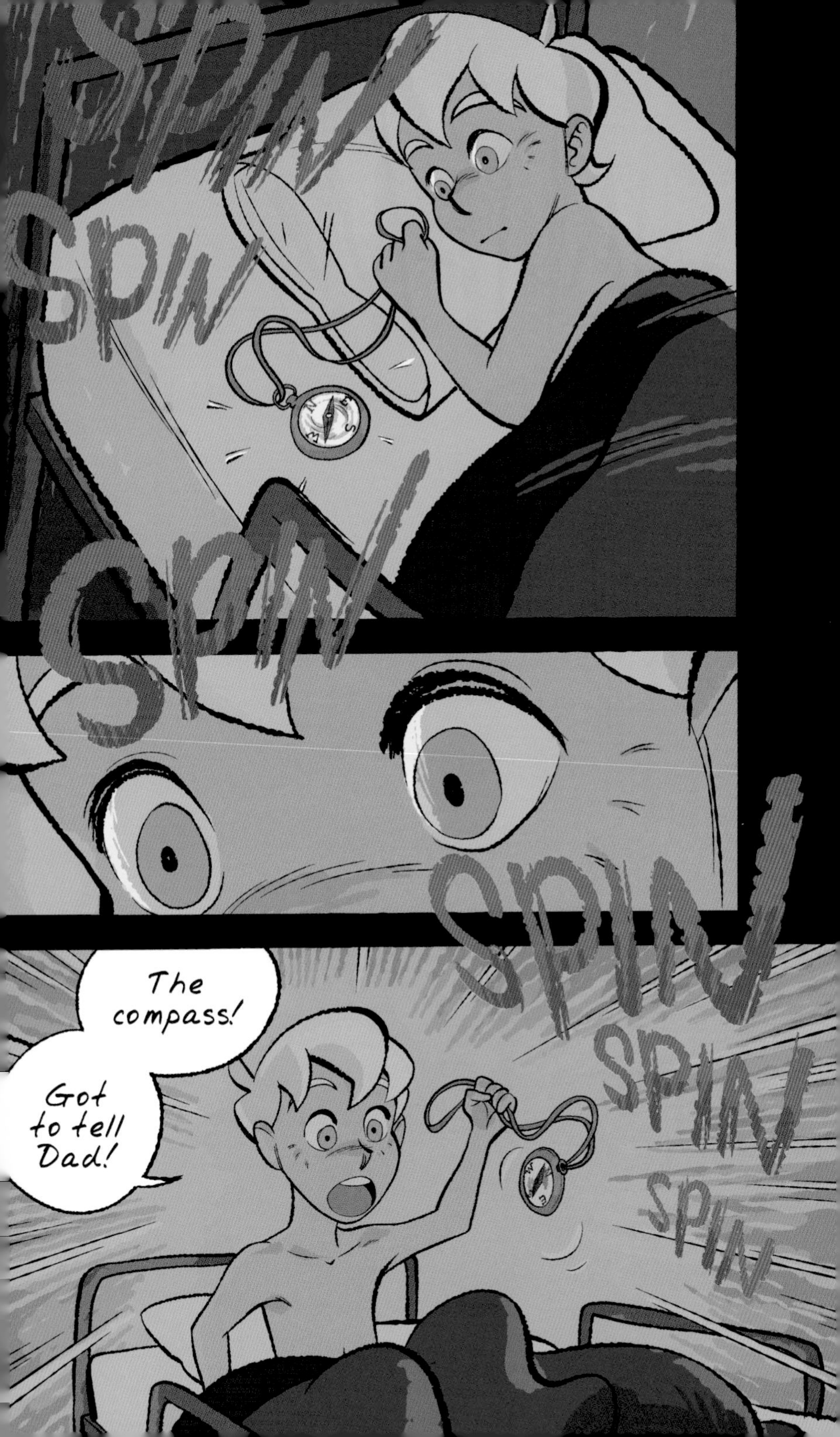
SPIN
SPIN
SPIN
SPIN
The compass!
Got to tell Dad!
SPIN
SPIN

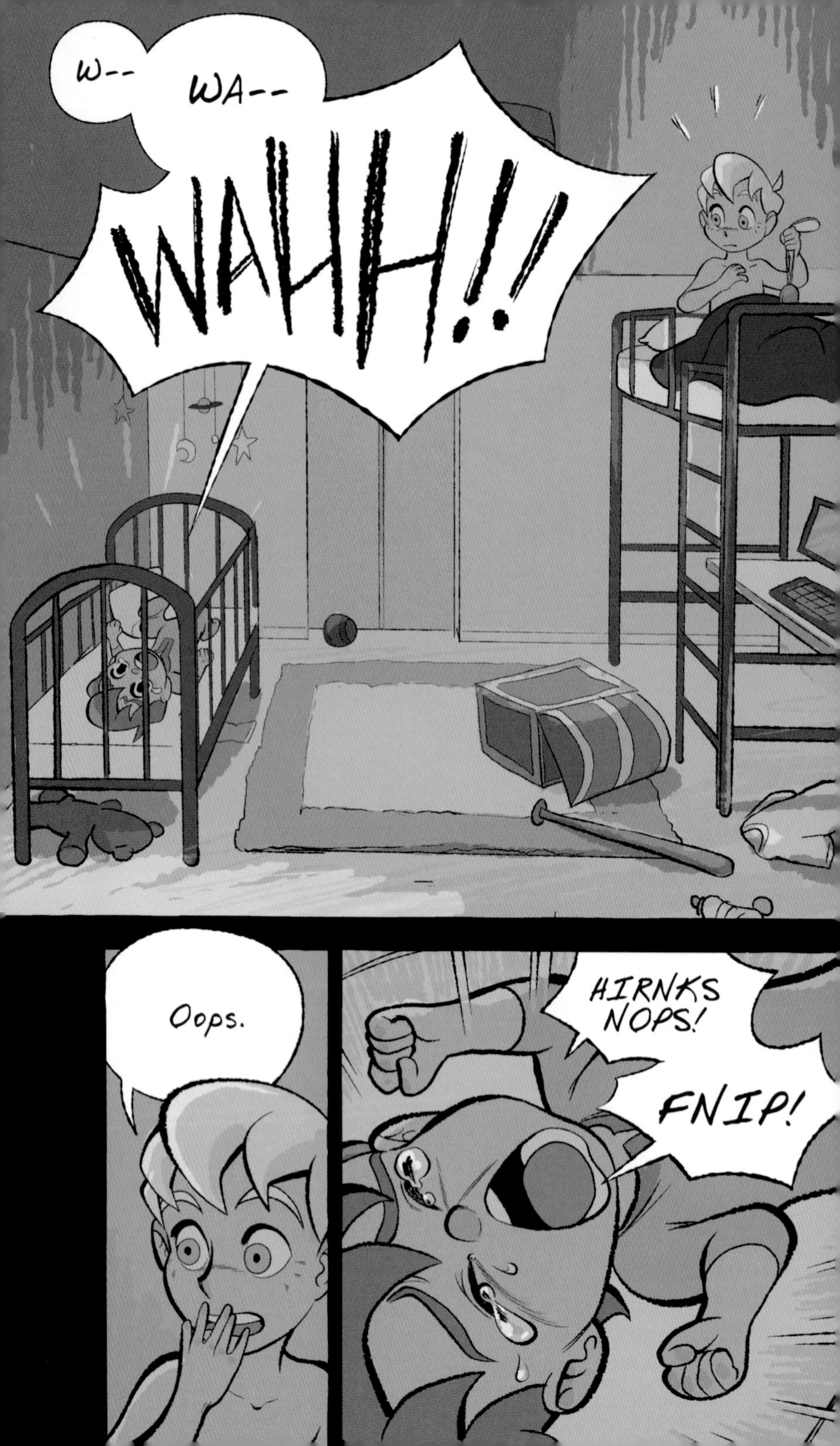
W--
WA--
WAHH!!
Oops.
HIRNKS NOPS!
FNIP!

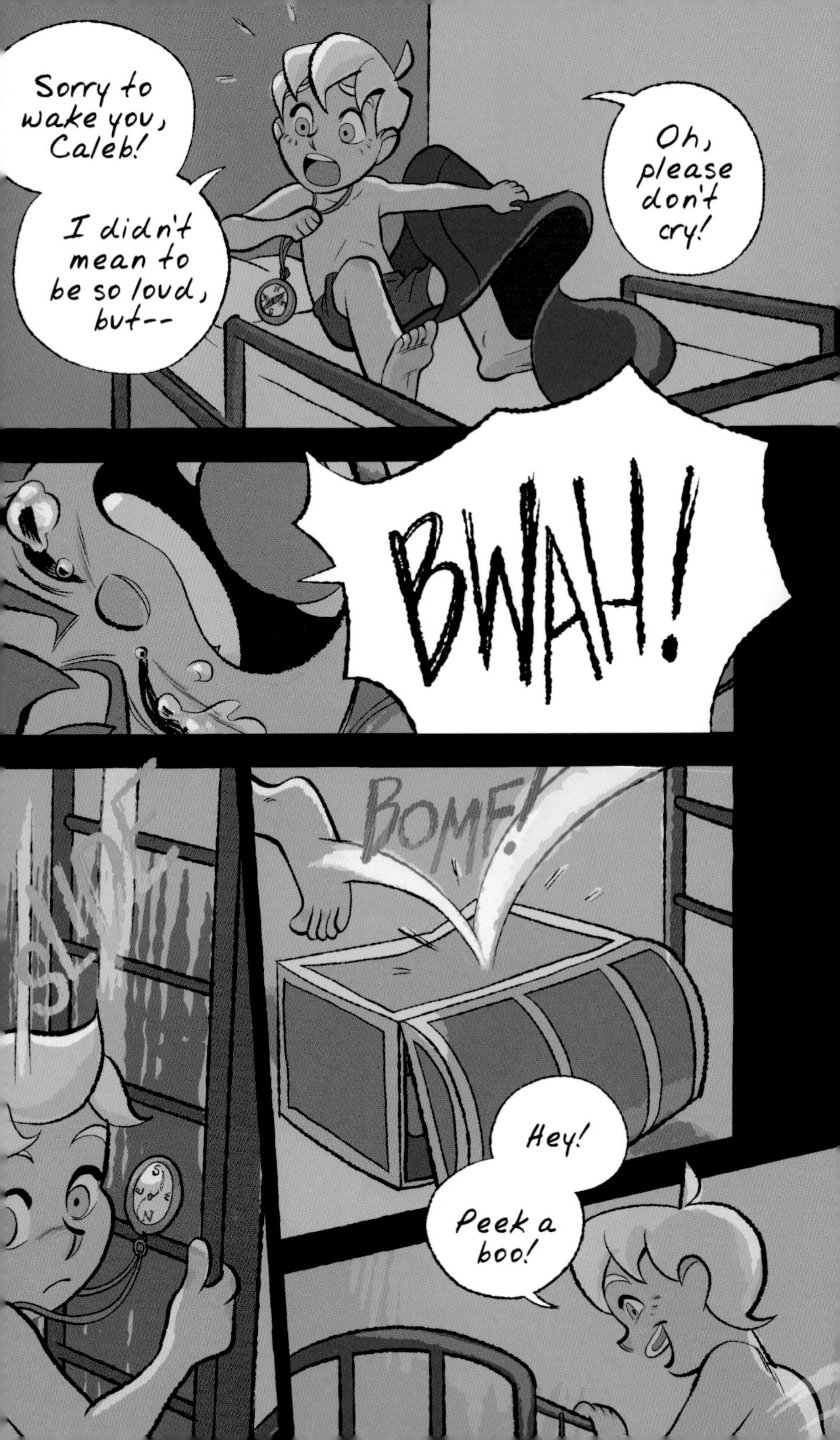

Sorry to wake you, Caleb!
I didn't mean to be so loud, but--
Oh, please don't cry!
BWAH!
BOMF!
Hey!
Peek a boo!

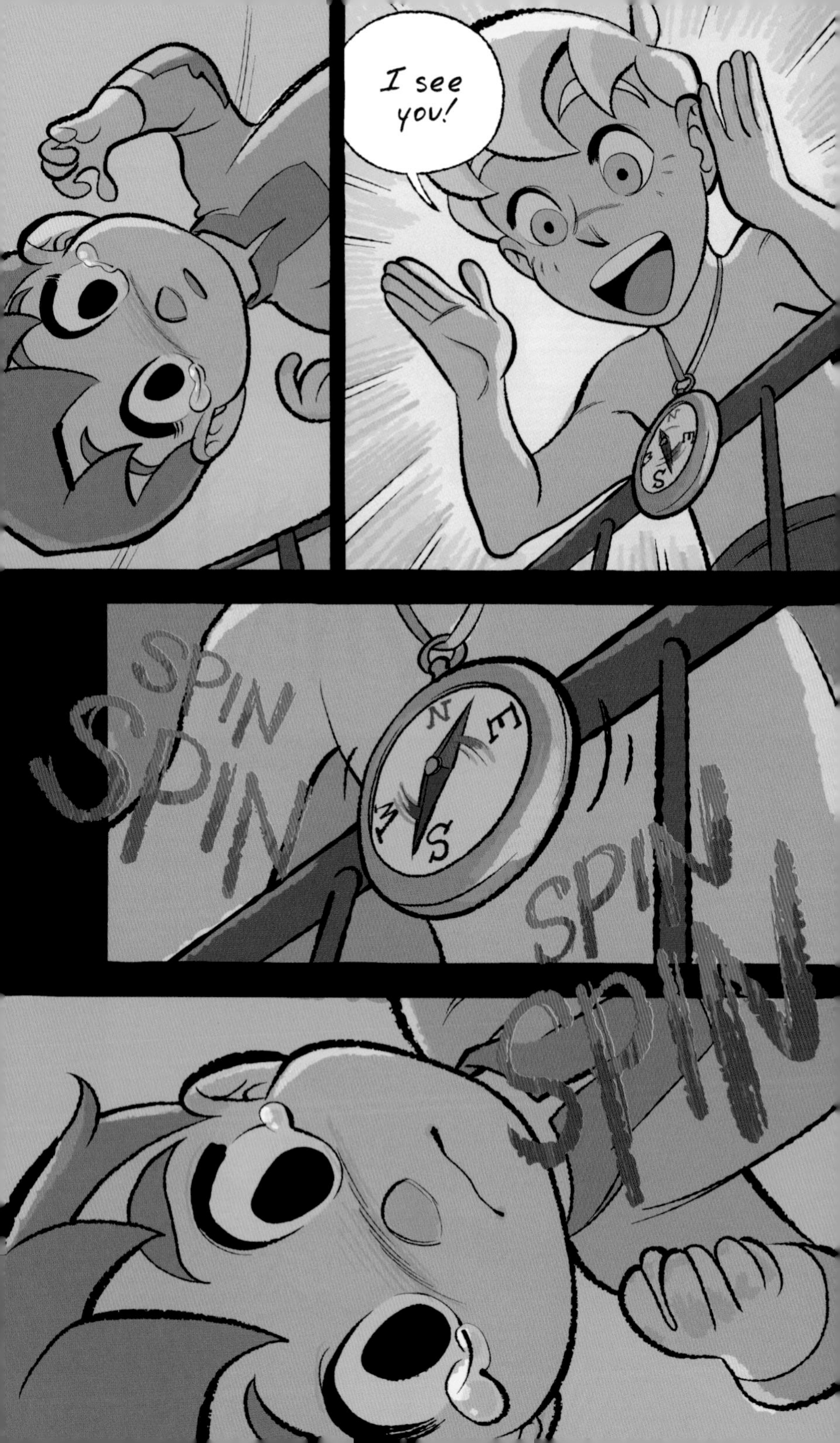
I see you!
SPIN
SPIN
SPIN
SPIN

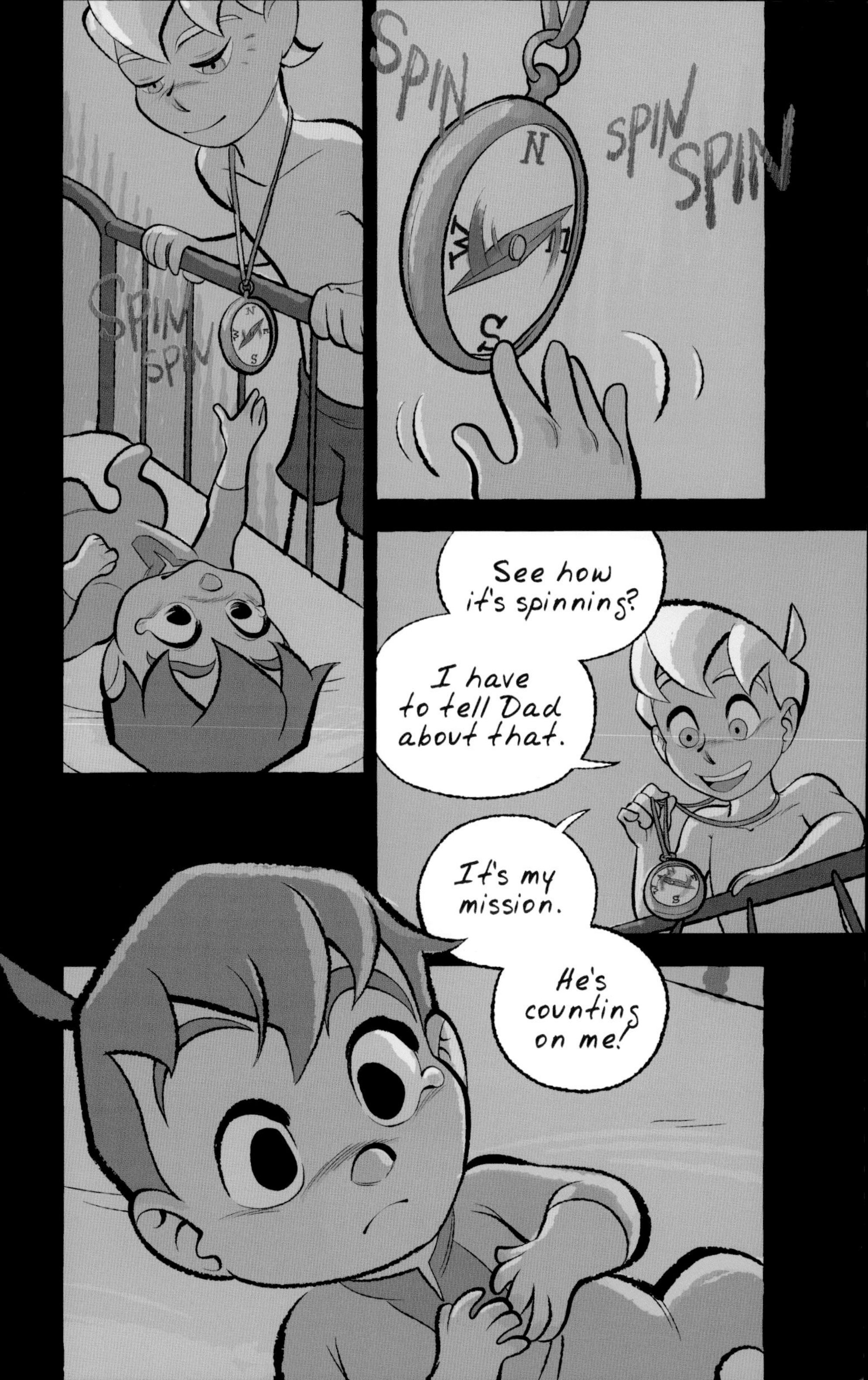
SPIN
SPIN
SPIN
SPIN
SPIN
N
W
E
S
See how it's spinning?
I have to tell Dad about that.
It's my mission.
He's counting on me!

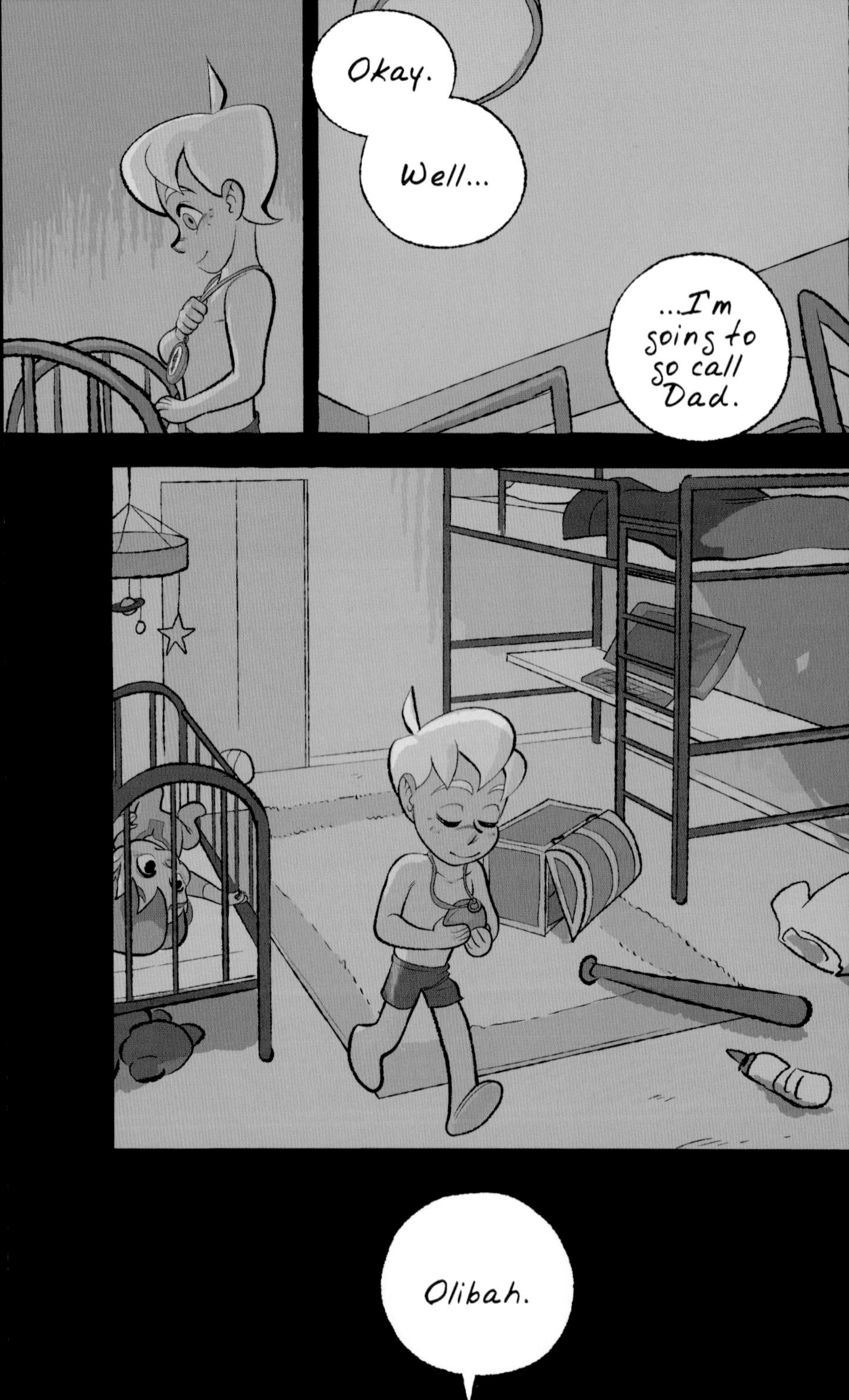
Okay.
Well...
...I'm soins to so call Dad.
Olibah.

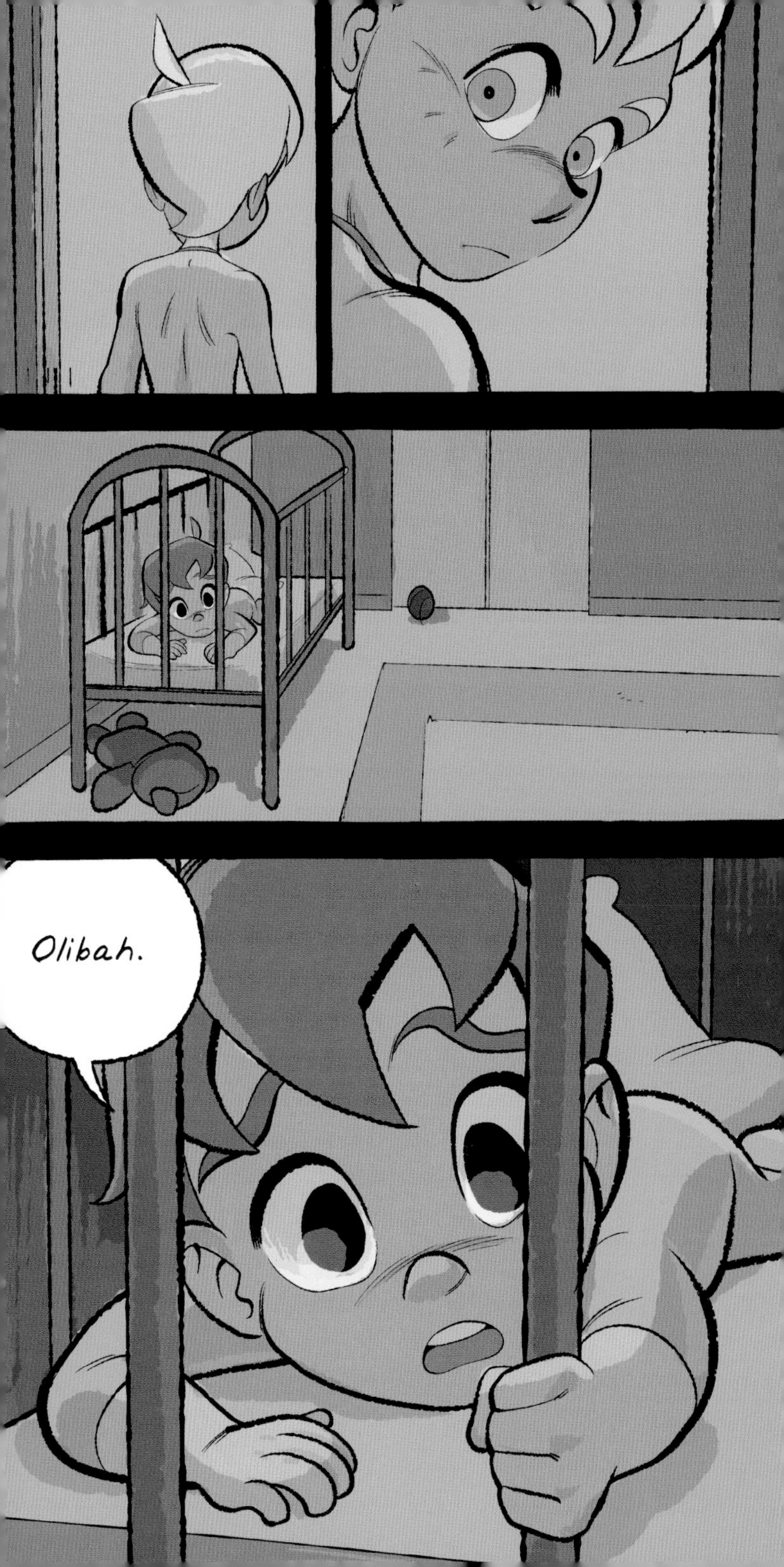
Olibah.

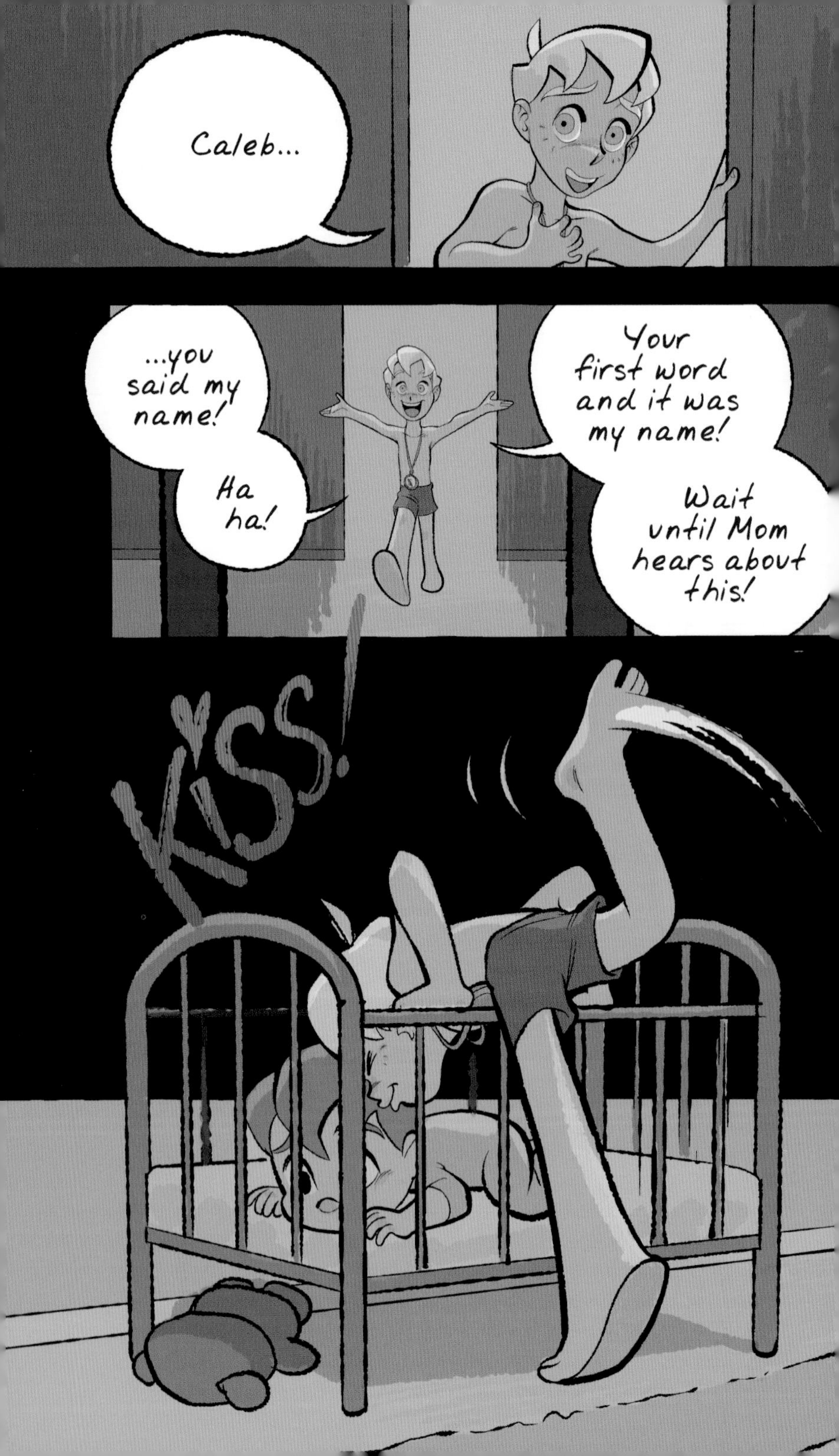
Caleb...
...you said my name!
Ha ha!
Your first word and it was my name!
Wait until Mom hears about this!
KISS!

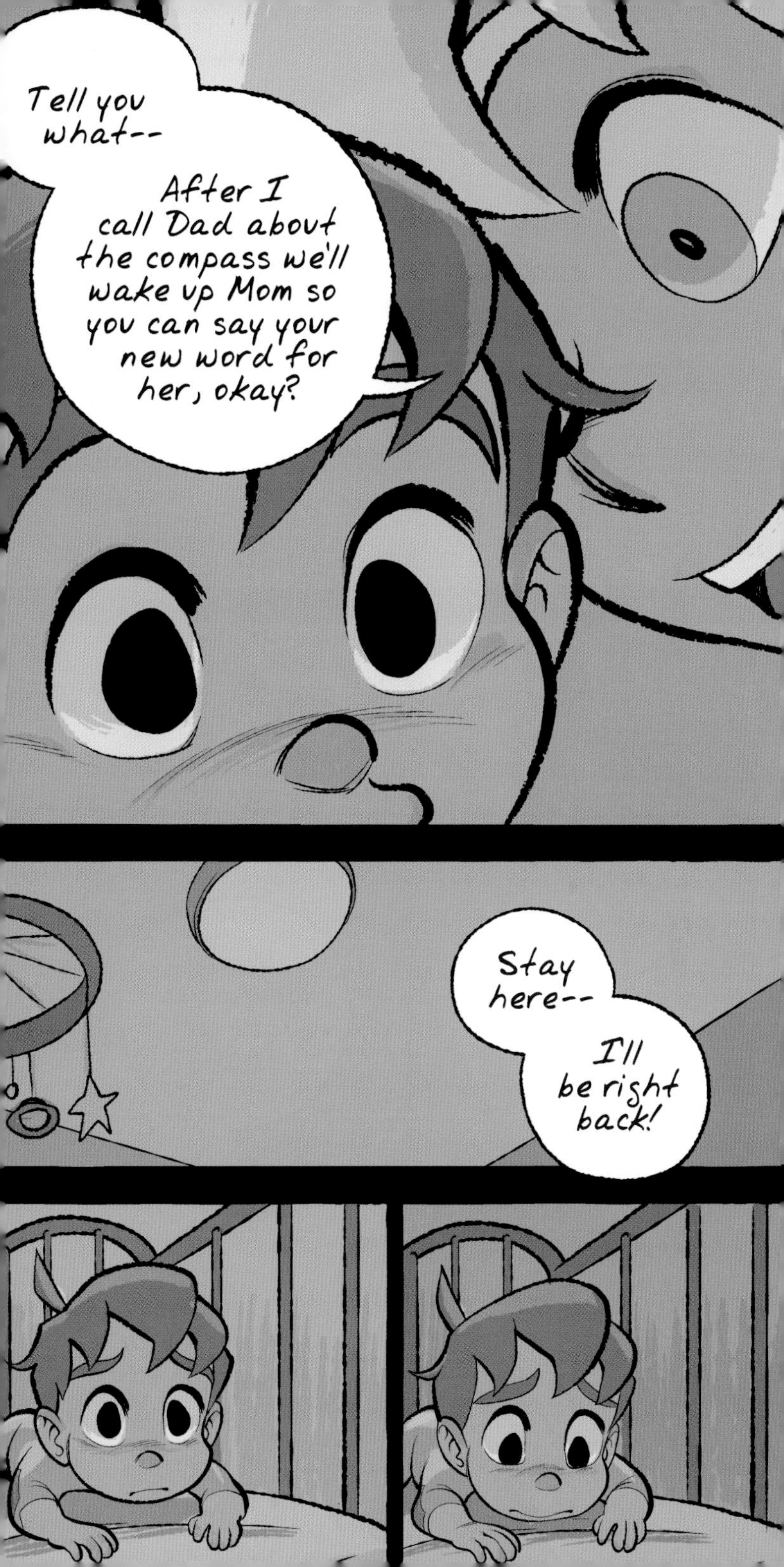
Tell you what--
After I call Dad about the compass we'll wake up Mom so you can say your new word for her, okay?
Stay here--
I'll be right back!

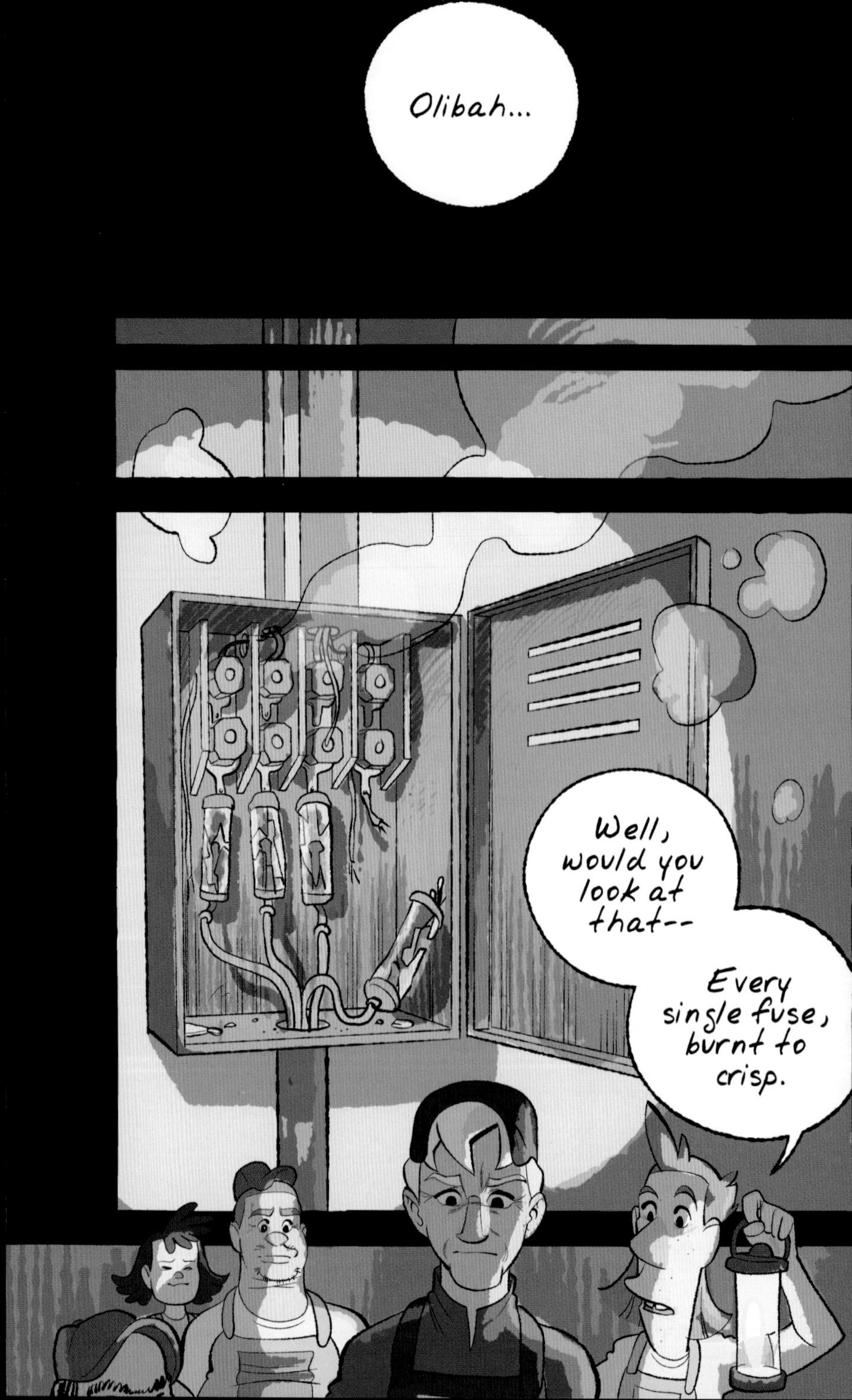
Olibah...
Well, would you look at that--
Every single fuse, burnt to crisp.

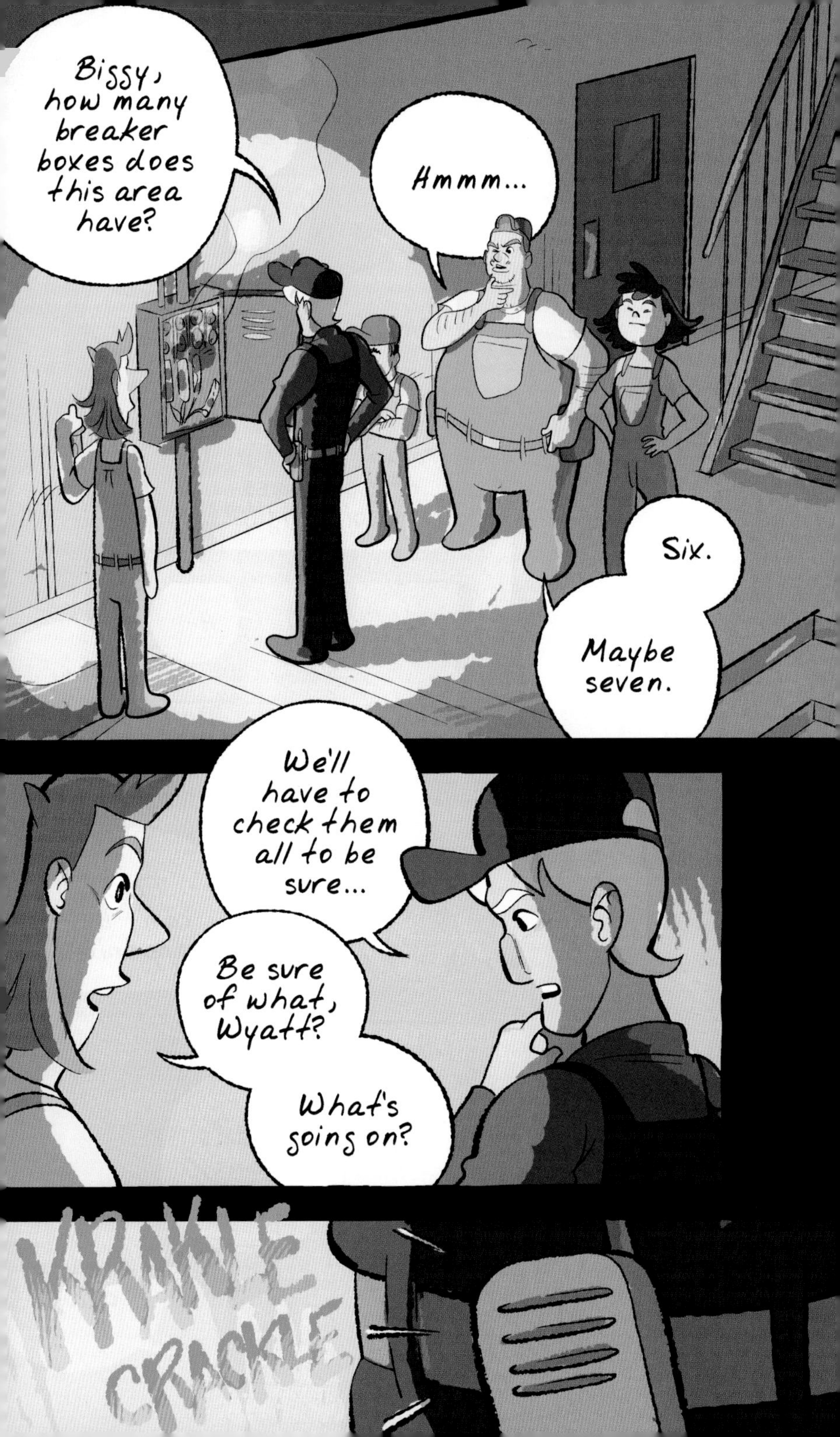
Bissy, how many breaker boxes does this area have?
Hmmm...
Six.
Maybe seven.
We'll have to check them all to be sure...
Be sure of what, Wyatt?
What's going on?
KRAKLE
CRACKLE

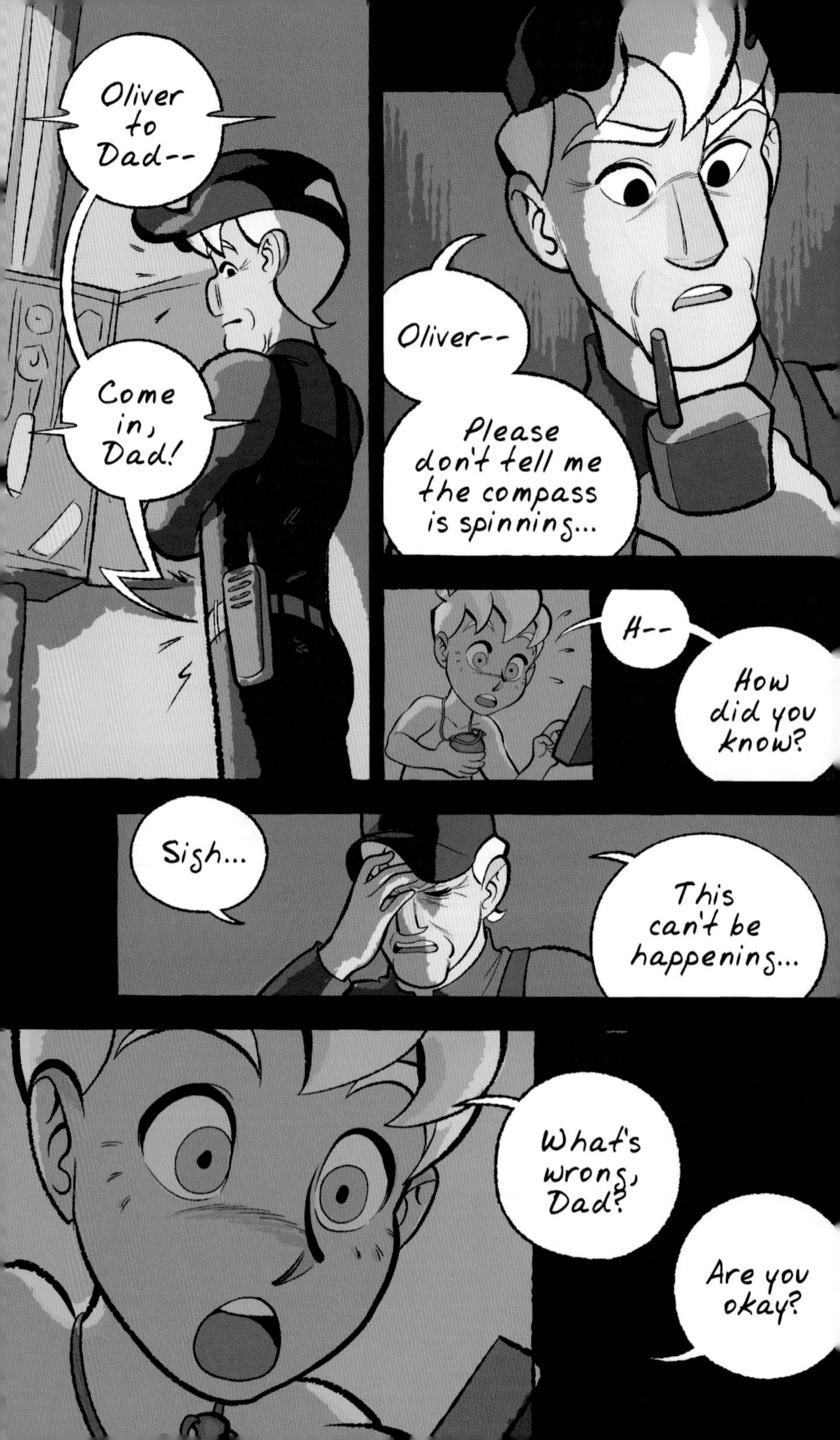
Oliver to Dad--
Come in, Dad!
Oliver--
Please don't tell me the compass is spinning...
H--
How did you know?
Sigh...
This can't be happening...
What's wrong, Dad?
Are you okay?

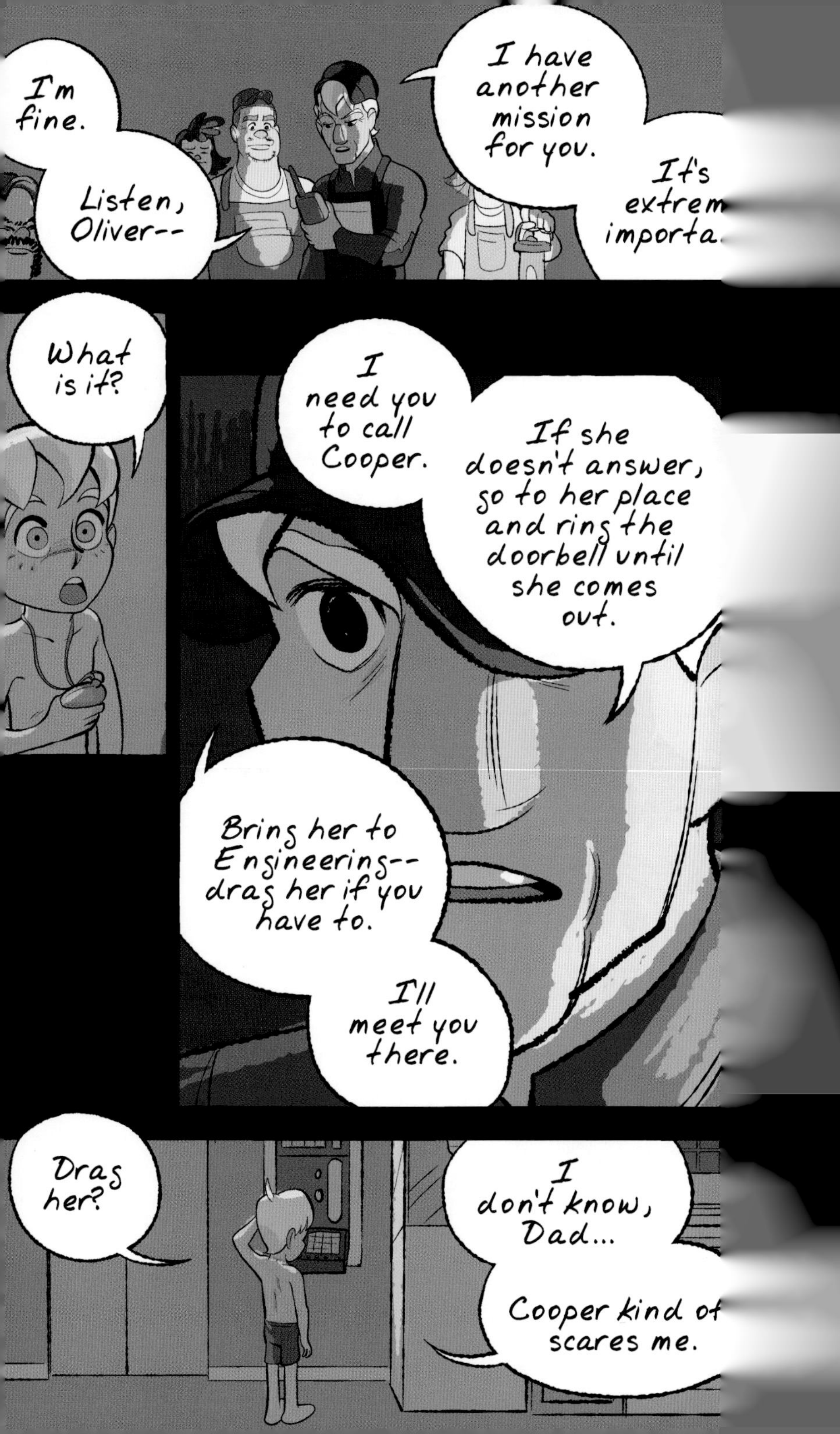
I'm fine.
Listen, Oliver--
I have another mission for you.
It's extrem importa
What is it?
I need you to call Cooper.
If she doesn't answer, go to her place and ring the doorbell until she comes out.
Bring her to Engineering--drag her if you have to.
I'll meet you there.
Drag her?
I don't know, Dad...
Cooper kind of scares me.

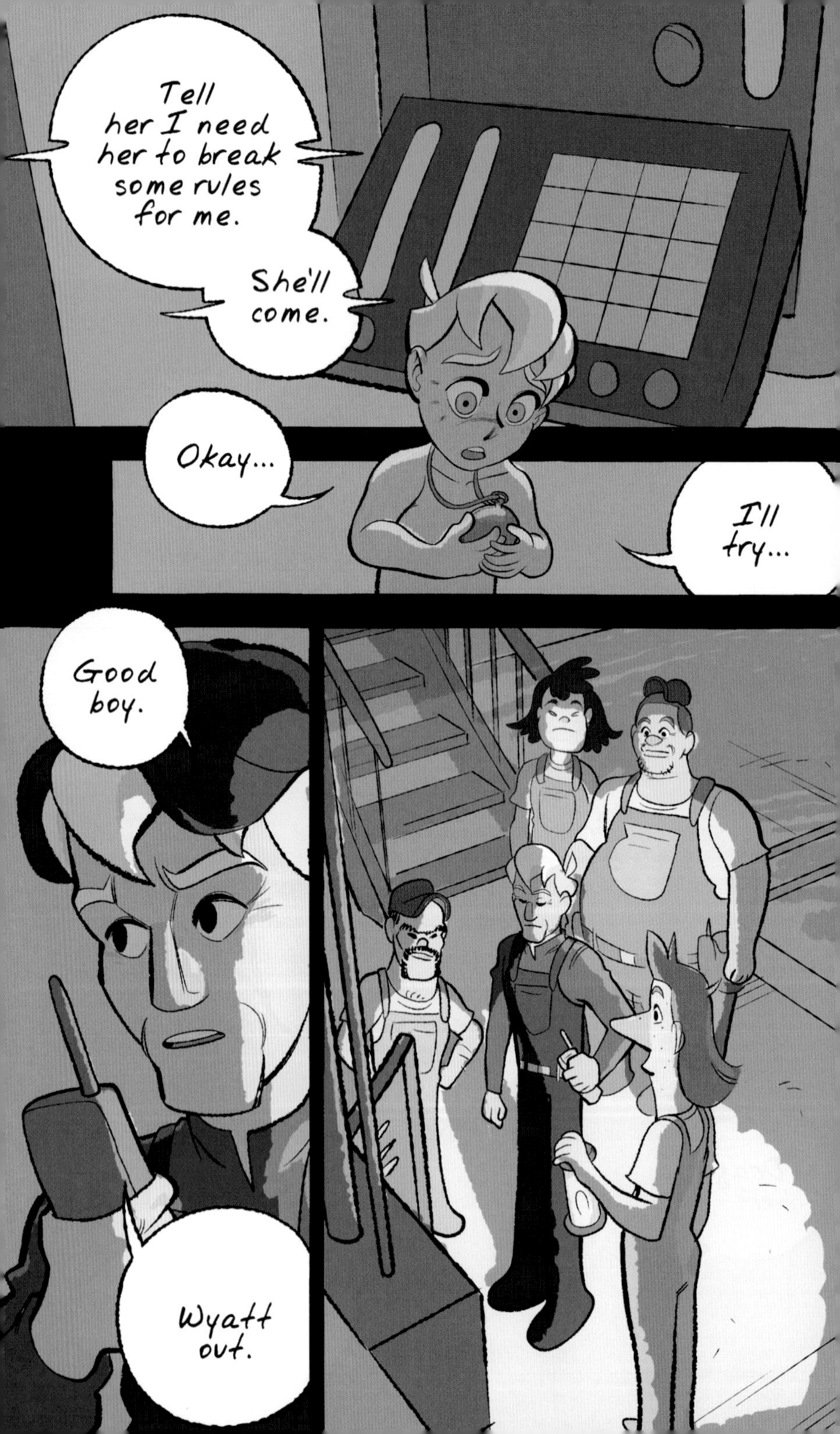
Tell her I need her to break some rules for me.
She'll come.
Okay...
I'll try...
Good boy.
Wyatt out.

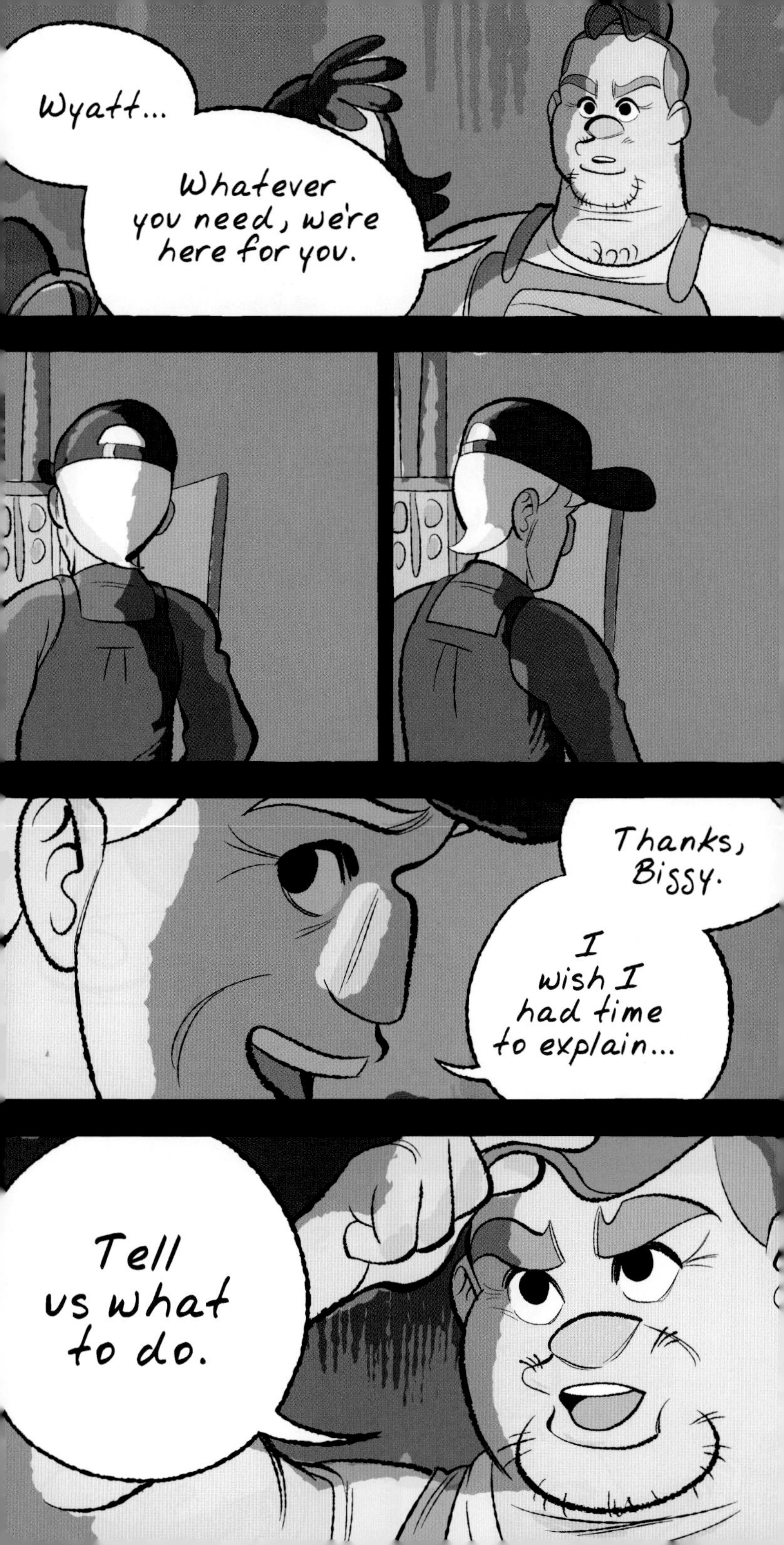
Wyatt...
Whatever you need, we're here for you.
Thanks, Bissy.
I wish I had time to explain...
Tell us what to do.

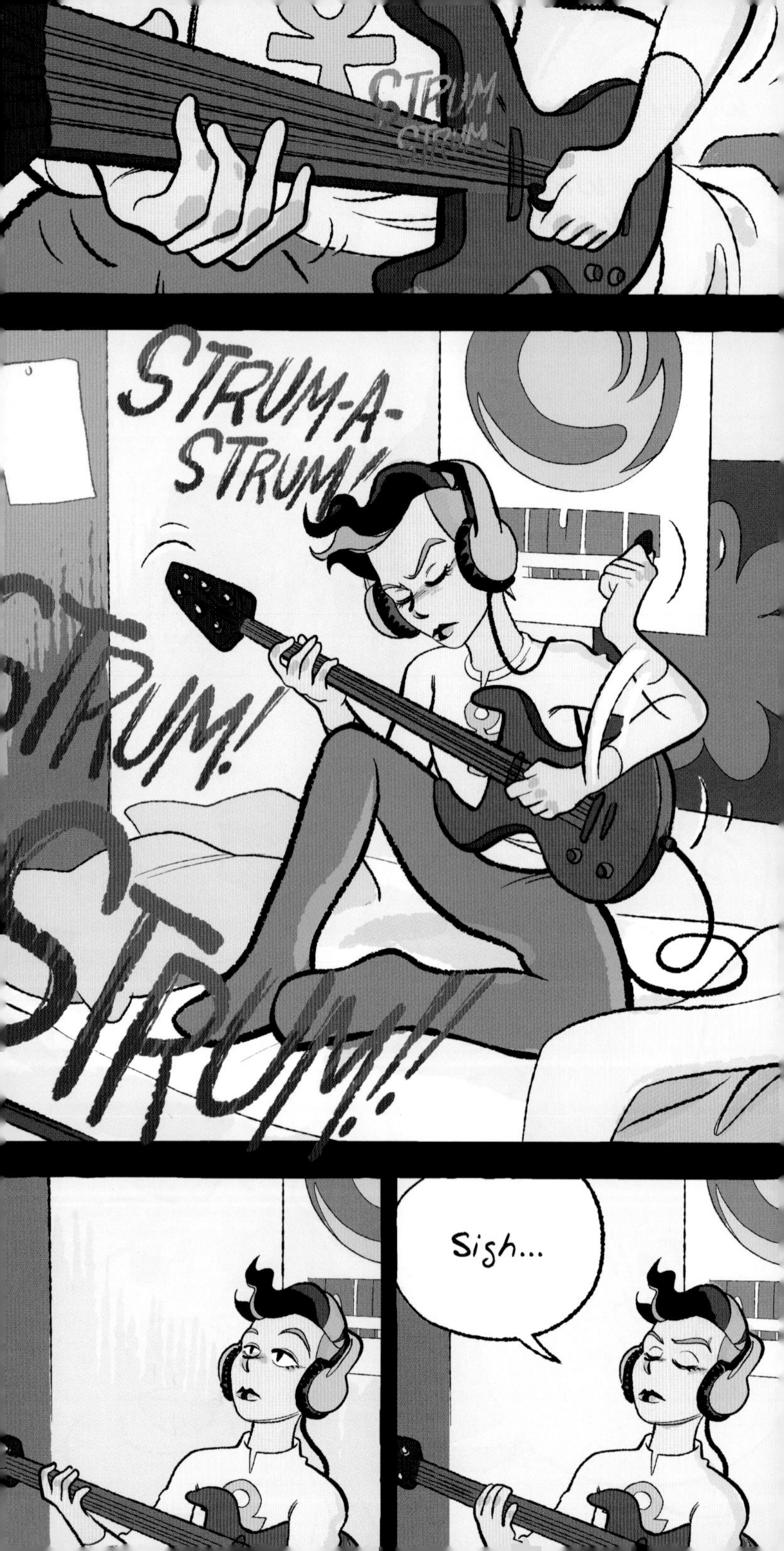
STRUM STRUM
STRUM-A-STRUM!
STRUM!
STRUM!
Sigh...

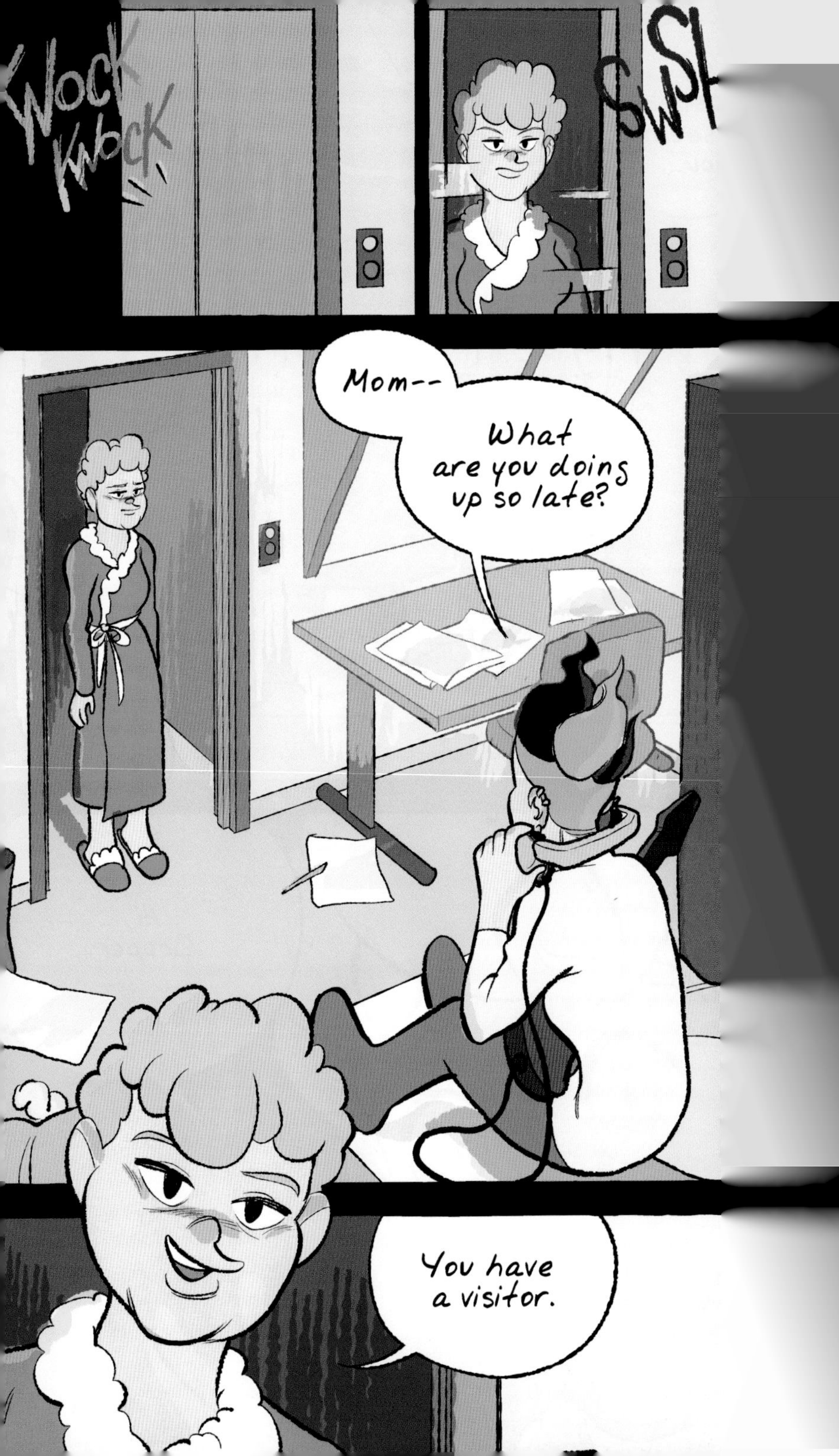

Knock Knock
SWSH
Mom--
What are you doing up so late?
You have a visitor.

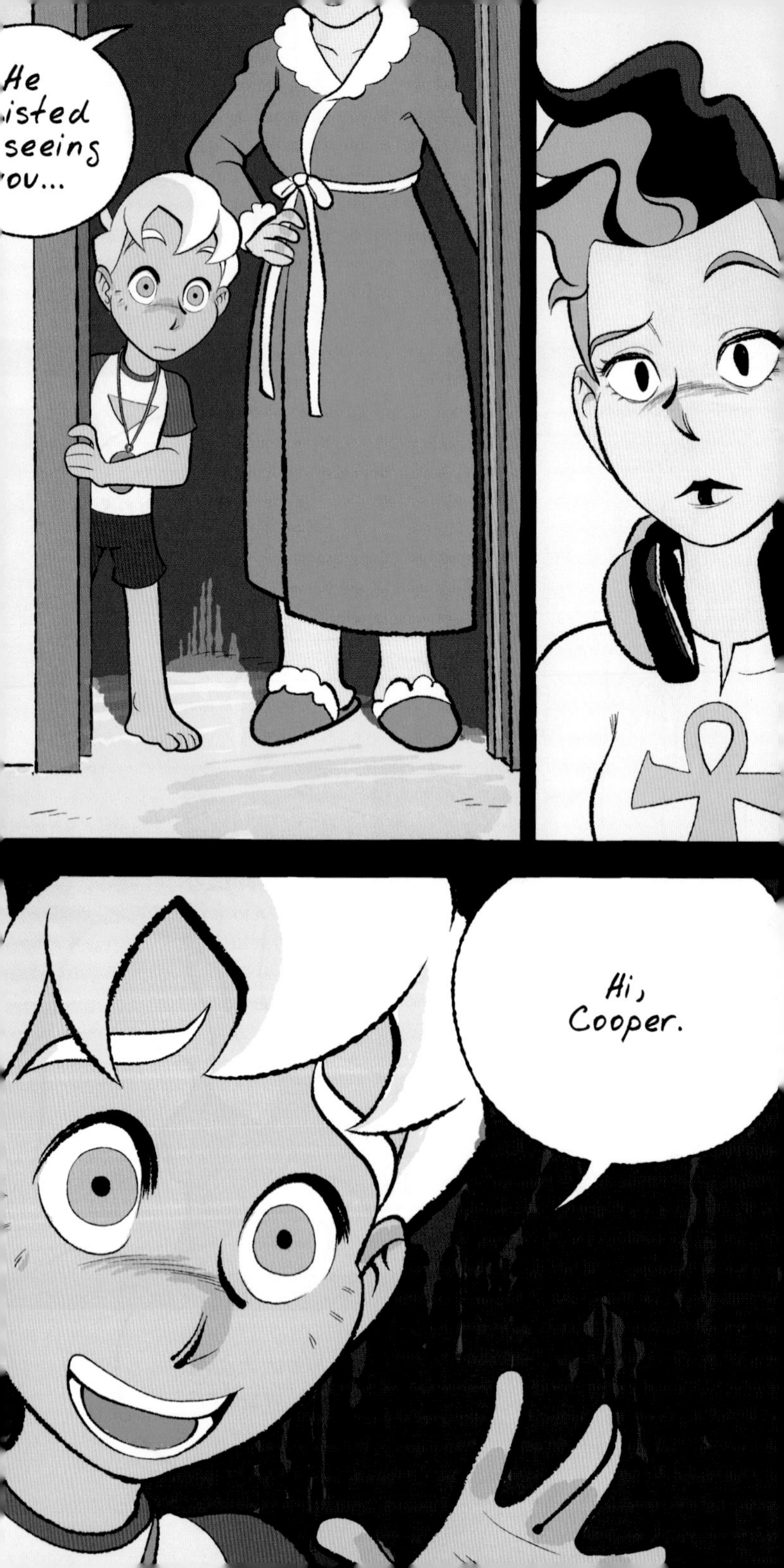
He
isted
seeing
ou...
Hi, Cooper.

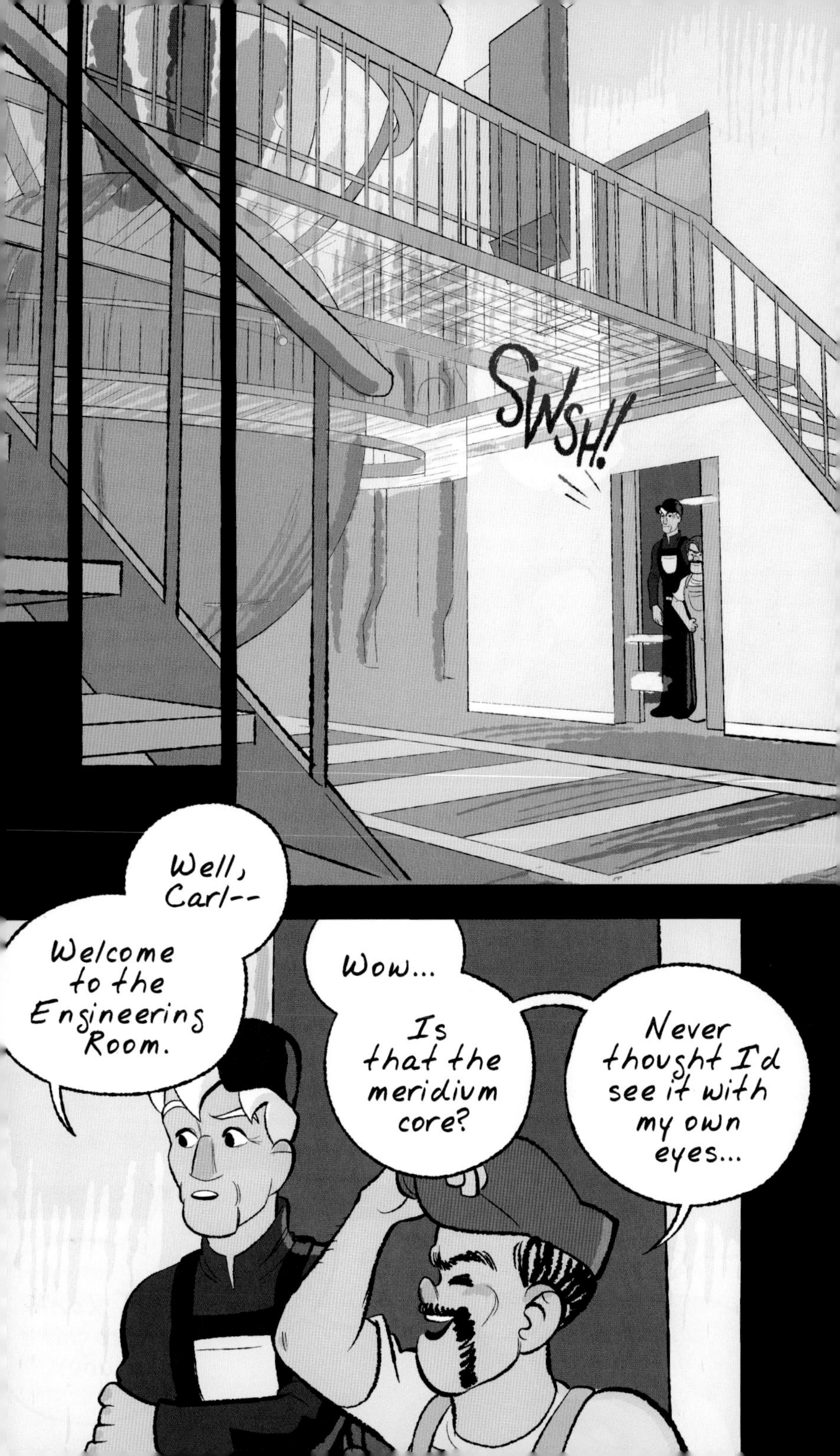
SWSH!
Well, Carl--
Welcome to the Engineering Room.
Wow...
Is that the meridium core?
Never thought I'd see it with my own eyes...

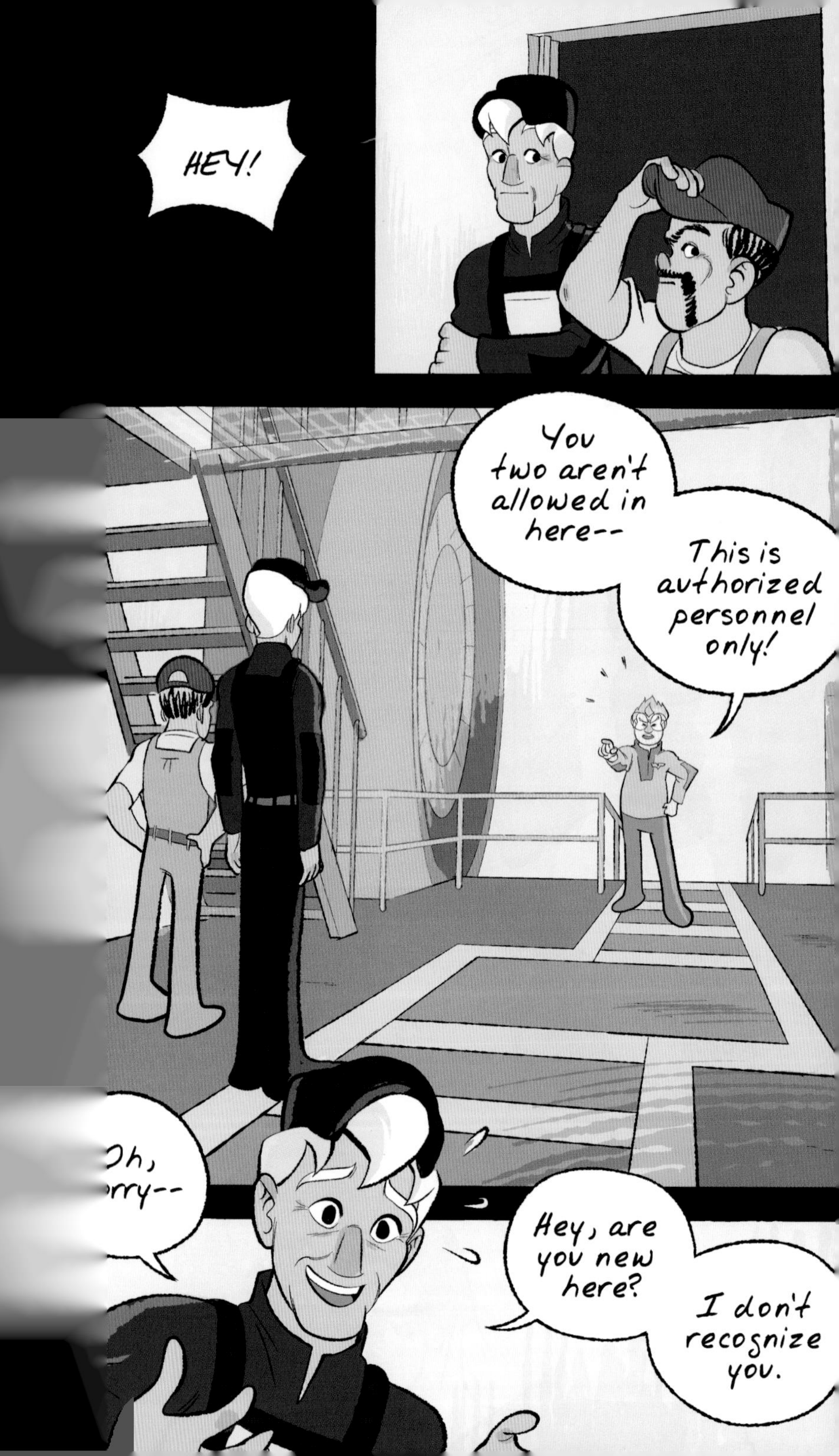
HEY!
You two aren't allowed in here--
This is authorized personnel only!
Hey, are you new here?
I don't recognize you.

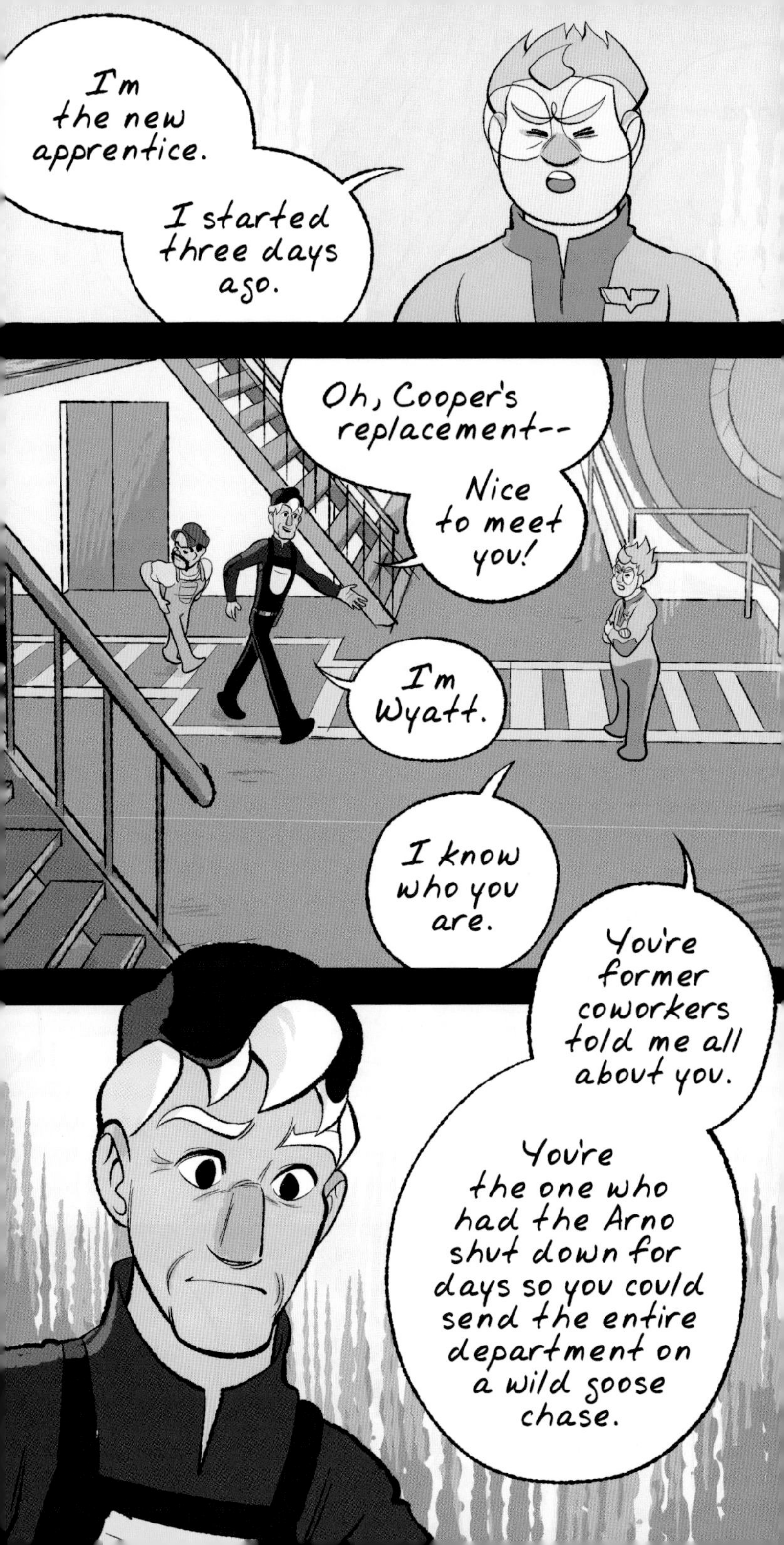
I'm the new apprentice.
I started three days ago.
Oh, Cooper's replacement--
Nice to meet you!
I'm Wyatt.
I know who you are.
You're former coworkers told me all about you.
You're the one who had the Arno shut down for days so you could send the entire department on a wild goose chase.

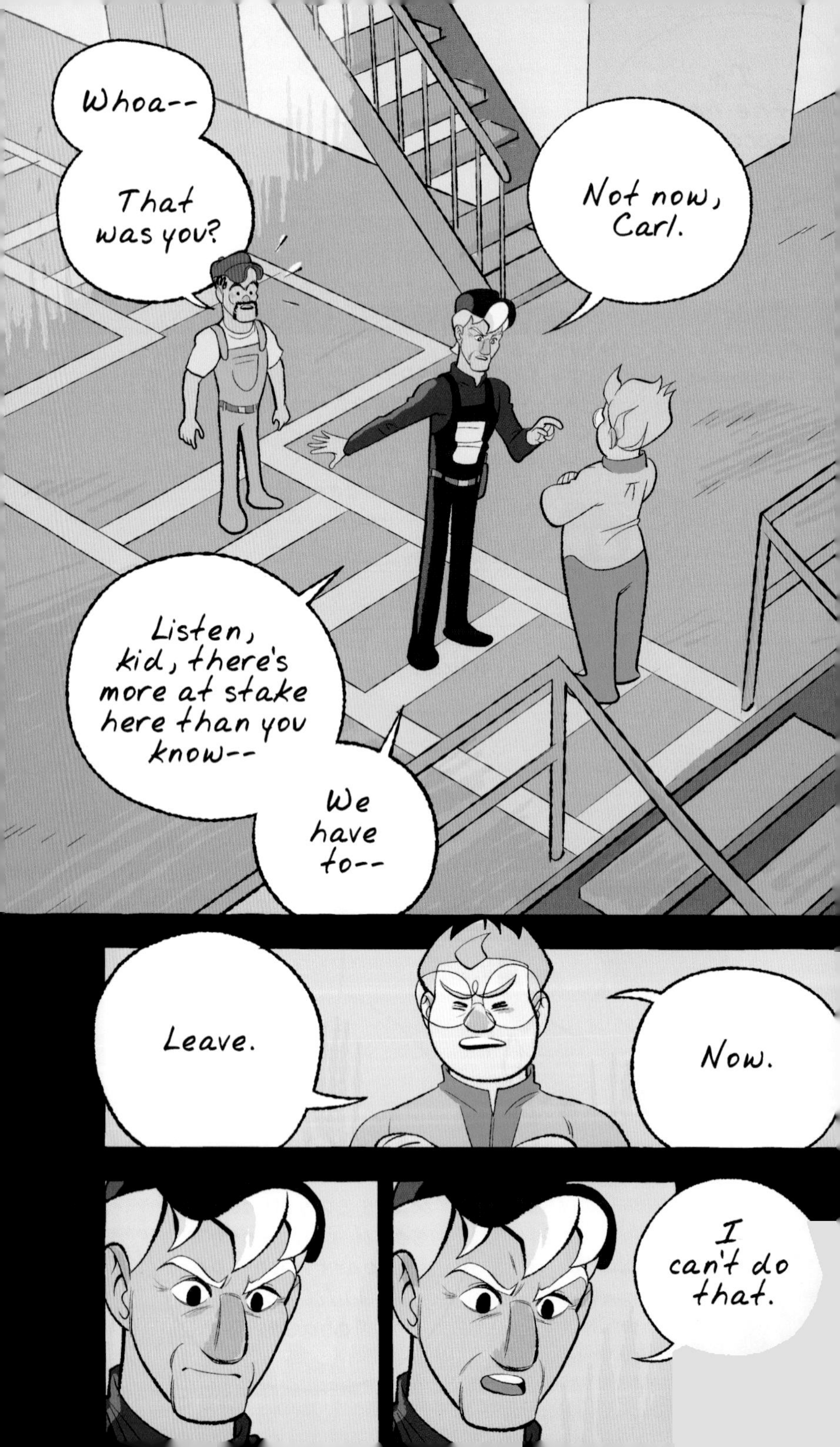
Whoa--
That was you?
Not now, Carl.
Listen, kid, there's more at stake here than you know--
We have to--
Leave.
Now.
I can't do that.

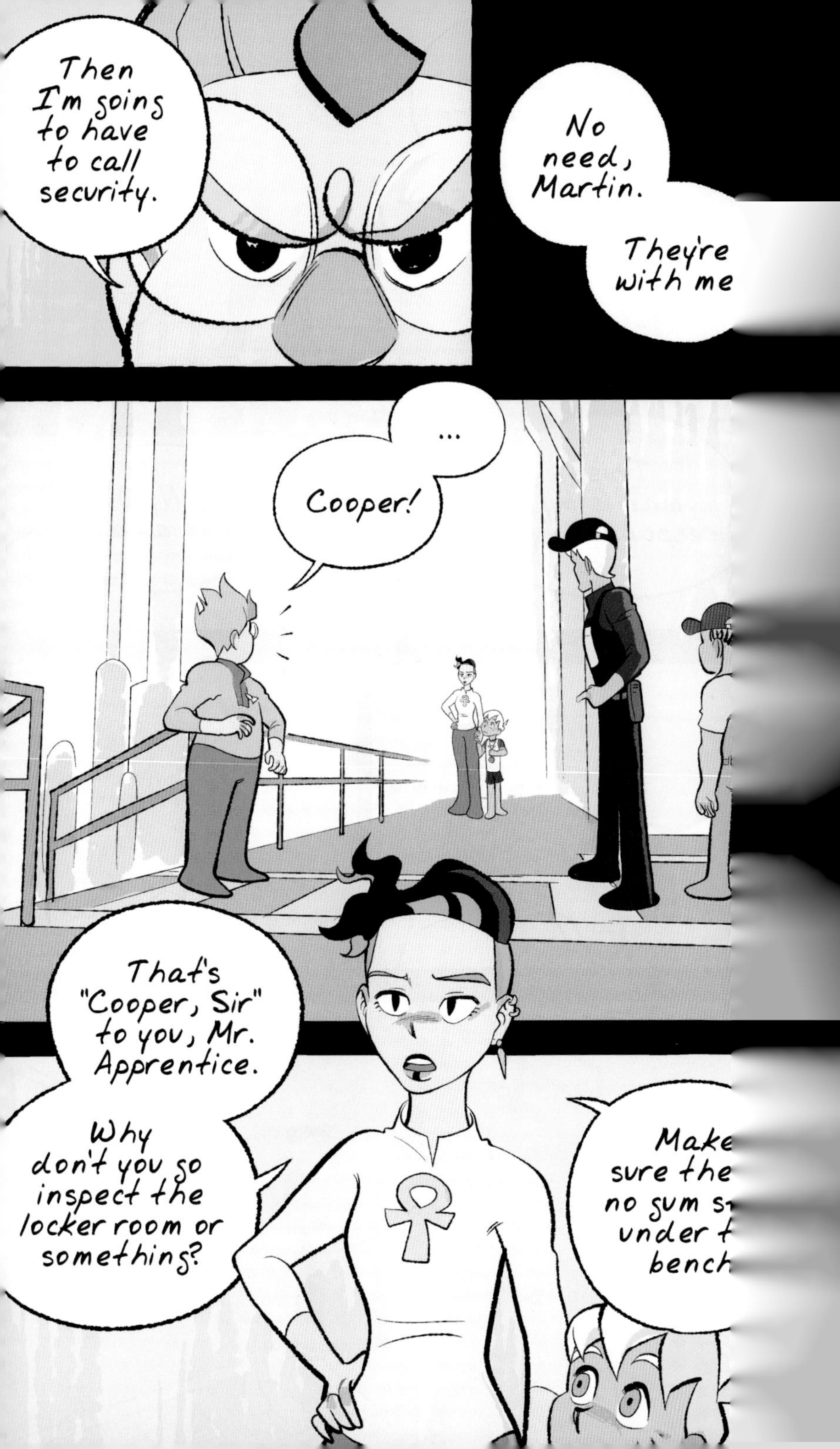
Then I'm going to have to call security.
No need, Martin.
They're with me
...
Cooper!
That's "Cooper, Sir" to you, Mr. Apprentice.
Why don't you go inspect the locker room or something?
Make sure the no gum s under t bench

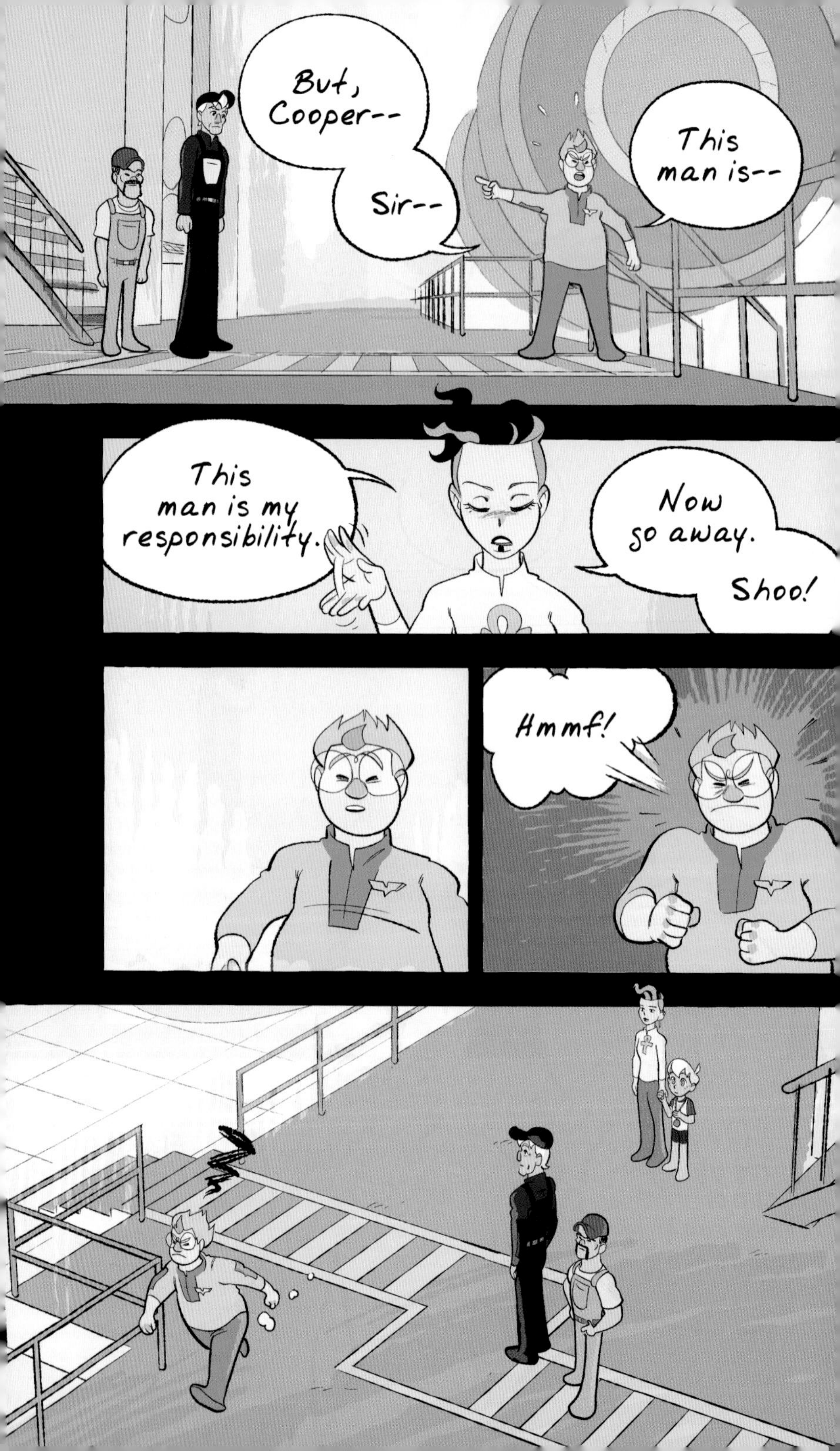
But, Cooper--
Sir--
This man is--
This man is my responsibility.
Now go away.
Shoo!
Hmmf!

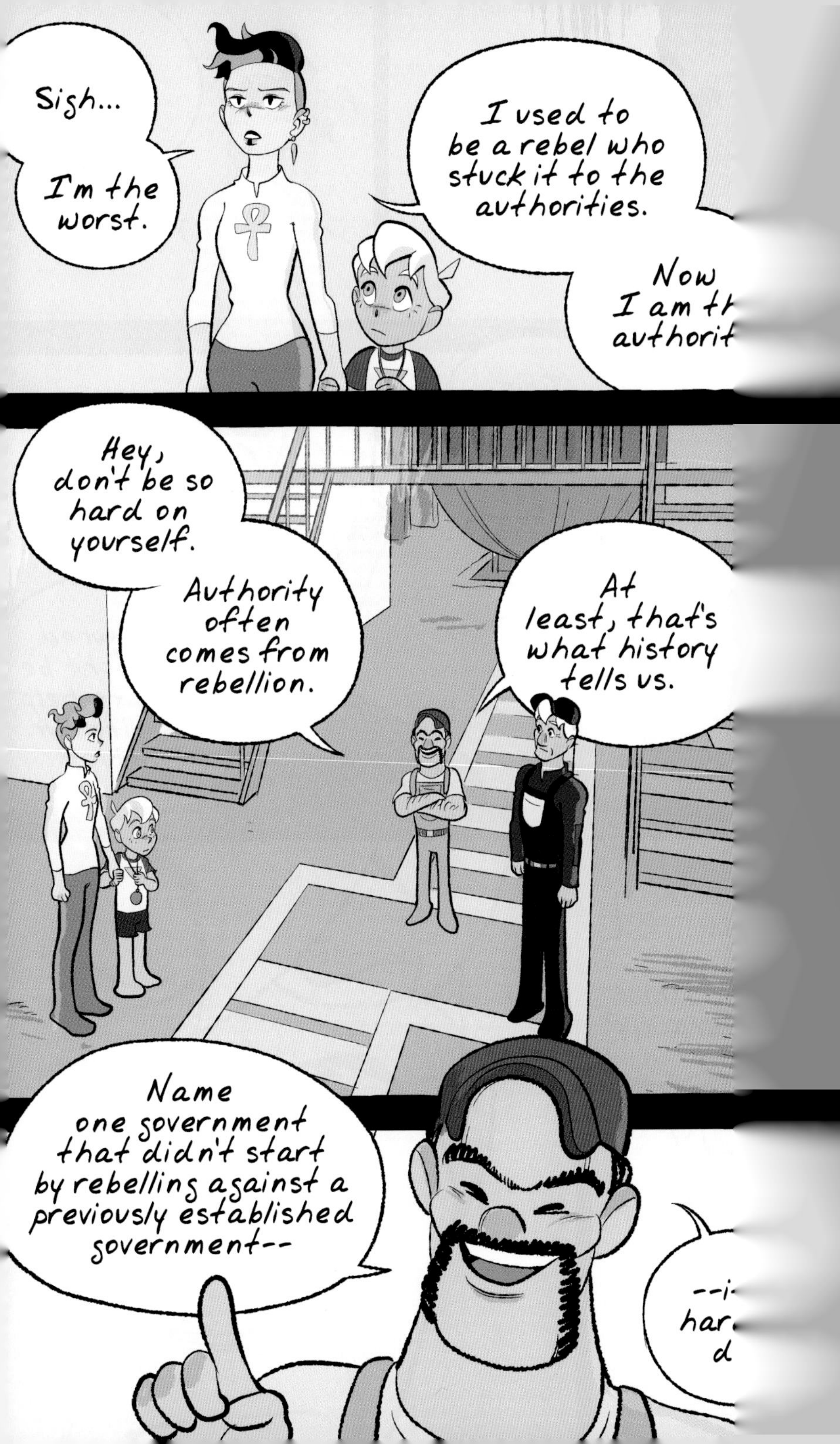
Sigh...
I'm the worst.
I used to be a rebel who stuck it to the authorities.
Now I am th
authorit
Hey, don't be so hard on yourself.
Authority often comes from rebellion.
At least, that's what history tells us.
Name one government that didn't start by rebelling against a previously established government--
--i
har
d

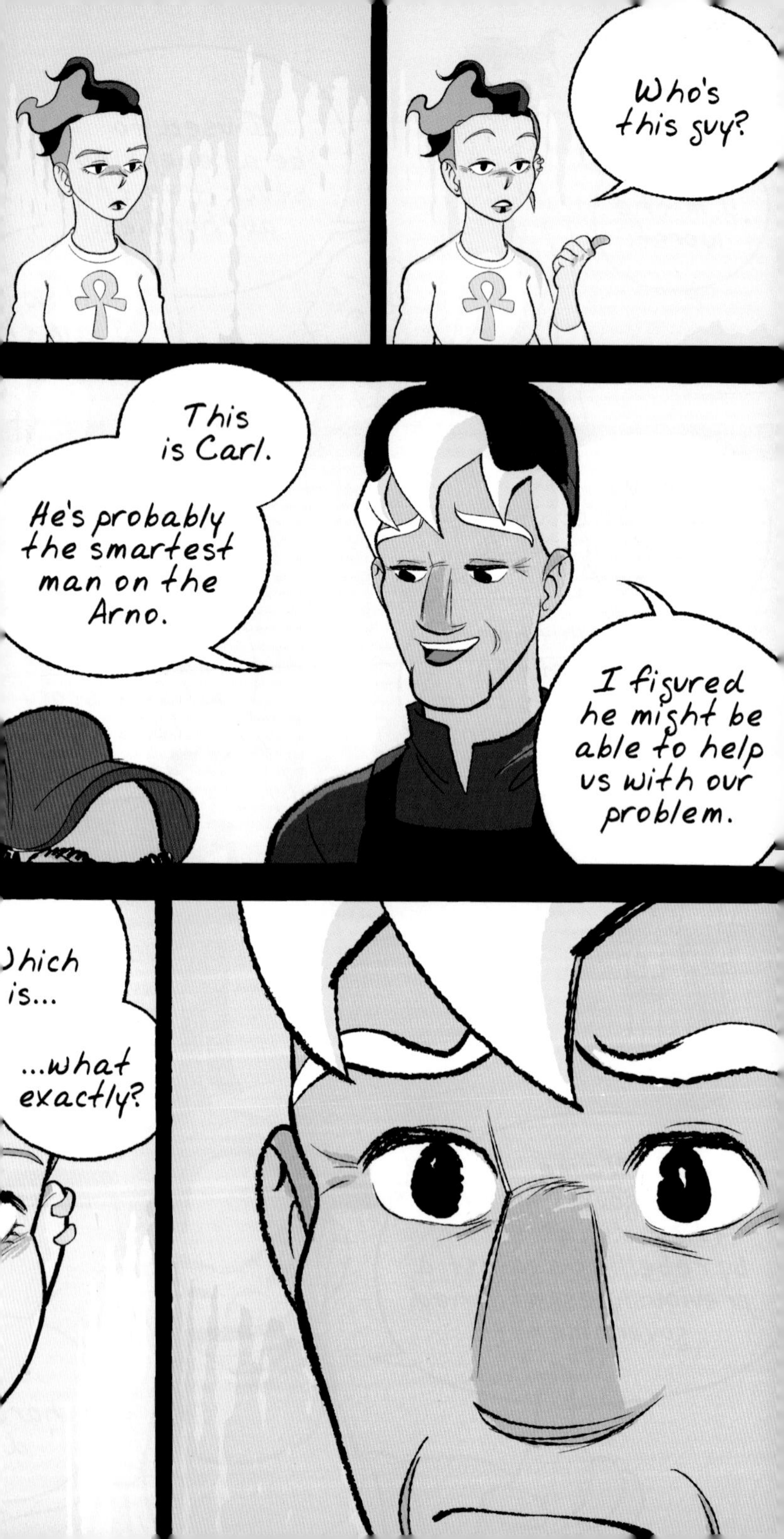
Who's this guy?
This is Carl.
He's probably the smartest man on the Arno.
I figured he might be able to help us with our problem.
hich is...
...what exactly?

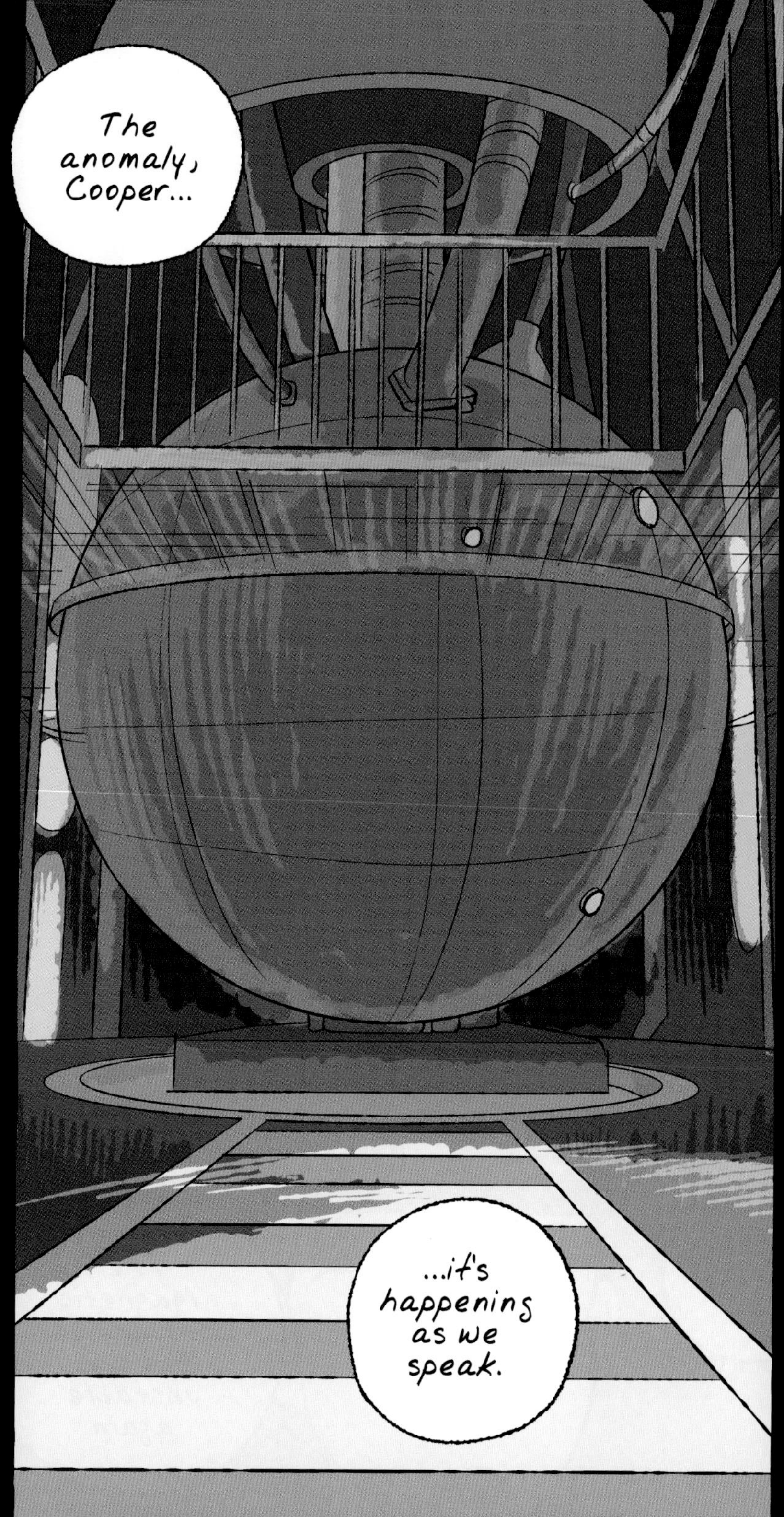
The anomaly, Cooper...
...it's happening as we speak.

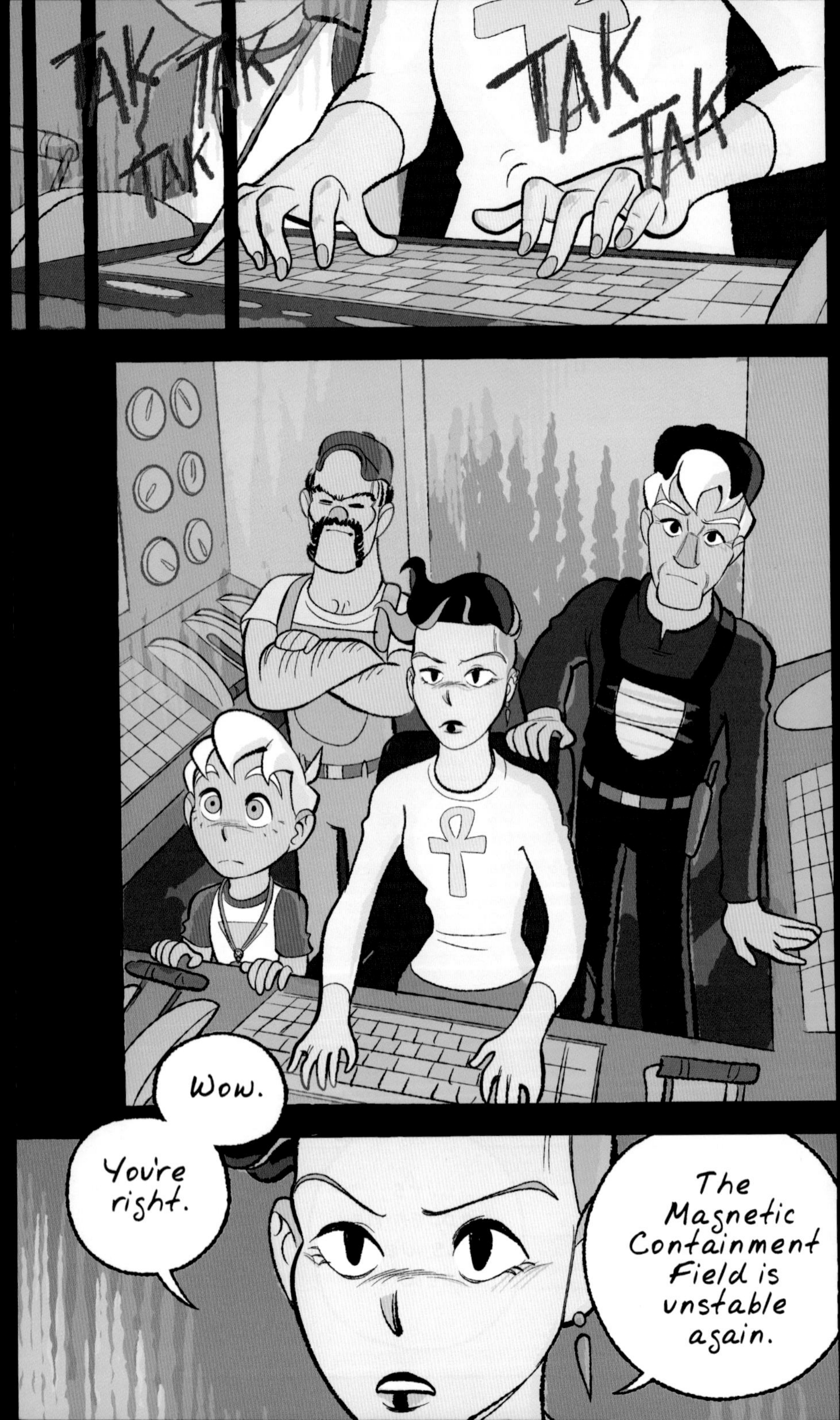
TAK TAK TAK TAK
TAK TAK
Wow.
You're right.
The Magnetic Containment Field is unstable again.

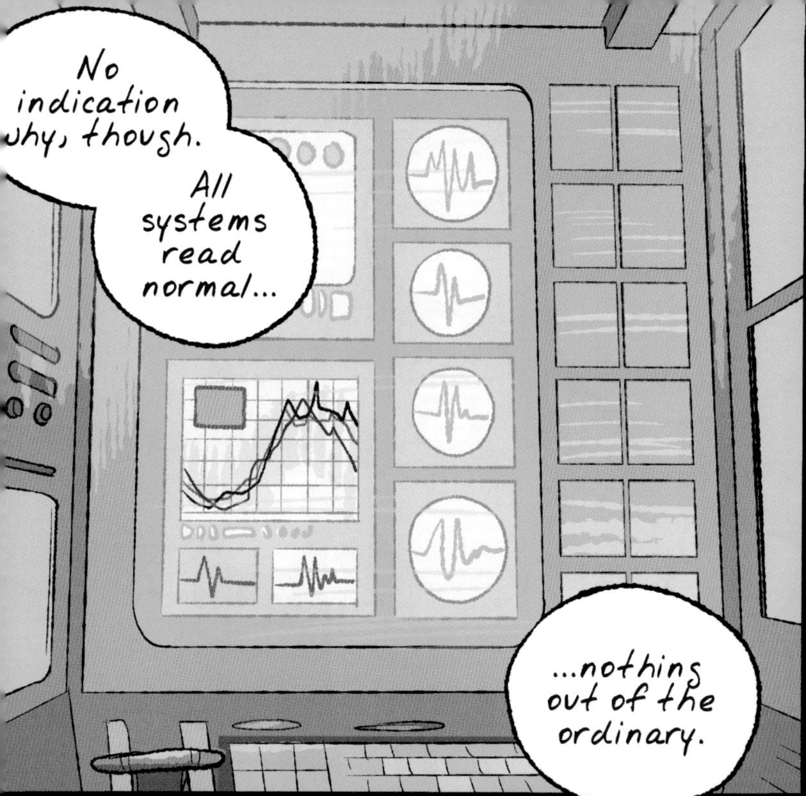
No indication why, though.
All systems read normal...
...nothing out of the ordinary.

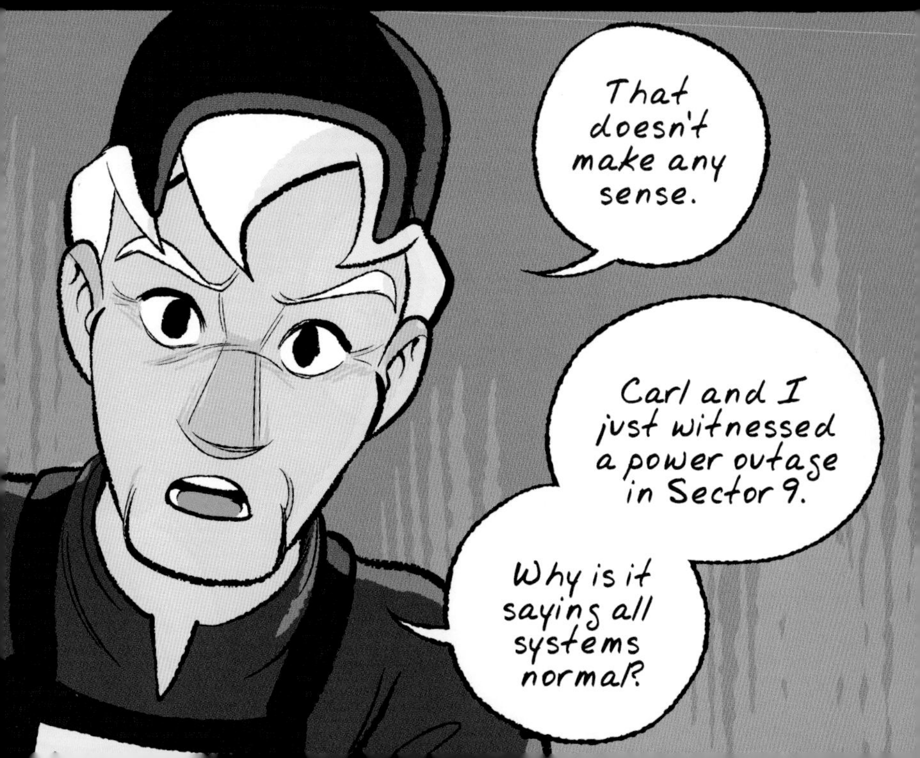
That doesn't make any sense.
Carl and I just witnessed a power outage in Sector 9.
Why is it saying all systems normal?

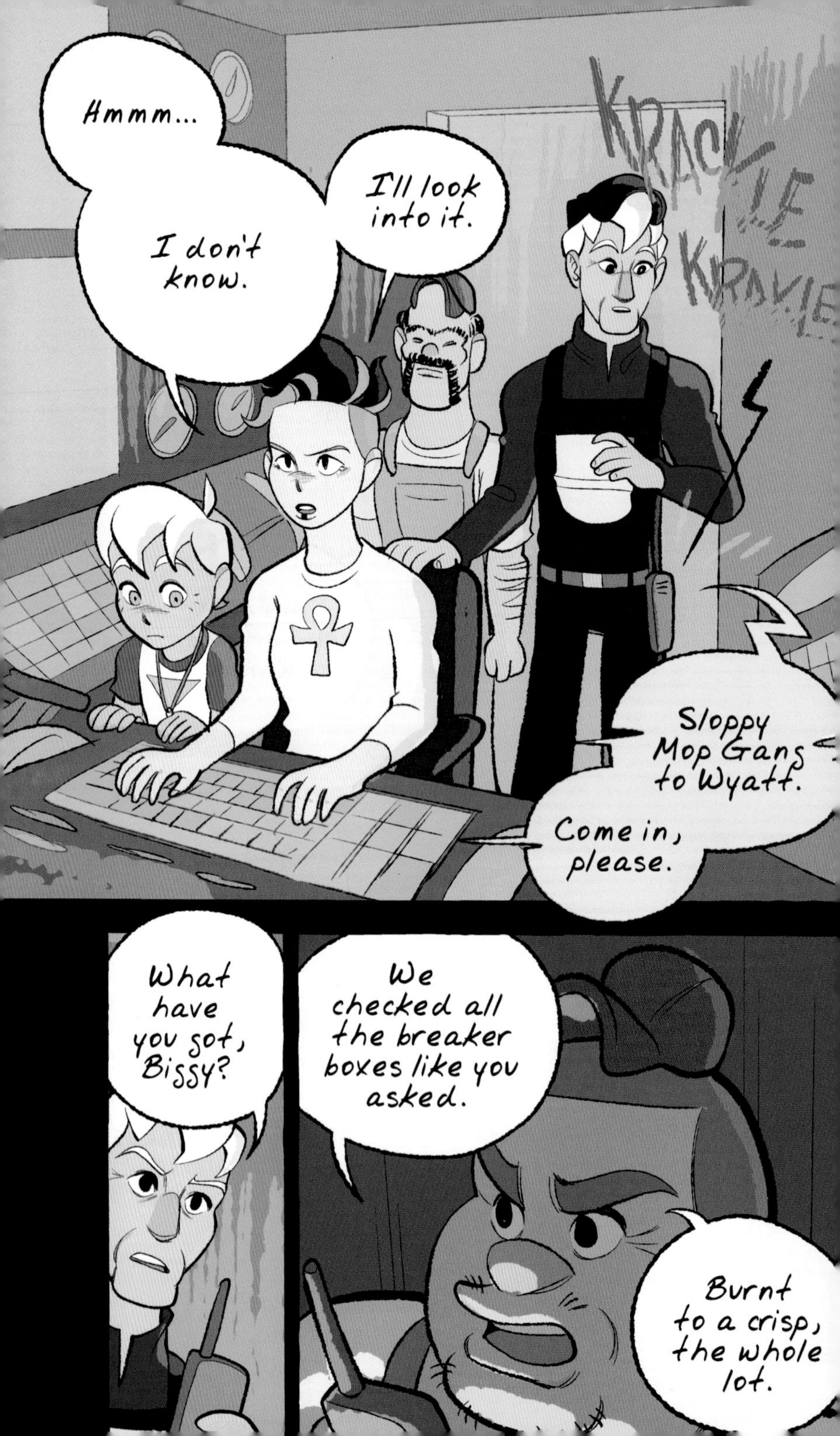

Hmmm...
I don't know.
I'll look into it.
KRACKLE KRAKLE
Sloppy Mop Gans to Wyatt.
Come in, please.
What have you got, Bissy?
We checked all the breaker boxes like you asked.
Burnt to a crisp, the whole lot.

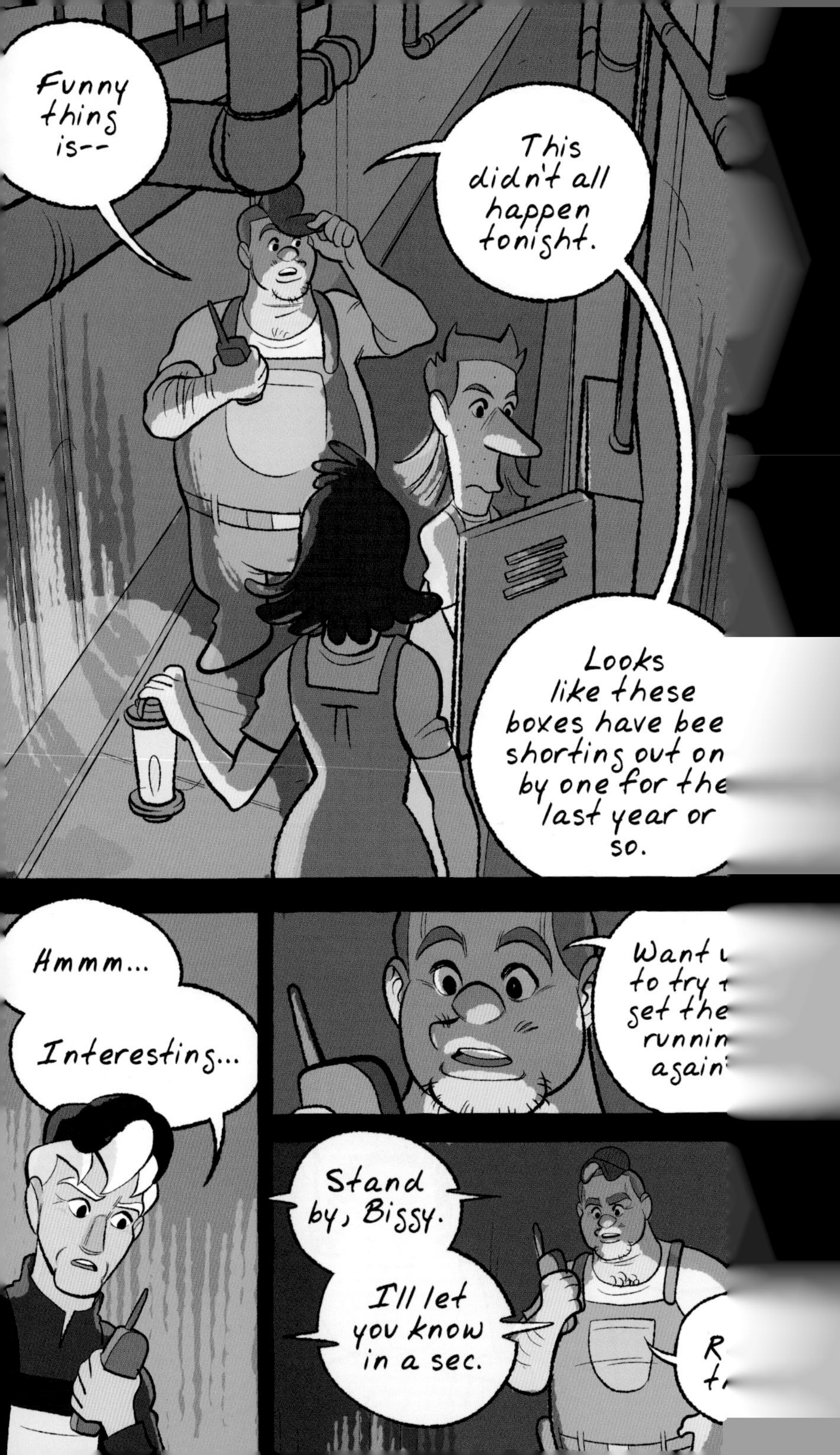
Funny thing is--
This didn't all happen tonight.
Looks like these boxes have bee shorting out on by one for the last year or so.
Hmmm...
Interesting...
Want
to try
set the
runnin
again
Stand by, Bissy.
I'll let you know in a sec.

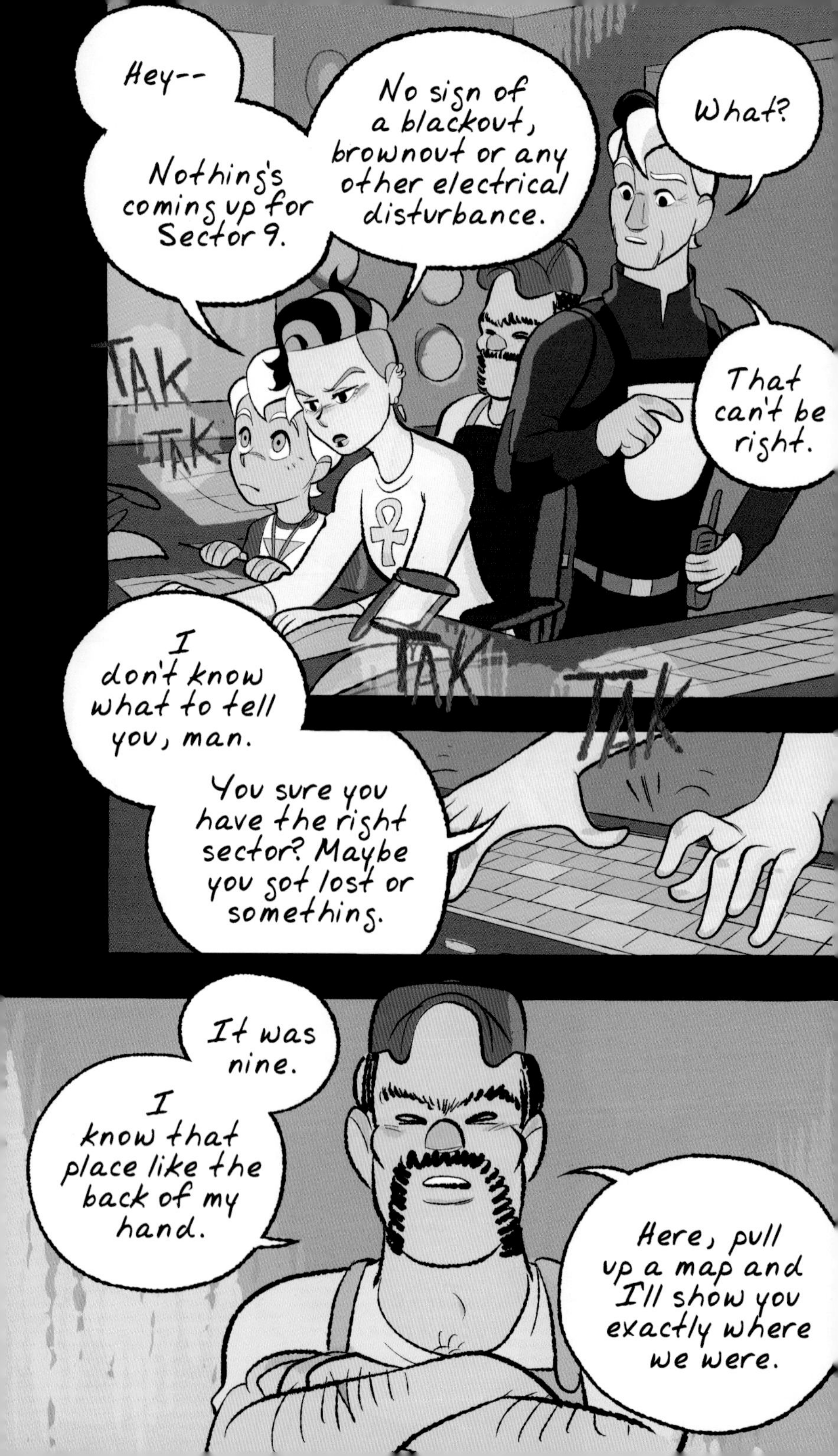
Hey--
Nothing's coming up for Sector 9.
No sign of a blackout, brownout or any other electrical disturbance.
What?
TAK
TAK
That can't be right.
TAK
TAK
I don't know what to tell you, man.
You sure you have the right sector? Maybe you got lost or something.
It was nine.
I know that place like the back of my hand.
Here, pull up a map and I'll show you exactly where we were.

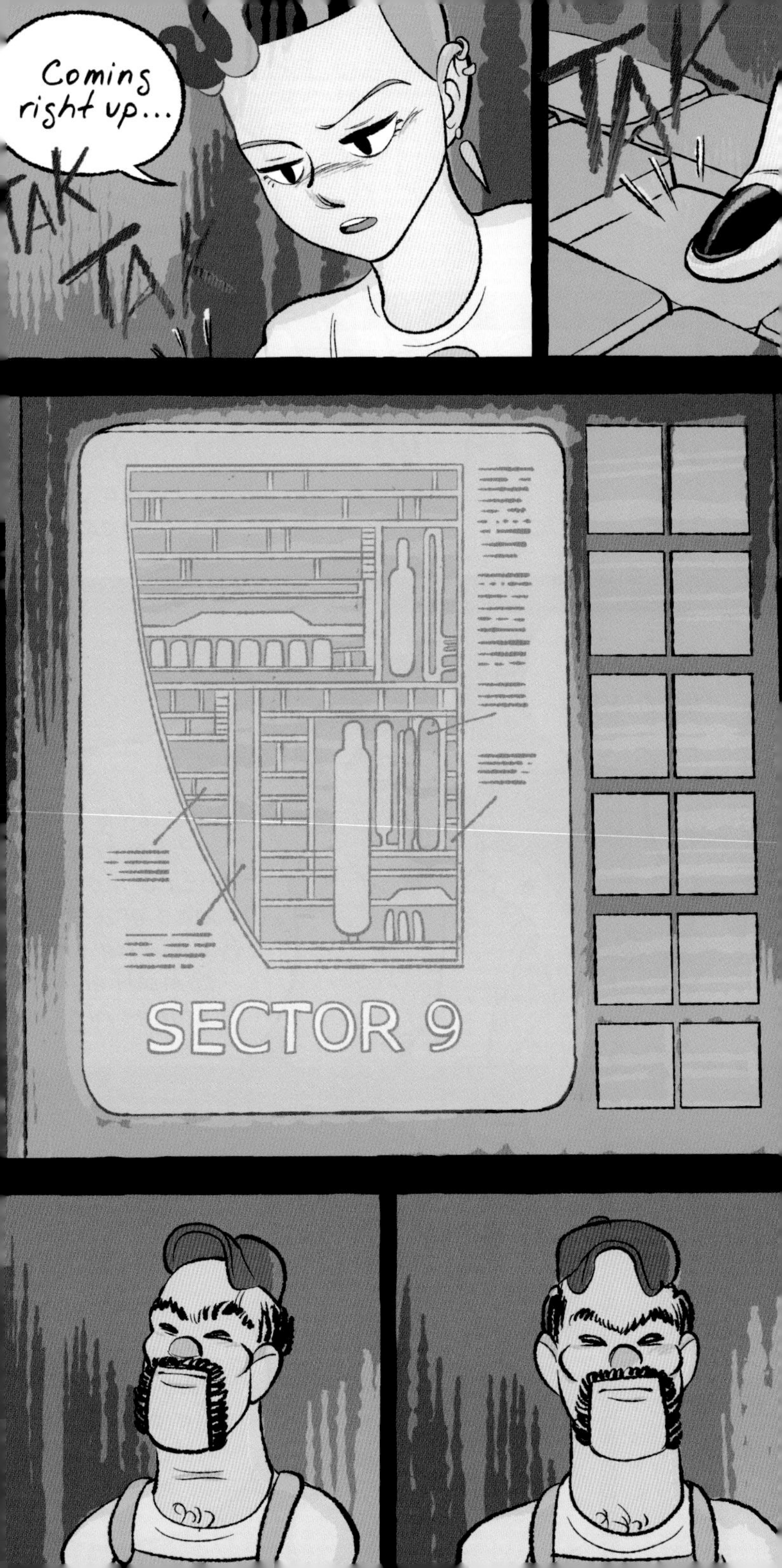

Coming right up...
TAK TAK
TAK
SECTOR 9

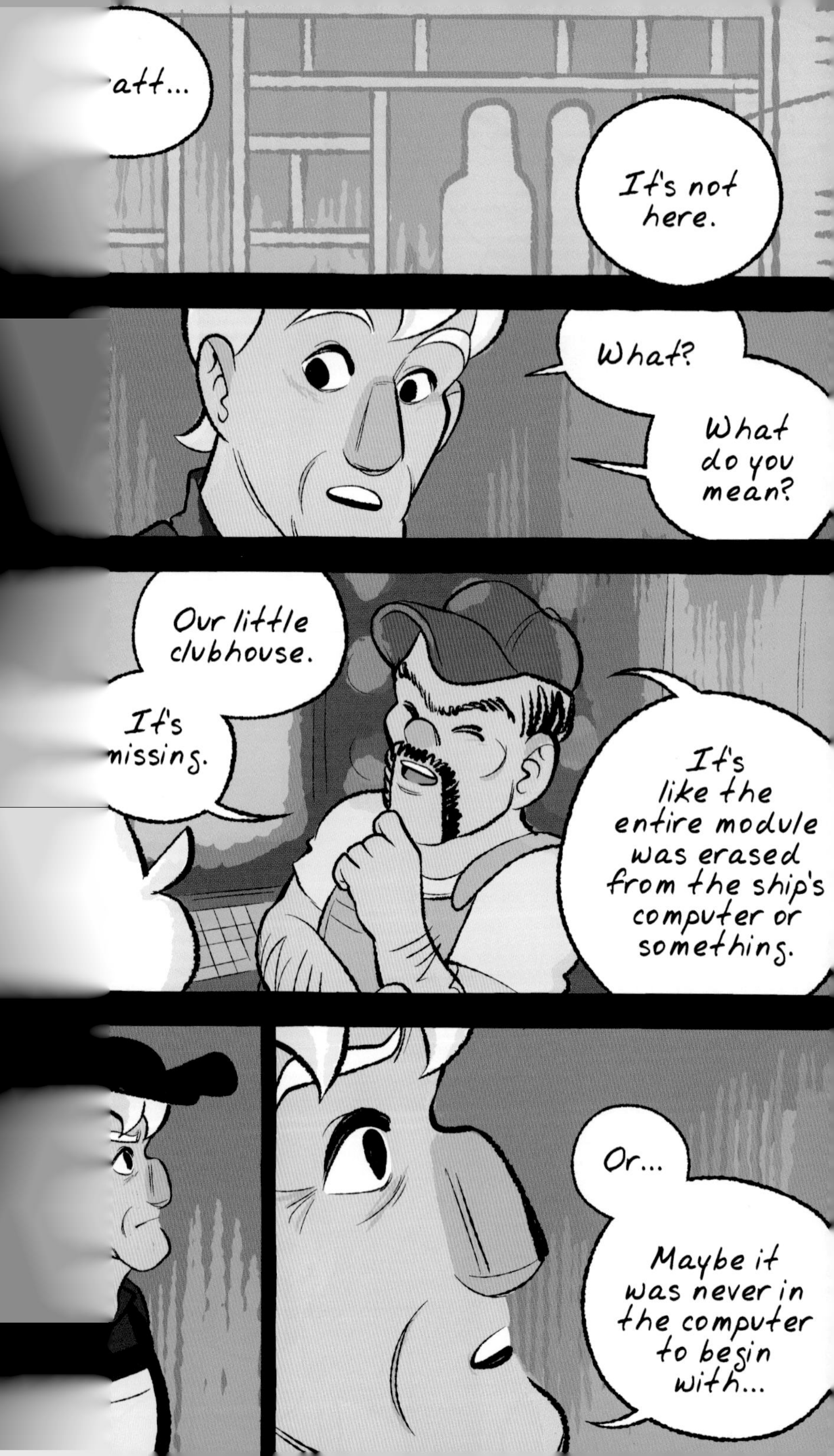
att...
It's not here.
What?
What do you mean?
Our little clubhouse.
It's
issing.
It's like the entire module was erased from the ship's computer or something.
Or...
Maybe it was never in the computer to begin with...

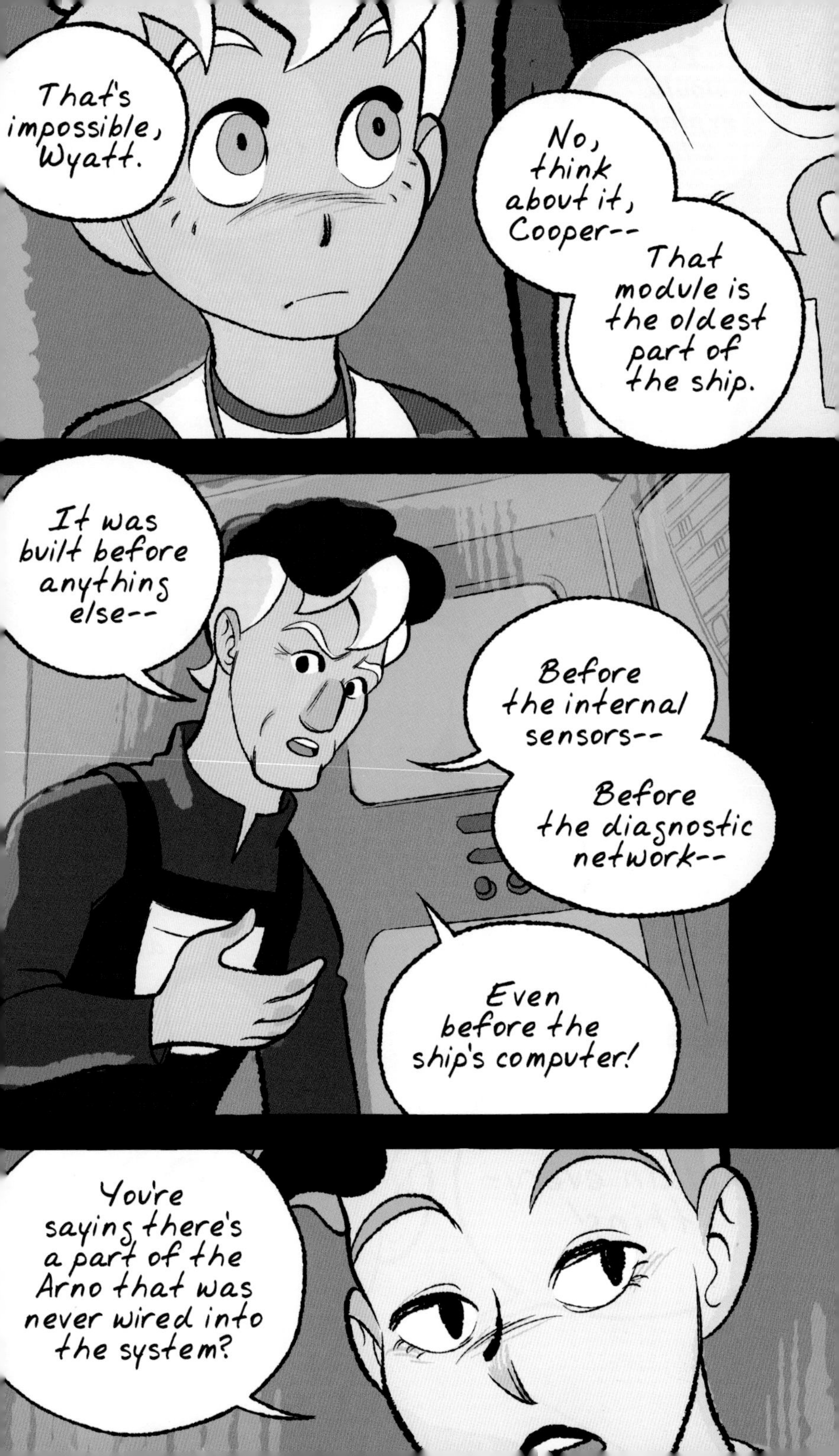
That's impossible, Wyatt.
No, think about it, Cooper--
That module is the oldest part of the ship.
It was built before anything else--
Before the internal sensors--
Before the diagnostic network--
Even before the ship's computer!
You're saying there's a part of the Arno that was never wired into the system?

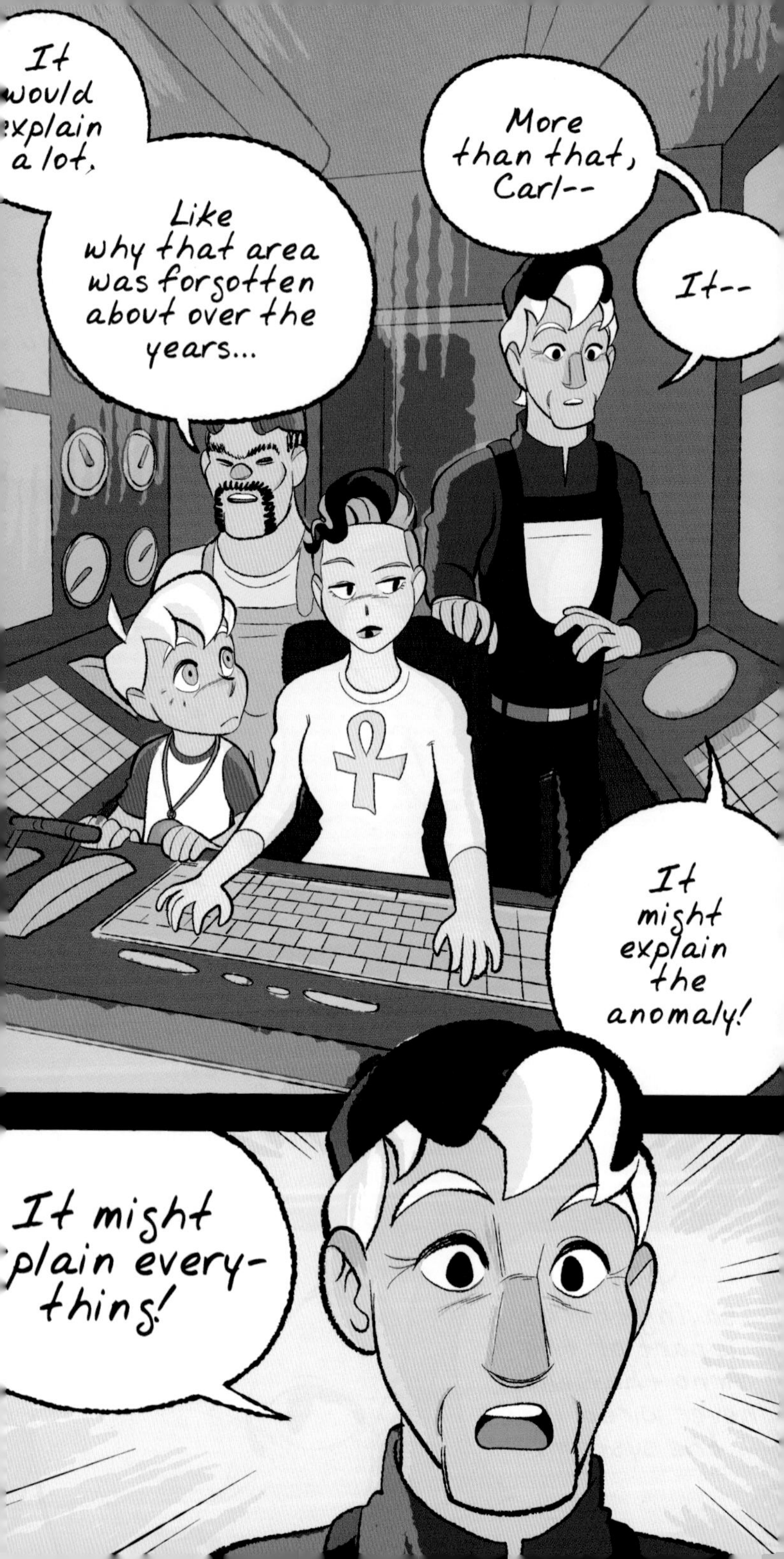
It would explain a lot.
Like why that area was forgotten about over the years...
More than that, Carl--
It--
It might explain the anomaly!
It might xplain every-thing!

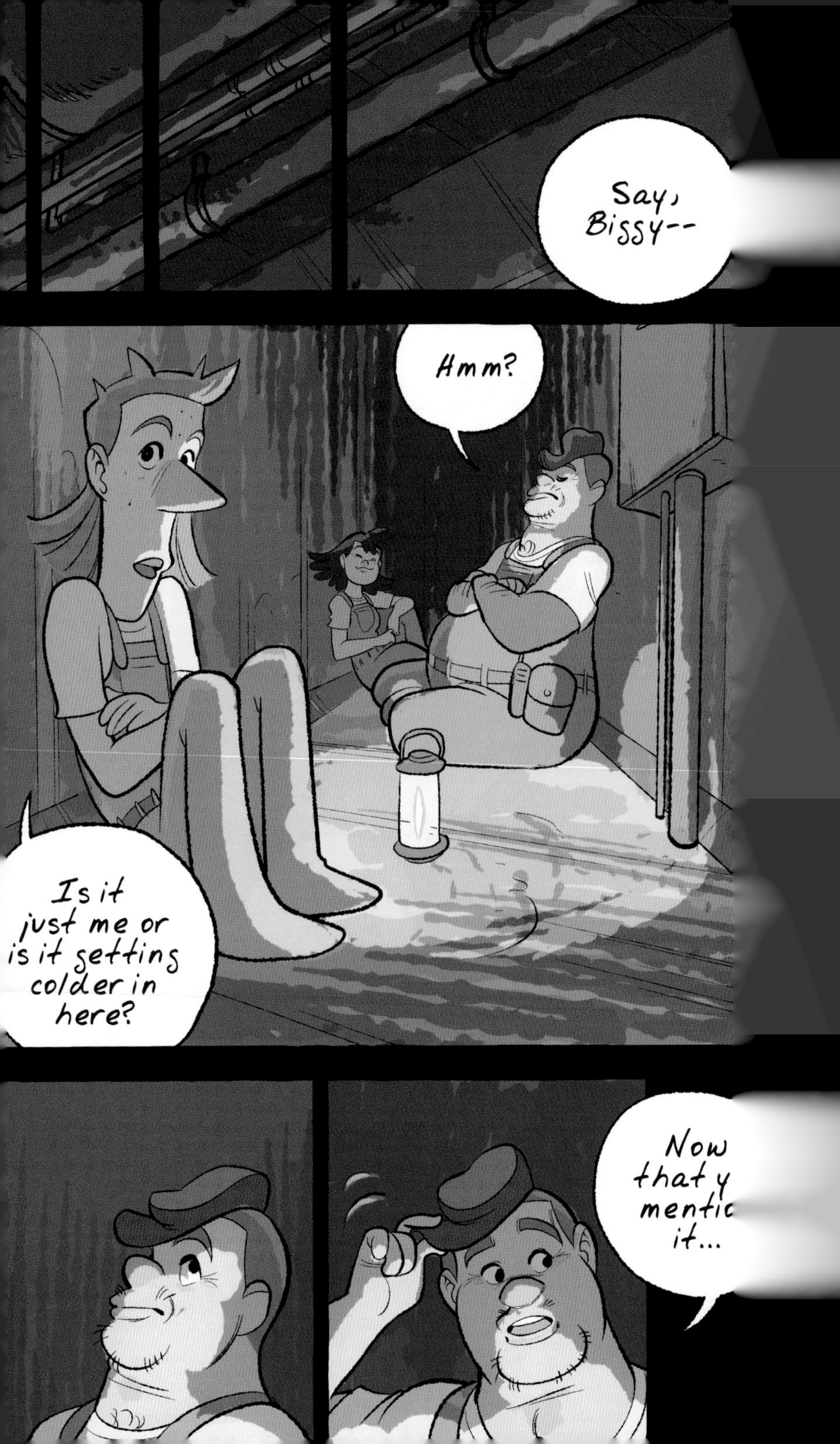
Say, Bissy--
Hmm?
Is it just me or is it getting colder in here?
Now that y
mentic
it...

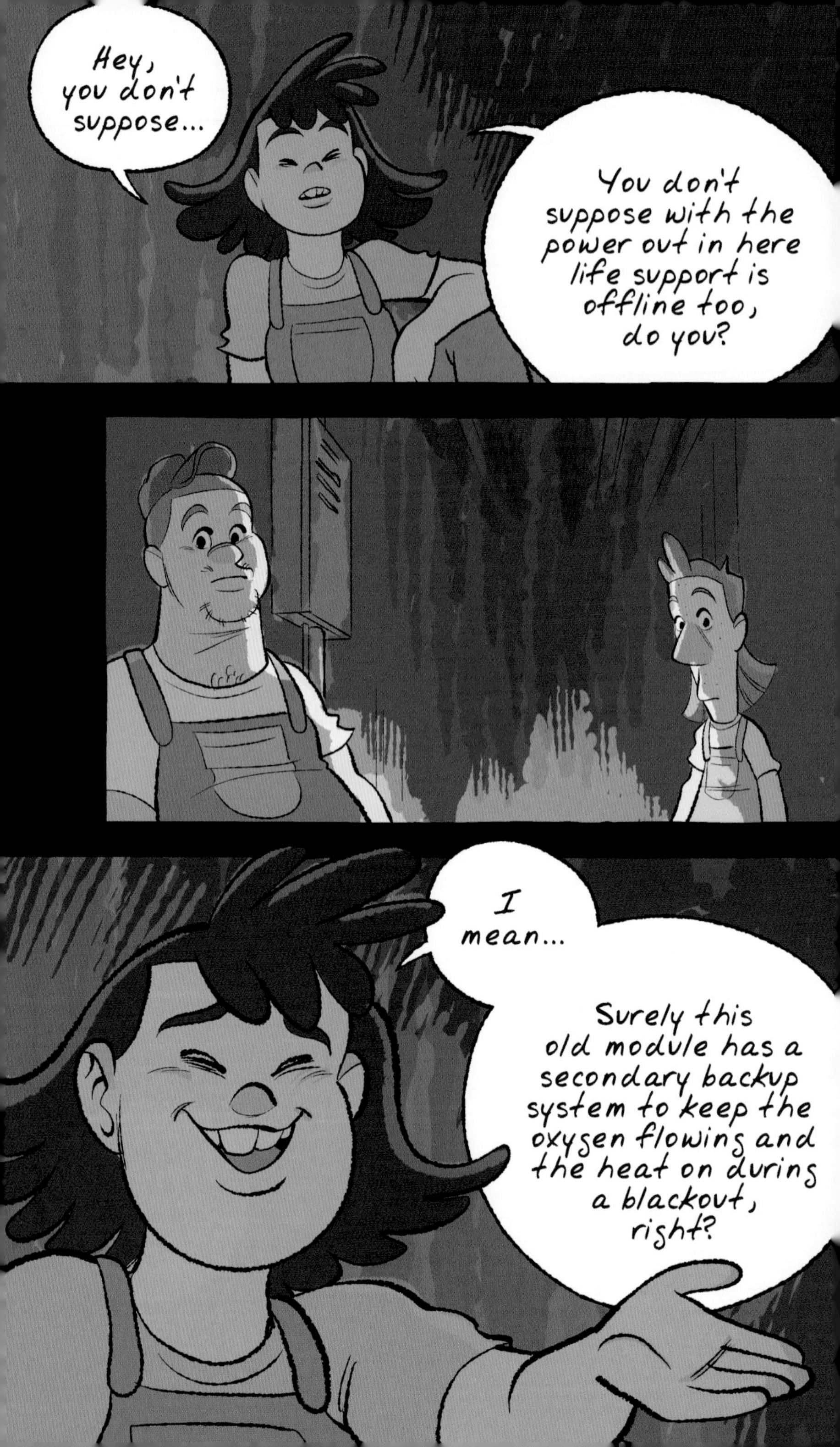
Hey, you don't suppose...
You don't suppose with the power out in here life support is offline too, do you?
I mean...
Surely this old module has a secondary backup system to keep the oxygen flowing and the heat on during a blackout, right?

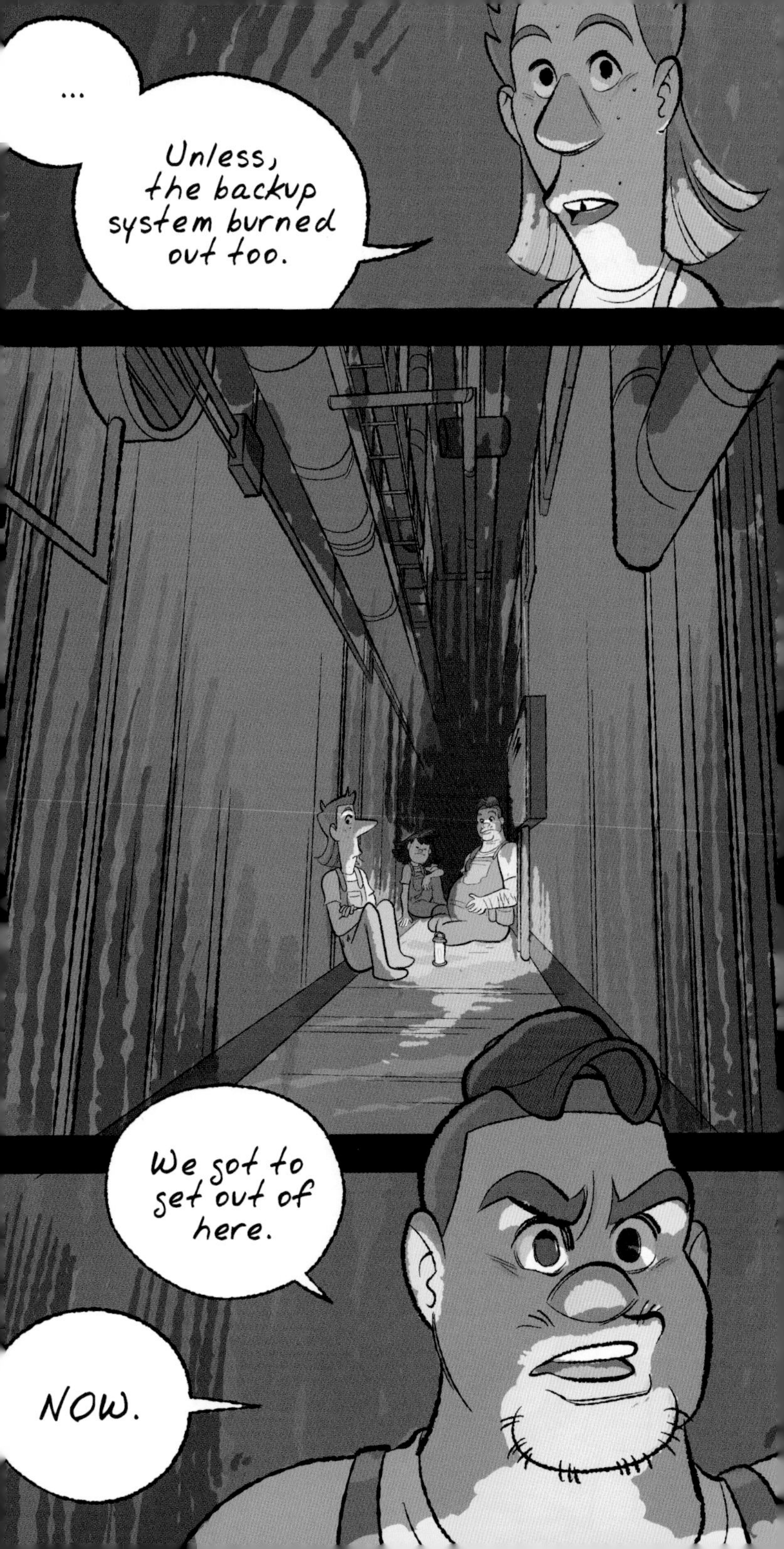
...
Unless, the backup system burned out too.
We got to get out of here.
NOW.

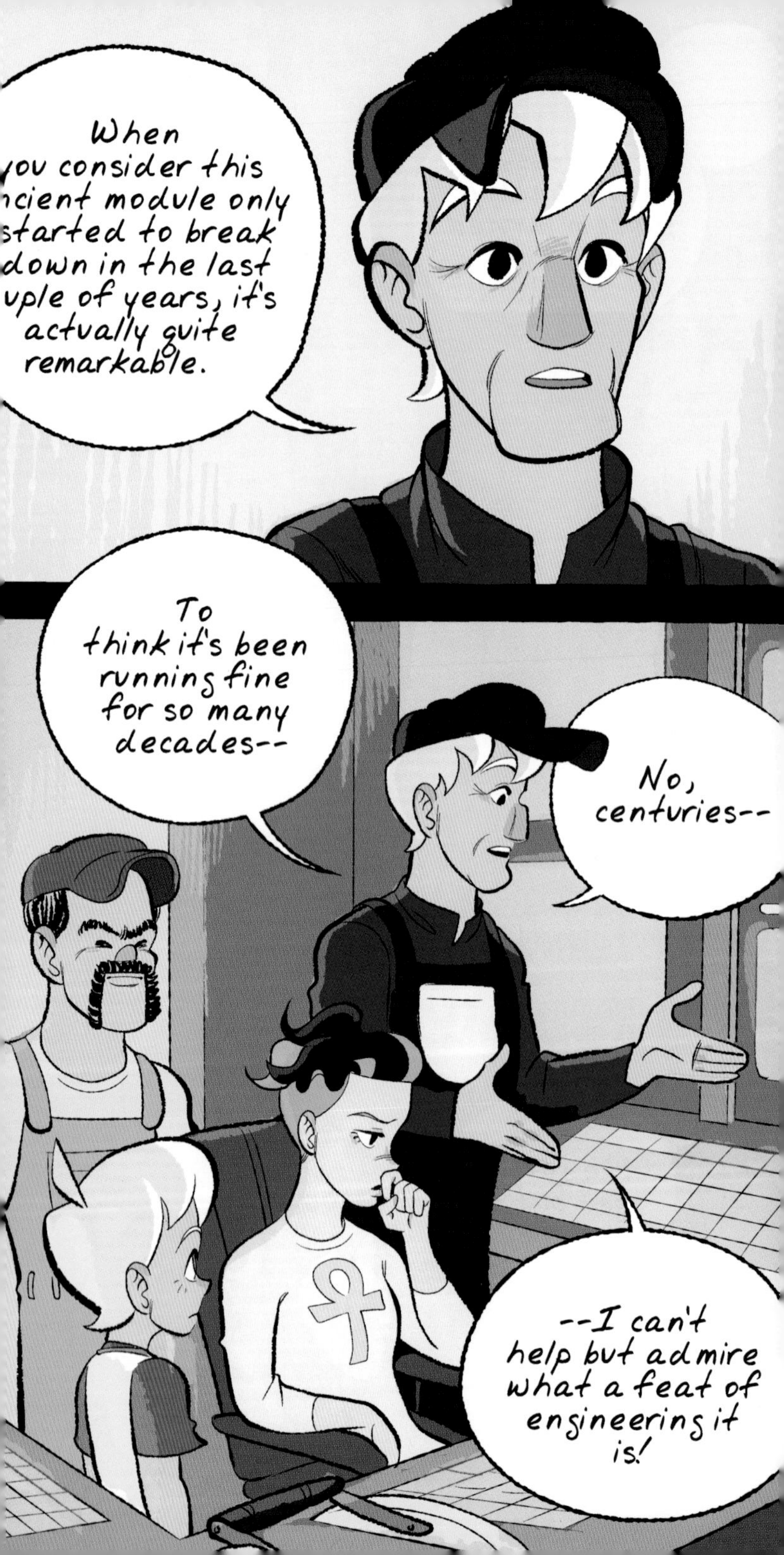
When you consider this ncient module only started to break down in the last uple of years, it's actually quite remarkable.
To think it's been running fine for so many decades--
No, centuries--
--I can't help but admire what a feat of engineering it is!

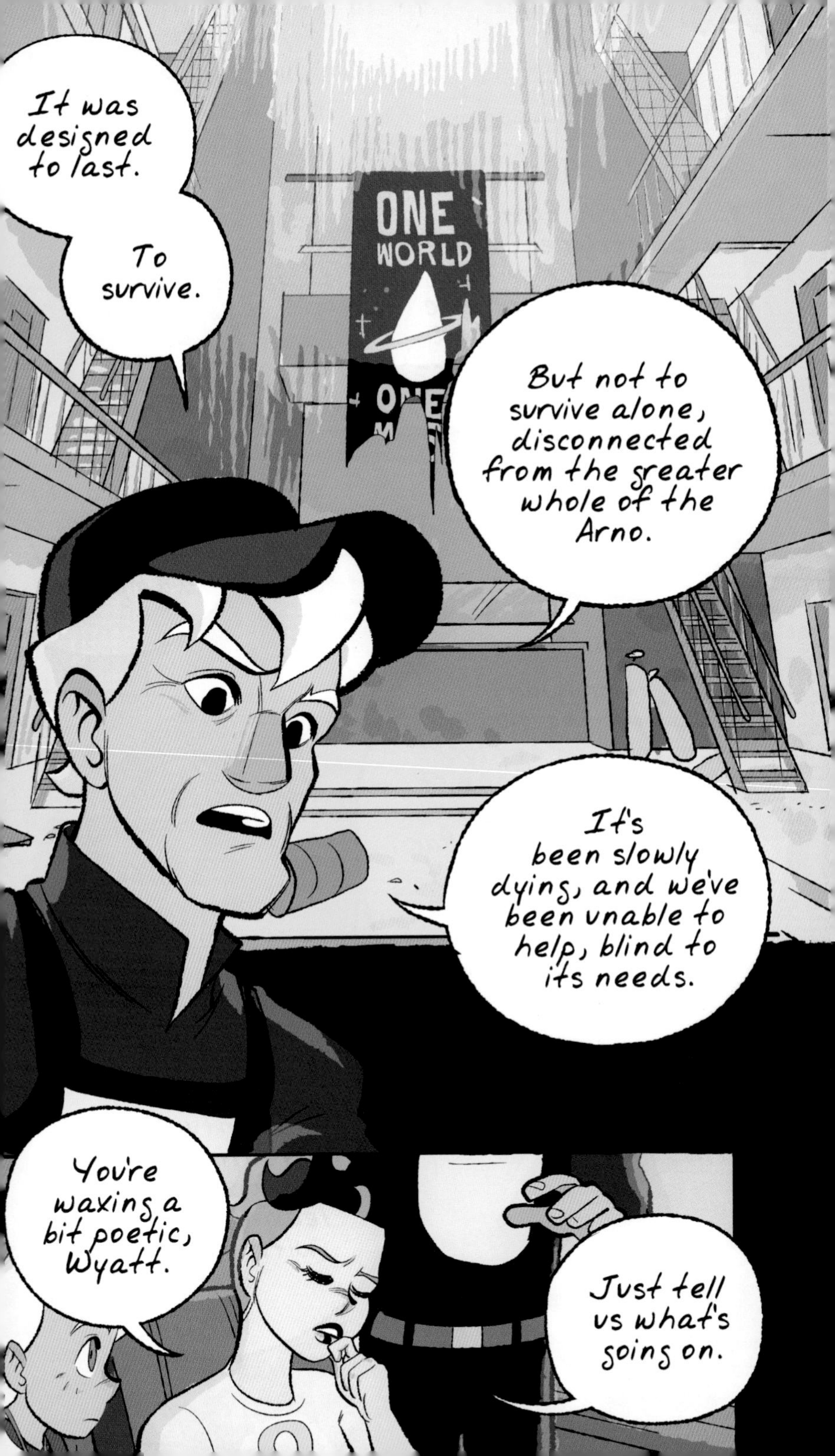
It was designed to last.
To survive.
ONE WORLD
But not to survive alone, disconnected from the greater whole of the Arno.
It's been slowly dying, and we've been unable to help, blind to its needs.
You're waxing a bit poetic, Wyatt.
Just tell us what's going on.

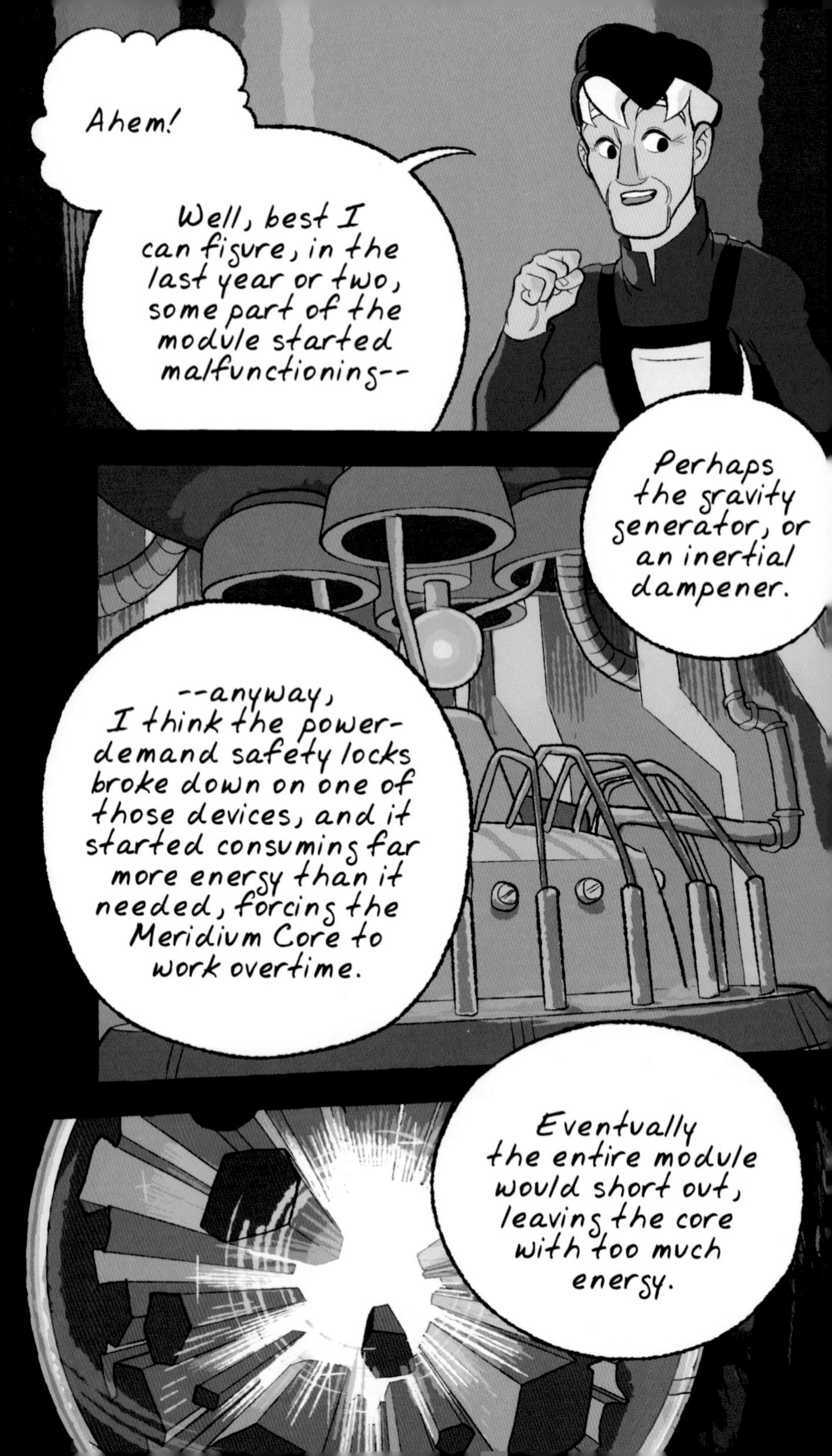
Ahem!
Well, best I can figure, in the last year or two, some part of the module started malfunctioning--
Perhaps the gravity generator, or an inertial dampener.
--anyway, I think the power-demand safety locks broke down on one of those devices, and it started consuming far more energy than it needed, forcing the Meridium Core to work overtime.
Eventually the entire module would short out, leaving the core with too much energy.

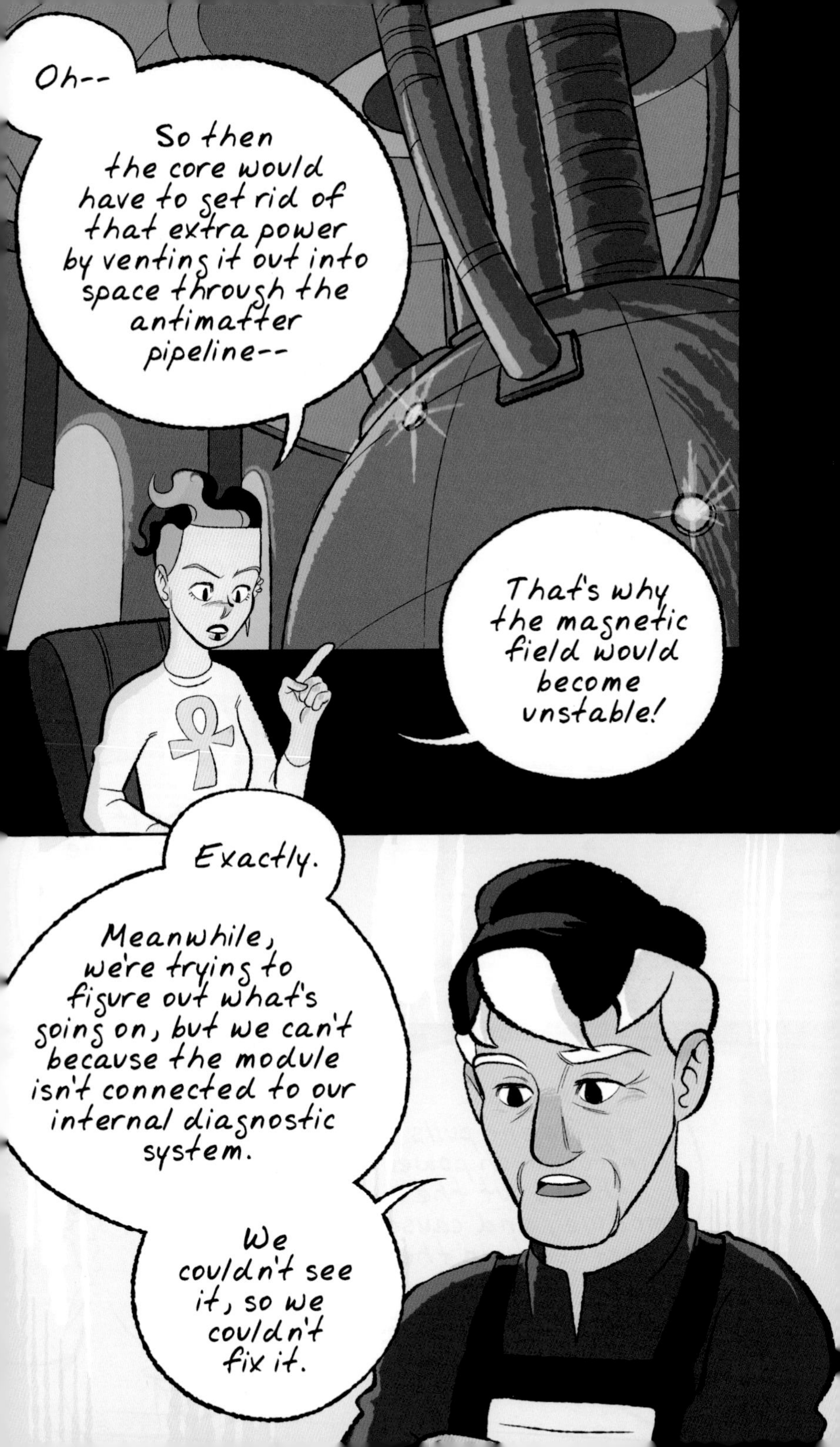
Oh--
So then the core would have to get rid of that extra power by venting it out into space through the antimatter pipeline--
That's why the magnetic field would become unstable!
Exactly.
Meanwhile, we're trying to figure out what's going on, but we can't because the module isn't connected to our internal diagnostic system.
We couldn't see it, so we couldn't fix it.

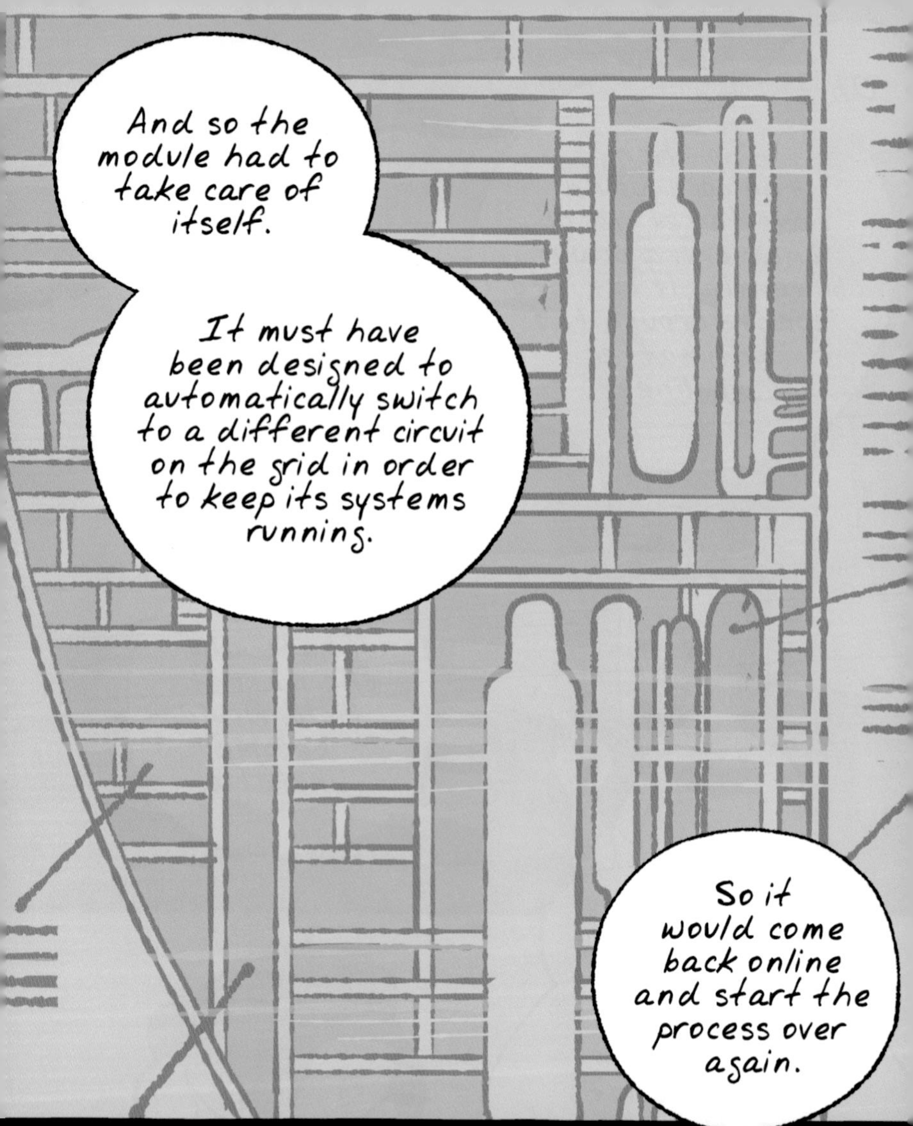
And so the module had to take care of itself.
It must have been designed to automatically switch to a different circuit on the grid in order to keep its systems running.
So it would come back online and start the process over again.

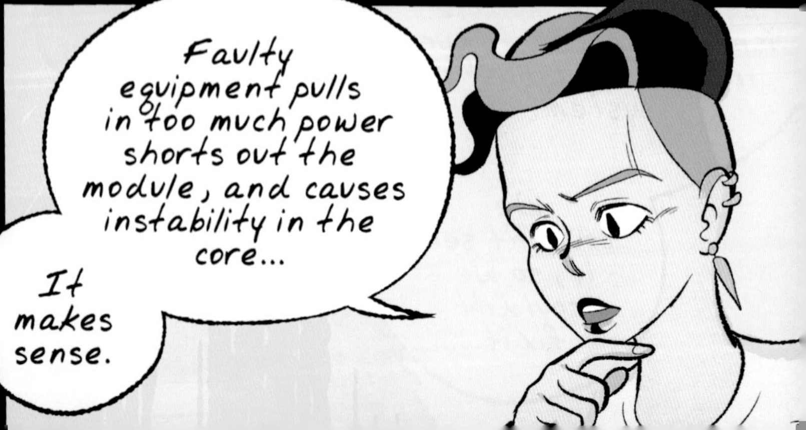
Faulty equipment pulls in too much power shorts out the module, and causes instability in the core...
It makes sense.

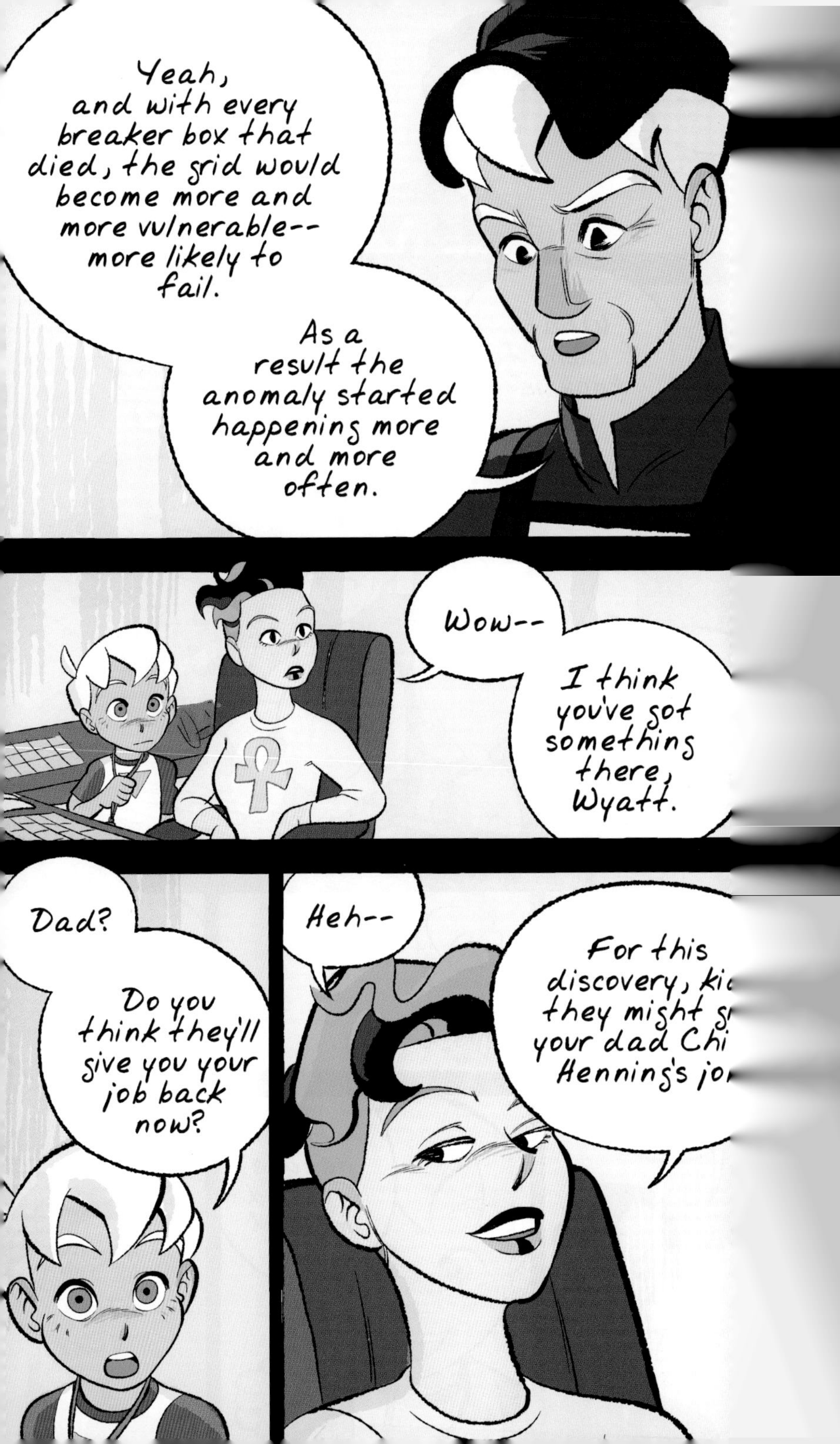
Yeah, and with every breaker box that died, the grid would become more and more vulnerable-- more likely to fail.
As a result the anomaly started happening more and more often.
Wow--
I think you've got something there, Wyatt.
Dad?
Do you think they'll give you your job back now?
Heh--
For this discovery, ki
they might
your dad Chi
Henning's jo

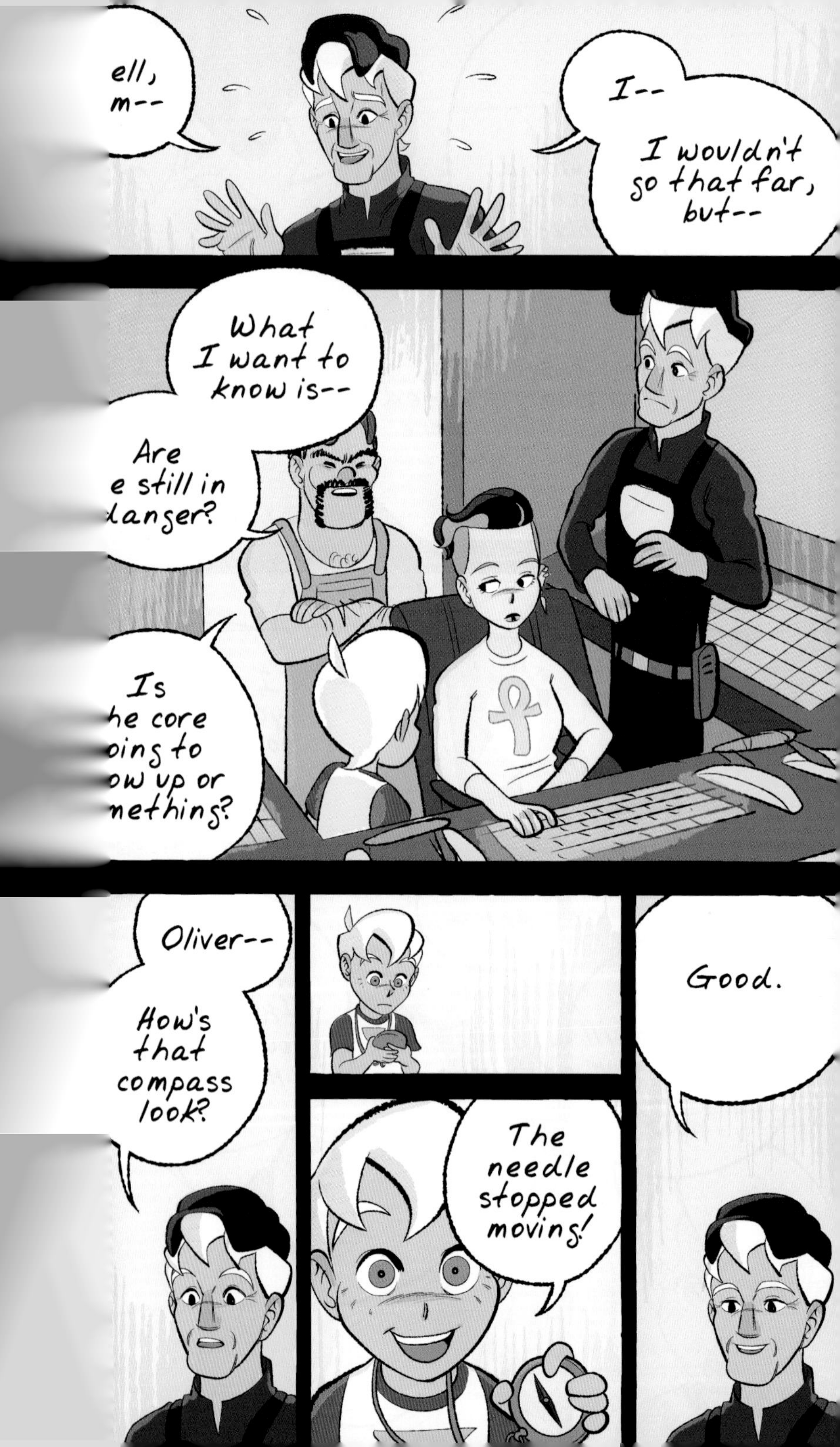

ell, m--
I--
I wouldn't go that far, but--
What I want to know is--
Are e still in danger?
Is he core oing to ow up or nething?
Oliver--
How's that compass look?
The needle stopped moving!
Good.

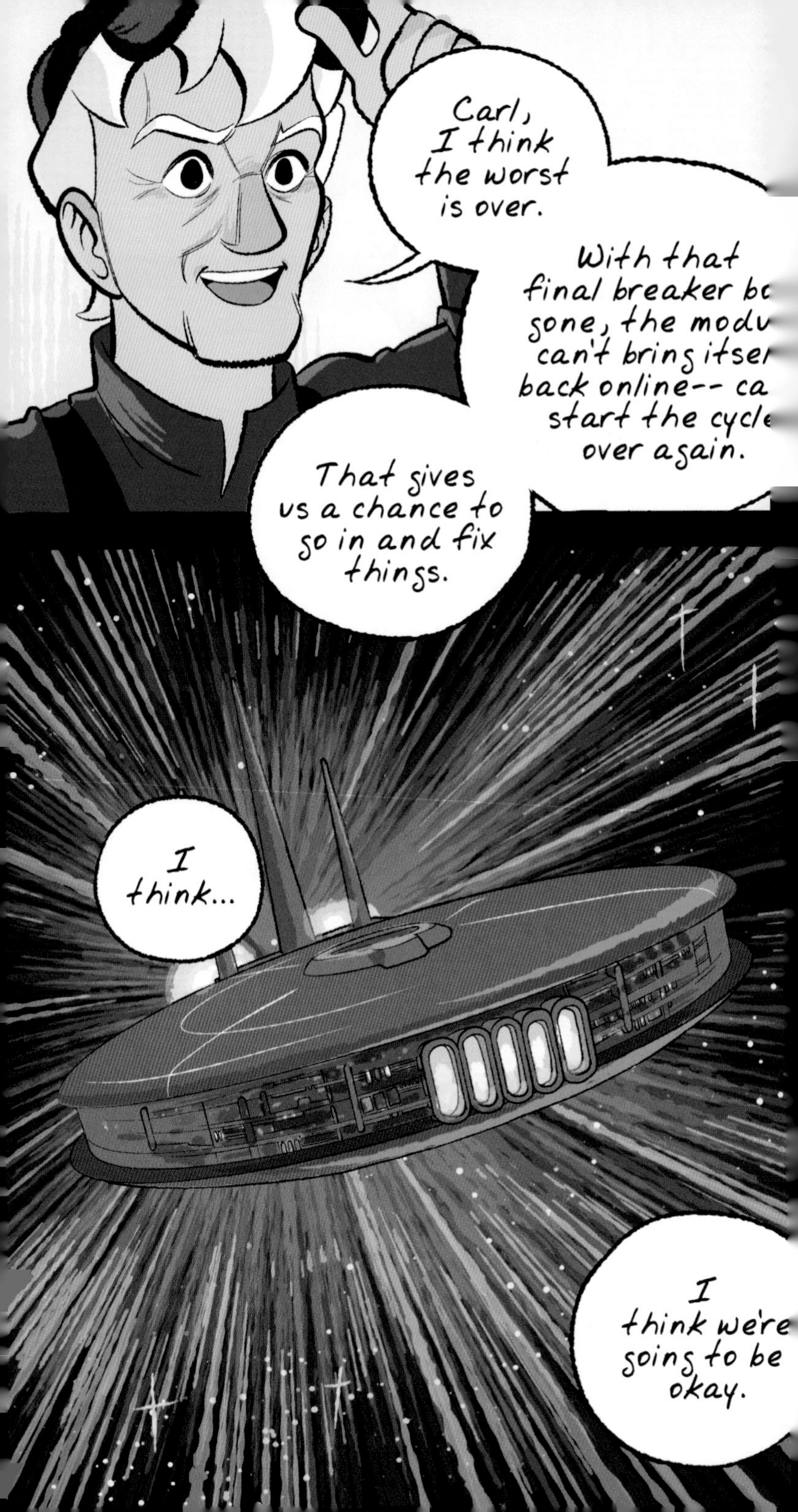
Carl, I think the worst is over.
With that final breaker bo gone, the modu can't bring itse back online-- ca start the cycle over again.
That gives us a chance to go in and fix things.
I think...
I think we're going to be okay.

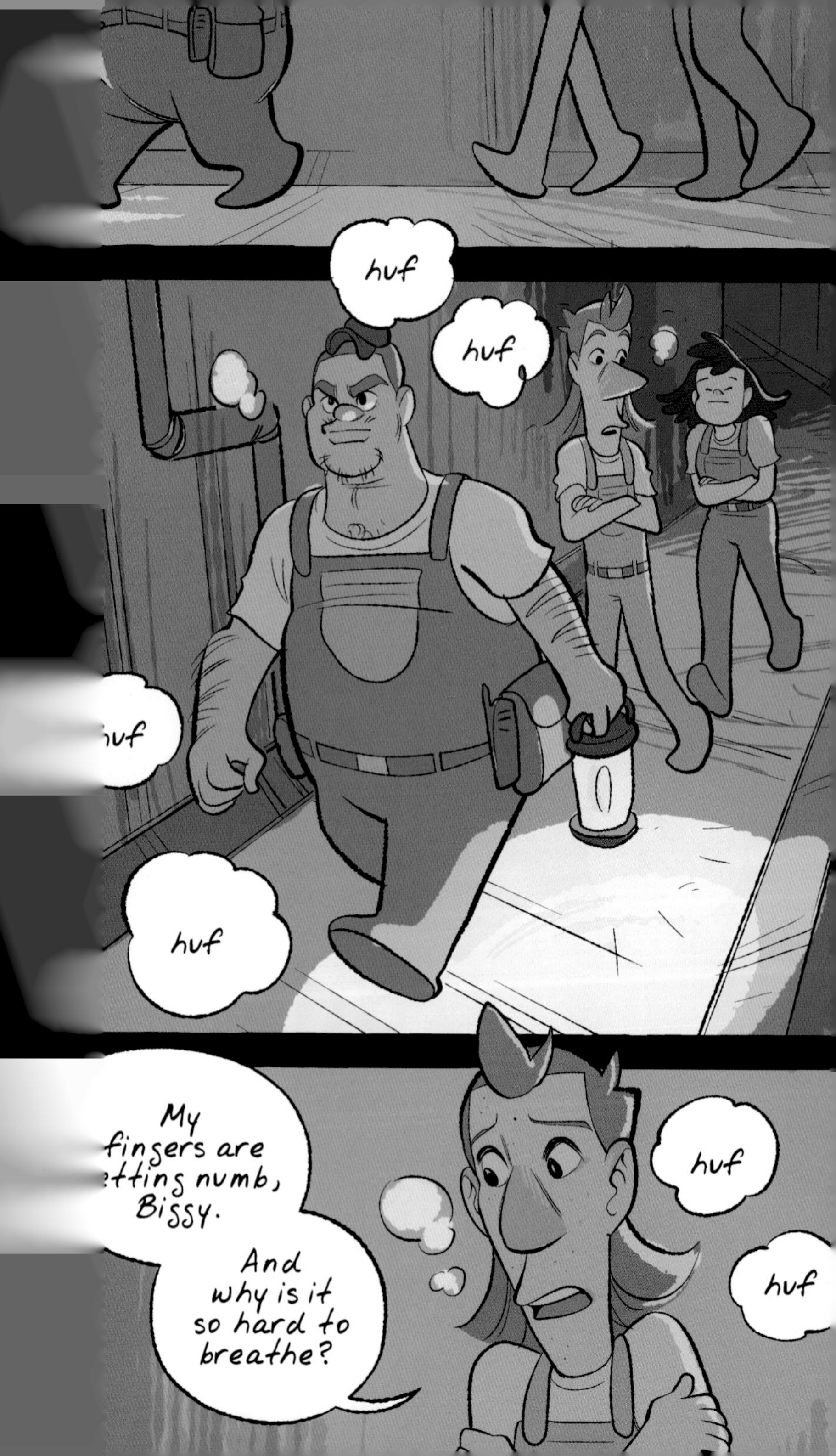
huf
huf
uf
huf
My fingers are etting numb, Bissy.
And why is it so hard to breathe?
huf
huf

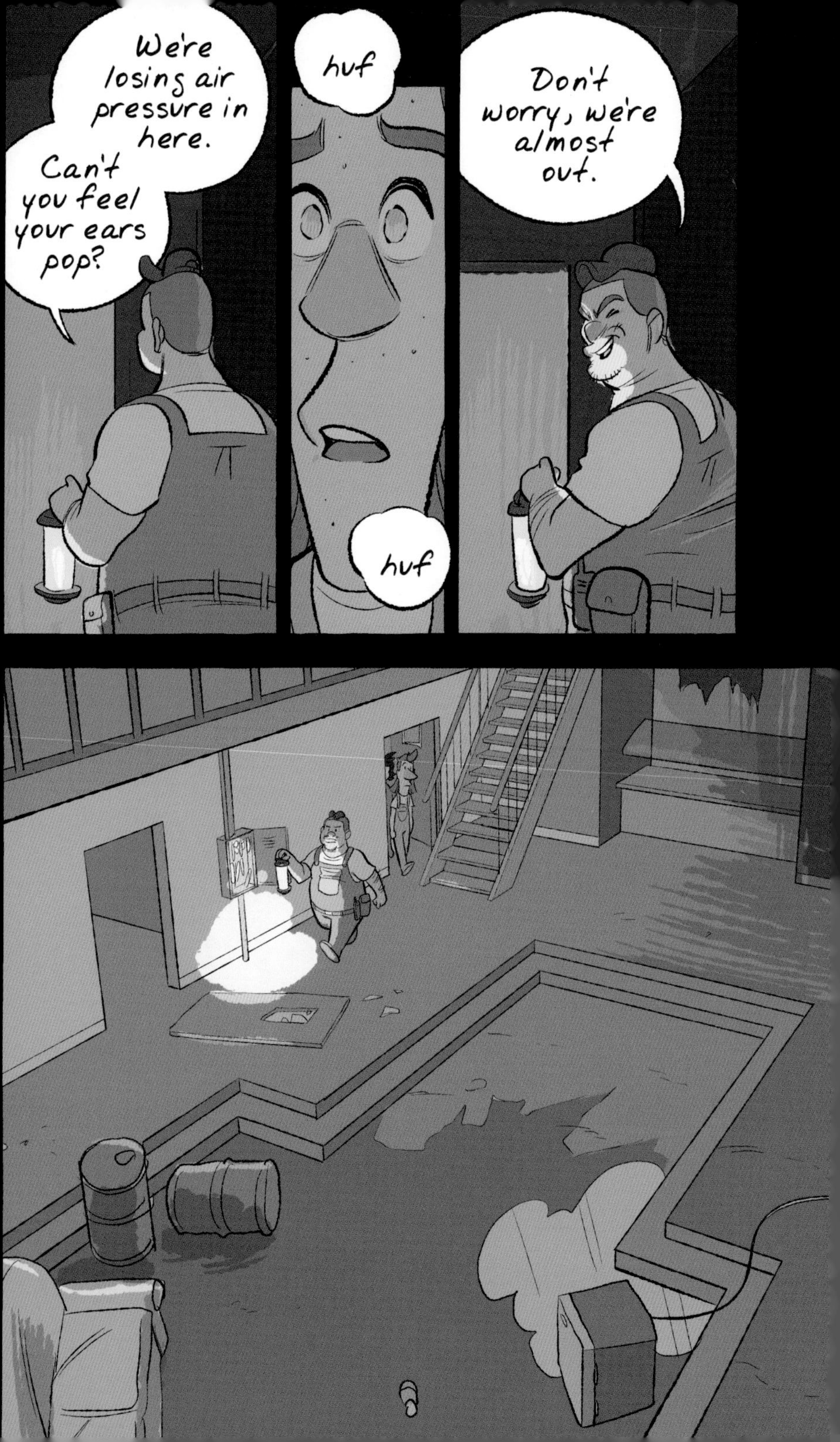
We're losing air pressure in here.
Can't you feel your ears pop?
huf
huf
Don't worry, we're almost out.

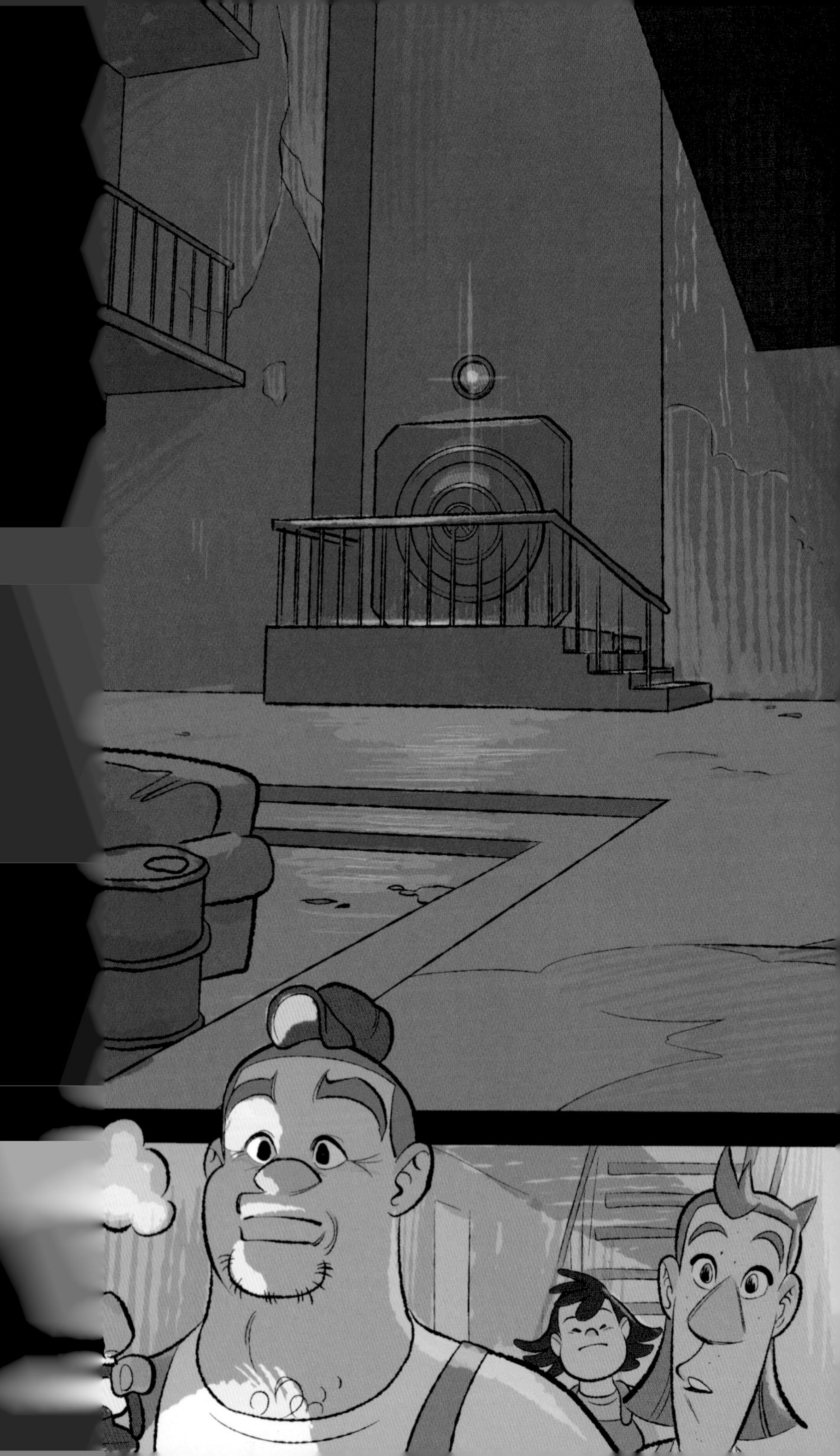

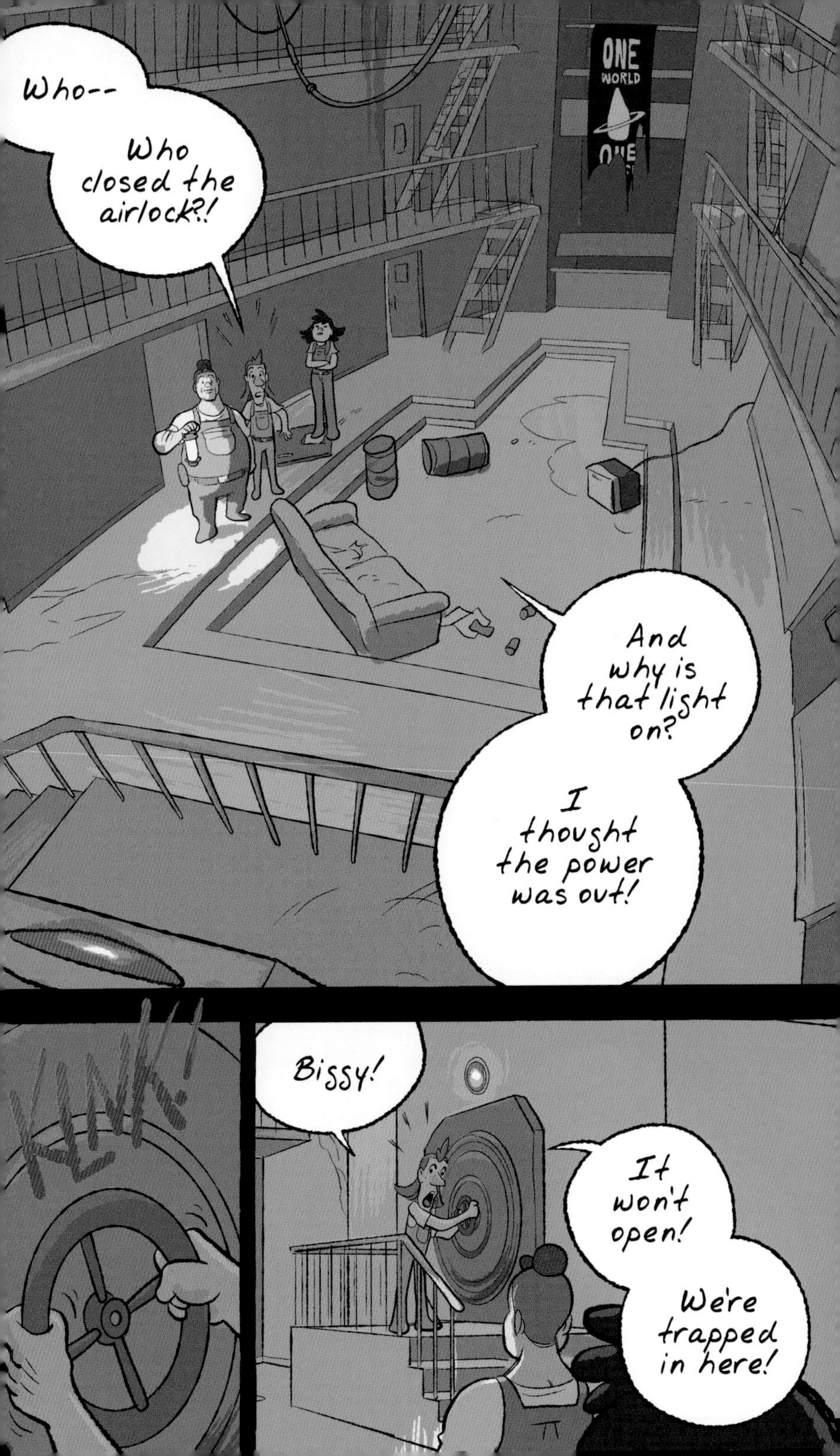
Who--
Who closed the airlock?!
ONE WORLD
And why is that light on?
I thought the power was out!
Bissy!
It won't open!
We're trapped in here!

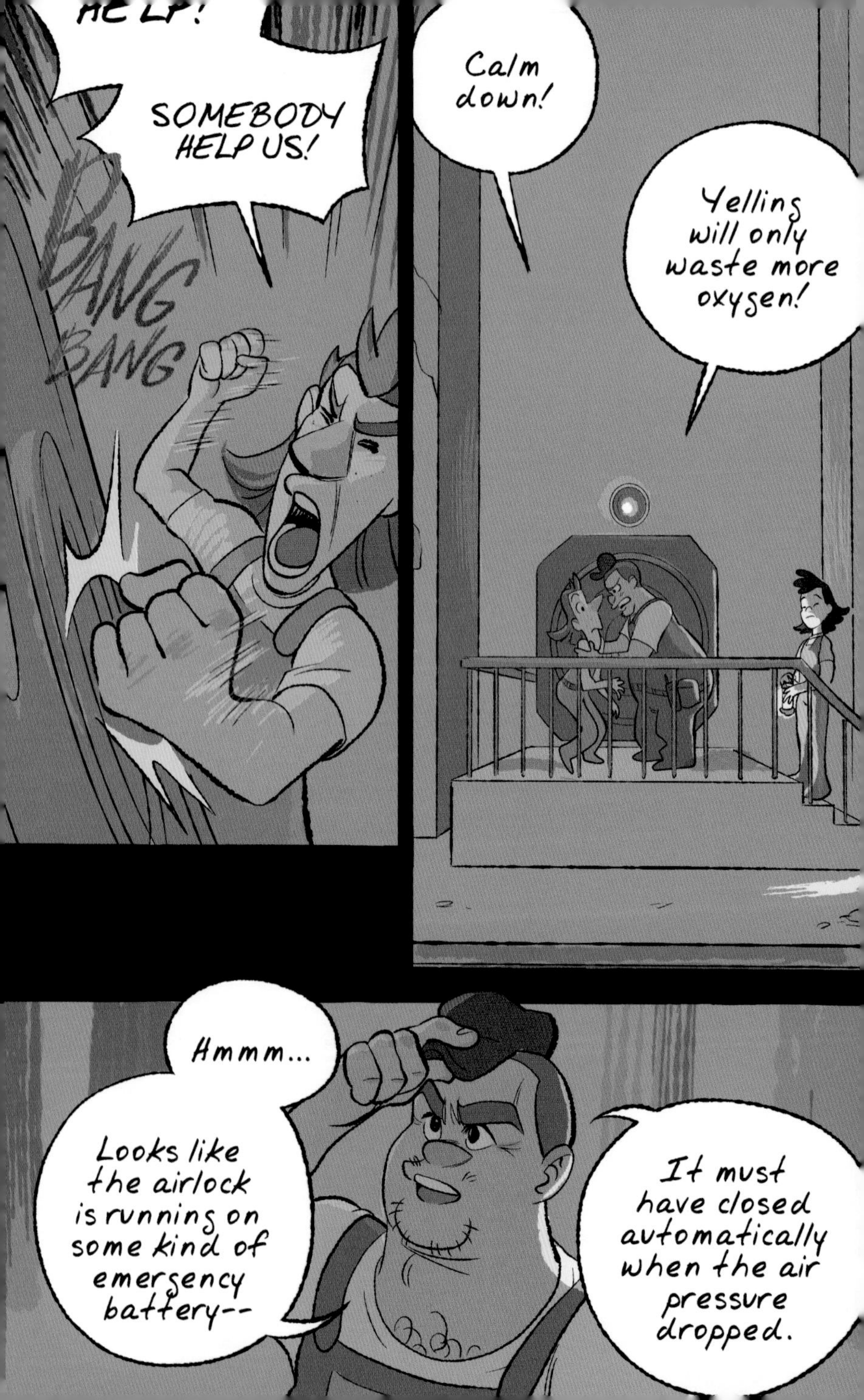
HELP!
SOMEBODY HELP US!
BANG BANG BANG
Calm down!
Yelling will only waste more oxygen!
Hmmm...
Looks like the airlock is running on some kind of emergency battery--
It must have closed automatically when the air pressure dropped.

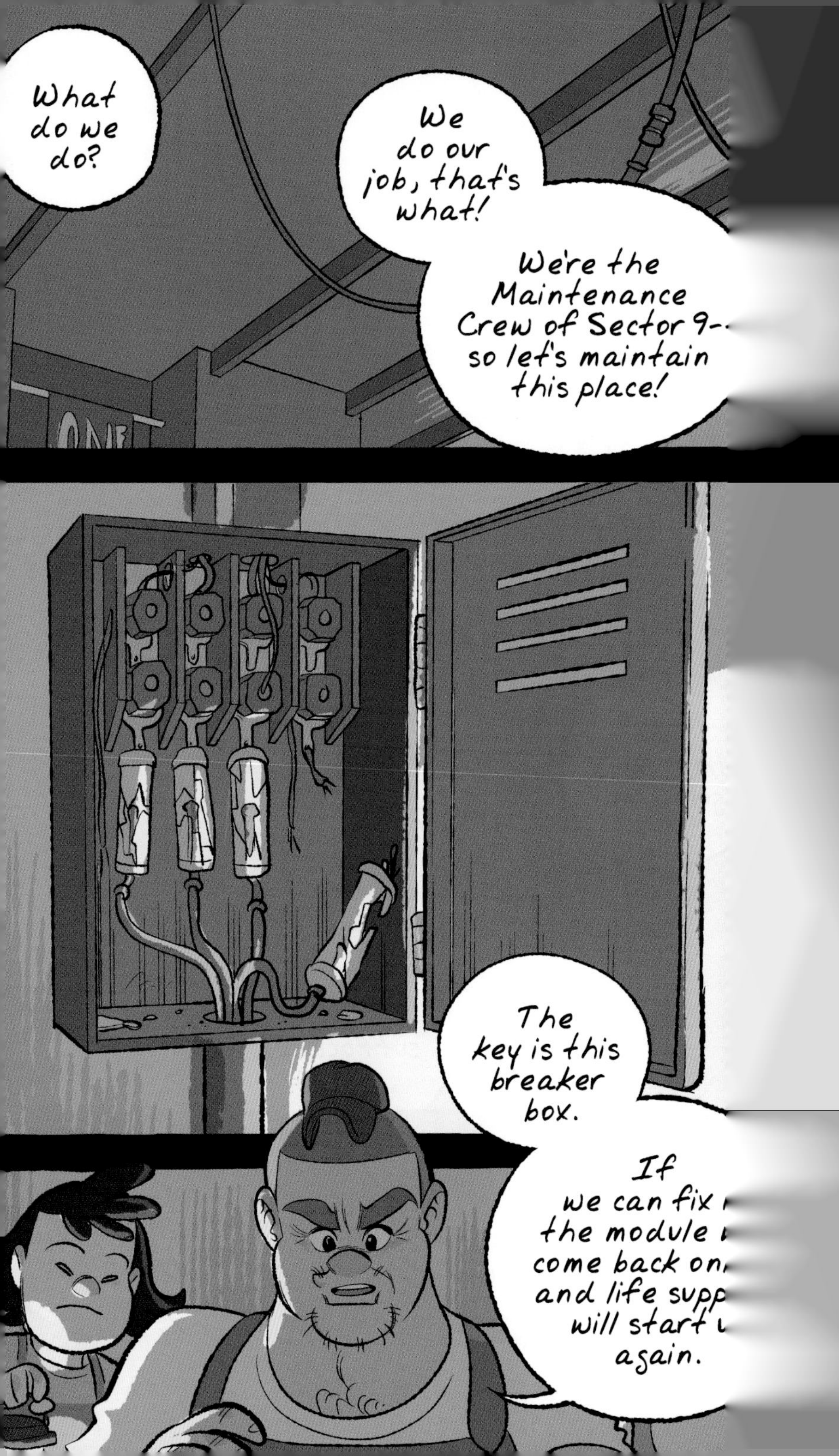
What do we do?
We do our job, that's what!
We're the Maintenance Crew of Sector 9--so let's maintain this place!
The key is this breaker box.
If we can fix
the module
come back on
and life supp
will start
again.

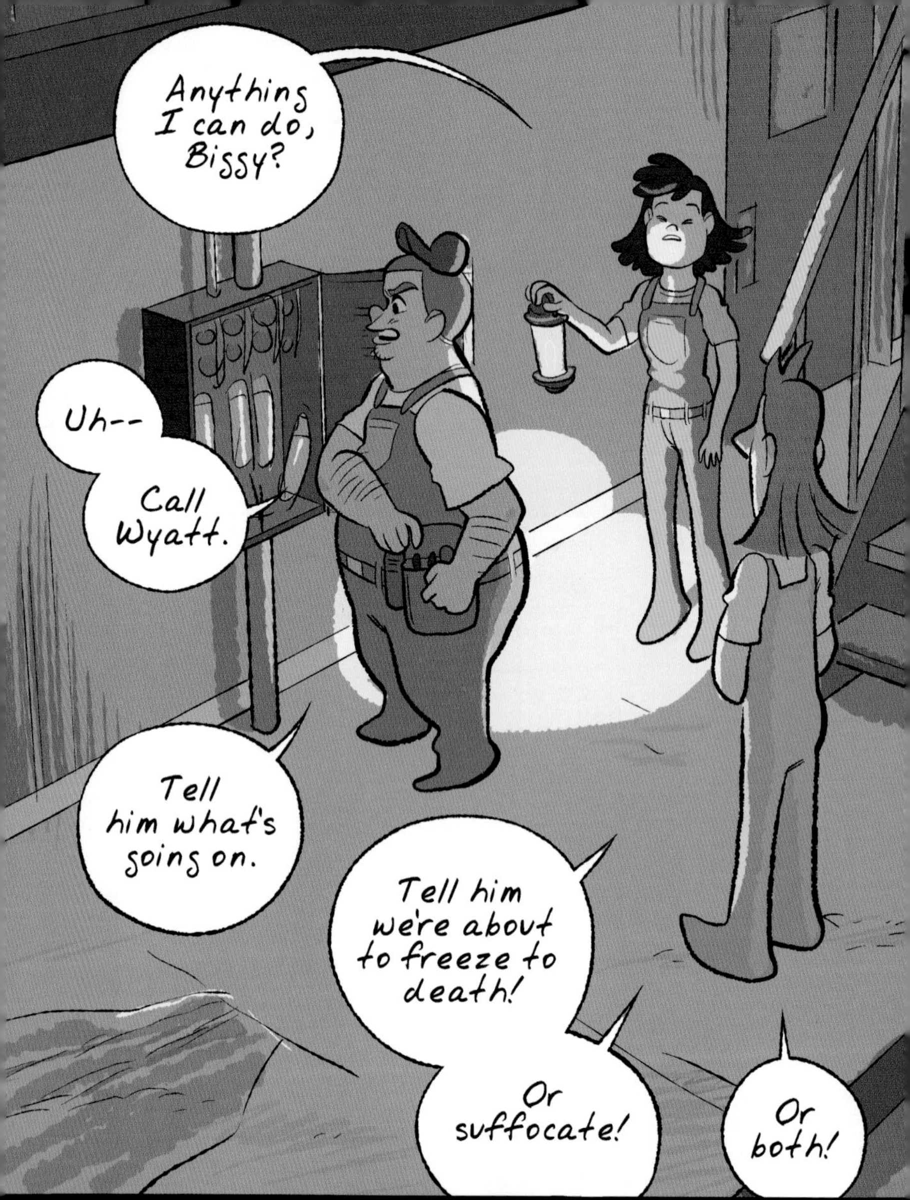
Anything I can do, Bissy?
Uh--
Call Wyatt.
Tell him what's going on.
Tell him we're about to freeze to death!
Or suffocate!
Or both!

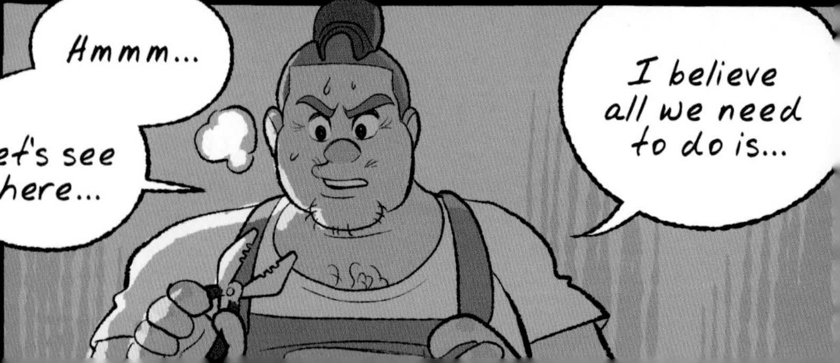
Hmmm...
Let's see here...
I believe all we need to do is...

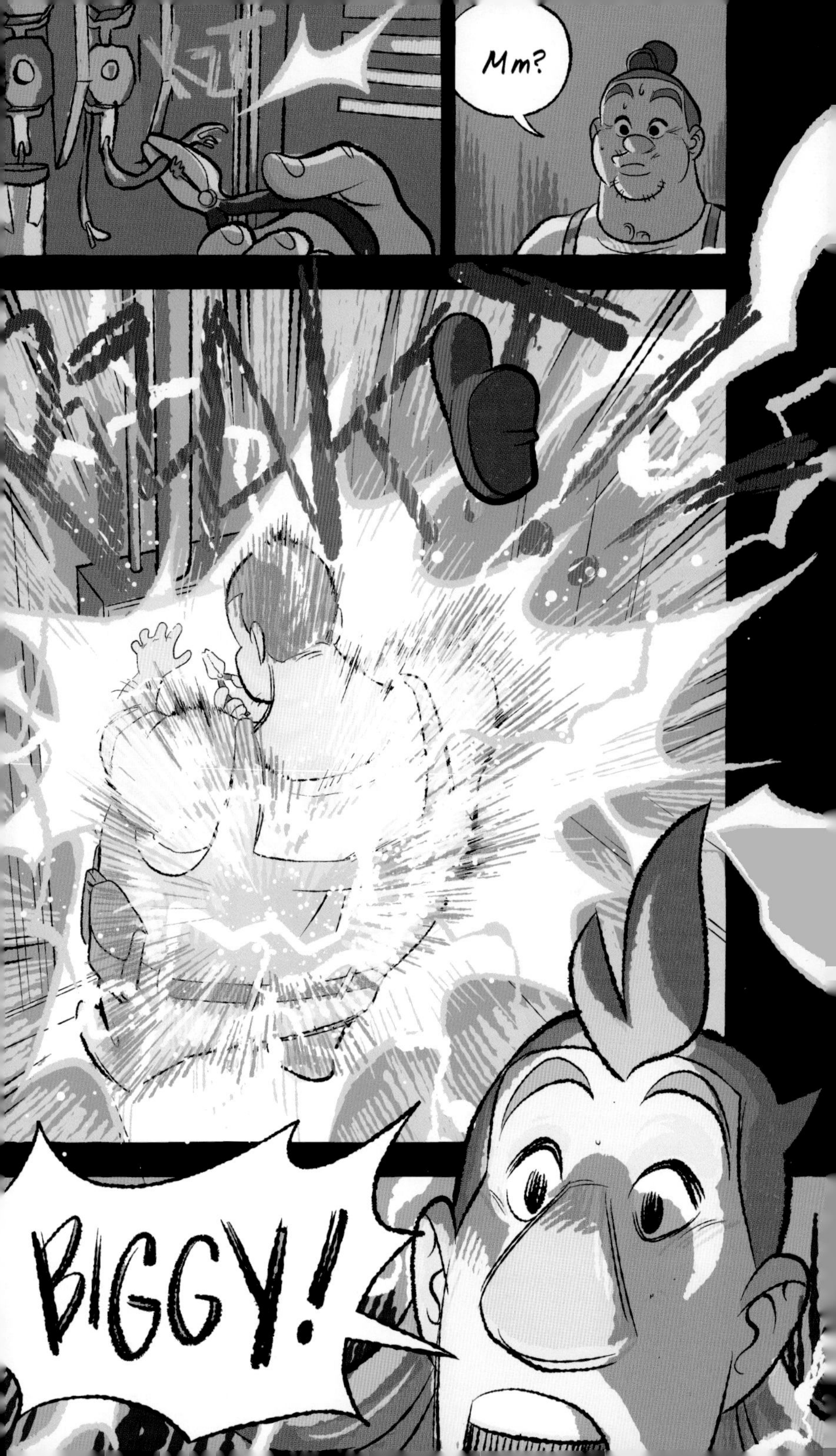
Mm?
BIGGY!

COMING SOON . . .

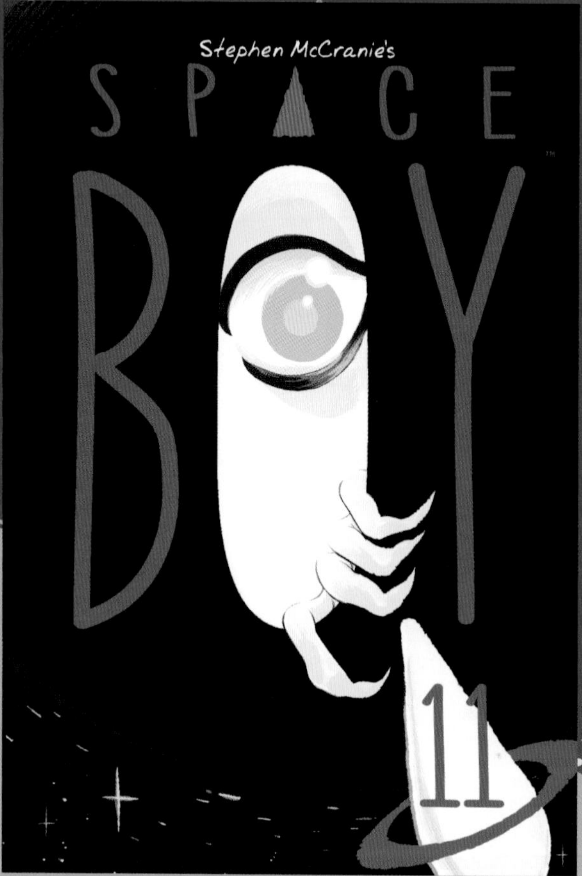
Stephen McCranie's
SPACE
BOY
11

THE ORIGIN OF SPACE BOY REVEALED!

Oliver is faced with the choice that will drive the course for the rest of his life! As the young boy learns to cope with the new world around him, the people on Earth struggle to find answers. Will Oliver make it to the mysterious artifact? And what is more important to the FCP?

With shocking reveals and moments that pull at your heartstrings, this is not a volume you will want to miss, available October 2021!

YOU CAN ALSO READ MORE SPACE BOY COMICS ON WEBTOONS.COM!

HAVE YOU READ THEM ALL?

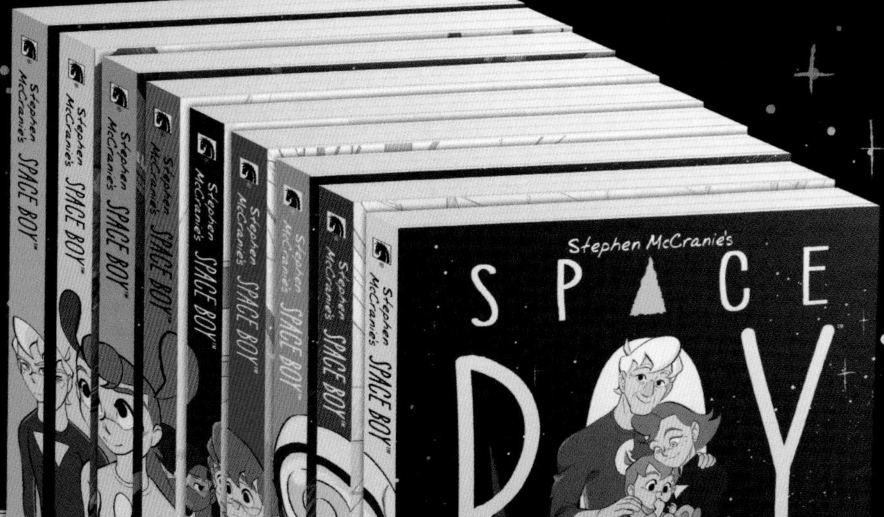

Stephen McCranie's
SPACE BOY
9
DARK HORSE

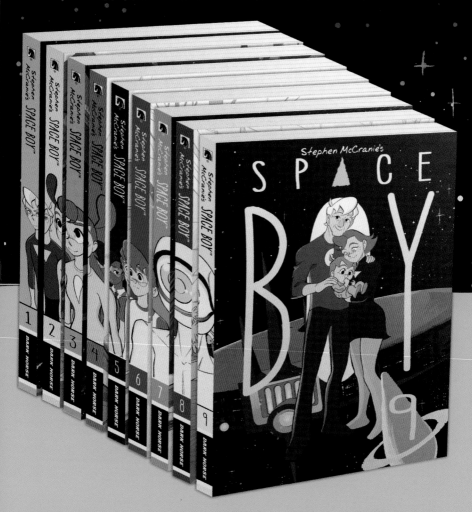

VOLUME 1
$10.99 • ISBN 978-1-50670-648-1

VOLUME 2
$10.99 • ISBN 978-1-50670-680-1

VOLUME 3
$10.99 • ISBN 978-1-50670-842-3

VOLUME 4
$10.99 • ISBN 978-1-50670-843-0

VOLUME 5
$10.99 • ISBN 978-1-50671-399-1

VOLUME 6
$10.99 • ISBN 978-1-50671-400-4

VOLUME 7
$10.99 • ISBN 978-1-50671-401-1

VOLUME 8
$10.99 • ISBN 978-1-50671-402-8

VOLUME 9
$10.99 • ISBN 978-1-50671-883-5

AVAILABLE AT YOUR LOCAL COMICS SHOP OR BOOKSTORE. TO FIND A COMICS SHOP IN YOUR AREA, VISIT COMICSHOPLOCATOR.COM. FOR MORE INFORMATION OR TO ORDER DIRECT, VISIT DARKHORSE.COM.